D0482415
JERUSALEM
IN THE DAYS OF LEHI
TO ASSYRIA
CITADEL
TEMPLE
JAWBONE INN
PALACE
KING STREET
UPPER CITY
GOVERNMENT ARCH
LABAN'S ESTATE
MARKET STREET
STREET
WATERSHAFT
MILITARY TRAINING GROUND
TREET
EAST GATE
GIHON SPRING

PILLAR *of* FIRE

PILLAR *of* FIRE

a historical novel

DAVID G. WOOLLEY

Covenant Communications, Inc.

Published by Covenant Communications, Inc.
American Fork, Utah

This is a work of fiction. The characters, names, incidents, places, and dialogue are products of the author's imagination, and are not to be construed as real.

Printed in the United States of America
First Printing: September 2000

07 06 05 04 03 02 01 00 10 9 8 7 6 5 4 3 2

ISBN 1-57734-722-6

Author's Note

Pillar of Fire, the first book in the *Promised Land* series, is the story of Jonathan the blacksmith and his family—fictional characters who moved to Jerusalem about 601 B.C. The stories of their lives were inspired by the insights of scholars and the events of history. Notes exploring the historical and fictional details appear at the end of the book.

It was the dawn of the sixth century B.C. in the declining years of the great monarchies of the ancient world. Nineveh had just fallen to the forces of Babylon, bringing the empire of Assyria to her knees. In Greece, Solon gave Athens its constitution. Socrates was gleaning his education amidst the residual glory of the schoolhouses of Egypt. And in a small and struggling kingdom along the eastern Mediterranean, a man named Lehi received his call from the Almighty to preach repentance to a doomed city.

His story comes to us from the Book of Mormon: Another Testament of Jesus Christ. The book's opening verses offer a narrow window onto the life of Lehi and his family. It is an intimately personal account. Lehi's scriptural story is bold in its authenticity, touching in its simplicity, and faithful in its witness of Yeshua the Anointed One, the Lord Jesus Christ.

To read the opening chapters of the Book of Mormon is to yearn to know these people, walk the streets they walked, hear what they heard, and feel what they might have felt. A wide gulf of centuries and unfamiliar cultures separates us, but the voice of Lehi rises as one speaking from the dust, reaching across the span of time like a bridge between civilizations to inspire us to live well our earthly probation.

Over the years since Joseph Smith translated the Book of Mormon, many writings have been unearthed that give a strikingly similar account of the desperate circumstances at Jerusalem in Lehi's day. Those compelling writings contributed ideas that led to the development of this story.

Amid the challenges of bringing a project of this magnitude to completion, my life has been blessed by the goodness of others who have made *Pillar of Fire* a far finer read than I could have ever accomplished on my own. Numerous authors, readers, and historians have spent hours poring over the manuscript, and their influence is manifest in the final product. It was Patty Jolley who first recommended I write this fictional work some years ago. She set my feet on the path of learning the craft of writing and this project would not have come about without her suggestion. Sherri Curtis deserves mention for her understanding of the writer's art. She and many other fine authors have inspired me, and their influence has contributed to this work. They are the masters and I am happy to be the apprentice. Many thanks go to Bonnie Arbon, a most able Soccer Mom and editor *extraordinaire*. Bonnie has served as the first reader and first hearer of this manuscript. Bonnie has spent countless hours listening to my reading of four versions of this manuscript, carefully sifting out the promising bits of writing from much that was poorly accomplished.

When my good friends Bill and Heather Bodine discovered that my computer was no longer able to accommodate a project of this size and I was unable to purchase another, they gifted me a PC along with their love and encouragement.

It is with admiration that I offer my thanks to the staff at Covenant Communications for their expertise and encouragement.

I express my thanks to Dean Bowen who posed for the cover portrait, and to Michael Lyons who is responsible for the beautiful maps of Jerusalem and the Mediterranean region.

I bow low in gratitude to the Almighty God of Heaven, the father of our spirits, for the Book of Mormon and for providing us with another testament of His Son, Jesus Christ. I have felt His presence, inspiration, and sustaining power throughout this project and I pray that it is acceptable to Him. Writing *Pillar of Fire* has drawn me back to read and read again the Book of Mormon. I pray that it will do the same for you. May God Bless your life as you search the Holy Scriptures.

David G. Woolley
Provo, Utah
June 2000

While Joseph Smith, Jr. translated the Book of Mormon from gold plates, he was also entrusted with an ancient sword and a Hebrew record written on plates of brass. This is the story of those treasures.

—Doctrine and Covenants 17:1; 1 Nephi 5:18-19

LIST OF CHARACTERS

While this is a work of fiction, and all of the characters have been fictionalized, many are based on what we know of the historical figures of the time period. In cases where the names of historical characters are not known, the author has created names for them. These are marked with an asterisk(*).

FICTIONAL CHARACTERS

The Family of Jonathan the Blacksmith
Jonathan, *Blacksmith*
Ruth, *Weaver*
Elizabeth, *Eldest Daughter*
Aaron, *Eldest Son & Firemaster*
Daniel, *Son & Forgingmaster*
Sarah, *Youngest Daughter*
Joshua, *Youngest Son*

The House of Josiah the Potter
Josiah, *Second Elder of the Jews*
Rebekah, *Josiah's Only Child*
Mima, *Rebekah's Handservant*

Others
Jesse, *Prince of Phoenicia*
Nimrod, *Jesse's Uncle*
Jonah, *Animal Trader*
Sephora, *Flutist*
Memphis, *Egyptian Teacher*

HISTORICALLY BASED CHARACTERS

The Family of Lehi the Olive Oil Merchant
Lehi, *Olive Oil Merchant*
Sariah, *Wife*
Rachel*, *Eldest Daughter*
Leah*, *Daughter*
Laman, *Eldest Son & Pressmaster*
Lemuel, *Son & Stablemaster*
Sam, *Son & Caravanmaster*
Nephi, *Youngest Son & Keeper of the Oil*

HISTORICALLY BASED CHARACTERS

The Royal Family of Judah
Zedekiah, *King of Judah*
Miriam*, *Queen of Judah*
Mulek, *Prince and Heir Apparent of Judah*
Dan*, *Prince of Judah*
Benjamin*, *Prince of Judah*

The Family of Ishmael the Vineyard Master
Ishmael, *Vineyard Master*
Isabel*, *Wife*
Nathan*, *Eldest Son & Master of Olive Culture*
Seth*, *Son & Watermaster*
Nora*, *Eldest Daughter*
Abigail*, *Daughter*
Hannah*, *Daughter*
Mary*, *Youngest Daughter*

The Family of the Prophet Jeremiah
Jeremiah, *Prophet of God*
Eliza*, *Jeremiah's Wife*
Zoram, *Adopted Son and Keeper of the Keys*

Military Personnel
Laban, *Captain of the Guard*
Yaush, *Military Governor of Fort Lakhish*
Elnathan, *Military Scout*
Hosha Yahu, *Mail Courier*

Other Major Characters
Zadock, *Chief Elder of the Jews*
Shechem, *King of Robbers*
Uriah, *Prophet of God*

PROLOGUE

1768 B.C., Egypt

It was a nightmare that drove Pharaoh to visit the debtor's prison. Royal protocol be cursed! Pharaoh was God in Egypt and when he wanted to speak with a man, he sent for him. And before he received his guests, he ordered them bathed in perfumed waters, rubbed in mineral oils until their skin glistened from head to toe, and dressed in robes befitting his royal presence. But none of Pharaoh's magicians and wisemen could interpret the dream. He'd gotten no sleep, he had little appetite, and last night when the dream returned, as it had every night for two months, he was certain he'd lost his mind.

Sometime in the wee hours between sleeplessness and insanity, Pharaoh's butler suggested he see a Hebrew incarcerated in the debtor's prison. Pharaoh departed the palace with such fury that he left his scepter on the bedroom mantle and his crown sitting on the head of an exquisitely cast bust that looked nothing like him. His only visible marks of royalty were a gold amulet around his neck and the ring he had worn since the day of his coronation.

He went to the palace stables without changing from his sleeping attire—a kilt of blue silks and an open vest. He ordered his chariot hitched and his menservants to follow on horseback. Only seven were able to keep up with his rampage through the streets of Tanis. He dropped the reins at the first sight of the prison gates and stepped from the chariot before it came to a full stop.

A rat skittered across the dungeon steps as a man emerged from the shadows. Pharaoh peered at him through the bars in the gate. "I will see the interpreter of dreams who was Potiphar's servant. The Hebrew they call Joseph."

The man spoke between the iron bars. "I am Joseph." He was thirty years old with piercing green eyes and deep black hair cut straight across his brow. He unlocked the latch, pushed open the gate and bowed.

"You're the prisoner?" Pharaoh stepped back. "What sort of man are you that the jailer entrusts you with the keys to your freedom?"

Pharaoh's servants arrived in time to usher Joseph away to the far side of the prison and prepare him for an audience with the king. They gave him a blade to shave his beard, and perfumed water and olive oil to clean himself. Before they let him stand before Pharaoh, they replaced his tattered robe with a brown leather kilt and a blue silk tunic.

The pharaoh asked, "Will you interpret my dream?"

Joseph set his gaze on him and in a calm, firm voice said, "It is God who will give you an answer of peace, not I."

A faint smile crossed Pharaoh's lips. It was peace he had come for. He said, "In my dream I was standing on the bank of the river. Seven cows, fat-fleshed and strong, rose up from the Nile, and while they grazed along the banks, seven lean cows emerged out of the depths of the river and ate them." Pharaoh told Joseph that seven ears of good corn grew up on a stalk and next to them seven ears of thin corn. When the dry east wind blasted the harvest and parched the ground, the seven thin ears devoured the seven good ears.

Joseph interpreted the dream to mean that Egypt would be blessed with seven years of bounty followed by seven years of famine. He advised the king to find a discreet and wise man to oversee the collection of grain in the plentiful years and see that it was stored in reserve against the lean years.

Pharaoh removed the gold amulet from his neck and placed it around Joseph's, saying, "There is not a man in Egypt who has the spirit of God in him as you have." He removed his ring, placed it on Joseph's finger, and said, "With this I make you ruler over Egypt and by your word my people will be ruled. Only in the throne will I be greater than you."

Joseph became viceroy of Egypt and ruled for forty years. He married the gifted daughter of an Egyptian priest, and two sons were born to them—first Manasseh and later Ephraim. And though Joseph was great in Egypt, he never forgot he was the son of Jacob, a Hebrew. Before Joseph died, he left two treasures to his sons to establish their birthrights, just as Pharaoh's ring and gold amulet established his own adoption into Egypt's royal house. For Manasseh he prepared a codex of brass plates, a book smithed from a mixture of Egypt's finest silver and copper. Upon its plates he inscribed the history of the Jews, from Adam down to the account of his own life. He entrusted them to Manasseh and charged him to record the prophecies of the Hebrew prophets. To Ephraim he gave his sword, a blade worth more than any amount of money, the same sword that had been passed down with other tokens of birthright through the generations from the time of Methuselah. Some even whispered that it had been given to Adam at the gates of Eden. It had come down through the centuries, touching the hands of Abraham, Isaac, and then Jacob, the Usurper. He passed it on to his favored son Joseph, Viceroy of Egypt. It was smithed of the ancient and secret metal Phoenician blacksmiths called steel, a metal finer and stronger than brass. The hilt was cast of pure gold and decorated with jewels. Before Joseph died, he anointed the sword with olive oil, and because his sons had the royal blood of two nations in their veins, he blessed the blade and inscribed it with the words of his prayer, that this sword should never be sheathed again until the kingdoms of this world become the kingdom of our God and his Anointed One.

Though Joseph ruled over Egyptians, he would be revered for centuries as the first monarch of the Hebrew nation, and his sword and plates of brass would stand forever as symbols of kingship.

The national treasures of the House of Israel were established.

721 B.C., Samaria, Capital City of Northern Israel

In the days when Israel was divided into two nations, the national treasures were retained by the kings of the Northern Kingdom. They were guarded at the royal palace until the kingdom fell to the armies of the Assyrians.

The two princes of Northern Israel marched through the great palace hall. Their steps echoed in the vaulted chamber that for two hundred and thirty years was the glory of their divided kingdom. Only the small lamps along the walls were burning, their timid flames offering little to discourage the shadows that loomed around the tall granite pillars and Syrian tapestries. The great lamps hanging from the ceiling had been dark for a month. Olive oil was difficult to come by during the siege, to say nothing of food and water.

When Israel's army fell back to the capital city of Samaria, the princes called for an emergency meeting with their father, King Hoshea—an unusual family gathering at a time like this, but since the princes were also the king's two most trusted generals, they had reason to meet. They went straight to Hoshea's balcony and pointed out the campfires of the massing Assyrian army. A rampart of earth had been raised in front of the main gate and, despite a showering of arrows and spears, the enemy had wheeled a battering ram into place. The pounding could be heard as far away as Mount Ebal. Assyrian infantrymen hacked on the smaller gates, and cavalrymen were called in to relieve the foot soldiers tunneling under the city walls.

The eldest prince said, "They've gotten through."

Hoshea asked, "Where?"

"Their first tunnel came up just inside the west wall."

"How many?"

"A few hundred soldiers so far, maybe more."

Cries of war filled the streets, and the clanging of swords on shields grew closer.

"We have our men in place to defend the palace."

Hoshea gripped the balcony ledge. "It's only a matter of time before all is lost."

"What are your orders, Father?"

"Secure the relics." King Hoshea scanned the darkness as flaming arrows arched over the walls. "We must preserve your birthrights." He began to pace. "We'll take the tunnel from the vaults to get outside the walls. From there we'll head east over the mountains and follow the Jordan."

"To the Southern Kingdom?"

"It's our only hope."

"They won't welcome us in Jerusalem."

"They won't turn us away." Hoshea nodded to his sons. "Not if we have the treasures with us. We'll be treated as royalty in Jerusalem, just as we are in Samaria."

They followed Hoshea into the main hall, then down four flights of stairs to the door of the royal vault. The sound of Assyrian soldiers breaking into the palace filtered down the stairwell. Cries of maidservants mixed with the fury of a sword fight in the main hall and Hoshea quickly locked the vault door behind them.

The glow from a solitary lamp cast a yellow light on a pedestal in the center of the treasury, atop which sat the codex of brass plates, a record given to Manasseh one thousand years before. It contained the prophecies of Israel's prophets and the genealogy of Joseph, who was Viceroy of Egypt, down to the reign of King Hoshea. On a red silk cloth next to the plates lay the royal sword Joseph gave to his son Ephraim. The relics had been passed from generation to generation for a millennium until they came to rest in this vault. Their possessor had natural claim to a royal birthright.

Hoshea wrapped the relics in sackcloth and the men escaped the palace by a subterranean passage that emptied into a forest of cedar. The trees gave enough cover to reach the summit of Mount Gerizim without being seen. From there the three men could see the fire that consumed the capital city. The Northern Kingdom of Israel was no more, fallen to the Assyrians.

Five days later, Hoshea and his sons arrived in Jerusalem with the relics. The ruler of the Southern Kingdom granted Hoshea a residence in the upper city and deeded him a thousand acres of land west of the capital, the largest single tract of land in all of Judah. It was suitable for growing olives, though nearly all of it sat uncultivated.

When King Hoshea died, the younger son lured his brother into taking the thousand acres as an inheritance, while he kept the modest estate in the city—and the relics. It was an easy bargain; with no kingdom left to rule, the older brother gladly took the estate and agreed to his younger brother's conditions, covenanting for full title to the land in exchange for the promise that his lineage and claim to the national treasures would forever remain their secret. Not even his children would know of their true birthright.

As time passed, the younger of the two princes was acknowledged as the sole heir to the relics. What he did not know was that God would raise up a righteous descendant of Joseph through the loins of his elder brother—a chosen prophet who would deliver the relics to a new land of promise.

120 Years Later, Jerusalem

The first time the Babylonians invaded, it was a short war that ended with a three-month siege of Jerusalem. Although the city was not destroyed in the conflict as it would be ten years later, it was not a peaceful takeover. There were fatalities on both sides and counted among the dead of the Jews were three heirs to the national treasures. They should not have perished in the conflict; they had no ties to the military except through their brother and son who survived them, a man by the name of Laban.

Laban was the only cavalryman in his family. His older brothers and father did not share his passion for military life and made their fortunes in the gold trade. But this morning it was Laban, youngest of three sons, who drafted his family into service along with fifty other men, none of them soldiers. He assigned each a sturdy horse from the king's stables and a sword from the commissary. They had little training and even less understanding of what they were about to face, with the Babylonian army surrounding the city and an oil fire burning the east gate to the ground.

Laban rode past the motley column of conscripts, down past his father and two brothers. He wished them luck before charging the entire company to keep the Babylonian soldiers from entering the city by the east gate. At the crack of his whip they galloped out of the livery and onto King Street.

Laban reined into stride behind them, but pulled up to watch his father and two brothers round the corner at the bottom of the hill, headed for Jerusalem's lower city. He hadn't told them the Babylonian army had already breached the east gate and massed two hundred men inside the walls. They were riding into an ambush, one he knew they would never escape. It was the last time Laban ever saw his family alive.

A man dressed in a black robe appeared out of the shadows. "So, the treasures are now yours and yours alone." He spoke with a voice that grated like nails on slate. The man's long thin nose and sunken features stood out in the moonlight. It was Zadock, Chief Elder of the Jews, and his graying hair poked out from under his turban and hedged about his neck. He smoothed the pleats in his costly black dress. "You are the last living heir to the relics." He grabbed the bridle and pulled Laban's horse in close. "You *are* the only one left, aren't you?"

Laban sat straight in the saddle. There was a distant cousin, but with his father and brothers gone, Laban was the only one who knew the blood relative's identity. The cousin himself didn't know he was related. It was a carefully arranged plan devised by Laban's great grandfather, the youngest prince of the Northern Kingdom. Laban nodded slowly, his eyes meeting Zadock's penetrating stare. "There are no others."

"Be off with you, then." Zadock let go of the bridle. "You must save the relics before the Babylonians reach your father's treasury."

"They know?"

"The Babylonians have their spies. They know where the most valuable spoils are hidden."

The sword and brass plates were legal proof, two witnesses testifying to Laban's royal lineage, and today he would claim them his, as long as he kept them from falling to the Babylonians. He was the only direct, living descendant of that Joseph who interpreted Pharaoh's dream. At least that was the story he would tell anyone who questioned his inheritance.

Zadock slapped Laban's horse on the rump. "Get to the relics before they're taken."

Jerusalem

Six hundred and one years before
the birth of the Anointed One

CHAPTER 1

Firemaster was Aaron's birthright. He was the eldest son of Jonathan the blacksmith and it was his chore to set the morning fire in the freshly bricked and mortared furnace that was to be the lifeblood of his father's newly built smithy. The smelting oven stood as high as a mule's head. Narrow air vents peppered the walls. A wide chimney vented more air than three men could pump with bellows. And a thick metal door sealed in more heat than ten open hearths could muster on this sultry August morning.

Only blacksmiths from Sidon knew the mysteries of steelmaking, and Aaron with his father and brother had worked for years among Phoenician smiths. They were members of Sidon's artisan guild and were sworn to keep the secret of the smelting oven from Jews in this part of the world.

Aaron filled a clay mold with iron ingots, placed it among the white-hot coals and latched the door to let the ore melt while he tended to other chores. There was wood to chop, a row of coal bins to fill and a grinding stone to repair. He filled the coal bins first while listening for the sounds of melting ore coming from the smelter. The iron was supposed to sputter like Mama's lamb stew, cracking now and again as it turned to a thick soup. Aaron picked up the axe and started chopping on a piece of wood when a loud blast shook the chimney and rattled the rafters. He set the wood aside, walked a quick circle around the oven, and checked for cracks in the new bricks. None had split; the mortar held and the chimney hadn't come loose. His smithing apron was hanging on its peg by the coal bins. If Papa were here, he'd insist that Aaron put it on to protect him from the heat, but there was no time to worry about what Papa would have him do. The smelting oven needed his tending, now!

Aaron swung open the thick metal door. The smelting mold had cracked; red-hot ore spilled out the sides and splattered onto the oven floor. A bad mold. The air pockets hadn't been properly pressed out of the clay before it was fired and the mold had burst wide open in the heat. Aaron had purchased the mold from the least expensive potter in the city and now, despite the savings, they had lost a full day of smelting. He reached the tongs into the oven to save the ore when another blast splintered what was left of the clay mold. A large fragment hit him in the belly, tearing through his tunic and charring his flesh. He slapped at the smoldering cloth as another blast shot a slug of clay into his right temple, slicing a gash three fingers wide in the side of his head.

He went to the ground, his vision blurred and his mind numb to the molten ore that poured from the oven and began to pool at his feet. The smell of burning flesh filled the air, and all he was able to do before he fell unconscious was offer a silent prayer.

God of Israel, save me.

In the months following the accident, Jonathan, Aaron's father, came to work alone every morning. Not a single strand of gray showed on his forty-year-old head of black hair, though the memory of Aaron's accident gave him reason for his age to show. He marched up High Street at a pace to exhaust men half his age. Walking any slower was too painful. It allowed far too much time to ponder his son's plight. Jonathan had moved his family to Jerusalem after the war with Babylon, thinking to make a decent living in a city that had lost all its blacksmiths. What he hadn't planned on was doing it without the help of his eldest son.

Jonathan paused for a moment at the clay yards of Josiah the potter. High stone walls surrounded the property and the firing yard within stood silent in the early morning. The potter never required his servants to start work before sunrise. If Jonathan had only purchased the man's expensive clay molds from the beginning, none of this would have happened. Josiah was the city's finest potter. He mixed white sand into his clay and cured his pottery before selling it. A mold from Josiah's firing yard would never have split open in the smelting oven and knocked Aaron senseless. But Jonathan was new in the city, and with his blacksmithing business struggling, he could hardly afford the potter's prices.

Beyond the pottery yard stood the entrance to the now abandoned blacksmithing district. Jonathan lowered his head as he approached, keeping his gaze on the cobblestones and stealing glances up at the shops lining his way. His own pain was deep enough; he didn't need to stare at the misfortune of others.

The men who once owned these shops were gone now, all of them taken captive after the war with Babylon. Broken chimney flues rose above the rooftops like sentries guarding these silent grounds where bellows, anvils, and grinding stones once echoed the cry of commerce. Hardly anything remained of the first shop on the corner. Not one stone remained of the north wall; the chimney was leveled and the hearth wrecked beyond repair. Jonathan would have offered a prayer for the unknown blacksmith; but he offered so few prayers, it was best not to stir heaven to a remembrance of him.

The door of the shop across the street whined on its hinges, surrendering to the wind like a white flag raised in defeat. Jonathan peered into the darkness beyond the door. The roof had fallen in, but all you'd need here were a few beams, some packed clay, and a hearty dose of ambition. The walls looked sturdy and when Jonathan tugged on the door frame it didn't budge, not even the width of a barleycorn. But this shop was destined to remain in disrepair, along with all the other shops in the war-torn district, until other smiths came to Jerusalem and laid claim to property just as Jonathan had with the last shop on the street, the one at the top of the hill. He marched toward it. The precisely rounded chimney flues he'd masoned last month rose from the clay roof like twin spires on a temple shrine, calling him to kindle a fire and make a smithing noise inside. Of all the shops in the district, he'd chosen to rebuild this one. The front door smelled of fresh olive wood cut with his axe and locked with a bright brass latch forged by his own hand. There were new ovens inside and three storage bins for iron ore, copper, and wood.

The only thing lacking was a pot of money left on the doorstep by an angel from heaven. With that kind of luck, Jonathan would have no trouble making this shop his shop. The Elders of the Jews hadn't lowered their asking price in three months, and it seemed he'd pay borrower's fees forever. In Sidon he'd owned his own property and there was always plenty of work for a blacksmith with the reputable distinction of steelmaker. But here, among the Jews at Jerusalem, he might never raise enough to purchase the property. He was the first smith to arrive after the war and no one could afford his ironwork—far less his steelmaking.

Jonathan crossed to the ovens and set three logs over a pile of kindling. He struck the flint over the wood, but stopped when he saw the marks on the floor. The flickering light danced over the dark blemish at the foot of the oven. He had to remove Aaron's bloodstains; he would never be able to buy this shop from the Elders if they became aware of what happened—especially concerning Aaron's rescue. If that story got out, he'd be accused of believing in miracles like the Rekhabites, and his business could ill afford such slander.

Jonathan took out a chisel and rasped it over the tile, but his scraping didn't remove the blood and he cursed the day it was spilt. Foolish boy! How did Aaron allow this to happen? If only he'd been more careful, he wouldn't be suffering the scars of his terrible accident, and Jonathan wouldn't have to live in fear of the Elders finding out how he was saved.

Footsteps sounded at the door.

"Who's there?" Jonathan stood over the bloodstains. "Is that you, Aaron?"

"Fine morning to you, blacksmith."

It was neither of his eldest sons, Aaron or Daniel, who darkened the doorway, but a gaunt man with flowing black robes, an even blacker turban tied with a white sash, and a grating voice that seared itself into Jonathan's mind—not because the words resonated from deep in the stranger's throat or because they fell from his mouth in labored breaths, but because a wretched feeling swelled in Jonathan's chest upon hearing the man speak. When the stranger stepped closer, moving the shadows from his face, Jonathan knew him immediately. He usually reserved his reverence for holy men, but the Chief Elder's visit bordered on holiness and he bowed. Before him stood Zadock, the noblest prince in the city, a man who sat in judgment with the Elders of the Jews and to whom fell the final word on every point of law, including the sale of this property. Why was Zadock here? It was not an Elder's task to collect rent.

Locks of gray hair poked out from under the rim of the man's turban. "How is Jerusalem's newest smith?"

Jonathan held the chisel behind his back. "I'm the only smith, sir."

"So you are." Zadock turned his gaze to the smelting oven. "I see you've built your invention."

"I learned the steel trade in Sidon."

"Living among Phoenician blacksmiths has served you well." Zadock's eyes were dark and impossible to read. "Tell me of your steelmaking skills."

"I can smelt anything you need, sir. Name the work and I'll see that it's done to your liking."

Zadock played with the oven door. It creaked open and shut on three metal hinges inlaid into limestone brick with alabaster mortar. "A peculiar piece of work."

"The door holds in the heat."

"I suppose it prevents accidents as well."

"I've built the oven to be safe," Jonathan said slowly.

Zadock trained his gaze on Jonathan. "I understand smithing can be perilous work."

"It has its risks."

"That's what I'm here to discuss with you."

"The dangers of smithing?"

"Risks." Zadock didn't flinch when he spoke, didn't even blink. "*We* have something in mind for you."

Jonathan looked past Zadock into the dark, predawn street to see who accompanied him. But he was alone, and since they had just met this morning for the first time, Jonathan had no way of knowing who *we* included. "What sort of risks, sir?"

"It's smithing work." Zadock leaned in close and Jonathan could smell the thick aroma of frankincense on his robe. "We hire only the finest artisans."

"You'll like my steel."

"I'm sure I will." Zadock shut the oven door. "You'll need your own shop. A respectable steelmaker like yourself shouldn't have to rent." He swept his arms over the expanse of the smithy. "See me in council chambers the first of next week with an offer for this, this . . ." The sleeves of his robe flapped about like a raven's wings. "This place."

Jonathan took a deep breath and blew it out slowly. The Chief Elder apparently didn't know about Aaron's accident. Zadock strode to the door but glanced back before going into the street. "By the way, my condolences to your son. It's a miracle he survived."

Miracle? That was the language of Rekhabites. Jonathan dropped his chisel and it clanged on the bloodied tiles until he silenced it with his foot.

"It was luck, sir," Jonathan said.

Zadock flicked away the ash that had settled onto his robe. "You're wise, blacksmith. Very wise." A subtle smile formed across his face. It was a smile that said Jonathan had passed his first test. "No reason to grant God credit for something he didn't earn." Zadock spun around and went into the street, his flowing black robes dancing about his ankles.

Jonathan followed the Chief Elder out the door to offer a parting word of thanks, but he was gone, vanished into the thick air of the alley running alongside the shop. He leaned against the doorpost, his head turned toward heaven. *Thank you, God, but no thanks.* He didn't need any divine luck to make this property his property. He could do without heaven sending an angel with a pot of money to leave on his doorstep.

He'd found his own angel.

Yaush, military governor of Fort Lakhish, stood outside the main gate in his military dress uniform to see to the delivery of wine. He

usually let the quartermaster deal with shipments, but with Laban, the new captain of the guard, expected this afternoon, he left nothing to chance. Yaush had new silver buttons sewn onto his tunic and new cloth sewn into the four stripes decorating his shoulders. His brass helmet was polished bright and a red plume dyed from the tail feathers of a peacock sprouted out the top. He had his sword sharpened on the fort's grinding wheel and he had purchased a new leather kilt that was delivered only last evening.

Fort Lakhish stood on the summit of Mount Jershon overlooking the southern leg of the trade route. Nearly two miles of winding switchbacks led from the valley floor to the main gate. Lakhish's impregnable double walls were built of solid limestone, each block ten cubits wide and weighing more than four oxen could rope-drag to the summit. There were towers at each turn in the wall, including the northeast jog built on the edge of a steep canyon where no sane invader dared attack.

The military spared no expense on the construction of their most important fortress. The watchtowers stood high enough to see into the next valley, and the signal station was the largest ever constructed by the Hebrews. The stone platform was stocked with dry timber ready to light and send a signal fire twenty-five miles north to Jerusalem.

Yaush scanned the outside walls of Lakhish. The fort was in good repair. There were no weak stones in the wall, the supply bins were well stocked, and the wells provided plenty of drinking water. Though to be honest, his men quenched more thirst down at the inn than they ever did from the well. And Yaush agreed with his men's tastes. Uriah the Innkeeper knew the secret to making sweet wines, fresh from the vine. So fine that Yaush ordered plenty for Captain Laban's inspection of Fort Lakhish.

Uriah steered his mule cart around the last bend and climbed to the gates. "Good afternoon, Governor."

"Is it all here?" Yaush walked to the sideboard and peered into the cart.

"Forty bottles of my newest wine." Uriah reined his mule to a stop. He was a thirty-one-year-old man who didn't look a day over eighteen. He had a thin but strong build with brown eyes, rose-red cheeks, and a smile that won over the heart of every customer who frequented his inn. He, with his wife and three children, lived with Uriah's father in a small home behind their inn. He was a good citizen and a fine father despite rumors that he had religious leanings that were not in harmony with those of the priests. The Rekhabites called Uriah a prophet. But Yaush didn't worry about the reports. He was old enough to remember living among the prophets of years gone by, and if he weren't the governor of southern Judah, he would have a mind to entertain some of Uriah's religious zeal.

"Excellent, son." Yaush slapped the sideboard of Uriah's cart. "That's exactly what Captain Laban will need to quench his thirst after the ride from Jerusalem."

"Laban's coming here?" Uriah spoke quickly, his brown eyes darting about and his broad smile fading.

"Do you know the man?"

"I've heard things."

"Laban is a clever soldier." Yaush tucked the ends of his tunic under his kilt and straightened the short sleeves over his upper arm. "He's only been captain of the guard for three months, and from what I hear, he's made some excellent changes at the other outposts along the trade route."

"I would agree that he's a clever soldier, but not a wise Jew."

"What do you mean, son?"

Uriah started the mule toward the gate. "I'll deliver the wine to the quartermaster and be on my way."

Yaush took him by the arm. "Tell me what you know about the man."

"Why not ask Captain Laban himself?" Uriah pointed toward the fort's approach, where a chariot and a company of riders were making their way up the winding trail.

Two black stallions led the two-wheeled vehicle, their sleek coats glistening in the afternoon sun. The driver cracked a whip and steered them around the sharp turns and up to the gate. When they came to a stop, Laban stepped out and gazed over the valley below.

Yaush took a bottle of wine from Uriah's cart, pulled the cork and handed it to Laban. "Welcome to Lakhish, sir."

Laban took a long drink. "It lacks bite, but it has a good flavor." He passed his tongue over his lips. "Where did you get this, Governor?"

"I make the wines, sir." Uriah stepped from behind the front board. "Down in the village."

"Qiryat Ye'arim, a quaint little place." Laban glanced north to the small town. "You make your home down there, do you?"

"My inn is that large building on the main road."

Laban stared over the lip of the bottle. "Uriah, isn't it?"

"Yes, sir."

"I've heard of you." Laban turned the bottle in his hand and smiled as he swirled the wine. "How do you make this so sweet?"

"Every family has its secrets, Captain."

"They do, do they?" Laban's smile disappeared beneath the thin line of his beard.

"Men who rise to power keep many secrets."

Laban threw the wine bottle down the hillside and it broke on the rocks below. "What do you know about my family?"

Yaush said, "Don't mind Uriah, he's just a local innkeeper."

"He better not be one of those Rekhabites."

"Oh no, sir. Uriah's not one of them." Yaush got another bottle of wine, pulled the cork and handed it to Laban. "He's a good fellow."

Laban pushed Yaush aside and turned the full force of his gaze onto Uriah. "Tell me what you know!"

Uriah held his ground, the end of his beardless chin brushing the captain's shoulder. "Thus saith the Lord, put away the evil of your doings." Uriah's eyes took on a certain light and Yaush looked around to see if the sun had come out from behind a cloud. It hadn't. Uriah was standing in full daylight, but his youthful face appeared brighter than before. He said, "It is written in the proverbs that treasures of wickedness profit nothing, but righteousness delivereth from death."

"What do you know about my treasures?" Laban took a step back, his calf rubbing against the winecart's sideboard. His glance flitted from Uriah, then to Yaush and back to Uriah. "No, don't answer that." He shook the wooden planks in the cart, cracking wine bottles and spilling the red liquid between the floorboards. "Take your wine and your foolish faith back to your inn." He stepped into his chariot and the driver whisked him through the gate, the wheels raising a cloud of dust.

Yaush stood with hands on his hips and watched the chariot disappear past the gatekeeper. "This isn't going to be an easy inspection."

"It's Laban's treasures that upset him." Uriah stood next to Yaush.

"Why do you say that, boy?"

"I sense he fears them."

"I didn't think Laban feared anything."

"He will learn to fear the treasures of his wickedness." Uriah turned his mule cart around and started toward Qiryat Ye'arim.

CHAPTER 2

A meadowlark chirped the arrival of morning. Its nest obscured the innocent faces of three cherubs chiseled into the facade of the stone arch that stretched above the east gate, like a cloud adorning the entrance to heaven. But this was not heaven's gate, it was Jerusalem's, and could hardly be mistaken for a cloud with its span of forty limestone blocks set without mortar and held in place by a keystone. It was thousand-year-old stone, badly quarried and with enough fissures to come crashing down under its own weight.

Ruth, Jonathan's wife, detoured across the square toward the gate, but pulled up before passing under the arch. She made a habit never to stand under it. Whenever she had reason to leave the city by this gate, and she found few reasons to do so, it was with a quick nod to the watchman and three brisk strides. Isaiah said not one stone in Jerusalem would be left standing upon another, and Ruth had no reason to doubt the prophet's word no matter how many years dead he was. Better to trust Isaiah and live than dawdle beneath the arch and suffer who-knew-what fate.

She ventured close enough to notice the new wooden gate was propped open with sandbags. Odd. The watchman never unlocked before daybreak, except on holy days when the large-bellied high priest bathed in the Gihon Spring—an immodest rite no matter how early the hour or how holy the priest. Odder still, the gate was left unguarded, but there were no signs the watchman had struggled with robbers. His were the only footprints in the dust.

A whinny drew Ruth's glance away from the gate and down along the wall. A powerful horse stood hidden in the shadows, pawing at the cobblestones. At this hour and with the gate left without a watch it could be the mount of a robber, just the sort she should avoid. She'd heard the stories about the robber band of Shechem. They lived in the hills around Jerusalem, sleeping in caves by day and doing their evil deeds by night, and a chance meeting with one of them was not a risk she cared to take. A robber wouldn't treat a woman alone in the streets at this hour with due respect.

If the animal or its dark-clothed rider saw her, they gave no hint. They faced the other way, leaving her free to slip behind the gatepost. Let the rider do what he would, but let her go unnoticed. She stayed crouched behind the gatepost, sharing her hiding place with the foul stench of rotted animal fat. The grease slicking the pivot stones hadn't been changed since the gate was rebuilt after the war. It wasn't enough she had to stand beneath the arch with stones that could fall on her at any moment, she had to endure that wicked smell. Why hadn't she picked a more suitable recess in the wall, an obscure crevice without stone overhead and with adequate ventilation? But she had no other choice than to remain there and pray the arch wouldn't fall, while holding her nose until the rider went his way so she could go hers. And heaven willing, he would go quickly.

She peered around the gatepost and caught a better view of the rider, judging him to be a military man, not a robber, though he didn't holster a weapon or girdle heavy breastplates. He was too slight of stature to be anything but a courier, and he had a mailbag strapped over one shoulder. His cap of short hair was combed straight back as if riding into the wind, and his tight-fitting tunic wrapped his torso as skin covers the body.

The courier was a young soldier named Hosha Yahu, assigned to mail delivery in southern Judah, his routes covering cities south of Jerusalem. He wore nothing that would slow his animal. They were a pair outfitted for speed, a fleet horse and a light rider.

Ruth would have abandoned her hiding place, relieved Hosha Yahu wasn't a robber, if only he hadn't reined about and straightened to attention as another horse approached at full gallop. A white Arabian raced into the square from the upper city. Its braided mane peaked, fell, and rose again in cadence with its stride. The saddle was all show, silver plates sewn into darkly tanned leather with threads made of the same precious metal. The owner's care of the animal was meticulous down to its tail, cut short and braided around a cord. Not a comfortable fashion for the horse, with its reach to shoo flies sheared in half, but certainly elegant as the captain of the guard's horse should look.

Ruth saw the Arabian owner's face when he slowed to a canter and reined in next to the courier. Captain Laban seemed a timeless figure, dressed in full brass armor. The leather cords of his breastplates strained with his every breath.

"Where's the watchman?" Hosha asked.

"I sent him off." Laban scanned the square, his gaze pausing on the gatepost where Ruth hid. She didn't move, and with a bit of luck Laban shifted his stare farther down the wall to the deserted guard station before turning across the square to the line of darkened shop fronts. "No one's to know of your ride until I catch the palace informant."

Ruth pulled the collar of her robe around her ears. This conversation was not intended for her and she would have plugged her ears with her fingers if it weren't for the smell. She kept a firm grip on her nose and prayed a childish prayer. Keep the stones from falling and the foul smell from choking her. And if there were enough blessings in heaven, let the angels stop her ears to keep her from hearing what she was about to hear.

"I'm getting closer." Laban leaned over the neck of his horse. "The informant is someone very close to me. Someone who knows my family well."

"I don't mean to trouble you, sir, but your father and brothers died in the war." Hosha glanced at the rebuilt gate with its new wooden slats and iron braces. "At this very spot."

"My only troubles come from men who question my inheritance." Laban tightened his grip on the reins. "The relics make me King of Israel."

"This is Judah, sir."

Ruth peered around the gatepost, careful not to draw Laban's eye. What did the captain mean? There had been no kingdom of Israel for a hundred and twenty years—the Assyrians had seen to that. There was no Northern Kingdom, not one acre of land over which to rule.

"I know our history, boy." Laban worked the tip of his beard between his fingers. "Do you know mine?"

Hosha met his stare. "You're descended of Joseph who was sold into Egypt. Everyone knows that."

Laban sat erect in the saddle. "I'm the only one."

"No one thinks otherwise."

"The enemy should honor my lineage."

"Sir, the war's been over nearly six months."

"I'm talking about the palace informant," said Laban.

Hosha checked his reins. "Oh, that enemy."

"He's a Rekhabite."

"Are you certain?"

"The informant is one of them." Laban's horse reared against his tight hold on the reins. "Cursed traitors."

The clap of the animals' hooves shook the wood planks that framed Ruth's hiding place. Rekhabites. She'd heard the stories about them, named for the religious vows they made, but until now she'd tried to convince herself they didn't exist, that they were conjured up by the neighborhood gossip. Now Laban gave life to the tale. She steadied herself against the gatepost until the rumbling underfoot and the whinnies stopped and she could forget what little she knew about the Rekhabites. Forget that they listened to the words of the prophet Uriah and his preaching of an Anointed One—with a common man's name no less. Yeshua the Anointed One. If that wasn't blasphemy she didn't know what kind of abomination was. She would never repeat that phrase. It was not in her to use profanity. Most of all she'd forget that the Rekhabites accused Laban of crimes against the people of Judah. What did she care? Let them accuse Laban of whatever sin they would and believe whatever foolish doctrines they wanted to believe, so long as she didn't have to endure their repulsive religious symbol. Of all the patterns on earth, none struck more fear into her heart than the mark of the Rekhabites.

Laban said, "You're to ride to Fort Lakhish this morning."

"A letter delivery?" Hosha asked. "That's what this is about?"

"What did you expect, a call to arms?"

"Your orders were unclear."

"My orders are secret."

"That's always the procedure for your letters."

"Is it?" Laban drew his horse in close enough to grip the courier's delivery bag. "Or do you read my letters before you deliver them?"

"I've been taught better."

Laban backed his horse, blocking passage through the gate. "Why don't you tell me exactly what you've been taught about Rekhabites."

"If you mean, am I one of them, no, sir, I've not been baptized by their prophet."

"I can get a record of washings and anointings from the temple scribe. What I want is your oath. There's no better assurance than a man's life."

Hosha tore the sleeve of his riding tunic. "As I now rend this garment, so will I lay down my life if ever I am found to be a Rekhabite!"

"See that you deliver this letter personally to Commander Yaush at Fort Lakhish. Don't leave it with the quartermaster." Laban handed Hosha a parchment scroll. The soft leather draped over his hand. "It's far too important."

"That's part of my usual route."

"It isn't your usual mail."

Hosha slowly fitted the letter into his pouch and slung the delivery bag over his shoulder. Twice each month he rode the fifty-mile round trip delivery route, through five small villages, the last one called Qiryat Ye'arim, then on to Fort Lakhish before turning back to Jerusalem. It would have been as unimportant as all of his other routes, except that the prophet Uriah lived in the village below the fort. Hosha was born there and when he rode through, he stopped for long visits.

Laban chewed cedar bark to sweeten his breath, and spat out a black cud, saying, "The letter has orders for Uriah's arrest. I want him silenced. I'll not tolerate him spreading rumors about me in the name of God." He reached over and slapped the courier's horse on the rump. "If it means anything to you, soldier, Godspeed."

Ruth would have abandoned her hiding place once Hosha bolted through the gate and onto the road leading south into the hills beyond Bethlehem toward Fort Lakhish, but she wasn't allowed that freedom. Another horse trotted out of the dark alley next to the carpentry, appearing out of the shadows like a dark spirit from another world. The rider's bare arms were thick rods and his loose-fitting kilt hardly covered his powerful legs. He untied his bandana and let his long hair fall in ratted thatches at the small of his back. It was like beholding the resurrected Samson of old, his long hair a symbol of uncommon strength—the same mark worn by the leader of the band of Shechem's robbers. Shechem was their king, a zealot leading them after the treasures of the world and the pleasures of the flesh.

"You scared your courier, Captain. Scared him good." Shechem reined in next to Laban. "Maybe too good."

"He'll go straight to Uriah with that letter now."

"He always goes to Uriah with your mail. And he will this time if you haven't warned him off with your threats."

"You can track him down. I pay you more than enough for that."

Shechem took out his dagger. "I don't do this for money."

Laban and Shechem were strange partners from unlike ways of life. The law Laban had sworn to uphold mandated the slaying of robbers without trial and without mercy, and now he worked in league with one. Thieves were bad enough: pitiful criminals, loners, working their craft among their neighbors. They stole bread from the baker, sheep from the farmer and coins from a blind man's purse. And for their misdeeds they were compelled to repay the stolen goods and make a sin offering at the temple. But robbers! They were the most ruthless of outlaws, burning farms and besieging villages, plundering the trade route, and raining terror down on whole cities from their mountain hideouts. With their oaths, they planted men on government councils and assassinated heads of state. And for their crimes, they were not tried by a judge, but simply beheaded by the first man to catch them.

"We have an oath between us." Shechem leaned forward in the saddle, close enough to lay the dagger's tip to Laban's chest. "I keep mine and I expect you to keep yours."

Laban scanned the horizon, watching the courier's trail of dust rise and spread like a cloud against the morning sky. Hosha Yahu was well onto the plains south of Jerusalem. "You're sure he's the palace informant?"

"Everything points to him." Shechem shook his head enough to make his long hair jump onto his shoulders. "He's the only man in your army who frequents the palace. He reads all your mail and he stops at Uriah's inn every ride through Lakhish."

"Report to Captain Yaush when you arrive. He'll help with the arrests."

"Arrests?" Shechem held up his dagger and grinned. It was like watching a hyena smile. "There are better ways to silence traitors."

"You'll do this my way." Laban handed over another set of orders. It was his eighteenth letter sent to Lakhish about the prophet. "Uriah and the courier are to be in prison before the week's out."

"I don't take orders, Captain." Shechem prodded his horse to the entrance and glanced back before going out. "You do things your way, and I do things mine." He reared his horse and bolted onto the road, chasing the courier's trail of dust.

Once Ruth was certain they must be gone, she stepped from behind the foul-smelling gatepost and unplugged her nose. Finally! She took a deep breath, grateful to be on her way and hopeful she could forget what she'd overheard. What she didn't plan on was Laban lingering, watching after Shechem until long after the dust settled. Her only recourse was to keep going, striding across the square with the determination of a shopper on the way to market, though the market didn't open for hours.

She kept close to the wall, but any hope to go unnoticed faded when Laban spurred across her path. He pulled so close, Ruth felt the warmth of the horse's breath on her face.

"Why, good morning, Captain." Ruth lifted the hem of her robe. "You're out early for a ride, sir."

"Did you overhear—"

"Nothing." She turned from his penetrating stare. "Nothing at all."

Laban blinked before inspecting each pleat in her robe, every contour of her form. "Treason will not go unpunished in this kingdom."

Ruth tried to step back to escape his stare but the wall stood firm. She was trapped there, bound by his gaze. "Are you charging me, sir?"

"I'm informing you that my commander at Fort Lakhish will have his orders before any Rekhabite can do anything to save Uriah."

"I'm neither a soldier nor a Rekhabite."

"You're Ruth, wife of Jonathan the new blacksmith."

Ruth caught her breath. How did Laban know so much about them? He wasn't the neighborly sort of man who enjoyed the sociality of friendships or the company of strangers. The captain kept commoners at a respectable distance, and since Ruth and her family were without any of the visible graces of wealth, it didn't seem possible he would know her from among any of the throngs of women who made Jerusalem their home. Laban's interrogation goaded her to silence but she couldn't restrain the impulse to ask, "Have we met?"

"You came to Jerusalem three months ago with your husband, who hopes to acquire one of the blacksmith shops abandoned after the war. And no, we've never met. Though I do make it my business to know the citizens who come and go. Just like your husband knows the secrets of steelmaking." Laban shifted his weight and the saddle leather squeaked. "He does know them, doesn't he?"

"Steelmaking is Jonathan's craft." Ruth answered with a calm voice before looking away. She would tolerate his probing gaze no longer. It wasn't proper.

"We have work for him."

Ruth checked the square. Laban was alone and after what she'd overheard she had no desire to inquire who else his *we* included. "Good day." She dismissed herself and started across the square, but Laban reined alongside again and pinned her against the wall. "If you'll excuse me, Captain." She pushed the horse's muzzle aside. "I'm on an errand to the tannery."

Laban didn't take her suggestion or his leave. He followed her, high stepping across the square and down Water Street to the tannery where he stopped across the street beneath the branches of a Joshua tree.

The tanner's shop stood between the masonry and a stable, a two-story limestone building with a roof large enough to stretch twenty pelts over cedar planks and dry them in the sun.

Ruth knocked. "Is anyone in?" She tried the latch. It was bolted. Under any other circumstance she would have left to come back another time, but with Laban scrutinizing her every move she determined it best to knock again. "Is anyone about?"

She was never so thankful than when she heard footsteps stir inside. The tanner unlocked the bolt and cracked open the door. His hair needed a good combing and his eyelids drooped.

"Good morning," Ruth said.

"It would be finer if it weren't for your knocking." He held his eyelids shut, fighting back the arrival of morning.

"If it isn't any trouble, I've come for my husband's smithing apron."

"Trouble, my good lady, would be to have the captain of the guard standing on my porch wanting to search my home."

Ruth worked her lower lip between her teeth. Of all the things the tanner could have said, why that? She glanced at the large door carved with an intricate lattice pattern. "What a lovely door."

"Everyone's a Rekhabite to Laban. We're all spies."

Ruth sniffed the grain in the wood. "Is this made of cedar or olive?"

"It's written that the leaders of the Jews are called by God, but Laban?" The tanner yawned. "Makes you wonder if God hasn't forsaken us for another chosen people."

Ruth sniffed again. "Has to be cedar."

"He's obsessed by those Rekhabites, and for no good reason."

"It has that scent."

"Who does he think he is raising a stir among us law-abiding people anyway?"

"It's the sap."

"Laban?" The tanner scratched his head.

"No, I meant the cedar wood. It has the scent of pine sap." Ruth let go of the door. "I'm sure Laban has good reason for his suspicions."

"He has one reason and it's—"

"It's best I come back another time."

"Nonsense. Your apron's finished drying. I can have it down from the roof in no time."

"Could we speak softly?"

"Don't worry about waking the family. It's time they were up and about."

"That isn't what's troubling me." Ruth shifted aside and let the tanner's gaze drift beyond her, across the street.

"Captain?" The tanner swallowed hard.

Laban reined over, edging the horse's hooves onto the steps and forcing Ruth out of the way. "I'll have a word with you."

The tanner half-closed the door, his beady eyes peering out between the plank and post. "Perhaps another time?"

"Obsessed over the Rekhabites, am I?"

"Concerned would be a better word."

"Everyone's a spy, are they?"

"You heard that?"

"I hear everything." Laban reared his Arabian, its powerful legs kicking open the door and ripping the planks off the frame. He spurred inside and pinned the tanner between the wall and the horse's haunches. "Take off your shirt."

"I don't wear the mark. I swear, I'm no Rekhabite."

"Don't make me undress you." Laban unsheathed his sword. "My hand isn't always steady when I'm on the back of a horse."

The tanner knelt at the horses' hooves with the animal's breath blowing his hair back in bursts. It was a degrading thing to watch, like a sinner begging forgiveness of a God who did not deal in mercy. He stripped to the waist, bearing his chest for Laban to inspect. No mark. He was free of the sign the most ardent of Rekhabites wore on a brass chain over their breast bone.

Laban sent the tanner to the roof to fetch the apron, then cantered out the front door, coming round in the street. He relaxed his hold on the reins, sat back in the saddle and tipped his head to Ruth. "We'll be by to see your husband." Then he trotted up the street toward the upper city, calm as a man out for a ride through his vineyards.

"Is he gone?" The tanner descended the last steps from the roof with the smithing apron in hand, his glance darting about the room.

"We're alone."

"Good thing. This door wouldn't stand any more of his interrogating." The tanner shook the latch and another plank fell off its nails. "Curses." He picked it up and fitted it back in place. "Laban's afraid of something. You look at him sometimes when he doesn't think anybody's watching. I say he's murdered men who got in his way. You can see it in his eyes." He tugged on the planks, checking each one.

"Most people think him a hero. He saved the national treasures from falling into the hands of the Babylonians during the war, but lost his father and brothers, God rest their souls. They were good men, nothing like Laban. Then all of a sudden . . ." He snapped his fingers. "Laban's made captain of the guard. It isn't common for a soldier to rise so quickly. Thirty years old and he's reached the highest office in the military. How does he do that?" The tanner clucked his tongue. "It's because of the relics he keeps in his treasury. The finest sword in the kingdom and a history kept on brass plates. They belong to Laban and that makes him royalty. Just the sort of man the new King Zedekiah should fear." The tanner stepped close enough to whisper. "You didn't hear me speak that before the coronation. If word got out I spread that rumor, I'd lose more than a good door." He looked at Ruth standing with the apron held close, like a comforting blanket that could protect her from all she'd heard. "I've gone and upset you, haven't I?"

"I'm fine."

"Don't worry about Laban. You're safe as long as you don't associate with the Rekhabites. They preach some foolish belief about the ending."

"I really must go."

"Rekhabites call it the fulfilling of Moses' Law, but it's blasphemy, pure and simple."

"How much for the apron?"

"You should hear me out. It's for your own good." The tanner nodded. "It was the prophet Uriah who accused Laban of conspiracy. Something about his lineage and those relics of his. I'd be careful before listening to any of those prophets."

"There are other prophets?"

"You are new here, aren't you?" The tanner took Ruth by the arm. "You should've stayed in Sidon. You'd have found more tolerance there."

Ruth pulled back. "We've not had any trouble since we came."

"That's because you've yet to take sides." He wagged his finger at her. "I don't support any of them. Side with Laban and the Elders of the Jews and you'll go to hell as sure as the night is dark. Side with the Rekhabites and you'll go to prison as sure as the sun rises. Why, I'll bet you three shekels you'll see Uriah in the palace dungeons before the year's out."

Ruth lowered her head. The tanner was right about prison, but it would happen much sooner. She opened her coin purse and handed over three shekels.

The tanner said, "I can't take that. It's a sin to wager on the life of a prophet."

"It's for the apron."

"That sells at six."

Ruth turned back her sleeve and pulled up the stitches until another shekel fell from inside her cuff. "Four and I'll take the apron."

"Done." Somehow the tanner knew she had no more money. He asked, "Is your husband's shop doing well?"

"There isn't a lot of money in the city since the war ended, but I'll not let my husband go another smelting day without a good apron. Not after the . . ."

"Accident?"

"You know about that?"

"Only that your oldest son was hurt." The tanner patted Ruth on the hand. "My sympathies."

"That's all you heard? No name?"

The tanner cocked his ear. "What name?"

"My son Aaron is healing well." Ruth bit her lip to keep it from trembling and to keep herself from saying any more about the name of the one Aaron said would heal him. If anyone learned he'd uttered that name the whole family could be accused of believing as the Rekhabites believed. And there was no name under heaven with that kind of healing power, no matter how much faith the Rekhabites placed in the Anointed One they called Yeshua.

"Tell me something." The tanner scratched his chin and leaned forward. "Which side do you favor? Laban and the Elders of the Jews or the Rekhabites and the prophets?"

Ruth tucked the apron under her arm. "On the advice of a good tanner, I've decided not to take sides."

She started home.

CHAPTER 3

Jonathan entered the yard from the street. He swung open the front gate with enough force to pull down the vines that clung to the wood planks, the same vines his sons should have trimmed back when they first arrived last spring. The grape harvest would have been double if the boys had pruned the leaders. He pressed the tendrils against the brick mortar hoping they'd take hold and the harvest would be saved. But the vines had grown far too gangly to offer much wine for the winter.

He scanned the rooftop where the boys slept during the hot summer nights. The olive trees next to the house had grown over the steps leading to their outdoor bedroom. The longest branches should have been cut and cleared, but his sons were too busy helping him rebuild the blacksmith shop to have been much help around the house. He called their names, Aaron first, then Daniel, but there was no movement on the roof.

Jonathan climbed the steps scaling the outside wall of the house, up to a large olive branch growing across his path. It was covered with fruit, but none of it sweet. The graft hadn't taken and the fruit had gone bitter. Daniel, Jonathan's second son, should have tended it better. Careless boy. It was his duty to score the ends and graft saplings into place, but he never got around to tying them down with cords. He was always busy with other things, always sneaking off to the military grounds to watch the soldiers train. He'd have to temper Daniel's ambition for wrestling despite his talent for throwing men. It was a gift he wasn't modest about. Not less than once a week, usually smelting day when the heat inside the shop was unbearable, Daniel threatened to join the army. Said he was good enough to beat their finest wrestlers, said he could feel it deep down in his soul. Jonathan rattled the branch with his foot and showered olives down over the steps. He didn't remember having time for a soul when he was Daniel's age. Next year he'd have the boy tend the trees properly. Next year. It was always *next year* in Jerusalem.

Daniel appeared at the top of the steps, tunic in hand and wearing nothing but his kilt. The outline of his strapping shoulders and thick arms stood out against the morning sky. He was a sturdy boy, even for a lad of sixteen years. He worked a forging hammer like a man of thirty and he never lost a wrestling match to the stoutest seamen and dock hands in Sidon, men twice his age. Jonathan enjoyed that part of Daniel's wrestling. The winning. In Sidon people knew their family for two things, Jonathan's steelmaking and Daniel's wrestling. But that was before they moved to Jerusalem, when they could afford the time away from the shop to practice something other than blacksmithing.

Daniel's dark eyes were half closed and his straight black hair was matted against his left ear like greased mule skin. He sauntered down, loitering a moment on each step.

"You were to be at the shop before first light," Jonathan said.

"Didn't sleep so well last night." Daniel stretched his arms overhead and yawned.

"Was that you last night, making all that noise?"

"I tossed some grain sacks for a while."

"You kept all of us awake."

"That's how the soldiers at the military grounds train for wrestling."

"You can do that swinging a forging hammer."

Daniel leaned over the edge and peered into the side yard where he'd drawn the boundaries of a wrestling pit between the rows of olive trees. "There'd be a lot more room to wrestle if we got rid of this tree close to the house. It's gone bad, doesn't put out any sweet fruit."

"We're not getting rid of any trees. Next spring I want this one pruned, spliced, and dunged until it's sweet again." Jonathan climbed onto the step next to Daniel, close enough to lay a hand on his shoulder. "We're not soldiers in this house. We're blacksmiths, boy. Do you understand?"

Daniel pulled free. "I'll see to the trees."

But he didn't understand. Not one word. Wielding a hammer all his youth had served him well, and he'd become a respected master forger. He could make a name for himself with his blacksmithing and there'd be good money for his skills as soon as their business started doing well. But Daniel's head had grown as mulish as his arms were strong. He'd find himself a foot soldier, fighting on the front lines of every war the Jews got themselves into if he didn't stay away from military men who recruited boys like Daniel.

Jonathan said, "You don't want to be a soldier."

"I could become an officer. I'm a good enough wrestler to prove myself."

"They don't need wrestlers. They need stout men like you to die for them. You get yourself mixed up with the army and all you'll become is a foot soldier wasting away in some distant outpost on Judah's borders."

"Maybe that's a chance I'm willing to take." Daniel pushed past him, hurdling the last five steps and landing in the courtyard next to the water cistern. He dunked his head, stirring it around like a ladle troubling a pot of water.

The door to the house creaked open and Aaron's tall, thin frame faltered out. He limped over, wincing on the uneven surface of the courtyard stones, each stride slow and teetering. It was like watching a baby take its first step. But behind the pain on his face, a fire of determination burned in his deep blue eyes, an inheritance from Ruth's family. All the women on her side had enough faith to turn mustard seeds into mountains. The men in her lineage were more Assyrian-looking than Jewish, with long bones, uncommonly light-brown hair, and eyes as blue as the Great Sea. The only thing Jonathan had bequeathed to Aaron was a legacy of common sense. If only it could temper the fierce faith that boiled deep in his soul.

Jonathan had always hoped Aaron would marry, build a wing onto their home for his own family and take over the shop one day. That's what the eldest son did as he grew to manhood. But those dreams were gone now, shattered in an instant by one horrible accident, and now Jonathan had to think of another future for his son—one that took into account a good share of the flesh on his feet having been burned away.

Aaron sat beside Daniel and leaned his back against his brother's legs to take the weight off his feet. He opened the cistern's spigot and let the water trickle down his shins and over his feet, washing away the blood. It was the last thing he did each morning before wrapping the bandages around the burns. The same routine he'd followed for two months. Scrape the scabs with a knife to keep the skin from scarring. Scarred skin wouldn't grow enough flesh to cover all the holes the physician had cut out. Next, he stretched the skin by flattening his arch on a board. If he could just grow enough to cover the largest holes it would keep the infections from swelling his feet to the size of melons.

The right foot showed some promise, most of the bone and sinew had pink skin attached. But the left one, well . . . Jonathan lowered his gaze from his son's wounds. That one couldn't possibly heal. The physician wanted it cut off. Too much infection, he'd said, and too little flesh to protect what remained. Aaron begged to keep both limbs, believing God would provide. But not even heaven could bless him with anything more than the life of a lame man begging alms, and the sooner Aaron realized that the better. He'd come to his senses soon. Then Jonathan would call for the doctor to come and remove the bad limb and Aaron could blame God for not sending a cure. Since the day Abraham offered Isaac, Jews had blamed the Almighty for their troubles. God always made the best scapegoat.

Daniel shook the water from his brow, but didn't move his legs from supporting Aaron. "Women like a man to be groomed." He brushed his fingers through his hair.

Aaron said, "There isn't one maid out this early to faint over you."

"I'll wake them up on the way to the shop and I'll cry; 'Here passes Jerusalem's finest wrestler!' And they'll run to the windows and—"

"Why don't you hand me that towel?" Aaron closed the spigot and dabbed the water off his feet. "Did you have a good match last night? That sack of wheat you were wrestling must weigh all of twenty pounds."

"It was a full bushel."

"Did you win or was it a draw?"

"Why don't you stay up and watch?" Daniel snapped the towel at Aaron's backside. "I'm wrestling him again tonight."

Jonathan marched down the steps and stood over Aaron. "Where are your new sandals?"

"Do you really want me to wear those stiff things?"

"I paid the cobbler good money to sew extra leather into the soles. You'll be needing them now that you're coming back to work at the shop."

"I'll wear them, Papa. Soon, real soon." Aaron raised his feet to the breeze.

Jonathan asked, "What are you doing?"

"The midwife across the street says the morning air is good for them. She says the skin needs to breathe."

"You're not giving birth."

"She knows about healing and such."

Jonathan stepped closer, hovering over Aaron. "You didn't tell her about the accident, did you?"

Aaron lowered his head. "There's a reason for what happened to me, Papa."

"God doesn't cripple men."

"He's going to heal me," Aaron said, his blue eyes wide open and pleading. Jonathan understood the boy's pain, but he blinded himself with faith. Aaron still hoped for a miracle, but two whole feet was an impossible cure—beyond what should be hoped for now. It was miracle enough he survived.

"We found you unconscious on the other side of the shop." He leaned over and gripped Aaron's knee. "You were nearly dead."

"I was saved." Aaron pulled away and tucked his knee under his chin. "Just like I told you."

"You don't know who saved you from the ovens. You could have crawled across the shop on your own. People do strange things to escape pain. You said yourself it was all a blur. For all we know, you dreamed the rescue."

"It was no dream. Someone saved me and he gave me a blessing. That part wasn't a blur. I heard it as plain as I hear you. He said my feet are going to heal so I can save the life of a prophet."

"No more of that talk." Jonathan rubbed his hand through his hair. "If that's what you want to believe, you're entitled, but don't go spreading around the notion that God wants you to save the life of a prophet. People hear you telling stories like that and they'll think we're . . ."

"Rekhabites."

"I said, no more." Jonathan's hands turned into fists at his side. He'd forbidden Aaron to tell of his accident. He wouldn't have to be so strict if the boy didn't cling to the childish belief that he would be healed. Even worse was the name Aaron's imagined hero had used in the blessing. It was a common man's name, but the way he used it, why, it bordered on blasphemy. Yeshua the Anointed One. It was the phrase Rekhabites used and it was not to be spoken in this house. Not now, not ever. Not if they wanted the blessings of the Chief Elder in their home. Aaron was not to speak the phrase—no matter how much he believed it had power to heal him.

Jonathan said, "The way you tell about the accident, it's more than enough to condemn us to prison. You're not to have anything to do with Rekhabites. Do you understand?"

Daniel snapped a thick olive branch. "I could break us out of the palace dungeons if I had to."

"No one's going to prison as long as Aaron keeps his accident to himself. If the wrong men hear his story it could hurt our family. Do you understand?"

"I can't deny what happened." Aaron dabbed the ooze from his feet and tied the bandages with a pin knot. "A man pulled me from in front of the ovens and gave me a blessing."

"You may not be able to hide your feet, but you're not to utter a word about the accident to anyone outside this family."

The gate swung open and Ruth stepped in from the street. Her robe caught the morning light and reflected it back. The garment was shot with a new weave she'd learned from an Egyptian tailor. How she crafted such fine clothing Jonathan wasn't certain, but he'd never mistaken it, even in a crowded market. It draped over her straight shoulders and wrapped about her waist with an uncommonly narrow sash. He always teased her that if she stood sideways she'd disappear. But she wasn't weak-boned as Hebrew men thought of thin women. When she had to, she could load a mule cart, swing a hammer, or dig a hole as well as a man.

Ruth rushed to Aaron's side. "What are you doing out here, young man?" She bent over his feet. The right one was fine but blood streaked the bandages of his left one. "I've warned you about doing too much too soon."

"It's nothing," Aaron said.

Ruth checked beneath the wraps. "I want you inside and off your feet."

"Not any more, Mama." Aaron stood and leaned on Daniel, his long, slender body hanging like a limp vine from his brother's shoulder. "Today's my first day back at the shop."

"It isn't good to be on your feet all day."

"I'll sit on a bench." Aaron stood away from Daniel, his feet bearing the full weight of his body. "I'll stand on my head if I have to, but I won't spend another day lying on my back, staring at the ceiling, waiting for the physician to give his permission."

"You lost your cane," Ruth said.

"I whittled a new one yesterday."

"It isn't long enough. You're taller than that and I won't have you bent over like a . . ."

"A cripple?"

"I didn't say that."

"I know what you're thinking. But I'm going to heal."

"Of course you are, son. Of course you are."

"I will." Aaron's gaze moved to Jonathan. "I was given a promise."

Jonathan bit on his lower lip. The story of his accident was not to be repeated aloud.

Ruth tugged on Jonathan's arm. "You'll see he wears his smithing apron, won't you?" She was pleading for his support, but he didn't answer; his gaze was riveted on Aaron. The boy would obey him, and that was his last word. If Aaron wanted to sleep on Jonathan's roof and eat his food, he'd learn to mind or find himself in the street. Well, maybe not the street. Ruth wouldn't allow him that. But the boy would suffer for his disobedience.

Ruth took Daniel's tunic and stuck her fingers through the burn holes in the cloth. Even good linen from her loom didn't last long next to the smelting ovens. "I want your aprons tied on the moment the ovens are fired." She took Daniel by one arm and Aaron by the other. "Is that clear?"

They nodded an obligatory yes and she said, "I have to speak with your father now." When Aaron kept staring at Jonathan she said, "And I'll do it alone." She scooted Aaron toward the front door, careful not to hurry his stride. He was to wake up Elizabeth when he got inside. At twenty, she was the oldest child, and the heaviest sleeper. Then he was to roust Sarah out of bed. Now nine years old, the girl could help her older sister with the early-morning chores. Ruth told him to use the new sandals she'd hung on a peg by the window and not to forget his new cane she half hid in the corner by the front door. She knew Aaron wouldn't tolerate the confines of home any longer.

Ruth took Daniel by the shoulders and pointed him toward the roof. She listed in order everything he was to do before leaving for the shop. She always had to give Daniel a list. Get himself dressed properly, shirt tucked in and hair combed, wake up his little brother, Joshua, who always sneaked out of the house at night to sleep with Aaron and Daniel on the roof, and roll up his sleeping mat before he came down for something to eat.

When the boys were out of earshot, Jonathan said, "Aaron's restless."

"He's been at home for two months." Ruth watched Aaron pull open the front door and disappear inside. "But I worry. The thought of him lying there, burning . . . It's too soon for him to go back to the shop and . . ." Ruth covered her eyes.

"It's time. Coops are for pigeons, not young men."

Ruth brushed away a tear before handing over the new smithing apron to Jonathan. "I bought this for you." The finely tanned leather was cut to fit his robust frame from chest to ankle, just the right size. "It should shield you from the heat. I got it from the finest tannery in the city. The one up the street from the east gate." She played with the sash on her robe the way she did whenever she had a burden that required his ear.

Jonathan asked, "What is it?"

"Nothing."

"I know that look."

Ruth took a deep breath. "This morning, on my way to the tannery, I happened upon the captain of the guard quite by accident. It was all very strange." She dropped the sash and clasped her hands. "Laban knew you by name and said he had some steel he wanted you to smith. He's coming to see you with another man."

"Zadock?"

"I didn't inquire."

"It must be him. The Chief Elder made the same sort of odd request. Something he needs made out of steel."

"You've spoken to him?"

"He'll sell us the shop for whatever we can afford to pay."

Ruth lowered her eyes. "I see."

"You should be happy. This is what we've hoped for ever since we moved here."

"I don't like taking favors from a man like that."

"A man like what?"

"I have a bad feeling about the men the Chief Elder associates with."

"You mean Laban."

"There are others."

"You'll have to put your feelings behind you. This is our chance, the one we've been waiting for."

Ruth turned away, her hands set squarely on her hips. "Once you accept Zadock's kindness, you're obliged."

Jonathan came around in front of her. "And what's wrong with being obliged to the Chief Elder of Jerusalem?"

"Quite more than I'm willing to risk."

"What am I supposed to do?" Jonathan reached for her hand but she pulled away.

"This morning the tanner asked, did we prefer the Elders or the Rekhabites? I told him we didn't take sides."

"I've told you before, we're with the Elders."

"Isn't it better not to take sides?"

"We have to protect our business." Jonathan straightened his shoulders. "And our business is with the Elders."

"But Jonathan . . ."

"Tell the boys I'll meet them at the shop. They're to have the ovens fired before I get there." He walked over and unlatched the gate.

"Is that your last word?"

"The fire box is empty. They'll have to split more wood."

"I don't feel good about this, Jonathan, not good at all."

"I sharpened the axe. Have them chop up the dry olive stump behind the shop."

"Jonathan!"

He stood at the gate facing the street. "I won't let religion keep us from doing what's best for our business."

"What about what's best for our family?"

Jonathan closed the gate without answering and left Ruth standing in the courtyard, alone. Her concerns would fade with time. A successful blacksmithing business was exactly what was best for the family. And until Ruth understood that, he'd suffer her fretting in silence.

He was doing the only sensible thing.

CHAPTER 4

The town of Qiryat Ye'arim was called Arim by the locals, who boasted the virtues of this village to every passing traveler: two streams with the clearest spring water in the hill country, the largest corral on the trade route for caravaneers to rest their animals, and twenty west-facing slopes growing some of the finest dates and nuts in the kingdom. Like all soldiering hamlets, Arim enjoyed the protective graces of Fort Lakhish; its towering parapets and high walls dominated the hillside above the village.

What the locals didn't tell travelers was that Uriah the prophet was the town innkeeper. Some virtues were better left unspoken so that, with the passage of time, Uriah would end his railing against Laban, and the captain would simply forget about him. Uriah was not the only holy man to question Laban's doings, but he was the most outspoken. Uriah had become Laban's enemy, proclaiming that God revealed to him Laban's wicked ways. And if truth was difficult to swallow, then Uriah's words were enough to choke Laban's entire cavalry.

Uriah's inn stood among the five mud-brick shops that lined the dusty road running through town. It was the largest building in Arim, larger than the wheat bins to the south, with enough space to accommodate fifteen men seated at tables. At this time of day, with the sun sinking below the western hills and casting a red glow through the windows, farmers from the valley's vineyards crowded inside to swill a mug of Uriah's finest. They'd grown accustomed to his sweet wines, prepared fresh from the vine to tantalize the tongue rather than cloud the mind. Farmers always asked Uriah why he didn't let his wines sit a season in his cellar and serve them in their strength. A little bite would help them forget the hot sun, the long days, and the sometimes poor harvest. But Uriah believed that anything strong enough to cloud the mind had kindred powers over the soul.

Two strangers entered the inn wearing the red and black striped robes of Benjamin's tribe—normal dress for Arim since everyone in town was related. Dust covered their clothes as it did the other vineyard owners, but there was no dirt under their fingernails and they had calluses in all the wrong places. From their hands, they didn't look to have dunged or digged or pruned a day in their lives.

The one whose long hair was loosely braided down to his waist answered to the name Shechem. He had a crooked nose that had been broken too many times to count and the scar under his left eye was a hook, received while raiding a caravan in the hills near Shilo. The only callus on his hand was the one at the base of his right thumb where the hilt of a dagger rests. He crossed the inn ahead of his hooded companion and took a seat below the window, as far away from the other patrons as possible. It was a quiet corner, a table with only two chairs, surrounded by three wooden pillars that blocked the view from the other tables. They could speak here and not be heard by the other patrons. Shechem pointed out the innkeeper to his mate. "That's him, the one serving wine."

"Not Uriah." Commander Yaush brushed the dust from the sleeve of the farmer's robe he'd picked up from the quartermaster before leaving the fort. "Uriah keeps a nice place. Always has. He's a respectable citizen, a fine innkeeper."

Shechem took out his dagger. The silver hilt and sharp edge were visible in the shadows. "I'll take care of him now."

"Put that away. Any killing will be done at the execution grounds in Jerusalem. The military pays spies for information, not murder."

"If you only knew what Laban really paid me for." Shechem leaned back, shaking his long tangle of hair, the ends sweeping the floor.

Yaush sat across the table, his posture erect.

Shechem said, "Don't sit like a soldier."

"I'll sit how I please."

"They'll recognize you." Shechem spat out a cud of poppy seeds and rubbed it into the floor with the heel of his boot. "These farmers live every day around your men. You sit like that and they'll see through your disguise like a dog picks out a scent."

"I never should have agreed to this." Yaush hunched his shoulders forward and set his elbows on the table. "I run this town."

"This is Laban's town and he pays you to run it for him." Shechem held up the scroll. "And these are Laban's orders."

"I don't need orders to tell me what I should do with Uriah. He's a good man."

"Laban wants Uriah silenced."

"I can't arrest him without reason."

"He's a spy."

"I want proof."

"Where do you think Uriah gets all his information about Laban?"

"You say he's a prophet. Maybe he hears things or dreams dreams. I don't know and I don't care."

"He isn't getting his information from little angel voices, commander." Shechem raised an eyebrow and the ends of the scar beneath his eye raised up in a smile, cackling back at Yaush. "He reads your mail."

"You don't know that."

"Every letter sent to you from Jerusalem stops at this inn before it goes on to the fort."

"That's impossible." Yaush straightened in his chair.

"Wait and see." Shechem leaned back on the legs of his chair. "As soon as the courier arrives with the . . ."

They fell silent as Uriah crossed the inn with long, buoyant strides. At only thirty-one years of age, it was hard to understand why anyone took him for a prophet. He was a tall, thin man with rose-red cheeks that turned the edges of his brown eyes upward. He wasn't even blessed with a prophet's beard, not a whisker on his unblemished face. For God to have chosen this man as His anointed, well, it was easier to believe that fish grew on olive trees.

"Evening gentlemen," Uriah said. "You're not from around here."

"Just passing through." Commander Yaush pulled the edges of his hood close around his face.

"Caravanning?"

Shechem said, "That's right."

"We get a lot of travelers through here. Caravanners, merchants, that sort."

"Any couriers?"

"Not so many." Uriah answered slowly, studying them as he held out a pitcher and two tankards. "Something to drink? Red wine today, fresh off the vine with a good flavor. Sweetest harvest we've had in three years."

Shechem plunked down two shekels, told Uriah to fill the glasses and move on to the farmers three tables over.

When he was gone Yaush said, "You fool."

Shechem rapped the tabletop with his finger tips. "You saw that, didn't you? White as a spirit he went. He's the man Laban's looking for."

"I want more proof he reads my mail than a pale complexion."

"That courier of yours, Hosha Yahu, he stops here every Jerusalem-Lakhish ride. I've tracked him for weeks. I know the routes he rides, where he lays his head at night and where he drinks."

The plodding of horse hooves carried in from outside. It grew louder until it stopped in front of the inn.

Shechem strained to see out the window where a man was tying up to a fig tree. "That's him now."

"It couldn't be," Yaush said. "He isn't due till late this evening."

"Do you think Hosha would tell you what time he really arrives in Arim? This is where your courier was born. He knows every man in town, especially Uriah the innkeeper." Shechem lowered the legs of his chair to the floor without a sound. "He's been passing your mail to Uriah for months."

The door swung open and Hosha Yahu hurried across the inn, his tight-fitting tunic soaked with sweat and his riding boots caked in dust. Uriah poured him a drink but he refused and sketched the mark of the Rekhabites into the droplets of wine spilled on the bar.

Uriah wiped away the mark, covered the spot with a wine glass and directed Hosha to step behind the curtain separating the inn from the back room. Uriah lingered at the bar, filling a farmer's glass to the brim. He turned to follow Hosha and tipped the glass over, sending it crashing to the floor. He picked up the broken pieces, his gaze flitting off the faces of the patrons like moths glancing off the flickering heat of an oil lamp. Whatever news Hosha Yahu brought, it was enough to convince Uriah he was being watched.

"You get the courier." Shechem reached for his dagger. "I want Uriah."

"Not yet." Yaush grabbed Shechem's dagger hand and forced it under the table. He waited until Uriah disappeared into the back room before he said, "Give them time. If they are traitors I want them caught reading my mail."

Yaush sat erect, watching the curtain where they had disappeared, ready to give the word. Three patrons pushed through the front door and took a seat at the bar and still Uriah didn't come out to serve them.

Shechem flicked his long bangs from in front of his eyes. "Something's gone wrong."

"Sit still and keep your dagger out of sight until I give the word."

A table of farmers across the inn drank their tankards dry and were tapping them on the table for another round when Uriah finally appeared from behind the curtain shouldering a keg of wine over to the bar. He took longer than usual to steady it on the table. And when he split open the cork with an axe he missed the mark, cracking the side of the keg and spilling his profits over the floor. It seemed odd that an innkeeper as experienced as Uriah would be so clumsy with his wine. Odder still was the way he'd veiled his face with the hood of his robe. How could he ever hope to wield an axe with that hanging over his eyes?

Shechem shifted to the edge of his chair, his dagger barely out of sight below the table edge. "This isn't right."

"Wait here," Yaush said.

"Where are you going?"

"To find out what isn't right."

Yaush marched to the bar, but the prophet didn't raise his head to greet him. "Uriah, we need to have a word."

Uriah mumbled something that sounded more like an animal's grunt than a man's speech and went to the floor with a linen to sop up the spilt wine.

"Son," Yaush hovered over him, "I want to know why my courier is hiding in the back of your inn?"

Uriah continued wiping up the wine without answering. Yaush leaned over, took Uriah by the shoulders, and raised him from the floor. He pulled back the innkeeper's hood to speak with him face to face and there, dressed in Uriah's robe, stood the courier.

"Good evening, commander," Hosha Yahu said.

"Where's Uriah?"

Hosha's horse whinnied outside and the clatter of its hooves pounded up the street, away from the inn.

"Why, you . . ." Yaush shook him. "Do you know what you've done?"

"Yes, sir. And I'd do it again."

"Do what?"

"I'm not the only one who feels this way about the prophets."

"I don't understand."

Hosha tipped his head toward the street where Uriah had escaped. "God speaks to his people again, sir."

Shechem pushed through the farmers and threw open the inn doors. Uriah was gone, and there was no telling which way. He came back through the crowd, gripped Hosha by the arm. "You fool. Did you really think you could trick us?" He shoved Hosha against a post. "Where did he go, east or west?"

"I'll die before I tell you."

"You'll die anyway." Shechem slammed Hosha's head against the wood post and ripped his tunic down to the waist. The cloth rent with a savage tearing of fibers and fell down his thighs. At the end of a brass chain, dangling against Hosha's breast bone, lay the mark of the serpent. It was the sign the most radical Rekhabites wore to show their faith in Yeshua the Anointed One, and it rose and fell with Hosha's short gasps as if it had come to life and slithered onto his chest.

Shechem leaned his head in. "Tell me where Uriah's gone."

"Never."

"I can leech information from the most stubborn of men." Shechem pointed the tip of his dagger into the brass serpent, pressing it against Hosha's chest. "Where's your Anointed One now to save you?"

"I don't tempt God."

"You should try. It may be your only chance at life."

Hosha kneed Shechem in the stomach and snatched his dagger. "Back away!"

But Shechem stood his ground and drew a sword from under his robe. The double-edged blade was four times the length of the dagger and heavy enough to cut a man to the ground. Shechem swung at Hosha, but missed and landed the full force of his weapon square across the wooden pillar. The beam split in half and the ceiling creaked.

Shechem brought the sword around. "When I finish, you'll beg to lead us to Uriah."

"I'll not betray my God." Hosha said the words slowly and as he spoke he lifted the dagger heavenward, his hand unsure, trembling. "Have mercy on my soul."

He turned the blade on himself.

CHAPTER 5

Aaron found his cane by the door, but ignored the new sandals that hung on a peg by the window. He'd rather swim the width of Galilee towing a millstone around his neck than break in stiff leather. Ruth always asked him why he didn't wear them and he would answer that they were for when his feet were whole again. He never told her that he sometimes doubted they'd ever heal. Two months had passed since the surgeon cut the burned flesh from his feet and he was just now beginning to walk with a cane and a hobbled gait. It was evil to blame God for his laggard recovery so he chided himself for losing hope.

He dropped to his belly and shimmied beneath the foot loom, feeling around the threading spools and carting board until he found his worn-out sandals hidden under a stack of newly shot linen. Ruth always hid what she didn't want him to find under her weaving, and she certainly didn't want him wearing these things. They were worn and wouldn't protect his feet like the new sandals. But the old ones pulled on easily, fitting around the burns that crisscrossed the undersides of his feet. The new sandals would hang on the peg for another day. Today was Aaron's first day back at the shop, his first chance to test his feet after the accident, and he wasn't about to wear those stiff things.

The front door opened and Daniel ambled in, head down. It was like watching an ox squeeze through, though beasts of burden didn't carry a hole-worn tunic in hand or wear a half-cinched leather kilt sagging at the hips. His broad shoulders hardly fit between the door posts and his wet hair stood on end like the mule hairs on a painter's brush. He only combed it in the presence of young women, and at this hour the only maids up and about were the ones he fancied in his dreams. He stretched his arms to the sky and yawned. "I'll get the mule and meet you in the street."

"I'm walking."

"You're riding." Daniel sauntered toward the door. "Mama's orders."

Aaron waited for Daniel to disappear around the corner of the house before heading to the front gate. He would walk, no matter who ordered otherwise, and he'd prove to himself his feet weren't growing worse.

The steep grade in front of the house was pieced together with cobblestones, worn smooth from a thousand years of hooves, clattering and pummeling them to a rounded finish. Aaron understood that kind of finishing. The uneven edges of his soul had worn smooth from pain, preparing him for what, he wasn't certain, but of his disgrace he was sure. A man in the prime of life shouldn't have to learn to walk again.

He didn't use his cane up the hill, at least not until he reached the cobbler's shop, and then only to soften his step down Main Street. Praise be to heaven there was no one about this early to point at him and say: "Look, there goes a cripple." Or worse, mistake him for a man begging alms, press a shekel into his hand and whisper that God would forgive his sins.

There was no light inside the oil vendor's shop and the perfumery next door was empty. He limped past the stone masonry before stopping at the corner to rest on his cane and, as always, to study the entrance to the property of Josiah the potter. He always checked the potter's gate to see if his daughter, Rebekah, stood between the posts, but all he could see was thick black smoke billowing from the kiln chimney. It swirled over the high brick wall surrounding the firing yard, before blowing into the street and filling his eyes with enough bite to force them closed.

He rubbed the smoke from his eyes and checked the gate again. There was no one selling pottery—"no one" meaning no Rebekah.

He could cross the street without risking her seeing him with a cane. He was halfway over when a sharp tingling shot through his feet. Not enough to stop him, but when he reached the other side, the full force of the hurt struck like lightning. The skin on the underside of his feet began to tear. A little at first, then a sharp splitting across the arch. It was a tearing he knew too well. He bent at the waist, bowing his cane to near breaking before falling to his knees like a man in prayer, begging not for relief but for privacy. He'd endured this kind of pain for months in the solitude of home, but never in public. He clutched the nearest cobblestones and let the warm blood ooze between his toes. The pain passed quickly if he held still and let the blood dry.

Another cloud of smoke blew down from the potter's chimney, thick enough to choke him to tears. He wiped his cheeks and, when the smoke cleared, found himself staring at a dreadfully beautiful sight that stood at the far end of the potter's wall in front of the gate to the firing yard. Josiah's daughter toiled in the shifting smoke, arranging pottery on the canopied selling tables. Thank heavens she hadn't seen him kneeling there. She disappeared inside the gate and returned with a stack of cups. It was like watching an angel do the work of humans. She dressed in a white robe, and had saintly black hair, a cherubic smile and deep jade eyes. But this wasn't heaven, it was Jerusalem. And there could be no curse more damning than to be seen as less than whole. What woman would have a crippled suitor?

The pain lessened and he stood and spread his weight from heel to toe. His stirring caught Rebekah's attention. She set down the cups and blinked, clearing her lashes of the ash that settled out of the smoke.

"Good morning." Rebekah nodded.

Aaron stayed downwind and shouted through the smoke. "Fine pottery you have there."

"I'm sorry." Rebekah leaned over the selling tables. "I didn't hear you clearly." Her apology echoed off the store fronts like music from a piper's flute. "What was that, sir?"

Sir? No one had ever called him that before.

"Beautiful pots," Aaron said.

"They're cups." Rebekah raised one through the smoke, glazed to a brilliant polish. "But we do sell pots. Would you like to see one? I have a stack inside the yard. Why don't you come over and I'll show you in. You can get a good look at the—"

"I can see fine from here."

"They're behind the walls." She motioned to the gate.

"I've heard about them."

"From Papa, no doubt. He's proud of his pots. He's proud of everything he's created around here."

"I don't blame him." Aaron admired her long black curls and high red cheeks until it wasn't proper to stare, and then he stared some more. "He has every right to be proud."

Rebekah cupped her hand to her ear. "Pardon me?"

"I was saying that your father—"

"Oh, he's gone for the morning. He has council meetings the first of every week."

Aaron nodded and kept nodding. He was searching his mind for what he knew about Rebekah's father. He'd nearly forgotten her connection to the princes of the city. Josiah the potter, Second Elder on the Council, second-most powerful man in Jerusalem next to Zadock, and both more powerful than the new King Zedekiah. Not as rich, but certainly more powerful. "I heard about your father's promotion," Aaron said.

"I can't hear you either." Rebekah waved him over. "Why don't you come closer?"

Another draft of smoke poured over the wall and when it cleared Aaron said, "I'm happy to make your acquaintance."

Rebekah eyed the distance between them. "I'd hardly call this a proper introduction."

Aaron curled his toes under, testing his feet. He'd move closer if he could endure the pain long enough to make it without limping, but the leather soles dug into his burns like a pound of salt in a fresh wound. It would be easier to swat every flea on a caravan of camels than walk without limping. And if he made it over, Rebekah would see the bloodied bandages. He leaned back on his heels, taking the weight off the worst burns. Not today. There would be no proper introduction this morning. He'd make a less-than-proper one from where he stood.

Aaron nodded again. "Good day to you."

"You didn't have a look at our pots."

"Perhaps another day."

"If I must, I'll carry the pots over there."

"Don't bother."

"I'm happy to oblige."

She turned to get a stack from inside the gate, but pulled up when Daniel turned onto Main Street, struggling with the mule. It whinnied loudly and would have wakened everyone for three hundred cubits if Daniel hadn't jerked on the reins and pulled the animal's muzzle. He was about to deliver the mule a firm kick when Rebekah drew his eye and he dropped the reins. Aaron picked them up while Daniel wandered closer to the selling tables, combing his hair and tucking the ends of his tunic under his kilt as he went.

"Is there something I can get you?" Rebekah said, motioning to the plates.

Daniel glanced at the gate. "Is that heaven in there?"

Heaven? When did Daniel start talking religion in public? Aaron shimmied belly first onto the mule and trotted over. His brother was philandering again, and he'd make sure he didn't overstep the limits of what was proper to say to a young woman, especially one as well-bred as the daughter of Josiah the potter.

"It's a pottery yard," Rebekah said in answer to Daniel's question.

"My apologies." Daniel tipped his head. "I thought you were an angel."

Aaron slapped the mule on the backside and reined over. Daniel had a habit of making them both the fool, and he wasn't about to allow him, not in front of a woman of Rebekah's upbringing.

"I assure you sir, we're only potters," Rebekah waited for Daniel to move on, but when he set his elbows down on the selling table, she began rearranging the pottery around him, moving the bowls away from his forearms and pushing the cups in front of his face.

"Pots," Daniel said. "That's what I need. A good pot."

"You and your brother both?"

"Did he say we needed one?"

Aaron pulled up beside Daniel, the mule's nose rubbing against his side. "Mother will send us for a pot when she needs one."

"Tell her we have a good assortment," Rebekah said.

Aaron said, "Better than most, I'm sure."

"You're too kind, young blacksmith."

"You know about us?" Aaron asked.

"What young maid doesn't know when two handsome brothers move to the city?"

"That's why we're here," Daniel said and winked.

Rebekah tilted her head to the side and asked, "Because you're handsome?"

Aaron pushed the mule's head forward, jamming the animal's nose into Daniel's back. His brother's vanity was only surpassed by his foolishness. It would have been better for both of them if they had never passed by the potter's gate at this hour.

Aaron reined in next to the selling table, the mule's powerful body pushing Daniel aside. "What he means to say is that we came to Jerusalem because we're blacksmiths. I'm sorry to have troubled you."

"Thank you, Aaron. It's not been any trouble at all." She blinked again, but this time there was no ash in her eyes and she dismissed herself with a bow.

The gate latched behind Rebekah, and Aaron could feel a wide grin cross his lips. Daniel laughed, but all the teasing Daniel could muster wouldn't change the fact that Rebekah knew Aaron's name. They hadn't exchanged a proper introduction, but she'd said Aaron. He'd heard it as clear as the Jordan is wet, and he sat up in the saddle to stare a while longer. Today he was less of a cripple, not because his feet were any closer to healing, but because Rebekah didn't know him as one. To her, he was simply Aaron, the young blacksmith from Sidon.

Nothing more, but indeed nothing less.

CHAPTER 6

Ruth and Jonathan's youngest son, Joshua, wrapped a blanket around his head and rubbed the warmth of the linen over his ears. He suffered the cool autumn nights in silence. At his first complaint of cold weather Ruth would insist he abandon his sleeping spot on the roof and move indoors.

At seven years, he was barely old enough to remember the animal-skin roof of the family's first house in Sidon. A shanty with a roof of leather was all Papa could afford until he learned the art of steel-making. During the rainy seasons, the leather mildewed and Ruth replaced the rotted parts with new hides each spring.

His new Jerusalem roof was strong enough to endure his play. It was reinforced with wood crossbeams. And the gaps between the beams were filled with a mixture of clay and straw, then troweled smooth and cured to a hard surface in the hot sun.

The roof was whatever his imagination conjured—a king's palace, a general's fortress, a merchant ship sailing the waters of the Great Sea. Last month, while imagining he was a soldier, he jumped onto a weak spot in the beams and showered bits of clay down on Ruth's loom. From then on, she forbade him to play on the roof.

Joshua's oldest sibling, Elizabeth, climbed the steps to the roof carrying a bundle of flax to set out for drying. She was skinny, though Ruth insisted Joshua use the word slender. The neighbors said Elizabeth was a sturdy, hard-working woman. Joshua peered at her from beneath his blanket as she walked across the roof toward him.

She didn't seem to be any more sturdy than on any other day. She was still skinny.

"Wake up, little idler." Elizabeth poked at his blanket with the tip of her sandals. "Your brothers are up and gone to the shop and you've chores to do."

He lay still. She'd leave him alone if he played dead.

"Up, up, and gird on your clothes." Elizabeth jabbed him with a stalk of flax.

"Girls gird their robes." Joshua pulled back. "Boys strap on kilts."

"Out of bed or I'll strip you of your kilt and gird you in a robe for the rest of the day." She grabbed the ends of his reed mat, dragged him across the roof and out of her way. "Papa will have extra chores for you if you sleep past sunrise."

He turned on his side, pulled the blanket around his ears and yawned. "Sun's not up yet."

There was still time before the sun came up to lay awake and imagine himself atop one of Jerusalem's watchtowers. Elizabeth was the chief watchman, ushering the bundles of flax up the steps, posting them to their watch. No. Elizabeth was his prisoner. That was better. And he would order the sentries of flax to bind her and set her in the corner of the roof. That was much better. Elizabeth didn't deserve to be a watchman today, not the way she was bothering him. Joshua's first line of defense, the wall dividing their home from the street, had weakened. It was run over with grapevines bearing Babylonian soldiers. And though the soldiers resembled bunches of ripening fruit, they were still enemies climbing the wall to enter his besieged courtyard city.

Joshua didn't daydream long. Elizabeth's stirring wouldn't allow him. He rolled over and watched her tear the damp flax fibers off their woody stems. She'd started the stalks soaking last night in water and olive oil, and now the white stuff came loose in her hand. She held up a clump of flax, then sighed. He'd heard that sigh before and he ripped back his blanket and sat up. "Elizabeth's thinking about the boys at the market. Elizabeth's thinking—"

"I am not."

". . . about the boys."

Joshua wrapped himself inside his blanket and peered out at her. She'd turned the color of wild rose petals and it served her right. She spoke about boys more than he ever remembered her doing in Sidon. Not just any boy, either, but a certain scribe who lived in the upper city. If she kept on about how a new robe would draw his eyes he'd hold his breath until he popped. What did she need a new robe for? Hers was clean enough and well-scented. Just yesterday she stuck it to his nose and asked how it smelled. What did he know about sweet-smelling things?

Her robe did show the wear of traveling the dusty roads between Sidon and Jerusalem. He agreed with her on that. All his things had taken a beating too. During the journey he'd broken his favorite stick and worn a hole through his sandals. At least he hadn't lost his lucky flat rock or he'd have to search for another just like Elizabeth searched for a man. Suitors made her a boring sister. Or was this the beginning of greater fun? He said, "Elizabeth has a suitor and I know his name."

"You keep your tongue quiet!" She came after him shaking a stalk of flax, but Joshua curled up into a ball, shielding himself with the blanket. Elizabeth wasn't shy with a stick and he'd felt her embarrassment across his backside before. He pulled back the edge of his blanket when he heard the front door of the house creak open.

Ruth called, "Joshua. It's time you were up. You've chores to do."

At the sound of their mother's voice, Elizabeth stopped coming after him.

Spared!

"Don't forget to fill the water clock," Ruth cried. "There'll be extra chores if you miss today."

Joshua unwrapped himself from the blanket and scowled. He wasn't completely spared. He sat up straight and looked over the neighborhood rooftops to see if morning really had arrived. The woman who lived farthest away—the one Ruth called a gossip and warned him about what to say in her presence—stood draping wash over a line. Was gossip another word for washwoman? He shifted his gaze one roof closer to where the wife of the brickmason set out figs to dry, his favorite. The last time he played in front of her home she gave him handfuls of dried fruit. Today would be a good day to play leapfrog outside her gate.

His gaze danced from rooftop to rooftop. Salted fish set out to cure on the fisherman's roof, nuts to be browned on the stonecutter's, dates waiting to ripen on the cobbler's roof, and green wood on the carpenter's. Next door, the sons of a vineyard owner poured buckets of water over their roof, softening the clay enough to mend a crack before the rainy season.

His wandering gaze stopped on the roof beam that hung out over the courtyard of their home. It was a fine place to climb, if only it weren't off limits. A hemp rope was lashed four times around the weathered beam and the end disappeared over the edge. He crawled out onto the wooden plank and looked over the side. The water clock hung suspended at the other end. Mama's most prized heirloom. It was her wedding gift from Grandma and his first chore of the day.

The clock kept track of the passing of time and its faithful use had become a family tradition. Joshua called it a bucket, and it did look like one except that it had a narrow hole cut into the bottom and lines etched on the inside wall to track the hours. At sunrise each day, he filled the clock, uncorked the spigot and let the water drip, hour by hour, out the bottom. Not too difficult a chore, but one that forced him out of bed with the rising sun. When the sun set each evening, he corked it and had his mother read the clock. She was the best reader in the family. Last winter she judged the end of the shortening of days even before the priests in Sidon announced the winter solstice, the day the sun begins to stay in the heavens longer.

"Joshua, did you hear me?" Ruth called.

"I'm awake, Mama." He inched back down the beam. Praise be to heaven she hadn't seen him perched above her. "I'll remember to fill the water clock today."

Without looking up she said, "And you'll not climb out on the beam to do it. It's far too dangerous for a boy your age."

He reached the safety of the roof and peered back over the edge. "Yes, Mama."

Ruth closed the door behind her as Sarah, the youngest daughter, flew around the corner of the house with a kettle in hand, filled with madder bulbs. Today was dye-making day. She stepped to the water cistern and poured the remainder into her kettle.

When Joshua saw her he threw on his sandals and pulled his shirt over his shoulders. "No. Sarah! Wait!" The cistern had held just enough water to fill the clock, but it was too late. She'd emptied it and he'd have to fetch more before the sun rose. He jumped down the steps and lugged the cistern into the street, pumping his legs as fast as the cistern would allow, then headed for the pool of Siloam at the end of the street.

Elizabeth had nearly finished pulling the flax off the stalks when he returned. He said, "Help me with this, else I'll tell everyone you dream about the boys in the market all day."

"You'll do no such thing."

"Will."

"Will not."

"Will so."

Elizabeth put away the flax. "You'd think I was your prisoner."

Joshua puckered his lips and let out a long, high-pitched whistle. How did Elizabeth know that? He'd never let her in on his imaginings, but somehow she knew. Grown-ups always had a way of ruining his fun, and though Elizabeth wasn't married, she had herself a suitor—or at least she was close to having one—and that made her almost like a grown-up.

Elizabeth carried the cistern up the steps and had Joshua sit in his usual place on the edge of the roof. His spindly, pliable legs wrapped around the cistern like the vines of a melon and he sat waiting for the sun to rise so he could fill the water clock and start tracking the hours. His gaze shifted between the eastern sky and the water clock below, searching for the first ray of sun to break over the Mount of Olives while balancing the water cistern on its side, ready to let go with a torrent of cool water. Ruth wouldn't give him extra chores now that he was taking care of the clock, but to be sure he stomped his foot on the roof to let her know he'd minded.

Over two, under one. Ruth wove the intricate twill that made her sons' shirts more durable and her girls' robes fuller. She was experienced enough with the foot loom to keep working the pedals while bending her gaze toward the sound of Joshua's stomping. Over one, under two. He'd better not be playing soldier on the roof again or he just might make Ruth miss a stitch and then she'd have him milk the goat, a chore that usually included a few swift kicks. Better to let the goat discipline him than his father. Over two, under one. He stomped again and his playful giggle streamed in through the window. There was no clay coming lose from the roof beams, at least not yet.

Over one, under two. With Ruth's old hand loom, twilling cloth took so much time that she used a simpler weave pattern, over one, under one. But now, with the foot loom freeing her hands to pull the thread, she twilled a boy's shirt in a few days, a man's tunic in a week, and a woman's full robe in just eighteen days. When the family lived in Sidon, Ruth's weaving had gained the notice of the noble class. She wove a shirt for the harbor master, a robe for the chief judge of the city, and before leaving to come to Jerusalem she was commissioned by the King of Phoenicia to weave a garment for his son, Prince Jesse of Sidon. Despite the fame her talents brought her, and to say nothing of the money it garnered for the family, she was never so happy as when she was weaving to clothe her own family. Her children would dress as well as any child of nobility if she could only find time to weave with so many chores from their move to Jerusalem demanding her attention.

Sarah burst through the front door, dye kettle in hand. Ruth didn't take her eyes off the beams in the ceiling but she could see Sarah from the corner of her eye. Her curly brown hair bobbed as she slapped her feet together and stood erect like a little soldier. She held the dye kettle between both hands. "Are these enough madder roots to make dye?"

"Is the kettle full?" Ruth asked.

"Mostly full." Sarah's voice trailed off as it did whenever she hedged the truth.

"I want it completely full, young woman."

"You could say it's completely full."

"How completely full is that?"

Sarah jostled the kettle. "Nearly half-way."

"I see, and that's mostly full, is it?"

"I don't have time to cut more."

"And what seems to be your rush this morning?"

Sarah hid a mischievous smile behind the kettle. "Joshua."

"You're not going to chase him about the yard with that stick, are you?"

"I found a small one that doesn't hurt nearly as much."

"Sarah!"

"Only if he deserves it."

"What am I to do with you, girl?"

Ruth threaded the spool of yarn over two spindles, found the pedal with her toes and stepped, shifting the upper spindles down and the lower spindles up. "See that the kettle is filled to the brim with madder bulbs before you start it boiling." She passed the spool under a single spindle, curled her toes beneath the pedal and pulled up with both feet. The wooden arms shook for a moment, followed by a deep groan before shifting.

"You didn't even look," Sarah said.

Ruth turned her eyes from the ceiling and the sound of Joshua's stomping to study the half-filled dye kettle. "Hurry along and get the kettle boiling."

Sarah pulled open the front door only to be greeted by Joshua's loud cry.

"Ima, Ima, the sun's up!"

Ruth loved to hear Joshua say the word *Ima.* Mother was the title every Hebrew woman prized. And there were five of her very own who called her Ima, five handsome sheaves in her basket. Ruth stood in the doorway next to Sarah, admiring the sunrise. Above them, Elizabeth held Joshua around the belly while he poured water into the clock, spilling more than went in.

"Mama," Sarah said, tugging on her hand. "Let's dance in the water."

Ruth resisted. It wasn't wise to play right now. Not with linen to be shot and dye to boil, but Sarah's smile beckoned. For a moment Ruth was a girl again and she stepped out under the stream of water, hand in hand with Sarah. They danced under the shower, laughing and singing the childhood song she remembered from her youth. Round and round in a circle we whirl, round and round merrily we twirl.

A rustling near the front gate drew Ruth from her dancing. She left the children and stepped to the gate to see a strange boy push aside the vines reaching across the entry. He wasn't dressed like other boys. Silk vents were sewn into the sides of his tunic to let air pass comfortably under the purple cloth. It was a costly color Ruth had used only once because of its tedious preparation. The dye was extracted from clams, and it took over eight hundred to color one tunic. What kind of boy could afford such clothing? His head was shaved except for a long braid on the left side, a style popular among young Egyptian boys and a must for the youth of Jerusalem's noble class.

"I'm sorry to disturb your playing." His brown eyes lighted with a sparkle. He was a child, but oddly comfortable with the etiquette and speech of an older man.

"It's a good thing you interrupted or I might play the day away." Ruth dried her hands on her robe. Who was this boy and what did he seek? "Did you come to play with the children?" She hoped to find more friends for her young ones and this boy seemed a fine lad.

His dark eyebrows gathered and he was studying the children. He looked first at Elizabeth who had climbed down the stairs from the roof and stood behind Ruth, a few paces off. His gaze fell next on Joshua who held Elizabeth's hand and stared back. His stare stayed longest on Sarah who popped her head out from behind Elizabeth's robe, then hid again. "Perhaps another day." He turned to the gate. "I must have the wrong house."

"I can direct you," Ruth said. "I don't know everyone on the street, but I've met most of our neighbors. Whom do you seek?"

He tilted his head to the side as if weighing out his answer against her worthiness to hear. A peculiar thing for one so much younger than she. He said, "I'm searching for the weaver from Sidon."

"Why, I'm Ruth the weaver."

Without another word he marched out the gate, leaving them as quickly as he had appeared.

Elizabeth stepped to Ruth's side. "Where did he go?"

Ruth brushed the wet hair off her face. "I must have given him a dreadful scare, looking like this."

"He's an odd boy," Elizabeth said. "So young to be versed in good manners."

"You think he's strange, do you?"

"Well, he's not a normal boy. Not by any measure."

The grape vines rustled again, louder this time, and the boy returned drawing a woman by the hand. Her face was half hidden behind a veil. She walked like the boy, long strides, shoulders erect, and she seemed taller than most women, though she was no taller than Ruth herself.

"I am Mulek." He announced his name carefully. "Prince of Judah, eldest son of King Zedekiah." He raised his hand toward the woman he escorted, his voice going as deep as a boy's voice can. "This is my mother, Miriam, Queen of Judah. She wishes me to thank you for seeing us."

Ruth bowed.

Mulek said, "Mama bids you. No, not Mama, what I mean to say is that the queen seeks . . ." Mulek took a deep breath. "What my mother intended, or rather, what the queen rehearsed for me to say, I mean . . ." He gripped his kilt with both hands. "Must I continue, Mother?"

"That will do for now," Miriam said.

He bowed, stepped aside, and let her take the lead.

"We seek your favor." Miriam's voice soothed. It was not overly harsh, and not so thick that it weighed heavily on the ear. Her words fell from her mouth as a queen's words should fall, like music from a harp. She lowered her veil and smiled as if it were a natural thing for her.

"I must beg your pardon." Ruth combed back the scraggly bands of black hair that hung over her brow and brushed away the chips of red clay that had flaked off the walls of the cistern and lodged on her cheeks. What a mess she must appear to the queen.

Miriam said, "I see you're having a wonderful time."

"We were playing." Ruth forced a smile.

"What lovely children." Miriam stepped to the side enough to see behind Elizabeth to where Sarah hid. "With only boys to raise in my house, I sometimes forget how beautiful girls can be. Especially young ones with freckles." How gracious of the queen to turn her attention to Sarah and allow Ruth time to wring the water from her hair.

"I believe Mulek is your age," Miriam said, stepping closer to Sarah. "Am I right?"

Sarah poked her head out. "I finished my eighth year this summer."

"I thought as much. Nine years old, the same age as the prince."

"Mother, must you?" Mulek stared at the ground.

"Don't be shy, young man. I've taught you to act properly around girls."

He shrugged as politely as a boy can by drooping his shoulders and said, "Good day, young lady."

Sarah jumped behind Elizabeth without a word in return and stayed hidden. Ruth motioned for Elizabeth to take Sarah and Joshua back inside. They were to eat a breakfast of bread left under a cloth from last evening's meal and pour themselves a glass of warm goat's milk from the pitcher on the kitchen table. Ruth ordered the children about in as pleasant a tone as she could with Miriam listening. She told Joshua to wash his hands immediately after spreading the honey on the bread or he would have to clean the walls and the table top of his handprints. Sarah was to eat without throwing crumbs at Joshua, and Elizabeth was to make sure they minded. Ruth knew it wouldn't be long before Joshua left the kitchen and returned to her side with tales of Elizabeth the taskmaster who made him eat all of his bread and wouldn't give him any more honey to make it go down easier. Joshua always had a taskmaster story and Ruth prayed that the Queen of Judah wouldn't have to endure another telling of it.

Once the children were away and the front door closed behind them, Ruth cleared her throat and asked, "What brings you to our home?"

"I need robes for my family."

"Certainly there are expert weavers in your court."

"These are special robes and I was hoping to find a weaver with your experience. I understand you've woven garments for the King of Sidon."

"How did you know?"

"Word travels quickly in this city." Miriam sighed. "Far too quickly for my liking."

Ruth gathered her hair into a tail behind her neck. "What kind of weaving did you have in mind?"

"Coronation robes."

Ruth felt her face flush and she brushed her wet apron across her cheeks to cool them. "For the king?"

"My sons and I will need one as well. I have three boys. Mulek's the oldest."

"I'm not sure I can."

"You'll be paid well."

"It isn't that, it's just, well, I . . ." Her words came out in a rush. They were like a gentle breeze telling her that this was meant to be. Miriam's offer came at a provident time. The family savings were nearly exhausted. But would Jonathan approve of this? It would remind him of their difficult circumstances. "I have to speak with my husband first." Ruth bowed to Miriam then turned to Mulek, but before she could offer the prince the same gesture she caught her breath and stepped back. A brass charm serpent had worked its way out from under Mulek's collar. It hung from a chain at his chest, catching the morning sun and reflecting fiery colors of red, green, and blue. Rekhabites. Ruth looked away from the charm but it was too late; the queen had seen her staring.

"Mulek!"

"I'm sorry, Mother." The prince hid the charm under his shirt. "I forgot to take it off."

Ruth said, "It's a fine piece of jewelry."

"It isn't an idol. I would never allow such a thing." Miriam said the words carefully, precisely. "It's a symbol of faith, given to him by good Jews."

"Of course." Ruth wrung water from her sleeve and let it gather in a pool at her feet, but she didn't step out of the puddle. She couldn't move with that horrible symbol hanging around the boy's neck. It was a dreadful thing to wear!

"You know about it, don't you?" Miriam laid her hand on Mulek's collar.

"Know what?" Ruth asked.

"About the people who wear the mark of the serpent."

"I've heard of them."

"Rekhabites are not traitors. No matter what you've heard, they live the laws of Moses better than most Jews." Miriam took Ruth by the hand. "Oh look at me, going on like this. Forget the charm; it's only a child's keepsake, nothing more."

"As you wish." But it wasn't a simple keepsake, not by the trembling Ruth felt in the queen's hand—deep-to-the-bone trembling.

"You won't say anything about it, will you?"

Ruth nodded, but it wasn't enough to keep Miriam from pressing. She said, "I must be able to trust you like a friend." She gripped Ruth's hand and the trembling stopped for a moment. "A very close friend."

Ruth let drops of water trickle down her brow and drip off the end of her nose without brushing them away. Could it be they would become friends? Ruth had prayed to find one here, but there was not another woman she trusted with simple things. No one she could talk to about Joshua's chipped tooth, Sarah's whining, or Elizabeth's unmarried state. And then there were her fears, the ones she didn't share with anyone, couldn't share with anyone. At least not any common friend. She needed a confidante, someone who would understand; she feared saying too much to strangers, saying too little to neighbors, feared hearing what wasn't intended for her to hear from men she never wanted to meet and hoped she'd never see again. She feared that the push and pull of powerful and menacing lives were tearing at her and her family. Oh, how she longed for a friend to give her balance, to share her bread-baking and jam-making and help her bear her newest burdens. But there was something distant in Miriam's face, not unfriendly, but reclusive. And if they were to ever become friends, true friends, Ruth feared she would have to climb the wall separating them and discover what lay behind.

"I won't say anything about the charm," Ruth said.

"To anyone?"

"Not a soul."

Miriam didn't let go of Ruth's hand immediately, and when she did her voice was decidedly withdrawn. "I'll await your word on the coronation robes." She veiled her face with the hood of her robe. "We'll go now, Mulek."

Ruth followed Miriam out the gate to tell her again that she could trust her, that she would keep their confidence, but the street was not the proper place. Not with six soldiers waiting to escort the royals back to their palace in the upper city. What would Laban's men think if they heard Ruth addressing the Queen of Judah about a Rekhabite charm no one was to know about?

Miriam climbed the hill toward the upper city with Prince Mulek by her side and the soldiers marching at her flank in a steady rhythm.

Ruth had just met Miriam for the first time, but she understood the queen's fears, felt her misgivings. She had similar worries and that was why she believed they could become friends.

They were of a kindred spirit.

CHAPTER 7

Shopping in Jerusalem was a different affair for Ruth than it had been in Sidon. The Jews reckoned their purchases by a confusing combination of weights, measures, and money—a system she had yet to decipher fully—and she was left to the mercy of the merchants. She walked on the side of the street opposite the moneychanger. Last week he weighed her honey jar at sixty-five shekels. What kind of counterbalance did he use? Her clay jar held precisely one pound of honey and that weighed fifty shekels, not one more. His measuring of her purchases was always a few shy of a fair balance, and she didn't need him to tell her the value of her purchases. She could reckon that without the help of his scales. She'd purchased a bekah of salt, just enough for the week's cooking, thirty shekels of dates, a pound of oats and about an eighth of a talent of wheat. Not a poor sense of Jewish reckoning for a newcomer from Sidon.

Ruth got as far as the cobbler before the shoppers ahead of her slowed to a stop. So many here to buy and sell today. When the market stood empty, five carts could drive through side-by-side, but today she couldn't find room to negotiate past the crowd. A commotion in the street ahead slowed shoppers to a standstill. Merchants down both sides ended their selling and strained to see. A maidservant hurried young children off a balcony then returned to bend over the railing. When the woman in front of Ruth removed the basket from her head she caught a glimpse of the reason for the delay.

The crowd swelled around a cart that had its wheels chocked with a brick and its bed leveled on a stack of grain bags. A man, his hair groomed straight back and his graying beard falling to his chest, stood on the bed of the open cart. Plain-looking. Just the sort of man who'd keep to himself and let others do the same. The kind she'd seen a hundred times walking the streets of Jerusalem.

His hands drew Ruth's attention, not because he held them outstretched as merchants do when they barter, but because they were calloused and cracked hands that knew the toil of cultivating a harvest. Ruth worked through the crowd until she was close enough to see inside his cart. Empty. No nuts, no dates, no figs or grapes, nothing that would attract so many. At least not until Captain Laban reared his horse out of nowhere. The animal's powerful body knocked Ruth aside. Laban swung around the cart, circling it like a hawk. He was dressed in a plain gray tunic, no breastplates or weapons. His reckless riding gave her reason to believe he'd been drinking. She'd heard the rumors about his overindulgence, and his bloodshot eyes confirmed the gossip.

Laban pulled up beside the cart. He said, "Here to sell olives, eh, old man?"

"I don't grow olives."

"Grapes, then? I don't see any. Has your quaint little orchard in Anathoth had a bad harvest?"

"I've not come to sell anything."

"Not even one of your sermons?" Laban kicked the side board with his boot, cracking two planks. "You and your wild notions." He lifted his powerful arm to the crowd. "This is Jeremiah, the man some call a prophet. He came here last year to tell us about the war with Babylon and now he's come back, no doubt with more rumors of another war. Is that what you want to hear?" He spurred around in front of Jeremiah. "More holy drivel?"

A jeweler stepped out from the last row of carts. "Go back to the lower city and preach to the poor. They can afford to listen to you. We don't want to hear any more of your preaching here. It isn't good for business!" His words silenced the whispering crowd. He held up a handful of silver chains. "I don't have any gold to sell because Egyptian gold merchants don't come to Jerusalem any more. Your preaching scared them away and they've yet to return." He spat at the cart. "The Babylonians are gone. They've left us in peace and I say you do the same. Then maybe Egyptian gold will flow into the city as it did before."

Jeremiah leaned over the sideboard. "It isn't my preaching that keeps you from prospering."

Laban swung around in front of the cart. "You know the secrets of wealth, do you? Tell me what trade will make me rich. Wine? Olives? Maybe the perfume trade? I want to get rich, just like any man."

"Only one thing can do that."

"Tell us, old man." Laban looked out over the crowd. "We all want to get rich."

"Only charity can bring you the blessings of heaven."

"Did you hear that? Love is the secret." Laban placed his hand over his heart and the crowd erupted in laughter. "No need to barter and sell. We can get rich by loving our neighbors."

"Hear me out." Jeremiah moved to the edge of the cart, his hands raised to the crowd. "There are men in this city who make secret oaths to gain power over this people. They gather wealth around them while the poor and the needy pass by, unnoticed." His voice deepened. "If you allow their selfishness among you, this city, the great city of Jerusalem, will be destroyed!"

The crowd erupted again, this time in cries against Jeremiah. Every good Jew knew Jerusalem could never be destroyed. God would not allow it, and it was blasphemy to speak of it.

Laban reined in close to the cart. "Why don't you tell me exactly who these selfish men are and I'll see them cast out of the city."

"You should know, Captain." Jeremiah lowered his voice to a whisper and only Laban and those standing nearest the cart could hear. "You're one of them."

Laban reared his horse and knocked the cart off its mooring. Jeremiah lost his footing and fell over the sideboard, his body sprawling over the cobblestones. Laban barked at him, "Get out! And if you ever come back within the walls, I'll have you hanged." He leaned forward in the saddle. "I don't allow *piqqeah* in this city!"

The stonemason standing next to Ruth chanted, "Piqqeah! Piqqeah! Piqqeah!" Others joined him, the chant spreading through the crowd until the entire market rang with the belittling slang for the prophets. It was a vulgar word and it burned Ruth's ears like a hot iron: *visionary, dreamer, lunatic.* Ruth didn't join the chanting. *Piqqeah* was a saying she would never suffer on any man.

Laban jumped over Jeremiah's body, the horse's hooves coming down next to him. He could have killed the prophet, but the animal steered away from his head, or was it God who kept the hooves from crushing his skull? The captain cursed Jeremiah's name and disappeared into the shadows of an adjacent alley that wound its way back toward the military grounds. It was an odd way for the captain to behave, but drinking men showed little public temperance.

The chanting quieted and merchants returned to their shops, calling out their wares and bartering for the highest price. The maidservant on the third-story balcony attended to the cries of a child within, and the woman next to Ruth lifted her basket to her head and picked her way around the fallen form of Jeremiah, never glancing down at his bleeding hands and torn robe.

Ruth stepped closer. She asked, "Are you hurt badly?"

Jeremiah stood and brushed his robe clean. "The captain's been drinking again."

"I've never seen him like that."

"You've yet to see him at his worst." Jeremiah adjusted his belt. "You're Ruth, the wife of the new blacksmith."

"Well, yes." She brushed a lock of hair from in front of her face. "We moved from Sidon a few months back."

"I sensed it was somewhere along the Great Sea."

"You've been to Sidon?"

"Only in my dreams." Jeremiah fitted the cracked sideboards back together. "You were sent here."

"I don't know that I would call it that. We moved to build a smithing business."

"Precisely the reason you were sent."

Sent? Ruth was beginning to believe the chanting crowd was right, that Jeremiah was a piqqeah.

He said, "We need your help."

Ruth checked about the cart. There was no one else standing by and she had no way of knowing to whom he referred.

"We'll pay you a good price."

"What sort of help, exactly?"

"Plates." Jeremiah harnessed his mule to the cart. "Brass plates, each one about the length of a forearm and wide as three hands."

Ruth glanced at the alley where Laban had left the market. "I'm afraid my husband has other work right now."

"It's simple work compared to steelmaking."

"Well, yes, but—"

"Certainly he can find time to smith a few plates for a poor farmer."

"It isn't so much the time as it is the timing." Ruth held her shopping bag close. "You should have come by the shop before my husband started work for Zadock."

Jeremiah peered at her as if he were looking into the past, into her past. After a long silence he said, "I did come by."

"My husband never mentioned it."

"I never spoke with him. I found your son, Aaron, in a pool of hot metal that morning. I pulled him to safety and went to find a doctor. When I returned you had already taken him."

"It was you?"

"And a good thing I arrived when I did."

"*You* blessed him to heal, didn't you?" Ruth held her hand to her mouth. "*You* gave him the blessing he's always speaking about. The one that makes him believe he's going to be healed."

"By the grace of God, he will be healed."

Ruth touched him on the arm. "I don't know how to thank you."

"Help me with my brass plates."

"I'm sorry." Ruth lowered her head. "I'm afraid Jonathan sides with the Elders now."

"He'll change his mind."

"He's a stubborn man."

Jeremiah walked to his cart and unchocked the wheels. "I'll be by to see him."

Ruth hurried to his side. "When did you have in mind?"

"As soon as God softens his heart."

Ruth slowly shook her head. "That may not happen."

"It will, my good lady, it will."

Ruth said, "Thank you for my son's life."

"God has a purpose for healing your son."

"He's to save the life of a prophet." Ruth said the words slowly, the same words Aaron had spoken in the delirium of pain that followed his accident and a hundred times since. She leaned against the sideboard of the cart. "When is it to be done?"

"Listen to your heart and you'll know when the time comes." Jeremiah patted her on the hand. "The Lord tells us in His own time and in His own way."

Jeremiah started the mule walking down the street and left Ruth standing alone, but his words remained, penetrating her soul to the center. Aaron had said that God was healing him so he could save the life of a prophet. But Jonathan had convinced her that Aaron was dreaming all that. And he had his reasons. The boy wasn't healing, despite his claims that God would send a miracle. She watched Jeremiah drive his cart out of the market, his tattered brown robe swaying in the breeze. He was banned from the city, a prophet without a place to preach. As he drove down Milo Hill, Ruth wished she could drive his words from her thoughts. She couldn't mention that Jeremiah was the stranger who came to the shop the morning of the accident, not to Aaron, not to anyone. Not if she were to obey her husband and side with the Elders. She would have to use wisdom in this matter and a short memory seemed the only wise investment. Jeremiah disappeared out of sight, but she couldn't forget what he'd said. Was God really healing Aaron to save the life of a prophet? The thought haunted the farthest retreats of her mind. If it were true, then she had to know one thing.

Which prophet?

CHAPTER 8

Adjacent to Solomon's Temple stood the Citadel, the great government headquarters. Within its walls the Elders held their councils, and today they would consider the sale of property left abandoned and without heirs after the war. The price for Jonathan's property was set at one talent of silver.

The sentries guarding the main entrance of the Citadel let Jonathan into the lobby without asking his name. He crossed the marble floors imported from Athens and scaled the stairs past gold lamps set on each landing. They were twice the size of a man, with an oil flame large enough to make a burnt offering of anyone who ventured too close. On the fifth floor, he found a line of twenty property buyers snaking around tall stone pillars. The line ended at the double doors to the council chambers where a scribe hunched over a small cedar desk.

"State your business with the Council." The scribe spoke without looking up. He dipped his pen in an inkwell and continued scratching numbers into his ledger.

"Property," Jonathan said. "I've come to buy the—"

"Money, please."

Jonathan handed over a coin purse and let the scribe count out the thirty mina coins. "There's only a half-talent of silver here."

"That's my offer." Jonathan spoke softly.

"Are you bartering, sir?" The scribe's voice echoed off the high ceiling, garnering the stares of every man in the hallway. He pushed the coins toward Jonathan. "I suggest you come back when you can afford property."

Sale of property in Jerusalem required more than the shake of a hand. It was a sacred rite, a hallowed exchange of Israel's soil, land given to Abraham as an inheritance forever, or at least for as long as the Jews deserved to live on it. The people of Jerusalem preferred not to remember that condition of property ownership. Less-flattering prophecies revealed that their land would be taken back if the city's dwellers turned into a wicked lot. But they trusted God would indulge them their most cherished sins. This was their land of promise and God could never barter it away to another people, no matter how deaf an ear or stiff a neck they turned to Him. For that reason, property in Jerusalem was never traded openly between buyers and sellers. The Elders set the sale price and the buyer paid. And it was near sacrilege to haggle over property, but that didn't stop Jonathan. He had come to see the Council of Elders this morning to make an offer for his shop. Traditions be cursed.

"How much do the Elders want for the blacksmith shop?" Jonathan asked.

"You're the new blacksmith?" The scribe stabbed the tip of his stylus into the ledger, blotting it with thick black ink. "I'm sorry, sir, I had no idea." He rifled through his ledger to the list of buyers. Jonathan's name was ahead of the others. The deed to the shop was already filled out except for an empty space for the sale price. He scribbled thirty mina onto the line and handed over the deed. It was a pittance of the price any of the men standing in line could hope to pay and they strained to read what the scribe had written. Jonathan stared back at them until they turned away, but they had already overheard. Exactly why he'd found favor with Zadock he wasn't certain. The Chief Elder had his reasons for the blacksmith to remain in Jerusalem, and who was a blacksmith to deny him his charity.

"Everything's in order, sir," The scribe reached down and began unlatching Jonathan's sandal, but he pulled his foot back and said, "I'll latch my own sandals if you don't mind."

"It's the custom, sir. Sole up if you're the buyer, sole down if you're the seller. Surely you know."

The purchase of property required the performance of the rite of sale. The buyer removed his right sandal, turned it upside down and placed his offer on the leather sole. If the seller accepted, he took the money and returned the sandal with the sole facing down.

The men in line grinned at Jonathan's unfamiliarity with the rite. "Of course I do." Jonathan unlatched both sandals.

"I only need the right one, sir." The scribe turned it upside down and laid Jonathan's money on the leather sole. "Give it to the Chief Elder like this. He'll take your money and return your sandal with the sole facing down. Then it's done. You own the property—ovens, chimneys, and all."

"You're certain of that?"

"Sole up, sole down. That's how we've done it for a thousand years."

"I meant my offer." Jonathan lowered his voice to a whisper. "Do you think Zadock will accept thirty mina?"

The scribe rolled the scroll around the sandal. "Money should be your last worry."

Josiah the potter stepped through the double doors of the council chamber. He wore a faded black robe cinched around his waist with a leather strap. A band of carefully combed gray hair rimmed the sides of his thinning scalp like a turban with a skin top. He spoke to the scribe in a soft but direct voice, which accounted for his longevity on the Council. Quiet men had greater staying powers. Twenty years he'd served, long enough to rise to the post of Second Elder on the highest council in the land, a council that rivaled the power of the king himself. Josiah was the only artisan on the Council. Jonathan regarded him as an honest man who never overcharged a customer, sold a broken piece of pottery, or extended his clay by mixing it with silt. He was the only Elder on the Council who hadn't purchased an estate in the upper city, preferring to keep his substantial inheritance in the lower city as a remembrance of his father. The same home and pottery shop had been in his family for generations. Two years earlier, he bequeathed a portion of his property to the Council to allow for the building of a through street where before there had been a dead end. The new street was a blessing disguised as a loss. The road had become the main street, busiest in the city and a perfect place to sell pottery. But today it was not pottery, but property that was at issue, and Jonathan's name topped the list of buyers.

Josiah stepped to the scribe's desk. "Would you be so kind as to point out the blacksmith to me?"

"Right here, sir." The scribe pointed his pen at Jonathan. "He already has the deed to the property. You should find everything in order."

Josiah wasted no time on an introduction. There was no handshake, no trivial talk about the weather, the harvest, or questions about Jonathan's blacksmithing. He took Jonathan by the arm and quickly pulled him behind a pillar and sat him on a bench. He sidled in next to him and said, "This isn't the usual property buying. You have one chance to impress the Elders. Disappoint any one of them and you'll be packing your smithing hammers back to Sidon on the next caravan headed north." He didn't speak in the soft, gentle tone used to address the scribe. His voice was firm and he spoke quickly, almost desperate to give advice Jonathan had never asked for.

"Why are you telling me this?"

Josiah didn't answer. He put half of Jonathan's money back into his coin purse and tied it shut. He scratched out the price on the deed and wrote in fifteen mina next to it.

"What are you doing?" Jonathan took back the deed and studied Josiah's writing. "The scribe will never allow me into the Council with the deed altered like this."

He said, "You could offer the Council nothing and still get your shop."

"They'd give it to me?"

"Zadock wants to keep you in Jerusalem."

"Why me?"

"I was hoping you could tell me that." There was something odd about the way Josiah hung on every word Jonathan uttered, his ear cocked to the side and leaning forward. "Perhaps it has to do with your blacksmithing."

"Zadock said he had some work for me."

"What kind?"

"Steel. He has a partner, a friend, someone he's working with. I really don't know much more than that. Why do you ask?"

Josiah stood and adjusted his robe over his shoulders. He glanced at the council chamber doors and said, "We should go now. Zadock is expecting us."

Josiah entered first and crossed to his seat at the council table. He kept his head down and avoided the glances of the other Elders. Jonathan paused at the threshold until he found Zadock at the head of the council table. He was studying Jonathan's every step. Why did his arrival merit so much attention from the man? He was here to buy property like all the others, not to address these princes of the city on points of the law. Jonathan took a seat in the first row of the gallery before the Chief Elder shifted his attention back to the business at hand.

A good buyer always versed himself in the ways of the seller, though Jonathan knew nothing of the eleven members of the Council, except that they were all merchants. Artisans like Jonathan were out of place among these men who were skilled in the arts of the marketplace, buying at the lowest price, selling to the highest bidder, and getting rich on the difference. They were all merchants, everyone but Josiah the potter, the second Elder on the Sarim Council.

The chamber was a prattle of loud voices, a blur of turbans. The Elders sat in order of seniority around a long cedar table. Eleven of the twelve chairs were occupied. The last stood empty and the Chief Elder had yet to select someone to fill it. The former Elder had suffered an unfortunate accident, drowning in the Gihon Spring in water less than knee deep. It was believed strong drink was the culprit, though it was rumored he had a tolerance for Rekhabites. The Elders dressed in matching black robes. White underclothes showed at their collars and cuffs and gold amulets hung on chains around their necks, a symbol of their status on the Council. Smoke hovered in a cloud above them, distilling the lamplight to a steamy yellow glow and dimming their formal dress to an ashen gray.

Above the fray of voices, the perfume-importing Elder made an urgent plea in favor of a vote to lower the import tax stifling his business. His suggestion raised the silk-dealing Elder out of his seat, arguing for a vote to increase the tax and use the money to finance the building of ships at the port in Aqaba. More vessels, he said, would lessen Israel's dependence on caravans. No sooner had he spoken than the caravan-owning Elder stood and locked stares with him. Shipping at the port in Aqaba had already decreased his caravan profits by half, and more ships would be his undoing. After an uncomfortable moment, the two Elders retreated to their seats, yielding the floor to silence.

The Elder who made his living in the gold trade took advantage of the lull to accuse the Elder who owned nearly all the money-changing tables in Jerusalem of falsely appraising his gold reserves. The moneychanger clucked his tongue like a hen searching for a safe roost. He'd find none among the Elders on the Council. Fair weights and measures were not the standard at his changing tables.

Zadock shifted on his red cushioned chair at the head of the table. He said, "It's time we consider the blacksmith's offer to purchase property."

The honey trader stood and said, "We don't accept offers for property."

The gold merchant rapped his ringed fingers over the table top. "We've never bartered for land."

"That's right," the perfume merchant said. "We've already set the price for the blacksmith at one talent of silver for a piece of property that's worth three times that. Surely he can pay what we ask. It's one talent of silver and not one mina less."

"Elders." Zadock raised his hand and they quieted. "This is a different matter, one we should consider under separate terms." He stood and came around the table to Jonathan. "What price did you have in mind, blacksmith?"

"This." Jonathan stepped from the gallery and offered his sandal sole-up with the deed and fifteen mina coins stacked on top. Zadock read down to where Josiah had scratched out the thirty minas and replaced it with fifteen. He glanced up.

"That's all you can afford?"

"These are hard times." Jonathan folded his arms over his worn tunic. Ruth would have woven him a new one for the occasion, but she was busy moving into their new home and a worn tunic was a sympathetic bartering companion.

Zadock said, "We accept."

The chamber erupted in a flurry of dissent. The honey trader slammed the back legs of his chair to the floor, the gold merchant made a fist with his ringed fingers and the perfume merchant spat on the floor.

"Silence!" Zadock's dark eyes were flints of coal shifting above pale cheeks, scrutinizing the face of each Council member. His glance quieted them, turning ten divided men into single-minded souls. "The sale of this property to the blacksmith isn't about money; it's about trust, and we have need to trust the blacksmith." He stepped closer to Jonathan. "We can trust you, can't we?"

"With what?"

Zadock began stacking the fifteen mina coins one by one, the sound clinking about the chamber. He spoke in a thin, rasping voice. "Swear that in your shop you'll never smith so much as a brass nail for a Rekhabite."

"I don't know any, sir."

"You will. They'll come to you." Zadock rolled up the deed and pointed it at Jonathan. "And when they do, you'll turn them away—if you want to keep your shop."

"How will I know who they are?"

"Interrogate them." Zadock flicked his index finger at the stack of coins, spilling them over the floor and filling the chamber with the sound of tinkling cymbals. "Trip them up in their words." He turned the sandal over and held it out to Jonathan, sole facing down. "You can find out a lot about a man by catching him in his words."

He was recruiting Jonathan to spy for him. The shop in return for his watchful eye over Rekhabites. It wasn't Jonathan's practice to meddle in the affairs of others, but it was a small price to pay for his own shop and Jonathan took the sandal. He shook Zadock's hand, bowed to the Council and dismissed himself from the chamber, waiting only long enough for the scribe to affix a seal on the deed before taking the five flights of stairs to the front doors. It was a glorious day with the bright midday sun shining down on him, warming him to the very soul. He was a property owner with all the rights and privileges accorded such.

Jerusalem's newest citizen.

CHAPTER 9

Except for a pale spot on her nose, Rebekah's face was black, covered with potash from the floor of her father's kiln. Josiah insisted she be properly disguised if she were to help with the underground and she obeyed, smudging the charred-smelling ash over her sensitive skin, despite the rash it raised on her neck and the dryness it caused. Her skin was better suited to the fine creams Josiah imported from the perfume houses of Egypt, but smuggling people out of Jerusalem had no grooming standards. She was to make herself over in potash and nothing else.

Since the war, Rebekah had helped her father smuggle seven families out of Jerusalem. Tonight they would add the stonemason's family to the number of Rekhabites believed dead. It would have been a simpler task to leave through the east gate by day. But that was a trail as wide as the Jordan River was long, and any trail that large could lead to their capture, or—more likely—their death. They couldn't pack the stonemason's possessions and leave the city under the watchful eye of Laban's men. If they were followed, they risked giving away the location of their secret colony of Rekhabites. Better to disappear under the cover of darkness and keep forever hidden the location of Qumran, the secret city of salt, nestled on the barren western shores of the Dead Sea.

Rekhabites didn't need to hide their strict observance of the laws of Moses or their belief in the prophets. A good number of Jews in Jerusalem still kept that part of the faith. Rekhabites were a small group with deep convictions, but hardly a threat and Rebekah had no way of knowing that it was their ties to the prophet Uriah that kindled Laban's hatred for them.

Among the thousands of citizens in Jerusalem, two hundred seventy-three called themselves Rekhabites. There were forty-two families, a carpenter and his three sisters, a blind man who gathered alms at the east gate (and overheard every word the soldiers spoke about Rekhabites), three prisoners they had yet to rescue from the palace dungeons, and the most recent convert to their number—the palace informant.

Rebekah finished covering her face with black ash before blowing out the lamp and pulling back the thick linen blanket she'd thrown over the front windows to hide the light. She searched the yard for the informant, but he hadn't arrived. The pottery yard stood vacant. Not a good sign, since he was expected much sooner with word about the night watch. They couldn't risk the escape without knowing if the south wall was to be left unguarded this evening. Without his help, they would have to abandon their plans and try again another night. Not that their plan to lower the stonemason and his family over the south wall in a basket wouldn't work. A number of Jews had escaped the Babylonian siege that way, finding safety and sustenance in outlying villages. But this was a different kind of war, a more patient struggle; the stonemason's family wouldn't starve tonight if the informant didn't bring word about their escape route.

Rebekah scanned the yard a second time, searching for any sign that the informant had arrived. The rounded roof of the kiln was visible against the night sky. It stood dark and silent at the far end of the yard save for the hooting of an owl perched on the chimney vent, warming itself on the bricks still tepid from yesterday's firing. The kilnmaster left early. There were no overnight firings to tend and he spent the early evening drinking at the Main Street Inn, his favorite drinking establishment in the lower city. He would still be there if Rebekah hadn't fetched him back to receive a delivery of sand he said he never ordered. He could have saved his breath; she'd requested the late shipment in order to get him home and into bed. Thank heavens he went to his quarters and fell asleep without complaint. The kilnmaster was always a more biddable fellow after a few hours at the inn.

The wedgers and turners had finished mixing tomorrow's clay and retired to the mud-brick dwellings behind the house hours since. They were well fed on a meal of pheasant that had the power to put them to sleep faster than other meats, especially when served with the strong wine Rebekah switched with their usual drink. The menu had worked its blessed task. The last lamp in the servants' quarters was out an hour earlier than most nights, and all the men were working on a good night's sleep.

Of all the servants at the estate, Rebekah worried most that her overly protective maidservant would not sleep early enough to allow them their getaway. Mima was the lawgiver when it came to Rebekah's education, her dress, and her suitors, and Rebekah could no sooner order her off to bed than part the Red Sea. But Rebekah would not be deterred. She started this morning before dawn, getting Mima out of bed to help with the bread baking. She ordered an unusually large delivery of wheat, unwinnowed and unground, which required the better part of three hours to ready for the ovens. By the time the loaves were baking, Rebekah had sent the cook off to market with a list of perishables for dinner and asked Mima to help with the servants' lunch. Mima normally prepared food only for Josiah and Rebekah, and lunch for so many was tenfold the work to which she was accustomed. When she went for a short nap at midday, Rebekah convinced her to help with the sewing of a new sash for her robe. When the cook arrived with Josiah's favorite vegetables, Mima had to prepare them for dinner or lose them to mold. Once dinner was done and the dishes cleared, all it took from Rebekah was the suggestion of retiring early. Mima was up the stairs and down the west wing to her bedroom before Rebekah could suggest another chore. She hadn't heard from her since just after sundown.

Rebekah's gaze drifted to the front gate. She'd left it unlocked for the palace informant. Four times servants had found it ajar and she had to venture across the yard and unlatch their latching. Hopefully, with the entire estate gone to bed, the gate would remain unlocked.

Rebekah replaced the thick curtain and hurried down the hall to light the lamp in the reading room when a knock sounded. Three quick taps that echoed off the stonework in the corridor, followed by the shuffle of footsteps hardly audible in the dark silence. How did the informant get to the door so quickly after she replaced the curtain? But it had to be him. No one else would dare knock at this hour—at least she hoped it wasn't anyone but their trusted friend from the palace. She put away the lamp, returned down the hall and cracked open the door, expecting to find the bright, smiling face of the palace informant peering back at her. She was wrong. There was no one on the other side of the door. The informant had vanished, but he'd left a small urn on the porch. His small footprints trailed across the side yard and disappeared through a hole dug beneath the limestone wall, hardly wide enough for a child to shimmy through. By now he was into the neighbor's gardens and on his way back to the palace.

The urn he left on the porch was cast of blue porcelain with an oriental flower brushed onto the side under the clear finish. Rebekah set it on the table in the hallway beside the steps leading to the second floor. A rolled piece of expensive Egyptian papyrus stuck out the top, the message written with hasty pen strokes, most likely under difficult circumstances. It had to be, with so many soldiers milling about the palace. It read: *Escape by the south wall, no watch on that tower till dawn. Godspeed.*

Josiah appeared at the top of the stairs leading from Mima's bedroom. "She's asleep," he said, and picked his way slowly down the steps, keeping the hem of his black council robe from dragging. "You certainly tired her. I thought she was going to fall asleep in her soup during dinner."

Rebekah asked, "Can't we tell her?"

"Not about this."

"She'd help us, I know she would. There isn't anyone we trust more than Mima."

"It's best this way. If we're ever caught, she can answer truthfully that she knew nothing of it." Josiah glanced at the papyrus in Rebekah's hand. "You should have invited him in."

"He was away before I opened the door." Rebekah handed over the urn. It was only the second time the informant had left a sealed message on the porch and vanished. The first time he left a written message was to warn Josiah that Laban had almost captured him and he would have to cease communications until the threat subsided.

After two months of silence, Rebekah believed the palace informant had been captured. But contact was reestablished soon after and their work continued.

Josiah marched down the hall to the reading room with Rebekah following close behind. He lit the lamp on the table and began to pace.

Rebekah asked, "What's wrong, Papa?"

"He doesn't usually slip away like that. He always comes inside for a word with me."

"Has he been found out?"

"I doubt it." Josiah turned the urn in his hand. "He never would have gotten word to us if Laban knew." His voice was steady but a tinge of concern jumped the darkness between them. "Next time I'll be the one to wait for him. He must understand I don't expect him to risk his life for us."

"I'm sure he already knows that."

"Not well enough to keep him from spying. And what he's doing for us is spying, plain and simple. He'll be hanged if he's ever found out."

"Laban would never do that, not to him."

"His standing in the palace won't save him if he's ever captured." Josiah burned the message over the lamp and threw the burning ashes into the hearth. A bit of black ash remained on his thumb and he smudged it over Rebekah's nose. "It's night already and I haven't told you about the day you were born."

"Papa, not now. We have too many worries to talk about that."

"Allow me my father's pride on this most glorious of evenings." Josiah stood beside her. "It was seventeen years ago tonight you were born."

"You don't need to tell me the story again."

"I'll tell it every year until I have no breath to tell it or until the day you marry, and hopefully it's the latter."

Rebekah sat on a cushioned footstool in front of the cold, dark hearth and peered up at her father. His disguise matched her own, with black ash covering his face, and she could only imagine the red that flushed across his cheeks as it did whenever he told the story of her coming into the world.

Josiah said, "You were a lovely little thing to behold, not a cubit long with sparkling blue eyes, rose-colored lips and that nose." He leaned down and smudged his finger over it again. "It curled up when you smiled just like it does now. But back then you didn't have such beautiful hair, not a single strand on your head. If only your mother had lived to see you become such a lovely woman." He leaned over and held her hand. "I made her a promise that night. I remember it as if it were yesterday. Your mother had a difficult time breathing and I leaned over her so I could hear every word. She begged me to make certain you married the right man. It was very important to her. She repeated it five or six times. They were the last words she ever spoke."

"Papa?"

Josiah lifted her off the footstool with both hands. "What is it, girl?"

"Oh, nothing really. I was only wondering how I am to know who the right man is."

"He'll be strong so he can make a good living for you, with a good heart to tend to your needs, and bright so that you'll enjoy each other's company. But most of all he'll follow the prophets. Only a man like that would be worthy of my daughter." Josiah laid his hand on hers. "Is there something I should know about?"

"Don't you mean, *someone?*"

Josiah stepped back. "Is there?"

"Papa, you would be the first to know." Rebekah turned her head to the side and smiled. "Well, possibly the second, but no less than second." She glanced over at the waist-high reed basket standing in the corner of the reading room. It was the largest one from the clay pit and it had taken most of the day to prepare—to say nothing of keeping it out of Mima's sight. "I've packed everything you asked."

"Are you avoiding my interrogation of your heart?"

"I'm telling you there's nothing more to interrogate."

Rebekah leaned over the basket's edge. She'd placed three bottles of yellow lamp oil in the bottom, the grade that took fire the quickest. They'd need that if they were to burn down the stonemason's home and escape without being seen. There was a coil of double hemp rope to lower the family over the wall, a jar of sheep fat to grease the rope, bedding for the journey, and enough food and water to get them safely across the desert to Qumran.

Josiah took a scroll out from under his robe. It was a long parchment with a binding stick made of pine. He read through it before rolling it up and placing it with the supplies. Then he quickly turned away from the basket and walked to the window to check the yard. Rebekah asked, "What's that for?"

Josiah turned back from the window. "It's nothing."

"You promised me you wouldn't send a letter this time."

"It's only a comforting word." Josiah bent back over the window sill and peered out into the night. "Something to buoy our people up."

"May I read it?"

"I don't want any objections." Josiah replaced the thick curtain and came back to her side. "I must send word."

"This isn't a good thing."

"Is that an objection?"

"You know it's true."

Rebekah unscrolled the letter, spread it under the lamp and began to read. Josiah peered over her shoulder, close enough that she could feel his breath on her neck. *"To my dear friends,"* it began, the words barely legible in the dim light. *"My position on the Council is still secure, but I suspect I do not have Zadock's complete trust. My greatest concern is that he will so alter the management of the affairs of the Jews at Jerusalem as to bring down the punishment of God upon us all."*

"You can't write that." Rebekah's head shot up, clipping Josiah in the chin. "If the stonemason's caught with this, there'll be fifty soldiers on our doorstep come morning."

Josiah rubbed his jaw. "I'll make sure he hides it well."

"It would be better if you didn't send it at all."

"You worry like your mother."

Rebekah placed her finger over Josiah's lips before turning back to the letter. "*The Chief Elder is transforming the entire Council into a den of thieves. And what they plan to steal, I can only guess. Zadock speaks often of Jonathan, a new blacksmith from Sidon. I'm not certain what his intentions are for the man. As best I can tell, the blacksmith is not particularly religious, but he is possessed of integrity, a noble trait that Zadock will no doubt subvert.*

"Be comforted that the Council has no knowledge of us. You are safe at Qumran to live the Law of Moses in its fullness, it pointing our souls forward to the coming of the Anointed One."

Rebekah paused at Josiah's signature. He'd signed the letter with the title the Rekhabites had given him: *Teacher of Righteousness.* Rebekah returned the letter to the basket and covered it with a length of rope. It was full of news, but hardly the kind that would buoy up the faith of the people at Qumran. But then, Papa was never a man to gloss over anything.

Josiah hoisted the basket over his shoulder and walked it out the door. They crossed the yard without making a sound and when they reached the gate, Rebekah cracked it open and peered out. The windows of the homes across the way stood dark and the chimneys cold.

Rebekah went out the gate first. She hurried down Main Street, her black clothing shrouded in the shadows. She felt her way along the outside wall of the pottery yard to the corner and checked to make sure the way down Water Street was clear before motioning for Josiah to follow with the basket. While she waited for him, she stepped back into a dark recess in the wall and pressed her body against the cold limestone block, hidden in the safety of the shadows.

From there she could not see that Mima stood in her darkened second-story bedroom window, watching them sneak away.

The stonemason's home stood on the corner of Tunnel Street and Hinnom Place in Jerusalem's new city, just inside Hezekiah's wall near the cheesemakers' district. It was a two-story limestone building, unattached to the neighbors and it could burn for hours without the flames jumping to the adjacent rooftops, though the hundred goats milling about the cheesemakers' pens at the rear would suffer if they stampeded the gate. But with hardly a breath of wind blowing this time of night, none of the fodder from the stonemason's home would fall into their corral. The interior of the home would take fire quickly. Wooden beams spanned the roof, spruce wood filled the staircase and banister, and the hardwood decorating the mantle was so ornately carved the stonemason could have found work as a carpenter.

When Rebekah and Josiah arrived, they found the stonemason's family already wearing black sackcloth. The father covered the young boys' faces with ash from the fireplace and stood them next to the door, ready for a march to the tombs south of the city in memory of a deceased loved one. But the only deaths they would celebrate tonight were their own, the ones they were about to invent.

Josiah handed the stonemason a bronze incense burner. It was shaped like a large metal ball on the end of a triple brass chain. He said, "You may need this."

"For what?" The stonemason hung the brass ball in front of his eyes and studied the inscription from the prophet Job: . . . *destroy this body, yet in my flesh shall I see God.*

"You must remember this is not an escape."

"But I thought—"

"It's a funeral." Josiah pressed the incense burner against the stonemason's chest. "You're going to the funeral of your wife's uncle in Bethlehem. All you have to do is wave this a few times in the air, have your wife wail a bit, and Laban's soldier's will leave you alone."

"I thought we were going over the south wall in a basket."

"You are, my good man." Josiah patted him on the shoulder. "But you must be prepared for anything if you hope to get out of the city safely."

"Do you really believe they'll catch us?" The stonemason pulled his sons close to him. The youngest boy grabbed his father by the leg and nestled his head against his thigh.

Josiah spoke in a quiet but firm voice. He said, "By the grace of God you go, and by His almighty hand you will be protected."

The stonemason ran his hand over his sackcloth clothing. "With God's help we don't need all this."

"God will protect you after you've done all you can." Josiah placed the incense burner around the stonemason's neck like a brass amulet. "Now we should get on with it."

They set hay and gypsum on the floor in front of the hearth for kindling and laid linen rugs, sleeping mats, and blankets around the base. The rest of the furniture was stacked on top, every possession the stonemason and his wife had worked their married life to accumulate. A cedar chest; a stone-cutting bench; a dining table with chairs; three standing cases for pottery; a tall fishing spear for the father, and a shorter one for the sons; a baking paddle with matching wooden bowls; and the frame of a bed the stonemason had yet to stretch with leather cords but would never finish.

The stonemason watched Josiah as he sloshed the oil over their belongings. He was a sturdy young man with enough life ahead of him to build a finer home at Qumran. But in spite of his strength, he couldn't keep his chin from trembling at the sight of Josiah preparing to turn his home to ashes. His wife sat in a solitary chair rocking the baby. It was the only piece of furniture they hadn't piled against the hearth. She cuddled the infant with trembling hands and all Rebekah could do was dry her tears and tie the infant into a satchel strapped to her mother's bosom.

Josiah waited until the woman composed herself enough to allow him to stack her rocker with the other furnishings. The stonemason's family would be remembered as good neighbors lost in a tragic accident. It was best this way. They would be believed dead and a proper funeral would follow without a single corpse to bury.

The flames caught the rugs first, spread up the table legs and danced across the chairs, reaching for the wooden roof beams. A stream of smoke chased the company of Rekhabites out the side door and into the alley. They traveled the back way, down Tunnel Street and under the arch onto High Street, then along Water Street before emerging at the south wall. It towered above them in the moonlight, its high precipice and mighty watchtower dominating the horizon, the tallest of the city's six major walls. And, according to the palace informant, it was the only one that would not have a watch tonight. The closest watch was stationed a good thousand cubits away, on the southeast turn in the wall. The way to the top of the south wall was worn smooth from years of use, the mortar cracked and crumbling. The aging steps had injured more men than any watch had saved. Little question why soldiers preferred to man any tower but this one.

Rebekah went up the steps first, holding the woman's hand. The stonemason followed, carrying his two sons in his arms, while Josiah quietly dragged the basket up the steps.

They climbed slowly past the roof line of adjacent buildings to where they could see the dark skyline of Jerusalem. The square rooftops of four thousand homes stood dark, except for the stonemason's residence. Smoke poured out the upper windows and filtered into the air. The walls had taken fire, and flames leapt through the sunken roof, lighting the home with an eerie orange glow. There were no voices crying "fire" or men running through the streets carrying buckets of water, though the quiet wouldn't last much longer. Not with the anxious cry of goats filling the air and the thick smell of smoke hovering over the neighborhood.

Rebekah reached the top of the south wall first. She crossed the catwalk and checked over the opposite railing. They stood two hundred feet above the Kidron Valley. From this height the road to Bethlehem was no larger than a farmer's furrow. A gusting wind swept through the valley and bent the tree branches along the roadside before turning up the wall and whistling between the stone parapets of the deserted watchtower.

Josiah lashed one end of the rope twice around the stone outcrop, wove the other end through the basket's grips and lowered it over the railing. The men held the basket steady while Rebekah helped the woman and her children over. When they were safely inside, she kissed the mother and pushed them away.

The rope pulled taut, slacked, then pulled again as the basket fought the stiff wind and lowered past two hundred cubits of brick and mortar to the floor of the Kidron Valley. They were lucky. The basket reached the ground with three coils of rope to spare. Two tugs signaled they were safely out, and the basket slipped easily to the top. The stonemason was next. Josiah tied off the rope and the man climbed in. Josiah whispered, "Watch yourself through the hills. The army patrols there at night." He leaned over the wall and clasped the man's hand. "Do you have the letter?"

The stonemason patted the small leather satchel tied around his belly. "I'll make sure it doesn't fall into the wrong hands."

"I've told you how to keep from being followed."

"We'll take the streambed until we're away from the city."

"And if you're caught?"

"We'll not be taken."

"But if you are, what will you say?"

"That we're on the way to the funeral of an uncle."

Josiah worked a swatch of the stonemason's black cloak between his fingers. "Tell them you're in mourning. They'll respect your grieving and leave you alone."

Josiah swung him away, letting him down hand-over-hand with Rebekah's help. He signaled his arrival at the bottom with two tugs, and

Josiah pulled the basket quickly back while Rebekah coiled the rope. They had most of it drawn in when a voice pierced the air. It came from the next watchtower over. A soldier raised an oil lamp to the night sky. "Who goes there?" The soldier started down the east catwalk, slowly at first, then breaking into a brisk march. "Identify yourselves!"

"Run, Papa," Rebekah said. "Drop the basket and run."

Josiah took her by the arm. "He'll only chase us and alert others." He positioned the basket just below the ledge, tied it off and threw the extra rope over the side. Josiah shimmied in first. Rebekah followed him over the ledge but her cloak caught on the parapet and she had to climb back onto the catwalk to free herself.

The soldier reached the last bend and turned onto the south wall. He was close enough that Rebekah couldn't get into the basket without giving away their hiding place. He sprinted toward her, his metal-plated kilt jingling with each firm stride. He raised his sword as he approached and asked, "What are you doing here?"

Rebekah lowered her head and offered a silent prayer. Dear God, how should she answer the soldier? She no sooner thought the prayer than her father's words came rushing into her mind. It was seventeen years ago tonight she was born. That's what he had said to her earlier this evening and it was the answer she needed to give the soldier now. It was the perfect answer. Rebekah raised her head, gazed at the stars and said, "What a beautiful evening."

Her answer forced the soldier back a step. "What did you say?"

"It must have been a night like this seventeen years ago."

The soldier sheathed his sword. "Why are your dressed like that?"

"Why it's my birthday, of course."

The soldier tipped his polished brass helmet back, exposing his sweat-covered brow. "Why do you wear sackcloth and ashes to celebrate birth?"

Rebekah pointed to the tombs on the plains south of Jerusalem. "My mother died giving birth to me."

"I'm sorry." The soldier sheathed his sword.

"Don't be. I find peace knowing I'll see her again, one day."

The soldier pulled his helmet down over his brow and looked away from her, away from her words of faith in a resurrection that many in Jerusalem had forsaken. "I can only leave you to mourn a few moments longer. You shouldn't be up here at all, you understand." He started down the catwalk when a gust of wind shifted the basket, slapping it against the wall.

The soldier turned back to face Rebekah. "What's that?"

"What was what?"

"That noise from over there."

The soldier started for the ledge, but Rebekah stepped in front of him. "I didn't hear anything."

He was a large man and he easily pushed past her and peered over the edge. Rebekah slid in next to him, his sword pressing against her side and a cold shiver piercing her soul. Josiah hung huddled in the basket, staring up at them with wide eyes.

"I can explain," Rebekah said.

"No need for that. I understand completely."

"You do?"

"I know what it's like to grow up without a mother. I lost mine when I was a boy." He kept staring over the wall without the slightest indication he'd seen Josiah. When the soldier pulled back from leaning over the edge, he said, "Must be the wind."

He was the night watchman, chosen for his keen eyesight, but he'd looked directly at Josiah and seen nothing. The soldier excused himself and marched down the catwalk toward his post on the east tower, leaving Rebekah to mourn her mother's passing, but all she could think to do was rejoice. The watchman's blind eyes were nothing short of a heavenly miracle, and she praised God.

They'd been spared.

CHAPTER 10

Aaron pried open the door to the smelting oven. The fire popped inside the logs and the wood fell in on itself with a thunderous crack.

Jonathan and Daniel kept watch from across the forging table, though they didn't need to stare. Aaron could tend the fire without them hovering over him. He didn't need their protecting watch or their help. Tending the fires was the easy part of blacksmithing as long as he could do it sitting down.

Jonathan said, "Let Daniel stock the oven with coal."

"I can do it, Papa."

"Not the hard coal. I don't want you near the oven when the hard coal goes in."

"It's not going to happen again."

"You don't know that." Jonathan motioned for Daniel to get the shovel. "Now, move aside and let your brother stock the smelting oven."

Hard coal was the steelmaking secret that nearly killed Aaron. He never told anyone outside the shop about the fierce temperatures hard coal produced inside the smelting oven. It was their secret and few blacksmiths had the good fortune of discovering the stuff. Hard coal was the purple ingot left over after a load of black coal burned down. It was hard as a rock and free of the impurities that made ordinary coal burn cold. With hard coal, the smelting oven was hotter than with black coal, hotter than with wood, hot enough to smelt iron ore to steel. And that made Jonathan and his sons more than blacksmiths.

They were artisans because they knew the secret to making steel that other smiths lived every day to find out and died never knowing.

Aaron shimmied down the bench away from the oven door and let Daniel shovel in the coal. The bench ran the length of the shop from the front door to the back wall. Before Jonathan built it, Aaron had to limp about the shop on his feet, kneel at the block to chop wood, and lie on the floor next to the smelter to set a proper fire. But now, with the bench legs fitted to the height of the forging table, and the last splinters sanded out of the long boards, the bench was a positive comfort.

Aaron slid over to the shop doors and pushed them open to let in a breeze. He took a deep breath of cool morning air as a grinning young man peered round the half-opened door. He said, "Good morning. Didn't know which shop was yours till you opened up. There isn't much smoke coming from the chimney."

"The smelting oven burns too hot to make much smoke." Aaron scooted off his bench and tried to stand with the help of a staff.

"Awfully warm day for blacksmithing."

"We're used to it."

"I never fire an oven after the sun gets over the hills. It makes for unbearable work."

Aaron scratched the side of his head. "You're a blacksmith?"

"I mend tools now and then. Only problem is I don't have time, not with the olive harvest on and fifty camels to outfit."

Mend things himself? The stranger didn't look strong enough to lift a forging hammer or work a pair of tongs. He was a swift-talking lad with the savvy of a man, but the body of a boy. His sandy-brown hair matched the patch of freckles that streamed across his cheeks. There wasn't a shekel of fat on his thin frame and he could have flown away with a flock of birds if he had the notion.

"I'm looking for the blacksmith named Aaron."

"What do you want with him?"

"I've got a caravan leaving for Egypt next month and there isn't time to mend everything that needs mending. You know, bridles, wheels, the usual things." He spoke like a caravan master, but he couldn't be. He was too young for anything more than a stable boy. "We used to have a blacksmith come out to the plantation this time of year to help us get the caravans ready." He glanced at the abandoned shop across the street. "He owned that place right there. Fine man, hard worker. The Babylonians took him captive with the rest of the blacksmiths after the war." He stared at the bandages wrapped around Aaron's feet. "Do you know where I can find Aaron, the son of Jonathan?"

Aaron turned his head and spat. "What kind of wage do you pay?"

"I'd go as high as five shekels a day and a talent of silver when the work's finished."

Aaron let out a whistle louder than a river crane at mating season. He said, "You've got yourself a blacksmith." He made his way over to shake on the deal, but the stranger didn't offer his hand. He was searching for a reason to tell Aaron he'd have to find a man who wasn't crippled. At least that's what Aaron thought until the stranger said, "I was told you'd have trouble with your feet."

"You know about my accident?"

"My father does. Said he had a good feeling about hiring the boy with the injured feet." The stranger brushed his hand across his freckled cheeks. "And whenever my father says he has a good feeling about something, he's usually right. We'll work things out somehow." He handed Aaron a string of broken camel harnesses and three horse bridles. "You'll have to ride out to the plantation for the rest of the work."

"Plantation?"

"Beit Zayit. Have you heard of it?"

"Who hasn't? More land than a man can walk across in a day, largest olive vineyards in Judah. You work there?"

Jonathan came to the door with a forging hammer at his side. He tipped his head and said, "Morning, son."

"Good to meet you, sir. I'm Sam."

"That's a good Egyptian name. Are you from that part of the world?"

"No, sir." He shook Jonathan's hand and flashed a grin as wide as the Nile Delta. "Our family made their fortunes caravanning olive oil to Egypt, so when I was born, my father insisted on a well-bred name from there. It means uniter of the lands, but the only thing I'll be uniting are stray camels unless I get your son to repair those bridles." A saddlebag hung from Sam's shoulder. The thick leather was double-stitched and the seams covered with silver clasps. He unlatched the buckle and rummaged through it until he found a plow bit under a coil of rope. He walked it across the shop and dropped it on the forging table next to Daniel. The low-grade iron had a crack across the belly two thumbs wide and was rusted worse than a nail in salt water.

"Can you fix this? We've got winter wheat that needs planting."

Daniel set aside the sickle he was sharpening. "I can put a hammer to it, but I can't promise anything. You'll be lucky if it doesn't crack."

"I always feel lucky."

Daniel buried it under the coals of the open hearth, turning it slowly with tongs until the metal softened. Sweat beaded off the end of his nose and spilled onto the sputtering coals before the bit was red enough for the hammer. He yanked it out, steadied it on the table and brought the forging hammer down with three careful strokes, pounding its cracked edges. On his last swing the plow bit split open on the table, the heart of it eaten by rust.

Daniel hung the hammer on its peg. "Your plow bit's seen its last furrow."

"How much for a new one?"

"A half-talent of silver."

The stranger could get two plow bits for that much, but Daniel knew when to barter up, and Sam was the first man in months who could afford to pay for their steel.

"Will you forge me a new one?" Sam asked.

"That depends on how soon you need it," Daniel replied.

"Two weeks."

"That isn't a lot of time."

Jonathan said, "He'll have it done for you." He spoke in a firm voice. "Daniel spends his strength wrestling men instead of metal, but I'll see he makes time for your work."

"Is he any good?"

Jonathan came around the forging table and squared his shoulders. There was no mistaking his pride. He said, "My son's the finest master forger in Judah."

"I meant his wrestling."

Daniel said, "I never lose, and I can prove it if you like."

"Very well, let's have a go right here."

Daniel removed his smithing apron and tunic. He said, "What do you say we put a small wager on this?"

"I don't like small wagers," Sam said.

"Then, what did you have in mind?"

"One throw, not the best out of five. If you win, I'll double what you're asking for the plow bit. You lose, and you do the work without pay."

Aaron let out another whistle, this one longer and higher than the first. Sam could get eight plow bits for that much money. How he could afford such a wager, Aaron didn't know.

Daniel strutted toward the door. "Let's step outside."

"You're not wrestling *me*." Sam walked alongside Daniel, matching him stride for stride. They pulled up at the shop door and Sam said, "It's my little brother Nephi I want you to wrestle."

A boy stood next to the shop holding the reins of two Arabians. By the breed of horse he steadied, he was from a wealthy family. Any Jew who could afford such an animal was rich beyond measure, and these boys owned two. Their black coats were freshly curried, manes cut short, and tails trimmed to the same length. Their hooves were shod with new shoes and their legs wrapped to the knees with silver-stitched cloth. They were fitted with high saddles for easy riding over long journeys and the flaps were decorated with silver studs sewn in the outline of an olive tree.

When Nephi saw them staring, he flashed a quick grin and it wasn't difficult to see the boys were related, though the rest of him hardly resembled Sam's feeble constitution. Nephi dressed as a mother would dress her youngest. His thick shoulders had long outgrown his light-blue Egyptian tunic and he stood with his feet together, his legs crowded by the boyish kilt he wore. His curly black hair was combed forward over his brow and tied in place under a blue silk headband. If it weren't for his powerful arms, he'd be confused for a child. He had a child's innocent clean face, with dimpled red checks, wide brown eyes that framed a square nose and straight white teeth. He said good morning, tied the horses to a post and walked over wearing a new pair of sandals freshly polished in beeswax. He strode past them, his thick frame bumping lightly against Daniel as he stepped inside. The two were about the same height, though Nephi's leaner frame made him seem taller.

Sam arranged a space in the center of the shop, moving the bench behind the ovens and spreading hay over the stone floor. He said, "This should do if we're only wrestling to one throw. Best of five and we'd have to do this in the street." He shook his head. "I've never liked a street fight. It always draws a crowd. You lose one time in front of a crowd and they never let you forget it."

Nephi leaned close to Sam and lowered his voice to a whisper, hardly audible over the crackle of the fire in the ovens. "Not another match."

"This is different."

"That's what you said about the soldier from Fort Lakhish."

"He was from Shilo," said Sam.

"He was twice my age." Nephi lifted the sleeve of his tunic, revealing a large bruise on his arm.

"Daniel's maybe two years older." Sam removed Nephi's headband and his deep black curls fell over his brow. "One throw and then we go home."

Nephi blew the locks from in front of his eyes. "One throw and then I go home—with or without you."

Sam pushed Nephi toward the makeshift pit and left him standing there alone. Nephi didn't remove his tunic like Daniel and he kept his sandals latched about his feet. It was a sure bet the boy didn't know the finer points of wrestling. Daniel never wore anything but a kilt when he wrestled. Said he couldn't move fast enough and the cloth always got in the way. But there Nephi stood, fully dressed from shoulder to toe. He did move with a powerful stride for a boy of fifteen. He tested his footing in the straw, staking a full circle around Daniel.

Daniel asked, "So, what happened to the soldier from Shilo?"

"You can't really judge my wrestling by that match."

"You lost?"

Nephi grinned. "I beat him in three straight throws."

They lunged at each other.

Daniel got hold around Nephi's waist, but he twisted free. He feigned for Daniel's arm, but grabbed his shoulder, turned him about and picked him up off the ground. He was good and he had the strength to beat Daniel. He took a step and started to hurl him from the pit when Daniel arched his shoulders with enough force to break free. He wrapped himself around Nephi and came onto his back, locking him in a standing cradle.

Aaron ducked as Nephi flew over the bench. He landed on his side and rolled three times before slamming against the shop door.

Daniel spoke to Sam in bursts, his chest heaving for breath. "That will be one talent of silver for a new plow bit."

Sam scratched the side of his head. "You'll get your money."

Aaron stood with the help of his staff and tried not to teeter. The less he looked like a cripple, the more Sam would treat him like a blacksmith. He said, "When do I start?"

"Three weeks. You can board at the plantation with the other men. The cooks put out three meals a day and you'll have a good straw bed with blankets. It should take about two weeks to get the caravan ready."

"What caravan?" Jonathan removed his smithing apron and hung it on a peg. He came around in front of Sam. "No one told me anything about my son working on a caravan."

Aaron said, "It's good money, Papa."

"Forgive me, sir." Sam handed Jonathan a talent of silver for the plow bit, more money than they had earned in weeks. "I thought you understood we came to hire your son."

"I didn't." Jonathan brushed the ash from his hands. "Not without my blessing."

Aaron said, "My feet are fine."

"This isn't about your feet, son. We have to be sure about the new customers we take on."

"Sure of what?" Sam asked.

Daniel leaned his head in and grinned. "The serpent people."

"He means Rekhabites." Jonathan pushed Daniel aside. "We don't work for them."

Sam raised his chin. "Are you accusing us?"

"I'm asking."

"We're the sons of Lehi." Sam nodded as he spoke, as if their father's wealth was enough to prove their innocence.

"I don't need an introduction, boy. I need your word."

Nephi stepped between them. "I can tell you, sir, we're not traitors. Not now, not ever."

"Tell me this, boy." Jonathan rubbed the talent of silver between his fingers. "Do you believe in the God they call Yeshua the Anointed One?" His eyes were a cold, tarnished copper and he didn't blink, not even the hint of a flinch in his stare.

Nephi dusted himself off and pulled the straw out of his sleeves. He said, "We believe the words of the prophets, but that doesn't make us Rekhabites."

Sam said, "If you doubt our allegiance to the kingdom, we'll take our business and our money elsewhere."

"I'm not turning you away." Jonathan slipped the talent of silver into his pocket. "When you come back for the plow bit in two weeks, I'll have an answer for you."

"It's my uncle who'll come for the plow." Sam walked to the door of the shop. "He'll want to speak with you about this."

Jonathan followed him into the street. "How will I know him when I meet him?"

"You won't miss him. No one ever mistakes Uncle Ishmael."

Sam mounted and reined a full circle around Jonathan while he waited for Nephi to untie and rein in next to him. He was a young man, but sitting in the silver-studded saddle of a fine horse, Sam looked like a king hovering over a commoner. He didn't break into his wide smile. His eyes had taken on a sullen look and his body sat rigid in the saddle. He didn't offer a parting word, not even a tip of the head. And once his brother Nephi was mounted, they spurred away at full gallop, their spirited Arabians tossing their heads and their shoes clattering over the stone.

Aaron stood watching in the street long after Nephi and Sam had disappeared around the corner at the top of the hill. The clapping of their horses' hooves filtered over the rooftops of the shops beyond the blacksmith district as they trotted down Main Street toward the west gate. It was a dull sound, shielded by brick walls and two-story facades and it mixed with the sound of rolling cart wheels and the cries of merchants selling their wares, but Aaron would never forget the sound of metal-shod hooves trotting over cobblestone. No one had ever come by their shop with such fine animals before.

The sound trailed off slowly, but as it faded, the voice speaking to his soul grew, telling him he should seek work with Lehi and his sons. It was like a whisper he heard with his heart, not his ears, and the longer he stood in the street staring at the place where Sam and Nephi's horses had disappeared at the top of the smithing district, the more the thought was a firm voice saying he *would* work for the olive oil merchant, no matter how impossible that seemed with Papa standing beside him, his teeth clenched and the muscles around his jaw flinching. He would have pressed Jonathan about the matter right there, but Aaron had seen that look on Papa's face before and now was not the time for words. Better to let the passage of time cool Jonathan's fervor like the spray of water on a hot smithing iron. He would have words with Papa later, and avoid the violent rush of steam that accompanied that kind of tempering.

CHAPTER 11

The sun slipped below the hills and painted shades of evening gray across the freshly mortared balcony of the Citadel. The new limestone railing trapped the heat of the sultry day and Zadock warmed his hands on it. After the war, he had ordered the renovation of the balcony along with the restoration of the entire government headquarters. Carpenters replaced the front entry doors with thick slabs of olive wood, reinforced with metal cross pieces, and stonemasons bricked over the windows on the first two floors to guard against the threat of robbers entering the city and taking the building hostage.

Evening quiet settled into the winding streets that sprawled below in a web of cobblestone paths, twisting around the homes of the forty-thousand inhabitants who knew Zadock as Chief Elder of the Jews at Jerusalem. At fifty-three years of age, it had taken him more than half a century to rise out of the depressed quarter of the lower city and sit as chief of Jerusalem's highest council.

The scuffle of sandals on stone broke the quiet, and Shechem hoisted himself onto the railing. His beardless face was flushed red and streaked with sweat from scaling the wall. He wore a leather tunic and kilt that no Jew would wear against the skin, but then Shechem was hardly a man to observe the laws of Moses. He was a rebellious soul with little patience for the laws of men or the gods they worshiped. He peered over the ledge and said, "I like the alterations you've made to the place." He jumped over the railing and landed on the balcony. "It's more of a challenge to break in."

"Did anyone see you?"

"No one ever sees me." Shechem leaned against the stone with his arms folded. "Where's Laban?"

"He'll be along soon."

"You've been preaching patience for months." Shechem spat into the alley that ran between the balcony and the palace. The lamps in the upper chambers where the royal family made their home burned brightly and danced shadows into the courtyards below. The first four windows graced the bedroom of King Zedekiah and his wife, Miriam. The next three windows marked the room of his eldest son, Prince Mulek. The last two windows stood dark. King Zedekiah's two youngest boys, Dan and Benjamin, were down for the night.

"Cursed sons," Shechem said. "There are too many heirs to this throne." He drew a dagger out of his boot and ran his fingers lightly across the blade. "I should take care of them tonight."

"Not until the relics are ready."

"How long will that take?"

"Do I look like a blacksmith?"

"Hurry him."

"I haven't hired him." Zadock primped the pleats in his robe. "I need to be sure we can trust the blacksmith before we tell him about the sword of Joseph."

The clatter of breastplates sounded at the balcony entrance. The curtains parted and Laban stood at the threshold. Lamplight from the council chamber silhouetted his form. At thirty years, he seemed a timeless figure, dressed in full brass armor. He looked toward Zadock and asked, "Did you tell him?"

Shechem stood away from the wall, his leather kilt sagging around his hips. "Tell me what?"

Zadock turned to face Shechem, his robes swirling on his sudden movement. "Your friend Uriah is going to be found guilty of treason. I'm going to see to it."

"What good will that do?" Shechem turned the pearl-covered hilt of his dagger in his hand. "You don't even hold the man in your prisons."

"We will." Laban moved away from the entry, the silk curtains raising on a stream of air behind his long stride. "And this time he won't get away." He leaned over the railing, his gaze reaching past the city walls to the dark countryside surrounding Jerusalem. "I'm putting Captain Elnathan in charge of the mission; he's my finest military scout. It shouldn't take him long to organize a search party and begin the task of flushing Uriah out of the hills."

Shechem said, "He isn't in our hills anymore."

Laban stepped back from the ledge and squared up to Shechem, his breastplates pressing against him. "Do you know where he is?"

"My men know every empty quarter in the hill country, and they've found nothing." Shechem backed away. "With the palace informant dying in Uriah's inn, we may have frightened him out of the country."

"The palace informant isn't dead." Laban gripped the stone railing and squinted across at the palace. A woman stood in the dimly lit window on the fifth floor. It was Queen Miriam and she was dressing for bed. "I used to think the palace informant was a military man, some low-ranking officer in my army. But I'm beginning to think it has to be someone of greater stature. Someone with access to everything that's going on in the palace." Laban slapped his fist against his chest. "The courier you saw die, Hosha Yahu, he wasn't the informant."

Shechem leaned forward, his long hair falling between them. "How do you know that?"

"Before his death there were only bits of information leaking from the palace. A few missed watches on the city gates we can endure, but now others know about us."

"Who?"

"Jeremiah." Laban turned back to the railing and peered out over the city. The streets stood dark and silent, except for the stir of soldiers changing guard below at the main doors of the Citadel. "I met him in the market a few days back. He didn't mention any of us by name, but I could tell he knew something about us."

"I'll take care of him." Shechem kissed the blade of his dagger.

"Not Jeremiah!" Laban removed his breastplates and slowly pushed them along the railing toward Shechem, scraping the metal over the stone. "It's Uriah who must be silenced."

Zadock stepped between them and grabbed the breastplates. The grating stopped and in the silence he asked, "Is there a reason you want Uriah put to death so badly?"

Laban raised his finger toward Zadock. "You make sure the Council convicts him of treason. I'll see to the rest."

Zadock's narrow chin moved slowly as he spoke. He said, "If Jeremiah knows about us, and you say he does, then it seems he's the one we should silence."

"We can't get rid of both of them; we need one alive," Laban said. "Or did you forget that only a prophet can anoint the sword of Joseph before the coronation?"

"Uriah can do that for us."

"Forget your Hebrew traditions!" Shechem waved his dagger in the air. "You should silence both prophets."

Zadock said, "The blade must be properly anointed."

Shechem tossed his dagger in the air and caught it by the hilt. "Have your maidservants do it."

"We'll do this my way." Laban began to pace and in a low voice, almost a whisper, said, "Jeremiah doesn't know what Uriah knows."

Zadock tapped his fingers together "Which is . . . ?"

Laban said, "I ran Jeremiah out of the city, banned him from ever coming back. That should keep him from interfering."

"That doesn't answer my question."

"I'm telling you that Uriah must be silenced." Laban brushed the sweat from his brow. "That's all I've got to say on the matter." He pushed away from the railing and crossed the balcony in three quick strides. The silk curtains lifted out of his path and he was gone into the light of the council chamber.

Shechem parted the curtain with his dagger and they watched Laban leave the chamber by a side door. "There's something he isn't telling us."

"Don't be a fool," Zadock said. "Laban wants the prophets dead as much as we do."

Shechem let go of the curtains. "Watch him." He straddled the railing as he spoke.

"I always do."

"He's our only chance to get what we both deserve." Shechem climbed down the face of the Citadel, the ringing of his words mingling with the scuffle of his disappearance.

CHAPTER 12

Elizabeth was on her way to market when curiosity begged her to stop at the pottery yard of Josiah the potter. She hid in the shadows of a fig tree across the street and peered between the branches to get a glimpse of the enchantress who had captured Aaron's fancy. A farmer's cart passed in front of the firing yard and Elizabeth had to stand on her tiptoes not to lose sight of the gate.

"Excuse me, but aren't you Aaron's sister?" The sound of a woman's voice spun Elizabeth around. Rebekah stood not three cubits away. She held a flowerpot fired in red clay and glazed to a brilliant finish. She'd come out the side gate and crossed the street without a sound.

Elizabeth switched her shopping basket to the other arm and arranged the skirts of her robe. "Why, yes, I . . . I am."

"I thought so." Rebekah pressed the flowerpot into Elizabeth's hands. "I planned to bring you this gift when you first moved to the city. I don't know how I let all these days slip away without making a proper welcome."

"You don't need to bother."

"It isn't any trouble. I had Papa fire this one especially for you."

Elizabeth peered into the pot and when she found her name inscribed into the fired clay with delicate Hebrew script and sealed under a coat of glaze she began to understand exactly why Aaron was taken by this woman. "My brother talks highly of you." She bit her lower lip. That was not something Aaron would have wanted her to say.

"He's a fine man." Rebekah's face flushed. "I'm sure there's a good number of women who have taken an interest in him since you moved to the city."

"They would have—if it weren't for the accident."

"I'm sorry about that."

"You know what happened to him?"

"Shouldn't I?"

"It's just that, well, Aaron seemed to think you might not."

"When I met him the other day he seemed to have healed well. He is healed, isn't he?"

Elizabeth switched her shopping basket back to the other arm. That was a question better left without an answer and she fell silent.

Rebekah took Elizabeth by the hand and they began walking across the street toward the gates of the pottery yard. She asked if Elizabeth liked it here in Jerusalem, how her family was getting along, and how the weather here compared to the coast of Sidon this time of year, to which Elizabeth answered yes, fine, and hot. It wasn't until Rebekah suggested they go shopping together that Elizabeth decided she'd found a friend. When Rebekah asked if any young men had caught her fancy, she explained that she had hoped to be courted by the son of a cobbler in Sidon, but after the move to Jerusalem she would never see him again, and she didn't have a robe fine enough to attract the attention of another. Her family had worked to build her father's blacksmithing shop in the war-ravaged smithing district and their income hardly allowed for her to weave a new robe to replace the frayed one she wore.

At the gate of the pottery yard, Rebekah turned before entering and said, "We'll talk again."

"I'd like that."

"Until then." Rebekah leaned over and kissed Elizabeth on the cheek. "Welcome to Jerusalem."

Jawbone Inn. Named for the day when Samson slew a thousand enemy soldiers with the jawbone of an ass. It was a fitting name for an inn across the street from the military grounds. Daniel turned the corner below the inn, and made his way toward the entrance, walking beneath the eaves of the shops lining the street. No one would recognize him in the long afternoon shadows that covered his face.

Mama said it would shame her if he ever patronized the Jawbone, but he wasn't going there to drink. He had a meeting inside, a very important one, though the scent of wines coming from the inn were lure enough. The law forbade serving strong wines before sundown, but the loud laughter that streamed through the dark windows convicted the innkeeper of beginning the unlawful merry-making early, a crime he committed nearly every afternoon about the time soldiers ended their training and gathered at his inn.

Daniel pulled open the door, greeted by a round of vile oaths. The afternoon sun filtered in with him and cast a dim glow on the patrons, all of them soldiers. They waved their mugs and cursed their fortunes as violently as they did their misfortunes.

The jawbone of an ass was nailed over the wine shelves and tankards hung from a rack overhead. The smallest vials held just enough to wet the lips. A good size for Daniel who had never taken strong wines before. The larger cups were for the regulars, men who came here to forget their lot for a few hours. The largest ones were for troubled men, the kind who lost their souls in the bottom of a mug.

The innkeeper stood behind the bar drawing wine from a keg and when he saw Daniel he corked the spigot. "Did you bring the money?"

Daniel tossed down the ten mina coins he'd gleaned from his father's purse. The innkeeper reached for them, but Daniel pushed his hand away. "Introduce me first."

"I agreed to let you come in here and talk to him. The rest is up to you." The innkeeper snatched the money and pointed out Captain Laban drinking at a table of officers. He was dressed down in a simple tunic, without any of the metal plates or buttons of his usual regalia. But Laban didn't need anything to set him apart. Everyone who drank at the Jawbone revered him as something akin to royalty; and despite Laban's blood-shot eyes and intemperate drinking moods, he was nobility in this inn.

Daniel reached across the bar, grabbing the innkeeper by the sleeve. "I paid you for an introduction."

"Let go of me."

"Not until I get what I came for."

"All right."

The innkeeper filled a tray with drinks and led Daniel away from the captain, toward the opposite corner of the inn where two men sat alone, their table half hidden between rough-hewn cedar columns. The light blue cloth in their tunics, stitched with gold-threaded hems at the sleeves and necklines, spoke of a wealthy Egyptian upbringing. Their kilts were tied with a knot at their sides like the merchants of Tanis, rather than at the small of the back as most Hebrew men dressed. They strapped their sandals up to the knee, a style common among men who had reason to cross the scorpion-infested deserts of the Sinai.

The innkeeper shoved a mug into Daniel's hand. "Drink with these men and they'll see that you get a proper introduction. They're friends of the captain."

"What kind of friends?"

"They always meet the captain at this table after the other soldiers leave. They spend a lot of time talking in private. You know, personal things. I try not to listen. I just serve the wine. If anyone can get you what you want, they can." The innkeeper stepped around the cedar pillars, gathered the empty mugs and replaced them with another round. He kept his head down when he spoke to the older-looking man and said, "This boy's buying your drinks."

"Who are you?" asked the larger of the two.

"My name's Daniel, the son of Jonathan the blacksmith." He pointed at the gold trim in their tunics. "What part of Egypt are you from?"

"Does Laman sound like an Egyptian name to you?" He sucked a long drink from the mug. At twenty-one years Laman had the face of a much older man. His robust frame filled enough of the bench on his side of the table that Daniel decided it wise to sit across from him, next to his smaller, younger companion.

"I didn't mean anything by it." Daniel leaned against the backrest. "By your clothes I thought you were Egyptian."

"I come here to forget we're only Hebrew." Laman wiped his mouth with the sleeve of his tunic, soiling the expensive cloth with a deep red stain. He said, "This is my brother Lemuel."

The younger man wasn't as threatening as Laman. He had the look of a nineteen-year old, without a hair on his red-flushed face or the strength to wrestle a bird. Lemuel's thin neck sprouted out of his tunic like a cattail by a river and his long, spindly arms draped across the table like wet reeds.

Despite the two men's differences, they followed the same fashions. Their eyebrows were trimmed in perfect semicircles like all good Egyptians though their dark complexions were nothing like the light Egyptian coloring he'd seen on men from the Nile. The only other particular that didn't look Egyptian were their nails. They were trimmed short like olive pickers to keep the green meat from lodging beneath them. Their hands were stained a light yellow green, leaving little doubt they earned their living working an olive press.

Laman asked, "Why did you buy our drinks?"

Daniel said, "I need to talk to you about the military."

"You're buying for the wrong people." Laman raised his mug toward the far side of the inn. "The soldiers sit over there."

"The innkeeper said you have the captain's ear." Daniel held his wine glass close to his chest. "He said you're good friends." He glanced across the inn at the captain then brought his gaze back to Laman downing his wine. Laban and Laman shared a resemblance as close as some brothers. But for all their similarities, they couldn't be family; everyone in Jerusalem knew that. The captain was the last living descendant of Joseph and he had claim to the national treasures, something no other Jew could boast.

The resemblance must have been due to the way Laman wore his beard. He shaved after the same style as the captain, a thin line starting at the ears, splitting around his lips and forming a point at the tip of his chin. That had to be the reason they were so alike. And though Daniel was certain they were not related, he couldn't keep from leaning over the table and saying, "You're either good friends or brothers."

Laman slammed his mug down, the wine sloshing over the brim. "Did the innkeeper say that?"

"I just meant you look alike." Daniel glanced once more across the inn to the captain's table and then back at Laman. "Quite a bit, alike."

Lemuel tapped his fingers rapidly on the tabletop until he got Daniel's attention. "Their names sound the same. You know, Laban, Laman." He laughed into his mug. "About this far into the drinking everyone calls them by the wrong name, but they're not related. That's all it is. A slip of the tongue. I'm the only relation Laman has here."

Laman said, "We have business with the captain. That's why we come here."

"Then you can help me." Daniel set both elbows on the table. "I need an introduction. Something that will impress the captain."

"What can I tell him?" Laman blew his wine-scented breath in Daniel's face. "I hardly know you, boy."

"Tell him anything a military man would want to hear."

Laman pushed aside his mug. "Can you track a man through the desert?"

"I can learn."

"What about sighting a bow at full gallop?"

"I don't own a bow."

"But you can ride, can't you?"

"My father owns a mule."

Laman scratched the back of his head. "What about swords? Can you handle a long blade?"

"I can forge one."

"Curses, boy." Laman picked up his mug and took a long drink. "What *can* you do?"

"I wrestle." Daniel nodded and kept nodding. "I can wrestle better than any man in the captain's army."

Laman asked, "Better than the captain himself?"

"Is he any good?"

"He never loses." Laman stared over the lip of his mug. "And you want me to tell the captain you're better than him?"

"I can prove myself."

Laman pointed to a boy vested in military dress sitting with his soldier friends. "Why don't you prove yourself with him?"

Daniel turned on the bench. "Who is he?"

"What kind of wrestler has never heard of Simeon? Of all the recruits training to become officers, he's the best wrestler the captain's got. They say he'll be better than the captain one day." Laman pulled on the thin point of his beard. "You prove yourself stronger than him and you'll get your chance to be an officer."

"How do I get a match with him?"

"Now that's something I can help you with." Laman raised his hand toward Simeon's table and waved him over. The boy didn't come at first, but when Laman said there was someone at his table who wanted to challenge him, he left his half-filled mug and marched across the inn with his friends following close behind. Simeon had a thick neck that pulled at the seams in his collar, and shoulders that hardly fit beneath the stripes on his tunic. He asked, "Who's the challenger?"

"Have a seat." Laman moved and let Simeon sit across from Daniel. He threw a stack of coins on the table. "I'm betting on Daniel here."

Daniel said, "Where do we wrestle?"

Simeon and his soldier friends erupted in laughter.

Laman said, "This isn't a wrestling pit, boy. It's an inn and you prove your strength by how well you hold your wine."

The innkeeper delivered twenty-four glasses of his strongest to the table and arranged them in front of the challengers.

Laman said, "The first man to go to the floor loses." He pushed a glass at Daniel. "You first."

Daniel took a sip. It burned his throat, but he swallowed the foul stuff in one gulp and turned the glass over. One down, eleven to go. He traded glass for glass with Simeon until the seventh—or was it his eighth glass? He couldn't remember and the harder he tried, the more Simeon's scowling face blurred into the mass of faces chanting Simeon's name and cursing Daniel. He reached for his next glass, but faltered forward, catching himself before his face struck the table top.

Simeon downed another round and all Daniel could do was reach for his next. He lifted it to his lips and leaned his head back as the front legs of his chair came up off the ground. He grabbed for the edge of the table, but lost his grip. He landed on his back, his skull banging against the stone floor. He tried to get to his feet and challenge the sneering soldiers hovering over him, but the ringing in his head kept him down. He got up on one elbow, then two. Stupid Egyptian, olive oil pressing brothers. Why did he ever agree to a drinking contest? Wrestling was his strength, not wine. He slipped off his elbows, his head slamming against the stone a second time.

The inn went dark.

Four legs of a chair framed Daniel's head like a prison cell, and a large bump had sprouted on the back of his skull. Simeon and his soldier friends were gone and the room stood empty except for Captain Laban. The toes of the captain's boots stared Daniel in the face. They were made of snakeskin with soles of corkwood nailed over with animal hide. The boots were close enough for Daniel to reach out and touch them, but that would not be a wise introduction if he were to prove himself fit for a commission in the military. What would the captain think if Daniel rose up from the floor in a half-drunken stupor and challenged Simeon to a wrestling match? Laban was speaking across the table to Laman and Lemuel and Daniel lay there waiting for them to say his name, to say anything that sounded like an introduction, but their conversation never touched his wrestling.

"Does Lehi know *anything* about his lineage?" the captain asked.

"Our father knows nothing," Laman replied.

Daniel closed his eyes. How could it be? These two Egyptian-looking men were the sons of Lehi, brothers to Sam and Nephi and they looked nothing alike, except that Nephi was nearly as stout as Laman.

The captain let go with a string of curses and said, "I've had to get rid of the keeper of the keys to my treasury because of you."

"Is the new man trustworthy?"

"Zoram?" Laban leaned against the table. "I can trust him never to read the lineage on the brass plates."

Laman worked his lower lip between his teeth. "You can trust us. We were your friends long before we learned of this."

The captain rapped his knuckles on the table. "I made you my friends because I had to know what you and your father knew."

Laman stepped closer to his brother. They stood on the opposite side of the table from the captain, as far away as they could, as if the thin piece of cedar could protect them from the most powerful man in Jerusalem, a man who commanded tens of thousands of soldiers. Laman said, "What about all the hours we've spent in this inn, all the drinks you shared with us?"

The captain said, "I do what I have to do."

"It wasn't our fault. Your servant had one too many drinks the night he spouted off what he knew about your lineage."

"He was a fool to have ever read the brass plates. I warned him of it time and again." Laban made a fist and pounded the tabletop. "Of all the people he could have told, why you?"

"We came to you with it, didn't we?" Laman pointed across the inn to where the captain usually sat. "The very next night Lemuel and I sat at your table and told you every detail."

"And I trust you to keep our secret because of that." The captain gripped the backrest of the chair that straddled Daniel's head and he closed his eyes until the teetering legs quieted on level stones. "Otherwise I would have been rid of you both."

"We'll tell you if father Lehi ever finds out anything," Laman said. "This is the same agreement our great-grandfathers made. You keep your relics and the estate in the upper city and we keep Beit Zayit as an inheritance."

The captain asked, "And what happens when you grow tired of cultivating olives?"

"We won't cross you."

Lemuel said, "We don't share your interest in the throne." He gripped the edge of the table. "All we want is to keep our land, the same land that's been in our family one hundred and twenty years."

Laman said, "You have the plates. If we were to ever cross you, what proof would we have but our word against yours?" He reached across the table and offered his hand.

"I'll allow it for now." The captain grasped Laman's hand, and didn't let go. "If your father ever finds out, I'll kill him—and you and your brothers with him. Your families will be stripped of their inheritance. I'll confiscate your vineyards, your caravan herds, and the deed to your thousand acres before you can ever lay claim to any sort of royal lineage."

Laman took back his hand. "Lehi won't find out."

Lemuel sat down, took a drink from his mug, and stared across the inn as if looking into his future—indentured to the captain by his own pedigree. He softly said, "We'll take this secret with us to the grave."

"You'll find yourself in the grave if you don't." The captain started across the inn, but the tip of his boot caught Daniel in the side. It was a painful kick and Daniel groaned but didn't open his eyes. Laban said, "You'd better take care of your friend. He's drunk out of his mind." The captain was nearly to the side door of the inn that emptied into the alley when Laman said, "He's a wrestler."

The captain stopped on the threshold, the evening breeze lifting his hair off his shoulders. "Is he any good?"

"I don't know, but they say blacksmiths make strong wrestlers."

The captain turned back. "He's a blacksmith?"

"His name's Daniel, the son of Jonathan the blacksmith."

"Walk with me." The captain motioned for Laman and Lemuel to follow him. "I want to know more about this boy."

The three men left Daniel lying on the floor and went out into the night. When the sound of their footsteps faded down the alley, Daniel pulled himself up and vomited over the table before slumping into a chair. His stomach was reeling like a ship on high seas, but his thoughts were anchored in the captain's words. Laban was the finest wrestler in Judah, and now he knew Daniel's name. Daniel wrapped his arms around his belly and curled up into a ball. He was better than any of the captain's recruits; he was certain of it, and all he had to do was challenge Simeon.

And win.

CHAPTER 13

Jonah the animal trader built his corral in the worst location for a large herd. No water within five miles, no hay or oats within six and only a leaning log fence to keep the animals from straying. But there it stood next to the trade route on the plateau above Jerusalem like a wart on a frog's back. And in spite of the lack of spring water and green pasture, his stockyards flourished on the highlands west of the city.

Jonah had seen an opportunity and seized it. Caravanners didn't risk riding their soft-hoofed camels through the rocky Hinnom Valley to Jerusalem. From this point, the capital was too far for a caravaneer to carry his wares on his back, but near enough that the market's lure of a good profit beckoned: "Come sell all your merchandise here." Jonah charged ten shekels a day for each mule he hired out; packs were extra. And he stabled the caravan camels for another ten, water and feed not included.

The only risk Jonah took by building his corrals this far from the protecting walls of Jerusalem were robbers, but he had an arrangement with the captain of the guard. He was the eyes and ears of the military along this part of the trade route, and for his information he was rewarded with protection. How the captain kept the looting bands off his property he didn't know, but Laban had a way with Shechem's robbers and Jonah was grateful for that. He'd never lost an animal to Shechem, while others in the hill country were plagued by the robber bands.

It was watering time and Jonah had finished lifting all but one of the buckets from his cart. He hoisted it to his shoulder and started for the water trough. He was an older man with slumping shoulders and an oversized paunch hanging about his middle like a sack of feed. The ends of the cord tying his robe barely reached around his waist.

A man riding a black horse trotted through the gates, past the mules and camels milling about the enclosure. Jonah stopped in the middle of the corral, waiting for the rider to come closer before offering a greeting. He had no way of knowing it was Uriah the prophet who steered the black horse toward him, but he could tell the man had ridden long and hard. His black courier's tunic was covered in dust.

"Evening," Jonah said, and lowered the water bucket to the ground. "That's a fine horse you've got there." Its mane was braided and cut short like the royal herd. He checked the legs. Strong and nothing lame. It would take a good barter to get it for anything less than a half talent of gold. "You looking to sell your horse?"

"Not today," Uriah said.

"You must be on your way back to Jerusalem."

"Just passing through."

"Never known a courier to pass through anywhere except on his way to Jerusalem."

"I didn't say I was a courier."

Jonah circled to the animal's backside and brushed his hand over its coat. On its hind end, beneath a layer of salt and dust, was the military brand, a lion's head, the emblem of the royal house. This horse was property of the king's army, Captain Laban's own cavalry.

Uriah spurred round. "I'm looking for the road to Beit Zayit."

"Are you lost?"

"I'm new around here." Uriah didn't blink, didn't flinch, didn't give anything away.

"See that trail leading up into those hills?" Jonah pointed a long thin finger toward the bluffs rising west of his stockyard. A trail switchbacked across the face and ended at a rift in the almost seamless wall of purple-gray rock near the summit. "That's the only way in."

Uriah circled his horse toward the gate, but pulled up when Jonah said, "I can make sure no one follows you." He strode over and laid his hand on the horse's brand. "The way I see things, my silence is worth about the price of your horse." He smiled a toothless smile and without a word Uriah dismounted and handed Jonah the reins.

He left the yard on foot.

At this late hour, and with an autumn rainstorm pouring down, Uriah could see nothing but the mud underfoot. It had taken him two hours to clear the pass and find the cluster of mansion homes nestled in a stand of trees.

Hidden in the hill country west of Jerusalem lay Beit Zayit, the valley of the house of olive trees. A suitable name for the nation's largest olive plantation. With hundreds of west-facing slopes and cool summer evenings, it was a perfect clime for olive culture, though the land had never produced much fruit until Lehi and his cousin Ishmael inherited the vast tracts. Their quick rise to prosperity had become the stuff of legends. How they accumulated so much land was a mystery, but with over a thousand producing olive trees and another thousand nearly to the age of production they were the kings of the oil trade, lords of the grandest olive operation in all of Judah.

The lights were out except in the main house, where an oil lamp burned in the window. Uriah scraped the mud off his sandals before entering by the front gate and making his way to the door.

A stout man answered his knock and he looked enough like the captain of the guard that for a moment Uriah believed himself captured. But it was only Lehi's son Laman, and he asked, "Is Lehi in?"

Laman said, "We don't want any problems."

"Just one word and I'll be on my way."

"Take your troubles somewhere else. We don't want them here." Laman shut the door and locked it.

Uriah turned and walked slowly back down the steps when the bolt unlatched, the door opened and Lehi stood in the entry, his son Laman glaring from across the foyer. Lehi held a lamp at shoulder level, the yellow rays lighting his windblown face. But his face wasn't leathery like most caravaneers who frequented the southern deserts.

His green eyes were as Uriah remembered them the last time Lehi had stopped at his inn. His chin ended in a well-trimmed tuft of black beard, without even a strand of gray. "Excuse my son's behavior. What do you need, sir?"

"I lost my horse."

Lehi raised the lamp to Uriah's face. "Why, if it isn't the innkeeper from Arim."

"I'd hoped you'd remember."

"How could I forget your sweet wines, the finest in all of Judah."

Uriah managed a smile. "You're very kind, sir."

"I've quelled many a thirst at your inn since making my first caravan to Egypt." Lehi rubbed his cheek. "It's been . . ."

"Twelve years this harvest, sir."

"And what prosperous years they've been." Lehi wrapped his free arm around the prophet. "How long will you stay with us?"

"I can't."

"Nonsense. We have plenty of warm beds and more food than my wife knows what to do with. She's wanted to learn the secrets of preparing your wines since the day I first told her of them."

"Send him away, Papa." Laman stood in the doorway. "He'll bring us nothing but trouble."

"What are you saying, son?"

"Ask him; he knows. It's all the soldiers in the city talk about." Laman took the lamp from Lehi and walked it to the end of the porch, holding it up to the storm. "It's a wonder he hasn't been followed."

Lehi said, "Calm down, son."

"You'd worry, too, if you knew what I know."

"I'll not allow your worries to send one of God's anointed back out into this storm, hungry and cold."

"The captain of the guard is searching for him."

Uriah said, "I don't mean to cause you trouble. I'll go."

"You'll do no such thing." Lehi put his arm on Uriah's shoulder and escorted him inside. Egyptian silks hung from the windows and thick rugs graced the stone floors. Blue porcelain vases stood at the base of the stairs that led from the lobby to a second-floor mezzanine. The room was finished in blackwood imported from the walnut groves of the north country. Lehi hurried up the steps and walked along the mezzanine to the master bedroom. He called softly to his wife, Sariah, and was only there long enough to repeat her name twice before she appeared, her long black hair combed in place and a ribbon tying it back over the collar of her sleeping robe. She was an elegant woman, with the same noble high cheeks as her husband, and skin soft as a rose petal. She wore only a dash of Egyptian makeup, a red pomegranate dye on her lips, and a flush of white powder on her cheeks. Her deep blue eyes were bright and penetrating as sapphire.

She invited Uriah to the kitchen, a room large enough to stable a herd of camels. Along the far wall stood wooden bins of milled wheat and barley, barrels of olives, pickles, nuts, and dates. The hampers were filled with onions, tubers, and spices to tantalize the nose.

Heat from three hearths still warmed the kitchen air, though the fires were long since dead. One was for boiling, one for grilling and the last for baking, its cooling shelf filled with the day's bread: ten freshly baked loaves.

"This family will eat through those before the morning is done," Sariah said in answer to Uriah's staring.

There were four young men still living under her roof, five grandchildren living in the home next door, and three more grandchildren living across the square from the marriage of her second daughter. Her two oldest girls were married to cousin Ishmael's oldest boys. No doubt there'd be many more loaves to bake once Laman, her eldest son, married Ishmael's oldest daughter. They'd have to consider planting another field of wheat, or at least adding another baking oven once they realized that marriage.

"You don't need to tell Uriah everything about us." Laman leaned against the oven bricks. "He isn't family."

Sariah said, "He's our guest. And if you can't be civil, then I'd prefer you keep silent." She girded up her robe to keep it out of the way while she cut the already cooked and salted lamb onto a plate, humming while she worked. She could have roused a host of maidservants to prepare the food, but she was happy to do it herself, and Uriah was happy to keep this meal between the four of them. And if Laman didn't behave, there was always the hope that she'd reduce the number to three. She broke the bread and filled a bowl with a generous helping of dates. She placed them at the table next to Uriah with a bottle of honey, a fig, and a cup of pure wine. "This should take the edge off your hunger. I'll have a proper meal ready for you by morning."

"Thank you, but I won't be staying the night."

"You're not going out in this. We've got five spare rooms and never a traveler to use them. We don't get many visitors out this way."

"We don't get any," Laman said. "And we don't want any."

"You're tired, son," Sariah said. "Why don't you go off to bed like your brothers?"

"I'll go when I'm ready." Laman folded his arms tight across his chest.

"Don't mind him," Sariah said. "He's been harvesting all day and you know how tiring that can be." She refilled Uriah's glass with fresh wine. "Now, tell me. Where did you say you were headed?"

"I don't know."

Lehi said, "Are you lost?" He drew a cushioned chair in from the reading room and sat across the table from Uriah. "I have maps."

"A few weeks back, two men came into my inn and—"

"He's a criminal," Laman said. "He's running from the captain of the guard. That's why he's here. We should never have let him in."

"Laman!" Sariah looked over at him.

Laman said, "Have Uriah eat quickly and be gone."

Sariah said, "He's staying the night."

"We're better off if he leaves now."

Lehi asked, "What's gotten into you, boy?"

"We don't need to hear who or what he's running from."

"We most certainly do." Lehi leaned forward in his chair. "Go on with what you were saying."

"The captain believes I know something about his lineage."

Lehi's eyes narrowed. "There's no law against that."

"Even if there were, I don't know anything about the man's family. But the captain believes I do, and he's come after me because of it." Uriah laid down his knife next to the plate of lamb. "Two men disguised as farmers entered my inn just after sunset a few weeks back. I knew the first one to be Captain Yaush from Fort Lakhish but the other . . ." Uriah paused and took a bite from the loaf of bread.

"He was a mighty man, with hair longer than any I'd ever seen and he answered to the name Shechem."

Sariah gasped. "That man's done more harm."

"The captain sent him after me and I've been running ever since. I spent a week in the hills outside Arim and another in the east desert near Jericho before riding this way."

Lehi said, "You risk your life coming this close to Jerusalem."

"I have to keep moving. Shechem and his men know this country better than I."

"The captain of the guard doesn't hire robbers to do his work." Laman crossed to Uriah. "He commands ten thousand soldiers."

"He didn't send a soldier after me." Uriah turned in his chair toward Laman. "He sent a murderer."

"What do you know about murder?"

"Son!" Lehi stood, nearly knocking his chair off its legs.

Uriah said, "I've told you the truth." He pushed the plate across the table toward Laman. "Whatever it is the captain's trying to hide about his lineage, it's damaging enough to drive him to have me killed."

Laman said, "You're a fool."

"I assure you, I'm not." Uriah stood and came around the table to Lehi. "I need your help to escape. It's God's will I go from here and leave to another prophet the task of stopping the captain. Someone more influential than I. One who is his equal."

"There isn't another prophet left in all the kingdom except for Jeremiah."

Sariah said, "That poor man is hardly influential with the captain of the guard." She offered Uriah more figs. "Laban banned him from ever preaching in Jerusalem."

"God will raise up a man to stop the captain; of that I'm certain." Uriah spoke in a low voice, his stare firmly set on Lehi. "He'll not allow the captain to cause our nation to dwindle in unbelief."

Lehi said, "Egypt's the best place for you. I have friends there, trading partners; they're men you can trust."

Uriah pushed the backrest of the chair up against the edge of the table. "I know a man at Elephantine. He's a good friend to my father. I knew him as Uncle Japheth when I was a boy. He commands the military outpost there."

"Can you trust him?" asked Lehi.

"He's employed by Pharaoh and he has little love for Captain Laban and his military."

"Then it's settled. Go to Elephantine. You'll be safe there among the other Jews." Lehi motioned to Laman. "Ready a horse with four saddle bags and two large water skins. Your mother and I will be along with food to pack in them." He took Uriah by the hands. "You leave at first light."

CHAPTER 14

The damp evening air hung like moss on a river tree. Jonathan made his way in the shadows opposite the moonlit fronts of the abandoned shops. The blacksmith district was empty, not a soul out this late, but he could feel the watch of unseen eyes follow him to the door. Chief Elder Zadock had asked for a late night meeting, and who was Jonathan to deny the man his request?

He turned the key in the latch, the bolt clicked, and the door edged open slowly. In the dark next to the window, a large man stood waiting. When he turned his face to the moonlight, Jonathan knew him immediately. Captain Laban stepped out of the shadows, the case he carried under his arm bobbing in cadence with his step. Ruth had told him he should expect a visit from the captain, but not tonight, not with Zadock coming to speak with him about his steelmaking.

Laban offered no apology for breaking into the shop and Jonathan didn't ask for one. He came near and Jonathan could see the scar on his left bicep, the wound everyone in Jerusalem knew he'd gotten saving the national treasures during the war. The captain had risked his life to keep the brass plates and the sword of Joseph from being taken by the Babylonian soldiers. He'd saved the treasures, but lost his entire family: a prosperous gold-trading father, a brother who was a highly regarded scribe, and another brother Jonathan didn't know much about. The captain was the only family member to survive.

Laban pulled the gold-trimmed sleeve of his tunic over the scar. "It's a war wound."

"Yes, sir. I knew that."

"Are we alone?"

Jonathan lit a lamp. "I'm expecting someone."

"Zadock's always late."

"You know about our meeting?"

"The Chief Elder had me bring this."

Laban rested the sword case on the edge of the forging table and ran his hand over the delicate palm branches carved into the walnut surface. It was sealed shut with polished brass latches that shimmered in the flickering lamplight. The captain freed the pin and lifted the lid, obscuring the view, but Jonathan already knew what lay inside. He'd imagined many times what the sword of Joseph might look like, never expecting to see it. Since the Babylonian war, Captain Laban never wore it in public and it was rumored he locked it deep in the vaults of his treasury to keep true to the prophecy. The sword was to remain unsheathed until God had worked all his purposes among the children of men. The captain did not seem the sort of man who gave heed to such traditions, but he never wore the sword, not even on feast days. When he did bring it out, it was locked away in its case with a servant bearing it behind him and a regiment of soldiers keeping watch. Why he brought it here at such a late hour without anyone to guard it was a mystery. This kind of valuable object was better left in the protection of Laban's vaults. He couldn't want Jonathan to work on the sword. Jonathan had a fine mixture of oils to polish the dullest metals, but the Captain had his own oils and chamois and resins and a host of servants to do that work. And he couldn't want it passed over Jonathan's grinding wheel. The metal was too fine for common sharpening.

Laban rotated the opened case toward Jonathan, exposing the outline of a sword fitted into an ivory setting. The blade itself lay hidden from view, wrapped in red silk.

Laban said, "Do you know of the sword of Joseph?" He laid his hand on the silk-covered hilt. "The same who was sold into Egypt for his robe of many colors?"

Jonathan leaned forward to get his first glimpse of the blade and all he could think to say was, "Has it kept well?"

"It's never tarnished."

"I've heard that legend."

"It's no legend."

"But sir, metal rusts no matter how fine a steel it is and your sword must be a thousand years old."

"One thousand one hundred sixty-seven." Laban picked up the corner of the silk between his fingers. "Joseph anointed it to be a symbol of kingship, and whoever possesses it rules with the power of God." He began to pull away the silk when a cry came from the doorway.

"Don't unveil it yet!"

It was Zadock. He reached Laban in three strides. "I'll do this." He closed the case, rapped his knuckles over the lid and spoke to Jonathan in a deliberate monotone. "I trust you're enjoying your new shop."

"Very much, sir."

Zadock raised his arms over the expanse of the shop. "You've settled in nicely."

Jonathan agreed, though it had been ten months now since they had moved into the shop. What else could he do, but agree? Before him stood the noblest of all the princes of the city, the man who had given him this property.

"We have need of your steelmaking skills." Zadock's lips hardly moved when he spoke.

"I was expecting that, sir."

Zadock lifted the silk-wrapped blade out of its casement and handed it to Jonathan. "Please, examine it."

He unraveled the cloth that had been wrapped seven times around the sword. When the silk fell away he held a piece of olive wood roughly hewn into the shape of a sword. Iron pellets were hammered along its length to disguise its weight. It was nothing but a worthless piece of wood.

Zadock opened a bag of jewels and spread them over the table. Five large diamonds split the lamplight into beams. Sapphires and rubies glowed deep blue and red, and the small green jade stones were rounded to a perfect finish. "These are identical to the ones that decorated the sword's hilt. We know the blade's dimensions and its weight. That piece of wood you hold should give you an idea of the size. It was a rather large, weighty weapon."

"Where do you keep the original?"

"We don't."

Jonathan came around the table and stood next to Laban. "I thought the relics were saved."

Laban pulled his captain's tunic off over his wide shoulders, exposing the full extent of his scars. One cut deep across his bicep then ran up his arm and over his shoulder. Another shot across his chest before disappearing under his arm. "I was able to save the brass plates from the Babylonians, but they got the sword and left me for dead."

Jonathan looked puzzled. "Every Jew believes you saved both treasures."

Laban stepped close enough that Jonathan could feel the heat rising off his chest. "That's exactly what they're to keep on believing. He pulled his tunic back on. "Not even the keeper of the keys to my treasury knows it was taken during the war."

Zadock took out three coin bags and a leather scroll. "There's enough gold here to smith the hilt, and this drawing marks the location of every jewel on both sides of the hand piece." Zadock leaned his head in. "You must be exact. We're hiring you to make a perfect duplicate; we'll accept nothing less."

"You want me to remake the sword?"

"You'll be paid when it's finished. Twenty talents of gold, enough that you'll never have to smith again."

Jonathan held the wooden hilt in both hands. That much money would make him a wealthy man. No, not only wealthy—he'd be among the noblemen of Jerusalem. He fitted the wooden sword back into its case. "You won't be disappointed with my work."

Zadock said, "There's one more thing."

"What?"

"Your silence."

Laban said, "Twenty talents of gold should be enough to buy that along with the sword."

Zadock continued, "We don't want anyone to ever know the sword was taken by the Babylonian army. It could damage the captain's reputation. He's a military hero now and if the wrong people found out about it, . . . well, we all have our enemies."

"No one is to find out about this." Laban drew the form of a serpent in the thin film of ash that had settled over the forging table.

It was the symbol of the Rekhabites, the sign of their Anointed One. Laban asked, "Do you understand?"

"I'll need the help of my sons."

"You'll do it alone or not at all."

"Laban." Zadock pulled his hood over his graying hair. "All we need is the good blacksmith's word." He turned to Jonathan. "You will swear on your life to tell no one, won't you?"

It was an odd request. Why would the Chief Elder require Jonathan to swear on his life? That was for robbers, men who lied and stole and whose word could not be trusted without a promise sealed with their life. Jonathan agreed to Zadock's request, but he needn't have bothered. These were dealings between respectable men. Zadock had an odd sort of manner, without the graces you'd expect in the Chief Elder. Aloof was the best word for him, and though Jonathan had dealt with him a number of times, he knew no more about him now than when they were first introduced.

Jonathan picked up the drawing of the hilt. "I don't know how long this will take me, working alone."

Laban said, "You have until King Zedekiah's coronation at the solstice."

"I'll do what I can."

"You will finish by the coronation or lose everything," Laban said.

"Don't threaten the blacksmith." Zadock stepped between them. "He's working with us now and I expect he understands our urgency." He laid his hand on Jonathan's shoulder. "You see, the sword represents the power of God on earth. It's been in the hands of Hebrew kings since Joseph was crowned Viceroy of Egypt, and even though it belongs to Laban, the people have come to expect that it will be present at the coronation." He patted Jonathan on the back. "We wouldn't want to disappoint anyone, would we?"

Jonathan said, "I'll have it finished."

"That's better." Zadock took out a carefully folded parchment from under his robes and handed it to Jonathan. "When you finish the blade, see that these words are inscribed on the metal."

Jonathan read through it slowly. They were the words of Rekhabites. Something only a Rekhabite would engrave into the sword. He looked up from the parchment. "You don't really want this on your blade, do you?"

Laban said, "Every word."

"But, sir."

"Do it."

Zadock and the captain left without another word. Jonathan could hear Laban go, his boots clicking over the cobblestones, but Zadock exited the shop without a sound, not even the swirl of his robes against the door frame or the shuffle of his sandals on the cobblestone. They were gone, but they'd left Jonathan with a wooden sword and the promise that he was working for them. Just the sort of men he must impress if he were to be successful in Jerusalem.

And his work *would* impress them.

CHAPTER 15

A juggler performed for the shoppers, his breeches ballooning around his legs and his sleeveless leather vest flapping about his shoulders. Market Street hummed with the chants of merchants working their trade, heralding the commerce of the upper city. Elizabeth peered across the street at the third servant's entrance from the corner, the one with two soldiers standing guard. A crowd of shoppers passed in front of her with tall reed baskets bobbing above a sea of white and brown robes. She stepped to the side and kept her sights on the back gate; she didn't want to miss her chance. The smell of frankincense drifted faintly across the street from the perfume shop on the corner. The fragrance was more enticing than the homemade perfume she wore, but that was all she could afford to impress the man who would step from the gate at any moment.

"Pomegranates! Ripe pomegranates!" The farmer in the closest cart beckoned her to come and examine his produce. By the dirt coloring the hem of his robe and dusting his sandals, he looked to have traveled the south road. Red-brown earth from Bethlehem's vineyards.

"I love the market," Elizabeth said to the farmer and took a deep breath, her attention still focused on the third gate from the corner. "Isn't it wonderful? And those expensive perfumes, how I love the smell."

"The perfume merchant charges too much." The farmer pointed to his pomegranates. "But you can have six of these for a mere shekel."

Elizabeth stepped as close as she dared without losing her view of the gate. She glanced over just long enough to see water droplets streak down the reddish skins of the freshly washed fruit. She asked, "Are you from Bethlehem?"

"What has that to do with the price of pomegranates in Jerusalem?"

"You're from the south, I can tell."

The farmer scratched the back of his head. "Did I sell you twelve pomegranates for a shekel in Bethlehem yesterday?"

Elizabeth turned her gaze back to the gate. "And if you did?"

"The price has gone up."

This was not the right time to buy fruit. Not when the man she waited for could walk out the servant's gate at any moment, but her father had taught her to never shun a good barter. "Why should food be more expensive in Jerusalem?"

"For you, pretty lady, eight for a shekel."

"I suppose I'll have to travel to Bethlehem to get twelve for a shekel."

"Ten, but not one pomegranate more." The farmer cut into the skin of one and exposed the tightly packed balls of red fruit inside.

"Such a needless journey for pomegranates."

"All right." The farmer threw his hands in the air. "Twelve for a shekel."

"You're certain that's the same price you sell them for in Bethlehem?"

"You should know."

"I would had I ever been there." She pointed at his sandals. "My brothers come home with the same red dirt on their feet after mining coal from the hills above Bethlehem."

"Why you odd little imp."

"You may call me observant, thank you."

"Are you going to buy my fruit or not?"

"I didn't come to barter."

"Moses have mercy on my soul, woman. What are you doing here?" The farmer picked out the red bits of pomegranate and popped three into his mouth. "You didn't come to market perfumed and bathed for no reason."

He was right. The reason she'd come was stepping out the gate of the largest estate on Market Street. The man nodded to the soldiers guarding the entrance, then started up the hill.

The farmer sidled in next to Elizabeth. "So that's why you're here."

"If you don't mind." Elizabeth pushed past him and turned her attention back to the man who walked up Market Street with a mature, confident stride. He was robed in expensive white linens worn by only the wealthiest scribes, though he wasn't really a scribe, not yet. Zoram was keeper of the keys to Laban's treasury, but as soon as he finished his training he'd be raised to the title of scribe, a prestigious thing for any man, particularly one so young. Zoram was Hebrew, though the coarse curls that crept from under his white turban were anything but Jewish. Some of the blood of Ethiopia coursed through his veins. He had green eyes that remade his glance into a penetrating stare and his beardless face was a shade darker than most.

Elizabeth dodged a mule-drawn cart, sidestepped three basket-laden women, worked her way past the jeweler, refused the beckonings of the cobbler and nearly ran down the juggler only to see Zoram disappear beneath the archway that separated the market from the government district. When she emerged from the shadows of the arch, she caught sight of him walking near the Citadel toward the entrance of the temple. It was just like him to walk like that, hands behind his back, a scroll tucked beneath his arm and whistling to the sky, though his whistle sounded more like chewing on a piece of day-old leavened bread.

If only she knew how best to draw Zoram's attention. Two months shy of twenty, she was a good two years past a proper marrying age and Elizabeth had yet to pique any man's curiosity. Was the farmer right? Was she really an oddity? Her inclination was for reading and writing, not promenading or perfuming, though in Zoram's case she'd made an exception. She bathed this morning in the finest perfumes she could boil from the petals of wild flowers and she washed her robe as clean as it would come, though to be honest the lye wasn't good for much beyond adding gray to her already drab clothing.

She slipped into stride behind Zoram, following him past the Citadel and skirting around the tax collectors who streamed out of the tall main doors of the kingdom's headquarters. When he started to cross over to the temple gates she whistled strong enough to spin him around in the middle of the street, his robes dancing at his feet.

"Elizabeth?"

"Why, Zoram, is that you?"

"I was on my way to morning readings."

"I thought I recognized your whistle."

"Do I sound that awful?"

"Awful isn't the right word."

"Like an ox, then."

"I've never heard an ox whistle," Elizabeth said.

"They don't, and if they did, I wouldn't imagine it to be a pretty sound."

Elizabeth volunteered to teach him to whistle, not expecting him to ask for a lesson right there—and in front of a constant stream of scribes on their way to morning readings. But there was never a better time than the present and she would rather give Zoram his first lesson in the middle of King Street than risk missing the chance altogether. It seemed such a simple way to get his interest that she chided herself for not thinking of it before. She spoke her instructions between puckered lips telling him to mimic her. He did and he blew hard, but only air sputtered from his mouth. And though they must have looked an odd pair, at least they were a pair. She was tired of waiting by his gate every day only to nod and exchange a few words out of the notion that he might begin to think of her as something more than a shopper passing by his back gate.

Zoram tried to whistle again but only a faint hollow sound came from his mouth. "I'm hopeless."

"No more than my writing is cursed."

"I can help you with that."

"Would you really?" Elizabeth looked into Zoram's deep green eyes. "I've wanted to learn to use a stylus."

"It's all in how you hold it between your fingers." Zoram took out a writing pen and lodged it between Elizabeth's thumb and forefinger. She fumbled with it so that Zoram had to hold it in place. His hand was steady and she found herself not wanting him to let go immediately, despite the temple priest who appeared at the gates and began calling for all the scribes.

Twelve pillars graced the entrance to the temple, each column as wide as a cart is long and higher than the head of an elephant. Zoram led Elizabeth over to the entrance and they stood there to keep the priests from pulling up the chocks and closing the gates.

Zoram said, "We'll have to finish this lesson another time."

"Really, you would do that for me?"

"Come to the treasury. That would be a good place for a writing lesson." Zoram removed his turban and brushed away the locks that curled over his brow. "Captain Laban doesn't usually allow visitors, but I'll make an exception this once."

"We can meet some other place if you'd like?"

"It must be there."

"Really, we can."

"The treasury." Zoram said the words with such force there was no mistaking he wanted her to meet him there. No other place would do. He lowered his voice and said, "There's something at the treasury I want you to see. Will you come?"

"When?"

"The first day of the week."

"How will I find you?"

"The back gate, do you know it?"

"The one that empties onto Market Street?"

"That's it."

"I can find it."

"I'll tell the guards to expect you."

Two priests with long beards began pushing the gates shut. Zoram replaced his turban, tucked his thick black curls beneath the brim and left her standing beneath the giant stone pillars, alone.

"Zoram." Elizabeth waved to him through the gates. "What time should I come?"

"For lunch," he said and disappeared into a crowd of white robes and turbaned scribes milling about the temple courtyard. She had an invitation to see him again, and for that she was grateful. But he didn't say if they were to eat lunch or only be there at lunchtime.

Why, he hadn't said if she was expected to bring her own papyrus for the writing lesson—a thing that she could hardly afford, but she'd find a way. And what did a woman wear to see the insides of a treasury? Elizabeth placed her hands on her hips.

It was just like a man to leave her with so many questions unanswered.

Zoram could still see Elizabeth straining to see him from outside the temple gates. He removed his turban again, but this time it was to feign a bow to the Babylonian idol standing near the entry. Conquering armies left behind their worst art, and Zoram could ill afford to offend. Better to bend before a piece of stone and live free than cause a stir among those who favored submission to the Babylonians. The war forced a good number of changes on the Jews and religion was not exempt. Even the reflective quiet of these grounds was gone, replaced by a musical band of priests parading so close Zoram could feel the blare of their shofar horns, the pulsing of their drums, and the lyrical strumming from the lyres. They had replaced the ordinances of the House of God for entertainment, but he could ill afford to offend the temple priests or the noblemen of Jerusalem. So he came here once each week—the sole member from Laban's house—and kept quiet his dislike over the loss of eternal covenants that once made this public place a holy place.

The courtyard was a blur of finely tailored robes and expensive turbans. Scribes and accountants from every treasury and merchant house in Jerusalem gathered here the fourth day of the week to study the covenants, though there were few covenants more studied than business. They discussed the price of gold and the merits of buying property more than they ever recited Isaiah. In this once sacred place, trafficking in the talents of men had replaced the redeeming of souls.

A priest fell in stride next to Zoram. His white-capped head bobbed like a gull on the surf of the Great Sea. He took Zoram by the arm and began to usher him to a seat on the far side of the gallery, away from the stir of the crowd.

Zoram lowered his head and followed without resisting. He couldn't draw attention to himself, or someone might take notice of his companion. If anyone connected them he could be released from his work in Laban's treasury, or even imprisoned. But he wouldn't avoid meeting with him. It was a risk he'd take as often as needed.

Walking beside him was Jeremiah the prophet, the man who had raised him from childhood. Zoram was born in Anathoth, in the house next door to Jeremiah, the orchard owner turned prophet. He was six years old when he lost his parents in the plague and Jeremiah raised him until he was old enough to find employment. Zoram would have given Jeremiah a warmer greeting, but in these troubled times the prophet could only lay claim to purity, not popularity.

"What happened to your beard?" Zoram asked.

"Resin oils." Jeremiah fluffed the whiskers he'd dyed from gray to black. A long, white coat hung from his shoulders, fastened down the front with brass buttons and a belt inlaid with rubies. His hands were the only thing that didn't look priestly. They were chapped and worn from working vineyards in the hills north of Jerusalem.

"Where did you get those clothes? You look like a—"

"A priest." Jeremiah adjusted his white horned cap and pointed to the dressing rooms. "It was open."

"What are you doing here? Laban has men everywhere."

"I think you know."

"You shouldn't risk your life for those brass plates."

"The work of God is not a risk, my boy, though things have gotten more difficult." Jeremiah sat on the bench seat next to Zoram. "The blacksmith sides with the Elders."

"You told me he came to Jerusalem to help you with the brass plates."

"He did." Jeremiah scratched the side of his head. "He just doesn't know it yet." Jeremiah turned his gaze to Solomon's Temple. "There was a time when men entered in those doors to make covenants with God that would turn their hearts to their fathers, but those days are gone." He turned to Zoram. "Have you ever read the record you care for in Laban's treasury?"

Laban had warned him never to read the genealogy recorded in the plates and Zoram obeyed. They were a sacred record, a family history, the captain's personal ancestry and intended only for him and his descendants.

"He won't allow it, not since he hired me to replace the last keeper of the keys."

"If you had, you would understand." Jeremiah looked up into the patches of clouds swirling across the blue sky. "One day, in a distant future and in a promised land far from this one, God will raise up a prophet clothed in prophecy and called to restore the lost ordinances and covenants of His Holy House. He will be called the chosen one, the anointed son of that Joseph who first began Laban's brass record."

"I know the prophecy."

"Then you'll help me."

"The prophecy doesn't mention anything about brass plates."

Jeremiah lowered his voice to a whisper. "Those plates will preserve the covenants of the Lord God until He raises up an anointed son of Joseph to restore them to a remnant of the House of Israel. Then we can rest assured that our children will not be cast off forever, and they will know that we knew of the Anointed One who will be called Yeshua."

"There's no safer place for the brass plates than locked away in Laban's treasury."

"I used to believe that as well, but if they stay with Laban much longer, he'll destroy them."

"Why would he do such a foolish thing?"

"All I can tell you is that the plates will be taken from the city before Laban or any other man can harm them."

Zoram lowered his voice and said, "I can't let you steal Laban's property."

"I'm not taking it."

"Then who?"

"The rightful heir." Jeremiah's eyes filled with a serious light.

Zoram said, "Laban's the only descendant of Joseph."

"There's another."

"Who?"

"God has preserved an heir. I don't know who, but I know I need to prepare the brass plates before they're taken."

"How many plates do you need?"

"I don't know. Four or five, but they must be identical to the other plates."

"I'm no blacksmith."

Jeremiah smiled. "Did you invite the blacksmith's daughter to come to your treasury?"

"Well, yes, but . . ."

"I think she's taken a liking to you."

Zoram fiddled with his turban. "She taught me to whistle, but I'd hardly call that a courtship."

"She wouldn't be opposed to one."

"Why do you say that?"

"I may not have brought you into this world, but I'm the closest thing you have to a father."

"I can't ask her to do this for us. I hardly know the woman. And what about her father?"

"What of him?"

"You said he sides with the Elders. We can't possibly convince him to help us."

"At least his daughter is willing."

"Not exactly." A group of scribes took their seats nearby and Zoram helped Jeremiah up. They walked together for a moment before Zoram said, "Elizabeth believes she's coming for a writing lesson."

"I was right."

"About what?"

"The girl has taken a liking to you."

"Must you keep saying that?"

"We'll talk more about the girl when I meet her."

"I hadn't planned on introducing you."

"You will, and very soon. There's little time to waste."

Jeremiah patted Zoram's hand. Then he was gone across the back of the courtyard and out the priests' gate.

Zoram felt for the keys to Laban's treasury he kept on a chain around his neck. It was his charge to guard the brass plates. They were Laban's property, but if Jeremiah was to be believed, then the brass plates had another, more powerful owner.

They belonged to God.

CHAPTER 16

The scent of warm bread and new cheese filtered up from Elizabeth's basket. She took a deep breath of the aroma before turning the corner onto Market Street and approaching the back gate to Captain Laban's estate. Lunch seemed a more womanly offering than teaching Zoram to whistle in exchange for writing lessons, though they both needed instruction. A white cotton cloth covered the smoked quail, berries, some of Mama's dates, and a loaf of leavened bread with nuts baked into the dough. If all men had a weak spot for bread and dates like Papa did, then Zoram was about to acquire another vice, if he had any to begin with. The long neck of a jar sprouted out of the basket, and spring water gurgled with each step.

The guards nodded and opened the small side gate off Market Street without asking Elizabeth to identify herself. Zoram must have described her to them and she wanted to ask exactly what he'd said, but she restrained the impulse. The narrow servants' alley was a world apart from the cries of merchants and the call of moneychangers.

Despite the midday hour, shadows darkened the back of Captain Laban's estate and a labyrinth of stone-walled passages posed a bewildering number of paths to choose from. Thankfully, Zoram had given her instructions to keep to the left. She went straight until she reached the date tree branches hanging over from the courtyard gardens. She turned left and the path narrowed and bent to the right. She was about to stop and go back to see if she'd taken a wrong turn when the alley opened onto the back door of the treasury, fixed with enough safeguards to discourage the most enterprising thief. It hinged on limestone pivots recessed so firmly that a battering ram carried on the shoulders of twenty men could not extract it from its moorings.

The massive door forbade her from seeking entrance, but Zoram had insisted on a writing lesson. She made a fist and knocked with the fervor of a tax collector. Oh that it were possible, that by some good fortune he did want to see her for reasons other than to trade his writing for her whistling.

The wood piece covering the peep-hole popped open, replaced by a solitary eyeball. It blinked twice and all she could think to do was smile. What an awful predicament to stand there with heaven knows who staring back. It could be any of the menservants or, worse, one of the fifty soldiers guarding the estate, whose minds rarely found reason to creep out of the mud-brick pits. Zoram insisted they meet at the treasury, but there were few days in late fall as beautiful as this one and it seemed a shame to waste it in these underground recesses. There was an abundance of perfectly private places for a writing lesson away from the watchful eye of society. The olive vineyards in the hills east of Jerusalem were more secluded, the Gihon Spring less forbidding, and a walk up the Hinnom Valley far more invigorating. Most of all, at another meeting place she could have discovered Zoram's intentions, if he had any at all, without having to endure the interrogation of the unknown eyeball that stared at her with shameless curiosity.

The peep-hole clicked back into place, the door swung open, and Zoram stood in the entry.

Elizabeth rested her basket on her hip. "That was you?"

"I scrutinize everyone who knocks."

"You didn't have to stare so."

"I wasn't really staring."

"What would you call it?"

"A moment of reflection." Zoram smiled. "An enjoyable one, of course."

Elizabeth relaxed the basket off her hip and he ushered her inside and locked the door behind them. "I mixed some new ink for your writing lesson."

"A clay tablet would have suited me fine."

"Not for a gifted student." Zoram took the basket from her and started down the steps. "We'll take the lesson in the main vault."

Damp air rose past Elizabeth's cheeks as they descended the stairs and turned the corner into a subterranean corridor running beneath the estate. Lamps flickered along the hallway that ended at the vault door, flanked on either side by thick limestone arches. Zoram slid his key into the latch and turned it until the teeth caught and the lock clicked. When he pushed open the door, a gasp of air rushed out. Inside stood row after row, shelf upon shelf of accounting documents, histories and genealogies. More writings than ten scribes could copy in a lifetime.

"I have a treasure I want to show you." Zoram squeezed her hand. "Wait here while I get it." He rushed off, calling over his shoulder, "And don't get into anything you shouldn't."

He disappeared down an aisle between shelves of sealed repository jars, leaving Elizabeth alone in the vastness of the vault. She removed a sandal and stroked the expensive rugs with her toes. Hopefully that didn't qualify as getting into something she shouldn't. Nor did lifting the red and gold tapestries away from the wall to feel the weave. And it couldn't be taboo to sit in one of the high-backed reading chairs that stood at the head of every aisle. Elizabeth took a seat and sat like the Queen of Judah with her elbows on the arm rests and her head tilted back to study the domed ceiling. It was finished with a mixture of white plaster and crushed sea shells that glittered like stars in the night sky. The ceiling arched upward to an apex above the heart of the treasury a few rows over, and Elizabeth could not resist the temptation to step down three aisles and peer around the last shelf to see what lay beneath such fine architecture.

A writing table stood in the center of the main room with a stylus and an ink bottle waiting for Zoram to write in the papyrus ledger. Elizabeth crossed the room, over beyond the table, to a purple curtain draped between two pillars. She ran her hand along the exquisite cloth until she found the seam. The treasure Zoram wanted to show her must be behind here, but where had he gone? She lifted the curtain aside revealing two porcelain urns that flanked a large empty pedestal.

"Not there, Elizabeth; you can't go back there." Zoram came through the curtain, stepped around her to the pedestal and ran his hand over the empty top. "Where is it? Where did you put it?"

"I didn't touch anything."

"The case. What did you do with it?"

"What case?"

"Laban's sword case."

"He must have it with him. You know how men are about their weapons."

"He never sheathes it." Zoram ran his fingers through his curly hair. "He never takes it anywhere."

"Could someone else have taken it out of here? Perhaps a servant is polishing the blade as we speak."

"Impossible. Laban and I are the only ones with keys." Zoram placed both hands on the wooden pedestal, his head down. "He hung these curtains up after the war and forbade me from coming behind them. I can't even tell him it's missing or he'll know I've been here." He turned from the pedestal. "You can't tell anyone what you've seen."

"I haven't seen anything."

"That's right. Forget what you didn't see, forget we ever spoke about the sword." Zoram led her from behind the curtain. "Come. There's someone I want you to meet."

Without making the slightest noise, an elderly man had entered the main vault and taken a seat at the head of the writing table. His common brown eyes sparkled with an unusual light, beckoning Elizabeth to step closer. His gray beard flowed over the collar of his dusty traveler's robe that hung limp on his shoulders like wash hung out to dry. Lines of age marked his hands, but his fingers were nimble enough to dance over a large wooden box, inscribed with palm branches, a sign of nobility in the kingdom of the pharaohs. Why did an elderly Hebrew man have a box like that? This was Israel, not Egypt. The lid rested half-open and a streak of orange-red light sparkled from the shadows inside. He removed it and lifted out a codex of brass plates. They were stacked uniformly one upon the other, bound together with three rings and inscribed with artistic Hebrew script. These were not standard accounting records that treasuries kept on leather or clay tablets or papyrus scrolls. They were brass, smithed to endure a millennia of aging.

"I asked Zoram to invite you here," the stranger said, casting a steady smile in her direction. "Please, sit down."

Elizabeth remained standing. "I thought I was here for a writing lesson."

Zoram said, "This is my father, Jeremiah." He spoke in a respectful tone and laid his hand on the prophet's shoulder. "After my parents died, he raised me until I came to work in this treasury." Zoram didn't move as he spoke. His hand was still on Jeremiah's shoulder, and he held his head as steady as the rhythm of his speech. He said, "My father's a prophet of God."

Elizabeth held the backrest with both hands. Zoram had never mentioned Jeremiah. What would Papa say if he ever found out that she had met the prophet? Elizabeth should have refused to speak with him, but his gentle voice and kind eyes drew her to sit in the chair next to him. He pressed his finger over the characters inscribed on the top plate and began to read in a low soft voice that soothed her soul. Elizabeth listened with more interest than she should have allowed herself.

Jeremiah read aloud, "I, Joseph, Viceroy of Egypt, make this record." Jeremiah's voice grew stronger and he continued reading the prophecy of Joseph who was sold into Egypt, detailing how the words written on the plates of brass would be restored by Messiah ben Joseph and were to be mingled with the words of another book to come forth out of the dust, the words of both books bringing men to a knowledge of their covenants with God. Jeremiah removed his finger from the record. He said, "More than a thousand years ago, Joseph began this record, writing down the words of Adam, Enoch, Noah, and Abraham. Moses brought them across the Sinai, and the prophet Zenos took them to the Northern Kingdom when Israel was divided into two nations. It was Laban's great-grandfather who brought them here to this treasury." He sat forward and rested his arms on the table. "Once my writings are added to these plates the record will be complete."

Zoram took a seat next to Elizabeth. "What he's asking for is your help." He reached beneath the table and brought out a sack of copper ore and another of silver. "This is to smelt plates of brass." He laid the bags on the table and inched them closer to her. "Will you ask your father to smith them for us?"

"Why don't you ask him yourself? He's the blacksmith, not I."

Jeremiah leaned close and his long beard brushed her hands. "It's God's will that we finish this record."

"We came to you," Zoram said, "because, well, your father can't know all the details."

"And why not?"

Jeremiah touched Elizabeth's hand. "Your father can't be trusted."

"Not trusted!" Elizabeth stood and arranged the pleats in her robe. No one had ever insulted her father like that, at least not to her face. He was the most trustworthy man she knew. She gripped her lunch basket. "I'll be going."

Zoram asked, "What about your writing lesson?"

"I'd rather not take one this afternoon." Elizabeth hurried down past the rows of records. Not this afternoon? She held the lunch basket close to her. She didn't want to take one ever, not from Zoram. She reached the door to the vault and found it locked. Her only choice was to wait for Zoram to catch up and let her out. No, not let her out, let her go. She wanted to be free of this humiliation.

"Would you please open the door?"

"You don't have to leave."

Elizabeth's lips trembled. "Is this why you had me come? To disobey my father's wishes?"

"I was only asking your help."

She wiped a tear from her eye. "I never should have trusted you."

"Trusted me with what?"

"You don't know, do you?"

Zoram turned the key in the latch. "Should I?"

Elizabeth held her hand to her heart. His thoughtlessness pierced like a sword. When Zoram pushed open the vault door, she hurried down the corridor, up the steps, and outside. The alley was quiet and she quickly made her way down its winding paths and through the servants' gate into the sunlight of Market Street. She should have stayed and told Zoram she had feelings for him, but she couldn't risk baring too much of her soul. Not if all Zoram wanted was her help with the brass plates. She could never go against her father's wishes.

Not even to win Zoram's favor.

CHAPTER 17

Zadock sat in his red-cushioned chair at the head of the council table. This was his chamber, decorated with silk curtains he'd ordered from the weaving mills of Egypt, mahogany tables caravanned from Phoenicia, marble floors from Athens, and gold-threaded tapestries from the Orient.

The tall chamber doors groaned open and Laban marched in. He wore a tight-fitting gray tunic with the sleeves cut out and a short wrestler's kilt that reached to the middle of his thigh. His feet were shod with single-strapped sandals, the ones wrestlers wore to a match and removed before entering the sand pit. The captain was on his way to train the recruits.

"What are you doing here during the day?" Zadock shifted on his cushion.

"I have business to discuss."

"Couldn't you at least wear something more dignified than that, that . . ."

"It's about the blacksmith."

Zadock came around the council table, the hem of his long robes sweeping the floor. "Has something gone wrong?"

"He knows too much."

"Nothing we can't deal with when he finishes the sword."

Laban said, "I want him kept alive."

"What are you saying?"

Laban circled to the lower end of the council table, gripping the backrest of the last chair with both hands. The twelfth and most junior post had remained vacant over the turbulent months following the war. "Put him on your Council and make him one of us."

"Don't be a fool. He's not the sort of man I'm used to dealing with."

"What sort of man would that be?"

"He has loyalties."

"To whom?"

"His family."

"Then we use his family." Laban took a seat across the table and set his boots up. "The blacksmith has a son."

"The crippled boy?"

"No, the second son, Daniel. He has a talent for wrestling."

"You've got fifty recruits with that kind of talent."

"This boy is special."

"Who told you that?"

"I have my sources."

Zadock waved his long, bony fingers in front of his face. "We already control the blacksmith."

"A shop and some silver aren't enough." Laban jerked his feet off the table and stood. "It won't keep him quiet forever."

"And you think his son will."

"With Daniel under my wing, his father will beg to join us."

"I'll have to think on it." Zadock returned to sit on his cushion and faced Laban.

The captain was an arrogant enough man that he could ruin everything if he wasn't cautious about who he brought into their circle. Laban could be right about keeping the blacksmith alive regardless of what he knew about the sword. And recruiting his son was a shrewd move, one Zadock would allow Laban, but on one condition. Zadock would decide how much they trusted the blacksmith and his son. And unlike Laban, Jonathan and Daniel were expendable. Everyone was expendable but the captain. There was no future without him. He was the last living descendant of Joseph.

Laban said, "I decide who joins my army."

The glow of a brass lamp overhead streaked Zadock's face with yellow light. "And I decide who becomes an Elder."

"Then make your decision quickly before I make it for you." Laban marched from the chamber without another word.

Daniel came by his strength swinging a forging hammer, but he'd never learned the wrestling hold men of his stature should master: the flying mare. Named for lifting an opponent over the head, like a wild horse rearing its hind legs, and throwing him into the sand. He'd tried the hold, but he was doing something wrong. He wasn't sure if he needed to bend lower at the knee or hold his opponent by the hip—or maybe it was by the thigh.

If only he had a sparring partner. He didn't ask Aaron, not with his feet the way they were. Elizabeth refused, saying it wasn't a dignified thing for a woman. Sarah agreed to let him try, but slapped him in the face every time he lifted her overhead. Joshua volunteered before he was ever asked, and he would have been a help if he weren't so small. Daniel didn't need any leverage to pick up the boy.

Since the day Daniel heard about the flying mare, he'd wanted to wrestle like the soldier who had invented the hold. Hercules was the greatest of all wrestlers and his fame reached from the Olympiad in Athens to the floating gardens of Babylon. Daniel first heard the tales of Hercules from Greek sailors at the docks in Sidon. And though they invented unbelievable stories of sea monsters fighting with pagan water gods, what they said about Hercules rang true. He was a Greek soldier who built his wrestling strength lifting large stones up hills and carrying cows across his pasture. The captain of the sailing vessel Zeus confirmed the stories, and, since he sailed out of the port at Thebes three times a season, Daniel found no reason not to believe him.

Nothing could keep Daniel from sneaking from the shop today, in spite of Papa's orders that he finish forging the plow bit before sundown. Captain Laban was the only man in Judah who knew how to throw a flying mare and he was teaching it to his recruits this afternoon. When Jonathan left with the mule cart to pick up a load of coal from the mine, Daniel hung his apron on a peg, put away his forging hammer and started for the military grounds. The plow bit could wait until morning.

The military training ground stood across the street from the Jawbone Inn. Swordsmen were training near the front gates when

Daniel arrived. Their blades clashed like great rams battering upon metal shields. Daniel entered under the archway, the deafening sound of metal on metal echoing off the brick. In the main yard, spear throwers launched long sticks at red clay targets. Daniel skirted past them and found a spot in the shadows, behind the trunk of an olive tree.

The wrestling pit lay down a small incline. It measured the same as every match-worthy pit, twenty-four cubits square, the length of six men laying head to foot. Captain Laban stood in the center. He widened his stance in the freshly raked sand and squared his powerful shoulders. He was the fittest man Daniel had ever seen, without the sagging belly or drooping shoulders that plagued many officers of lesser ability. The captain warned the recruits that only the strongest among them could execute a flying mare, and he selected one of the boys to help him demonstrate it. He was shaped like a pyramid turned on end and Daniel knew him immediately. His shoulders were as wide as an ox yoke and his arms thick as mason's bricks. Of all the recruits gathered around the pit, Laban chose Simeon, the soldier Daniel had met at the Jawbone Inn, the boy with a tolerance for strong drink.

Simeon strutted to the center of the pit and lowered his body in a wrestler's stance. Laban circled him like a leopard closing down on its prey, kicking at the sand to find his footing. He struck like a cobra, wrapping his arms around Simeon's waist and hoisting him to his shoulder. The flying mare lasted only as long as a man can blink, but Daniel held the image in his mind. The finest hold he'd ever seen and he memorized the shift in Laban's stance, the angle of his grip, the dip of his shoulders, every detail down to the twist of his wrist and the grimace on his face.

Laban hurled Simeon out of the pit, the boy's arms and legs waving to the sky. It was like watching a sack of wheat flung from a mule cart. Simeon jumped to his feet begging for another chance, but Laban told him to clean the sand off his body at the oiling table and sent the young wrestler marching up the rise.

The oiling table was equipped with a metal trowel to scrape away the sand. Daniel stayed behind the trunk of the olive tree and watched Simeon clean off the grit, wipe his arms and legs with a linen, then uncork a vial of olive oil to slick his body. He started at his ankles, worked the oil up his shins and around his thighs. It spread easily onto his belly and he palmed it up onto his chest, along his shoulders and down his arms.

Two powerful arms wrapped around Daniel. It was Laban. He'd come up the rise, staying along the west wall so that Daniel didn't see him. He said, "What are you doing here?" His voice was a low, deep growl, his grip a vice. He stood the same height as Daniel but he seemed larger and stronger than any man he'd ever known.

"I was only watching, sir."

Laban spun Daniel around. "You're the son of the blacksmith, aren't you?"

"I'm one of his sons." Daniel stepped back against the trunk of the olive tree. How did Laban recognize him? They had never been introduced, despite Daniel's failed attempt at the Jawbone. Whatever the reason for Laban knowing him, Daniel couldn't let news of his coming to the training ground get back to Papa, not with the plow bit left unfinished. He said, "I'll go, sir. I have some forging to do."

"What sort of forging?"

"Nothing, really."

"Tell me." Laban gripped Daniel's arm. "I need to know what kind of work you help your father with."

"A plow bit." Daniel twisted his arm free and stood away from the tree trunk. "Any more questions?"

"Not right now, son."

Son? Laban never called any of his recruits by that name. He wasn't that kind of man, but his voice had taken on a gentler tone and he was smiling back at everything Daniel said. Why did Laban treat Daniel with the trappings of friendship? It was his duty to train the men in his army, not befriend them.

Laban glanced at Simeon oiling his body. "I understand you and my recruit have met."

"We had a few drinks."

"I could arrange another match."

"I've sworn off wine for now."

"A wrestling match, boy. They tell me you know how to wrestle."

Who told him? Daniel glanced around the yard. There was no one here who knew of his wrestling skills and he could only believe it was Laman and Lemuel who had advised the captain.

Daniel said, "I've tried my hand before."

"Then oil up and you can try your hand on Simeon."

Daniel had never greased his body for a wrestling match, but it seemed the best way to ensure a fair one with Simeon already strutting to the wrestling pit, his oiled skin glistening in the afternoon sun. Daniel peeled off his tunic and covered his skin with olive oil. When he finished spreading the last of it down past his elbows, he marched to the center of the pit and squared up across from Simeon.

"This is a full match." Laban held his hand between Daniel and Simeon. "The first man to throw his opponent three times, wins." He pulled his arm back.

"Wrestle!"

Elizabeth would never have come to fetch Daniel back from the training grounds on her own, but Papa's disposition at midday meal persuaded her. He had stopped back in at the shop and found it empty. If Daniel would only get his work done, Jonathan had said over a cold leg of lamb and fresh bread, he wouldn't mind that the boy had other interests. Papa hadn't used the word "interests," but it was not Elizabeth's nature to use the word he used. It wasn't any vile cursing, mind you, but close enough that she decided someone should go after Daniel. And, since no one else did, that someone was her.

She entered the training grounds by a small gate off the alley and stayed in the shadows along the west wall while she searched for Daniel's brown tunic among the recruits who wore nothing but a kilt to cover their nakedness. He was nowhere to be found until a cheer, fifty voices loud, turned her gaze down an incline to a wrestling pit nearly out of sight below the swell of earth. It was surrounded with recruits, all of them mesmerized by every movement, every hold, every throw made by . . .

Daniel? What was he doing in there?

Laban stretched his arm between Daniel and his opponent. "Two falls for Simeon and two for the challenger. The next man to throw his opponent to the sand wins." He drew back his arm and said, "Wrestle!"

Simeon lunged, but Daniel dodged the strike, grabbed hold of his unguarded left side and hoisted him over his shoulder into a flying mare. The cheering stopped as Daniel heaved Simeon across the pit.

Laban didn't move from his place along the edge of the pit, didn't flinch, didn't give any sign he was angry with Daniel for throwing his best recruit three times into the sand. And he'd done it with the hold Laban was trying to teach to Simeon and the other boys. The murmuring among the recruits quieted, and Laban stepped to Daniel's side. "You're a strong lad."

Daniel bent over and between gasps for breath said, "Seven years of forging, sir."

"I can see that. And you learn fast."

"You're a good teacher." Daniel raised his dark brown eyes from staring at the sand.

Laban tugged on his beard as if he hadn't heard the praise; but he had. His lips turned up into the slightest of smiles and Elizabeth wanted to run from the shadows of her hiding place, down the incline to the wrestling pit and tell Daniel it wasn't wise of him to befriend the captain of the guard. He could end up a soldier if he wasn't careful and what would Papa say then? Daniel was their best forger and if he left the shop, who would help Papa with that part of the business?

Laban said, "I want you to train with my men."

"I'd like that, but my father . . ." Daniel brushed the sand off his hands. "I don't think he'd allow it."

"Your father should be your last worry."

"You don't know him like I do."

Laban picked Daniel's tunic out of the sand and handed it to him. "You'd be surprised what I know, son."

"I'd be grateful for anything you could do to convince him."

"Consider it done."

Daniel pulled his tunic on over his shoulders, thanked Laban, and started out of the wrestling pit, past the recruits who parted to let him pass up the incline. He was near the west wall when Elizabeth said, "Daniel, over here."

He squinted through the afternoon sun. "Elizabeth?" He hurried over. "Women aren't allowed in here."

"Papa sent me."

"He knows you can't come in here."

"He doesn't exactly know that I'm here."

"You could get us both in trouble." Daniel took her by the arm and started her toward the side door that spilled into the alley running between the training grounds and the palace.

"Papa said you had forging to finish before tomorrow."

"Can't you see I have more important things to do than forge a plow bit?"

"Don't say that, Daniel." Elizabeth lowered her head and walked beside him. "You're a blacksmith. Papa raised you to be the best."

Daniel pulled open the gate and hurried Elizabeth into the alley. It was cool in the shadows of the high walls towering over the training grounds. They were alone, but Daniel didn't let go of Elizabeth's arm. He tightened his grip and said, "You shouldn't have come here."

Elizabeth pulled free. "Are you going to tell Papa what happened?"

"Don't you understand? This is my chance to be more than a smith."

"Don't say that." Elizabeth touched his lips with her finger. "I can't bear to hear you say that."

"And why not?"

"Because it means we could lose you."

"You're not losing a brother, you're gaining a soldier."

"Papa needs you at the shop, especially with Aaron's feet the way they are."

"Swinging a forging hammer hasn't gotten me anything." Daniel began dressing in his tunic. It had three burn holes in it. "I don't even dress well." He yanked it on over his head and ripped another hole in the cloth. "Cursed thing!"

"Would you really leave us to become a soldier?"

"I'm not leaving the family."

Elizabeth stepped to Daniel's side and took him by the hand. "You don't want to work for Laban."

"What do you know about him?"

Elizabeth's voice dropped to a whisper. "I've heard things." She looked past him into the shadows dancing about the foundation of the palace walls and when she turned back to him she said, "Laban's killed men."

"He's a soldier."

"Soldiers don't murder."

"Where did you hear that?"

"People talk."

"Don't say any more about Laban." Daniel continued scanning the alley. "Not until we're away from here."

"I just don't want you to get in with the wrong sort of men and Laban is—"

"I said no more." Daniel's eyes took on a wild look.

Daniel was the first out of the alley and into the sunlight of King Street. He didn't speak a word as they walked down past the Citadel toward the lower city. It was quiet enough that Elizabeth could hear the hem of her robe brush the cobblestones. When they were well past the entrance to the military grounds, she asked, "You're going to speak with Papa about what Laban told you, aren't you?"

"Not right now." Daniel jabbed his finger at her. "And you keep silent as well."

"You shouldn't keep this from him."

"Why do you care about this anyway?"

Daniel was covered in sand and Elizabeth brushed his arms clean. He was a strong boy. No, not a boy. He'd become a man these past few years. He was no longer the little brother who played with her on the beaches in Sidon, or the mischievous lad who hid a frog in her bed or chased her about with a garden snake. And it didn't seem so long ago that he was more interested in collecting rocks and climbing trees than he was in wrestling a man to the ground. But there he stood, her younger brother, his powerful shoulders rising and falling with each breath, and his deep brown eyes filled with the determination to be a soldier in Laban's army.

"I care . . ." Elizabeth leaned over and kissed him on the forehead, ". . . because I love you."

CHAPTER 18

"Air for the fires!"

Aaron pried open the smelter door with tongs, letting a stream of air rush out and nearly searing his eyebrows. Bubbles formed on the surface of the molten ore like steam boiling from a pot of thick stew. It was ready for ash, the last ingredient transforming the ore to steel, returning just enough of the carbon that had burned away in the smelter to make the metal hard as diamond. That was the other secret to steelmaking, a riddle most smiths never deciphered, just like the mystery of hard coal.

Aaron leaned forward off his bench, his leather smithing apron protecting him from the heat. He tossed in a handful of ash and let it work its miracle, mixing with the ore and hardening as it cooled.

"Not so close, son!" Jonathan barked the order.

"I know how to work the oven, Papa."

Jonathan lowered his head. "It's just the sight of you in front of the door."

Aaron pulled away from the sparks showering out the oven. "I'm not going to let it happen again."

Daniel shuffled through the shop doors with his head down and shoulders forward. It was a walk that said he didn't want anyone to bother him about coming late to work.

"Hand me that, will you?" Daniel said.

Jonathan handed over the newly smelted plow bit that waited for the finishing touches of Daniel's forging hammer. "Why did you wait till the last moment, son? This plow bit was to be finished for the vineyard owner."

"I'll have it ready."

"He's coming by today."

Daniel stabbed the plow bit beneath the hot coals of the open hearth and held it steady with tongs. "I always get my work done."

Aaron filled a scoop with ash, but didn't measure it as he should have before mixing it with the smelted ore. He shimmied back down the bench toward the oven and threw far too much of the black powder over the molten steel. A shower of sparks shot out from the oven and he swung the door shut to keep from getting burned. The metal latch banged shut and Aaron looked over at Daniel. "You were at the military grounds yesterday, weren't you?"

"Did Elizabeth tell you that?"

"She didn't need to."

Daniel hefted the plow bit onto the forging table and brought the hammer down smartly, dancing it up off the table. The hammer connected for three more ringing blows, followed by one strike that snapped deep inside, cracking off a thin layer of shavings and spraying them over the table. "What do you care about what I was doing?"

Aaron said, "You're getting behind in your work."

Daniel waved his hammer at the storage shelves. "Do you see anything up there I didn't forge?" He stuck the bit under the coals and let it heat to a red glow, then he purged the weak spots, turning it with tongs and bouncing the hammer rapidly over its surface in a flurry of sparks. The bit rang, and rang, and rang again, sloughing the outer skin onto the table in a pile of tailings. Daniel said, "I'm the master forger in this shop."

Aaron sat up high on his bench. "Then you best act like one."

"Boys." Jonathan stepped between them. "I won't have you talk like that."

The chimney flue began to rattle against the rafters, the same shaking Aaron knew all too well. He yelled, "Papa, step away from the oven." But it was too late. The excess ash Aaron had thrown over the ore blasted the oven door open in a flash of light. The force of it sent Jonathan reeling onto his back, reaching for his legs to smother the flame in his apron. The thick leather shielded him from the worst of the sparks, but his shins were scorched red and the skin lifted up into blisters.

Aaron limped to his side. "Papa, are you all right?"

"Give me a moment." Jonathan struggled to his feet.

"It was my fault."

"It was an accident." Jonathan touched his fingers over the shins.

"We never should have come here," Daniel said. "There's no money in Jerusalem for blacksmiths."

Jonathan's head came up. "You're wrong. I have work that will make us richer than . . ."

"Than what?"

Jonathan lowered his head back into his burns.

Daniel said, "I could make more money than ten blacksmiths if I were an officer in Laban's military."

Aaron sat on his bench next to Daniel. "They make boys like you foot soldiers." He turned back to the oven and fitted the hinge into place. "They'd give you a rusted sword left over from the last war, and a dented helmet, and tell you stories about the glory of getting killed."

"Laban wouldn't do that, not to me. I'm a wrestler."

Aaron swung the oven door open and shut, testing the hinges. "Captain Laban doesn't even know you."

"He does. He knows I can wrestle better than . . ." Daniel stepped back to the forging table and fell silent.

"Better than who?"

Daniel tapped the hammer over the plow bit, though it didn't need any more forging. It was finished. "I was just saying that I could make a good living as a soldier, if I had reason to."

"You don't have reason." Jonathan stood, his face twisted into a painful grimace. "There's enough blacksmithing work in Jerusalem for us to make a good living."

"When?" Daniel folded his arms across his chest. "In time to hire wailers and incense burners for your burial?"

"Don't speak like that to me, son."

Daniel untied his smithing apron and started out the door.

"Where are you going?"

Daniel threw the apron in a heap on the ground. "To get a load of wood for the ovens." He kicked the apron out of his way and disappeared into the street.

Ruth hurried toward the blacksmith shop with a lunch basket. Joshua followed a few paces behind, straining to carry a full jar of goat milk. The poor child had carried the heavy load from home and it was all he could do to keep it from dragging on the ground. Ruth would have stopped to help him, but there were more pressing thoughts on her mind than spilt milk. Daniel had stopped by the house to get the mule cart to haul wood and told her about the accident. It frightened her and she decided it best to bring midday meal to the shop. All she wanted was for their life to be good and for Jonathan to be healthy—the same strong-willed, resolute husband she had known these twenty-one years. What would she do if he were injured?

She turned into the shop and waited for her eyes to adjust to the darkness before glancing at Aaron. He managed to smile and she motioned to him, silently telling him to take the milk from Joshua and go outside while she spoke to Jonathan.

Aaron nodded to her in a way that said he understood.

"Come along Joshua." Aaron set the milk on the forging table and directed his little brother to wheel the pushcart out into the street. "You can ride down the hill in this."

Aaron followed him out the door, leaning on his staffs. He knew her son was going to need more support than those two small sticks of wood. He ducked under the door beam and there was a hitch in his gait that hadn't been there before. He needed a crutch. Ruth had seen a lame man with one at the east gate last week, begging alms. It reached from the ground all the way to under the shoulder and she remembered enough of the design that she could get Jonathan to craft one right here in the shop. He wasn't a carpenter, but he was good with his hands and then Aaron could…

What was she thinking? Ruth turned from the door and peered across the darkened shop. It was Jonathan who needed her comfort right now, not Aaron.

Ruth said, "Jonathan?"

"Over here."

"Are you hurt?"

"I'm fine."

She could tell he wasn't. Wives knew when their husbands hurt and Jonathan was hurting. He knelt at the door of the smelting oven, chiseling away at the hardened steel they had lost this morning. At forty years old, he still had the stamina of youth. Blacksmithing had kept him lean and agile enough that she silently admired his vigor. His calloused hands were spotted with white burns from years of blacksmithing and she wanted to hold them and tell him she had worried over him until she couldn't weave another stitch.

"It's early for lunch," Jonathan said.

"I thought you'd be hungry. You know how you drive yourself and the boys."

Jonathan stood and tipped the jar of goat milk to his lips. "No one was injured." He slapped away the burnt pieces of leather that still clung to his apron, exposing his blisters. They'd gone white, filled with a watery pus.

Ruth turned away. "It was the ash this time, wasn't it?"

"Did Daniel tell you?"

"He was upset about something."

"The boy is too temperamental."

"The move's been hard on us all." Ruth sighed.

"He's not entitled to act like he did. He can't speak his mind whenever it pleases him."

Ruth emptied dates, nuts, a loaf of her homemade leavened bread, and a bowl of figs from her basket. The figs were Jonathan's favorites, especially the way she prepared them soaked in goat milk. The cream turned the sugars sticky brown and coated the fruit with a caramel taste. "Daniel's a good boy, he's—"

"He's lacking respect."

"Be patient with him."

Jonathan chewed on a fig. "I'll not endure his outbursts."

Ruth set out a linen over the forging table and arranged the food on it. It was best to change the subject when Jonathan was like this.

"We had a visitor at the house a few weeks back. I've been meaning to tell you, but you've been busy with other things."

Jonathan stared at the wall and Ruth could tell he was only half listening, hearing her words but thinking his own thoughts.

"That boy is trying my patience."

"It was a visit from the wife of Zedekiah."

Ruth served him a portion of still-warm bread, then hurriedly told him of Queen Miriam's visit. "Oh, it would be wonderful to weave the robes for the coronation and it would bring us enough money until you're paid for your new work. What do you think?"

Jonathan scratched the side of his head, took a drink of goat milk and a bite of bread before he said, "Daniel's without respect for our good name."

"Have another fig." Ruth pushed the bowl closer to him and broke more bread. He'd heard her. He'd gotten every word about the queen's visit. He just wasn't ready to discuss it while he had other things on his mind. Ruth leaned on the knife, pressing with both hands until it found its way into the bread's soft dark middle, then cut the loaf in two. It must still be hard for Jonathan, remembering less prosperous times when he was a traveling blacksmith, wandering from vineyard to vineyard mending farmers' broken tools. If it weren't for the money she'd earned weaving, he never would have been able to purchase an apprenticeship with the steelmakers in Sidon and learn the art of steelmaking. He might still be a traveling smith if her weaving hadn't brought such a high price in the markets. She'd become so expert that even the noblemen of Sidon sought her out to weave their most expensive garments.

"This weaving for the queen." Jonathan turned back from staring at the wall. "Will it be like before?"

"Just until the coronation at the first of the year, then it would end." Ruth put away the bread knife.

"Maybe Daniel's right. Maybe we never should have moved here. It's been nothing but pain for all of us."

"We've been worse off. Remember when we were first married, how you'd travel to every vineyard between Sidon and Tyre mending tools."

"That was twenty years ago."

She laid her hand on his chisel arm. "We can start all over again if we must."

"It wasn't supposed to be this way."

"I've never blamed you for the money we don't have. Moving here was the right thing." Ruth took a deep breath and let it out slowly. "But now that we're here, I have this feeling that—"

"I'm not going to start traveling again."

"I know." Ruth looked through the front doors of the shop, past the broken chimneys of the blacksmith district, beyond the rooftops of the lower city toward home. "It's just that ever since we moved here I've felt there's something pulling us apart."

"Nothing in this city is going to divide our family. I'll not allow it."

"I'm scared for us, Jonathan."

Jonathan fell back to his knees and worked his chisel over the hardened metal. "Mothers have that right when they worry."

"It isn't worry; it's a thought, like a memory only that it has yet to happen." Ruth held her hand over her heart. "And it keeps coming back."

Jonathan grated the chisel over the floor, dislodging bits of slag. "I've found some new blacksmithing work."

"Will it be enough?"

"If it doesn't bring us a good deal of money, then we'll go back to Sidon."

"We're not going back." Ruth folded her arms and held them tight around herself. "This is where we belong; it's where we're supposed to be right now."

"Didn't you say you wanted to start over again, like when we were first married?"

Ruth turned back from looking out the shop doors. "That was twenty years ago."

"We've done it before; we can start over again."

"Do you really mean it?" Ruth knelt beside him. "You'll allow me to weave for the queen?"

"See that she treats you right." Jonathan set aside the chisel and held her hand. "You're too good a weaver not to have her respect."

"That doesn't matter; I've yours."

"You have mine always."

"An angel, Aaron! Look over there; it's an angel!"

It wasn't proper to point at strangers, but Aaron couldn't stop Joshua from jumping out of the pushcart and jabbing his fingers in the direction of the strange man who reined his mule cart down through the district. Aaron sat up straight, his back braced against the outside wall of the shop. He said,

"It isn't proper to point." He waved for Joshua to come close, but he didn't mind Aaron. Hadn't Mama taught him better? If she were to come out of the shop and find Joshua acting like this, she'd tan his backside.

Joshua kept pointing at the stranger as if he were a spirit from another world. And he did look something like an angel with his round red cheeks and brown eyes that sparkled as if he knew Aaron before he met him. He wore a red, yellow, blue, and green tunic—definitely from Egypt, not heaven, though the hem did sway about his feet as if he were floating. His full head of snow-white hair lay back in well-combed furrows and his white beard was trimmed close to his cheeks resembling foam atop the surf of the Great Sea.

"That's no angel," Aaron said. "And put your fingers away before you hurt someone."

Joshua stuffed his hands under his tunic. "How do you know he's no angel?"

"Angels don't drive carts."

By the dull yellow color of the stranger's box frame, his cart couldn't have been more than a few weeks old, cut from fresh olive wood. He had to be a vineyard owner; who else owned enough trees to afford an entire cart out of olive wood? He walked alongside the mule with an easy stride, not like other older men.

Joshua asked, "Have you ever seen an angel?"

"Of course not."

"Then how do you know angels don't drive carts?"

"The plow, silly." Aaron pointed it out to him, the handles rising above the sacks of winter seed piled in the cart.

Joshua said, "Angels could be farmers."

"That's Ishmael, the vineyard owner, come to pick up his plow bit."

Joshua left Aaron sitting against the door of the shop and sprinted across the street to Ishmael. "Are you a man?"

Ishmael lashed the mule reins once more around the post. "What do you think I am?"

"I say you're someone close to God, like an angel."

"I've never been mistaken for that." Ishmael scratched his beard. "My wife calls me 'husband' and when she does, I come running."

"I have a sister who shouts names at me, but I never come running when Sarah calls else she'll hit me with a stick."

"Joshua." Aaron struggled to get to his feet and leaned against the wall of the shop. "Leave the poor man alone."

"Good morning, son." Ishmael crossed to Aaron. "Your feet are causing you some pain today."

"No more than usual." Aaron didn't move, didn't want Ishmael to know how bad they really were. He couldn't, not if he wanted to get the job Sam had offered him for three talents of silver. That kind of wage was impossible to earn in two months and the vineyard owners were offering it for two weeks of work.

"I hope they're healing well." Ishmael laid his hand on Aaron's shoulder and immediately a calm feeling swept over him. For a moment Aaron believed the pain in his feet had disappeared. He wiggled his toes and the pain was still there. Tomorrow he'd wear two wraps on both feet instead of one.

Jonathan came through the shop doors with the plow bit. He braced his knee against the sideboard of Ishmael's cart and hoisted it onto the floorboard, setting it flush against the base of the plow handle and tying it on with leather cords. Planters turned harder to the right when they dug furrows, and he lashed extra cords around the opposite side to hold it against the strain: three around the left horn, two around the right.

Jonathan shoved the plow back into the cart. "This bit will turn rock-filled soil where iron bits would crack."

"Fine piece of work." Ishmael stepped in next to Jonathan and slipped a talent of silver into his hand.

"Sam already paid for this."

"That's for Aaron's work preparing our caravan. Part now and the rest when he's finished. I always like to pay our good help in advance. We have fifty head of camel to get ready to caravan to Egypt. We've never taken more than thirty at a time, but we've got a larger than usual order for olive oil and Sam's determined we take the entire herd. There's a good deal of work for your son. We need all the harnesses mended, saddle hitches gone over, and wheel hubs fixed before we leave."

Jonathan scratched the side of his head. "Aaron's feet aren't healing well and it's—"

"It's a miracle he survived at all."

Miracle? Aaron lowered his head. Why did Ishmael have to use that word in front of Papa?

Joshua tugged on Ishmael's flowing robe. "You sure you're no angel?"

"No, son, but I know a prophet who is about as close to an angel as you or I'll ever get."

Jonathan's lips flattened and his jaw tightened. It was a look that said he wouldn't stand for much more of that kind of talk. He shooed Joshua inside to eat lunch with Ruth. The boy walked slowly to the shop door, turned back once, then darted inside. Jonathan said, "I can't let Aaron go right now. I need him here with me."

"I can pay you more, double what Sam offered."

"It isn't the money."

Ishmael nodded slowly. "Sam and Nephi said there might be a problem."

Jonathan dusted the metal tailings from his hands. "I'm sorry."

"I wish you would trust us."

"I have to do what's best for my family."

"Very well." Ishmael untied the mule from the post. "I'll be off; it takes a good three hours to walk this mule home with a load like this and our planters are expecting the plow this afternoon." He tugged on the reins and the mule took a lurching step forward. "My offer for Aaron still stands."

Jonathan didn't answer and Ishmael had enough sense not to press further. He drove his cart up the hill, his robe stiff about his feet, walking without the same easy gait that had carried him into the blacksmithing district and it made the climb look steeper than it really was.

Aaron limped over next to Jonathan and they watched Ishmael go. Papa stood with his chin up and shoulders back, resolute and firm about his decision. When Ishmael finally rounded the corner at the top of the district, Jonathan turned back to Aaron and said, "Are your feet well enough to go by the potter's?"

They weren't, but if it meant a trip to Rebekah's home he'd find a way. "Which pottery yard?"

"Josiah's. He's a man we can trust."

"Don't you mean he's not a Rekhabite?"

"I didn't accuse Ishmael or his cousin of anything."

"You didn't need to."

"Don't question me on this, boy."

"What do you need from the potter?"

Jonathan disappeared inside the shop and when he returned he carried a long piece of pine hewn into the shape of a sword. "The clay mold needs to be pressed to precisely this size."

"When did we get an order for a sword?"

"We didn't."

"It looks like a sword."

"I'm smithing it for good luck."

"Luck?"

"That's right." Jonathan reached down, gathered a handful of sand that had lodged between the cobblestones and threw it into the breeze. "Here's to a more prosperous future."

Papa's words rang like bells on a feast day, but smithing a sword for luck was hardly reason to celebrate. He should have agreed to Ishmael's offer. Working for the olive oil merchants would bring them more money than a hundred lucky swords. What was Papa thinking? There wasn't much reason to dream about a prosperous future. Not with Papa wasting their resources on a sword they weren't going to sell. They didn't need luck.

They needed work.

CHAPTER 19

Aaron stood across the street from the potter's yard leaning on a new crutch, an invention Ruth said would support his weight better than two staffs ever did. Papa had just finished lashing it together this morning from the longest timbers in the firebox. It came up under his left arm with enough support that he could get around just fine with one.

He strained to catch a glimpse inside the pottery yard, but the servants closed the gates as soon as the clay and sand carts rolled inside. The only thing he could see was the same skyline he'd seen every day on his way to the shop. There were shovel loads of potter's clay arching above the wall and landing on the summit of a growing pile, the square cement roof of the estate at one end and the domed roof of the kiln at the other. No smoke billowed from the kiln's chimney today, but the cries of wedgers and turners confirmed there was work afoot.

In front of the gates, shoppers moved between the selling tables, handling the merchandise like a farmer examines a melon. They tapped the sides of pots to check for cracks, spat on glazed plates to examine their watertightness and shook cups by the handle to test their strength.

Mima, the potter's Ethiopian maidservant, sat on a bench beside the selling tables, twirling an umbrella of reeds to stir an idle breeze out of the stagnant air and calling to shoppers as they passed. Her colorful striped shirt was hardly Hebrew, but it didn't cause near the stir her skirt had sparked among the respectably dressed women of Jerusalem. It hardly covered her knee, far too much leg to be within the law. No one ever complained that she pressed the limits of modesty, except during the last feast celebration when she wore an empty grain bag of sackcloth to cover her head instead of a linen veil, a breech of etiquette for which she had yet to be forgiven.

Beads of sweat streamed down Mima's brow and she used a newly fired plate to fan herself. Her waving exposed rolls of skin hanging from her arms like fruit left unpicked on a sultry day. Her nostrils flared with each breath, but the afternoon heat didn't seem reason enough for her round face to draw into a scowl. And it wasn't. It was Aaron she glared at with the dander of a wild boar protecting its young. Mima guarded Rebekah from undeserving suitors, and Aaron was fast becoming the object of her disapproval.

"Fine pottery for sale!" Mima's selling voice took on a deep, harsh tone and she shifted her weight on the bench. "Bowls! Drinking cups! Saucers!"

Buying a mold from the potter was the best excuse he'd had in weeks to come by Rebekah's home. Aaron tucked the wooden sword under his arm and limped across the street, Mima or no Mima.

"Plates and water jars for sale." Mima dropped her umbrella and stared at him with a gaze strong enough to bore a hole in his chest. He lost himself among the shoppers to wait until the gates to the pottery yard opened. He picked up a wine bottle and tapped it, spat on it, shook it a bit, and held it up to the sun. The glaze reflected the light into his eyes, blinding him for a moment.

"You can't pick out a wine bottle with your eyes closed."

Aaron blinked three times before the glare disappeared and he found Mima standing in front of him, her arms swaying at her waist like bags of wheat. He held out the wine bottle. "Very nice work."

"That will cost you four shekels."

Aaron returned the bottle to the selling table. "What I really came for was a mold, a clay blacksmithing mold."

Mima took a deep breath and blew the air out her nose. Her white teeth gleamed between black lips when she spoke. "You sure that's all you're looking for?" She looked him over, starting at his sandals, moving up his legs and past his leather kilt. She must have recognized the twill weave in his tunic. Her gaze paused there and she reached out and pressed the cloth between her thick fingers. "Awful fine clothing for a lower city boy."

"My mother's a weaver."

"Every mother's a weaver, boy. But this is something special."

"She uses a foot loom."

Mima nodded as if his finely woven tunic had somehow convinced her to be civil. She said, "Follow me."

Aaron obeyed, all the while scanning the pottery yard for Rebekah. He couldn't let her see him using a crutch and luckily she was nowhere to be seen. The place was busier than he'd thought it would be between firings. A boy servant shoveled clay into a pushcart then wheeled it across the yard to the wedgers who mixed in a portion of white sand, pinched away the lumps, and pressed out the air. The wedgers' muscular forearms bulged out of proportion with the rest of their bodies from years of wedging. A pack boy hauled the wedged clay over to the turners. They threw it onto stone wheels set between their sprawled legs and spun the red mud into recognizable shapes. On one turner's wheel sat the beginnings of a large vase, on another wheel an urn. There were three wheels with cups, and four more with bowls spinning and sputtering wet clay between the turners' fingers.

The kiln stood at the far end of the yard, ten cubits high and wide enough to stable three elephants if you could have fit them through the waist-high door. The red and yellow brick walls curved inward near the top like an oversized beehive and the slits cut into the wall for ventilation weren't much larger than a duck's egg.

Mima stopped at the kiln door. "This is as far as I go. You'll find Josiah somewhere in the darkness, but you'll have to find him on your own." She stepped back from the small opening, hardly large enough for her body, with the cross beam set so low she'd have to crawl to get inside. "I don't go in the kiln very often."

Not very often? She should have said she couldn't go in the kiln ever. The sight of her squeezing through the opening was as likely as sheep sprouting wings and flying with a flock of gulls. Aaron didn't laugh. He didn't dare. Not with Mima hovering over him. He quickly thanked her and ducked through the door, shimmying inside on his hands and knees and dragging his crutch alongside.

Except for a glimmer of light streaming past the chimney flues, the kiln chamber was dark and Aaron coughed at the smell of charred wood. He couldn't see the ash, but he could feel the powdery stuff gather around his sandals and he kept still, not letting it dirty his bandages. His eyes began to adjust to the darkness, and the tall stacks of pottery appeared in front of him less than an arm's length away. Stacks of bowls, plates, cisterns, and urns sprouted out of the floor and sat awkwardly one atop the other. Lucky for Aaron he hadn't taken another step or he would have brought them crashing to the floor.

"Is anyone here?"

A rattling sound echoed just behind the stacks. The potter was working on the chimney flue.

"Josiah?"

"Over here, boy. Come help me yank this pipe out of the vent. It's sprung another leak."

"Over where, sir?"

"You know your way around."

Josiah gave another tug on the chimney pipe, and a loud crack shot through the kiln. The pipe pulled free and the end knocked up against the stacks of pottery, starting them swaying. Aaron dodged the first falling pot, but the next one caught him on the shoulder, and, before he could use his crutch to back away, three full stacks fell on him, smothering him face down in the ashes.

Josiah cleared away the largest broken clay off Aaron's back. "Are you hurt?"

Aaron blinked his eyes until he could see Josiah standing above him. He was a fatherly looking man with only a touch of gray in his beard, though it was hard to say how much in the darkness. The man looked like Rebekah's father: high, smiling cheeks and very thin lips. But it was his eyes that most resembled Rebekah's, filled with the same light he'd seen in hers.

Aaron spat out the chalky taste of ash and said, "I'm fine."

"Glad to hear it. I can't afford to lose good men around here." Josiah helped Aaron over to a stool. He pointed at the flue pipe rising out of the fire box and disappearing through the back wall of the kiln. "We've work to do on that chimney. Can't keep the fires lit with it leaking smoke back into the kiln. It'll take three of us to fix it. You go bring the kilnmaster."

"What does he look like?"

"Must you always tease me, boy?" Josiah slapped a cloud of fine pot ash from Aaron's shirt. "Off you go and fetch your father."

"But . . . ?"

"What is it now?"

"My father's Jonathan the blacksmith. He sent me to see you."

Josiah peered through the haze. "Lord have mercy on my soul, you are the blacksmith's son. Did I give you a scare?"

"Only a few bruises."

"I've never entertained a customer in here."

"If it's all the same to you sir, I'd rather not attend another of your celebrations."

Josiah glanced over to where Aaron had fallen. A crutch lay in the powdery ash. "Is that yours?"

"I use it sometimes." Aaron lowered his head. The truth was he used the crutch all the time. He couldn't get around without it.

"I see." Josiah looked at the dirty bandages covering Aaron's feet. "What does your father need?"

"A smithing mold shaped like this." Aaron held out the wooden sword.

Josiah walked back to the chimney and began tinkering with the hole. "Can he wait until the end of the month?"

"That should be fine."

Aaron stood and was about to excuse himself when a young woman ducked through the opening carrying a water jar. She stood next to Aaron, the hem of her robe brushing his leg and gathering over his feet. "Father, where are you?"

"Over here, Rebekah."

She blinked, trying to focus her eyes in the darkness. "I've brought you a cool drink of water from the spring."

"Give some to our customer."

"What customer?"

Aaron leaned over and spoke in her ear. "Hello, Rebekah."

"Who's that?" She stepped back and searched the darkness, her nose wrinkling up her narrow bridge and her brow gathering into tiny furrows while she focused her eyes. It made Aaron laugh inside, not in a humorous way, but a joyful one, as if he'd found a treasure that could make him forever rich. He wished her blindness would last long enough so he could study her without her studying him. Then he could remember every nuance in her smile, every line around her eyes that spoke of feelings he sensed she kept from others, not hidden, but preserved deep in her soul, waiting to share them with someone she trusted.

"Shalom, son of the blacksmith," Rebekah said.

Aaron turned toward the ground. She'd caught him staring and he immediately felt as if he'd trespassed.

Rebekah said, "Would you like a drink?"

"Thank you, but I'm not really . . ."

Rebekah tipped the jar to his lips and the water kept him from refusing her offer. "I believe I'll have to visit the kiln more often if Papa insists on entertaining our customers in here." She laughed and the sound was as Aaron had imagined: carefree, happy and full of kindness.

"Can I help you find some pottery?" Rebekah asked.

"The boy doesn't need to see any more." Josiah came around the broken pots and had Rebekah pour some cool water over his sweaty, balding head. By the way he stared at Aaron between the streams of water pouring off his scalp, he wasn't comfortable with their flirting.

"Well actually, sir, I could look awhile—that is, if Rebekah has time to show me. Maybe find something for my mother."

"I have some very nice flower vases." Rebekah lifted the drinking jar to Aaron again. She steadied its base so he could press his lips against the vessel's opening when Mima's face appeared at the entrance, and Aaron pulled his head back from the drinking jar. Maybe sheep really could fly.

Mima said, "Come with me, child. I need you inside."

Rebekah said, "I'm helping the men with a drink."

"Leave the jar and let them help themselves."

Mima grabbed Rebekah's arm and scurried her off through the door leaving Aaron alone with the potter.

Josiah said, "She's a difficult woman, she is."

"Maybe a little odd." Aaron said.

"Rebekah is anything but odd, boy."

"I meant Mima, sir."

Josiah watched the low-lying entrance where Mima had gone out and he smiled. "Now there's a strong-willed woman." He turned from looking out the door. "You have an eye for her, don't you."

"Mima?"

"No, boy, my daughter."

"Well, I . . ."

"Women are a different animal."

"I don't doubt that."

"More difficult to understand than any other creature."

"Whatever you say, sir."

"You'd have to be a prophet to decipher my Rebekah's thinking."

"Do you know any?"

"Prophets, boy?"

"Men who can decipher her thinking."

"I'm no prophet. Are you?" He stood beside the flue, his frame silhouetted by the light that entered through the hole in the wall. But his face remained shrouded in darkness, and there was no way to tell from his expression if he was speaking a bit of humor or if he was serious. There should be no question of how Josiah felt about the holy men. The Elders of the Jews did not take kindly to the prophets.

"Me a prophet, sir? Not likely." Aaron cleared his throat. "My father would never allow a prophet in his shop. He wants nothing to do with visionaries or with zealots."

"You mean Rekhabites."

"Them more than the prophets, sir."

"Do you agree?"

"I don't have an opinion one way or the other."

"I suggest you get one."

"What sort of one, sir?"

"My Rebekah is a sensible woman and any man who has an inkling to court her should make wise choices about who he supports."

"If you don't mind my asking, sir, who do you suggest I support?"

Josiah hefted the wooden sword. "A mold this large will cost you an extra piece of silver." He turned it in his hands. "I'll send the mold by your shop as soon as it's finished."

"But . . ."

"That will be all."

Aaron picked his crutch out of the ash and ducked through the kiln door without asking another question. He should have stayed until he was certain exactly what kind of opinion the potter expected from him on the matter of Rekhabites. It would be easier to court Rebekah if he knew how the potter felt. But Josiah didn't want any more questions. Not by the way he stood at the door and motioned for Aaron to take his leave. It was an odd way to end their conversation, but Josiah had left him with little doubt. If he were to court Josiah's daughter he would have to make the right political choices. And in these times the only right choice was with the Elders of the Jews.

Anything else was foolishness.

CHAPTER 20

Ruth smelled the faint aroma of mint leaves burning in the oil lamps that lit the north wing. The royal family's living quarters were located where she believed they'd be, on the upper floor of the palace, each room with a view of the temple grounds.

"You can fit the king for his robes last." The robust palace maidservant shuffled toward the door at the end of the hall. "Now is not a good time."

"Is something wrong?" Ruth asked.

"Nothing that tea and a short nap won't cure."

"Has the king been ill?"

The maid shook her head. "He's upset."

"I can come back another day."

"That's all right, he's expecting you. He'll be tolerable once he meets with the captain of the guard and clears up the matter of the prophet Uriah and the palace informant once and for all."

"Laban's coming here?"

"Of course, dear. He's responsible for the royal family's safety. Do you know him?"

"We met once. Briefly."

"A handsome man, don't you think?"

"I hadn't noticed."

"He's coming to speak to the king about Uriah's tie to the palace informant. You knew the prophet escaped, didn't you?"

"Is that so?"

"Oh dear. You really should spend more time at the market. It's all they talk about these days." The maid slowed. "Laban's obsessed with capturing the man who passed information to the mail courier."

"You mean Hosha Yahu."

"Killed himself, he did. A dark thing if I do say so myself."

"I thought he was the informant."

"Where do you shop, woman?"

"I make a practice never to dally at the market, especially early in the morning."

"If you did, you'd know that Captain Laban believes there's another, more powerful informant here in this very palace and he won't rest until he's caught him. You can see it in his eyes whenever he comes to discuss the matter with the king."

"I've seen that look before." Ruth walked a half step behind the maid and she would stay there until their discussion of Laban ended and she could forget the morning at the east gate where she'd first met the captain of the guard face to face.

The maid leaned in close. "Laban questioned me about who in the palace might be carrying warnings to the prophets."

"Does he suspect you?"

"No dear, he spoke to all the help. I gave him the name of a Rekhabite who works in the palace kitchens, just the kind of information he wanted to hear. The next day my wage increased two shekels a week and they moved me to a private room overlooking the courtyard gardens. They don't want any trouble with this."

"And the kitchen help?" Ruth asked.

"We're always replacing the cooks." The maid's glance flitted about the hall. "If he could, Laban would be rid of all the holy men tomorrow, but he's going to take care of them quietly, one at a time. I heard it from the gardener, who heard it from the night watchman who heard it fall from Laban's lips." She held Ruth by the arm and pulled her close. "I try not to get involved with the intrigue."

"A wise choice," Ruth said.

"It is if I want to keep my private room over the gardens. I don't take risks like the queen." The maid wagged a feather duster at Ruth. "You didn't hear this from me, but Miriam's got what you might call other allegiances." She lowered the mass of feathers long enough to clean a day's buildup from the urn in the hall then pointed it at Ruth again. "I heard Miriam speak kindly of Jeremiah." She nodded. "It's true—not that she outright supports the prophet you understand, but it isn't wise for a woman of her station to say such things. Next thing you know, someone will accuse her of being a Rekhabite, and they're nothing more than a scourge Laban will no doubt ferret out." The maid tucked her feather duster under her arm and bustled down the hall toward the bedrooms. "Did you bring enough to measure all the boys?"

Ruth counted the cords draped over her arms. The longer ones for measuring height from shoulder to floor, the shorter ones for the arms and the reach around the waist. "Three sons, isn't that right?"

"Benjamin is four years, Dan is eight and Mulek's ten," the maid said.

"My what a young family."

"They're all well-behaved."

"I sensed that."

"You know the boys?"

"I met Mulek."

"Ah yes, he's a fine young man." The maidservant stopped outside the first bedroom. "You can begin with him." She turned the latch and pushed open the tall cedar doors. "Call when you've finished."

Mulek's room boasted three windows overlooking the temple grounds, fourteen lighted brass lamps that flickered in the sunlight for no other purpose than show, seventeen chairs to entertain heaven knows who, and four entry doors, no doubt employed by Mulek for games of chase. Ruth walked to the bed and ran her hand over the quilts. The bed was large enough to sleep the entire royal family. The billowing mattress spilled over its cedar frame and hung down around the ornately carved wooden legs. A canopy of white linen was suspended between the bedposts like a cloud shading a riverbank where the prince could dream of dangling his feet in make-believe water. But why would anyone need a rain canopy for sleeping indoors? The worst rainy season could never produce a storm inside these vaulted chambers.

Next to the bed stood a table spread with four arrowheads, a bowl filled with bird feathers, and a sealed cedar box, no doubt for Mulek's most intimate keepsakes. Ruth smiled and shook her head. Not keepsakes, they were treasures. Boys didn't collect keepsakes.

She picked up the only game among Mulek's things, a wooden cup with a long string and a rock tied to the end. She tried to catch the rock in the cup, missed and tried again.

"Do you like games?" Mulek's quiet voice came from the other side of the bedroom.

Ruth spun around to see him standing by the window, his broad smile touched by the morning sun. She swung the rock and caught it this time. "Now and then."

"Have you played beneath your water clock since we met?"

"I'd hoped you'd forgotten about that."

"I wish we had such a thing on the palace grounds. It did seem fun."

Ruth put away the toy. "We'd best be about measuring you for your robe."

This wasn't the first time Mulek had been measured for new clothes, not by the way he walked to the center of the room, straightened his shoulders and held out his arms. Ruth handed him the first measuring cord and he already knew to hold the end to his shoulder. She tied a knot where the rope met the floor then wrapped a second cord around his chest. He took a normal-sized breath and held it without Ruth asking him; and when she asked to measure his wing span, he took the cord in a tailor's hold between his middle fingers while she strung the other end up his arm, behind his neck and down the other arm, working the cords as if he'd done this a hundred times with a hundred royal weavers.

"If I must wear a robe to the coronation," Mulek said, "I'd prefer a short one. I can't give chase when my garment drags on the ground."

"I suppose your father wouldn't notice if I cut a few hands off the length."

Mulek's eyes widened and his eyebrows shot up. "You will, really?"

"If your mother approves, of course."

"What about the sleeves?" Mulek said, raising his arms to let Ruth tie a knot at the end of the third cord. "Can you make them wider than usual?"

"That would look odd."

"Just enough so I can hide a game to pass the time."

"I'll see what I can do."

Mulek fell silent when Ruth held the end of the last cord to his collar bone. It was the same silence as when she'd seen the charm around his neck the day he came to her home.

Ruth took back the cord. "Do you have it on?"

He didn't say a word, only glanced at the table near his bed.

Ruth said, "Tell me about your treasures. Those feathers are wonderful, and the arrowheads, my how polished you've kept them. And that well-crafted cedar box, what do you keep in there?"

When Mulek didn't answer she knew she'd asked the wrong question. She tied the last cord at his wrist. "There you go, all finished. I'll make sure your sleeves are large enough to hide a treasure or two."

"I've only one treasure." Mulek went to the cedar box and returned with a small brass serpent dangling at the end of a chain. It was a frightening trinket to wear around the neck. How could anyone wear such an abomination? There were others in Jerusalem who followed the teachings of the prophets and they didn't wear the mark of the serpent. It was a sign of membership among the Rekhabites, but why did Mulek have it? Rekhabites were far too zealous a community of believers to allow royals into their ranks.

Ruth said, "I don't think you should show me this."

"It's all right."

"What would your mother say?"

Mulek held up the charm. "I can share it with anyone who has a good heart."

"And you think I have such a heart?"

"I feel it right here." Mulek pointed to his chest. "The feeling Mama taught me to judge by." He lifted himself onto the window ledge and dangled his feet against the wall. "The charm has to do with the story of Moses. The one about serpents that attacked our fathers in the deserts of Sinai, and Moses held one up nailed to a stick and told the people to look and be saved."

"How nice. Your charm is a remembrance of the story of Moses." Ruth rubbed it between her fingers and would have thrown it out the window if it weren't for Mulek watching her study the trinket. It was a simple brass charm, but it was still a serpent. She let it fall to her palm. At least it wasn't as dreadful a religious symbol as she'd heard. She took a deep breath. All those rumors about Rekhabites perverting the Hebrew religion.

"That isn't everything," Mulek said.

"There's more?" Ruth returned the charm.

"Do you believe you can know the future?"

"You mean the prophecies."

"It's more than that." Mulek pulled his knees up to his chest like a young boy, but his words were those of a wise man. "It's God sharing a part of the future with you, because it's so important that your life . . ." He paused and searched for a better word and when he found it, he said it slowly. "Your soul depends on it."

Ruth patted him on the head. "Everyone believes the prophecies are important."

"It's not about blessings for doing good or cursings for doing evil. I mean to really know the future, to know a man before he's ever born, because knowing him can save your soul."

Ruth stepped close enough to see the seriousness in his eyes. "Who has power to save the soul?"

"He'll be born six hundred years from the year my father's crowned."

"It isn't for us to know these things, young man."

"The prophets say his birth will be at Jerusalem, to a mother named Mary."

"No one can know that."

The sunlight danced over Mulek's brown hair, turning it gold. He lifted his charm until it caught the light and shimmered with reds, greens, and blues like a precious stone. "The prophets call him Yeshua the Anointed One."

Ruth backed from the window. That was the name, the one Rekhabites used freely enough to be stoned. Surely, pairing a common name with deity was unspeakable blasphemy in every tongue and in every nation on earth: Yeshua ha-Mashiakh—Joshua the Anointed One—a blasphemy punishable by death, and no good Jew would dare utter such a phrase, no matter the language or country.

Mulek dangled the charm in the air. "The prophets tell us to look to him, just as our fathers looked to the staff Moses held up in the wilderness."

"Mulek!" Queen Miriam stood at the door. "What have you done?"

He jumped from the window ledge. "You said I could share my charm if I—"

"Even your father doesn't know about that." She crossed the room in long, brisk strides.

"Ruth isn't like the others, Mama." Mulek hid the charm in the sleeve of his tunic. "I felt the peaceful feeling. The one you said wasn't in the whirlwind or the earthquake or the fire, but the still small voice."

"Join your brothers in the gardens."

"But, Mama . . ."

"Now."

When he disappeared into the hallway, Miriam began to pace. After her fifth pass she asked, "What did he tell you?"

"Only about his charm."

"Nothing about the Rekhabites?"

"Not a word."

"But you've heard things, haven't you?" Miriam walked to the window and set her hands on the sill. "You're wondering if I'm a Rekhabite, aren't you?" She stayed by the window until enough time had passed that it was not improper to answer her own question. "I'm no traitor to the kingdom. But I'll not stand by and watch men of God hunted like wild beasts, even if my husband allows Laban his little revenge."

Ruth gathered her measuring cords. "I have your other sons to measure."

"What I've said troubles you, doesn't it?" Miriam asked.

"No, it's . . ."

"What?"

"This seems a very personal matter. I'll go now."

Miriam stepped in front of her and closed the door. The well-oiled hinges hardly groaned under the enormous weight of the cedar wood and once it was latched, Miriam said, "When we first met in the courtyard of your home I felt I could trust you as Mulek does."

Ruth lowered her head. "I'm flattered."

"Mulek and I joined the Rekhabites a year ago." She waited for Ruth to say something, but there was nothing to say. Not with

Miriam baring her deepest secrets, her greatest fear and to Ruth, someone the queen had only met under the oddest of circumstances, soaking wet from the water clock. "We were baptized in a secret washing pool outside the city gates." Miriam took Ruth by the hand and seated her on the edge of the bed. "When I stepped from the water, I felt a peace descend over me. It was as a gentle breeze passing over my heart, so real that I thought for a moment I'd glimpsed the heavens where God dwells. And I knew for the first time in my life that the *Mashiakh* was mindful of me and would always be mindful of me."

"Mulek called him Yeshua, Yeshua the Anointed One."

"He *will* be the Mashiakh, the Anointed One all Jews wait upon. It's His name, Yeshua, that I've covenanted to take upon me, to always remember, and I look forward to the day of His coming when He will be lifted up—like the serpent Moses nailed to a staff—to redeem us." Miriam closed her eyes. "Do you see why I feel as I do? Why Mulek keeps his charm close to him?"

"Everything's new to me. I've lived my whole life in Sidon among the Canaanites." Ruth held the measuring cords close. "How can I judge when I know so little of what we Jews believe?"

"I used to ask the same questions, but I always knew I would recognize truth when I found it, like the memory of another world reminding me of the way things should be. And I've always watched, so that when I found it, I'd recognize it like meeting an old friend."

"Have you found that friend?"

"Once, when I joined the Rekhabites." Miriam placed her hand on Ruth's arm. "And again when I found you soaked in water from your water clock."

Ruth smiled. The memory of their first meeting welled up inside her and she remembered it as if it were yesterday. "Since the day we met I've wanted to ask where you find the serenity I see calming your soul."

"You'll find that same peace, my friend."

Ruth gathered the cords over her arm. "I have more measurements to take."

"Wait." Miriam stepped to the door, blocking the way into the hall. "Promise me you'll tell no one. If this were known, even to my husband, Mulek and I could be . . ." She brushed a tear from her eye. "Look at me, crying. I'm sorry."

"You can trust me." Ruth held Miriam's hand until the trembling stopped.

"I don't want you to suffer my fears."

"I'm supposed to help you bear this." Ruth laid a hand over her chest. "I feel the peaceful feeling."

"Sit here."

The palace maidservant directed Ruth to a bench in the lobby outside the king's chamber. "Zedekiah will see you after he meets with him." She dusted the bench down near a man seated at the opposite end.

He was dressed in expensive clothing, but dreadfully out of fashion. His robe was all wrong, the cuffs so wide they showed far too much of his white undershirt. No doubt Prince Mulek had some influence with the man's tailor. He stared at Ruth between spikes of gray hair that poked out from beneath his turban. It was a look that said this bench wasn't large enough for both of them, particularly a woman. But the maidservant had allowed it and Ruth wasn't about to give up her seat because of a venomous stare from a stranger she would never meet again. He nodded to her, but his eyes warned her off so that she determined to sit as far away as possible rather than divide the bench equally between them. Thankfully it was a wide bench with planks cut almost as long as a cedar is tall.

The maidservant came back down the bench, her feather duster dancing over the wood planks. "I have to get the king some . . . ?"

"His tea?" Ruth said, draping the measuring cords over the back rest.

"Oh my, that's what I was going to prepare." The maidservant's hands were all aflutter. "I'll bring you a cup of tea while you wait."

"With a touch of honey, if that isn't asking too much?"

"Hardly, dear. We have jars brimming with the sweet stuff." The maid hurried down the hall to the kitchens.

The lobby's majesty drew Ruth's attention from the stranger. The double doors reached eight cubits high with two lion statues gracing either side, reposing on their haunches in peaceful contrast to the swords and spears hanging on the walls. The noble creatures weren't ferocious in the least bit. More likely to purr than roar; and if given life, they'd lounge about the colorful rugs and curl up to sleep beneath the warmth of the giant oil lamps.

But despite the lobby's splendor, Ruth couldn't keep her eyes from coming back to study the man at the other end of the bench. He had pouches under his eyes, dark cavernous half circles, as if he'd died and been resurrected only to be refused by an angel and turned back to the grave to wait for a second chance. His long nose protruded between his eyes like a diviner's stick pointing toward the front doors of the palace. He was waiting for someone and Ruth found herself wanting to ask—

"Zadock!" Laban threw open the double front doors and marched across the marble floor in company with another man. Ruth veiled her face to avoid another interrogation at the hands of the captain.

"You're late," Zadock said. "It isn't wise to keep the king waiting."

"There's something you should know before we see the king."

"Not now." Zadock glanced at Ruth. "Not here."

Laban stepped aside and motioned to his companion, a middle-aged man with only a touch of gray hair. But he walked with a stooped gait and his rounded belly nearly fell out of his loosely tied robe. His nose was a stick, a very long stick, long enough for a fowl to roost, and his eyes were narrow and dark.

"This is Jonah," Laban said. "The animal trader from the western plateau. He keeps his eyes on the trade route for me."

"Fine day to you, sir." Jonah's long fingers wrapped completely around Zadock's hand. "Very fine day."

Zadock took back his hand and turned the full force of his gaze onto Laban. "Why did you bring this man to see me? I don't need to purchase a mule, Captain."

"Jonah brought me a horse this morning." Laban said the words slowly, carefully. "A black Arabian with a military brand on its hide."

"Mules, horses. I don't need either. Now come along, Captain; we have business with the king." Zadock started toward the royal court chambers.

"A man left the horse at my stockyard," Jonah said, his nose jabbing at the air when he spoke.

Zadock kept walking as he spoke to Laban. "We must convince His Royal Highness to have you order a search party to go after the prophet Uriah and bring him back to stand trial."

Jonah said, "The rider was dressed like a courier."

Zadock reached for the door to the king's chambers and stood waiting for Laban to join him before going in. "There won't really be a trial, of course. At least not the usual sort of trial with witnesses. You know how that can drag on and since we already know what the final vote will be, it seems a pitiful waste of time."

Jonah said, "The courier's name was Uriah."

Zadock let go of the latch and hurried back to Jonah in three longs strides. "Where is he?"

"Beit Zayit."

"The olive oil merchants? Why would he go there?"

"That isn't important." Laban stepped between them. "Knowing where he went is."

"Every detail is important, captain." Zadock pushed Laban aside and stood next to Jonah. "Tell me what you know."

"Uriah came by my corrals about three, maybe four weeks back."

"Why didn't you come to us with this earlier?"

"I didn't think anything of it. I just thought the captain would be happy to get his animal back, that's all."

Laban said, "We need to silence Uriah. He's more dangerous than any other."

Zadock took Laban by the arm. "You've never told me exactly why Uriah is any more dangerous than Jeremiah or the others."

"Trust me, he is."

"Not unless you tell me the reason for your obsession."

"Not here." Laban glanced at Ruth and a chill shot through her. She pulled the veil farther over her face, thanking heaven for the thick weave.

"Very well, captain, but we will discuss it." Zadock turned and disappeared through the doors leading to the king's chambers.

Ruth waited until she heard Laban and Jonah go out the front doors and click the latch behind them before she started across the lobby, leaving her measuring cords draped across the bench. They'd be safe there until she returned. She was only going upstairs to see Queen Miriam.

"Don't run off, I've got your tea." The maid shuffled down the hall from the kitchens. "It's good and sweet. I stirred in two spoonfuls of honey."

"Will it keep?" Ruth asked.

The maid set the mug on the bench. "It'll go cold sitting here."

"I've another measurement to make for the queen's garment."

"I thought you were done with her."

"I forgot something."

"You certainly did." The maid held up the measuring cords. "You'll need these. You go searching for the queen without a good reason, and the guards won't hesitate to march you right to the dungeons. They're a suspicious lot. We've all been on our toes since learning there's an informant among us."

Ruth came back and took the cords from her.

"Shall I tell the king where you've gone?"

"No!" Ruth's voice echoed about the lobby and scared the maid back a step. She quieted herself and said, "I mean, I should be back before he requires me."

"Very well."

Ruth waited until the maid returned to the kitchens before climbing the steps to the fifth floor. She had to tell Miriam what she'd overheard.

It could save the life of a prophet.

The royal court stood quiet and dark with only the light of day filtering in through the three-story arched windows that opened onto a view of Jerusalem. Marble columns adorned with gold lanterns held up the vaulted ceiling. Zadock shut the doors as quietly as he could, but the sound of his entrance danced off the walls of the oval room like the palace crier announcing his arrival and he feared he'd roused Zedekiah from his pensive pose. But the king remained seated into the angle of his throne and facing the windows.

Zadock picked his way down the steps to the sunken floor. He held his robe up off the marble and quietly stole across the long chamber, up the steps at the far end and in behind Zedekiah. The king sat staring out over the city. It was midday and he seemed entranced by the carts streaming down Main Street and the bustle of shoppers along Market Street. The sun's rays caught the silver thread in his blue cape, and the cloth shimmered on his narrow shoulders. The cape was buttoned with one silver clasp near Zedekiah's neck, and hung open, revealing his matching blue tunic and kilt decorated with the same silver threads. The king's brown hair was cut level with his shoulders and his bangs level with his eyebrows as if the palace barber had placed a helmet over his head and cut away the hair that wasn't protected from his clippers. He had fine trimmed eyebrows that formed a half-circle above each of his brown eyes. His thin lips and the narrow bridge of his nose were delicate features that most citizens believed was a regal look, though Zadock preferred to think of them as weak, just like Zedekiah's other traits. He had long, spindly legs and arms. The only thing that wasn't weak about the man was his position. This boy of thirty years would be crowned king in two month's time, and Zadock was the only man who had power to rectify that error.

It was a twist of fate that brought Zedekiah to the throne. His older brother, Jehoiakim came to power ten years before and he had an heir, a son named Jehoiachin. When Zedekiah's brother died of a heart attack during the war with Babylon February past, his seventeen-year-old son was made king in a short wartime ceremony. Three days later the Babylonians took Jerusalem, carried the new boy-king off as their prisoner and named his Uncle Zedekiah vassal king of Judah. But since Jews never crowned their kings until the first of the year, Zedekiah would have to wait for the coronation to begin his official reign.

Zadock said, "What a wonderful view, sire."

"It's a large city to rule over." Zedekiah spoke without looking away from the window.

"You rule the kingdom of Judah, not this city."

"Jerusalem is part of my kingdom." Zedekiah adjusted his cape over his shoulders. "Or did you forget the Council of Elders answers to the throne?"

"Of course we do. I didn't mean to speak otherwise." Zadock came around the throne and bowed.

"What business do you bring from the Council that couldn't wait?" Zedekiah offered his hand and Zadock kissed it.

"Uriah, sire."

"The prophet?"

"That's what he calls himself."

"And what do the Elders call him?"

"A traitor."

Zedekiah asked, "You're not a religious man, are you?"

"I'm a Jew, sire."

Zedekiah stood from his throne. "My brother who was king before me was a Jew, but he was not a religious man."

Zadock lowered his head. "God have mercy on your brother's soul."

"I doubt there will be much of that wasted on him." Zedekiah gripped the backrest of the throne. "It was God who removed him from ruling over this people."

"Must we remember the dead so poorly?"

Zedekiah walked to the windows, the light silhouetting his tall frame. "I'll not offend God in this matter."

Zadock stroked his thin forefinger across his chin. "Uriah's a traitor and it's your duty to see that he's punished according to our law, not our religion."

"Can you separate the two?" Zedekiah pulled his cape tight around his shoulders. "I won't have anything to do with this."

"Then let the Council deal with Uriah."

"What are you proposing?"

"Send a company of soldiers to search him out and bring him back to Jerusalem. The Elders will determine his guilt and you will be free of any responsibility in the matter."

Zedekiah took a deep breath.

Zadock said, "Does that mean you approve?"

"Have Laban organize his search party."

Zadock bowed. "Your will be done."

"I'm counting on the Council to see that God's will is done." Zedekiah sat on the throne and looked out over the city with his arms folded and his face without expression.

"Of course, sire. That's exactly what we'll do." Zadock left the king alone in his chamber.

CHAPTER 21

Jonathan spread the papyrus drawing over the forging table. He'd never fashioned a sword after a picture, even less after a piece of wood. Hilt first. That's how to craft a fine sword. He held a lamp over the drawing, illuminating every stroke of ink. Once he finished the hilt, he could fit the weight of the blade to the gold hand piece. Jonathan took the jewels from the bag and placed them over the drawing. Twelve rubies beveled around the crest, six sapphires inlaid along the grip, and diamonds the size of acorns fixed to the butt. That would be the most difficult. The hilt came to a point at the end, and fixing the diamonds without embedding them too far in the gold would take a delicate hammer stroke and a bit of luck.

A large man stepped into the doorway, blocking the light breeze that filtered through. Who could that be at this hour? No one ever came by the shop late at night and Jonathan stuffed the jewels in the bag and scrolled up the drawing. When the stranger stepped closer and the light of the fire shone on his face, Jonathan relaxed his hands on the forging table. It was only Captain Laban, and his square shoulders pitched in cadence with his step.

Jonathan laid the jewels and drawing in a box he'd dug beneath the floor and sealed them with a flagstone. "Your sword won't be ready for weeks."

"I don't expect it finished until the coronation." Laban approached Jonathan with the formality of a general marching into battle. "Can you mend this?" He held out a common-looking single-edged blade. It was a short sword, not much longer than a dagger and if Jonathan hadn't mended a good share of these, he would have thought it one. It was short enough to wear under the belt or hide in a boot, but most men sheathed them at the hip. And no good soldier carried a short sword any other way. The steel had a grainy complexion, probably fired at too low a temperature. There were cracks along both sides from impurities in the mother ore. The brass hilt was nothing to speak of, without any decoration except an engraving that read: *the king's army.*

"Is it yours?" Jonathan asked.

"The quartermaster gave this to me the day I was commissioned in the military." Laban handed the poorly crafted military-issue sword to Jonathan. "I haven't used it in years and won't be needing it or any other sword once you've finished your work."

Jonathan walked it over to the grinding stone. "I can sharpen it, maybe take out some of the cracks." After four passes, the steel began to growl, but it would never have a clear ring like finely smelted ore. Only the kind of steel Jonathan planned to smelt to replace the lost Sword of Joseph would have a clear, resonating ring. Jonathan asked, "Is there a reason you want this mended?"

"It's for your son, Daniel."

"You're giving my son a military man's sword?"

"He's a fine boy."

Jonathan turned back toward the grinding stone. "I've got three fine sons."

"True, but Daniel, he's a wrestler."

"He likes it. Spends a lot of time at it. Maybe too much."

"It shows."

Jonathan turned the sword over and kept the grinding wheel spinning with his feet. "Have you ever seen Daniel wrestle?"

"I haven't seen any better."

"Really?"

"He beat my best recruit."

On the last pass the blade gave up its growl for a hum, though it still didn't resonate. Poorly smithed metal never did, no matter how finely ground it was. "Daniel didn't say anything about his victory to me."

"Let me be the first."

"You were that impressed with him, were you?"

"I want your son in my army."

Jonathan set the blade over the open hearth to gather heat. "He's a blacksmith, not a soldier."

"Blacksmiths make the finest soldiers."

"Foot soldiering isn't what I want for the boy."

"He's what I want in an officer." Laban's face lifted into the slightest of smiles. A smile that Jonathan had hoped to see, a slip of emotion admitting how much he really wanted Daniel in his army. Smiling and bartering didn't mix; it was a costly luxury Jonathan never indulged in, but one Laban afforded himself.

"I'm sorry," Jonathan said. "I need Daniel in my shop. He's my best forger."

"I'll pay you a soldier's wage for the time Daniel's in training. That should cover the loss of his labor."

"No wage could cover that." Jonathan took the hot blade from the coals and began pounding out the cracks. The first five taps were muted deep inside the steel. As it cooled, the tapping should have rung clear. It didn't and Jonathan could only believe that this blade would break in battle.

Laban said, "I'll send one of my servants to work in Daniel's place, two days each week."

"Smelting is private work." Jonathan dipped the sword into a water bath and let the steam rise in a cloud around them. "I only trust my sons with our secrets."

"You can trust my servant."

"Not with steelmaking."

"At least meet him, see what you think." Laban stood at the door and waved his servant in from the street.

Zoram's dark-skinned face peered around the shop door. He removed his turban and let his cap of tightly curled black hair shine in the lamplight.

"Are you Hebrew?" Jonathan asked.

"Mostly, sir."

"Where are you from?"

"The village of Anathoth, a morning's walk north."

"And your family?"

Zoram lowered his head. "Dead, sir, taken by the plague."

"I'm sorry."

"I was very young when it happened."

"How old are you?"

"Twenty-four, sir."

Jonathan leaned forward and squinted. Zoram was much older than his young face and childlike green eyes showed. There was red in his cheeks. A good sign. The boy had his health and could endure two days a week in a blacksmith's shop without tiring. He had the look of a working man, long arms, wide shoulders, though they were lacking strength. Jonathan took Zoram by the arm. "Blacksmithing isn't easy work."

"I understand that, sir."

"He doesn't do a lot of heavy lifting," Laban said. "But don't believe him soft. He works as hard as the next man, even harder." He slapped Zoram on the back. "The boy's a scribe, has a good head, picks things up quickly. He knows Egyptian and some Babylonian."

"We don't have much need for that here," Jonathan said.

"What I'm telling you is that I trust Zoram more than any of my servants." Laban ran his hand under the neck of Zoram's tunic and pulled out a set of keys chained around his neck. "These are to my treasury. Zoram's the only one I trust to keep them. I've turned everything over to him. He accounts for my money, keeps all the records, and he cares for my most valuable possessions. If it's blacksmithing secrets you're worried about, you can trust them to Zoram."

"He's your servant, not mine." Jonathan polished the blade with a chamois until it shone as brightly as poorly smithed steel can shine. "How do I know I can trust him?"

"I swear you an oath that if Zoram breathes even one word of the secrets of your trade, he'll pay with his life."

Jonathan nodded. He was becoming accustomed to the captain's frequent use of oaths. "Very well, have him here to the shop on the first day of the week."

Laban took his sword from Jonathan and held it in the air. "I plan to have this issued to your son on his first day in my army."

"It isn't a very good blade."

"It was good enough for me."

Jonathan cleaned the metal tailings from around the base of the grinding wheel. Why was Laban gifting this sword to Daniel? Did he think the lad was going to follow in his footsteps, take the same path to the top posts in the military? Laban was captain of ten thousand soldiers, certainly a position of power worth considering for Daniel, though it was impossible to hope the son of a blacksmith could achieve such a thing. Best for Jonathan to get as much money for Daniel's work in the military as possible. They could deal with Daniel's future later. "How much of a wage for my son?" Jonathan asked.

Laban directed Zoram to get him the gold from his purse. He held it out and immediately Jonathan recognized the eight-sided medallion impressed with the seal of the royal house of Judah. He'd seen the large Hebrew currency only a few times. Wealthy men kept gold talents locked away in their treasuries. The glow from the open hearth shimmered over the coin like the yellow flames of a fire. "Consider this Daniel's first month's wage." Laban slapped the talent onto the table. "You can bring it back if you decide otherwise." He marched out of the shop taking Zoram with him, the sound of the captain's boots mixing with the popping of coals in the open hearth. It was a confident stride, like a man who always tipped the balance in his favor. The sort of stride Jonathan wanted for himself.

And for his sons.

CHAPTER 22

Miriam had received no more than a five-day notice before the Prince of Sidon was to visit the palace. He had changed his traveling plans and sent word by messenger he would stay in Jerusalem for an undetermined number of days. It was a complete surprise to Miriam, and she had no experience hosting royalty. She asked the cooks to prepare fish in lemon sauce, a good meal for a prince who lived by the sea and a kosher choice for any Jew. But since Jesse was no more a Jew than he was the prince of Egypt, she ordered crab and crayfish despite their uncleanness, and at the last moment requested any other seafood the cooks could muster this far from the sea, kosher or not. The watchmen raised the ensign of Phoenicia over the palace this morning; the maidservants trimmed and polished every lamp, dusted the columns in the entry, and scented the rugs and tapestries with frankincense.

Twenty shofar horns sounded the arrival of Jesse, Prince of Sidon, son of the King of Phoenicia. He drove the lead chariot into the palace courtyard where Miriam, Zedekiah, and Prince Mulek waited to greet him. Jesse's chariot was the largest of five in the royal traveling party. It had a gold-trimmed shield across the front and silver-plated wheel hubs. Forty soldiers from the Phoenician cavalry followed double file into the yard. The prince handed the reins to his driving companion, an uncle named Nimrod, and walked up the palace steps to the main doors.

Zedekiah said, "We're honored to have the Prince of Sidon visit us."

The prince shook Zedekiah's hand. "Please call me Jesse and leave the formalities to older royals." He stepped aside and let his uncle pass.

Nimrod studied the ornate stonework arching overhead and ran his hand over the brass latch on the large double oak doors. When his glance fell back to his nephew, he said, "You can call the prince whatever you like, for now."

Miriam would have honored the boy's request, but since this was their first introduction and Nimrod such a formal sort of man, she could only bring herself to call him Prince Jesse. He didn't stand taller than any other boy his age; neither his height nor girth were traits that would draw one's eye in a crowded market. It was his golden brown hair, his eyes as blue and deep as the sea beside which he lived, and his sweet grin that must have had all the women in Sidon taking notice. At fifteen years, he was of an age to enjoy that sort of attention, but far too young to understand the responsibility that came with a woman's interest.

Jesse stood on the porch and looked out over the courtyard. "My father wanted me to ride straight to Aqaba, but I wouldn't miss a side trip to see this place."

Nimrod ordered the envoy of soldiers to unpack their clothing and deliver it to their room. He turned a full circle, a leather satchel in one hand and a snuff box tucked under the other arm. He took one last look over the courtyard, his gaze stopping for a moment on the large brass lamps, lion-head statues, and flowing artesian fountains that gurgled into the shallow blue pools lining the far wall. "I am impressed by the way you live." Nimrod turned back to Miriam and bowed. "I believe I will enjoy myself these next few days." He waved to the soldiers carrying his things. "Follow me."

When he disappeared inside, Jesse said, "He'll be back." He leaned against the porch railing. "He doesn't like to ask many questions; he thinks it makes him appear weak. But he doesn't know where to find his room."

Nimrod's head popped out between the double doors. He cleared his throat, but before he could ask, Miriam saved him the embarrassment. She walked to the door, and pointed toward the main palace stairs. They were lined with twenty maidservants who stood with their heads bowed, waiting to receive Nimrod and his nephew. Miriam said, "It's on the fourth floor; the servants will direct you."

"I knew that." Nimrod slipped back inside, with the company of soldiers following him up the steps. They marched quickly behind him, suffering his commands in silence.

Mulek stepped out from behind his father and stared at Jesse until it wasn't proper to stare any longer, then he stared some more.

"Son," Miriam said. "This is Prince Jesse."

Mulek bowed exactly as Miriam had rehearsed him, bending at the waist and getting as low to the ground as he could. He said, "Would you like to see the palace? I can show you all the best hiding places."

"Mulek," Miriam said, "The prince is tired from his journey."

"No, really. I would enjoy a tour." Jesse ordered the soldiers not to follow and the two princes disappeared around the north side of the palace. And though they were separated by six years, they understood the pressures of each other's princehood and spent the day in a very unprincely manner. They were boys destined to become friends and Miriam allowed them their play.

Miriam sat in the chair facing the vanity and leaned her head back to let the maidservant braid a veil into her hair. The bedroom door swung open and Zedekiah walked in. He wore his white tunic for this evening's reception, a cape draped over his shoulders and a long kilt that went to his knees. He was a tall, thin man, and longer clothes presented a more domineering figure than a short kilt without a cloak. Especially if his knees showed. They weren't his most distinguished feature.

Zedekiah's hair lifted and fell about his shoulders as he walked to Miriam's side. "Let me do this." He took the veil from the maidservant, and she dismissed herself without another word to let him finish tying it into Miriam's hair. He did such a good job with the first braid that if the lace weren't white and her hair brown, she would never have been able to tell where the veil ended and her braids began. Zedekiah said, "You don't usually wear this veil."

"We don't usually entertain royal visitors."

Zedekiah carefully pulled her hair through the veil. "You have two of these, don't you?"

"You know my mother. She wanted me to have a choice of which to wear."

Zedekiah began to laugh.

"What do you find funny?"

"The two veils she gave you are identical."

"Don't say anything to her."

"I would never think to embarrass your mother." Zedekiah leaned over her shoulder. "But why she ever wove identical veils, I'll never know."

"In case one should tear, of course." Miriam adjusted her veil over her shoulders.

"You don't wear them enough to be concerned about that." Zedekiah finished one braid and began on the next. "Why, I've not seen you wear either since the day your mother gave them to you."

Miriam's veils weren't like ordinary linen veils women laid on their hair to cover the tops of their heads on feast days. And they were nothing like the long modesty veils that hid her face. This veil was made of thin, almost transparent white lace, and the snowflake pattern added a measure of elegance to her robe and flaunted her beauty more than it ever hid it.

Zedekiah finished braiding. "I need to warn you that Captain Laban has called an entire regiment in from the field to guard the palace this evening."

Miriam stood and pushed her chair back from the vanity. "That's five hundred men."

"I didn't think you'd approve."

"How are we to host a reception with so many soldiers milling about?"

"There's nothing we can do about it now."

"Order them to take their leave."

Zedekiah kissed her on the cheek. "I'll see that they're well behaved."

"I've never known Captain Laban or any of his men to behave well." Miriam caught her husband by the sleeve. He was still a young man, not as naive as when they were first married, but at thirty years he was far too young to have the responsibility of leading a nation. They could never have known when they were first married they would be King and Queen of Judah.

Miriam said, "I wish you wouldn't let Laban bully you."

"I've allowed him this show of strength. Laban believes Prince Jesse is here to assess the strength of our military and report it to his father."

"He's a fifteen-year-old boy. What does he know about military strength?"

"I have to trust Laban's opinion on the matter. He understands these things."

Phoenicia was the only country with shipbuilding docks along the east coast of the Great Sea; but despite their powerful navy, they were known for avoiding wars, not fighting them. The range of coastal mountains lining their shores protected them from most advances. And for those armies not deterred by geography, the Phoenicians forged alliances. Over the years since their kingdom was formed, they had prevented war by sending their blacksmiths, stonemasons, and architects to engineer the building of temples and palaces in Assyria, Babylon, and Egypt, and lending their expertise to the construction of Solomon's temple in Jerusalem. The royal court where Miriam and Zedekiah were to host this evening's reception was designed by Phoenician artisans.

Miriam said, "Laban is always lurking about the palace."

"He's only performing his duties."

"That doesn't give him license to order the palace servants about as if he were king."

"The man is concerned with our safety."

"I wish that were true."

Zedekiah folded his arms. "I've never heard you speak like this before."

"I've never had reason until now."

"Is there something wrong?" Zedekiah pulled her close to him.

"It's nothing."

"I know better when I hear that tone of voice."

Miriam straightened Zedekiah's collar and brushed her fingers through his hair. Her husband was a man without guile, a trait that Laban had used to his advantage on every decision affecting the daily operation of the palace and its security. Zedekiah's youthful humility had only encouraged Laban to overstep, and it was time her husband exercised a degree of control over a palace that Laban had spun out of his control. After the coronation, Miriam would insist he keep the man away from her.

Miriam said, "I worry Laban may try to hurt you."

"My, you have an imagination."

"And with good reason."

Zedekiah offered Miriam his hand. "We shouldn't keep the guests waiting any longer."

"Aren't you worried?"

"I'll let you do that for both of us." Zedekiah escorted Miriam out the bedroom door and down the corridor to the main hall. The anteroom quieted as Miriam and Zedekiah began their descent from the upper chambers, their hands clasped and raised between them. The steps were lined with Laban's men. They were dressed in formal attire, at least as formal as the army issued their foot soldiers, each with plumed helmets, brass breastplates and swords which they drew and raised toward Zedekiah in a loud clinging and clanging of metal.

Miriam didn't let Zedekiah stop and speak with any of the arriving guests. They quickly made their way through the crowded entryway to the royal court chamber and found Jesse and his uncle Nimrod already in their places at the head of the cavernous hall, flanked on either side by more of Laban's men. Soldiers lined the perimeter of the chamber, starting at the main doors, and running down both sides of the hall with the last man standing behind Miriam's throne.

The entertainment began as soon as Zedekiah and Miriam took their places next to Jesse. A muse recited the history of the docks of Sidon, followed by a band of musicians and a troop of dancers. The jugglers were next, ten Scythians with ballasts and balls and streamers kept aloft as if they had wings to fly.

Miriam would have enjoyed the jugglers' routine more if it hadn't been for Laban showing up at every turn. He walked in behind her when the jugglers began with the ballasts, lost himself among the guests when they changed to throwing balls, only to appear from behind a pillar and stare across at her between the streamers before disappearing for a moment, only to reappear standing next to her. He was supposed to be her protector, but he was nothing more than a nuisance and she would have sent him away if it weren't for Zadock marching through the entrance at a pace far too undignified for the

Chief Elder. He hurried over to Laban and whispered something in the captain's ear that sent them both rushing out of the palace.

Miriam waited for the jugglers to switch from streamers to swords, just long enough that Laban wouldn't suspect her of following. She went out a side door into the courtyard and moved in the shadows along the north wall, careful not to lose sight of the captain's black-cloaked figure hurrying along beside Zadock. She stayed back so she could jump behind the pillars lining the courtyard walls and hide from their quick glances. They ducked under the archway leading to the livery where Laban stabled his finest horses, and maintained his office. She would have preferred he perform his duties outside the palace precincts, but his highest duty was to ensure the safety of the king and royal family, so she kept silent her dislike of his constant presence.

Miriam followed through the same dark stone tunnel and emerged near the moonlit stables. They turned into the first stall and Laban began to curry the mane of his white Arabian. She would have left them alone to care for the horse and do whatever these two men did late at night in a horse stable when she heard a third voice.

"Close the gate." It was Shechem's low, rasping voice that gave the order. He'd come here twice to meet with the captain, but never in company with Zadock. He was Laban's accomplice and she knew the legends. Shechem, king of robbers was a murdering, power-seeking rebel and he had come to speak with Laban, the man charged with protecting her husband.

Miriam slowly stepped to the wooden gate and knelt in the shadows of the stable door. The lace cascading from her veil kept her from hearing clearly. She pulled it aside and pressed her ear to the wood next to the hinge. This time she would get every word.

"What about Uriah?" Shechem asked shuffling across the straw to stand next to Laban.

"He came through Jerusalem and sold his horse to the animal trader."

"Jonah?" Shechem asked.

Laban said, "The man's been a good investment for both of us."

"True enough." Shechem slapped the hind end of Laban's horse and the animal gave up a soft whinny. "Have you sent your men after Uriah?"

Laban said, "I'm assembling a search party."

"What about the trial?"

Zadock said, "There isn't need for one. I have all the votes I need."

Shechem said, "You need all twelve to behead Uriah. One dissenter and—"

"I know the law." Zadock's footsteps were muted as he walked across the fresh hay. "If any of the Elders on my Council vote to acquit Uriah, I'll deal with them."

Shechem asked, "What about the king?"

"He won't oppose me."

Oppose him? Miriam felt her face flush. She'd make certain her husband opposed him. Laban's horse bumped the gate, forcing Miriam to pull her ear back, but she couldn't move farther than a few hands. Her veil was caught in the hinge, pinched between the boards and post. She tried to pull free but the cloth stuck firm between the cedars.

Laban said, "By the time we bring Uriah back to Jerusalem, the Council will have ordered the executioner to prepare his block and sharpen his axe."

"Enough, gentlemen," Zadock said. "We all agree this is the way to proceed."

"We have to get back." Laban was the first to move toward the door, kicking the hay out of his way as he came. "We can't be missed at the reception."

Miriam tore her veil free.

Laban stopped mid-stride. "Did you hear that?"

"What?" Shechem asked.

Laban turned his head to listen. When nothing but the grunting from the next stall met his ears he jumped to the gate, kicked it open and marched out to the watering trough. The yard stood empty with only the drip, drip, dripping of water from a crack in the clay tank. Had he imagined the tearing sound? It was as loud as the rending of the high priest's robe on the day of Atonement, or at least it seemed that loud. He shook his head, rubbed his eyes and scanned the yard again. There were no servants hauling feed, no one tending the stables and no strays loose in the grain bins. He must have been hearing things and he bent over the trough and splashed water onto his face. That's what it was, his imagination playing another trick. He turned back toward the stall. Hanging from the hinges was a scrap from a woman's veil, not just any veil, but a piece of a finely woven lace. It felt soft between his fingers and smelled of perfume.

The same veil and perfume Miriam wore at the reception.

Miriam huddled behind the water trough. She peered around it to see Laban scanning the yard. Her hands trembled at the memory of kneeling with her veil caught in the hinges and Laban marching across the stable. He would have caught her listening to them if she hadn't hid here—and she prayed he didn't look any further.

Laban stood above her and she could feel the heat rise off his legs. The captain turned back to the gate and paused. He was staring at the torn lace stuck on the hinge and she wanted to run over and take it down and pretend this had never happened, but it had and with the help of God she would find a way to cover this unfortunate mishap. She had to find a way! There were too many lives at stake.

Laban pulled the lace free of the hinge, rubbed it between his fingers and smelled the perfume before returning to the stable and resuming his conversation with Shechem. Once the sound of their voices filled the air and Miriam was certain they wouldn't see her, she gathered the skirts of her robe and hurried across the livery and under the archway into the palace courtyard. There was one duty she had to attend to, and heaven willing she could do it and return to the reception before Laban found her missing.

She must send the palace informant with a message to Josiah the potter.

The crisp evening air streamed through the bedroom window, chilling Mulek's cheeks to a frosty red. The stars came out earlier now that late autumn had come to Jerusalem, and adventure waited in the dark streets below, lit only by the twinkling night sky. Not one boy in the city had gone to bed this early. Mulek was certain of it; he'd been out after sunset, and despite the dangers lurking in the streets, he'd never been held up by a thief. Though he did purchase three arrowheads for his collection from a Bedouin who'd remained inside the city after the gates were locked. He never told Mama where he'd gotten them, or she'd never again send him out with a message. She told him never to speak to Bedouins because they hid small daggers under their dirty robes, never bathed, and they ran off into the desert with little boys and made them slaves. That was Mama's way to scare him, but it never did. He was ten years old and she still treated him like a babe. Despite her warning of robbers jumping the walls to plunder and murder after dark, he'd never run into one in all his late-night adventures. The only scare he'd ever had was last month when one of the palace soldiers nearly caught him on his return after a run through the streets into the lower city and back.

"Must I go to bed now?" Mulek asked the maidservant who was busy turning down the top cover and fluffing his feather mattress.

"You're to follow your mother's orders."

Mulek leaned out the window. "I'll jump."

"If you insist on escaping, wear this." She held out his nightshirt. "There's a nip in the air."

"Mother doesn't care that I'm up late." Mulek threw on the nightshirt that reached to the floor before dropping his kilt and handing it to the maid.

"Your mother isn't here."

The maidservant unlatched his sandals and placed them at the foot of his bed when the bedroom door flew open and Miriam slipped inside. Her face was pale and she was short of breath.

"My lady." The maidservant tucked the blanket ends under the feather mattress. "What of the reception?"

"The jugglers were fine."

"And the musicians?"

"Wonderful." Miriam's fingers trembled as she untied her veil.

"Why, you've torn it." The maidservant reached to help undo all her braids and free the veil from her hair. "Let me help you."

Miriam pulled away. "That will be all."

"I haven't put Mulek to bed."

"I'll see to that."

"As you wish."

As soon as the maidservant dismissed herself into the hall and closed the doors, Miriam hid the torn veil under Mulek's feather mattress, then hurried through the side doors to her room and returned with the other veil made of the same cloth and the identical lace pattern of snowflakes. She braided it into her hair with Mulek tying the veil in place. Miriam said, "You must take a message to the potter."

"When?"

"Tonight." Mulek guided his mother's fingers as she tied the second veil into her hair. He could feel her words on his ear when she said, "Tell the potter he must vote in favor of beheading Uriah or they'll kill him. Do you understand?"

Mulek repeated her message word for word and Miriam kissed his forehead. "This is a most serious message, young man."

"I've never failed you before."

"No, you haven't." Miriam ran her hand through his hair. "Now change into your clothes and be off with you."

"Shall I go out by the front gates?" The gold insignia sewn into Mulek's shirt flashed in the light as he pulled it on.

"Go out through the kitchens and sneak through the servants' gate. With all the preparations going on over there, no one will question you."

Mulek took his soft sandals from the closet, the worn ones that made hardly a noise on the stone streets. Getting past the well-lit Citadel building undetected wouldn't be as difficult as descending the narrow street down Milo Hill to the potter's house. If pursued, he'd lead his assailant on a chase through the winding streets of the lower city before doubling back and sneaking through the hole in the back wall of the potter's property. Mulek buckled his sandals tight to keep them from clapping against the cobblestones. This was more exciting than riding in his father's chariots! But he wasn't foolhardy. He understood the risk and he drew courage from the promise given him by

Jeremiah. After his baptism, the prophet laid his hands on Mulek's head and blessed him that if he remained faithful to his covenants he'd be preserved to rule over a nation in a promised land. Preservation was exactly what he needed tonight. Every soldier in Laban's army hunted him, a ten-year-old informant with a contagious smile, an unbounded enthusiasm for adventure, and a heart pure enough that he prayed God would judge him worthy of divine guidance.

"Don't worry, Mama," Mulek said. "I'll be fine."

Miriam squeezed his hand. "I know you will."

A knock came at the door. "My lady." The maid called from the hall. "The captain of the guard is here and asks for a word with you."

Mulek backed into the corner when the door swung open and Laban pushed past the maidservant.

Miriam spun around. "How dare you!"

"There's an intruder in the palace and I feared for your safety."

"Then I suggest you be after him and leave us alone."

Laban reached under his tunic and drew out a shard of veil. "I believe the thief made off with the rest of this."

"It certainly looks like mine, but as you can see . . . ," Miriam turned her head and let Laban examine her veil closely. "I'm wearing all of it."

The frayed ends of the torn piece of lace coiled around Laban's hand like a weed and he held it close to Miriam's veil, searching for where the scrap had torn free. When he couldn't find it he took it back. "There's been a mistake."

"I suggest you mount a search among the guests and see if another woman has been robbed of her veil."

"Do you think a thief could get past my men?"

"It wouldn't be the first time, but then you do have five hundred gathered this evening. It shouldn't be a difficult task to check veils at the door."

Mulek lowered his head to hide a smile. Mama was calm under pressure, but this was her finest show.

Laban wadded the cloth into a ball and threw it on the floor. "Have the maidservants do it." He dismissed himself, but before going out into the hall he turned back and said, "You'll be under my constant watch."

"I wouldn't have it any other way, Captain. With my husband's coronation ceremony drawing near, we can hardly afford a breech in security. I understand the large coronation feast attracts robbers to the capital in droves."

"I'm well aware of that."

Miriam nodded. "That will be all."

Laban marched out and left them in peace. Mulek straightened his tunic over his shoulders. Well, maybe not peace, but at least they were alone and free of Laban's meddling, for now.

Miriam said, "I'll keep checking until you're safely back." She went around pinching out the flames until the room went dark.

"If I don't return," Mulek said, "Give my arrowheads to Dan and my slingshot to Benjamin."

Miriam laid a hand on Mulek's shoulder. "Are you afraid to go out tonight?"

"I can do this."

"You're certain?"

Mulek didn't want her to think he was anything but a man in a child's body; and since she couldn't see him in the darkness, she wouldn't know he brushed away a tear. Tonight's message wasn't like any of the others. It was a matter of the potter's life, a man who had befriended Mulek with the gentleness of a grandfather. Mulek couldn't be seen leaving the bedroom with Miriam, and before she went into the hall he held her hand longer than usual. It was a grip that firmly said he would return safely.

He would live to collect arrowheads and fire his slingshot another day.

CHAPTER 23

Joshua dangled his feet over the edge of the roof. He leaned forward, stuck his head between his knees and sniffed at the uncommon smell of pheasant filtering up from the kitchen. The last time Papa brought home a bird butchered for roasting was the day Sarah had stolen Elizabeth's hairbrushes and was sent to bed without even a taste of evening meal. Joshua wasn't about to tell Papa about his thievery. That would ruin tonight's feast. Only God knew about the honeycomb he'd taken from the sweet jar and there was no way Papa knew. God was no snitch.

Maybe the pheasant was for a freewill offering, though there wasn't anything free about buying the largest bird in the market. And this was the wrong time of year for a shewbread offering, save that the loaves baking in the oven smelled good enough to please the most jealous god. With so many offerings to decide among, Joshua ticked off the names on his fingers. It wasn't a ram offering, a bullock, pigeons, or doves; none were as grand as what roasted in the oven below. Maybe it was a peace offering, but that was for giving thanks and there was nothing to be thankful for except tonight's pheasant.

There was another offering, the most dreaded one of all. He sat up and sniffed at the chimney. Not a burnt offering! That meant Mama would leave the sweet smelling bird on the spit until it burned to ashes. You couldn't eat a burnt offering, only watch the smoke rise and mix with the clouds to remind you of where God lived, somewhere in the heavens high above the earth. Luckily it was only the scent of wood smoke filtering up the chimney. No burnt pheasant. The angels would have to wait another day for their dinner.

"You'll make yourself sick breathing in that smoke."

Joshua rolled over to find Aaron standing above him leaning on two crutches. Papa made him a second one after his feet were infected with ash from the potter's kiln. They swelled to nearly double in size before the fever broke.

"Why did Papa bring home such a large bird for dinner?" Joshua asked.

"I suppose he has a reason to celebrate."

"I knew it." Joshua shot his hands in the air and began to giggle. "It's a feast."

"Not exactly a feast."

Joshua stopped giggling. "Say it isn't a sin offering."

"You've been dipping into Mama's sweet jar, haven't you?"

"Have you been talking to God?"

"I have, and He says you're to ask Mama next time you get into the honey." Aaron patted him on the shoulder. "But you can eat pheasant tonight. We'll call it the feast of good luck."

"What luck?" Daniel asked, clearing the landing at the top of the steps and placing two chairs next to the dinner table. "It's been eight months since we moved here and we haven't made half the money we could have if we'd stayed in Sidon."

Aaron said, "Don't talk like that in front of Joshua."

"Somebody needs to tell him there are better ways to make a living in Jerusalem than blacksmithing."

"I've had enough of your preaching about the military."

"I'd walk away from the ovens tomorrow if the chance came along."

"Don't be a fool. Blacksmithing's been good to us."

"There's no future in it."

"The future is all there is. We have to count on things getting better." Aaron sat in a chair and laid his crutches across the armrests. "If you'd spend a little more time on your forging, instead of always running off to the military grounds, maybe we'd have a better future."

Daniel hovered over Aaron. "If you weren't a cripple, I'd teach you to mind your own business."

Their voices rose, becoming louder and meaner. Joshua rolled onto his belly, leaned over the edge of the roof and cupped his hands around his mouth.

"Hurry, Mama, and bring the food! Please hurry!"

"Dinner's nearly ready."

Elizabeth closed the door and hurried back to tend the hearth. Would Joshua ever learn any patience? She ladled the basting sauce of minced onions, pepper herbs, and vinegar over the pheasant. "It's only Joshua," she said to Ruth. "He's hungry."

"Those weren't hungry voices I heard." Ruth stared at the ceiling with a look intense enough to bore holes through the thick clay and wide wooden cross beams. "Here, take this before you burn yourself." She handed a thick cloth over to Elizabeth.

"Whatever got into Papa to buy this?" Elizabeth drew the pheasant off the spit and laid it on a platter.

"I'm not sure."

"He didn't tell you?"

"Not a word."

"It isn't like him to spend money foolishly."

"You know how your father likes to surprise us and it must be quite a surprise or he wouldn't have asked to eat on the roof."

"Must we? It's terribly cold this time of year."

"Your father insists on it. He said we always pass feasts on the roof."

"This isn't a feast."

"Humor him."

"There's nothing humorous about freezing."

"Try." Ruth handed the wooden bread paddle to Elizabeth. It was a long pole with a flat head attached to the end. "The bread's ready. Why don't you get it out of the oven."

Elizabeth paddled out seven loaves, carefully placing each one into the basket Sarah held. She said, "Don't go picking at the bread before dinner."

Sarah said, "I never do."

"You always bore holes in the loaves like a wild beast."

"I'm no beast."

"All right then, a little girl." Elizabeth turned back to the oven, her voice echoing off the hot bricks. She'd gotten out all the loaves save the one at the very back, the one she couldn't reach without leaning inside. "Come closer and keep me from falling in." She waited until Sarah took hold of her robe before raising up on her toes and sticking her head inside. She had to trust Sarah to keep her from falling into the fire that burned beneath the bustle, a trust she would have preferred not to have endured. She held the paddle by the tip of the handle and pushed it along the floor, scraping the end against the bricks. It slid under the last loaf and she was bringing it out when Sarah cried, "Fire, Elizabeth! Fire!"

Elizabeth dropped the paddle and pulled her head out of the oven to find her skirts had brushed near the coals and caught flame.

"My robe!" Elizabeth jumped back from the hearth, beating at the cloth.

Ruth doused the fire with a pot of cold water.

"Mama, look at this." Elizabeth held up her skirts; a hole the size of a lemon smoldered at the hem.

"It isn't so bad we can't mend it."

"A hole this big?" Elizabeth poked her fingers through it.

"A patch should cover it."

"Not on the front."

Elizabeth batted at the burned edges. It wasn't the hole that bothered her. Not as much as the clips and stings of a hundred glances from women whose names she didn't know and never cared to know. Elizabeth lived in the shadows of others with finer clothing and perfumes and prospects. Why had she hoped Zoram would be hers? At least the family didn't know about him. She loathed explaining away her failures to her brothers. She flicked at the bits of ash that blackened her robe. How could she ever hope to draw another man's eyes dressed in a perfectly ruined robe? But then, it wasn't really a man's eyes she fancied. It was his heart.

"You needn't bother, Mama." Elizabeth lowered her head. "I'll mend it."

"This has been hard on you, hasn't it? Moving to a new place, building a new life."

"No more than on anyone else."

Ruth stepped back. "My, you're a beautiful woman."

"Nothing's changed; it never will. I understand that now. I'm odd and I'll grow old and never marry and be left alone. I've seen other women like that."

Sarah let out a giggle, the girlish sort intended to rile Elizabeth's feathers, and they would have if Ruth hadn't sent Sarah to the roof with the basket of bread. When she disappeared out the door, Ruth wrapped an arm around Elizabeth. "I used to feel the same way before I met your father."

"Not you, Mama."

"It's true. I thought I'd never be blessed with children and now look at the five wonderful arrows in my quiver."

"It doesn't bother me that I'll never marry." Elizabeth raised her head and fought back a tear. "Not as much as it used to."

"Don't talk like that. Of course you will. You're as beautiful as any."

"We don't even need to mend the hole." Elizabeth touched her burnt robe. "Unmarried women dress like this."

"It isn't like you to talk this way."

"How should I talk?"

"You'll have the blessing of a good husband and until then you'll have to cultivate the beauty that's deep inside."

"I can only hope there is something worth harvesting inside of me for I've no visible graces."

"Listen to me, young woman." Ruth held both of her hands. "Womanhood is more than a fine robe or the sweet scent of an expensive perfume. The way to find a husband is to share your talents with others, then you'll know how to weave your life into the cloth of another's life."

"I don't feel like weaving my life into anything. Not after what he's done."

Ruth arranged the pheasant on a platter. "This wouldn't have anything to do with a certain young scribe, would it?"

Elizabeth's glance darted around the kitchen, avoiding her mother's penetrating stare. How did she know about Zoram? She said, "He's selfish, scheming, and unkind."

"You've changed your mind about him, have you?"

"Oh, Mama, I don't know what to do." Elizabeth wrapped her arms around herself.

"Have patience, daughter."

"How can I?"

"Peace doesn't come in a whirlwind or in an earthquake or even in the flash of a fire. It comes when you know that what you're doing is right."

"But I'm so confused."

"Maybe your confusion is telling you something."

"What?" Elizabeth asked.

"That you've chosen the wrong course."

"Do you really think I should trust Zoram?"

"I don't know what you should do, but if you believe you'll find some peace in that, then yes, you should trust him with all your heart."

"How will I know?"

Ruth stepped close and took Elizabeth by the hand again. "You're blessed with it a little at a time, until you're filled with the peace that God grants to your soul."

"I've never heard you speak like this before, Mama."

"I never have."

"Why now?"

Ruth ladled out a broth, bathing the bird in the simmering liquid. "Because I'm just now learning about that kind of peace."

"From who?"

"We'll talk about that later."

"When?"

"When I'm able." Ruth handed Elizabeth the platter of pheasant. "Take this to the roof. I'm afraid that if we don't feed the boys, we'll never have peace in this house."

Halfway up the steps, Elizabeth met Joshua barreling toward her faster than a log rolling down a hill. He stopped at her side, his eyes the size of river stones. Between panicked gasps for breath he asked, "Did you hear them? It's mean stuff." He rubbed his eyes before jumping down the steps and hitting the yard on a dead sprint to the front door.

Elizabeth climbed to the landing and marched over to her brothers. She dropped the pheasant on the table in front of them. "Did you threaten to throw Joshua over the roof again?"

Daniel leaned back in his chair and grinned at her.

"You be good to him. One day he'll be bigger than both of you and he may just throw you off the roof—if he survives that long."

Sarah giggled through a soft dark lump of bread. She sat draped in a chair at the head of the table and reached into the bread basket for another.

"Sarah, no bread until dinner." Elizabeth wagged a finger at her. Why did she have to be everyone's mother?

"I never pick," Sarah said.

"You'll never convince me the bread basket is infested with weevils the size of a little girl's fist."

"It could be."

"Not this time, young lady."

"Why don't you pick on *them*?" Sarah pointed a loaf at the boys. "They're the ones arguing."

"We weren't," Daniel said.

"You were and it was awful," Sarah said between bites. "Wait until Mama finds out. She'll tan your hides."

Sarah was right. Mama would do just that if she found them arguing. Well, maybe she'd have Papa do it.

"Fire! Fire!" Daniel sneaked up behind Sarah and lifted her out of the chair. "The house is on fire and the stairs are blocked. What should we do to save our Sarah?"

"Over the roof with her!" Aaron propped himself up on his two crutches and took Sarah by the feet.

Daniel cried, "One!" and they swung her.

"No, please don't throw me over the edge!"

"Two!"

"Were we arguing?" Daniel asked.

"You were."

"Two and a goat's hair," Aaron said.

"Please let me go."

Daniel asked, "Did you hear us arguing?"

"I did and Mama did too."

"Three!"

Aaron let go and Daniel kept hold of her hands, swinging her through the air. She jumped from his arms, bolted to the stairs and disappeared.

"She loves it when you do that." Elizabeth peered over the roof and watched Sarah dart inside.

"She hates it," Daniel said.

"You're seventeen years old and still haven't figured out women."

"And you don't know a lot about men."

Elizabeth arranged and rearranged the warming cloth over the bread basket. So what if Daniel was right. She didn't want to know anything about men right now, particularly one named Zoram. And if Daniel teased her any more she'd place his name at the top of her list of unfeeling, shallow men who possessed the judgment of a frog.

Elizabeth said, "Deep down, Sarah knows if she ever stops screaming and going off like that, you'll stop teasing her."

"Who gave you power to read her thoughts?"

"It's something women do."

"Tell me." Daniel tapped the side of his head. "What am I thinking?"

"You're thinking I don't know what I'm talking about."

"Maybe you haven't lost your senses completely." Daniel slouched into a chair and grinned over the armrest. "That is, unless you pass up this fellow."

"What are you talking about?"

"Zoram."

"How do you know about him?"

"He came by the shop asking after you."

Elizabeth couldn't help but let her mouth hang open and if it had been summertime a hundred gnats would have found a new home. "What did he tell you?"

"Maybe you'll catch a husband with your reading and writing and intelligent conversations," Daniel said. "I'm sure Zoram likes a woman with a good head about her."

Elizabeth turned away. "I haven't any interest in Zoram."

"I don't blame you." Aaron made a long whistle that came down off a high pitch like a slow falling feather. "Zoram can't whistle."

"Who told you that?"

"The same sparrow that flew by our shop."

"Why you!" She stomped her foot. "Moses said, 'thou shalt not kill', but I can always repent and make a sin offering at the temple." Elizabeth folded her arms. Brothers. What good was explaining her feelings to them? They'd only tease her. Instead, she'd fight back. She raised on her toes and kissed Daniel, then bent over and planted another on Aaron's cheek.

"What was that for?" Daniel said.

"I love it when you tease me," said Elizabeth.

Daniel held his cheek where her lips had touched. "You do?"

"Of course."

"I misjudged you, Elizabeth," Daniel said. "Maybe you will catch this one with your mind."

Elizabeth tossed the bread cloth over Daniel's head. "I'll cast my net wherever it suits me."

She left the roof.

The rest of the family sat waiting for Jonathan to finish evening meal, except for Joshua who circled the table swatting at the few fireflies that lighted this late in the year. Jonathan broke a piece of bread and sopped the pheasant broth off his plate. The meat was tender, the yams held their honey and the bread was soft and light, at least the bread that Sarah hadn't mauled. Now seemed the perfect time to break the news. Even Daniel, who rarely stayed at the table after eating, sat with an expectant look on his face. Conversation wasn't one of his talents, but there he sat waiting to hear the reason for tonight's feast. What he didn't know was that he was the reason.

Jonathan washed down his last piece of bread with a drink of goat's milk before tapping the side of his cup with a knife. He didn't need to attract anyone's attention, except maybe Joshua who went on chasing fireflies despite Jonathan's call to order. Ruth was reaching for Jonathan's plate when he said, "I met with the captain of the guard."

Ruth dropped the plate and it broke on the table in front of

Jonathan. She gathered the broken pieces without looking up and Sarah broke into a giggle that Ruth silenced with one quick glance.

"I was saying . . ." Jonathan tapped the butt of his knife on the table until the family quieted. "The captain of the guard came by the shop to discuss business."

"What did he say?" Daniel asked.

"He said that you were the finest wrestler he'd seen in some time."

Daniel shot to his feet. "I took his best recruit and put him right out of the pit. You'd have been proud of me."

"I am, son. You'll make a fine officer."

Daniel leaned over the table. "Then you approve?"

"That's what this feast is all about."

Aaron pulled himself to his feet with the help of his crutches. "Daniel's our best forger. We can't afford to lose him, not when the shop's struggling."

Jonathan waved off his protest. "Laban's agreed to pay a full wage while Daniel's training."

"We'll have to hire help to replace him."

"That's exactly what I intend to do."

Ruth stood close to Jonathan with the stack of dishes in her arms. "Can we afford to pay someone?"

"It won't cost a shekel."

"We don't have anything to barter but your blacksmithing. I could do some more weaving, but you—"

"You'll never have to weave again." Jonathan leaned back in his chair. "I have an arrangement with Laban."

Ruth asked, "Is that wise?"

Jonathan said, "Of course it is. He's agreed to send one of his servants to work in the shop two days a week."

Aaron said, "You can't teach a stranger about our steelmaking secrets. He could sell them."

"I have Laban's word he won't."

"Do you really trust the captain?" Ruth washed her hands clean on her apron.

"I won't have you speak ill of him."

"What's the servant's name?" Ruth asked.

"He's a young man named Zoram."

"No, Papa!" Elizabeth shot up from the table, her voice trembling. "Isn't there anyone else?"

"I thought you'd be happiest of all."

"I'm not. At least . . ." Elizabeth covered her mouth. "Oh, Papa!"

"I spoke with the boy. He's a fine young man."

Elizabeth said, "You don't understand."

"What is there to understand?"

Elizabeth took the plates from Ruth. "I'll clean those." She left the roof with a hurried stride and a hurt look, deeper than any Jonathan had seen on her.

"What's gotten into that girl?" Jonathan asked.

"Nothing, dear," Ruth said.

"It isn't right for her to act like this in front of everyone."

"I'll take care of it." Ruth followed Elizabeth to the landing with an arm full of dirty dinner plates.

Jonathan asked, "Do I have your blessing?"

Ruth stopped on the top step. "We should have spoken first." There was a numb look on Ruth's face and it chased away any thanks Jonathan had hoped to glean from his announcement.

Jonathan asked, "Aren't you at least pleased for Daniel?"

"Of course I am." Ruth switched the plates from one arm to the other and offered Daniel a weak smile.

Jonathan said, "It's a fine day for our family."

"We'll talk later." Ruth lowered her head and took Joshua by the hand. "Come with me, son."

Somehow Joshua knew he should stop chasing fireflies and he went quietly. The sound of their sandals fell lightly on the steps and grew softer until only silence remained. Why didn't they understand? Jonathan did this for the promise of a brighter future for all of them.

"Daniel shouldn't work for Laban," Aaron said, breaking the silence.

Jonathan turned on him. "And why not?"

"Because we don't take sides. Isn't that what you've always said?" Aaron swayed on his crutches. "I don't work for the vineyard owners at Beit Zayit and Daniel doesn't join Laban's military." He shuffled closer. "Isn't that right, Papa?"

"For the life of me, boy, don't you understand? Laban's captain of the guard, not some visionary divining the future."

"Ishmael and his cousin aren't prophets."

"I didn't say they were, but they don't speak against the prophets and that's enough for me. We can't work for that sort of men. It wouldn't look right."

"They say Laban's a murderer."

"Where'd you hear that?"

"In the city."

Jonathan's lips flattened. "I won't have you speak lies about the captain of the guard."

Daniel stepped between them. "You can't bear to see me win a commission. That's what this is about."

"What this is about is you and Papa taking sides while the rest of us are expected to sit on a fence and watch."

"You sound like a Rekhabite yourself." Daniel raised his fist to Aaron's face.

"Daniel," Jonathan said, "I don't even want to hear mention of those people in this house."

Aaron leaned forward. "I hope you rot standing watch on some desert outpost."

"Enough!" Jonathan separated them. "We'll sit down and finish this celebration as it was intended. Your mother has a dessert ready for us and when she brings it we're going to eat it."

"I'm not hungry." Aaron worked his crutches over to the landing and began lowering himself one step at a time. It was such a slow, painful thing to watch but Jonathan wouldn't let the boy speak to him like that. He said, "Aaron!" But the boy kept going, lowering himself farther down the steps, his tall, thin frame gone out of sight below the roof's horizon. "Come back here!" There was no response but for the tapping of his crutches on the courtyard stones. Jonathan ran his hand through his hair. "Did you hear me, boy?" He stepped to the edge of the roof and watched Aaron push open the gate and start up the street through the shadows toward the upper city. When the gate banged shut, Jonathan felt a wall rise between them, one he wasn't sure he knew how to climb.

Daniel went to the kitchen to get the dessert, figs soaked in milk, and left Jonathan alone with Sarah. She sat at the far end of the table, nibbling on the last loaf of bread and completely uninterested in anything else.

Jonathan tapped the side of his cup until Sarah's head came up with a snap. Jonathan asked, "Are you finished eating?"

She took a bite out of the last loaf of bread and chewed on it.

"What are you looking at?"

Sarah took another bite.

Jonathan said, "I've never seen Aaron like this." He leaned over the table and took the loaf of bread from Sarah. "Aaron's always minded before. Never given me one bit of trouble." He took a large bite of bread. "The boy's growing up, and that's the way boys are when they become men. They need to be alone and think things out." He tapped the table with the end of the loaf. "That's all it is. Aaron's gone off to cool his temper. He'll come around and see things my way. It'll just take the boy some time."

Sarah hopped from her chair, came around the table and snatched back the loaf. She stood beside Jonathan and took three large bites. Why didn't she take the bread and leave him in peace? He didn't need a silent scolding from his youngest daughter, but there she stood, her cheeks filled with bread and puffed like a toad. She leaned over, gave him a bread-crumb kiss before skipping down the steps, leaving him alone with an empty table set for six.

What had he done wrong?

Aaron negotiated the well-worn steps of the water shaft with only moonbeams guiding his crutches. It was a good thing he wouldn't meet anyone on the stairs at this late hour. He couldn't move his crutches far enough out of the way to allow anyone to pass, and he lowered himself so slowly that anyone stuck behind him was doomed to go mad from thirst.

Around the last turn of steps, the water shaft opened into a limestone cavern. The sound of water lapping against the landing echoed inside the chamber, drowning out the tapping of his crutches. It was spring water from the Gihon: cool, clear, and without any of the murkiness that spoiled the water of sedentary pools. Down here, far below the surface, it was as if he'd traveled to a different land removed from the troubles he left above. He unraveled his bandages and laid them with his crutches against the cavern wall before crawling to the edge of the landing and leaning over for a drink.

Hezekiah's Tunnel, named after the king who directed its construction, was an underground aqueduct running under the streets of Jerusalem. It carried water from the Gihon Spring just outside the east gate through one thousand winding cubits of tunnel to the Pool of Siloam in the lower city. In times of peace, the water source saved women the trouble of going outside the protecting walls of Jerusalem to draw water. In times of siege it saved lives.

As Jerusalem's wealthiest residents built their homes further up the slopes of the city and away from the Pool of Siloam, drawing water became an unbearable inconvenience and a shaft was dug in the upper city. The water shaft connected the upper city with the head-waters of Hezekiah's tunnel where the spring waters entered under the east wall. The circular shaft was lined with stone, and steps were chis-eled into the wall, down to the water's edge where a landing provided women a place to kneel and fill their jars.

"Aaron, is that you?"

A woman descended the steps with a water jar tucked beneath one arm and a lamp held in the other. The low angle of the flame darkened her face with long shadows. He stood to greet her, but without the help of his crutches he lost his footing and stumbled back.

The woman rushed across the landing and reached for his hand, but she came too late to save him from falling off. He hit the water, his arms swinging wildly.

When he came up gasping in waist-high water the woman asked, "Are you all right?"

"I'll manage."

She laughed, and immediately Aaron knew her kindly voice. He asked, "Rebekah?"

She held the lamp to her face. "I didn't mean to laugh, but you made quite a splash."

Aaron lifted himself onto the ledge and unlatched his sandals. Sores formed quickly on his feet if he left them in wet leather. In the dark she wouldn't notice them; but to be sure the lamplight never revealed their repulsiveness, he lowered them over the edge. "What are you doing here?"

"I come here nearly every evening." Rebekah sat beside him despite the water that dripped off his shivering body. "Father likes a cool glass of water before he retires."

"Do you think it's safe walking through the streets this late?"

"I don't worry about that. I like coming here when there's no one around." Rebekah brushed the dust from her robe. "You can be alone with your thoughts down here."

"Why not send one of your maidservants?"

Rebekah began to laugh. Slight at first, but it grew louder until the cavern shook with merriment. "I can only imagine what Mima would do if she found us together down here."

"I'd rather not."

"She likes you."

"Like the plague, she does."

It didn't require an imagination to know what Mima would do if she found them together. Mima would sit on him until she squashed the breath of life from his lungs. And if he survived she'd cover him in honey, tie him to a desert rock and leave him for the scorpions to nibble away whatever life remained. Mima might have the title of maidservant, but she was well versed in the duties of a sentry, guarding Rebekah from every suitor who showed the slightest inclination to storm the potter's palace.

Aaron offered to fill Rebekah's water jar. He knelt on the landing, perched there like a crane on the edge of a pond and pushed the jar deep to let the water flow into it. It gurgled full and he was about to draw it out when he heard Rebekah let out a gasp. A slight one, but enough that Aaron knew he never should have let her see the bottoms of his feet.

She raised the lamp and it cast a yellow glow over them. They were like hole-worn sandals in need of a new sole. The burned flesh reached from his ankles, ran along both arches and disappeared into hollow spaces where there should have been muscle and sinew. He didn't try to hide their ugliness and he didn't stand and feign they weren't as bad as they really were. The lamplight had already exposed him and for the first time he saw his lameness through her eyes. He was a cripple because Rebekah had seen him as one.

"There you are." Aaron plucked the jar from the pool and held it up between Rebekah and his feet. "Filled to the brim with sweet water for your father. I'll carry it out for you."

"Let me." Rebekah reached for the jar but Aaron wouldn't let her have it.

Aaron said, "I can do it."

"I only thought it would be easier if—"

"If you helped a lame man?"

Rebekah shook her head. "I didn't say that."

"But you thought it."

"I would never . . ."

"I'm going to heal, I've got to heal. I was given a promise of healing."

The water sloshed past the stones, and the longer Rebekah stared at him, the louder the water seemed to rush through the shaft. Rebekah asked, "Is that what the doctors say?"

"They told me what they tell everyone who's burned like I am." Aaron steadied his hands around the water jar. "They say my feet have to be cut off or the infections will kill me."

Rebekah knelt beside him and lightly touched the wounds, but her caressing couldn't make the pain disappear. "Tell me how it happened."

Aaron got off his knees and sat, dipping his feet and letting the water nurse gently over them, numbing them. It was the perfect salve to forget his imperfection and remind him of his promise. The one he'd received at the hands of the stranger who saved his life. But with his feet getting worse, it seemed the promise would never be fulfilled. The spring water flowed cool around his feet and the memory of that day came drifting back. He wanted to tell her the story, but she was sitting too still to be thinking anything but the worst. Did she believe him less handsome, or less hard working, or worse: less of a suitor? His cursed, maimed feet!

"Please tell me." Rebekah inched the lamp back behind them, hiding his feet behind a long, dark shadow.

"You don't want to hear it."

"Is it that painful?"

Aaron took a deep breath and when he let it out he said, "It was bad clay molds."

Rebekah gasped. "From . . . from our pottery yard?"

"It was from another yard. Papa left me alone to tend the smelting and once the molds were heated, they burst."

"How did a bursting mold injure your feet?"

Aaron began to describe the accident, and once the tale was begun, he couldn't keep the story from flowing out of him like the water that coursed over his burned feet. "I lay half conscious when a stranger entered from the street and pulled me to safety. I was hardly able to think for the throbbing in my head and the pain screaming at my feet, but the man laid his hands on my head and promised me my feet would be made whole. It was real. I felt the power of God in him."

Rebekah asked, "Who was it?"

"I don't know. When I came to my senses he was gone; but I knew my feet would be healed, no matter how many doctors wanted to cut them off." Aaron reached down and touched his swollen feet. "I won't let them do it, not until I'm finished."

"Finished with what?" Rebekah took his hand. "Please tell me."

"The stranger said my feet would heal so I could save a man's life."

"Whose life?"

"There's a man out there somewhere who needs me to save his life. Aaron squeezed her hand. "I'm not frightening you, am I?"

"Please, go on."

"The stranger didn't give a name. He only said I would save the life of a prophet in order for God to preserve His covenants for a remnant of the House of Israel."

Rebekah didn't speak. She dipped her feet in the water next to Aaron's, stirring them back and forth. The seconds turned to minutes and only the quiet sounds of moving water, low and faint, filled the silence. When she spoke it was in a distant voice.

"You'll catch cold wearing those wet clothes."

"I'm fine."

"We're only a short walk from my home. I'll have my father get you a dry robe."

"I have to be on my way."

"Papa will have a warm fire lit. You can tell him what you've told me while you wait for your clothes to dry."

"I could never do that."

"Trust me, you can."

Aaron searched her eyes for something that would tell him he could, but how would he recognize trust if he found it staring back at him? He said, "I can't speak to him about this; your father's an Elder." He got up onto his crutches and he would have gone up the steps if it hadn't been for Rebekah, hurrying ahead of him and blocking his way.

"Please, Aaron, speak with him" Rebekah pleaded.

"He would never understand."

"You don't know that."

"He'll think me a Rekhabite."

"Is that so bad?"

"He could send me to prison for less than that." Aaron rubbed the back of his neck. "I never should have told you any of this."

Moonlight streamed down through the shaft past Rebekah's face, turning her skin white like that of an angel resurrected to some higher place. "Please, you have to trust me. You can tell my father. He can help you make sense of all this."

"I won't do it." Aaron spoke with such finality that Rebekah took the water jar and started for the steps, leaving him at the bottom of the shaft.

Aaron watched her climb to the surface, his good judgment telling him it was best he didn't go with her. He could never tell her father about his accident. But his heart forced him to call after her and ask her to wait. He worked the crutches up the steps and when he got close he took her hand and said, "The stranger who saved me . . ."

"I'm listening."

"He gave me the promise in the name of the Anointed One the Rekhabites call Yeshua."

They went to see the potter.

Jonathan stood in the shadows across the street and down from the main gates of Laban's estates. The fires of ten cauldron lamps danced shades of yellow onto the towers of the estate. Hot oil vapors rose past the porch columns and swirled beneath the portico before filtering through leafless winter vines crisscrossing the building's face. The tendrils were so withered and dry they should have fallen to the ground long before, but they clung to the limestone facade like parasites, dormant and waiting for longer, warmer days to subdue their host in leafy foliage.

None of the soldiers guarding the residence took note of Jonathan, or if they did it was too cold for them to bother ordering him away—a good thing, since he left the house immediately after dinner, not stopping to speak with Ruth. She wasn't ready to listen to him, not with Aaron gone and Elizabeth in need of a mother's ear. Daniel was the only child who didn't react badly to the feast. By now he would have eaten most of the figs and gone to bed believing that all was well. Jonathan rocked back against the stone wall and pressed the eight-sided gold talent between his thumb and forefinger, the same coin Laban had paid him for Daniel's first month's wage in the military. It was more money than he'd ever held at one time and more than a recruit would garner in a year of work. Was Daniel really so fine a wrestler that Laban would pay so much for his military service?

Jonathan moved from the shadows and immediately the watchman ordered him to halt. On his signal the sentries closed rank, forming a human wall across the entrance and forcing Jonathan back a step. The watchman said, "What do you want?"

"I have business with Laban."

"He didn't say anything about a visitor."

"He'll see me."

The watchman turned to one of the soldiers. "Tell the captain it's the blacksmith, but wake him slowly. You know how he is after he's had too much."

The soldier dispatched into the warmth of the estate, leaving his mates to endure the cold evening. They were an impressive lot, not because of their brass helmets plumed with red feathers or the breastplates that made their sturdy frames stouter, and not even for the long swords holstered about their waists. It was their stillness that drew Jonathan's curiosity. They stood at attention without the slightest flinch, no chattering teeth or rubbing hands. Steam rose from their nostrils like the living dead, though dead men didn't have power to take life as they did. They were boys trying on manhood, and soon Daniel would wear the same helmet, holster the same sword, and share their hopes for glory.

Laban appeared on the porch and stood beneath a lamp. His mussed hair confirmed the late hour as did his creased sleeping robe that hung open to the navel. Dew-covered leaves pealed off the stone landing and stuck to his unshod feet as he crossed to greet Jonathan. The guards stepped down and let him pass. "What's the meaning of this?" He coughed the sleep from his throat.

Jonathan climbed the steps. "I've come about Daniel."

"At this hour?"

"Would another time be better?"

Laban leaned close, the wine on his breath fouling the air between them. He said, "Come inside."

The captain caught his foot on the trim of the striped rug in the foyer, lifting the colorful pattern of red, white, and black off the floor. The rug matched the thick linen curtains and there was no mistaking the owner's lineage. Laban was descended from the tribe of Manasseh. They moved from the hall into the ready room and the decor shifted to that of an Egyptian temple honoring the god of harvest. Impressions of wheat were pressed into the white plaster ceiling, a golden bundle of grain sprouted from a marble urn on the table, and a stand of wheat bending toward the sun was etched into the mantle above the fireplace.

The room harked back a thousand years to the day when Manasseh's father, Joseph, interpreted Pharaoh's dream to foretell seven years of famine. Joseph's memory lived on in this ready room, his kingliness bequeathed to Laban, bestowed by the blind luck of pedigree.

"Have a seat." Laban directed Jonathan to the chair nearest the hearth where the dying embers of a fire warmed the cushion.

"I have some reservations."

"I'm finished bartering for your son." Laban poured two mugs of wine and handed one to Jonathan. "I expect Daniel at the military grounds first thing next week. His career is important to your future." He took a swig of wine. "I'll release him from training long enough to attend your induction ceremony."

Jonathan choked on the wine and he held his hand to his mouth to keep from spraying the drink on the furnishings.

Laban said, "Zadock should have told you."

"Told me what?"

"Your appointment." Laban slowly circled Jonathan's chair and when he came around, he offered his hand. "It isn't every day a blacksmith from the lower city lands a seat on Jerusalem's highest council."

Jonathan stared past Laban at the flicker of flames dying in the hearth. Jonathan an Elder? He should be flattered, but what did the Council want with him? Certainly there were lawyers and doctors and a host of temple priests more qualified to pass judgment. He said, "I don't have any training in the law."

"We'll advise you on how to vote." Laban cupped his mug with both hands and took a long drink. "Just make sure you don't mix with the wrong people."

"That's what I came to ask you about." Jonathan inched to the edge of his chair. "We've been doing some work for the owners of Beit Zayit." He peered over the lip of his mug. "Are they the wrong sort of people?"

"Not at all." Laban leaned back in his chair and forced a yawn, but his body was stiff and his jaw tight. "They're not Rekhabites." He took another longer drink, this time directly from the bottle. "What did they tell you?"

"Only what everyone already knows about them."

"What was that?"

"They own the largest olive oil operation in Judah."

"That's all?"

"Is there anything more I should know about them?"

"Nothing." Laban's lips were a straight, tight line.

"Then you don't mind us working at the plantation?"

"Who will you send?"

"Aaron."

Laban asked, "The crippled boy?"

"They trust him."

"I'll want a report."

"On our blacksmithing?"

"On Lehi. I want your son to watch him carefully."

"Is the oil merchant in some sort of trouble?"

"None, but have your son watch him just the same. I want word back on everything he says about me. I always like to know what kind of support I have from our wealthiest citizens." Laban forced a smile, raised his wine bottle, and took a long drink. "Now, a toast to your new place on the Council, and to Daniel, the newest officer in my army."

Jonathan leaned back against the cushion and raised his mug. To Jonathan the Elder, and Daniel the soldier.

The late night walk from the water shaft to the pottery yard took longer than it should have, and Aaron would have apologized for his slow stride, but he wanted to enjoy Rebekah's company as long as she would endure him. She kept her hand near his to steady him over the potholes, and when they passed under the oil lamps of an estate she didn't walk ahead or behind him, but next to him without any concern for who might see her with a crippled man.

Along the way, their conversation turned to Rebekah's life in a wealthy potter's house. With her mother passed away these seventeen years, she suffered the fretting and pampering of seven maidservants, one being Mima, whom she mentioned only by her girth. Still, there was no question whom she meant. The fine clothes Rebekah's father could afford were nice, but the cook's attempts to fatten her with expensive foods were a bother. The kitchen help insisted that no proper suitor would ever marry a woman with such a small waist and they were duty bound to add three fingers to Rebekah's midsection.

Aaron told her about his first smithing job in Sidon. He'd smelted a latch to lock the pens of a wealthy sheepherder. When the metal didn't hold, he spent two days rounding up the herd in the hills above the city. And he never should have told her about losing his kilt diving off a busy fishing dock. They could hardly breathe from laughter when he explained that Daniel dived in after it and as a prank took it home and left Aaron to tread water until a fisherman threw him a net. Not his first choice in clothing, but he wrapped himself ten times in it and walked home by the back roads.

Aaron was savoring their walk so much that Rebekah caught him off guard when she pointed to the front gate and announced they were home. The potter's residence stood as far upwind from the kiln as possible, nestled beneath a stand of date palms. Smoke rose from the hearth inside the home and lamplight bent around the thick blankets thrown over the windows, casting an orange glow across the porch. Whoever was awake this late had done a hasty job of hiding it.

Round-bottomed flowerpots hung from the roof, each one full of red winter blossoms cascading to the porch. Aaron stuck his nose into a bouquet that spilled from a long-necked urn at the front door.

"Crane's bill," Rebekah said. "They're from a desert mountain near Aqaba. They don't freeze if I keep them on the porch near the door."

Their beauty would have served as a welcome to the home if it weren't for Rebekah's father lurking on the other side of the thick cedar door and blanketed windows. Well maybe not lurking, but he was inside, and Aaron was going to have to explain why he was out late at night, alone with his daughter and soaking wet. He never should have consented to come and speak with the potter. The man already knew Aaron had lame feet, but he didn't need to know the story behind them. Better to speak with him of less damning things. The run of cold weather, the rise in taxes. Men of the potter's distinction talked about that sort of thing.

Rebekah lifted the bolt and swung open the door, but there was no one waiting to greet them. He'd been spared, if only for the moment. Rebekah put a finger to her lips and directed him to wait quietly in the hall while she hurried off to pour a drink for her father.

The entry was decorated in hard wood with a stairwell at the far end leading to the second floor mezzanine. A wooden pedestal stood to one side of the entry with a copy of the laws of Moses resting on top. The new papyrus was scrolled around a stick of mahogany with a red tassel hanging from one end. It was a costly thing to own, but something the Second Elder of the Jews would possess. No doubt Josiah used its words to rule on whatever it was an Elder ruled on.

Aaron took a few quiet steps down the hall admiring the wall hangings, when he heard soft voices coming from the reading room behind him. He turned around to see Josiah reposing in a large chair in front of the hearth, collecting the warmth of the fire. The light flickered in his eyes and seemed to say he was in the company of a good friend. He leaned over the armrest and spoke in soft tones to the child occupying the second chair. The boy's spindly, bare legs reached clear to the floor, a long stretch for one so young. He wore a purple tunic like no other in Jerusalem and he bore a profile as recognizable as was his dress. It was Mulek, the prince of Judah. What was a young boy of his birthright doing outside the palace grounds and without any guards to protect him? Could he be the reason the blankets were thrown over the windows? Immediately Aaron felt as if he had intruded, but he couldn't back away. He feared his sudden movements would only draw their attention. He stood still and prayed for a chance to make his disappearance.

Josiah leaned over and patted Mulek on the hand. "Don't you worry about me, son. I know how to deal with the Chief Elder and the Council. It's you and your mother I worry about."

Mulek said, "No one knows anything about us."

"What about Laban?"

"He suspects we might have something to do with the Rekhabites, but Mama covered it well and set him straight. He won't bother us again."

This was a conversation not meant for Aaron to hear and he should have backed down the hallway out of earshot. But the slightest movement could draw their glance. Better to stay in the shadows of the hall and endure whatever treason they were plotting. And it was treason; there was no doubt about that. Before him sat the second Elder on the Council and the Prince of Judah, two faithful Jews who should have been discussing anything but sedition.

As Aaron huddled in the shadows, his crutch slipped on the stone floor. Mulek spun toward the sound and Aaron saw a brass charm dangling from the boy's neck. It was a serpent, the mark of the Rekhabites, and it sparkled before the light of the fire. When their eyes met, Mulek immediately stiffened against the high back of the chair and hid the charm beneath his tunic.

Josiah jumped from his seat and stood in front of the prince. "Who let you in?"

"I did." Rebekah returned down the hall with a glass of water for her father. "I didn't expect to find you in the reading room this time of night."

"What have you done, daughter?"

"Aaron was kind enough to dip the water for me."

"Did he pour it over himself?"

Aaron said, "I slipped in the water shaft."

Rebekah said, "I offered him a warm fire to dry his clothes. It's the least I could do for a guest."

"We already have one." Josiah stepped aside and let Rebekah see into the reading room.

Mulek sat peering around the backrest. He blinked his long, dark lashes. "Good evening," he said, in a soft, steady voice, as if he'd greeted her a hundred times before. He got up out of his chair and stood beside the potter, his shaven head nestled against Josiah's arm and his hand reaching for Josiah's hand.

"Oh, Papa, I didn't know." Rebekah pulled Aaron toward the hall. "Come with me. We can talk in the kitchen."

"The damage has been done." Josiah stepped in front of them and Aaron could feel the rush of the potter's breath on his face. "Your guest has seen too much."

"It's my fault," Rebekah said. "I invited him."

"I'll go." Aaron said.

"You're not going anywhere."

"Papa, please," Rebekah said. "He's here to speak with you about our beliefs."

Josiah grabbed Aaron's arm. "What did she tell you about the Rekhabites?"

Aaron pulled free. "She didn't mention them."

Rebekah said, "Oh, Papa, I didn't tell him anything."

Josiah reached for Mulek's collar. The prince resisted at first, but Josiah nodded and placed his hand on the boy's shoulder. Mulek removed the charm and passed it to the potter's hand, scattering the firelight about the room as a diamond splits sunlight. Josiah held it out to Aaron. "Is this what you came to ask me about?"

"I don't know anything about that charm." Aaron stepped back from the brass necklace. "And whatever you have to do with Rekhabites, I don't care to know." He turned his crutches towards the door.

Josiah asked, "How do I know you'll not tell anyone what you've seen here tonight?"

"You'll have to trust me."

"Swear me an oath or you'll not see my daughter again."

"Don't say that, Papa." Rebekah backed up against Aaron and he could feel her body tremble.

"Why didn't you tell me?" Aaron said softly.

"I would have, but not like this. You must believe me."

Josiah said, "Leave us, daughter."

"But, Papa . . ."

"Now."

Josiah pulled Rebekah away and shooed her up the stairs. She went quickly, her shoulders lifting and falling in quiet sobs.

Josiah said, "You have feelings for her, don't you?"

Aaron watched Rebekah disappear beyond the railing at the top of the landing. She was gone, and under the worst circumstances. Why had he come here? He didn't need to know the potter was a Rekhabite. But now that he knew, he couldn't put it away and forget it. Even if it meant losing Rebekah.

Aaron said, "I think I love her, sir."

"If you ever want to see her again, you'll swear an oath not to speak a word about Mulek."

"I'll tell no one what I've seen here tonight." Aaron set his jaw and spoke between straight lips. "But I'll not swear an oath to traitors."

"Is that what you think we are?"

"Good evening, sir." Aaron pulled open the door and a cold breeze shot into the hall. He turned on his crutches and headed out the gate and into the street. The skin ripped with each labored stride, but he couldn't feel the pain for the ache in his heart. He left the potter standing in the doorway and a splotch of his blood staining the porch next to the Crane's bill blossoms. He never should have told Rebekah about his accident, never should have come here believing the potter would help him understand the blessing he'd been given. There was only one person he could trust with the story of his accident, only one person he would ever trust again.

Himself.

Sleep did not come to Ruth though the house stood quiet and the children were in bed long ago. Aaron and Jonathan still hadn't returned and she decided to do the only thing she could to bring them home. She descended the steps from the bedroom, took down the largest oil lamp from the shelf above the hearth and lit it from the dying embers. She rattled the lamp across the window sill all the way to the edge, as far out as she could place it without it falling into the yard. The flame scattered its rays in every direction, lighting the farthest reaches. There would be no darkness in her family, not while she had a seed of faith to pray them home safely.

"He'll be back."

Ruth spun around and peered across the room. "Jonathan?"

"Over here."

He'd been watching from the corner of the main room, hiding from her in the shadows. He leaned against the wall with his arms folded, chewing on a mint leaf.

Ruth said, "Where have you been?"

"Out."

"Did you look for Aaron?"

"I didn't see him."

"Do you think it was wise to surprise him with news about Daniel? Can't you see it's hard for him to watch Daniel win a commission in the military while Aaron suffers with his feet?"

"He should tan himself a thicker skin."

"Jonathan!"

He stood away from the wall. "Our lives are changing."

"Too quickly for me, I'm afraid."

"We have to establish ourselves with the right people."

"Exactly who do you believe are the right people?"

"I don't want Aaron telling his tale of prophets and healings to the wrong people. He could ruin everything we've worked for."

"There was a time I believed we worked for the same things."

Jonathan took Ruth's hand and led her to a chair. There were no cushions, but she'd grown accustomed to the hard planks. He said, "I've been offered a seat on the Sarim Council."

"You, an Elder?"

Jonathan spoke quickly as he explained the details of his meeting with Laban. He finished by saying, "This is best."

"Best for whom?"

"For all of us."

Ruth lowered her head. "Maybe Aaron's right."

"Don't go siding with him."

"No one's siding with anyone." Ruth laid her hand on his shoulder. "Aaron's trusted you until now."

"I'm not taking sides, can't he see that?"

"It's hard for any of us to tell what you're thinking."

"What do you mean?"

"The way you've embraced Laban."

"The captain of the guard has dealt fairly with us."

"Then deal fairly with Aaron. You owe him that much."

The flame grew weak and Ruth took the lamp from the sill and filled it with oil before bending her gaze out the window and into the fog that had settled over the yard. The chill collected the dew and hung it in the air like smoke. On a sudden breeze it began to swirl around the stiff form of Aaron moving his crutches slowly toward the door. Ruth fumbled at the latch and when the door swung open, he stood in the frame, his long body shaking in the cold. His hair fell in wet bands over his brow and his robe hung on him like seaweed. He wasn't wearing his bandages and his toes were red with blood.

"Your feet!" Ruth snatched the lamp from the window and held the light close. "What have you done with your wraps?"

"I left them at the water shaft."

Tears welled up in Aaron's eyes and she ended her questioning before it began. This was not the time to hound the boy with her fears. He was a tough-minded lad but with a tender disposition and a general dislike for displaying his emotions in private to say nothing of public soul-baring. He'd hardly cried since the day he cut his finger at age seven and tonight he would act no differently, though she could see he was fighting back the urge. The tears weren't over the bandages. There were plenty of linens in the pantry. Aaron was suffering a deeper hurt and she would have sat him down and asked the reason for the hurt she saw in his eyes. But not now, not with Jonathan upset with the boy. All she could do was welcome him home and pray Jonathan would see what she saw.

Ruth opened her arms to embrace him, but Jonathan warned her off with his eyes and stepped between them. He was going to finish the interrogating where she'd failed. He asked, "How'd you get yourself wet?"

"I fell in."

"Is that how you split your feet open?"

"That's most of the reason."

"You'll never heal carrying on like you do."

"I'm sorry, Papa."

Jonathan straightened, his shoulders back and his chest raised. "You acted poorly tonight at evening meal."

"I didn't mean to disobey."

"Do you have anything to say for yourself?"

"I spoke to Rebekah tonight."

"The potter's daughter?"

"That's right."

"Well, isn't that something?" Jonathan relaxed his stance and the hint of a smile turned at the corner of his lips, but only a hint. "Was the Second Elder pleased by your interest in his daughter?"

"I don't think so."

"What?"

"Our conversations went poorly."

"You didn't tell him about your feet, did you?"

"Not exactly."

"We've been over this a hundred times. You don't say anything about the accident or people will have reason to think things."

"The potter doesn't think ill of us, only of me."

"What did you say to him, boy?"

"It's between us."

"We can't have the potter upset with our family."

"Jonathan." Ruth touched his arm. "You were going to work this out."

"The boy has to learn."

Ruth said, "He isn't a boy anymore."

"As long as he lives under this roof he'll behave like our son."

Aaron widened his stance between the crutches. It was like watching a prisoner preparing to be sentenced. He said, "I'll do whatever you ask to make up for what I've done."

"You've not done anything I wouldn't have done myself." Jonathan's voice was softer than before and Ruth immediately sensed he was going to find a gentler solution until he said, "I'll expect a sin offering of sorts."

"Jonathan!" Ruth raised her shoulders and her voice. Did he have no feelings for the boy's situation?

Aaron asked, "What did you have in mind?"

"Two week's hard work from sunup to sundown."

"I'm used to that."

"I'll want you to earn every shekel you can while you're away at Beit Zayit."

Aaron's head shot up.

"That's right," Jonathan said. "I want you to impress Lehi with your work."

"You're letting me go?"

"With my blessing."

"I don't understand."

"We can use the money."

"Thank you, Papa." Aaron shifted his weight forward on the crutches. "You won't regret this."

"I'll want a full report about Lehi." Jonathan rubbed the nape of his neck. "If we're going to work for him in the future I need to trust him. Keep your eyes and ears open while you're there. I want to hear about anything that might be, well, you know, odd." He turned to Ruth. "Are you coming to bed?"

Ruth said, "I'll be along," and took the lamp from the window sill. Why did Jonathan want a report on Lehi? He'd never asked for such a thing with any other customer. His request was strange, very strange. She smiled at him for offering Aaron an olive branch instead of a sword. She wanted to thank him, but now wasn't the time. Aaron was the one who needed her attention. She waited for Jonathan to climb the stairs and disappear into the bedroom before she wrapped her arms around him, crutches and all, and held him close. "Everything's going to be all right."

"It isn't." Aaron pulled free and ran his hands through his hair twice, the second time holding wet bangs between his fingers.

Ruth said, "You're upset."

"I won't be seeing Rebekah again."

"I'm sorry, son." Ruth held the lamp up to Aaron's face. The yellow light streaked the lines of a much older man across his smooth cheeks. He'd suffered so much in his short life; must he also endure the cruelty of a woman? Aaron was a good boy and if Rebekah could see beyond his injured feet she'd find a handsome man with a heart as fine as gold is pure. But this was most likely a sign of the way things would be for Aaron, and Ruth had to begin to prepare him for the disappointment of a woman's rejection. She held the lamp close to his face. If only his feet would heal, Rebekah would see him as she saw him; in the full light of his eternal soul.

"It isn't fair," Aaron said.

"Oh, Aaron." Ruth held his hand. "You feel badly now, but you'll get over this. There will be other women to court."

"I should have thrown a punch."

"Aaron! Don't speak like that." Ruth let go. "You're not that kind of man."

"I'm sorry, Mama, but I wish I'd broken Josiah's nose."

"The potter?"

"He has no right to keep me from seeing her again."

Ruth began to laugh so loud she had to cover her mouth to keep from waking the family. Aaron wasn't rejected by Rebekah, but by her father. And there was no better assurance that a woman had intentions on a man than for the father to intervene. This was good news, and between laughs Ruth caught her breath and said, "I thought you were going to take a swing at Rebekah."

A smile played at Aaron's lips, then a grin, and finally he and Ruth fell into each other's arms laughing as quietly as they could. Ruth held Aaron close and felt the warmth of his neck on her cheek. And for a moment everything was all right.

Her son was home.

CHAPTER 24

Sephora, the royal flutist, held the highest note on her delicately carved ivory instrument for nearly five counts. The dancers rushed across the main court of the Citadel in a burst of pirouettes. They gathered in circles of five at the far end of the hall in preparation for her second refrain of David's nineteenth psalm, the melody Sephora reserved for this sort of ceremony. Today Jonathan the blacksmith would be seated on the Sarim Council as the twelfth Elder. She tilted the end of her flute down to see the blacksmith lead his family to their seats. Passive, that was the only word for his appearance. He was dressed in newly woven black linen with white cuffs and a ceremonial turban, a stiff high-brimmed affair ending in a point like the horn on a bull. Jonathan was as calm as a sacrificial lamb before the temple altar, shaking hands with the senior Elders.

How a man like Jonathan ever got himself appointed to the highest council in the land was a mystery, but these were changing times and who was she to deny the blacksmith his good fortune? It wasn't until Captain Laban left his entourage of soldiers and crossed the room to shake the blacksmith's hand that Sephora saw Jonathan's apprehension. His body stiffened, an unmistakable tension between them, like the strain of a debtor meeting his creditor, but since Sephora knew nothing about the men's relationship she could only conclude it was the blacksmith's tight-fitting collar that caused the strain. She never wore anything tight around her neck. It might interfere with her breathing and a rasping flutist could never get steady work.

Some said Ruth had gained the pleasure of Queen Miriam, and if Sephora were to choose a friend it would be someone like Ruth. She seemed a plain-spoken, kindly woman, following Jonathan in silence. But you would have thought there was a gulf between the couple as wide as the Red Sea the way she avoided looking directly at her husband when he introduced her to Laban, and she took her seat nearly a cubit's length away. She folded her arms beneath her neatly pressed robe and half lowered her head, deflecting the glances from her husband like arrows off a brass shield. It was obvious she didn't want to be here. And who could blame her? What woman would want her husband on the Council? You'd never know which of the other eleven Elders had planted the dagger in your husband's back, figuratively speaking of course. But then isn't that the price Elders pay for a seat on the Council? Peace of mind exchanged for a little power and glory. Sephora took a deep breath between the second and third refrains and played a little faster. The dancers always raced through this part of the psalm.

Ruth's son Daniel took the seat next to her, his head held high. He was all the talk among the unmarried women at the market. They all knew he had proven himself as a wrestler and found a place in Laban's favor. What maid wouldn't have an interest in the silver stripes that would soon decorate his broad, powerful shoulders? With that black hair, straight jaw, and those brown penetrating eyes, he'd make a fine catch for any woman lucky enough to get an officer for a husband. His gaze was riveted on Rebekah, the daughter of Josiah the potter, seated in the next row over. She smiled and returned a quick nod, and Sephora would have thought she was competing for his affection if she didn't know Rebekah had an interest in the older brother.

Aaron sat down next to Daniel and leaned his crutches on the bench between them. When his stare met Rebekah's, her eyes turned away like moths flitting from the searing heat of an oil lamp. Wounded she was, by a simple glance from Aaron. The potter pulled his daughter in close, away from Aaron's stare, but then, that made plain sense. To provide for Rebekah in the manner she was accustomed, well, it would require more sweat than a boy with crippled feet could ever muster. Sephora took a long breath, played through a series of high-pitched runs and finished with a trill, but with so many still not seated she repeated the music from the top with the dancers following her lead, at a slower more tasteful tempo.

Elizabeth came last, struggling with her two youngest siblings, Sarah and Joshua. She was her mother's shadow, slender, but not weak. Sure, but not pretentious. She was a beauty above reproach, with her mother's rose-colored cheeks, short nose, and delicate eyelashes, and her father's curly hair, cascading to her high shoulders. She was a desert flower waiting to bloom, and the word at the market was that a certain scribe named Zoram made the perfect gardener. You never could trust what you heard at the market, though the pair did make a handsome couple. When Zoram crossed the aisle to assist Elizabeth with the children, she flatly denied his offer and settled Sarah and Joshua into their seats on her own. She didn't appear at all willing to be plucked by his public advances.

The dancers finished their last pass about the chamber and it was time Sephora began a more melancholy melody to quiet the guests in preparation for the procession. She soloed Solomon's twenty-third psalm as Zadock entered from the back with two assistants holding the train of his robe and a third carrying a black shawl draped over a pillow. It was the official mantle to consummate Jonathan's appointment to the Council. The Chief Elder directed Jonathan to join him and walk with the entourage to the front of the hall.

It was a simple ceremony. No words, only Sephora's flute playing in the background while Zadock placed the mantle over Jonathan's turban. She had to admit, it did make him look the part of an Elder, though he was more handsome than most with his dark hair showing on his brow below the headdress and the robust color in his straight cheeks. He put in an honest day's work and it showed. His robe draped in a straight line across his sturdy shoulders and he was out of place with the other, less fit Elders.

Zadock pronounced the words of the prayer with little emotion, then proclaimed Jonathan an Elder of the Jews. That was Sephora's signal to begin an up-tempo rendition of the river song. The dancers heard their cue, and the guests stood to offer a round of applause and a reserved cheer for Jonathan the blacksmith.

Jerusalem had its twelfth Elder.

Elizabeth inched to the threshold of the blacksmith shop, but refused to go one step inside. Not with all that dirty wood smoke back-drafting from the ovens and out the doors. The pungent odor would spoil her new robe. Just this morning she stitched the last hem, tied on the sashes, and sprinkled the cloth with perfumes. And she'd let nothing mar it, least of all the smell of blacksmithing. After dropping off the basket of food with Papa, she'd walk home by way of Jerusalem's upper city market. That was the best place to show off her pleats and skirts and ballooned sleeves that narrowed to delicate cuffs at the wrist.

She inched up on her toes and said, "Papa, I have your lunch."

"Bring it in, daughter." Jonathan's voice bellowed out the smoky entrance. "Set it on the table."

"Can't you come out and get it?"

"I'm busy, girl."

Another cloud of smoke swirled out the door and she stepped back into the street. All she could see inside was the shadowy outline of a man passing in front of the orange glow of the ovens. "Oh, Papa, please."

The clang of the forging tongs rattled into their resting place in the rack. Thank heavens. Her request had been granted. She waited while sandals brushed across the shop floor and a draft of smoke surged ahead of a man wearing Aaron's smithing apron and gripping Daniel's forging hammer at his side. The smoke cleared from his face and she found herself looking into the deep green eyes of . . .

"Zoram?"

"Good morning, Elizabeth."

"I didn't know that you, well, that you had started."

Zoram took a long breath to rid his lungs of the smoke. "Today's my first."

"Papa didn't say anything."

"He said you might be upset with the idea of me working here."

"He said upset?"

"Well, not upset."

"What exactly did he say?"

"I believe he used the word furious."

"That's ridiculous." Elizabeth turned toward the street, the skirts of her new robe swaying about her ankles.

Zoram came around and stood in front of her. "He didn't seem to think so."

"Papa doesn't need my approval to hire a laborer."

"What does he need?"

Elizabeth held the lunch basket against her hip to free her hand. She touched the forging hammer Zoram held. "I see you've made yourself useful."

Useful? Was that the harshest thing she could think to say? "You've found your way into my father's blacksmith shop without my help."

"If you mean he hired me, yes."

"You know exactly what I mean."

"Here." Zoram reached for the lunch basket. "Let me take that for you."

"I'm perfectly capable." Elizabeth pulled away. "How did you ever convince him to take you on?"

"I had nothing to do with it." Zoram removed his turban and brushed his hand through his dark hair. "Laban made the arrangements with your father."

"You could have declined."

"Is that what you want me to do?" Zoram peered at her from behind thick black bangs that flopped over his brow. He was begging her to trust him with that innocent look of his, but he wasn't innocent, not with his intentions on her father's blacksmith shop.

Elizabeth said, "Did you tell him why you're really here?"

"He knows about the brass plates."

Elizabeth dropped the lunch basket to her side. "He does?"

"He said I can forge as many as I like, just as long as I do it before work in the morning. He doesn't want me around here in the evening. Said he has other work to see to then."

"What about Jeremiah?"

"I didn't mention his name."

"Papa deserves to know who ordered the smithing."

"You're the only one who needs to know that."

"Why?"

Zoram hung the forging hammer from the strap in his apron. "Because you and Jeremiah are the only ones I trust."

"Don't say that."

"It's true." Zoram reached for the lunch basket and this time Elizabeth let him take it, but when he smiled with those pleading eyes she looked away. He was only making it more difficult to tell Papa of Zoram's relationship to the prophet Jeremiah. And if she told him that, she'd also have to tell him why he was smithing brass plates, and that was a story she was just beginning to understand herself. Jeremiah planned to add his writings to Laban's record; that much she understood. But the idea of Laban's record becoming part of another record that would somehow bring Jews to a remembrance of their covenants with God, well that was something strange indeed. If Jeremiah wanted his words preserved for generations yet unborn, who was she to deny him his vanity. But he didn't need to make up stories to persuade her cooperation. She could only hope that telling Papa all this wouldn't upset him enough to dismiss Zoram. As difficult as it was to admit, she liked having him around.

Elizabeth asked, "Why do you listen to Jeremiah? Working for him could get you into trouble, and he's so . . ."

"Odd?" Zoram asked.

"I didn't say that."

"Jeremiah has his weaknesses and no one knows them better than I. He speaks his mind when he should keep quiet. He's not educated. He can hardly read. I've had to do most of the writing for him and when I'm not around he has a friend help him. Jeremiah was raised as an orchard keeper, not a scribe and . . ." Zoram lowered his head. "I know what he's told you about the brass plates and his prophecies may sound foolish, but I help him because he's a prophet of God." He took Elizabeth by the hand. "If you knew what I knew, then you'd help him too."

Before Elizabeth could answer, Jonathan sauntered out of the smoke-filled shop. He cleared his throat and said, "I see you've met our new apprentice."

Elizabeth pulled her hand away from Zoram. "I have."

Jonathan said, "He's a might stronger than he appears on first sight. He's a hard worker, picks things up quickly, and already smelts a good brand of brass and a fine grade of iron."

She glanced at Zoram. "I wouldn't doubt that."

"He'll do steel as well as your brothers as soon as he puts a few callouses on those delicate hands of his and learns how to fire an oven."

"I'm sure he will, Papa."

Jonathan smiled at her. "You seem more approving of the arrangement than before."

"Did you think I'd be furious?"

"I've been thinking that for some time, girl."

Elizabeth straightened her collar. "Whatever for?"

"The other night at evening meal you were as close to furious as I've ever seen."

"There's something I should have told you about Zoram."

Jonathan folded his arms. "I'm listening."

Zoram stood behind Jonathan on the steps leading into the shop and peered over Jonathan's shoulder, his green eyes narrowed, his lips drawn tight. Must he look at her that way, as if she was expected to trust him like he trusted her? Why did she ever allow his misplaced faith to get a foothold in her heart? She said, "You should know that Zoram is . . ."

"Speak, girl."

"He's a fine worker."

"Is that all?"

"Well . . ." Elizabeth loosened the collar of her robe. "It is."

"I've been saying that for a week."

"I only wanted to agree with you."

"Women." Jonathan headed back inside shaking his head, but before disappearing into the smoke-filled shop, he said, "Tell your mother we'll have Zoram to dinner the end of next week. I want the whole family to meet the boy."

He left them alone, staring at each other, and they would have kept staring if Zoram hadn't broken the silence. He said, "Thank you for not mentioning Jeremiah."

"I want to keep you working in the shop so I can keep an eye on you."

"That's a fine robe you're wearing." Zoram said.

"I didn't think men took notice of such things."

"You're not the only one keeping an eye on someone."

Elizabeth felt the warmth of a blush rush through her cheeks and she looked away. "Shall I tell Mama you're coming to dinner?"

"I'd like that."

"Very well." Elizabeth lifted the skirts of her robe off the ground. "Good day, sir." She spun around and started home, her white robe catching the full light of morning. A walk through the upper city market to show off her pleats and cuffs and collars could wait for another day, maybe forever, now that the man she really wanted to see it had noticed. There was something about him that drew her affection, not just his handsome smile or his intelligent words, but something deep in his soul. She would watch him closely and find out why he kindled such strong feelings in her.

What was that light she saw shining in his eyes?

CHAPTER 25

"Just a moment. I'm coming."

Ruth finished straining the goat's milk, set out a bowl of fruit and a quarter-paddle of bread, then left the chores in the kitchen and started into the main room to answer the knock at the door. Who could that be at this hour? It was well before sunrise, and Joshua and the girls were sleeping.

She walked by the window of the main room and leaned on the sill. The caller wore a formal robe flaunting more pleats and skirts than a man's, though with fashions these days it was hard to know. Whatever was wanted, it was not to borrow a jar of milk or a cup of milled wheat.

Ruth brushed her hair back off her forehead and untied the apron string that girded her robe off the floor. She walked through the main room, gathered in Joshua's sandals, folded a blanket, arranged the sitting chairs flush against the wall and fluffed the cushion on the bench seat. She smoothed the wrinkles in the throw rug with her feet before opening the door and offering a kind greeting.

"Delivery." The girl held out a wood sword and clay mold shaped like it.

"My husband left not more than a moment ago for the blacksmithing district. If you hurry you can catch him."

"I saw him go." The girl's eyes took on a certain timidness. "Aaron wasn't with him, and I thought he might take these to your shop for me."

Her hair was brushed to a shine and braided around an ivory bar, and she smelled freshly bathed in perfumes. The girl wasn't here to make a delivery, not by the way she carefully selected her words. And she wasn't a girl. She was a woman, the one who'd captured Aaron's heart. Ruth was certain of it and she said, "You must be Rebekah."

"And you're Ruth." She offered a slight bow. "Good day."

"Is Aaron expecting you?"

"I doubt that."

"He's out behind, milking the goat." Ruth took the clay mold and showed her into the main room. "Why don't you make yourself comfortable while I fetch him in."

There was no need. Aaron's familiar whistle filtered through the windows. The door swung open and he stood in the threshold, a jar of goat's milk strung over his left crutch. He smiled that timid smile of his and said, "Morning, Mama." Thank heavens he'd been up and combed comb his hair and washed his face. He was presentable enough to see Rebekah. No, it was more than that. His dark hair, large eyes, and cheeks touched red from the cool morning were handsome features. It was an odd feeling to see him that way. Aaron was her son and she didn't need another reason to love him, though she had noted his loveliness from time to time. He was pleasing to look upon, but for the first time she saw him the way Rebekah must see him. A handsome man, worthy of a fine woman. In Aaron's eyes, Ruth saw the shadows of her husband as he was twenty years ago when they first met and she immediately knew the feelings Rebekah held for her son. Only the crutches were different.

"There's another jar behind the house." Aaron lowered the milk to the floor. He hadn't noticed Rebekah seated on a chair in the corner of the room. "I'll fetch it in before I leave."

"I'll take care of that." Ruth motioned for him to come inside.

"You will?"

"You're in a hurry, son."

"I am?"

Ruth set both hands on her hips. Would the boy ever notice he had a visitor? She said, "Come inside, I've packed a jar of olives, two loaves of bread and a pound of honey for the journey. Ishmael expects you at Beit Zayit by midday."

"Do I really need that much?" Aaron came back to the threshold. "It's only a few miles, Mama."

Ruth turned toward Rebekah, but Aaron still didn't understand she was telling him he had a visitor. He said, "Tell Papa I finished everything at the shop last night except for the . . ."

Aaron fell silent. He brushed away the hay that clung to his sleeve and stood straight, his long body facing Rebekah like a watch pole with a banner waving from its top heralding what Ruth hoped would be a glorious reunion. But this was not to be a celebration, not by the way Aaron lowered his voice and said, "What will your father say?"

Rebekah folded her hands on her lap. "He doesn't know I'm here."

"Oh."

Oh? Was that the only thing the boy could think to say? It was not Ruth who taught him that diction. She excused herself to get Aaron's things from the kitchen, but mostly to keep herself from blurting out a better word for him to use than *oh.* He was more articulate with Hebrew than any of her other children, though his tongue was now void of even a syllable of eloquence. Ruth returned from the kitchen with a full pack and the family's largest water skin to find Aaron still standing in the doorway and Rebekah still seated in the corner chair. They hadn't uttered a word or moved a cubit closer than when she left and her only recourse was to force them together.

Ruth handed the water skin to Rebekah. "Would you help Aaron fill this on his way out of the city."

"I'll do it myself." Aaron reached for the skin, but Ruth warned him off with her eyes and placed it in Rebekah's hands. Ruth pecked a kiss on Aaron's cheek and invited Rebekah and her father Josiah to come share a meal with the family another day, then she ushered them into the courtyard and closed the door. She held the latch shut and leaned against the wood planks. Only time would tell if forcing them to be alone was a wise choice. Under any other circumstance she would have monitored their conversation, but this was for younger hearts to resolve. At least it was until she heard another voice call down the steps from the loft.

Elizabeth asked, "Why are you standing there?"

Ruth spun around to see her daughter parting the curtain that divided her bedroom from the rest of the loft. She flew down the steps like a bird taking flight, tying her robe as she came. "Don't you want to hear what they're saying?"

"It's only a delivery girl." Ruth raised the smithing mold. "She brought this by for your father."

"Not dressed like that she didn't." Elizabeth hurried across the room to the window.

"What do you think you're doing, young woman?"

"I'm going to listen to every word you're afraid to hear."

"Afraid, am I?" Ruth stepped in front of Elizabeth in time to win the best spot at the window sill. "I'm the mother in this house."

"That's a shame."

"Why?"

"Because mothers don't enjoy this nearly as much as sisters."

They shared the window sill, leaning out together and peering across the courtyard as if their indiscretion would go unnoticed. It was an outright trespass on the couple. For Elizabeth a breach of etiquette didn't require a reason, but for Ruth it wasn't curiosity that forced her to the window. A mother had to exercise a certain degree of supervision and she was simply being motherly, no matter how improper her spying.

Aaron kept his head down, tinkering with the stirrups. Rigging the mule for his journey to Beit Zayit didn't require any talk, and he didn't even glance at Rebekah while he fitted the foot straps. He wrapped each stirrup with eight strips of linen to keep the leather from cutting into his feet, three more than Ruth said he'd need. And he secured the pack onto the mule's haunches with no less than ten lashes of hemp when three would have done. On the last loop over and around the slipknot, he glanced under his arm. Rebekah stood a few paces behind him with the water skin in hand, waiting for him to finish. Why did she have to be so patient? It only served to make her more beautiful, though she didn't need any help with beauty. Not with her hair pulled back and tied around an ivory bar, soft and full and touched by the golden light of early morning. He wanted to take her in his arms and tell her to listen to his advice. But not enough time had passed since he found out her secret, and he didn't know exactly how to say what must be said. If there was ever a time for honor, it was now, and saving her from her father's religion was the only honorable thing.

The crutches fit snug behind the saddle, but to be sure they didn't fall, he secured them with a pull knot and two slips. Tied that way he could get them out and be on his feet as fast as a sparrow hops from a stoop. Well, maybe not as fast as a sparrow.

Aaron kept fiddling with the knots. They were secure. He'd checked each one three times, but to fritter away more time he checked them again.

Rebekah said, "I came to see you off to Beit Zayit."

"Who told you I was going there?"

"No one in particular." Rebekah glanced over at the house. Ruth was leaning out the window along with Elizabeth. They waved, then disappeared inside the kitchen only to stand at the table in plain view of the courtyard. To end their eavesdropping, Aaron untied the mule from the olive tree, swung up into the saddle belly first and trotted out the gate with Rebekah following. He said, "You didn't need to bother."

"You're not upset with me, are you?"

"It's your father I worry about. He's playing a very dangerous game." Aaron carefully fitted his feet into the linen wrapped stirrups.

Rebekah said, "You've given him reason to worry as well."

"He sent you to check on me, didn't he?"

"I told you he doesn't know I came." Rebekah walked ahead of him. "He trusts you."

Aaron said, "He doesn't have a choice."

"You won't betray him, will you?"

"No one will learn of his treason from me." Aaron slapped the mule on the rump and got her moving alongside Rebekah. Aaron said, "But someone is bound to discover it, and then . . ."

"I'm not in any danger." Rebekah lengthened her stride to keep up.

"Not until the Elders find out who your father really is."

Rebekah leaned in close to the mule and Aaron felt her press against his leg. "You'd never do anything to hurt us, would you?"

Hurt her? Aaron was trying to save her. "It's your father's secrets that will hurt you, not mine." They walked in silence past two women balancing water jars on their heads, past the carpenter's home and down the hill to the great Pool of Siloam.

Jerusalem's south wall formed the back of the pool and a waist-high masonry wall squared the remaining sides. Drinking water poured from Hezekiah's tunnel into the largest pool, then by overflow duct to the second and third pools where animals drank, and from there through a pipe bored into the south wall and out to the vineyards on the plains south of Jerusalem. At this time of day with so many women drawing their daily supply, the pool never rose high enough to spill over past the second pool.

The plaza was abuzz with the chatter of women. Nearly one hundred had come to get their morning supply, dipping their jars deep into the blue-green waters. Storytelling was the only chore practiced here more than water drawing; and to avoid becoming part of their next tale, Aaron steered the mule to the least crowded spot along the pool's edge. Aaron was in the company of the well-known and very eligible daughter of Josiah the potter and the glances from these women told him to beware else he'd end up fodder for their fiery gossip.

Rebekah pushed the water skin under and a cascade of bubbles rushed to the surface, clouding the water around her hands. She plucked it from the pool and replaced the corkwood cap. "There you go. Cool water for your journey."

Aaron gazed past her to the ripples gently troubling the surface of the pool. He asked, "Can we forget?"

Rebekah wrinkled up her nose. "Forget what?"

Aaron got down off the mule and leaned on the pool's edge. "Everything you haven't told me."

"What do you want to know?"

"That you don't believe like your father believes."

"Why do you say such a thing?" Rebekah slid in next to Aaron and they stared at the water together. He could feel her shoulders rise and fall with each breath.

Aaron said, "I want you to believe like other Jews."

"I do."

"Then you aren't a traitor like your father?"

"He's not a traitor."

Aaron lowered his voice to a whisper. "He's a Rekhabite." He closed his eyes and held them closed for a long moment. When he opened them, Rebekah had backed away from him.

"You should distance yourself from him."

"I can't do that."

"You must." Aaron leaned forward on his crutches. "Whatever he is . . . whatever he's done, it's going to harm you; it could kill you."

"Nothing's going to hurt us."

"There are men in this city who will stop at nothing."

"I know the risks." Rebekah wiped a tear from her cheek. "I live with them every day."

"You can escape the fear; I'll help you."

"You don't understand."

"I'd like to." Aaron ran his fingers through his hair.

"You should at least find out what Rekhabites believe."

"Why would I want to do that?"

"Because I'm a Rekhabite like my father." She lifted the skirts of her robe and started across the plaza.

"Rebekah!"

She hurried away from the pool and up the steep hill of Water Street without turning back—not even a glance over her shoulder to acknowledge Aaron's call.

The dipping ceased. Women balanced their jars on the pool's edge and stared at Aaron. He mounted up in his awkward belly-first way and swung the mule around, the glares from women piercing him like arrows. He trotted up the rise from the pool, but Rebekah had gone down any one of a hundred side alleys spilling off Water Street. When he returned from Beit Zayit he would talk sense to her.

He had to protect her from her father's foolishness.

CHAPTER 26

None of the guards at the west gate stopped Aaron and he steered past them without so much as a nod of their brass helmets. He was the son of the new Elder and they never questioned the reason for his leaving the city—a fortunate thing, since Jonathan had warned him to be careful whom he told about his trip to Beit Zayit. An Elder's son shouldn't work for the wrong people, and to Jonathan, Lehi and his family still may be the wrong kind of people.

Aaron steered the mule down from the gate and onto the road leading through the narrow Hinnom Valley. It was a steep, rock strewn path that led to the plateaus west of Jerusalem. The mule took its time picking its way around the largest stones and Aaron would have gotten out of the saddle and walked if it weren't for his feet.

The sun worked its way overhead as Aaron made his way up from the valley floor and it was midday when he finally reached the trade route. He headed northwest and made good time traveling the loosely packed dirt until he came onto a thirty-camel caravan headed north to Phoenicia. A thick cloud of dust kicked up under their hooves as the long line of animals lumbered up the trail, tethered together with long ropes. The caravan master led on horseback, followed by a band of Ethiopian caravan hands walking alongside the camels and swatting at strays with reed poles. Aaron kept back thirty cubits from the last camel and breathed through the cloth in his sleeve. He was never so thankful for a poorly groomed trail than when he reached the fork in the trade route and turned onto the seldom-traveled path leading over the bluffs to Beit Zayit. Aaron had to coax the mule through the first fifty cubits of bushweed and thistle with a firm hand on the rein and a slap on the rump.

The mule settled into a careful, lumbering rhythm around the switchbacks leading through the foothills. Aaron gazed back at the view of Jerusalem, rising to view over the brush that lined the lower turns in the trail. He was free of the troubles he left behind in the city, if only for two week's time. At Beit Zayit he wouldn't have to face Rebekah, though he couldn't protect her from the dangers of her father's religion this far away from the city. The mule balked at a large rock fallen in the path and Aaron carefully steered the animal off into the high brush and back onto the trail before returning to gaze back toward Jerusalem. The perimeter city walls were built of thick, impenetrable limestone and they rose and fell with the lay of the land. They stood taller than any of the inner-city walls. The highest in the city ran cross-ways, dividing the lower city of David from the upper city of Solomon like a rampart separating the estates of the wealthiest citizens from the commoners. The next largest wall ran east along Main Street before turning down the hill and coming in behind the family's shop. It was made of bricks and from this far away, it was a jagged seam in a patchwork of isolated walls separating neighbor from neighbor. Aaron sat high in the saddle and strained to see the wall around Rebekah's home. It was made of the same thick clay brick, but washed in a white plaster, and it glowed like pearl in the sun.

Aaron settled back into the saddle and reined the mule around a switchback that turned him away from his view of Jerusalem, but the image of the city flooded his mind. There were walls around buildings, walls lining the streets, and still more surrounding every home. Thick gray stone, brown brick, and red clay walled off everything from everyone in Jerusalem. Aaron prodded the mule over a sharp rise in the trail and down through a dry gully then up again toward the bluffs. Was that what the Rekhabite religion would do, separate him from Rebekah like a wall he was forbidden to climb?

If he could only climb the wall that surrounded Rebekah's soul and see what made her believe so fiercely in the faith of the Rekhabites, then he could help her, and bring her back to her senses.

She believed in the words of the prophets like all Rekhabites, and that didn't worry him, no matter how many men in the city called them traitors. The Almighty had sent prophets into the world since the beginning and He could still send them. But prophets weren't Rekhabites, with secret societies to divide father and son. Aaron wrapped the mule reins around his hands so tight his fingers went numb. What was he to do with Rebekah and her father? They were good people, nothing like the nameless traitors Papa railed against.

Aaron unwrapped the reins and let the blood flow through his hands. He shouldn't let the Rekhabites rile him so. He didn't really know much about them beyond his father's insults. Did their faith have anything he should consider? Aaron bent low to clear the branch of a solitary Joshua tree hanging over the trail, then righted himself in the saddle. And what about his blessing of healing? It was in the name of the Rekhabite messiah that he was to be healed, made whole to save the life of a prophet. He had to believe in the blessing; it was his only hope for a cure. But didn't that mean God had sent a Rekhabite to pull him from the fire?

Aaron came around another switchback that faced him back toward Jerusalem. Homes lined the hillsides and the afternoon sunlight danced over the orange clay roofs. Solomon's Temple shone in the skyline. It sat high on the temple mount above so many Jews who believed in the messiah, but could not agree on who he would be. The temple's heaven-pointing capstones trimmed the roof's edge like the many points on a king's crown. If only Aaron could find out which points of doctrine were true, the prophets' or the Elders'. Aaron would come back this way once he finished his work for the olive oil merchants and then he would begin his search for a blessing of peace to calm his troubled soul. Were the prophets men of God or traitors? If he could know that, then he would know if he could trust the men who believed on their teachings. Only then would he find peace with Rebekah and her Rekhabites.

The trail flattened at the summit, ending at a wall of rock with no way through except a narrow cleft barely the width of a cart. A steady cool breeze flowed through the passage where the sun never reached and Aaron eased the mule into the shadows, leaving behind the walled city of Jerusalem for the open vineyards of the valley that lay ahead. He patted the mule's neck, careful not to let the towering sandstone walls startle the animal. He prodded forward slowly, toward the blue sky at the other end, leaning over the animal's mane and searching for his first glimpse of the valley called Beit Zayit, the valley of the house of olive trees.

It was a long passage, nearly fifty cubits; but when the rock walls gave way to bright afternoon sun, he knew he'd found the place. Straight rows of olive trees lined every ridge top, hillside, and level plain, blanketing the land in green. Roads wide enough for a driver to turn an olive cart around ran between the vineyards and spread out from the center of the valley like strands in a spider's web.

Down on the flatlands, a settlement of white limestone homes, barns, and corrals stood by the shores of a spring-fed lake. A breeze raced across its waters, raising caps of white off the blue-green surface before pushing to shore and rustling up through the groves.

Aaron leaned his head back and let the wind play through his hair. What a fine place, this valley of the house of olive trees, fifty square miles of heaven, give or take a few acres. It was a pristine valley, secluded from the stir of society, with only the families of Lehi and Ishmael to divide the serenity between them. He'd heard tell of the size and beauty of this place though no one he knew ever claimed to have visited. Not even the war had reached this spot. No barns were charred to the ground; the roofs and walls and gates of the estates stood firm, and the vineyards lay undisturbed.

For all Aaron could tell, Beit Zayit was a forgotten paradise, protected from the war by the hand of—

"Angels, boy?"

Aaron turned in the saddle to find a man standing across the road beneath an olive tree, the highest tree in all the vineyards.

"Excuse me, sir. What was that you said?"

"I was just asking if you and your younger brother Joshua are still looking for angels." He dropped an olive into his mouth and chewed on it before spitting it out. "I say angels could find no prettier place in all of Judah to spend their days."

Aaron reined over, ducking the low hanging branches. He knew Ishmael's cap of white hair and matching beard immediately. He'd almost forgotten how white—angel white.

Ishmael circled the tree, searching out another olive to test. "I've been waiting for you."

"For me, sir?"

"Thought I'd check this vineyard while I waited. Don't get up here as much as I should." Ishmael circled the tree a second time. "I was a bit worried. Thought you'd be along sooner."

"The mule doesn't climb so well."

"I've set aside one of our stallions for you. You'll need it with your feet like they are."

"I've got this." Aaron patted the mule's mane.

"This is a large plantation and I want you to get around quickly. We're paying you too much to spend your day on a mule."

"I can't afford a horse."

"It comes with the job."

Aaron sat back onto the mule's haunches. "Blacksmithing, sir?"

"Caravanning. That's what built this plantation and we only use the finest animals." Ishmael tried another olive. It was bitter. You could tell by the way he puckered his lips on the first bite. He spat out the green meat and stabbed the toe of his sandal round the tree trunk like a spade airing the soil. "Better not be the roots. If they've gone bad I might as well cut down these trees and take a torch to them. I planted a hundred seedlings in this high ground ten years back and I'm still waiting for the first crop." He shook his head. "I'm just not having the same luck I did with the lower vineyards."

"It's a fine place you have here, sir." Aaron looked out over the valley. "Quite an inheritance."

"Didn't inherit any of it. Our family never owned this land before great-grandfather came by it and I can tell you he didn't have the money to buy it, either. He never spoke a word about how he got the land, God rest his soul. Said it was best we didn't know the story." The lines around Ishmael's eyes hardened. "To tell the truth, boy, I don't even know if he was a full-blooded Jew. But he got claim to this land some way and we're grateful for it, no matter how he came by it."

Aaron said, "You've done well growing olives."

"Caravanning, son. That's where we've done well. Shipping olive oil to Egypt." Ishmael stroked the well-groomed hairs on his chin. "When cousin Lehi and I first started, we didn't even own a camel, but back then we didn't need one. Didn't have any olive oil to caravan. It was Lehi who said the only way to prosper was putting everything in olives. Not wheat, not flax, not even grapes to sell to the winemakers. Olives, Lehi said, and he made sure we had the animals to caravan every drop of oil to Egypt." Ishmael nodded. "Lehi was right, he's always been right. I took to planting olive groves, acre by acre until, well, you can see for yourself."

"You're a fine farmer, sir."

"Anyone can grow olives. I did it and I'd never dunged an olive tree in my life. But it takes a man with vision to open trade with a nation on the edge of the world."

"You mean Egypt?"

"I mean Lehi. He's the reason we put everything into olives back, what, twenty years ago, when olive oil in Jerusalem was cheap as water, give or take a few shekels. But in Egypt it's worth more than gold. Olive trees don't grow along the Nile, no matter how much air and water you've got, and Cousin Lehi knew it. Too low, too hot, too Egyptian. He bought a herd of camels, took to caravanning and he's gotten a good price for our oil ever since." Ishmael stepped out from under the olive tree and pointed to the groves growing on the plains around the lake. "That used to be a wheat field, but now you couldn't winnow enough out of there for a loaf of bread. I put the first new saplings on the plains, moved onto those ridges a few years later, then up the sides of these mountains. We've done well. Never had a bad harvest until I planted this orchard." Ishmael tapped the tree trunk with his foot. "For all I know, it could be the thin air up this high. I tried everything to save these trees, but still can't figure out why the branches grow so fast." He picked up a handful of reddish brown soil and sifted it between his fingers. "That's the secret to growing olives, you know."

"Dirt, sir?" Aaron asked.

"Pace. Everything's got to grow at the same pace. The roots, the branches. Everything grows together. You play a little game with the tree. Dig about the roots four times a year, gives them just enough air to breath. Prune the branches every spring. Fertilize with rotten olives at the start of winter, and dung them once in three years, no matter how bad it smells. Gives them that little push they need. In the summer you watch them real close. If the leaves get too yellow you haul in a little water. Just enough to shake the dust out of the soil or you'll rot the fruit. You do all that and then you do one more thing."

He raised his index finger. "Pray the roots grow the same pace as the branches. That's the secret to sweet olives. Pace. And it's all a guessing game."

"What if you guess wrong?"

"Graft, boy. Never give up on a tree so long as there's hope for the roots. You chop the ends off the branches, tie in sweet shoots and leave the rest to God."

"I thought you were going to cut these trees down and set a torch to them."

"I was encouraging them. You have to scare them every once in awhile. Give them every chance to grow good fruit, just like a parent with a child." Ishmael circled the trunk to the lowest branch, plucked off an olive and worked it between his teeth. "This one's got some sweetness to it. We can save the roots with some pruning, a few grafts on the highest branches, and enough horse dung to keep them strong." He looked up at Aaron. "Now where were we?"

"Horse dung, sir."

"That's right. I'll have your new horse at the corral by evening. Riding one's no different than a mule once you get used to the faster pace and longer strides." Ishmael spat out the seed. "It's time we headed in. Cousin Lehi's expecting you."

Ishmael mounted his brown steed, pulled onto the trail, and waited for Aaron to come alongside. When he didn't, Ishmael turned back and asked, "What's keeping you, boy?"

Aaron said, "I was wondering about my work."

"Most of it's back at the smithy. Sam will bring the rest of it by in the morning."

"Thank you, sir, but what I mean to ask is why did you hire me?"

"You're a blacksmith, aren't you?"

"A crippled one."

Ishmael swung around. "Lehi doesn't see it that way."

"What does he see?"

"A hardworking young man who was injured for a reason."

"What do you mean, for a reason?"

Ishmael swung around. "I don't want you getting any ideas about the man, but Lehi feels things deeper than most men. He senses things before they happen." He sidled his mount in next to Aaron.

"Lehi said there was a reason you were injured like this. He's a dreamer and I suppose you could say he dreamed you here."

"Why me?"

"That's something you'll have to bring up with him. I'll see that you're introduced properly."

Ishmael leaned over his saddle and swatted Aaron's mule on the flank, sending them both lurching down the trail. They rode out of the highest vineyard and crossed a dry creek bed just below the ridge, then continued down through a stand of picked-over olive trees, bare of a single olive. Ethiopian servants worked the next ridge over, gathering in the harvest. The stick men kept time with long hickory poles, rattling them against the branches in a mesmerizing beat and bringing down bundles of fruit with each swing. Basket men crawled behind them gathering the fallen olives and humming a rhythmical chant. And once their baskets were full, they shouldered their loads to the road like dancers costumed in wicker, appearing on stage long enough to dump their olives in mule carts and head back into the groves to the beat of the stick men.

Aaron rode through the lowland vineyards without any resistance from the mule. The animal balked up a short rise, but eased when they came out into a clearing past three barns and a corral where the main road transformed from dirt to a cobblestone lane, an unlikely surface for any country road, but this was no ordinary country. The lane passed between rows of square, one-story servants' quarters. The homes boasted white lime plaster fronts finished with crushed sea shells that caught the sunlight and reflected it back in twinkling flashes. It was a stonemason's extravagance most vineyard owners could hardly afford, let alone their servants. Instead of blankets, a wooden door graced the entrance to each home and tailored linens draped the windows. The homes stood so close that the woman on the first roof hanging out her wash could have jumped to her neighbor's. And below, in the yard, a pack of children scurried about in a spirited game of chase.

Past the last home the lane turned up a hill, through a stand of trees and into a plaza paved in limestone block, cut and fit together without mortar. A pool flowing with fresh water piped from the lake graced the center of the square and would have been enough to capture the attention if not for the baskets of white, purple, and red poppies hanging from the opened gates of two large estates. Gardeners flitted about the grounds like bees, trimming hedges, plucking off the last brown petals of autumn and sweeping away the falling leaves almost before they lit on the maze of garden paths.

The estates stretched back into the trees so far Aaron couldn't see where they ended. Arching windows graced the upper floors, and a host of balconies were shaded by a canopy of vines.

"The map room is the last one down the main hall." Ishmael steadied Aaron's mule outside the gate of the larger estate. "You'll find Lehi in there."

Aaron dismounted slowly and stuffed the crutches under his arms. "You're not coming in?"

"You can find it on your own. It's just past the main stairs. Lehi leaves the door ajar. I'll see that your things are put in your room." Ishmael coaxed Aaron's mule down the path and disappeared behind the estate, leaving him standing outside the front gate.

So much for a proper introduction, but then Aaron didn't need Ishmael's help to get by the gardeners. They were busy weeding, pruning, and trimming. They didn't raise their heads when Aaron walked past, lifted the brass door latch, and slipped inside the main hall. The entry was adorned with blue porcelain Egyptian vases filled with fresh cut flowers, and gold lamps hung from the wide stone columns supporting the vaulted ceiling.

Aaron found his way along the west wing, past the tapestries and rugs to the map room door. When he opened it, a young girl stepped from behind a long series of shelves. She cleaned a scroll with a feather duster and said, "You must be Aaron." She placed the scroll back on the shelf and came out into the hall. "My name is Mary." She was a fifteen-year-old girl dressed in a blue wraparound robe that made her appear much older. Her dress was the newest style of clothing popular in the cities along the Nile, without any pleats or bows but with the sheen of finely woven silk. It was far too elegant for servant clothing, but this was an elegant place and Aaron was beginning to expect the unexpected. "Lehi can't be disturbed this afternoon. He left word he would see you in the morning." She closed the door to the map room behind her and pointed the feather duster down the hallway. "Come, there's fresh bread in the kitchen and I'll show you to your room." When they passed the main stairs, she handed Aaron a large brass key. "Your bedroom is up there, third door on the left. The maidservant will see that your things are unpacked." Odd that he was to sleep in the main house. Odder still was that she'd said the maidservant would get his things. Wasn't she the maidservant?

Aaron asked, "Do you work for Lehi?"

"Oh, no. I'm part of the family, almost."

Aaron followed her past the stairwell down another corridor leading to the kitchens. How could she be *almost* part of the family? They passed a dining hall large enough to seat forty. A lamp hung above the oak table, and each chair was crafted with armrests and an intricate flower pattern carved into the backs.

Aaron said, "You must be Lehi's daughter."

"Not yet."

Not yet? What did she mean by that?

"Tomorrow night you'll dine with us in here. We're having baked lamb and lentils." Mary stepped into the dining hall, dusted the table and chairs then came back into the corridor. "Father Lehi's been talking about your arrival for some time and we all want to meet you. With the grandchildren there will be nearly thirty." She looked about the dining hall. They were alone and she said, "Once all my sisters and I are married to the sons of Lehi, why, there won't be room around the table for all the children. There's talk of building a larger dining hall."

"Aren't you a bit young?"

"I'm not getting married, at least not yet." Mary directed Aaron toward the kitchen doors with her feather duster. "Nephi won't marry until he's at least twenty, and that's . . ." She ticked the years off on her fingers. ". . . a good five years from now, so far away I don't think about it much."

Aaron hurried his crutches to keep pace with her. "Did your mother arrange this?"

"Ishmael's the matchmaker in our family. Mama doesn't like the task of marrying off her children. I suppose it's difficult to see her little girls grow older." Mary continued down the hall toward the kitchen. "But with so many daughters advising Papa on the matchmaking, he never lacks for a woman's opinion, though he does like to think he knows best, and we allow him that. He's never really made a mistake."

"Never?"

"Well, he's only married off my two brothers." Mary waved her feather duster in front of her. "My oldest brother, Nathan, is happily married to Lehi's oldest daughter Rachel. And when Seth married Leah, you'd have thought he wedded the Queen of Israel." She wrinkled her nose and smiled. "Don't tell Papa I said this, but he really doesn't need my advice. I wouldn't change his mind for all the gold in Israel. Nephi's the perfect match for me." Before Aaron could ask any more about the marriage arrangements of her sisters, they reached the kitchen doors and Mary held them open for Aaron.

Bread baking at Beit Zayit was a family affair and the kitchen was filled with the bustle of women and children attending to the task. Mary joined her mother, Isabel, and three sisters, Nora, Abigail, and Hannah, and the two daughters of Lehi, Rachel and Leah, pressing and kneading dough at the baker's table. Four young grandsons lifted sacks of freshly milled flour from the storage bins to the table while two granddaughters worked brooms across the floor, barely able to keep pace with the mess.

Mother Sariah stood with a bread paddle in one hand and the oven door in the other. She was a small woman, but with a firm constitution much like Aaron's mother. Her long brown hair was tied back under the jeweled collar of her work robe, though with so many pleats and bows you could mistake it for a coronation garment. Her smooth skin was softened even more by the flush of baker's powder that had settled on her cheeks. She directed her daughters about the kitchen with a kindness in her eyes and a gentle voice. When she saw Aaron enter the kitchen, she quickly paddled a loaf of bread from the oven and carried it over to him, scooting her grandchildren out of the way as she came. "Be careful now, it's a bit hot." She inched the bread off the paddle with a shake and fetched a jar of the finest honey from the pantry. She placed them together in a leather pack, draped it over Aaron's shoulder and said, "This should be enough to hold you until dinner." Her hands were covered with flour and she brushed the hair off her brow with the back of her hand. She said, "Come with me."

Sariah held open the kitchen door and let Aaron shuffle out into the hall, the click, click, click of his crutches reverberating off the stone walls. She said, "My husband will be pleased you're finally here with us. He's told me so much about you."

Aaron leaned over the ends of both crutches, but he still towered over Sariah. He looked down at her and said, "There isn't much to tell. We've never met."

"It isn't so much what he knows about you." She adjusted her apron about her waist and rubbed the flour off her palms. "It's what he expects from you."

"I'm a good blacksmith, ma'am. All of us in my family are expert smiths. He won't be disappointed."

"I'll have none of that." Sariah wagged a finger at Aaron. "It isn't 'ma'am'." She placed her hands on her hips. "All of my sons and grandsons call me Mother Sariah, and if that's good enough for them, then it's good enough for you."

Aaron felt a smile well up from deep within, a smile with such power that, try as he might, he couldn't keep it from spreading across his face. Sariah was like his mother, and if he hadn't been standing there looking at her, he would have believed Ruth was standing there lecturing him. He nodded and kept nodding. Coming here was, in a way, like coming home. Not that this was his family or that they could ever replace his own flesh and blood. But he felt comfortable in the company of Lehi's family and he said, "Very, well," the ends of his smile still tugging at his cheeks and his head still nodding. "Mother Sariah it will be."

Sariah stooped to her knees and lightly traced her fingers over the bandages on Aaron's feet. The leather straps of his sandals didn't keep her from a close inspection and she said, "I'm going to start with Jasmine powders. My husband imports them from Egypt and they do wonders to soften the skin and help the healing. If that doesn't work, I've got a rare box of himony from the Orient. Soak in some water with those powders and you'll never know you've been injured."

"That's very kind of you, but you needn't bother. The doctors have already done what they can."

"Nonsense." Sariah stood and dusted her hands. "Lehi said your feet have gotten worse and I'm to see if I can reverse that and heal them for you." She clasped her hands. "I'll serve you a good portion of hyssop tea in the morning. It does wonders for the skin."

Aaron asked, "How does Lehi know so much about my feet?"

"Don't underestimate the man." Sariah folded her arms over her baking apron. "I married him because he was wise enough to marry me, you know." She winked and said, "When Sam first stopped to hire you, he said you were using a single cane to get around. But now . . ." She reached her hand over the knotted wood.

Aaron said, "They're called crutches."

Sariah took her hand back. The light in her eyes faded, replaced with darkness that flashed across her eyes for only a moment, but it was enough to know she had concerns about the crutches. She was a fast-speaking woman, but the pace of her words slowed and she lowered her voice. She said, "Lehi mentioned them to me."

Lehi mentioned them? Aaron stood as stiff as the wood in his crutches. How did Lehi know anything about them?

Sariah brushed her apron and started back to the kitchen door. "I have bread to bake. Will you be able to find your room?"

"Mary showed me the way."

"So good to have you with us." Sariah pushed open the kitchen door and the voices from within filled the hall for a moment then fell silent as the door came shut. Aaron stood by the entry, the door still swinging on the pivot. How did Lehi know anything about his crutches?

Aaron turned and started down the hall when he came across a maidservant sweeping the stone floor. And, since he had just met all the women in Lehi's and Ishmael's family, he was certain she was a maidservant. She had to be. He nodded as he passed and he was nearly to the stairs leading to the second floor when a monotone voice boomed from the reading room. It was a strange sound and Aaron came back down the hall and inclined his head to listen. It was Egyptian.

The maidservant noticed his interest in the foreign tongue. She stopped her sweeping and leaned on the wicker broom. She said, "That would be Memphis. He teaches Egyptian. I suppose that's one of the advantages of wealth." She pushed the broom toward the door.

"Who does he teach?" Aaron asked.

"The younger boys are taking their lessons. You know, reading, writing, that sort of thing. The stuff the older boys don't have patience for." She swept her way toward the reading room and Aaron followed. "You can listen in," she said, "but don't let Memphis badger you. He's new here and he thinks he owns the place." She whisked inside and over to the back of the classroom, then disappeared into the hall through another door, leaving Aaron in class and very much out of place.

Memphis paced between two pillars. His scalp was shaved and rubbed in olive oil. A frown graced his face, cemented there from years of teaching. The tone of his voice was an eternal hiss, like steam escaping from a narrow-necked herb pot. He read from a scroll while Sam and Nephi furiously transcribed his words onto papyrus.

Sam sat on a hard wooden chair, his body perched on the edge of it like a child ready to bolt. He gripped the writing stylus with long, thin fingers and made a fist with his other hand. He was never one to relax, always bartering a business deal, which usually meant bartering his way into and out of trouble. He was the first to see Aaron standing near the back of the classroom and greeted him with a grin before turning his head back into his writing to keep up with the constant stream of Egyptian dictation Memphis spouted at them.

It wasn't until Nephi got to the end of his scroll and his head came up to dip the pen in the inkwell that he saw Aaron. His thick-shouldered frame cast a wide afternoon shadow across the writing table. His hair was tied back neatly with a headband of blue silk, except for a bang of curls that hung over his brow. No doubt an Egyptian style his mother insisted upon. He had the same dimples as his mother, but not as deeply cut into his jawline. A smile came easily and he nodded before starting down the next column of the scroll.

Memphis stopped pacing between the pillars. His sandals slapped the stone floor and his oversized ears bobbed like ostrich feathers. He rolled his scroll, waved it around the room and immediately Aaron felt he'd intruded. But Memphis didn't see him. He was checking on his pupils' writing.

Memphis asked, "Did you get all that?"

Sam nodded. "Everything but the part about the Egyptian god called Sam, the one your people have an entire city named for."

"I didn't read anything to you about that."

"Are you sure you didn't?" Sam read back down his page.

"Absolutely certain."

Sam said, "Here it is, right here."

Memphis leaned over Sam's shoulder. "That was yesterday's lesson, young man."

"I would have bet a talent of silver it was today."

Memphis shook his head slowly. "Not another of your wagers."

"I'll bet there are more boys in Egypt with the name Sam than any other name."

"That wager has nothing to do with your writing lesson. Now back to the alphabet."

Memphis strode behind Nephi and ran his finger over the letters on the papyrus. The straight lines of the demotic alphabet took much less space than the flowing curves of hieroglyphic letters or Hebrew script. "Notice how much easier demotic letters are to write," Memphis said. "Reformed Egyptian will be the hallmark of your education." He droned on about the advantages of the new writing—how hieroglyphics were beautiful, but required far too much costly papyrus while demotic took little space. The Egyptians were a proud lot, especially of their alphabets. Memphis ended his lecture, reminding the boys how fortunate they were to have him as their teacher, probably the most qualified man in all the northern provinces. And Sam reminded him he was also the most expensive. Only Sam had the nerve to say that to his teacher, but then Sam was the family's accountant, tracking his father's wealth, paying the bills and tallying the profits. And it was Sam who paid Memphis. Ten pieces of silver a month, room, board and all the olive oil he could use. More than a fair price for any teacher.

Memphis stopped lecturing and turned his head toward Aaron. "Well, well, I finally meet one of the older boys. Have a seat next to your brothers."

He had mistaken Aaron for one of Lehi's sons. Aaron said, "I'm sorry, sir, I'm headed for my room."

"Not another step, young man. I'm not letting you go that easy."

Sam said, "He gets three more pieces of silver if you stay." Sam made a note in his ledger to pay Memphis, then pushed a chair between himself and Nephi. "Sit down Lemuel." He winked at Aaron. "It's time you had your first writing lesson."

Memphis said, "Do you know demotic?"

"I've heard of it, seen it used by some Egyptian merchants. We employed an Egyptian fireboy in our shop in Sidon. He taught me how to read a few lines."

"You've been to Sidon have you? Your father never mentioned anything about that to me."

Sam said, "We run a caravan up north from time to time." He lowered his head to hide a grin.

Memphis tapped the side of his head. "What about your writing?"

"Nothing, really," Aaron said.

Memphis scratched the word "welcome" in Hebrew. Next to it he wrote the straight, small letters of the demotic translation. "I want all of you to do the same."

Sam's characters were poorly formed and hard to follow. Nephi was more precise, his thick fingers were comfortable with the small stylus and his strokes were neat and flowing. Aaron tried to form the first letter, a ceantum, three lines stacked on top of each other and connected by a crossways slash.

"That's good." Memphis pushed the ink bottle at Aaron. "You have a sense for writing."

Aaron dipped the pen and formed the next letter, a half-circle with three dots placed above the arc. His pen scratched over the papyrus like a chisel over stone, slow and cumbersome. Not like Nephi, but still good enough to impress Memphis.

"You keep writing like that," Memphis said, "and you'll be hired out to scribe for that prophet friend for whom Lehi's always praying at evening meal." He snapped his fingers. "What was the man's name?"

Sam said, "That's enough, Memphis." Sam was staring at his teacher, at what he had just said. He put down his pen, leaned over and set his hands on the table in front of him. "What you mean to say is that my father has friends who have need of a scribe, like a prophet has need of one."

"I know very well what I mean to say." Memphis picked up Aaron's papyrus and waved it in the air to dry the ink. "I was referring to that man Uriah, the one your father always prays for God to protect."

Sam said, "That will be all, Memphis."

"You've not finished with your lessons."

"We're done for today."

"I'm going to speak with your father about this. He isn't going to approve of your behavior."

"Go see him if you will, but the writing lesson is done for now."

Memphis had no other choice. And since Sam paid his wage, he immediately gathered his pens and scrolls and disappeared into the hall.

Sam sat back into the angle of his chair, no longer perched on the edge of it ready to go anywhere he pleased or say anything he thought. It wasn't normal for him to sit like that, but Memphis had given him reason. Without looking at Aaron he said, "Be at the smithy by midmorning tomorrow. I'll have the first round of work ready for you." He stood and pushed his chair back, the legs grating across the stone floor. Without another word he followed Memphis into the hall.

Nephi put away his brother's pen and corked the ink bottles. He said, "Uriah was an acquaintance of my father." He came around in front of Aaron. "That won't keep you from working for us, will it? I mean, with your father having so many concerns about us."

"Should he be concerned?"

"We're not Rekhabites."

"You talk like Rekhabites."

"We follow the prophets like all good Jews and we've all been baptized by them. But that isn't a reason for your father to think ill of us."

"My father has his reasons for believing the way he does."

"And you?" Nephi stepped closer, his sturdy frame casting a shadow over Aaron.

"Siding with Rekhabites isn't wise; it could get a man hurt."

"Do you side with the Elders?"

"I don't take sides."

Nephi said, "You must at least have an opinion."

"I don't." Aaron patted Nephi on the arm as he limped past. "But if I ever form one, I'll let you know what it is."

Aaron left the reading room.

Aaron followed the shortest route to the stables, down the path behind the estate and across the ridge above the pressing yards. The horse barn was built of limestone block and each of the forty stalls was washed and spread with fresh hay this late in the afternoon. A stable boy carried feed from the barn and a water boy filled the troughs in the corrals. The wide swinging door to the last stall pushed open and Ishmael stepped out leading a white Arabian, the only one among the brown- and black-coated animals in Lehi's stock.

She was a fine animal, the pride of the stables—the finest from a large herd. Horses were rare in Israel, far too expensive for the common man and not nearly as practical as a strong pack mule or a seasoned camel. But they were fast beasts, spirited and swift as the wind, and any man who could afford to breed that kind of speed was blessed of heaven.

Ishmael said, "This is Lehi's horse."

Aaron rubbed the animal's mane. "Does she have a name?"

"Lehi calls her Beuntahyu."

"She's a fine animal."

"Why don't you ride her? She's a fast one, fastest horse in the herd, but she'll show you her kind streak if you rub her ears and speak softly. Just the sort of animal that will have patience with your feet the way they are."

Beuntahyu stuck her nose on Aaron's shoulder and nudged him in the side of the head. He laughed and when he did, Beuntahyu snorted a powerful blast of air through her nostrils, standing his hair on end.

Ishmael said, "It's better you learn to ride on her than the one I'm giving you. She won't be spooked by a man who doesn't know how to ride." He led a brown steed out of the next stall over. "I'll ride your horse—help her get accustomed to you. Once she sees you on Beuntahyu, she'll let you onto her back without a fuss." He handed Aaron the reins to Beuntahyu. "Now for a ride around the plantation."

Ishmael helped Aaron mount up, tied his crutches onto the saddle bags, then saddled his brown steed. He led out down the path from the stables and they rode by the stockyard where Sam and Nephi were feeding the camel herd, then past the storehouse where menservants hauled cisterns of olive oil into underground vaults. The pressing yard was surrounded by a high stone wall and they rode up the rise and in through the gates to get a good view.

Servants sorted the harvest from a line of waiting mule carts. Choice olives for pickling in one basket, bruised olives for animal feed in the next, rotten olives for fertilizer in another. The rest went to the press, a large circular stone near the gate used to extract oil from olives.

The watchman of the yard stood inside the pressing bowl, knee-deep in oil-grade olives. He bent over a ball of limestone, a rounded rock that circled the bowl and was heavy enough to crush a man, if he didn't have the sense to keep clear. His hands were busy lashing a rope to the end of a pole that sprouted from the stone. A harness hung from the other end of the rope, fitted with a yoke and waiting for an ox to come and walk the stone around the press and crush the precious drops of oil from the olives.

The watchman jumped to the ground, his hand gripping the side of the pressing bowl, and green olive pulp clinging to his thighs.

Ishmael leaned over his saddle and said, "That's Lehi's eldest son." Laman's dark skin was tanned from a summer of work in the orchards. His thick arms and shoulders knew the burden of hauling olives, though his preference for city life over the strictures of country living betrayed him. The close-shaven beard that came to a point at the end of his chin did not fit these surroundings. Neither did the leather kilt with silver-threaded pleats, or the boots that he laced around his calves up to the knee. Fashion was not a farmer's convention; but for all his country living, Laman was a city boy and he wasn't shy about dressing the part. He stepped back from the press and brushed the olive pulp from his legs. His was a booming voice and when he called his younger brother to bring the ox from the stable, the head of every servant in the yard turned. They were quick to obey his voice, or at least jump every time they heard him bark a command.

Lemuel appeared from inside the shaded barn, clinging to the ox harness like a bird clutching a worm. For a nineteen-year-old man he did not endure the heat well. He scowled at the sun. His beardless face was flushed from the afternoon heat, and his glazed green eyes drooped like rotten olives. His legs were thin as harvest sticks and he led the ox to the press with a gangly stride.

Ishmael got down off his horse to inspect the olive press. The bowl was full, the crushing stone secure, and the drain grates set in place ready for the oil to flow into underground vats.

"Is that him?" Laman pointed the tip of his beard at Aaron.

"His name's Aaron," Ishmael said.

"We don't need outsiders to do work we can do ourselves."

"Your father already made the decision."

"He never asked me." Laman lashed the yoke to the ox's shoulders with a double king's knot.

"When Lehi needs your opinion, I'm sure he'll ask for it." Ishmael brushed his hand over the grate to clear it of some pulp and let the oil flow free.

"Can he walk, or do we have to carry him around? He's lame, you know."

"I'm injured," Aaron said and sat up in the saddle. He tapped the wooden crutches tied to Beuntahyu's haunches. "I'll be using these till I'm healed."

"I'm showing him the plantation," Ishmael said.

"Why the Arabian? There are thirty other horses he could ride."

"He's learning to ride on her before I give him this steed." Ishmael stroked the mane of the horse he was riding.

"Why does he need a horse?"

"Your father wants him to get around quickly. It's part of his wage."

Laman studied Aaron from his head down to the bandages. "It should be all of his wage for what that animal would cost him."

"Don't mind him," Lemuel said, stepping his thin body in front of Laman and offering Aaron his hand. "He's not fond of paying anyone what they're worth. Thinks you get your wage out of his inheritance."

"Whatever I inherit," Laman said, tying the last lash around the ox, "is thanks to my own hard work."

"He's worried," Lemuel stood beside Beuntahyu and played with the animal's bit. "You can see it in his eyes. My brother Laman is the oldest son. He'll get the best orchards, the largest home, and most of what's in Papa's treasury when he dies. That is if he's a good son and does what Papa says." He shook his head. "All that and he's still the most frugal one in the family. He'd rather fight a stranger than hire one."

"What's all this talk about inheritance," Ishmael said. "Your father may well outlast both of you by the way you drink and carry on when you go to the city." He plucked the ropes to test Laman's lashings like a harpist picking out a melody. "You should worry more about the olive harvest and less about your inheritance, or there will be precious little of either."

"We may never see it, if Papa isn't more careful with how he spends it." Laman dropped the ox reins in the dust and marched off to prepare another press for olives.

Ishmael mounted and reined in next to Aaron. "Graciousness is one of Laman's subtle traits." He coaxed his horse over to Lemuel. "We'll have to press until sundown to keep up with the pickers."

"Don't worry. We'll have the day's harvest pressed and stored before we come in for evening meal." Lemuel prodded the ox forward, starting the stone over the olives and crushing them to a meaty pulp. A drop of oil fell through the drains and into the vat below, then another and another until a stream of thick, clear-yellow liquid flowed out the base of the press. Aaron glanced over his shoulder at Laman. He was standing in the other olive press, across the yard, setting the pressing stone. Olive oil was the life-blood of Beit Zayit, and the source of all their wealth—a fortune Laman would never let go.

Not without a fight.

CHAPTER 27

Except for a light in the upper windows, the Citadel stood dark. The night watchman let Josiah inside and he climbed to the council room, his breath rising past his cheeks in short, steamy bursts. The main doors to the chamber stood open and the glow from the hearth found its way into the corridor. At least someone had the sense to set a fire and take the chill out of the air. Josiah turned into the chambers, crossed to the hearth, and stood next to the moneychanger.

"Evening, potter." The moneychanger raised his cup of wine to Josiah and stepped aside to share a place next to the fire.

"It's a cold one, to be sure." Josiah rubbed his hands near the flames. "Do you know what this is about?"

"Didn't the messenger tell you we're voting on Uriah's guilt this evening?"

Josiah pulled his hands from the flames and stuffed them under his robe. "He didn't say anything; no one said anything about this."

"You shouldn't be surprised." The moneychanger sipped on his wine. "Zadock's never been fond of Uriah."

You're certain we're to cast our votes tonight?"

"Absolutely." The moneychanger held his cup out until a chamberservant passed and filled it to the brim. He stirred his finger in the wine and licked the end of it. "Is something wrong, potter?"

Josiah removed his hands from under his robe. "Nothing at all." He quickly counted the members of the council present. Nearly all the Elders had arrived and there wasn't time to walk among them and discover their position on the matter of Uriah's treason. No time to form a coalition in support of the prophet. Josiah pulled the collar of his robe close around his neck. Why now? They didn't even hold Uriah in their prison. This was the meeting Mulek had warned him about; he was to side with the Chief Elder or risk his life.

"You look distressed." The moneychanger retrieved a wine glass from the chamberservant's tray and offered it to Josiah. "Here, have a drink. The red wine has a powerful nip to it, but after a few drinks, it won't bother you."

Josiah refused the glass and walked slowly to his chair at the council table. He didn't take his seat next to the Chief Elder. Instead, he held the backrest like a crippled man holding a cane and stared at the back of Zadock's head. In all his years as an Elder he had never crossed the man, never dissented from his opinion, never done anything that would draw the notice of the Chief Elder, and he prayed that tonight would be no different.

Zadock wore the most expensive council robes, with enough pleats to hide the moon under his raiment. He had gold rings on his fingers, a silver amulet around his neck, and emeralds embedded into the brass bands around his wrists. Did the man not have better things to do with his money than decorate his limbs and hang precious metals about his neck?

Zadock turned in his chair. "Welcome, potter. So good to see you this evening."

"Likewise, sir." Josiah lowered himself into the chair next to Zadock.

"It seems everyone has arrived but the blacksmith." Zadock clapped his hands and ordered the Elders to take their seats.

The chamberservants poured three more rounds of red wine before Jonathan the blacksmith appeared at the door. His hair was combed back and his face freshly washed, though a smudge of ash from his smelting oven blackened one cheek. A new robe sat awkwardly across his broad shoulders and the hem caught on the heel of his sandal as he crossed to his chair. He set his turban on the table in front of him, his hair too wet for the headpiece. A chamberservant poured a cup of wine and pushed it into his hand.

Jonathan took a sip, cleared his throat of the strong wine and said, "I was tending to some smithing when the messanger brought me word."

"I understand." Zadock nodded slowly. He stood and opened his hands like a mother welcoming her children home. "I'm sorry to have gathered you here on such short notice, but this matter requires our immediate attention and I have invited Captain Laban to inform us on the matter."

A soft murmur of consent fell from the lips of the Elders and it mixed with the rhythmical tapping of Laban's boots as he entered the chamber from the hallway. He circled the council table and stopped behind Jonathan. "Before the war, Uriah claimed to be a prophet; but I come to you with evidence that he is nothing more than a traitor. He sided with the enemy during the war. All of you heard him preach peace with the Babylonians even as their armies marched toward our borders." He laid his hand on Jonathan's shoulder. "We are duty bound to convict Uriah for the crime of treason." His hand fell from Jonathan's shoulder. "When the Babylonians strung their first arrows, it was Uriah who urged our submission; and when Jerusalem was put under siege, it was Uriah who encouraged our surrender. He did it, not as a prophet, but as a traitor, making sure his preaching had weakened the resolve of my fellow soldiers." He planted his fists on the hard wood between Josiah and Zadock. "There is no honor in Uriah's words of peace, just as there can be no honor in his treason. He betrayed us, he betrayed an entire nation, and now it is our solemn duty to hold him accountable."

Zadock pushed his chair from the table and stood beside Laban. "The captain is sending a search party to bring Uriah to justice."

The moneychanger asked, "Where will you begin your search?"

"Beit Zayit." Laban rested his hands on his hips.

"The olive oil merchants?"

"Our spies tell us that Uriah may have gone that way."

"That's absurd." The silk dealer rested his chin in his hand. "Why would Uriah go to Lehi's plantation? He's a fine merchant, one of the wealthiest in Judah. He would never help a traitor."

"Hear me!" Laban took a deep breath while the murmuring quieted. "What Lehi did or did not do isn't important. Our mission is to find Uriah and bring him to justice."

"Enough questions, gentlemen." Zadock turned on his cushioned seat and faced Jonathan. "We begin with the last Elder first. How do you vote, blacksmith?"

Jonathan cleared his throat and said, "I'm not as familiar with the matter as are the rest of you."

"Laban has explained Uriah's guilt." Zadock said the words slowly, his high-pitched voice ringing across the chamber.

"How should I vote?"

"Yea or Nay."

Jonathan fitted his headpiece over his still wet hair. "You say he committed treason?"

"He did."

"And exactly what do our laws say about that crime?"

Zadock tightened his grip on the chain of his amulet and it pulled taut around his neck. "Death by beheading."

Jonathan's gaze flitted about the council room, but there was no one returning a sympathetic gesture. He leaned back into his chair and said, "Guilty."

Zadock asked for the vote of the silk dealer next. The man mumbled his thanks to Zadock for reducing the tax on imported goods before agreeing to Uriah's guilt. Two votes to execute, none to stay. The gold merchant owed Zadock his appointment to the Council. The caravaneer owed him nearly ten talents of gold for new stock. The moneychanger was a calculating man with a narrow stare, whose vote Josiah could never predict with any degree of certainty. But there was the matter of his weights and measures, and Zadock was the only man in Jerusalem with power to revoke his scales. The moneychanger sat in silence long enough that Josiah thought him a dissenter, but he sided with the others, and the final junior Elder immediately registered his vote. The tally stood at six in favor of beheading, none to stay.

The silver trader, the owner of the granary, the spice trader, and the mill owner were all supporters of the Chief Elder, and who wouldn't support a man who offered gold in exchange for a vote now and again? Bribery was a costly way to do business, but Zadock could afford the price. They quietly agreed to Uriah's guilt and the vote stood at ten in favor, none to stay. Only the potter's vote remained untallied. He pulled on his chin with thumb and forefinger and said, "I'm not convinced of Uriah's guilt."

A flurry of murmurs passed through the chamber, which Zadock quieted by waving his thin fingers, wisping narrow shadows over the table. He said, "I'll have your vote, potter. How say you?"

Josiah rubbed his palms together and said, "All we know about Uriah are rumors."

Zadock said, "The man escaped."

"What does that prove?"

"His guilt."

Josiah said, "There's so little evidence."

"Treason is a simple crime."

"Does not the law require at least two witnesses to make a case against a man?" Josiah leaned over the table. "We've heard only Laban speak to his guilt."

Laban said, "All of us here heard him preach and we all stand as witnesses to his treason."

Josiah inched to the edge of his chair. "We don't even hold Uriah in our prison."

Zadock stood beside Laban and said, "We will."

"Then I say we wait until then and convene a proper trial."

"The matter will be decided tonight."

"Without a trial, sir?"

Zadock ruffled the pleats in his robe. "You're stretching what little patience I have."

"Is there a reason to have so little?"

"Do you support Uriah?"

Josiah gripped the armrest. "I only question the timing of our vote."

"Traitors in this kingdom should be dealt with swiftly."

"The war's been over for eight months."

"I know that." Zadock walked to Josiah's chair. "How do you vote?"

"I suppose I have little choice."

"Then you agree with the rest of the Council?"

"I've always followed your lead."

"Very wise of you, potter."

Josiah stood, pushing his chair away, the legs grating on the floor, "I say Uriah is innocent."

Zadock stood by the hearth, warming himself until well after Josiah and the council members had taken their leave. Laban poured a glass of wine, gently rocked it in his hand and said, "I thought you had the Elders under control."

"I do." Zadock kept his gaze turned toward the flames. "The potter was the last one I would have suspected."

"I'll find out what I can about him."

"No need, Captain." Zadock stirred the coals with a brass poker. "I already have someone watching him."

"Who?"

"His maidservant, the Ethiopian woman they call Mima. I've been paying her to keep an eye on the potter."

"Has she ever reported any suspicions?"

"Nothing."

"Apparently you haven't been paying her enough." Laban rocked the glass one last time before downing the wine.

Zadock adjusted the amulet around his neck. "I'll arrange a meeting. She can help you."

"With what?" Laban asked.

"Ridding us of the potter."

"You need his vote to behead Uriah."

"There are other ways to make it unanimous." Zadock hung the fire poker from its hook beside the mantle. "Make it look like an accident."

Daniel leaned out the commissary window and sized up the recruits marching past in double file columns. Nearly a hundred from front to back, but only a handful were to become officers, while the rest would end up foot soldiers, rotting in distant outposts along Judah's borders.

"What's your rank?"

Daniel pulled back inside the musty storeroom and faced Jedediah, the quartermaster, whose tunic hardly covered his round belly. "Do I need one?"

"That's not an answer." An impatient tapping sounded under the table. It was Jedediah's boot on the floor. "You foot soldiers are a brash lot. You grow out of a uniform before you wear it out, lose it before you put it on or tear it to shreds before you've gotten a month's use out of it." He leaned over the table and examined Daniel's sandal-shod feet. "You've gone and lost your boots, have you?" He waddled to the shelves and rummaged through the supply of leather footwear. "What's your size?" He looked at Daniel, but didn't wait for an answer. "About a palm and five fingers, I'd say." He found a pair and dropped them on the table in front of Daniel. "What else?"

"I suppose a tunic and kilt like the others."

"You suppose? What did you do with yours, lose it in a game of chance?"

"I was told to report here first thing this morning."

"Name?"

"Daniel, son of Jonathan the blacksmith."

Jedediah's head came up. "Why didn't you say so, boy?"

"I just did."

"I mean, why didn't you say you were the officer to be outfitted for the mission?"

"I'm not. I've come to train with the recruits."

"There's been a change." Jedediah hefted to the table a leather saddlebag packed with bedding, an officer's cloak with hood, a leather kilt with metal plates woven into the seams, and four military tunics with silver officer's stripes along the shoulders, one blue the other three brown. "These should last until you get back."

"From where?"

Jedediah pushed the plume over the papyrus ledger, itemizing the riggings next to the title, Daniel son of Jonathan the blacksmith, officer, first class. "Just don't go around wearing that blue tunic anywhere you please. It's for dress. The three brown ones are for riding."

"Riding?"

"Your new horse. The stable master will see that your mount's rigged and ready for you when you leave." Jedediah bent under the table and came back up with a bridle, a riding kilt with leather chaps to keep a man's legs from wearing raw in the saddle and a length of new rope. "You know how to use these, don't you?"

"Don't all the officers?" Daniel slowly passed his hand over the riding gear. He'd never ridden a horse, never saddled one, never stabled one, and never known anyone who had.

"You've never ridden a horse, have you?" Jedediah said. "I've seen that look before."

"What look?"

"Laban had it when he picked up his first set of riggings." Jedediah nodded. "The captain never rode a horse before he mounted his white stallion in front of the entire regiment. There he was, outfitted in full dress with a red plume in his cap. Nearly got himself pitched right into the mud. But he was sturdier than most boys, strong enough to stay in the saddle that day and savvy enough to break and ride the most stubborn horses in the king's cavalry over the last fourteen years. He made an animal respect him, he did." Jedediah took down a blade from the weapon rack. It was a short sword, not much longer than a dagger. He'd mended a good number of them, but not for many soldiers. They hid well under a kilt and down a boot leg, but military men preferred broad swords. Longer blades kept men at a respectable distance. Daniel took the weapon from Jedediah and hefted it in his hands. He knew why he was issued the shortest sword on the rack. He'd have to prove himself to Laban before he got a broad sword. Only the finest officers sheathed long blades at their waist.

The short sword had a newly sharpened single edge and a hilt bearing the inscription: *the king's army.* It was smelted of low grade ore, not an impressive-looking blade and hardly reliable enough not to break in battle. "Your father sharpened this a few weeks back. It was Laban's first sword. Issued it to him on his first day, but he doesn't use it any more. He brought it in and told me to issue it to you." He handed it to Daniel. "It's yours. There's bound to be trouble where you're going."

"Exactly where is that?"

"I'll let the captain explain." Jedediah stood to attention as Laban turned in to the commissary and marched over in three long strides.

Jedediah leaned over the table and the two men shook hands. "You're here early today, Captain."

"Have you given the boy his things?" Laban asked.

"Everything but a horse."

"I'll take care of him from here." Laban took the old sword from Daniel's pack and held it in both hands. "I was about your age when Jedediah here issued me this sword."

Daniel said, "I can't take that from you, sir."

"I'm giving it to you." Laban handed it to Daniel and he ran his finger over the sharpened edge. Laban said, "It isn't much of a blade, but it should do for your first mission."

"What sort of mission?"

Laban motioned for him to gather his equipment. "Come with me."

Daniel followed Laban down the hall and through the main lobby to a tall cedar door with sheaves of wheat carved into the wood. Laban ushered Daniel inside to a straight-back chair set before a long desk. He sat against the backrest while Laban circled him. After the Captain made his second pass he said, "I'm taking a risk with you." He circled the chair again. "I don't normally do this, but I want you working with my best men." He glanced toward the window. The cries of recruits training on the grounds streamed through the opening. "Not with the other boys."

"I'll handle this from here, Captain." A man standing in the shadows spoke with a voice to make goat's milk curdle. He wasn't a soldier, the outline of his form was too frail and officers didn't wear cumbersome turbans like the headpiece capping his brow. Daniel recognized Zadock from his father's induction. The Elder's black robe was all cuffs, pleats, and skirts, the kind of frills a weaver like Mama would have studied endlessly.

Zadock had dark rings below his eyes like a man who never slept and he walked over with a rigid stride. "In order to make the rank of officer in this army you have to be more than a great wrestler or an expert horseman. You have to know someone or be something special. That's how Laban got where he is."

Daniel braced against the backrest. "Which am I, sir?"

"Both." Zadock bent close, the smell of fatted lamb on his breath, and Daniel willed himself not to recoil. The man said, "You look as I remember Laban the day we first met. I gave him his chance in this army and look where our friendship has gotten him. Only thirty years old and he's captain of the guard."

"Do you train soldiers?" Daniel asked.

He smiled a flat sort of smile, the kind that barely turned the corners of his mouth. "Let's just say I know a good soldier when I see one. You'll do well in this army as long as you know who gives the orders." He glanced at Laban. "Isn't that right, Captain?"

Laban didn't answer. He crossed to a waiting room off the main office and reached for the latch. "You're going on a mission, under the command of Captain Elnathan, my finest scout." He opened the door and there, framed between the posts, stood a man wearing a thick leather tunic and kilt. The guards on his forearms protected him from the recoil of a large bow he carried strapped to his shoulders. His eyes were dark and piercing like those of an eagle, and he scanned Laban's office before entering and standing next to the Chief Elder. "I didn't expect to see you here."

"This mission is more important than the others," Zadock said and plucked the string of Elnathan's bow. "If Uriah gets away this time, there will be an enormous price to pay."

"I understand."

Zadock lifted the hem of his robe. "Are there any other questions, gentlemen?"

When no one said a word, Zadock slipped into the hallway and disappeared around the corner without a sound. It was an odd way to leave the room, but the Chief Elder was an odd sort of man without the pomp you'd expect in a man of his standing. Mysterious was the best word for him. Not even his sandals made a shuffle on the stone hallway. No, he wasn't mysterious, he was powerful and he didn't need to make a dramatic parting. One day Daniel would leave a room like the Chief Elder left this room. The silence of his power left a thundering impression.

Elnathan closed the door. "Is this the boy?" He laid a hand on Daniel's.

"Sir." Daniel raised out of his chair, clipping the captain's bowstring arm with a hard shoulder. "Sorry, sir."

Elnathan held his forearm and turned to Laban. "The boy's untrained."

"He can wrestle."

"Does he ride?"

"He'll learn."

"Can he shoot?"

"He's strong enough to pull ten bowstrings with one hand."

Elnathan leaned on the desk with two fists. "You've been drinking again."

"Why don't you wrestle the boy and find out how strong he is for yourself."

"I need experienced men for this mission."

"Daniel shows promise."

Elnathan slid his fists across the hardwood toward Laban. He said, "Promise can get us killed."

"He learns quickly."

"I won't be his nursemaid."

"Take him under your wing and train him like a son."

"I don't have any sons, sir."

"You do now."

Elnathan stood straight. "Is that an order?"

"You're my finest scout." Laban came around his desk. "I want the boy to hear what you hear and smell what you smell and see what you see when you track a man across hundreds of miles of desert sand."

"I'm not tracking anyone anywhere until I investigate this matter further."

"I've already done that for you. The search for Uriah begins at Beit Zayit."

"The olive plantation?"

"Uriah went through there a few weeks back."

Elnathan turned to Daniel. "What do you know about riding?"

"My father owns a mule."

"Curses, boy! We don't ride mules." Elnathan went to the door. "Be ready to leave the first of next week."

"Yes, sir." Daniel stood to attention. "I'll have everything in order."

Elnathan circled Daniel and he didn't flinch, didn't even take a breath. Daniel tightened every muscle and set his jaw steady as a soldier should.

Elnathan spoke with a scowl. He said, "Break in your horse by then." He turned with a click of his heels against the stone floor and marched into the hall.

Laban took the blue tunic from Daniel's pack and tossed the newly woven officer's shirt at him. "You'll have to prove yourself to Elnathan if you want to keep this."

"How do I do that?"

"Capture Uriah." Laban sat and rested his boots on the table. "Dismissed."

CHAPTER 28

Why was Aaron allowed to sleep on such a fine bed? There was plenty of lodging in the servants' quarters down the road from Lehi's estate. But here he slept, on a bed with enough quilts and pillows to sleep five, and Aaron was without any of his brothers to divide the comfort among them. The guest bed was raised off the floor with legs of cedar, and the mattress was supported by a hundred cords crisscrossing the frame like threads on Ruth's loom. It was soft as the clouds with cedar bedposts sprouting from the corners like columns holding up a canopied sky of lace and linen.

Aaron turned onto his side and the wooden joists creaked. The sound startled his eyes open. This was not a dream, no matter how much it felt like one not to have the hard ground and reed mats he slept on at home cut into his slumber. Bright yellow rays of sun filtered through the slats in the balcony shutters, and through the windows the sounds of carts clattering over the cobblestones in front of the estate worked their way into his consciousness. The whisk of the gardeners' brooms and the rustle of leaves carried up from the yard on the crisp air as did the distant chanting of pickers harvesting the last olive vineyards high on the foothills. Aaron sat up in bed and rubbed his eyes. Was he the only one in all Beit Zayit still idling away in bed?

Aaron rolled out and doused his face in the water basin before stirring in three spoonfuls of jasmine powders. Sariah promised they would soften his skin and Aaron was willing to try anything to lessen the pain of changing bandages. She was right; the remedy soothed his burns and he tied on fresh linens with hardly a shot of pain.

A firm knock came at the door and a maidservant called through the wooden slats. Aaron was to see Lehi before going to work in the smithy. That was a fine thing. He'd slept well past a proper waking time, his eyes were still filled with the sands of sleep; and since today was his first full day at Beit Zayit, he hadn't a single piece of smithing work he could report finished. Even if he'd started, he wouldn't have gotten nearly as much finished as other smiths. Why had Lehi even bothered to hire a crippled blacksmith? Papa swung a firmer hammer; Daniel possessed arms strong enough to forge for a full day without tiring, and both of them walked about without crutches. It was pure nonsense to believe Aaron was as fit as they were for hire. Lame men did slow work.

When Aaron didn't open the bedroom door immediately, the maidservant knocked again and said Lehi would see him now. Aaron quickly eased his feet into his sandals, unlatched the bolt and followed her down the stairs on his crutches, stopping once to comply with her request that he comb his hair with his fingers and a second time to tuck his tunic under his belt. It wasn't every day he would be permitted to speak with a man of such wealth and it was only proper he be presentable.

The door to the map room stood open and Aaron went in ahead of the maidservant. Rows of tall shelves divided the room into narrow walkways, each one stacked with colorful Egyptian storage jars. She explained there were sales agreements down one row, accounting records down another, and on the third were maps for caravanning olive oil. The last row of shelves held jars of a more personal nature. Diaries and family records, each one embossed with the name of a child—Rachel the oldest, Leah the second child, then four sons, Laman, Lemuel, Sam, and Nephi.

She directed him past the last stand of shelves, over to where the room became a storied mezzanine of high ceilings with a large window opening onto a view of the plantation. The morning sun cast a good reading light over a gentleman seated in a wicker chair. It was Lehi, and his arms spanned the width from armrest to armrest like the long branches of a sturdy olive tree. He had a straight jaw that ended in a well-groomed tuft of healthy black beard covering his chin, the only growth on his otherwise beardless face. His thick black hair was neatly parted to one side, reaching to just above his left ear in the style popular among Egyptian businessmen. He had dark, tanned cheeks stamped with two deeply cut dimples that gave the appearance of a permanent smile. His green eyes were dry wells drinking in the words of the scroll he cradled in his hands.

Aaron was careful to stay on the rugs to keep the sound of his crutches from disturbing Lehi. But now he was unsure whether the man even knew he was there. He stepped closer, peered over the plantation owner's shoulder and read the reformed Egyptian scrawled on the papyrus. It was an order for olive oil signed by the pharaoh of Egypt himself.

Lehi took a pen from the inkwell, lodged it between his thumb and forefinger and noted the size of the delivery in his ledger. Fifty camels, each one bearing six cisterns of the highest-grade olive oil.

"You're a lucky man if you know how to read demotic." Lehi spoke without looking up from his scroll. He dipped his pen in the inkwell. "Memphis couldn't have taught you to read in one day. He's a good teacher, but not that good."

Aaron turned away from the scroll. "We had an Egyptian fire boy in our shop in Sidon."

"Good for you, son. It's the language of business, the language of the future. And there's no greater blessing for a Hebrew boy like yourself than getting a talent for reading it." Lehi put the tip of the pen to the papyrus and continued writing. "After work's finished, I'll expect you tonight for evening meal with the rest of the family."

"But, I—"

"You're my guest."

Lehi leaned over the armrest, took his first studied look at Aaron, and his smile immediately disappeared. The lines around his eyes flattened, his red cheeks fell and he stared for such a long time that Aaron would have backed his crutches a step if Lehi hadn't reached and taken him by the arm. His were worn hands, the only visible signs of age on his youthful, forty-six-year-old frame. They were leathery and creased from years of reining caravans over miles of untamed desert lands. He studied every contour and line in Aaron's face before he said, "It is you, isn't it?"

"I'm Aaron, sir." He straightened on the crutches as best he could without putting too much weight on his feet. "I'm the man you hired as a blacksmith."

"I knew you'd come. I was certain of it."

"It was mostly my father's decision. He has the last word on the smithing I take on away from the shop."

"How is the work going? Do you have any idea how long it will take Sam and Nephi to ready our caravans for Egypt?"

"Not exactly." Aaron paused, searching for the right words to explain his late start on the day. "Sam was to bring the first round of work by the smithy this morning." He scratched the back of his head. "I should have a good idea what it will take by midday."

Lehi tapped the tip of his pen on the ledger. "What about your feet?"

"They won't get in the way. I smith from a bench. It's really quite simple once you get used to swinging a hammer sitting down. If you'd like I can show you how it's done." Aaron gripped the handholds on his crutches. "If you're worried about me finishing before you and your sons head to—

"Egypt," Lehi said and raised his hand to stop Aaron from speaking. "We're caravanning to Egypt and I want you to go with us, but that's something we can discuss another time."

Go with them? Aaron rubbed his palms over the hand-hold on his crutches. If Lehi only knew how difficult it had been for Aaron to get permission to come here, he'd not ask more. It would have been easier to raise Moses from the dead and have him part the Red Sea a second time than to convince Jonathan that Aaron should accompany Lehi on a caravan to Egypt.

Lehi said, "What I want to know right now is about your accident. How did it happen?"

"Oh, that." Aaron rubbed the back of his neck. "There isn't much I remember." That was the best answer, one Papa would approve of. He would never allow Aaron to tell a stranger what he did remember. He'd already done that with Rebekah, and a secret shared isn't a secret at all.

Lehi set down his pen, put aside his scroll and leaned over the armrest to run both hands along the double cedar poles in each crutch. They were crafted out of dried timbers, none of them smoothed with a carpenter's lathe, and if Aaron wasn't careful with his stride he could pierce his skin with slivers, something he'd done not less than once a day. The top end of each crutch was batted with a white linen cushion that had gone yellow from sweat, but he had never removed them; he didn't want his underarms to rub raw against the bare end. The wooden handholds were lashed too high for his long arms, though he never had the inclination to remove the leather lashings and lower them a few fingers down the poles. Instead, he carried himself with his arms, strengthening them with every step. And he did seem to be getting stronger. Aaron's arms filled the sleeves of his tunic more than before and Ruth said they didn't look nearly as spindly as they did last year at harvest time.

For all their inventive design, these knotted timbers didn't merit Lehi's admiration; but there he sat, leaning from his chair and quietly considering the workmanship. In a breathless whisper he said, "Sam didn't mention these."

"I was using a cane when he came by looking to hire me. They're an invention of my father's making. It's easier to get around on these." Aaron didn't tell Lehi that he couldn't even walk without them, a fact more painful than the burns or the bleeding or even the infections that swelled his feet. It was his limp, his horrible limp that he cursed most—and the crutches reminding him every day that he was not a whole man.

Lehi raised himself from his chair nobly, like a king standing from a throne, his flowing blue robes draped over straight shoulders and gathered in a train on the ground. He stood at Aaron's side and said, "Nahum was the first to be treated like the prophets of old."

Aaron glanced around the room. There were expensive rugs, finely crafted reading chairs, and shelves filled with writings that only the wealthiest merchants could acquire. This was the estate of a prosperous businessman, not the dwelling of a man who fretted about the plight of a few holy men. Certainly not in these days and Aaron couldn't keep from asking, "Excuse me, sir. What does that have to do with crutches?"

Lehi left him and walked to the window, his long blue train following him over the stone floor. "The Chief Elder said the crime was blasphemy." He shook his head. "But Nahum never spoke a word of evil except to point out Zadock's crimes." Lehi was looking out the window, the back of his head turned to Aaron; but by the sadness in his voice Aaron could tell he was not pleased with the treatment of that prophet. Lehi said, "Men will do evil when they have evil to hide." He folded his arms across his chest, the long cuffs from his robe hanging down to his waist. "Zephaniah lived longer than the other prophets. I think he was sixty when he disappeared. No one ever knew what happened to him. Some say he was taken to heaven in a chariot of fire like Elijah, but there was no chariot. There's never been a chariot for any of these dead prophets." He pressed the cloth of his cuffs between his fingers. "The prophet Habakkuk would still be alive if the people of Jerusalem had enough courage to put an end to this slaughter of the men of God. And now that Uriah has escaped, Zadock will surely go after the prophet Jeremiah. And it won't end there."

Aaron crossed to the window and stood at an angle where he could see Lehi's face. It was a solemn look, his lips pressed lightly together and his eyes turned down. Aaron said, "I thought Jeremiah and Uriah were the last prophets left in Judah."

"If they are, then I pity the people of Jerusalem. The wrath of God is not a pleasant thing."

"And what if Uriah and Jeremiah aren't the last prophets?"

"Then I pity the man God sends in their place." Lehi raised his head and cast his gaze out over the vineyards, but he was really looking past the olive trees toward the capital, beyond the steep yellow sandstone hills that framed this valley. "These are dark days in Jerusalem, son. The darkest I've ever known."

A cool breeze streamed in through the open window and Aaron folded his arms to warm himself against the chill. "Why are you telling me this?"

Lehi took hold of the left crutch and Aaron felt his trembling. It passed through the wooden pole, and into the leather-strapped handles. The shaking was hardly visible, but Aaron could feel it as powerfully as if he were holding Lehi's hand. Behind the olive oil merchant's strong, tanned face and striking green eyes there was fear and it had something to do with the recent deaths of the prophets.

Lehi said, "God will send another prophet to face the Elders, and I fear it will be . . ."

Aaron leaned over his crutch. "Who, sir?"

Lehi removed his hand from Aaron's crutch. "Look at me, keeping you from your work. You have blacksmithing and I have ledgers to fill." He returned to sit in his chair and take up his pen, but he didn't go back to writing. He was gazing out the window, beyond the bluffs that separated Beit Zayit from Jerusalem.

Aaron quietly dismissed himself, but when he reached the threshold, he stopped with the end of one crutch in the map room and the other in the hall and asked, "Will that be all, sir?"

Lehi kept staring toward Jerusalem.

"Excuse me?" Aaron tapped the end of the crutch against the floor once. When Lehi didn't respond he tapped twice more and asked, "Is there anything else, sir?"

"There is one thing." Lehi turned his head slowly from the window. "Your presence here comforts me."

Aaron stayed in the threshold until Lehi turned back to his ledger, then he moved out into the hall and started toward the back door, placing the ends of his crutches quietly against the stones. What troubled Lehi that he would need anyone's comfort, least of all Aaron's? He reached the back door and stepped out into the frigid morning air, his breath visible with each step. He started down the path through the line of trees toward the smithy. What sort of peace did Lehi think Aaron could provide?

He was a blacksmith, not a priest.

A stand of trees hid the irregular lines of the smithy's roof, keeping it out of sight from the estate. Aaron came down the path and around the last tree to find a line of smoke pouring from the chimney and hovering over the roof like a dense fog. The door stood ajar, but when Aaron got inside, the smithy was empty except for the stack of tools that needed mending. This late in the year, morning frost gripped the earth and he warmed his hands near the flames, thankful for whoever shaved the kindling and sparked the flint.

The smithy had nothing but a dirt floor to catch the metal tailings; there was no coal hamper or ore bin and little room to move about, though all Aaron needed was a forging table close to the fire so he could reach both without standing from the bench. He took a deep breath and drank in the morning air that drafted between the wood slats and out the door. Thank heaven the chimney didn't leak. There was nothing worse than working inside a smoke-filled smithy all day.

Aaron laid his crutches on the bench next to him, sat up to the forging table and picked up the axe, not for any reason in particular except that it sat atop the pile. It had a large crack and there wasn't much he could do to salvage it. Tomorrow he'd smelt ore for a new one. He examined the swathing lathe next. It didn't have anything wrong except a few nicks, nothing a good heating and hammering wouldn't cure. Sam had told him the servant who brought it in was too lazy to harvest the last stand of hay. He said something about having enough in the barns to last three winters. Aaron would heat the lathe next, hammer out the nicks, maybe grind a new edge and polish it with a greased cloth to make it shine so bright the servant wouldn't have any excuse but to finish the swathing.

A movement in the darkest corner, over beyond the tong racks, drew Aaron's eye. Light from the fire danced across the face of a young man with black bangs hanging over a blue headband. It was Nephi and he'd been there all this time, not saying a word, not making a sound. Aaron said, "You didn't need to go to all that work of setting a fire. I need to earn my keep."

"You're a guest here."

"Why do you and your father say that?"

Nephi came around the open hearth, his powerful fifteen-year-old frame lit by the flames. Coals fell from the charred logs, drafting heat up in waves and lifting Nephi's hair off his brow. "Did he tell you why you're a guest in our family?"

"We talked about blacksmithing." Aaron set the lathe over the coals. "He wanted to know about my accident, that's all."

Nephi was kind enough to pump the bellows until the metal took on a deep red glow. "Is that all he said?"

"Is there more?" Aaron turned the lathe with tongs.

"It's just that, well . . ." Nephi stopped pumping the bellows. "My father worries about the way things are in Jerusalem."

"He shouldn't talk about the prophets the way he does if he wants to keep out of trouble with the Elders. My father would never allow it. He says it isn't a wise thing to be doing."

"And what do you say?"

Aaron took the lathe from the coals and began tapping the forging hammer over the hairline cracks in the metal. "It doesn't matter what I say."

"They're dead you know, at least most of them."

Aaron set down the forging hammer, pushed aside the lathe. "Must you and your father keep reminding me of that?"

Nephi laid his hand over the head of the hammer, pressing the stock against the forging table. "My father could be the next man God calls to preach repentance to the people of Jerusalem."

"You don't really believe that." Aaron stirred the coals with a poker. "Your father's an olive oil merchant, not a prophet."

"I didn't say he was, only that he could become one." Nephi sat on the bench next to Aaron. "He's not been shown the *Sod*, like the other prophets."

"What are you talking about?"

"The Council of Heaven." Nephi raised his hands and they danced like a storyteller's in front of him. "The place where God meets with his holy angels to discuss the doings of men on earth." He inched closer to Aaron, his shoulder pushing against his side. "Angels are messengers sent to earth to reveal to men what they hear fall from the lips of God during the meetings of the Council."

"Your father speaks with angels?"

"God doesn't always speak to his prophets through angels." Nephi's hands moved faster and he quickened the pace of his words. "You see, many of the holy prophets since the beginning of the world have been carried away in vision to see the Council of Heaven. And once they've been shown the *Sod,* they're prophets of God—because they know His will and heard it fall from His lips."

Aaron inched down the bench, placing some distance between them. He said, "And you think your father will be called like the other prophets?"

"He worries about it. He had a dream his life was in danger because he was called to preach repentance to the people of Jerusalem."

"It isn't a good time to be taking up that sort of work." Aaron moved farther down the bench and stabbed the lathe back into the coals.

"What I've told you troubles you, doesn't it?"

Aaron turned the lathe hard, knocking coals from the open hearth onto the floor. "I have work to do."

"You need to hear me out; you need to know this."

"Maybe some other time." Aaron turned away, took the lathe from the coals and began pounding the metal, filling the shop with a loud ringing. He brought the hammer down again and again, the lathe bouncing up from the table with each blow. He intended to find out more about the prophets, but not now, not here, and not from these people. They weren't Rekhabites, but they were enough like them he wasn't sure he could trust them in religious matters.

Nephi stood up from the bench and walked to the door of the smithy. The morning sun had broken through the fog and light filtered through a crack in the door. He pushed the door full open, the creaking hinges mingling with the steady clang of Aaron's hammering. Nephi started into the yard, but turned back when Aaron stopped pounding on the metal. The smithy fell silent and Aaron asked, "Why do I need to know?"

"In my father's dream . . ." Nephi came back to the door, the sun casting a golden light over his broad frame. "His life was saved by a man who had once walked with crutches but had been made whole."

Aaron's arms went limp and he dropped the forging hammer to his side. It wasn't Uriah or Jeremiah he was to save, but Lehi. A man God had yet to call as a prophet. He brushed the ash off his brow, stood on his crutches and slowly picked his way to the door. There was a reason he'd come to Beit Zayit to work for the olive oil merchant, but it had little to do with blacksmithing. Lehi was the answer to healing his feet, the reason for his blessing.

Aaron reached for Nephi's hand, but his right crutch came loose from under his arm and fell on the ground between them.

Nephi steadied Aaron with a firm grip. "Do you understand why my father thinks of you as his guest?"

"If only I weren't a cripple."

"Injured," Nephi said, and picked Aaron's crutch out of the dirt. "You're going to heal."

"Is that why Sariah wants my feet dipped in powder baths?"

"Mother feels it's her duty to do what she can." Nephi fitted the crutch under Aaron's arm. "We all do."

Aaron never should have started heating another bridle bit if he wanted to arrive on time for family dinner. Sariah said evening meal would be served promptly at sunset. He quickly finished mending the cracked metal and when he emerged from the smithy, the sun slipped below the western hills. The lamps inside the estate were burning brightly as he entered. Certainly the families of Lehi and Ishmael would be gathered and waiting for him. But thankfully all he heard was the voice of one of the servants. They were setting out the food before the families arrived and Aaron hurried over to ask them how much longer before dinner. He could still go to his room and clean up. And he did need a good bath after his first day of work. Elizabeth and Sarah always teased that he looked like the angel of death at the end of a workday, his face and arms covered with soot, his brow salted and his white teeth shimmering in contrast to the dark ash. It usually took two or three dunkings in a washbasin to get his hair to sit down after sweating into his scalp all day. Aaron ran his fingers through his hair. Tonight would be no different. The rising heat from the open hearth had blown his hair on end and it had dried as firm as a pillar of salt on the shores of the Dead Sea. It would take more than three dunkings before his hair was civil enough to attend evening meal with the families of Lehi and Ishmael.

The dining room stood directly on Aaron's path to the stairs and the servant's voice droned from inside. Aaron stopped at the threshold, stood between the open doors and leaned inside to ask the servant when he should come to dinner, but it wasn't a servant at all. It was Lehi. He sat at the head of the table next to his cousin Ishmael and addressed the members of both families. But when Aaron appeared at the doorway, all eyes turned toward him.

Aaron said, "I was on my way to wash up." He pointed to the stairs that led up to his room.

The small head of Lehi's grandson, Simon, began to rise from below the level of the tabletop. He had light brown hair like his mother Leah and when his brow crested over the wood horizon, Aaron could see his high hairline. Simon leaned over his plate and studied Aaron's bandaged feet, and when Aaron shifted his stance, Simon's gaze followed. Without a cry, or scream, or any warning, the boy jumped from his chair. His mother was helpless to stop him with her arms wrapped around her newborn babe. Simon came down behind the line of chairs, his short three-year-old legs pumping in a furious rhythm with his arms. He filled his red cheeks with air and puffed his way past the outstretched arms of his father then past Uncles Laman and Lemuel, giggling as he went and swinging his arms more wildly with each adult he eluded. Sam tried to scoot his chair out from the table and block the boy's way, but Simon jumped through the narrow opening between the backrest and the stone wall. Uncle Nephi caught the boy in his powerful arms and it seemed his game had come to an end. Simon groaned, then twisted free with the determination of a fish swimming upstream and headed around the foot of the table at full speed. Grandma Sariah and Grandma Isabel were ready to pick him up in their outstretched arms, as if his run around the table was a mealtime ritual. Simon darted under Grandma Isabel's arms and when Grandma Sariah reached to rein him in, Simon turned sharp to miss her. He fell flat, belly first with arms and legs spread like a bird in flight and slid across the floor.

Simon's nose stopped three fingers shy of Aaron's bandages. With a near-sighted stare and a gentle forefinger stroking the side of Aaron's feet, Simon asked, "Are these what Grandma Sariah asked us to pray about?"

Aaron looked down at Simon, his tiny legs sprawled out behind him and his gentle finger barely touching the bandages. Aaron said, "I need all the prayers I can get."

The family erupted with laughter—all but the two eldest sons. Laman turned his head into his plate and Aaron could only assume that he was less than pleased with his family's warm reception of the blacksmith from Jerusalem. To Laman, Aaron must seem a parasite, feeding on the family fortune.

Lemuel wasn't as interested in Aaron as he was the bowl of cut melons set in front of his plate. He stole two pieces of fruit and washed them down with a quick drink from his glass before the laughter quieted.

Aaron said, "I'll wash up and be down in a moment."

"Pray with us first." Sariah took Aaron by the arm and led him to sit between her and Isabel. "You can wash up after." She settled into the chair next to Aaron, and Lehi stood at the head of the table and asked the servants to bring in the roasted lamb he had prepared. An offering like this was a gesture usually reserved for moments of deep gratitude or to welcome the most honored guests.

It was a good-sized fatted yearling, cleaned and skewered by Lehi himself. It would have been simpler for him to order his servants to prepare the meal, but he insisted on a peace offering and he was obliged to do it with his own hands, a rite of preparation all good Jews observed. He had tended the fire during the afternoon and turned the lamb on the spit. And now it was his duty to mix the drippings with a bowl of garnish and sprinkle it over the lamb.

The family bowed their heads and Lehi said, "We thank thee, Lord, for the goodness of this food." His voice was soft, but steady. He thanked God for the blessings of family and friends before Aaron realized he was the only one with head not bowed. Papa had never offered a family prayer in their home and he found himself struck by the scene of every member of Lehi's family praying together. It was as if, for a short moment, twenty-odd people were joined as one through prayer and all Aaron could do was memorize every word—every inflection that testified this was not the first time Lehi had raised his voice to heaven.

Lehi said, "We thank thee for having Aaron in our midst, for his talent at blacksmithing and ask a blessing upon him." Lehi opened his eyes and glanced up at Aaron. Their gaze met and immediately an unspoken bond formed between them. Without closing his eyes, Lehi prayed, "Bless our friend with thy healing power, and return to him his feet, whole and well so that he may walk without crutches and live without pain."

The amen sounded. Lehi's lips turned up into a smile and his dimples returned, cutting deep into his cheeks. It was a prayer from the olive oil merchant's heart, a gesture of his thanks to God for Aaron.

It was Lehi's peace offering.

CHAPTER 29

Ruth steered the mule cart through the gates of the palace delivery yard without the guards questioning her or the children. Only merchants, farmers, and craftsmen were permitted to pass—and of course Ruth, "the weaver" as she was known to the gatekeeper. She held her head high and accepted the man's hails, letting him believe she was here to see the queen about weaving and nothing more than weaving.

Inside the delivery yard, another shipment of food for the coronation celebration had arrived. Burlap sacks brimming full of olives, nuts, dates, and figs were stacked higher than a camel's head along the receiving deck, waiting to be hauled into the cool preserving recesses of the palace's underground storage bins. A farmer unloaded sacks of wheat, winnowed until not even a hint of chaff remained. Only the finest harvest was sold to the royal family and its court.

With the coronation drawing closer, Ruth came and went no less than three times a week, picking up deliveries of silks from the Orient, gold buttons from the mines of Arabia and always another measurement for the queen's robe. It was always one more measurement for Miriam, though this trip she decided on a different tack to avoid suspicion. Today she'd use the delivery of shellfish as cover. No one would question a side trip inside the palace to discuss with Miriam exactly how dark a purple dye should be prepared from the newly arrived shipment of clams.

When the overseer saw Ruth and the children, he left his post and offered to hoist the cisterns of live shellfish onto the bed of her cart.

He strained against the weight of the first water-filled jar, pushing it past Sarah and Joshua and sloshing water over the floorboards. The salty smell reminded Ruth of the docks of Sidon where sea birds hung on the coastal breeze and where there was never a winter's day as chilly as this one in Jerusalem.

"Mighty large shipment." The overseer leaned his shoulder to the cistern and gave it a final push against the front boards. "Twenty-eight jars just like this one."

"There are a good many robes to dye," Ruth said and plucked out a shellfish. She pried it open and squeezed the animal's spongy gray belly where it stored a cache of deep blue dye used to color the clothing of royalty. "I'm surprised it took this long to arrive."

It had been almost three months since she sent to Sidon for the shellfish. She'd expected them to be harvested and caravanned to the palace long before the silk arrived from the Orient. But no matter, the silk came weeks ago and she'd nearly completed the coronation robes, all but Mulek's and Miriam's. She had yet to decide on the style for the queen's collar and there was still time to weave the prince's larger-than-normal cuffs.

Ruth dropped the clam back into the seawater and handed the reins to the overseer. "I must speak with the queen about the dye."

He nodded, tied the mule to a post and went on loading the shellfish without a word.

Ruth took Joshua by one hand and Sarah by the other. She hurried them up the gangplank, checking one last time to make sure they weren't followed before slipping inside. It would have been simpler to leave the children in the cart or let them play about the yard. She used to do that on her earlier visits, but not any more. Not since she saw how the gatekeeper and the guards watched their every step and noted every word. She didn't mind them watching her, but the way they looked at the children, it was as if her innocent little ones were the enemy.

Mima stood in the inner courtyard near the steps of Solomon's temple. Her bright green and red shawl was a wild affair compared to the somber white robes of the groundskeepers. Everything about her announced her presence and the longer she waited here for Laban the more she became an oddity. She scanned the yard; and when she couldn't find him approaching from any of the gates she adjusted the colorful shawl over her shoulders. That should disguise her until he arrived. Women weren't allowed inside the temple courtyard proper, but Laban had left word with the gatekeepers to let her pass before the sanctuary opened for the day. The captain had best not be late this time. The sun was high in the morning sky and her master, Josiah the potter, would expect his lunch at the same hour he always took it.

A groundskeeper struggled past her with a heavy cistern of fresh spring water. He carried it up the steps to the brass font set on the backs of twelve oxen. Mima turned her back to him and he obliged by not offering a word in greeting. The less she spoke the less he'd remember her. He poured the water into the pool and returned down the steps. This time Mima drew the shawl over her face. But who was she trying to fool? Every groundskeeper in the yard would remember a black woman alone in the temple court.

Another groundskeeper stood a few rods off filling an oil flask. He nodded to Mima, but she looked away. He mumbled a greeting that she ignored, then carried the oil up the temple steps and waited while a host of priests carried out the seven-branched menorah from inside Solomon's Temple. It usually sat inside the chamber of the Holy Place, but the priests were preparing the grounds for the coronation and since Zedekiah would be crowned on these steps, the flames of the menorah would burn near the temple doors for the weeks leading up to that sacred day.

The groundskeeper tipped the oil flask into the reserve chamber below the first flame, the one honoring the first day of creation when light was divided into day and night. He proceeded to the chamber below the second flame, the one remembering the creation of land and sea, then to the flame recalling the bringing of seeds and plants to the earth. It appeared to be a menial task, but it was a job laden with anxiety since these flames had been kept lit for nearly seven hundred years. Who could endure the shame of the menorah running dry on their watch after such a long unbroken run? Without spilling a drop of oil, the groundskeeper carefully filled the chambers below the flame for sun, moon, and stars, for moving creatures, and for the creation of man. Mima nodded her head slowly as he finished trimming the oil in the last flame, the seventh one commemorating the Sabbath, the day God finished His work and rested from His labors. Not that she was strict to observe that commandment, mind you. She had offered many a sin offering to absolve herself from walking more steps than were allowed. But she used an occasional fire for her Sabbath cooking, for which she made neither apology nor offering. None of the potter's neighbors ever mentioned the smoke that rose from her kitchen chimney on the Sabbath day, and the potter never complained about a roasted Sabbath lamb. Mima stared at the groundskeeper as he filled the seventh golden chamber in the candelabrum. The Sabbath was holy and she would have to plead for eternal rest after what she was about to do, at least that's what she wanted Captain Laban to believe.

Smoke rose off the menorah and up around the two pillars that graced the entrance to Solomon's temple like great palms shading an oasis. The images of pomegranates carved in the pillar tops were reminders of the bounties of God's blessings. Mima could use a little divine bounty if she were to get the best price for what she knew. Laban had money and she had information, or at least she wanted the captain to think she knew something about Josiah the potter and Queen Miriam. He was obsessed with both of them and Mima had only enough information to speak about one.

If only Laban hadn't insisted she meet him here, in view of the overhanging balconies and porticoes of the palace. It seemed the wrong hour and place. Their business was better done in the dark of night down a narrow alley in the lower city, not in full view of the royal family's living quarters, to say nothing of the House of God.

Mima lowered her face behind her veil when Laban came through a side gate from the military grounds and crossed the entire length of the courtyard, greeting each groundskeeper in turn with a loud, jovial voice. A foolish showing right before their discreet meeting, and the captain was the one who had arranged it. His full officer's dress was even less discreet, bright brass belt buckles, gold officer's stripes glittering in the morning sun and his silver-buttoned tunic tinkling about his chest like the bells of hell. You'd have thought he was raising an army for battle with the stir he made.

Mima waited for him to get close enough so she could speak softly. "Couldn't you have selected a better place? Someone could see us."

"This should be more than enough for your trouble." Laban handed over a purse of coins that Mima quickly hid under her shawl.

Laban didn't suggest they leave to stand in the shade over behind the temple. He faced the fifth-story palace balcony, the center bedroom directly above the women's court, the one Queen Miriam would use to observe the coronation ceremony of her husband. He asked, "What did you find out about the potter?"

"He works with the Rekhabites."

"Is he the informant?"

"Absolutely."

"What about the queen?" Laban kept his shoulders squared to Miriam's balcony. "How is she involved?"

Mima said, "She's had no contact with the potter."

"You're certain?"

"You paid me to watch."

"It seems I didn't pay you enough."

"If it's fables you want, I can dream them up, but Queen Miriam's not the one you're searching for." Mima adjusted her colorful shawl on her shoulders. "The potter works alone."

"There's got to be some sort of connection." Laban rubbed a silver button between his fingers. "The prophets know things Josiah could never know without someone telling him."

"You'll have to look elsewhere for the source. It isn't the queen."

The curtains draped across the queen's portico moved ever so slightly and Mima shifted her stance to see if Miriam was looking out. It wasn't wise for her to be seen—not now, not if Mima were to be believed.

Laban said, "I'd like to know exactly who Josiah's source is."

Mima said, "Josiah knows many powerful people."

"He's a potter."

Mima stepped between Laban and his view of the queen's balcony. "Do you still want a fire?"

"Do it the day of the coronation."

"Wouldn't it be better another day? The streets will be filled with people."

"I want a show."

"Very well, Captain. I'll send you word when it's done."

Mima started toward the gate, but Laban caught her by the arm. "That shouldn't be necessary, not with the large fire I want you to set. The smoke and ash of the potter's misfortune should fall on every citizen in Jerusalem."

"The kilnmaster is due for his next round of firings about the time of the coronation. No one will question an accident with the large fires he sets." Mima folded her wide arms across her front. "Is there anything else?"

Laban straightened, his four-cubit frame towering above her. "That should do for now."

Mima turned to go a second time, but Laban stopped her again and said, "See that the potter's last meal isn't anything different than usual. I don't want him to become suspicious."

"Don't worry about that, Captain." Mima pulled her shawl close and tightened her grip on the coin purse. "I've already planned something for the potter."

Ruth kept Joshua and Sarah close about the skirts of her robe as they made their way through the less traveled passages of the palace. Near the back of the kitchens, half hidden by the door to the pantry, stood a narrow corridor. It ran along the east wall to a dark stairwell that led to the fifth floor. The last time Ruth came to the palace, the cook showed her the secret passage used to take food to the royal family's living quarters without parading through the main hallways and grand stairways of the palace. There were no lamps to light the way along the damp passage, only a small window near the ceiling that allowed for an uncomfortably cold draft.

Joshua pulled his hand free and jumped onto the first step at the end of the passage. "This is a perfect hiding place, Mama. Can we play here?"

"I won't stay another moment!" Sarah shook her head at Joshua. "There could be monsters around any corner."

"Do you really think so?" Joshua jumped onto the second step and peered up the stairwell. "Come out monsters and show yourselves."

"Joshua!" Ruth's voice echoed off the stone. "There are no monsters in the palace. At least not that kind of monster."

"But, Mama . . ."

"I told you before we came, no chasing about the palace."

Joshua glanced about the stone passageway. "This really isn't part of the palace."

"Then what is it?" Sarah asked.

"It's a robbers' den and look over there . . ." Joshua pointed to the shadows on the wall, opposite the high window. "They're coming to get us right now." He started up the stairs, his small feet pattering around the first turn. "Follow me and I'll lead you to safety."

Joshua was the first to reach the fifth floor and sit on a bench in the hall. His little chest rose and fell in rhythm with his breathing and he slumped into the angle of the bench, his head nestled against the hardwood where the small of a man's back should have rested, one hand gripping the armrest to keep him from falling onto the floor. His feet dangled well above the ground and he beamed up at Ruth with the smile of a triumphant mountain climber at the summit. Sarah sat on the opposite end of the bench, as far away from Joshua as she could sit, with her toes skimming the floor. The girl was growing a bit. A month back she could never have reached that far with her legs. Ruth let them play with her long measuring cords. She wouldn't need them today. All she really needed were small swatches of purple silks, linens, and cottons as an excuse for meeting with Miriam, but to be sure, she kept back one measuring cord and placed it inside her satchel. She kissed Sarah on the cheek, patted Joshua on the head and left them with instructions not to leave the bench and not to say a word to any stranger, except that they were waiting for the queen's decision on the fabric colors.

Ruth quickly found her way to the last bedroom on the right, the one with the large lamps burning on either side of the closed door. Miriam would be inside. Ruth knocked, but no one answered. She knocked again and still no response. When she opened the door, the room stood dark and the chamber was without the usual stir of maid-servants fussing about. The curtains to the portico were drawn closed and Miriam stood holding them shut. She peered through a slit out onto the temple courtyard. It was past midday, but the queen was still dressed in a white morning robe accented with sequins crushed from the shells of abalone. She gave no hint she heard Ruth enter the room until, still peering through the curtains, Miriam whispered, "He's up to something." She drew the curtains tight. "Laban's out there with the potter's servant."

Ruth asked, "Mima?"

"Do you know her?"

"Who couldn't help but notice her in the market?"

"I wish I could hear what they were saying." Miriam clasped her hands under her chin. "I only hope it hasn't anything to do with the potter."

The potter? What did Miriam care about Josiah or his maidservant Mima? Ruth would have asked, but she didn't want to pry too deeply, not with Miriam acting so strangely. She crossed the room and began to draw open the curtains, but Miriam wouldn't let go. Ruth said, "You shouldn't fret about Laban's doings. He has more pressing things to worry about than the beliefs of two women."

"He thinks I'm a traitor."

"You're tired, dear. You didn't sleep well."

"It's Laban's soldiers who tire me. They wait around every corner, down every hallway, watching me when I sleep, when I rise, when I eat, and what I eat. If I miss a meal they want to know why. If I leave the palace they have to know where I'm going. If I have a visitor they want to know who." Miriam backed away from the portico. "Laban's plotting something awful and I can only pray it has nothing to do with the potter or with—"

Miriam stopped speaking so abruptly that all Ruth could think to do was fill the silence. "The dye for the coronation robes arrived today. How deep a shade do you want in your robe?"

"I can't think about that now, not with Laban outside my window looking up at me." Miriam began to pace in front of the curtains. "I'm a prisoner in my own home. He'd put Mulek and me to death if he had good reason."

"Don't talk like that." Ruth's hands began to tremble and she hid them beneath her robe. "You're only upsetting yourself."

"Don't you see the way he has his men treat you when you pass through the gates? The soldiers watch you and your children as if you were criminals."

"I try not to." Ruth stared at the floor. She knew the fear, but it hadn't stopped her from coming to the palace to see Miriam. At least not yet. She steadied her hands at her waist and said, "Laban's men always bow and open the gate, and I walk through on the wings of their greetings."

"He pays them to speak kind words."

"What does he want with us?" Ruth glanced toward the hallway where she could hear the faint sounds of Joshua and Sarah playing about the bench. "What do they want with our children?"

"I'm sorry, I didn't mean to burden you with my fears." Miriam touched Ruth on the arm. "I never should have brought you into this."

"Into what?"

Miriam held both of Ruth's hands in hers. "My deceptions."

"What are you talking about?"

"Laban believes Mulek and I are spies."

"That's absurd. Laban suspects everyone."

"No, Ruth." Miriam pressed Ruth's hands between hers. "I'm the one he's searching for." She let go and began to pace with long, firm strides. "After we joined the Rekhabites, they asked Mulek and me to pass them information about Laban."

"Who asked you?"

"I can't tell you that. It would place you and them in too much danger."

"You're the spy Laban's been looking for all this time?"

Miriam fumbled with the flint to light an oil lamp. She raised it between them, and Ruth could see the seriousness in her eyes. Miriam said, "I would have told you sooner, but I didn't want you in the same peril I find myself. You have your children to worry about."

"And you have yours."

"Do you think Laban would harm the princes?"

Ruth listened a second time for the sounds of her children playing in the hallway. Sarah was lecturing Joshua on his posture, telling him something about walking on his hands like a sheep if he didn't learn to sit up straight on the bench. It was the same lecture Ruth had given the girl not two days before. Ruth took a deep breath. The children were safe and she said, "Laban wouldn't dare harm your children."

"I hope you're right. I pray every night that I'm alone in this, that I'm the only one who has reason to fear."

"I'll not let that prayer be answered." Ruth walked to the portico and pulled open the curtains. On her sudden movement the guards stationed on the palace turrets and catwalks began marching. They'd been watching the balcony. Mima was gone now, but Laban lingered in the courtyard below.

Miriam ducked behind a pillar. "What are you doing?"

"I need more light if I'm to measure your collar."

"Laban's out there."

"You need another measurement."

"This is foolishness."

"Are you questioning my judgment or my weaving?"

Miriam straightened her morning robe and slowly stepped out from behind the pillar. "I only question your sanity."

"Come, you need a breath of fresh air."

Miriam hesitated in the shadows of her bedroom. But Ruth led her onto the balcony, telling her to look past Laban over toward the temple and think pleasant thoughts. Sunlight streamed between the two tall stone pillars gracing the main doors and shimmered over the surface of the washing pool, its twelve oxen glowing like a brazen fire. It was here faithful Jews performed their ritual washings much like the Rekhabites did their baptizing along the Jordan in the dark of night. It was a splendid view, and the rare warmth of the winter sun touched Ruth's face and filled her with a sense of calm, but it was only a fleeting peace. Her gaze drifted to the center of the courtyard where Laban stood and she immediately turned back to fuss over the measuring cord, and thank heavens she'd thought to bring one in with her. If she'd left it in the hall with the children, Laban would have reason to suspect her.

Miriam lowered her head for Ruth to wrap the short cord around her neck. "We shouldn't be seen together like this."

"Don't be silly." Ruth tied the knot where the two ends met at the back of Miriam's neck. She could feel the weight of Laban's gaze on her back, but she'd felt his scrutiny before and she finished the knot.

Miriam said, "You must go and never return to see me, ever. You can deliver the coronation robes to the maidservants once you finish."

"I'll do no such thing." Ruth draped the lone cord over her shoulder and stood straight, her shoulders back. "The first day I measured you for your robes I promised I'd not let you suffer this alone."

"You didn't know who I was then, at least not everything about me."

Ruth steadied her hands and adjusted the collar of Miriam's morning robe up about her cheeks. "That's what I'll do with this measurement. I shall weave a new collar for your coronation robe. A collar like no queen has worn before."

Miriam said, "Stop trying to make things right."

"Isn't that what friends are for?"

Ruth bowed like any of the other servants would, despite Miriam's request she not be so formal. But formality was their best defense.

Protocol would be their only cover to protect them against Laban.

CHAPTER 30

The evening chill rushed into the room when Elizabeth answered the knock at the door and found her dinner guest waiting to come inside. Rebekah was dressed in a blue, pleated silk robe. The pleats fluttered on the breeze like peacock feathers and the sash about her waist was a strand of silken lace. Her hair was wrapped around a comb of pearls and ivory and she wore the slightest hint of Egyptian pomegranate coloring on her soft red lips. She smiled and entered the main room as if she'd been here a thousand times, though she'd only been once. And that was not the best of meetings between her and Aaron. News of Aaron's indiscretion at the pool of Siloam traveled faster than a herd of sheep to water. The entire lower city buzzed over the spat, though no one knew what caused the commotion. When Elizabeth invited her to dinner, she didn't say anything about the incident, though there was no mistaking the wounded look in her eyes. Most likely it was Aaron's mouth that did the piercing. If his brain had not been attached to it, he wouldn't have created nearly the stir. Aaron had a way of speaking his mind, but that was his dilemma, one he would have to resolve once he returned from Beit Zayit. Tonight there were other troubles that needed tending—Elizabeth's troubles. And inviting another woman to help solve them, a woman like Rebekah whom she could trust, seemed the only wise investment.

"I brought you some combs to wear with your new robe." Rebekah handed over the gift.

"You shouldn't have."

"Maybe you could try them on before he arrives."

Elizabeth glanced over at the dark corner of the main room. "He already has."

"Good evening." Zoram stepped out of the shadows, like a nobleman should, and spoke up before Rebekah could say anything that could embarrass them further. It was the only proper thing to do and Elizabeth added his discretion to her list of Zoram's graces. But despite his gentlemanly behavior, Zoram was the trouble Elizabeth needed help solving and she had invited Rebekah for an opinion about the man. She'd already told Rebekah everything about his kindly disposition and disarming smile, not to mention his prosperous traits. His skillful use of the pen and knowledge of three languages had earned him employment in Laban's treasury, and once he was named scribe over the estate he'd be a wealthy man to be sure. What she didn't tell Rebekah was that Jeremiah was Zoram's father. But in keeping silent, she lived under the constant fear that Papa would find out about Zoram's ties to the prophet, and her future would unravel like a ball of yarn fallen from a loom.

Zoram sat on one end of the bench seat, and Elizabeth seated herself at the other end, far enough away not to give Zoram reason to believe he'd been forgiven, but close enough that he wouldn't lose hope. Rebekah sat in the chair directly across from Zoram. She said, "How good to meet Captain Laban's scribe."

Elizabeth gripped the armrest and an inaudible groan welled deep inside. Rebekah could have said anything but that. Zoram was sure to know how much they had spoken about him in private.

Zoram said, "I'm not Laban's scribe."

"Not yet, but I've heard what people say about your skill."

Elizabeth raised the hair comb to the side, where Rebekah would see it, but it would be shielded from Zoram's quick glances. She waved it ever so slightly and stared at her friend with eyes opened wider than an owl at midnight. She was signaling Rebekah, hoping to keep her from saying any more.

Zoram asked, "Which people?"

Rebekah's gaze flitted from Elizabeth's waving comb, to Zoram and then back again to Elizabeth. Her face flushed red, bright red. "Oh, you know, scribe people."

"Who exactly are scribe people?"

"Very fine men."

"I see."

Rebekah folded her arms in her lap. "I understand you speak three languages, isn't that right?"

Elizabeth dropped the comb in her lap and stared at it. That was not a question that had power to change the direction of their conversation. Zoram's skill with language was the other thing he didn't tell anyone and Elizabeth's cheeks began to burn.

Zoram asked, "Who have you been talking to?"

"No one really. I must have heard it in the market." Rebekah rubbed her brow. "You know, I'm sure I may have heard it there. It's absolutely possible that's where it was."

"The market?" Zoram held back a smile, but his straight white teeth showed from behind the rising edges of his lips. "I didn't know they talked of such things there."

"You'd be surprised."

"I'm sure I would."

Elizabeth stood between them, blocking Zoram's view of Rebekah. She said, "Zoram is working as a blacksmith with my father. He's a very quick apprentice."

Rebekah leaned around Elizabeth and asked, "And why is it that Laban's scribe would have need to work as a blacksmith?"

Elizabeth lifted the hem of her robes off the floor. That was something she should have warned Rebekah not to ask. The room fell silent and it would have remained that way if Ruth hadn't entered from the kitchen, a cooking apron draped down her front. She took Rebekah by the hand. "How good of you to come. And what about your father, will he be joining us?"

"No." Rebekah answered so abruptly, so absolutely there was no mistaking her father's resolve. Josiah the potter would not be coming to dine at the home of the blacksmith.

"I see," Ruth said, "Maybe another time?"

Rebekah said, "Possibly."

"It's eating me! It's eating me!" Young Joshua dashed into the room, running about in circles and waving the red body of a baby crab from the end of his thumb. He'd been playing in the jars of shellfish stored behind the house and found more than clams.

Sarah darted out of the kitchen in step behind him. She said, "Shellfish don't have any teeth."

"They do so!" Joshua stuck the crab in Zoram's face and said, "Save me, sir, before it eats me!"

Sarah set her hands on her hips. "Don't be such a fool."

Joshua cried, "Help me someone, anyone, please help me!"

Zoram yanked the crab free, and it spun out of his hand and into the air before falling into Sarah's hair, its claws catching hold of her long brown braids. Her freckled face lit up and she screamed, "It's eating me!"

"Settle yourself, young lady." Elizabeth removed the crab. "Hold it like this." She placed Sarah's thumb and forefinger around its belly. "Now off you go, both of you, and put it back in the salt water barrels." She turned to Zoram. "It isn't usually like this."

"It's sometimes worse," Jonathan said and marched into the room. He shook Zoram's hand. "Good of you to come, boy."

"Thank you, sir."

"Did you finish with the last of that ore?"

"Three barrels cleaned and ready for smelting."

"You're a hard-working soul. Just the sort of man a woman would be lucky to have for a husband." Jonathan nodded to Elizabeth, but when all she did was stare back into his brown eyes, he cleared his throat and said, "Shall we eat?" He quickly retreated to the kitchen where the table was set for seven.

It was too cold to eat on the roof. Evening meals were taken inside this time of year. The cedar dinner table brought down from the roof fit between the hearth and window with just enough room for Ruth and Elizabeth to stand at the fire and cut the roasted lamb. Elizabeth served Jonathan first, a thick slice of lamb with an onion garnish, lentils and a generous portion of freshly baked bread. She served Zoram, then Rebekah, and was finishing with Sarah and Joshua when the clatter of horse hooves roared into the courtyard. There was hardly enough time to lay down the cutting knife when the door flew open and Daniel marched in. He stumbled over the doormat and bumped into both chairs in the outer room before steadying himself on the bench seat. The children began to giggle, but Elizabeth warned them to silence with a stiff stare. It was all she could think to do to save her family the embarrassment of a drunken brother.

Daniel carried a hastily packed satchel over his shoulder. It hung half open with a gray tunic, the laces of a boot and the end of a bridle spilling over the top. His sword had shifted around to his back and he nearly tripped on it as he marched into the kitchen. He fumbled with the sheath until it slid around onto his hip where it belonged. He said, "We're headed out."

Ruth pushed the spitted lamb back over the fire and leaned close to speak in his ear, "Have you been drinking, son?"

"I was thirsty." Daniel tried to whisper back, but with everyone sitting in silence the guests heard every word.

Ruth said, "Why don't you go outside and wash up."

"I said I was thirsty." Daniel rubbed his eyes. "Not dirty."

"You need to clean up for dinner. You've been riding that animal of yours."

"It's a horse, Mama." Daniel dropped his pack on the floor. "A mare, a brown mare."

"Daniel," Elizabeth said, "we have guests."

"I see them." Daniel sauntered past the table and steadied himself against the window sill. It wouldn't have been so bad to have him falling over himself if it weren't for the smell of wine on his breath, strong putrid wine.

Elizabeth said, "Papa, do something."

Between bites of lamb, Jonathan said, "I've told you not to socialize with the other soldiers. Your mother and I disapprove of your drinking."

"We were packing for the journey."

Jonathan sopped up the broth with a piece of bread. "Did they tell you where you're headed?"

"Can't say."

Ruth served Zoram and Rebekah some baked yams, steaming hot out of a kettle. "Daniel's not allowed to speak about that part of his soldiering, you understand. You know all those rules military men follow."

Rebekah and Zoram nodded far too many times to be thinking anything but the worst. Zoram took a small bite of lamb, and poked the yams with his knife. Daniel leaned over the window sill on his belly and looked up at the full moon rising over the mount of olives.

He was drunk, bone drunk and acting like a child. He raised his fist to the moon and said, "You hear me Uriah? You can hide all you want, but we're coming after you tomorrow."

"Daniel!" Elizabeth pulled him back from the window.

Ruth came around the table wiping her hands clean on her apron. She took him by the shoulders and steered him to the stairs. They were halfway up when he fell against the banister. He said, "I'm going to get Uriah, Mama. You'll see. And I'll bring him back so they can take off his head and they'll make me an officer for it."

"Son!" Ruth scurried him up to his room, behind the curtains hung over the loft, but it was too late. Zoram pushed his plate away and stared at the table, his head down and hands clasped in his lap. It was like watching a man pray and Elizabeth was certain he was begging God to lead Daniel and his company of soldiers on a wild chase as far away from the prophet Uriah as the driven winds could carry them.

Zoram said, "I have to go."

"Why you've hardly touched your food, boy." Jonathan downed the last of his lamb and handed Elizabeth his plate for another serving.

"Thank you, sir, but I have some business."

"At this hour?"

"It's urgent." Zoram started for the door. "I'll be gone for a few days."

"Is it something to do with your work in Laban's treasury?"

"Something like that."

"Why didn't you tell me sooner?"

"I didn't know until now."

"Very well." Jonathan picked a morsel of meat from between his front teeth and pointed his knife at the spit where the lamb roasted. It was his way of telling Elizabeth to cut him more, but she couldn't, not with Zoram leaving like this. She handed her father's plate to Rebekah with a look that begged her to cut the lamb while she went after him. Rebekah obliged and Elizabeth caught Zoram at the front door. She leaned against it, keeping him from unlatching it. She said, "Please don't go."

"I must."

"I'm sorry about Daniel's behavior. There's no excuse for it."

"It isn't your fault." Zoram stiffened when Daniel's voice streamed over from the loft, uttering oaths against Uriah, vowing to chase the prophet to the ends of the earth. Zoram said, "It's Laban who's behind all this."

Elizabeth lowered her voice to a whisper. "Does your father know?"

"That's where I'm going." Zoram brushed back the curls from his brow and fitted his white linen turban over his head. "He must know how serious things are. I don't want him sneaking into the city any more."

Elizabeth said, "Don't let what Daniel said upset you. He's been drinking."

"Is that what you're going to tell me when Daniel comes to cut off my father's head?" Zoram popped the latch and pulled open the door, forcing Elizabeth out of the way. He went out into the chilly night and Elizabeth followed. "Can't you do something to stop this? You work for Laban."

Zoram spun around at the gate. "I wake up every morning wondering if today will be the day Laban finds out who I really am, who my father is. That he'll think me the enemy and that my father has placed me in his treasury to spy."

"Are you a spy?"

"You still don't trust me, do you?"

"I want to."

"I've been loyal to Laban."

"Tell me who you would choose if you had to choose?"

The full moon lighted Zoram's dark complexion and his eyes were filled with an uncertain look she'd not seen before. "I don't have to choose."

"Can you be loyal to two masters, then?"

Zoram opened the gate, but before going into the street he said, "God is my only master."

He left her standing in the moonlight and disappeared in the shadows at the top of the street. After a moment, the door to the house opened with Rebekah at the threshold. She crossed the yard and asked, "What did he say?"

"He's going to Anathoth." Elizabeth brushed a tear from her eye. "He has family there."

"Your brother upset him." She touched Elizabeth's arm and asked, "Does Zoram believe in the prophets?"

"It's more than that, and you must promise not to share this with anyone." Elizabeth raised one hand near her mouth to try to soften what she was about to say. "Zoram has divided allegiances."

"Laban and who else?"

Elizabeth closed her eyes and when she opened them, she said, "Jeremiah the prophet."

"Laban would never hire a man with ties to Jeremiah."

Elizabeth held open the gate and looked up the street where Zoram had disappeared. "Laban doesn't know he's Jeremiah's adopted son, and I don't know what to do about it." She shook her head. "Zoram's a good man, but the son of a prophet? It's his only flaw."

"Having a prophet for a father is no flaw." Rebekah pulled the gate shut. "Zoram has the courage of ten lions to endure this."

"Do you really believe that?"

"You care about Zoram, don't you?"

"You know I do."

"Then you're going to have to open your heart to his way of thinking."

Elizabeth lowered her head. "We side with the Elders in this house."

Rebekah laid her hand on Elizabeth's shoulder. "You can't love a man and hate what he believes."

"We shouldn't be talking like this." Elizabeth folded her arms. "Both our fathers are Elders."

"It's your heart, not your father, you should follow in this matter."

"What does your heart tell you?"

"It tells me that Zoram is a fine man." Rebekah lifted her skirts and started into the street, but Elizabeth stopped her and asked, "How will I know if I believe in the prophets?"

"Pray, my dear friend. Pray like you've never prayed before and the answer will come." Rebekah went into the street, leaving the gate swinging in its pivot and her words ringing in Elizabeth's ears. She'd wanted to believe that Zoram was a courageous man, not a traitor. Rebekah gave her hope; she was the first witness that Elizabeth's faith in the man and his beliefs was not unfounded. Only one question remained.

Would God be the second?

Aaron shut the door to the guest room and started down the landing to begin another day of work at Beit Zayit when he came across Sariah climbing the stairs with a basin of warm water, an urn of powders under her arm, and fresh bandages draped over her shoulder. She stopped on the top step, blocking Aaron's way down, threw her head to the side to flick away a long strand of hair that hung over her brow and said, "You're not going anywhere until I see to your feet."

"Out here?" Aaron leaned over the railing. Two menservants and Sam were headed out the front doors, speaking about watering the camel herd and hauling hay to the corrals.

Sariah said, "I can't think of a better place." She ushered Aaron away from the railing to a chair along the mezzanine hallway." Soak your feet awhile before you go out to work." She patted the urn. "These are the finest healing powders from Egypt. And I mixed in some frankincense to keep your dressings fresh." She set the basin at the foot of the chair, untied the old bandages and set them aside. "You really shouldn't use these more than once. I'll have fresh ones ready for you every morning."

A pounding noise filtered through the open windows of the foyer and echoed off the vaulted ceiling. It was slight at first, but the sound grew louder; horses' hooves clattered over the stone square in front of the estate and shook the basin, troubling the water around Aaron's ankles.

A loud knock sounded at the door. No one answered and the knocking turned into a furious pounding.

Sariah said, "Who could that be?" She measured the powders into the water basin, stirred them with her finger and set Aaron's feet into the warm bath. "You sit there while I see to the door." She hurried down the steps, holding the railing as she went, and Aaron lost sight of her below the level of the floor as she turned across the foyer.

The doors swung open and Aaron could hear the boots of a man march inside. He said, "Where's Aaron?"

Sariah asked, "Whom shall I say is here to see him?"

"Fetch him here, now."

"What's the nature of your business, sir?"

A maidservant hurried past Aaron, down the steps and across the foyer to Sariah. She asked, "Do you need help?"

Sariah said, "Go fetch Ishmael and Lehi. They're at the stables. Quickly, girl." The sound of the maidservant's feet running down the path from the front filtered back inside the foyer.

The man raised his voice and said, "I want to speak with the blacksmith, not the olive oil merchants—or do you want me to fetch him myself?" Aaron knew the voice, but sat in silence as the man walked across the foyer. When his face cleared the level of the mezzanine, Aaron stared through the railing at his brother.

"What are you doing here?" Aaron asked, but he didn't need an answer. Daniel's new leather boots, officer stripes and the sword sheathed at his side were enough. He stopped in the center of the foyer, erect and with a seriousness about him that Aaron had not known before. He peered up at Aaron and said, "You need to come with me."

"Why?"

"Captain Elnathan is waiting to speak with you."

"About what?"

"You stay there." Sariah hurried to the base of the steps. "I'll take care of them."

"It's all right. I have no reason to fear this man." Aaron quickly tied the bandages around his feet, strapped the sandals on, and lowered himself with crutches to the main floor. Sariah walked beside him as he cleared the threshold and stepped into the yard. Thirty cavalrymen were saddled on light brown horses. The animals pawed at the ground near the gate and they were readied for a long journey. Each had a water skin, filled and corked with gumwood, hanging over its mane; and a supply bag bulged at their hinds.

Aaron asked, "Why does your captain want to speak with me?"

Daniel laid his hand on Aaron's shoulder. "I told him you weren't one of them."

Aaron pulled free. "What do you mean, one of them?"

Daniel lowered his voice. "I told them you weren't a traitor."

Aaron could tell by the way Sariah bristled that she'd heard Daniel's words. "How could you do this?" Aaron turned his head away from Daniel and spat on the ground.

"They were coming here with or without me. I told them you could help us."

"Why?"

"I don't want anyone thinking you're one of them." Daniel glanced at Sariah then back at Aaron. "I did it to protect you and me and Papa."

Aaron shook his head. "These people grow olives. They don't have time to be traitors."

"We're not going to bother them." Daniel leaned his head in close to Aaron. "All they want to know is if you've heard anything that could help us track Uriah."

"I don't know the man."

"Then tell that to Captain Elnathan and we'll be on our way." Daniel ushered Aaron down the path and through the gate onto the square with Sariah following a few cubits behind them.

The soldiers closed rank around Aaron, cutting off his retreat. He was trapped there, hemmed in by the powerful animals. The swords holstered at their waists and bows with arrows slung over their shoulders were the first instruments of death Aaron noticed among them. But they weren't as ominous as the prisoner cart rolling into the yard. A camel drew it, bouncing and clattering over the potholes like a fishing boat on stormy seas. There were no captives aboard, but its use for carrying a man to meet the end of his mortality made it an ugly reminder of the times. From front board to back gate it wasn't long enough for a man to lie down and the roof came so low that a prisoner would have to hunch.

"It's for Uriah's execution," the lead rider said and leaned over his saddle. It was Captain Elnathan and he reined a circle around Aaron.

Aaron asked, "Don't you worry about what could happen?"

"I know how to track a man." Elnathan chewed on a piece of gumwood.

"I was talking of God's curse."

Every good Jew knew the Almighty cursed men with the same punishment they carried out against his holy men. And if Uriah was a prophet, whatever Elnathan did to him was a type and shadow of his own future.

Elnathan inched back in his saddle and swallowed his spit. "When did Uriah come through here?"

"I wouldn't know the man if I saw him."

"Help the boy remember." Elnathan snapped his fingers at Daniel.

"What do you know about Uriah?" Daniel shoved Aaron against the prisoner cart face first. The crutches fell from under his arms and the full force of the stones pressed against his feet, shooting pain up his legs.

Aaron said, "I don't know anything." He braced himself against the bars, keeping his weight off his feet.

Daniel stuck his chin on Aaron's shoulder, his mouth next to his ear, and whispered, "Tell the Captain what he wants to know and he'll order me to leave you alone."

Sariah slapped Daniel on the back. "Leave him alone, he's done nothing wrong."

Daniel pushed her away and pressed Aaron's chest into the metal bars. "Say something."

Sariah pulled on Daniel's arm, trying to free his grip on Aaron. "Have you no mercy?"

Elnathan reined the horse's haunches against Sariah, pushing her aside. "Don't interfere, woman."

Ishmael cleared the rise from the stockyards and pushed past the circle of horses. "Leave the boy alone. You're not welcome here." He scanned the faces of the thirty soldiers in the company. "None of you."

"We don't need an invitation," Elnathan answered. "The king sent us to track the traitor, Uriah."

Sariah stood in front of Elnathan's horse, her small body dwarfed by the animal's powerful frame, its nose poking at her face. She pushed the animal's head aside and said, "Uriah isn't a traitor."

Elnathan leaned over the horse's mane. "You know the man, do you?"

"He came by to see my husband."

"When?"

"You'll have to speak with Lehi about that."

Elnathan stepped his horse forward, knocking Sariah to the ground in front of the animal's hooves. A woman's scream sounded near the front door of Ishmael's estate across the square. It was Isabel. She'd been watching from a distance; and when she saw Sariah fall, she sprinted down the path, flanked by three maidservants, each one carrying a broom. The troop of women waved the reed ends of the brooms at the animals and spooked them out of the way. Isabel knelt beside Sariah and helped her up. She asked, "Are you all right?"

Sariah brushed her robe clean. "Where are the men?"

"They're coming."

Ishmael said, "Let the blacksmith go."

Elnathan said, "Not until he tells me what I want to know." He snapped his fingers at Daniel. "Have the boy stand on his own feet."

Daniel said, "But, sir, you said you wouldn't do anything to—"

"Have him stand away from the cart."

Daniel carefully placed his arms on Aaron's shoulder, but Aaron pushed him away and said, "I don't need your help." He let go of the bars, his feet taking on the full force of his body. Immediately Aaron could feel his skin tear. He hadn't wrapped the bandages more than once around the skin, and the blood colored the white linen red. His legs began to tremble from the pain and he was about to tell Elnathan again that he knew nothing about Uriah, when a powerful voice filled the square with the words, "In the name of God, leave the boy in peace." The horses parted, and standing at the top of the rise where the road from the vineyards emptied into the square was Lehi, dressed in a working robe. He was flanked on his right by Sam and Nephi, and on his left by Laman and Lemuel. Their arms were covered in olive pulp up to the elbows and their faces flecked with bits of green olive meat. Lehi led his sons past the soldiers without looking at them. His gaze was focused on Aaron. He picked the crutches off the ground, steadied them under Aaron's arms and helped him over to a low-lying wall of rock where he could sit down. He tied the bandages tight around the burns before leaving him alone and coming back to Elnathan. He didn't speak a word, only stared up at the captain until the man reined back a stride.

Elnathan said, "Tell me what I want to know about Uriah and you'll have your peace."

Laman stepped next to Elnathan's horse. "Can we talk about this in private?"

"I don't see any reason why we should."

Laman spoke slowly, deliberately, as if he were trying to tell Elnathan something that he couldn't speak aloud. He said, "Tell Captain Laban that Uriah isn't a threat."

"Did he come through here?"

"A month or so back, looking for food. We fed him, let him rest a while then sent him on his way."

"Where?"

"I told you he's not a concern to you any more."

"Captain Laban believes he is." Elnathan reined around the prisoner cart. "Where did Uriah go?"

Laman said, "He took enough supplies to cross the Sinai."

"Can't you tell me any more than that?"

"He may have gone to Egypt."

"Son!" Lehi took Laman by the arm. "You've told them all they need to know."

"We have to help them."

Ishmael said, "We don't have to do anything for them."

"You don't understand, Uncle." Laman pulled free of Lehi's grasp and stepped toward Ishmael. "We could lose Beit Zayit."

"This land is ours; we have the deed to it."

"A deed won't keep Captain Laban from taking this land if he wants it." Laman turned to Elnathan. "There's a Hebrew colony up the Nile in the southern mountains near Ethiopia. A place called Elephantine. Uriah took one of our Arabians, a midnight black with a white spot on the muzzle. If he went that way, people will know. You don't forget that fine a horse."

Lehi said, "That's enough."

Laman ignored his father and said, "Uriah knows nothing." He chewed on a yellowed grass stem and spat it at the feet of Elnathan's horse. "Make sure Captain Laban knows that Uriah only came to our plantation for food, nothing else."

Elnathan leaned over his saddle. "Seems a little strange Uriah would travel all the way north to your plantation for no other reason than food when Elephantine is due south of his home in Arim."

Lehi said, "There's nothing strange about hunger."

Elnathan asked, "You're sure there isn't another reason he came to see you?"

Laman stepped between them. He reached over Elnathan's saddle and gripped the reins. "My father knows nothing. Do you hear me? Uriah told him absolutely nothing."

Elnathan pushed his boots into the stirrups and spurred his horse forward, the force of the animal knocking Laman back. He raised himself in the saddle and circled Laman as he scanned the olive vineyards that spread out in every direction and up every hillside. "All this will be yours one day, won't it?"

Laman glanced at Lemuel, then Sam and finally Nephi. He said, "A portion of it."

"Then I suggest you do everything you can to keep it that way."

Elnathan swung around and galloped from the yard, his cavalrymen falling in line behind him. Daniel was the only soldier who didn't leave with the others. He mounted up, reined over by Aaron and said, "Get home, before you get both of us into trouble."

"These are good people."

"They're friends of Uriah, just the sort Papa doesn't want any of us to mix with." Daniel spurred out of the yard to join his company.

Sariah sat down on the stone wall next to Aaron and took his hand in hers. "Are you all right?"

"I'm sorry for what happened."

"This wasn't your fault." Sariah bent down and examined his bandages. "And that soldier who pushed you about." She began to rewrap the linens. "There should be laws against such behavior." She raised her head and watched Daniel ride alongside the prisoner cart until he fell out of sight among the vineyards. Sariah asked, "Who is he?"

Aaron closed his eyes and said, "My younger brother."

CHAPTER 31

Aaron had forged out the crack in the lathe and sent it out for the harvest of winter wheat nearly two weeks back. Since then he had repaired the wheel hubs on the three caravan carts, mended twenty cubits of camel chain and prepared every bridle but the one he held by the tongs. He dipped it in the cool water bath and let the steam rise past his cheeks. He'd spent the better part of his time at Beit Zayit in the small confines of the smithy, two days more than his contract required. But he'd agreed to stay on until the caravan was readied to leave for Egypt. Aaron heated the bridle-bit for the last time, hammered the last nicks out of the surface and dipped it again. Steam hissed into the air, forming a cloud around the outline of a man who walked through the door of the smithy and stood across the cooling barrel. When the mists faded, Aaron was face to face with Lehi. He was dressed in a finely woven robe of blue linen. His hair was freshly washed and combed back in perfect lines and if it weren't the middle of the week, Aaron would have thought he was washed and dressed for the Sabbath.

Aaron fished the bridle bit from the barrel and held it up between the clamps. "I'm finished."

Lehi said, "I was afraid of that."

"I thought you'd be pleased."

"I was hoping it would take longer." Lehi removed the bridle bit from the tongs and cradled the metal piece in his palm. "Are you ready for the ride home?"

"Once I finish with that, I'll be on my way." Aaron took back the bridle bit and tied it into the leather straps. "All I have left is to saddle my horse."

"I've taken care of that." Lehi tipped his head in the direction of the estate. "She's tied to a post out front waiting with the family to see you off."

"See me off, sir?"

"It was Sariah's idea. She's planning a surprise farewell and she sent me out here to tell you."

"Doesn't that ruin the surprise?"

"She knows I'm telling you." Lehi sat on the bench next to Aaron and held out a piece of ivory. It was delicately carved in the shape of a mason's trowel, except that it had fine long teeth, and the gold-plated spine was decorated with silver flowers. "I brought this back from the Orient."

"A comb?"

"It's a gift." Lehi tucked it into Aaron's hand. "Sariah insisted you be groomed for the occasion."

Occasion? Aaron ran the ivory teeth through his hair, laying the strands back in straight furrows. What kind of farewell had Sariah planned?

Lehi asked, "You can act surprised, can't you?"

"I suppose I could."

"I'm afraid you'll have to." Lehi patted Aaron on the back. "I don't want to spoil her fun."

"Let me see . . ." Aaron closed his eyes, leaned back and raised his hands in the air. "Oh, Sariah, you should never have gone to the trouble to see me off!" He opened one eye. "Is that good enough?"

"Maybe too good."

Aaron lowered his arms. "I'll keep these down."

Sam rounded the doorpost, whistling like a morning lark. He was dressed in a blue tunic with silver-threaded cuffs and collar. His face was freshly washed, his hair still wet from the water basin and there was no doubt Sariah had a hand in his grooming. He stopped at Lehi's side and said, "Did you ask him?"

"Not yet."

"But Papa, you know a good blacksmith will save us days, maybe a week or more."

Aaron turned on the bench and faced Sam. "Ask me what?"

"You're going to Egypt with us."

Aaron handed the finished bridle to Sam. "I can't."

"We leave first thing in the morning and we'll pay you well."

"It isn't about money."

"It's your father." Sam leaned against the forging table with his arms folded across his chest. "He thinks we're Rekhabites."

"Are you?"

"I think your father should fear Zadock more than he does any Rekhabites. I say Zadock put your father on the Council because he needs a blacksmith."

"What would he need a blacksmith for?"

Sam twisted his face into a hideous grin and pulled down on his cheeks until they sagged like Zadock's. "The Chief Elder is going to need an awful lot of balls and chains for all the Rekhabites he plans to find lurking in the streets of Jerusalem."

"You've gone mad."

"I was born mad." Sam grinned. "And now that you know we aren't a threat to your father, you're going to ride home this afternoon and ask his blessing on your trip to Egypt. And if he asks, you can tell him we're not Rekhabites."

"But you believe what they do, don't you?"

"Well, not exactly the way they do—"

"Sam, that's enough." Lehi stood up from the bench, the sleeves of his blue linen robe swaying about his wrists. He faced Aaron and asked, "Is it so awful that we share with the Rekhabites a belief in eternity?" His voice was firm and his question was not really a question at all. For the first time he was opening his soul for Aaron to see the faith that burned within.

"I'm sorry, sir." Aaron lowered his head. "I didn't mean to offend you."

Lehi came around the bench and stood beside the open hearth, the coals casting a yellow glow onto his face. "Is there a woman that you court?"

Aaron's head shot up. Of course there was. Rebekah was the most beautiful woman in Jerusalem. At least he thought her so and he hoped she would return the sentiment after their troubled parting.

But what did Rebekah have to do with Lehi's faith? He didn't know she was a Rekhabite. That was Rebekah's secret, her deepest darkest secret. Aaron said, "Why do you ask?"

Lehi said, "Come with me."

Aaron stood on his crutches and followed Sam and Lehi out the doors of the smithy and up the rise of earth toward the estate. They stopped short of the willows surrounding the back gardens and bent over to see through the branches. Sariah was out picking the last rose blossoms of the season. She hummed a quiet melody as she bent over a small bush and gently pealed away the brown petals to reveal a deep red blossom the killing frost had not claimed.

Lehi said, "She always comes to the gardens on days like this."

"Days like what, sir?"

Lehi pulled aside a branch. "The flowers are for you and if you watch closely she's about to close her eyes and take a deep breath of their scent."

Aaron leaned forward on his crutches and it was exactly as Lehi had said. After smelling the rose, she added it to her growing bouquet then raised her head to the morning sun and let it warm her soft skin. Her cheeks were touched red as was her nose, and the smile on her face radiated a peace from within.

Lehi picked up a small round stone from the ground and he was about to throw it up into the branches of the willows, but he stopped when Aaron whispered, "You'll startle her."

"I'm making a bird. She loves to have them visit her gardens and nothing will make her happier than to report that they have returned early this year." Lehi tossed the stone high into the branches and immediately Sariah turned her gaze toward the sound. She stood for a long time studying the trees before she went back to picking roses.

Aaron asked, "How do you know when you love someone?"

"Thirty-two years Sariah and I have been married," Lehi said. "She knows the worst thing about me and it doesn't matter."

"What is it?"

"It isn't any one thing, it's just that she knows all my weaknesses, all my shortcomings, and they don't matter to her."

"Does she know that you make the birds in the trees?"

"She suspects me." Lehi laid his hand on Aaron's shoulder. "We share each other's deepest secrets and that's why I can love her and why I'll keep loving her forever."

Aaron asked, "How do you know that it will be forever?"

Lehi stood straight, his eyes watering. "The greatest secret Sariah and I share is a knowledge that the Messiah, the man the prophets call Yeshua the Anointed One, will offer himself as a sacrifice to answer the ends of the Law to all those who have a broken heart." He glanced back into the gardens. Sariah was dipping the blossoms in a fountain. "She does that to keep them fresh and full of life." Lehi's voice took on a low, reverent tone. "She and I know, just as the Rekhabites know, that we will pass from this life one day. I don't know if she'll go first or if I will, though I'd prefer we went together." Lehi backed away from the willows and Aaron followed. The view of Sariah picking roses was lost among the branches, but they could still hear her soft humming. Lehi said, "However we leave this earth, I know that we shall live again because the Messiah will lay down his life according to the flesh, and take it up again by the power of the spirit. And we will be united with our family beyond the grave and enjoy the same sweet association we enjoy now."

Aaron whispered, "Rebekah."

Lehi asked, "What was that, son?"

"You asked me if I courted a woman. Her name is Rebekah."

"Do you love her?"

Aaron worked his lower lip between his teeth. "I know her deepest secrets."

"Does she know yours?"

"I thought she did." Aaron glanced at the ground. "But so much has changed since I last saw her, I'm not sure exactly what I feel any more."

"If you love her you'll tell her."

"Everything?"

"Reveal yourself to her and let her decide if she can love you." Lehi turned up the path that led between the willows and into the gardens. He crossed to Sariah's side and took the bouquet from her arms. She pointed to the branches, her face lighted with a smile, and she spoke quickly like a child with a new toy. She must have been speaking about the birds and Lehi nodded his approval as he picked the last blossom for her. He held it to her nose. She closed her eyes and took in the scent and while she was blinded, he leaned over and kissed her on the cheek.

Sam tapped Aaron on the shoulder. "You don't have to tell your father all this. You only need to ask his blessing to go with us to Egypt."

Aaron didn't answer immediately. He stayed bent over his crutches and peered through the willows. Sariah and Lehi were headed up the path to the estate now. They were olive oil merchant and wife, but right now they were king and queen, walking hand in hand to their palace, and Aaron knew for the first time he wanted to love Rebekah the way Lehi loved Sariah. He wanted Rebekah's secrets to be his secrets, her faith to be his faith. Before he'd come to Beit Zayit that would have been impossible, but now everything had changed. Aaron straightened on his crutches, turned to Sam and said, "I wish I could tell my father everything."

Aaron's hair was combed and scented with the frankincense Sariah had left beside the washbasin. He checked his pack to make sure he hadn't forgotten anything. His hammer, flint, and chisel were at the bottom with the water skin on top, filled and corked for the ride home. Aaron carefully wrapped the delicate teeth of the ivory comb in a cloth, cinched the pack closed and slung it over his shoulder.

The main hall was empty, but the voices of Lehi and Ishmael's families filtered in through the window. The muffled tones of older conversation mixed with the unbridled cries of the children.

Sariah was the first to greet Aaron as he pushed open the door. "These are for you." She held out a bouquet of roses.

Aaron said, "You shouldn't have gone to the trouble."

Sariah placed her arm around his, careful not to trouble his crutches. "Are you surprised? It would make Lehi happy if you were." Her husband stood at the gate, between the pillars and iron bars. "This was all his doing. We've been married thirty-two years and I've never known him to grow tired of a surprise."

Aaron smiled. "I'll be sure to thank him."

Ishmael's eldest son, Nathan, stepped into stride next to Aaron. He'd been away most of the week and arrived home last night from a vineyard north of Jerusalem where he'd bartered a deal on a new breed of olive tree that produced sweeter olives than any at Beit Zayit. Come spring they'd clear the virgin acres across the lake and put in the trees. Walking with him was his younger brother, Seth. Aaron had seen him around the plantation, but never had much reason to strike up a conversation. He was the watermaster, always digging an irrigation ditch up one of the small canyon gullies or hauling water to a faraway field. Sariah smiled at her sons-in-law and insisted that the greatest achievement of the marriage of her two oldest girls to the two eldest sons of Ishmael were the grandchildren. She was the proud grandmother of seven, a fact she rarely kept secret, despite never getting all the names right. She blamed her misnaming on old age, though Nathan and Seth were quick to suggest it was simple confusion for the sheer size of her family. She thanked them and said she wished her own sons were as kind with her age.

Ishmael stood with his daughters-in-law, Rachel and Leah. They wished Aaron a safe journey back to Jerusalem while ignoring the screams of Leah's girls who were chased around the grounds by Rachel's three boys. Both mothers could easily distinguish the cries of play from the screams of pain.

Laman and Lemuel stood off by themselves in the shadows of the west wall. They hadn't said much to Aaron since he arrived at the plantation and this afternoon they didn't look to be any more cordial. They were alone and they were drinking. Exactly what, Aaron didn't care to know, though Sariah wouldn't allow anything stronger than spring water in her home.

The families gathered around the gate. Lehi offered a parting handshake and said, "We will miss you, Aaron the blacksmith." He stepped aside and behind him stood Beuntahyu. The ends of a thick red, white, and black blanket poked out from under the edge of a worn leather saddle. Beuntahyu's white coat glimmered in the afternoon sun and she pawed the courtyard stones as if telling Aaron it was time to head home. But this wasn't his horse and he scanned the yard to find the brown steed he was given as part of his wage. There wasn't another animal in the yard except for Beuntahyu.

Lehi said, "I want you to have her."

"She's too fine a horse."

"Precisely why you'll need her. She'll look after you if you decide to come with us to Egypt."

Aaron asked, "And if I don't go with you?"

"She'll take good care of you all the same."

Sam hurried up the rise from the corrals with Nephi. They were the last of the family to join in wishing Aaron a safe journey. Sam slapped Beuntahyu on the rump as he passed around her sturdy frame. He said, "I put new shoes on her this morning."

Aaron rubbed his brow. "I . . . I don't know what to say."

Sariah leaned her head in close. "Say that you're surprised."

"I am, completely." Aaron nodded his head. "You've been far too kind."

Beuntahyu held still while Lehi helped Aaron up into the saddle and tied his crutches crossways behind him. Somehow the horse sensed Aaron needed more help than other men and she was happy to act as his surrogate feet.

Sam said, "She shouldn't need a drink until you get to Jerusalem. I watered her with the camels this morning and then again with the goats."

Lehi asked, "Is the herd ready?" His attention immediately shifted from Aaron's departure to the business of the caravan, as it should on the eve of their departure for Egypt.

Sam said, "We leave at sunrise."

Lehi turned to Nephi. "What about the olive oil?"

"All hundred cisterns filled, corked, and waiting in the storehouse." He spoke with precision and detailed the most important preparation for the caravan. The high-grade olive oil was ready for loading on the camels.

Lehi asked, "You took oil from the sweetest vats, didn't you?"

"Only the best for Pharaoh Necho, Papa. None of it rancid and every drop strained for pulp."

"Can't you men wait on your business for a moment? This is supposed to be a farewell." Sariah took out a white linen tunic embroidered in silver with the pattern of an olive tree and handed it to Aaron. "I want to see you in this."

Aaron asked, "Right now?"

"Don't be shy. With four boys of my own, I'm not startled to see a young man's chest."

Aaron pulled off his worn, brown tunic and quickly changed into the white linen.

Sariah motioned for Aaron to lean over Beuntahyu's mane and she kissed him before turning away to brush a tear from her cheek and direct her daughters to gather the grandchildren in the yard for games. Three-year-old Simon was the last to obey. He jumped down from swinging on the gate and stood in front of Beuntahyu as if his tiny frame could keep the powerful animal from moving. He stared up at Aaron with a serious look and said, "I prayed for your feet." Then he sprinted off to join his siblings.

Sam cinched the linen-wrapped stirrups under Aaron's feet. "Have you decided?"

Before Aaron could answer, Laman stepped through the gate. "We don't need him on the caravan. We can't afford his work."

"You've seen what Aaron can do," Sam said. "He repairs three bridles in less time than it takes you to drink a glass of wine."

"We didn't take a blacksmith to Egypt last year."

"There weren't any for hire—or did you forget there was a war?"

"Boys." Ishmael silenced them with a wave of his hand. And though he never made the caravan trips to Egypt, at fifty-four years of age he was the oldest man at the plantation and the sons of Lehi respected his wisdom. "Last year's caravans took two weeks longer than they would have with a good blacksmith along."

Laman said, "Can we trust him?"

"We're hiring him to mend things," Sam said. "Not stand guard over our gold."

Lehi said, "Is there a reason you don't want Aaron with us?"

Sam said, "Don't listen to Laman. He's never wanted to hire outsiders."

"He's entitled to speak his mind."

Laman stared at Aaron with his dark, brown eyes. It was a stare that said Aaron was going to cause Laman more trouble than he was worth. He said, "Hire him if you must."

Sam gripped Aaron by the leg. "What do you say?"

"You shouldn't have much need of me. I've mended everything with the finest ores."

"We'll pay you double for your work."

"Double?" Laman stood next to Sam. "Are you mad?"

"We need him."

"You might as well pour our olive oil in the sea."

"It's already settled." Sam reached up and shook Aaron's hand. "You're coming with us."

"Hold on, boys." Lehi stepped between Sam and Laman. "This is up to Aaron, not either of you." He laid his hand on Aaron's bandaged right foot. "If you're not back by sunrise tomorrow, we'll know your answer."

That was all Lehi said. No pleading or begging. And despite how much Aaron sensed Lehi wanted him to be part of the caravan, he would not force his hand. Lehi walked back through the gate with Ishmael at his side. Sariah would have a warm cup of mint tea ready for them in the kitchen as she did every afternoon about this time.

Nephi, Nathan, and Seth followed their fathers. They hadn't said a word for or against Aaron coming with the caravan. They were happy to let their fathers do that for them. If only Laman were as respectful. The two eldest sons left together, headed for the stables to curry and feed the horses, leaving Sam and Aaron alone in the courtyard.

Sam said, "I'll see you in the morning." Then he walked toward the corrals to tend to the afternoon feedings.

Sam wanted Aaron on the caravan for his blacksmithing. But if he went, it would be because of Lehi. Something told Aaron he should stay close, not that anything would happen to the man, but Lehi may need him.

Or was it Aaron who needed Lehi?

CHAPTER 32

The night watch had already taken its post at Jerusalem's west gate when Aaron arrived by way of the Hinnom Valley, riding Beuntahyu and stringing the family mule behind on a rope. He would have been back before sundown if Sariah hadn't stopped him on his way out of Beit Zayit and insisted he wait on a basket of her fresh bread and a bottle of pickled olives for Ruth.

The night duty officer at the west gate didn't know Aaron like the day shift and he suffered him to answer all the questions, his name, where he lived, the nature of his business outside the city and where he'd gotten such a fine horse. He told him he'd been blacksmithing in the hill country—no mention of Beit Zayit, or the man would have reason to make a report. He never answered the question about the horse. That would cause even more of a stir. When the guard asked why Aaron was traveling at night he told him it was cooler, a poor answer since it was plenty cool for traveling during the day this time of year. The soldier raised his eyebrows into the brim of his brass helmet and Aaron gave him a loaf of Sariah's bread so that he let him in without further questions.

Aaron passed under the archway and immediately steered toward the potter's home. He had to speak with Rebekah and make things right. His words to her at the Pool of Siloam last week were all wrong, and he had to tell her why and ask her forgiveness.

The gate to the pottery yard stood open and Aaron spurred Beuntahyu through without having to raise a cry for someone to let him in. The kilnmaster tended the fires late tonight. He stood on a ladder outside the kiln and reached to open the iron door to the wood chute halfway up the outside wall. Stacks of wood leaned against the kiln wall and spilled out into the courtyard. More stacks were nestled neatly against the north wall of the estate like an irregular wall of tinder, dried, cut, and ready to fuel the kiln for five days. The firing would last until every bit of soft clay inside the kiln transformed into the hard pots sold in the market. Aaron reined past as the kilnmaster opened the wood chute and a rush of flames filled the night sky with an orange blast. Each log he threw into the kiln raised a spray of sparks and he turned his head away from the heat before tossing in the next.

The rest of the yard stood quiet. The flowers that usually graced the porch were gone, all of them freshly uprooted and the pots empty, waiting for spring and the touch of Rebekah's hand to plant another stand of colorful blossoms.

A lamp burned in Rebekah's second story bedroom window and he called to her. When she didn't answer, he came around under the window, leaned over Beuntahyu's mane and said, "Rebekah, please! It's me, Aaron."

The curtain parted and she stood at the window, the moon lighting her face. "Aaron?"

"Down here." He raised up in the saddle.

"I hadn't heard you were home." She spoke slowly as if seeing him reminded her she would rather not see him. "Is your family well?"

"I haven't seen them. I came straight here from Beit Zayit."

"Oh."

Oh? Was that all she could think to say? Ruth had lectured Aaron a thousand times about his poor choice of words, and now his careless diction had become Rebekah's. He was telling her that she was the first person he thought of on his return to the city, and all she cared to say was "oh"?

Aaron steadied Beuntahyu with a firm hold on the reins. "Why don't you come to the door and we can talk?"

Rebekah leaned on the sill. "What did you say?"

She hadn't heard him clearly, just like the day they first met in front of the selling tables in the street outside the gates of the pottery.

She looked as much like an angel now as she had then. The morning sun lit her smile that day, though tonight it was the moon that caressed the lines of her face. That day the reason for their misunderstanding was a few hundred cubits of cobblestone, but now they were separated by much more than a window curtain and sill. It was Rebekah's secret that tore them apart and it was her secret that had the power to bring them together.

Aaron asked, "Can you come down?"

"Like this?" Rebekah was dressed in a sleeping robe, her hair unbraided and flowing past her shoulders. She removed a red blossom that had come loose from her hair ribbons and gotten stuck in her hair. "I'm hardly presentable."

"You look beautiful."

Rebekah glanced over her shoulder, inside her bedroom, and spoke a few words to someone. A muffled voice responded and Aaron was certain it was Mima checking on her. Rebekah waited for a moment before turning back to the window and whispering, "This isn't a good time."

That was not the answer Aaron had hoped for, but he shouldn't expect a warmer reception, not after what he'd done. He'd already reduced her to tears once, and a burned child dreads the smallest of fires.

Aaron glanced at the kilnmaster. He was throwing another cord of wood down the chute, and the flames roared like the rush of wind out the top of the kiln. Aaron said, "It's about your faith."

"We've already discussed that." Rebekah pulled back from the window.

"Rebekah, no, at least hear me out." She shut the curtains and Aaron knew he had to say something, anything to bring her back to the window. He dismounted and stood on his bad feet, steadying himself against Beuntahyu's powerful body. He said, "I want you to keep your faith. Do you hear me? I want to know what you know, I want to believe as you believe."

Rebekah's shadow disappeared from the window. She was gone and Aaron had himself to thank for it. He'd hurt her too deeply to ever hope she would trust him again. Why hadn't he listened to his heart, telling him to trust her. It was so much easier to see that now after his time at Beit Zayit. If only the time he'd spent with the olive oil merchants were enough to heal the wounds he'd inflicted on Rebekah. Aaron steadied Beuntahyu close to him and he was about to pull himself up into the saddle when the door inched open and Rebekah stood on the porch. The hem of her robe brushed the stones like the raiment of a queen as she stepped from the doorway.

Rebekah stood on the top step and asked, "What did you say?"

"I said I want you to keep your faith." Aaron untied his crutches and walked to the porch. He looked up into her eyes and said, "Isn't that what you want?"

"The other part." Rebekah held her hands over her heart. "The part about you."

Aaron lifted himself up the steps and stood beside her. He leaned down on his crutches to see into her eyes and said, "I don't know where to start telling you about how I've changed."

"The beginning would do," she said quietly.

"Everything's happened so fast. I've only been gone two weeks." Aaron cleared his throat. "It was the olive oil merchants and, well there was Nephi and Sariah too and, well, all of them had a part in it."

The soft skin on Rebekah's brow furrowed into small lines. She turned her head slightly to one side as she did whenever she was trying to understand something that was difficult for Aaron to say. She reached out and touched his hand. "What about them?"

"They believe all that you believe."

"In two weeks they told you everything they believe?"

"They didn't have to; I saw it in the way they live."

Rebekah held his hand and her eyes began to water. "Go on."

"Well." Aaron took a deep breath. "I know for the first time in my life that I want to find the love that doesn't fade with time." Aaron reached his hand onto Rebekah's shoulder. "The kind of love your Yeshua promises." He looked up into the sky and when his gaze came back to her, she was brushing a tear from her cheek. "Lehi said it was eternal love and because of the sacrifice of the Anointed One it was available to any man with a broken heart."

Rebekah was staring at him. Was she searching his eyes to plumb the deepest secrets of his soul? She took a short breath, smiled between her tears and asked, "What do we do now?"

Aaron slid his hand down her arm. "Teach me." His voice was pleading, begging her to understand how much he wanted to know the things of eternal life.

"Oh, Aaron." Rebekah fell into his arms and they stood on the porch, holding each other close with the orange light of the kiln dancing about them.

Aaron placed his lips next to her ear and whispered, "Will you forgive me for hurting you?"

Rebekah dried her tears on the cloth of his shoulder before stepping back and looking up at him. She was about to answer when the front door flew open and Mima burst out, her dark skin glistening in the moonlight. She took Rebekah by the arm, pulled her inside and sent her to her room. Then she stood in the threshold and shooed her hands at Aaron as if he were a fly flitting over evening meal. "Leave this house before I fetch the potter!"

"Rebekah!" Aaron strained to see past her, into the darkened entry. "I need an answer."

"Not right now you don't." Mima scurried him off the porch, crutches and all. "She's gone to bed."

"Rebekah! Please tell me that you forgive me."

"Away with you before I call the potter." Mima hovered above him on the top step.

"I'll go." Aaron stood up as high as he could on his crutches. "But not until I know she forgives me."

Mima placed her hands on her hips. "If she does, will you leave her alone?"

"I will."

"Then she forgives you."

"I must hear her say it."

"The potter's forbidden you to ever speak with her and the sooner you understand that, boy, the happier we'll both be." Mima latched the door behind her and she was gone, leaving Aaron alone in the yard. He hobbled back to where he could see Rebekah's room. The lamp was put out, her room dark, but Aaron waited, hoping Rebekah would come back as soon as Mima left her alone so he could hear her say he was forgiven and he could tell her face to face that he loved her, not for her beauty, but for what he felt was anchored deep in her soul.

When Rebekah never returned to the window, Aaron pulled himself up in the saddle and steered out of the pottery yard. The street was silent and as he trotted over the cobblestones, he lowered his head and offered the most childish of prayers. *Dear God, keep things as they are until my return.* But deep in his soul he knew he'd prayed the wrong prayer.

Things never stayed the same.

Ruth lay in bed alone when the front door creaked open and shut. It must be Jonathan. She didn't approve of his working this late, but tonight would be his last. Whatever it was he was smithing for the captain of the guard, it had to be finished by morning. She pulled the blankets up around her neck. Laban. Why had she ever allowed her husband to associate with the man?

Ruth turned on her side and listened for Jonathan's sandals on the steps leading to the second floor, but they never sounded on the wooden slats. She opened her eyes and scanned the darkness. It couldn't be Joshua or Sarah. She'd put them to bed hours ago. They were asleep in the loft and they would have passed by her opened door to get downstairs. And it couldn't be Elizabeth. She slept like a wintering bear. The girl had never gotten up during the night since she was three years old, unless of course she was sick—and that was near to impossible. Elizabeth was stubborn and she scared away an illness before it dared infect her. Sickness and plague knew better than to trouble with her.

The sound of wooden pegs on stone tapped over the floor to the kitchen. Was Aaron home? An oil lamp threw dim shadows across the door to Ruth's room and then she heard the steady scratching of a pen on papyrus. He and Elizabeth were her only children who knew how to write. She'd tried to teach Daniel his letters, but he didn't have the patience and the younger ones were just that, too young. She got out of bed, draped a shawl over her shoulders and hurried to the top of the stairs.

Aaron's crutches leaned against the table and his head was bent over a small piece of papyrus. Whatever he was writing, it had to be important. They could hardly afford to waste what little papyrus they owned. Aaron was dressed in a new white linen tunic and his hair was combed neatly in place, an odd thing, since the boy preferred his old, worn, brown tunic to the new one Ruth had woven for him. And he never combed his hair except to run his fingers through it. Whoever convinced him to improve his grooming habits had more influence over the boy than she.

Ruth leaned over the railing. "You're home."

"Mama?" Aaron turned in the chair. "I didn't mean to wake you."

Ruth pulled the shawl close around her shoulders and hurried down the stairs to stand over him. "Look at you. You've changed so much."

"It's only been two weeks, Mama."

"Your hair, and that tunic." Ruth pressed the cloth between her fingers. "You look so much older."

"It was a gift from Sariah."

"Lehi's wife?"

"You'd like her, Mama. She reminds me of you."

"I'm sure I would." Ruth leaned over the table and quickly scanned the words on the papyrus. She didn't read to the end; there was no need. Aaron was saying goodbye without ever having said hello. "You're leaving us?"

"I don't know what I should do."

Aaron was troubled by something. Ruth could tell he was confused by the way he kept rubbing the back of his neck. She asked, "What is it, son?"

"It's a hundred things."

Ruth sat in the chair next to him and set the lamp between them. "I have time to hear them."

Aaron set aside the pen and wiped the ink off his fingers. "Before I left for Beit Zayit I spoke with Rebekah." He swallowed hard. "I hurt her with some of the things I said."

"I wondered what happened."

"Did Rebekah tell you?"

"She didn't need to. There were more than a hundred women at the Pool of Siloam."

Aaron lowered his head. "I wish I hadn't said what I said." He reached out and held Ruth's hand. "I went to Beit Zayit a blacksmith and I've returned a . . ."

Ruth lowered her voice to a whisper. "Is it Rebekah's faith that caused the troubles?"

"You know about that?"

"I know enough."

"Before I left, I was worried about her. I thought she was in danger."

Ruth spoke slowly. "All who believe like the Rekhabites have reason to worry." Ruth stood behind Aaron's chair and gently rubbed the strain out of his neck. "These are difficult times to grow to manhood. So many conflicting voices drowning out the truth."

"I've never heard you speak like this before, Mama."

"I never have, until now." Ruth touched Aaron's cheek. "When you were a little boy I used to repeat a psalm at the side of your bed as you fell asleep. Do you remember the words?" She came around the chair to Aaron's side. "God is our refuge and strength, a very present help in trouble. Therefore will we not fear. The Lord of Hosts is with us and—"

"And he saith," Aaron finished the psalm for her, "Be still and know that I am God."

Ruth said, "You do remember."

"Only the words, not the meaning."

"Be still and you will hear the voice of heaven, the still voice within." She held her hand to her breast. "It is that spirit, the spirit of God that speaks to your soul."

Aaron glanced at his bandaged feet. "While I was at Beit Zayit I found the answer to my blessing." He took Ruth by the hand. "Lehi is the prophet I'm going to save."

"But, son, he's a merchant."

"I know, Mama. And all I can tell you is that somehow, sometime soon, he will be called as a prophet, just as Moses and Isaiah were called. And when that day comes I need to be by his side."

"Is that why you think you should go to Egypt?"

"I can't deny what I feel."

"Then you should go." Ruth took a deep breath. "But you should ask your father."

"Can't you do that for me?"

Ruth shook her head. "You'll find him at the shop. He's working late this evening." She picked up Aaron's crutches and steadied them under his arms.

"Will he allow me to go?"

"I don't know." Ruth held him close. She could feel him tense and she asked, "What is it now?"

"I don't know what to say to him."

"Be still and God will provide the answer."

Ruth walked Aaron to the door and held it open while he lifted himself over the threshold and into the night. Her son Aaron, the boy with the blue eyes as deep as the faith that had burned inside him. But he was no longer a boy. He was a man and she could only pray that one day, God willing, the right woman would see past his crippled feet and into his heart. Ruth watched long after he disappeared through the gate. She didn't worry about his feet or the dangers of associating with Lehi, not anymore.

He was her son and he would always be her son.

CHAPTER 33

The stone sealing the strongbox was moored tight and Jonathan had to leverage it out with a bar. He slipped the end of it in the groove and pried the stone free, raising a cloud of ash and soot that had collected in the cracks. Iron plates lined the sides of the strongbox and the edges were trimmed with a thick layer of mortar rising up in the gaps between stones so that when the cover was set in place it gave the appearance of a solid limestone floor without any breaks. It was Jonathan's fear of being found out by his sons that had convinced him to dig the secret compartment in the floor of the shop. Aaron and Daniel never knew they had been working all this time standing atop something more valuable than they would ever own in a thousand lifetimes.

Jonathan raised the sword case from the hole and secured it on the forging table as far away from the edge as possible. He opened the brass latches and lifted the lid, exposing the ivory casement where the original sword had rested all these years in the captain's treasury and where the sword of his own creation now took its rightful place. With Aaron gone to Beit Zayit, Daniel with the military, and Zoram gone to Anathoth, Jonathan spent day and night smithing the sword. He'd finished everything but the inscription. None of his chisels pierced the steel surface, but he had to engrave the words into the blade before Aaron returned. It wasn't that he didn't trust him, but the less Aaron knew about the hidden treasure, the more Jonathan kept faith with Laban.

The door flew open and Jonathan threw the red silk over the sword. It was Laban and he crossed the room to Jonathan's side.

"I didn't expect you this evening, Captain."

Laban stood across the table from Jonathan. "Is that it?"

"Yes, sir, but it isn't finished."

"Does it match the pattern I gave you?"

"Well, yes."

"Every detail?"

"See for yourself."

Jonathan lifted away the edge of the silk, exposing the narrow neck at the hilt. He pulled free the cloth to show how the blade grew wide as a man's hand just before it came to a point at the tip, nearly one-and-a-half cubits long. The hilt was of gold, not just dipped and plated over a steel end, but fashioned of solid gold with emeralds and jade inlaid along its length, and the largest diamond embedded in the end. Jonathan raised it by the hilt, holding it in the air in front of Laban, the luster of the steel reflecting the captain's image.

Laban lowered his voice to a breathless whisper and said, "It's a remarkable copy."

"It's more than a copy."

"You'll be paid well for it."

"You don't understand, sir. Something happened while I was smithing it." Jonathan stroked the blade. "I don't know how to explain it, but I believe this is the finest sword ever made."

Laban smiled. "You exaggerate your skills, blacksmith. But we've already agreed upon the price and I'm not about to pay one shekel more."

"I didn't smith this sword."

"What?" Laban slammed his fist on the forging table. "I warned you about your sons helping."

"No one assisted me."

"What are you saying?"

"Something happened when I smithed the sword."

Laban passed his finger over the blade. "Is the metal bad?"

"No, sir, but making good steel is part skill and part luck."

"I'm not paying you to be lucky."

"But I was. You see, steel always takes on small air bubbles in the smelter when it heats and over time, the air rusts the metal from within, but not this metal. There's not a single pocket of air in any of the steel I smelted for the blade." Jonathan spoke faster, the words rushing out of him. "And there's always some dross left in the ore, no matter how long or how hot you fire it, but this steel has a shine to it like no other. There's no blemish from hilt to point. I haven't even polished it, but look." He held the blade near Laban's face. "You can see a perfect image in the reflection, clearer than the calmest reflecting pool."

Laban looked up from his reflection. "It's a better replica than I expected."

Jonathan held up his hands like a priest offering a blessing. "It's like no steel I've ever worked with. It was as if . . ."

"As if what?"

"It was very odd, as if an unseen power controlled the ovens at the perfect temperature and kept out all the impurities. And when it came time to forge the blade, my own hand seemed guided. Every swing of the forging hammer landed square on the metal so that I didn't have to keep heating and reheating it while I forged and lose the finish that came from the smelting. I don't know how else to tell you that this sword is different from other swords, except to say that it's the finest steel I've ever known." Jonathan rested the sword across his arms like a mother holding a newborn. "The legend says the sword of Joseph will endure forever."

"Don't you think I know that?"

"This is the sword of legends." Jonathan cradled it with a rocking motion. "It has a finish as clear as water, but hard as diamond. Not even oils penetrate the surface and I believe it won't rust."

"For how long?"

"Forever."

"That's impossible. Everything has an end. Nothing survives the passing of time."

"No smith I ever knew in Sidon achieved this."

"Achieved what?"

"Here, let me show you." Jonathan flicked the blade with his fingernail. "You have to listen to the metal, check to see if the outer layer is hard and the inner layer soft." He flicked the blade again and again until it shook in his hand, but it was so finely balanced that Laban wouldn't see the shaking that Jonathan felt in his hand, only hear the ringing in his ears. The brittle outer surface rang crisp and clear as if it were a bell that could chime for eternity without cracking.

Jonathan flicked it again, this time with the soft side of his thumb to test the inner metal. Its ring was muted, like a distant echo, supple, workable, and flexible. It was a ring that said this sword would never break, even after clashing upon a thousand breastplates. He held the blade with both hands to silence it, like a priest holds a vessel of sacred olive oil. This was more than a weapon, it was a soldier's treasure and when Jonathan handed it over to Laban, the captain couldn't keep a smile from lifting the point of his well-trimmed beard. He held the sword on his palms, examining the polished steel, the jeweled settings, the hilt's golden luster, every contour and line of the metal down to running his thumb over the sharp edge of the blade.

Laban said, "I'm taking it with me tonight."

"I haven't done the engraving."

"Here." Laban handed the blade back to Jonathan. "I'll wait while you do it."

"I can't."

"Of course you can, that was part of our agreement. You were to engrave the words into the metal."

"I've tried a hundred times, but I can't get any of my chisels to make even a scratch."

Laban knocked three hammers off the rack in his rush to retrieve a chisel. He laid the sword out on the table and scratched the edge of the tool over the steel blade, lightly at first, but when he couldn't form the slightest mark of a Hebrew character, he pressed harder, the chisel slipping over the steel surface. He got one of the hammers off the floor and tamped the chisel into the steel, but not even a scratch appeared on the surface. He swung harder, raising the hammer higher and higher with each stroke and still no mark. When he raised the hammer overhead to inflict the heaviest blow, Jonathan grabbed his arm. "You'll break the chisel, Captain."

Laban lowered his arm, sweat forming on his brow. He took a deep breath and said, "It's—"

"It's eternal," Jonathan said and took the chisel from Laban's grip.

The galloping of horse hooves streamed in from the street and an Arabian passed by the opened shop doors in a flash of white. The rider dismounted and the sound of him lashing to the post outside filled the air.

Laban asked, "Who is that?"

"I don't know. No one ever comes by at this hour."

Laban fitted the sword into the ivory casement, latched the lid and started for the door.

Jonathan asked, "Where are you taking it?"

"To have it anointed."

That was the other part of the legend, and Jonathan could only assume that the captain was taking it to the temple priests. Joseph anointed his sword to endure forever—a symbol of divine kingship—and it seemed a noble thing that Laban didn't want to miss a single detail before it was used in the coronation of King Zedekiah. The metal in the sword did have the character to withstand the corruption of time, but divinity, well that was a superstition he never expected from the captain.

"When I bring it back, I want you to find a way to write the words into the blade." Laban tucked the case under his arm and marched into the night to meet the man who had arrived by horseback.

Jonathan huddled over the strongbox and retrieved the parchment with the words that were to be written into the blade. He unfolded it and slowly read: *this sword will never be sheathed again until the kingdoms of this world become the kingdom of our God and his Christ.* Why did Laban want this engraved in his blade?

They were the words of his most hated enemy—the words of the prophet Uriah.

Aaron reached the top of the smithing district as the moon fell behind a thick bank of clouds, darkening everything but the entrance to the blacksmith shop. The light of a fire danced through the open doors and cast a glow on another white Arabian tied to the post, one exactly like his.

Aaron slid off his mount and peered through the narrow slits cut into the brick walls for ventilation, just large enough to see without being seen. Jonathan stood by the forging table while Laban locked an elegant-looking sword into its case. He mumbled a few words to Jonathan before heading to the door. Aaron limped over to the entrance in time to bump shoulders with Laban, who knocked a crutch from under his arm. The captain didn't offer a word of apology. He returned the crutch and went straight to his horse, pausing long enough to study Beuntahyu. They were kindred animals, though it wasn't difficult to tell the difference between Laban's silver-studded saddle and Aaron's plain leather one given him by Ishmael. Both had a white coat with a black spot on the muzzle. The captain mounted and spurred toward the upper city.

Aaron turned in the doorway and asked, "What was he doing here?"

Jonathan quickly folded the parchment he was reading and dropped it into a hole in the floor. "Laban and I have some unfinished business."

"At this hour?"

Jonathan immediately placed the cover stone over the hole and said, "I didn't expect you by here tonight."

"What's that for?" Aaron pointed to the hole in the floor.

"This?" Jonathan stood atop the stone that was still marred by the brownish red stains from Aaron's accident. "I'm replacing it with a new stone. It isn't a pretty memory to keep around the shop."

If Papa really wanted to get rid of the stained limestone, he should have pounded it out with a hammer instead of carefully chiseling around the edges and digging a hole beneath it. Aaron asked, "Do you need some help?"

"I'll be fine." Jonathan stepped to the door and stood next to Aaron. "That's a fine horse you're riding."

Aaron turned on his crutches and faced the street. "It was a gift from Lehi."

Beuntahyu's white coat shimmered in the moonlight. Her mane was curried and her powerful haunches bristled against the cool evening air. Jonathan said, "You shouldn't be accepting things from a man like him. There must be a reason he wants you to have such a fine animal."

There was, but Aaron could hardly tell Jonathan what it was. In Papa's eyes, Aaron's rescue was a dream and his burned feet a result of bad luck—not a sign of divine deliverance.

"They want me to caravan to Egypt," Aaron said in answer to his father's staring. That was an answer Jonathan could bear. Aaron handed over a talent of silver. "I can earn more if you'll let me go."

"We don't need their money. Not once I finish my work with Laban."

"It isn't just the money, Papa."

"You like this Lehi, don't you?"

"He does well with his merchant business; that's something you've wanted me to learn. And he knows how to read and write in the language of the Egyptians."

"So you're telling me he's an intelligent plantation owner."

"Well, yes."

"Then go." Jonathan walked back to the open hearth and gazed into the fire, but he was really staring past the flames to the shadows on the dark side of the shop. "Go to Egypt if you must." He stabbed the poker into the coals. "I have blacksmithing to finish for Laban."

Aaron left Jonathan standing by the open hearth. He mounted up and came trotting past the door when Jonathan appeared in the entry without offering the slightest gesture of good-bye. He leaned against the doorpost and Aaron quickly rode away. As soon as Papa regained his senses he might forbid him from going with the caravan.

Aaron reached the top of the hill and was about to turn onto Main Street when he heard a voice. It was the same still small voice he'd felt at Beit Zayit, but this time it was telling him to go back and finish speaking with Jonathan. Hadn't he said everything that needed to be said? If he went back, Papa might keep him from going with the caravan. He coaxed Beuntahyu onto Main Street and she picked up her stride toward the west gate. They rode past Milo Hill and around the bend near the cheesemakers' district when the voice came again, stronger than before. Go back and say what Jonathan needs to hear. Aaron pulled up in the empty street. There were no shepherds herding goats about the cheesemakers' pens, and no mule carts streaming up from the west gate. There was no one standing in any of the darkened second story windows overlooking the street. Aaron knew he was hearing with his soul.

Aaron came around in the street and spurred back down over the cobblestones toward the shop. Jonathan was still standing at the door.

He was without his usual vigor, as if he'd been sapped of his strength. He asked, "What is it, boy?"

"I thought you might have more to say."

"Do I look like I have more?"

"I wasn't sure." Aaron reined Beuntahyu around and pointed her nose at Jonathan. "Lehi told me—"

"Enough about Lehi."

"He's a good man, Papa, and he has a deep faith in God."

"You came all the way back to tell me that?"

"I don't know why I came back. I thought you could tell me."

Aaron held the reins firm and sat straight in the saddle. Why did he bother with this? Papa didn't need to hear anything from him; he said so himself. And the longer he waited, the greater chance that Jonathan would keep him from leaving again. A cool breeze blew down the Mount of Olives, chilling Aaron to the very center.

"Go with Lehi and leave me to do what I must to feed and clothe this family. You don't need me now. You've found a father more to your liking."

"You think Lehi—"

"I've tried to do right by you, son. Teach you a good trade, see that you've never wanted for anything, and now . . ."

Jonathan turned away and clasped the doorframe. Papa never allowed his emotions to show, not even in the privacy of his own family, and tonight would be no different. He didn't utter another word.

Aaron leaned over Beuntahyu, laid his hand across Jonathan's shoulder and softly said, "I only have one father. And I'll only ever love one father."

Their conversation was over. Aaron had come back and said what Jonathan needed to hear. He spurred around and started up the hill toward Main Street. The words he'd spoken were his own, but it was the spirit of God that brought him back to say them. For the first time in his life he had been still.

And he knew that God was God.

CHAPTER 34

The village of Anathoth lay four miles northeast of the capital city on the leeward side of the Mount of Olives. It was a quiet farming community with some of the kingdom's sweetest date groves and most fertile vineyards, though the produce hadn't achieved a notoriety to compare with Zoram's father. The prophet Jeremiah criticized the nobles of Jerusalem enough that Anathoth was known more for his railings against the Elders than for the harvest.

There were no walls to protect the sixty-odd mud brick homes spread over the high valley plains, painted with a coat of red clay wash and scattered among the groves and vineyards of Anathoth. Each dwelling marked the end of one man's orchards and the beginning of another, except for the home of Zoram's youth, the one at the east end of town. The well-manicured vineyards he once tended with his father stood away from the other orchards, down the hill where he used to chase the wind as fast as his legs could carry him. He fell not less than once a week, skinning his knees and hands so often his mother Eliza warned him she'd stop bandaging the wounds and let him bleed to death if he didn't stop. He never did and she never did, until one day he found he couldn't catch the wind and turned his imagination to older boys' dreams. The irrigation ditch where he used to float seaworthy gourds and melon-rind rafts still flowed around the property like a moat around a castle. But the small brick home no longer seemed as large as a king's palace, dwarfed as it was by a forest of date palms on the east, olive trees to the north and west, and twenty-seven grape arbors to the south.

Zoram had grown tall and wise in this home; the thick cedar door he had struggled to open as a boy had given way more easily as he grew to manhood. The wood planks and latch seemed smaller than before, and he had to duck under the door beam. He swung the door open and went inside to find that his parents' love for him hadn't waned.

Eliza had prepared his favorite meal. Lamb stew simmered in a pot over the hearth, and Zoram was hardly able to refuse her insistence that he sit and eat his fill. She was a plump and hardy woman who looked nothing like her adopted son. He was tall and slender; she was short and stout. And Zoram's dark skin, curly hair, and green eyes bore no resemblance to her own. She had light-colored cheeks, flushed red from standing near the hearth, and penetrating brown eyes that seemed to see through things; at least that's what he used to think when she caught him in his childhood mischiefs.

Doting was Eliza's most visible talent and she exercised it on Jeremiah first. She filled his plate with another helping of thick broth and lamb before she circled the table to Zoram's side, stirring the pot with a large spoon and insisting he was far too thin to refuse a fourth helping. He declined, but she filled his plate anyway and placed a small loaf of bread on the side. Last came the fig and pomegranate salad. She always saved the best for last. She was filling Zoram's glass with another round of sweet wine when the bottle went dry.

Eliza said, "Sit right there while I fetch another."

"I'm fine, Mama." Zoram pushed his glass away. "Sit down and eat with us."

"And let my boy go without a good drink? Nonsense. I'll be back before you can finish your stew." Eliza placed the empty bottle under her arm and headed to the wine cellar. "There's more bread on the hearthstone." She pulled open the back door and went into the yard.

When the door shut, Jeremiah leaned over his plate and asked, "Did you bring it with you?"

Zoram picked up the leather satchel from the floor and carefully removed a bright brass plate, three hands wide, four hands long, and thick as a barleycorn. It was thicker than most plates used for writing, and Zoram used both hands to take it out of the satchel. It was a perfect match to the plates Laban kept in his treasury. The ends were scored and the surface polished and ready for engraving.

"It's wonderful, son." Jeremiah picked up the plate and held it in front of him, his reflection shimmering over the brass. "How many did you bring."

"That's all I was able to smith."

"Only one?"

"It requires much more work than we thought. And there's another problem." Zoram laid his hand on the brass plate. "I'm nearly out of ore."

"I gave you more than enough."

"You didn't take into account the thickness. The brass plates in Laban's treasury are three times as thick as any I've seen and twice as wide. You should be able to get more writing on each plate, but I'm afraid we'll need more copper and silver to smith as many as you wanted."

"I need them now."

"This one should keep you busy for a while. You know how tiring it is to engrave. You'll be weeks, maybe months, working on this one."

"I have a friend, a scribe who is going to help me with the—"

"You didn't tell Baruch about this, did you?" Zoram shook his head. "The more people who know, the greater danger you stir up for us."

"We can trust Baruch more than we should have ever trusted your friend Elizabeth."

"She's not going to betray us."

"How do you know that?"

"Don't worry about her."

"I hope you're right, son."

Jeremiah laid the brass plate on the table between their dinner plates. He said, "I'm going to bring you a larger supply of ores."

"You can't go back to Jerusalem."

"I'll go wherever I please." Jeremiah sopped up the stew with a piece of bread.

Zoram pushed away his dinner plate. "It's too dangerous for you to come to the treasury."

"I won't let Laban's soldiers discourage me."

"He's not using discouragement, Papa. He's going to kill Uriah." Zoram gripped the edge of the table. "Don't you understand? If you love Mama and me, you'll stay away from all that."

"It's my love for family that drives me to do this." Jeremiah came around the table. "You do believe we're a family, don't you, son?"

"I've never thought otherwise, but what does that have to do with the brass plates?"

"Everything." Jeremiah sat in the chair next to Zoram. "Laban's brass plates are to become part of another record." He touched Zoram's arm. "It will be a record for the last days. A book to show the Jews and Gentiles what great things the Lord has done for our fathers. And it will teach them the covenants that can bind their families forever, just as our family will be united forever." He held Zoram's long, thin fingers in the palm of his hand. "God is raising up a prophet to see that His will is done with Laban's brass plates, and you and I must prepare the way for that."

The door swung open and Eliza rushed in, bolting the latch behind her and waving the empty bottle of wine at Jeremiah. Her hair had come loose from its ribbon and danced about her shoulders like wild hyssop in a strong wind. Sweat flowed from her furrowed brow and stung tears from her eyes. She spoke in short, breathless gasps and said, "Soldier, coming down off the road."

Jeremiah stood. "How many?"

Eliza took another deep breath. "Only one."

Zoram started for the window. "Are you sure it was a soldier?"

"Well, I . . ." Eliza held her face in her hands. "I don't know."

Zoram parted the curtains to see a man riding toward the house. The moonlight shone on his brass armor and cast a glow onto his purple riding cape buttoned to his shoulders. He leaned forward over the horse's mane, reins held in both hands and his thick forearms moving up and down in rhythm with the animal's long sleek neck. The rider leaped the last arbors, clearing the wooden crossbars with a cubit to spare and hitting the ground on a dead gallop toward the house.

Zoram turned from the window and whispered, "It's Laban." But his mind was screaming his master's name. Laban had tracked him here and now he had to face his worst fear, that his master would find out his deepest secret, that Jeremiah's family was his family, the prophet's faith his faith.

Jeremiah said, "Hide, son!"

Next to the dinner table stood a large wicker basket set on the steps leading to the loft. Zoram returned the brass plate to the leather satchel and carefully placed it in the bottom of the basket. He lifted himself inside and huddled over the brass plate, his long-boned body barely able to bend below the rim of the basket while Jeremiah covered him with the lid. The basket's thick weave hid his white robes, but it wasn't so thick he couldn't see between the reeds.

The pounding of the animal's hooves thundered up in front of the house. Then came the clicking of Laban's boots up the path. He knocked hard enough to rattle the door on its hinges and the sound sent Zoram crouching low in the basket, still as a mongoose in a snake's pit. Jeremiah hid Zoram's dinner plate under a cloth then slowly lowered himself to sit at the table and finish his stew. He motioned with both hands for Eliza to open the door, but to do it slowly as if Laban's arrival were a common thing. She cracked open the door and Laban said, "Where is he? I know he's here."

Eliza asked, "Who, sir?"

"You know who, woman." Laban pushed open the door, knocking Eliza back. He marched to the table, his cape whipping about his knees and it brushed the wicker basket where Zoram hid. From under the purple cloth, Laban produced a wooden case, the same sword case that had gone missing from the treasury last month. He unlatched it and took out a sword. The metal in the blade shone in the lamplight with a new luster. It was without any scratches and the hilt didn't have even a hint of tarnish. The jewels were brilliant and set in the same circular pattern along the hilt. But for all the sword's splendor, it wasn't the same blade that had gone missing the day Elizabeth visited the treasury. It couldn't be. There were no scratches, the steel was untarnished, and the prophecy was missing. The words Zoram had been told were engraved into the metal were nowhere on either side of the blade.

Laban raised the sword above Jeremiah's head and for a moment it seemed the captain was going to take his life. He said, "Anoint this."

"That's a rite a prophet performs at a coronation ceremony." Jeremiah said.

"You won't be attending this one. You or anyone who calls himself a prophet will never be allowed in Jerusalem."

"Why have me anoint this sword, if you doubt me a prophet?"

Laban pushed the blade across the table at Jeremiah. "Just do it, old man."

Jeremiah lightly touched his fingers over the finely crafted metal. "Is this the sword you keep locked in your treasury?"

"It's mine."

"Well then, you don't need me to anoint it." Jeremiah pulled on the end of his beard. "It's already been done."

"I want it done again."

Jeremiah backed his chair from the table and stood. "There's no reason for me to repeat what Joseph of old did many hundred years ago."

"It has to be anointed by a . . ."

Jeremiah closed his eyes and said, "A prophet?"

"Bless this sword or I'll use it to cut off your head." Laban slammed his fist onto the table and Jeremiah's eyes shot open as if he were awakening from a dream. No, it wasn't a dream, it was a nightmare and his eyes were filled with fear. He said, "Don't say that."

"I'll say whatever I like."

"If I anoint this blade, you will have spoken your own fate."

"Save your cursings for those who cower to such things."

"Very well." Jeremiah took the sword and laid it on a white cloth. He poured droplets of olive oil over it, then worked the liquid over the metal, his fingers gentle but firm, feeling their way over the blade. He turned the sword over and over in his oiled hands until it was covered with a thin coat from point to hilt, but when he tried to pronounce a blessing the words didn't come.

Laban slammed his fist to the table. "Say the words!"

Jeremiah reached for a small knife that sat beside his dinner plate.

Laban grabbed his arm and said, "Don't try anything foolish."

"I need something sharp if I'm to anoint this."

Laban let go. "I'm watching you."

Jeremiah held the knife between his thumb and forefinger. The point pierced the blade's surface like a stylus passing over a scroll and he etched the words of his anointing into the metal. With bold, flowing strokes he wrote: *This sword will never be sheathed again until the kingdoms of this world become the kingdom of our God and his Christ.*

Jeremiah laid the sword on the table. "You have your anointing."

Laban pushed Jeremiah aside and tried to etch his own words into the sword. The metal resisted even the smallest scratch. He tried again and again, but not even the hint of a mark appeared on the blade.

Laban said, "The metal is too hard to do what you did."

"Your heart is what's hard, Captain."

"Enough of your preaching." Laban placed the sword in its case. "How did you know what to write on the blade?"

"I think you already know, Captain."

"Tell me where you got these words."

"The same place Joseph of old received them. From God."

"I've heard enough of your foolishness." Laban latched the case and when he spun around for the door, the end of his cape snapped at the basket where Zoram crouched. It was divine providence that he didn't see the sudden movement of the lid as Zoram lowered his head back below the basket's brim.

When the door slammed shut behind the captain, Zoram stood, his white robe creased and wrinkled about his waist. He had concealed his relationship to Jeremiah, but now there was a new secret he would have to keep. The sword that graced the treasury all these years was gone, replaced by another seemingly finer blade, anointed this very night as the sword of kings. Zoram stepped out of the basket and held the brass plate close to his chest. The sacred record begun by Joseph was going to be altered with his help, and if that wasn't enough to give him pause, the sword in his charge was no longer the sword of Joseph, the patriarch of old.

It was the sword of Laban.

CHAPTER 35

"Cover your faces, men!"

Captain Elnathan shouted the order as the company of thirty cavalrymen and the prisoner cart rode through a column of dust. Daniel tied on a bandana and peered over the top of the linen. In Egypt the wind blew upstream, no matter how many hundred miles they had ridden south of the Great Sea. It whirled around Daniel, raising so much dust off the trail he lost sight of the riders ahead of him and all he could do was keep the blue waters of the Nile to his right. The trail hardly ever strayed from running alongside its banks. Daniel shielded his eyes with one hand, lowered his head to the swirling dust and drove his heels into the horse's haunches. The river was his guide now just as it had been over the two-hundred-mile ride up the Nile River Valley.

It had been one week since the cavalry crossed the Sinai and rode across the borders into Egypt near the city of Pelusium, northeast of the Nile Delta. It was a swampy place, with more belly-crawling creatures than people. They camped on the highest dry ground they could find outside the city and stayed long enough to buy supplies, and for Daniel to barter a pair of crocodile-skin boots from a cobbler and win a belt crafted of snakeskin in a game of pitch and toss. The next day they headed southwest to Tanis and laid over two days while Captain Elnathan secured Pharaoh's blessing to search the country for Uriah. While there, Daniel concluded that Egyptian and Hebrew women did not share the same views on modesty. The women of the

Nile wore nothing but silks, a cloth that allowed more than air to pass through it, and Daniel's gaze found its way through more than once. The men in his company encouraged him, and Ruth wasn't around to keep his eyes from wandering. From Tanis, they followed the main channel of the Nile River south. The blue waters turned colder, the banks steeper, and the current swifter with each bend in the river. The only constants were the boats and the cries of rivermen. Ships headed for the Great Sea lowered their sails and let the current carry them downriver to the delta, while ships navigating upriver set their reeds to the wind and sailed against the current toward the gold country of Africa.

They passed through Thebes yesterday, and Daniel would have stayed a few days to relax at the large outdoor inns along the city markets and bask in the warm winter sun; but they were getting too close to their destination and Captain Elnathan pushed on to the southernmost fortress in Egypt, the capital of the first district of the kingdom, the governing city of Pharaoh's largest territory, the military outpost called Elephantine.

When the wind died and the dust settled, Daniel removed his bandana and took a deep breath. He could see the trail now. It divided just ahead, the left fork turning away from the river and crossing a wide, fertile plain. There were only five mud-brick farm homes where there should have been hundreds dotting the rich soil, but few Egyptians dared raise crops here. Gold trade, not wheat, was the business of southern Egypt, and it attracted robbers from far and near. Daniel spurred closer to the fork in the road. If he were an Egyptian farmer he wouldn't choose this place. Robbers he could deal with, but the threat of warring African tribes was too much of a deterrent to raising crops. Tribesmen refused to accept that Pharaoh's kingdom extended this far south. Necho was God in Egypt, but this was African soil and it would always be Africa, no matter how many soldiers Pharaoh sent to keep the peace and the land in his kingdom.

The company reached the fork in the trail and Elnathan led his men to the right, following the Nile past a stand of willow that grew up along the steep rock banks. The Nile's blue water flashed between the branches; and when they cleared the last tree, Daniel sighted the island fortress at Elephantine. Its redrock shoreline rose out of the

Nile's cold waters and stood a hundred and fifty cubits from the east bank and nearly five hundred from the west bank. The island reached up from the river bottom like the back of a giant hippo, slowing the river's current after its twelve-mile run through the cataracts. This was as far south as the wind could carry the merchant ships, the southernmost port on the headwaters of the Nile.

Daniel followed his company down an incline to the river's edge. A small dock was moored into the bedrock and a boatmaster operated a ferry from one end. He was an older man with gray hair and a potbelly that hung over his belt. He talked into a mule's ear as if the animal understood his grumblings, and when he saw Daniel and the company of soldiers thundering down the bank, he tied the animal into its harness and prepared to shove off.

The boatmaster asked, "You men looking to cross?"

Captain Elnathan reined to the dock, his horse pawing the first wood plank. "I'm going over along with that soldier there." He pointed to Daniel.

The boatmaster chewed on a single shaft of wheat. "What of the others?"

"They'll wait here."

"It won't cost you anything to haul them all over." The boatmaster yanked the wheat from his mouth and his words whistled through the gaps in his teeth. "Pharaoh pays the toll for his soldiers."

"We're not Egyptian soldiers."

"None of the military men around here are." The boatmaster slowly passed his gaze over the cavalry. "They're all Hebrews, just like you." He blew his nose on the sleeve of his tunic. "How much is Pharaoh paying you?"

Elnathan got down from the saddle and walked his horse onto the dock. "We're soldiers of the King of Judah."

The boatmaster turned his head and spat with the wind. "You could make more money working for Pharaoh; just ask your Hebrew friends on the island. No wars, just a bunch of vile-mouthed, gold-hungry river traders to protect."

Elephantine was an outpost, a fortress built by Pharaoh to safeguard the African gold trade from robbers. And since Egyptian soldiers refused to bring their families to live in the southern reaches of Egypt, Pharaoh hired Hebrew mercenaries. The Jews of Elephantine preferred the remoteness of this fortified island city to the crossroads of Israel where the trade routes from east, west, north, and south brought together as many armies as they did caravaneers and merchants. When Egypt declared war on Assyria, which they did whenever Pharaoh had a strong enough army or large enough ego, the Egyptians tore through Israel, drafting Jews into their ranks at the point of a sword. And the Babylonians were happy to fight their wars with Egypt on Judah's soil, halfway between the two nations. It was no wonder that these Jews at Elephantine were content to live their lives in the solace of the southern mountains of Egypt, on an island in the middle of the Nile.

"You'll be right at home over there." The boatmaster pulled his mule forward three strides and took the slack out of the line. The rope snapped out of the water, taut and ready to pull the ferry across the channel. "Nothing but Jews, give or take a few African cooks and an Egyptian cobbler. Then there are the wives and children, all of them good Jews as well."

Elnathan reached into his purse. "How much for the ride across?"

"I only charge the Nubians. They pay in gold." The boatmaster refused the offer. "Pharaoh takes care of the other tolls."

Elnathan held out a piece of silver. "We're not mercenaries."

"To them you are." The boatmaster pointed across the east plains and up into the hills. "There's a good number of robbers out there, and once word of your arrival reaches them, they'll think again before bothering those of us who live along the river." He nodded and said, "Come aboard, sir."

Daniel got down off his horse and carefully walked his steed over the dock and onto the ferry behind Elnathan. When both horses and their riders were aboard, the boatmaster cracked the whip and the mule started up the road away from the river. The boat lurched out into the channel, pulled by three sets of ropes tied to large wooden wheels on the island. The ferry tipped hard upstream against the current and Daniel steadied his horse on the opposite side to keep from taking on water.

A large cave came into view as they neared the island. It stood halfway down the shoreline, and a great upswelling of water surged out of it like a large fresh water spring. The Nile flowed past the cave, its currents fighting the upswell of eddies. The ancients believed the Nile was born at Elephantine. Legends said the river flowed out of the mouth of a serpent god that lived deep in the water cave of Elephantine, but Daniel knew better than to believe the old stories. He'd lived around waterways and seas long enough to know the mind and will of a river. The waters gathered in the mountains and flowed into the riverbed without any help from the fabled creature. The high water marks on the island's redrock shores were due more to spring rains than the vengeance of a reptile god. And no serpent could flood the plains to the east of Elephantine like the runoff after a good storm in the hill country.

The wood planks in the floor of the ferry creaked against the current's drag and lurched with each of the mule's strides, pulling them toward the downriver end of the island. River-trading vessels were moored there, bobbing in the afternoon sun with wooden masts reaching into the sky. Only one of the vessels was as large as the ships that docked at Sidon. She was a gold-trading vessel from Tanis and her hull was a blade—long and sleek, and able to slice through the river's current. No vessel Daniel had ever seen had such a narrow build. A blue flag waved from the highest of four masts and sail riggings hung stern and portside for the twenty reed sails that had carried the riverboat upstream. An odd-looking set of riggings hung down from her wooden prow like a beard of rope and chains. It was a water sail for the voyage downstream. Once the ship put in downriver, the large underwater sail captured the current and carried her home to Tanis faster than ships half her size.

A group of Nubian gold traders stood a little way off from the ship, their black skin glistening in the afternoon sun. They wore leather loincloths to cover their nakedness and colorful green and yellow shawls wrapped over their shoulders. The tallest men rested long spears at their sides, while the others carried bows and quivers. Thick gold and ivory bracelets studded with rubies and emeralds decorated their wrists and forearms. Three rings pierced the nose of the chief among them and hung down to his upper lip. He stood beside the dockhands and carefully watched them weigh the gold. For each bag of the precious metal they loaded into the bow of the ship, the dockhands returned with chests filled with olive oil, knives, swords, silks, linens, and wine. They hauled the cargo down the plank and up the dock to a waiting mule cart.

A company of Hebrew soldiers looked on like a mother watching over her children, but they weren't really soldiers—not like Daniel was a soldier. They were Hebrew mercenaries hired to patrol Pharaoh's gold trade. And though there were Egyptian gold mines upriver from Elephantine, they never produced anything but granite for building. It was the gold from Africa that made Elephantine Egypt's greatest trading port.

The ferry came alongside the dock and Daniel tied up to the pier and steadied the craft with his foot. The fishermen stopped casting their nets, and the soldiers watching over the Nubian gold traders glanced over as Daniel guided his horse off the ferry, adjusted his military tunic, and got up into the saddle. He rested one hand on the hilt of his sword, then followed Elnathan up the pier to the city gate. It was a double wood door the width of five camels standing side-by-side with pivot stones cut into the island bedrock. A line of merchants snaked down in front of it. There were yams and apples in one man's bag, wheat and flax in another. A pearl vendor held out a handful of white beads to Daniel as he passed, begging him to purchase his wares, and a fisherman shoved the end of a spear at Daniel's nose with something stuck to it that smelled like a fish but looked nothing like one. The guard glanced up from the sack of melons he was inspecting. When he saw them dressed in Hebrew military uniforms, he waved them past the merchants and through the gates.

The temple at Elephantine stood on the island's brow, surrounded by the rooftops of three hundred homes. It was patterned after Solomon's temple, though not nearly as large. There were no columns at the entrance, no ornate carvings of pomegranate and only one ceremonial chamber instead of three. Governor Japheth's estate stood just below the temple. It was a small two-story brick building without a wall to protect the front courtyard.

Captain Elnathan sat back in the saddle. He wiped the sweat from his brow and turned to Daniel. "We start looking for Uriah there." He tipped his head up the street toward the governor's estate. "If anybody knows where we can find the man, he'll know." He dug his heels into the sides of his horse and they were away, galloping up the rise between rows of square mud-brick homes and leaving a cloud of dust behind them.

The governor of Elephantine took his tea at the same time every afternoon. It wasn't a difficult task for Uriah to lift the kettle from the fire and pour the steaming water into a cup, but then none of the work Uncle Japheth assigned him was unlikable. Uriah swept the stables, fed the horses, and hauled water from the river. The rest of the day he worked the kitchens, picked up deliveries of food at the docks, and did whatever his uncle asked of him.

Uriah mixed in three spoons of crushed cypress root, stirred it into the water and strained the tea through a piece of linen stretched over a warming bowl. Governor Japheth wasn't really an uncle, but Uriah had called him that since he was a young boy in Arim. He and Uriah's father were childhood friends and everyone in Arim thought them brothers. They were born in the same month and lived out their childhood in adjacent homes at the south end of town. The old mud homes were gone now, replaced by stone dwellings, but even after Japheth left Arim to join the military, Uriah's father never doubted they would somehow renew their friendship. Uriah poured the strained tea from the warming bowl into a large cup, stirred in three drops of honey, and set it on a tray with a bowl of figs and a biscuit, just the way Uncle Japheth preferred his afternoon tea. Uriah never expected to renew his father's friendship under such odd circumstances, and he never told Japheth he was a runaway. What would the governor do if he knew Uriah were a man fleeing from the Elders of the Jews? He had kept the secret from Japheth these past three months, thankful to be many days journey from Judah, secluded in the southern mountains of Egypt and employed by a family friend.

Uriah steadied the tea on his tray and started out of the kitchen. He passed by the window and glanced into the yard. The sun was about to set and its warm glow bathed the stables in an orange light, the same stables where he hid Lehi's Arabian. He kept the animal out of sight. The less others saw it, the less they would ask how he came to have such a fine horse.

Two men rode into the yard and Uriah stayed by the window to get a glimpse. They were dressed in gray Hebrew military tunics. Uriah set the tray down and stepped closer to the window. Cursed Laban. The captain had sent his men after him. They tied their steeds to a pillar along the porch and marched to the door. Their knock was powerful and it echoed through the home.

Uriah hurried down the main hall away from the knocking. Tea sloshed from the cup and stained the belly of his white tunic. He found Japheth sitting at the dining table. He was a tall, lean man and he sat erect in his chair as if he were at attention. He was dressed in an Egyptian military uniform, a kilt with silver studs at each seam and a blue tunic that wrapped around his middle and over his right shoulder. He shaved his head and beard like a good Egyptian, but his dark hair left a shadow across his red cheeks and along the top of his brow.

Uriah dropped the tray on the table in front of Japheth, sloshing tea over the brim of the cup. He was breathing hard and he held his hands behind his back to hide the trembling.

Japheth asked, "What is it?"

"They're here, sir."

The knocking sounded a second time and Japheth said, "I'm not expecting anyone."

"They're here to see me."

Japheth leaned over the table and peered down the hall. "Invite them in, why don't you?"

"I thought it best to speak to you first."

"What's wrong, son, do you owe them money?"

"It's nothing like that."

"Then what is it?" Japheth blew over the surface of the tea and with one swallow he downed what was left of the hot liquid.

"They're Hebrew soldiers." Uriah steadied himself against the backrest of an empty chair. "They're the reason I came to Elephantine."

Japheth pushed the empty cup away. "You told me it was because you had fallen on hard times."

"I did, but the difficult circumstances had nothing to do with my innkeeping."

Japheth stood from the table. "What do they want from you?"

"They want to put me in prison for my beliefs."

Japheth came around the table, his penetrating gaze set on Uriah. "Are you a Rekhabite?"

"No, sir."

Japheth relaxed his stance and laid his hand on Uriah's shoulder.

"I'm a prophet," Uriah said quietly.

Japheth took his hand back and raised his brow. "You're too young for that kind of work."

"I know, sir. Young and foolish and very much afraid for my life." Uriah closed his eyes and stood silent. When he opened them he said, "There's more."

The soldiers knocked a third time and drew Japheth's glance down the hall toward the sound. "Tell me quickly."

"I believe Laban sent them after me because of his lineage."

"No sane general would send his men halfway across the earth for such, such—"

"Such a personal matter?"

"It doesn't make any sense." Japheth shook his head. "None at all."

Uriah spoke softly. "He thinks I know some dark family secret."

"Do you?"

"I know the spirit of God is not with Laban."

"That's hardly a family secret." Japheth started out of the dining room. "I'm going to have a word with them."

"No, Uncle." Uriah took him by the arm and stopped him in the hallway. "They won't listen."

"They'll hear me or I'll see them escorted off the island. I'm the governor of this city." Japheth pulled free of Uriah's grasp and continued down the hall. "You go upstairs and stay there while I see to these men."

"But—"

"Don't question me, Uriah. I know how to handle military men. I've lived with them all my life."

They walked down the hallway to the main entry and Uriah started up the steps to the second floor. He said, "Thank you, Uncle."

"I've not done anything yet."

"You have and I'm grateful for it."

"Don't go off talking like that, son. You sound like a priest blessing the feast at your own funeral."

"I feel like one, sir."

"I'll find you a way out of this." Japheth stood by the door and waited for Uriah to scale the steps.

"I'm sure you will, Uncle." Uriah nodded and turned down the second-floor hallway to his room. Japheth's intentions were noble, but Uriah couldn't stay here any longer and place the man and his family in danger. He swung open the door to his room, changed into a riding kilt and tunic and packed his things. The low rumble of men's voices filtered up the stairwell and their footsteps trailed off toward the reading room. When they were gone out of the main hall, Uriah climbed back down the stairs and slipped into the yard, latching the door shut without a sound.

Uriah crossed to the stables and quickly ducked inside. The horse Lehi had given him stood in the last stall. He threw on her saddle and tied the straps around her middle without combing through her mane or currying her coat. This was not the usual ride about the island and he could ill afford the luxury of his usual riding rituals no matter how much the animal stomped her hooves for the feel of a comb across her coat.

Daniel stood at the entrance to the reading room while Captain Elnathan settled into a high-backed chair. He said, "This is a fine estate you have, here."

Japheth remained standing. He said, "It serves its purpose."

Elnathan removed his riding gloves and laid them over the armrest. "You must have a wonderful view of the river."

"It hasn't dried up yet."

Elnathan began to laugh, but Japheth didn't join him. He stood beside his chair and asked, "What business brings you here?" His voice was tense and he asked the question as if he already knew the answer. Daniel stepped back into the hall and checked to see if anyone was listening. They were alone, but all was not right. Japheth was hiding something.

Elnathan rested his hands on his thigh. "I'm looking for a certain Jew."

"I'm afraid you'll have to tell me more than that." Japheth stepped behind the chair like a shield, hiding him from Elnathan's questions. "There are nearly four hundred Jews living here."

"I'm interested in one from Arim; it's a little farming village near Fort—"

"I know the place."

Elnathan smiled. "I'm sure you do, sir."

Daniel left them to finish their conversation and walked back down the hall to the front door. He quietly opened the latch and stepped into the late afternoon twilight. Clouds swirled above the rocky cliffs west of the Nile, capturing the last rays of sun and reflecting the light over the city gates. The gold merchant's vessel was away, the water sail open across her bow, and she was headed north toward Tanis. The soldiers guarding the dock had returned back inside the city, and the Nubians were unloading their mule cart from the ferry onto the east bank, chanting their good fortune like temple priests celebrating a high holy day. All appeared normal and Daniel was about to return inside when a breeze blew open the door to the stable. It banged against the outside wall and Daniel's curiosity drew him toward it.

Daniel lifted the gate around the pivot stone and was about to close it against the post when he noticed a horse out of its stall. The animal stood peering at him from the shadows and when his eyes adjusted to the dimness he saw a man mounted in the saddle of a mighty Arabian. The horse matched Laman's description; midnight black with a white spot on the muzzle. A stable was an odd place for a rider to mount up, hunched over to keep from banging his head against the roof beams, but hunted men did odd things. Daniel stepped in the animal's path.

Daniel said, "That's a fine horse you have."

The rider said, "The governor stables three fine horses here."

Daniel counted three other horses chewing on hay. He said, "Don't you mean four?"

"That's right, four fine horses."

Daniel stroked the white spot on the horse's muzzle. "How much did you pay Lehi for this animal?"

"Step aside, sir." The rider pulled on the reins and his horse inched forward, pawing at the ground.

Daniel widened his stance and held his ground. He grabbed the bit that stuck out the side of the horses mouth, yanked the animal's head down and held his hand between the horse's ears, jabbing his finger at the rider. He said, "Come with me and you won't be harmed."

"I'm not going back to Jerusalem."

Daniel let go of the bridle and reached for his sword. Those were the words he was searching for. He'd captured Uriah on his own and without a struggle. Daniel pointed the tip of his sword over the horse's head. The blade was only a few fingers longer than a dagger and he had to stand on his toes to reach it close to Uriah. He said, You'll have a fair trial."

"You don't know the Elders like I know them."

"I know them better than you think." Daniel reached the sword close to Uriah's chest.

"All the more reason not to trust you." Uriah tightened his grip on the reins. "Forgive me."

Forgive him? Did Uriah really think Daniel would show him mercy? He wasn't about to let him go free, no matter what kind of penance he offered.

Daniel said, "You'll have to come with me."

Uriah dug his heels into the horse's flank and the animal bolted, its powerful body throwing Daniel across the stable. He landed on his back and rolled against the gate, his stomach slamming into the planks and his head snapping against the post. He reached for the pain at the side of his head and his hand came back bloodied from a cut over his temple. Curse him! How did he ever let Uriah get away? He'd held him at the point of his sword just as he'd been taught by Elnathan and look what had come of it. Daniel wiped the blood from his brow and turned on his side to see the cloud of dust behind the galloping horse. Curse Uriah! Daniel struggled to his feet and steadied himself against the gate until the rushing in his head stopped and his vision righted. He should have pulled Uriah from the saddle. Daniel was a wrestler, not a swordsman, and he could have taken Uriah with his strength.

He untied his horse from the post and pulled up into the saddle. He should go inside to fetch Elnathan, but not like this. He'd allowed Uriah to escape and he was going to get him back, on his own.

Daniel reined across the yard and into the street at full gallop and turned down between the rows of houses. Uriah was putting his horse aboard the ferry when Daniel raced through the city gates and onto the docks. The fool! There were thirty men on the east bank who could catch Uriah when he landed. But Daniel wouldn't let him get that far, not if this prisoner was going to be his prisoner. Daniel came down the dock, his horse's hooves pounding over the wood planks. He left his sword sheathed at his side, let go of the reins and leaped from the saddle, throwing himself at Uriah. The man's body was a weak branch in Daniel's grip and he could have broken him with his bare hands. Daniel rolled on top of Uriah and shook him by the shoulders, the prophet's head banging against the dock. He said, "You're a fool if you think you can escape me!" Blood streamed into Daniel's eyes and he let go to wipe the sleeve of his tunic across his brow.

Uriah grabbed for the short sword and held the tip to Daniel's neck. He said, "Get off me!"

Daniel slowly stood and Uriah stood with him, keeping the cold metal edge against his throat.

Uriah said, "Take off your tunic."

Take off his tunic? Did Uriah think a gray shirt could disguise him from thirty soldiers? Daniel said, "Have you gone mad?"

"I don't want to hurt you." Uriah pressed the short sword into Daniel's skin. "Just do as I say."

"You won't get away." Daniel slid his head out slowly, and held up the gray tunic.

Uriah undid his sash and pulled his own white tunic over his head with one hand, tossing it at Daniel. "Put that on."

"I don't need your shirt."

"I said put it on." Uriah turned the blade, scraping the edge against Daniel's throat, and he obliged.

Uriah said, "Get up in the saddle."

"You can't escape." Daniel mounted Uriah's horse, the fine Arabian bristling under the weight of a strange rider and the bobbing of the raft underfoot.

Uriah said, "You'll come ashore downriver."

"What are you talking about?"

"You'll be safe as long as you don't jump in until you're well past the first bend. There's a strange current that runs down past the island." Uriah pulled the blade through the ferry's ropes, cutting the first of four lines. It snapped free and ricocheted into the river. Uriah slashed through the remaining ropes. They slithered out of the wooden pulleys like a hundred whips, their ends hissing above the surface of the water. The ferry put out into the channel, towed quickly away from the dock by the current. Daniel swung down from the saddle and stood on the edge of the ferry, helpless to do anything but drift away and watch Uriah sprint to the safety of an outcrop of rocks on the opposite side of the island with Daniel's gray tunic flapping in his hand.

The raft floated near the first bend in the river and listed to one side in the current. Daniel steadied the horse and moved her to the center when he saw Uriah dart out from behind the rocks and dive into the river, headed toward a low-lying ledge on the west bank. It was the only place a man could put out along the steep rocky shore. He was getting away, and once he cleared the cliffs on that side, there was no telling which way he'd head. Africa sprawled to the south and if he didn't like the jungles of the dark continent, he could track west along the coast to Alexandria, or cross the Great Sea and lose himself among the cities of Greece, or double back to Tanis and find refuge in the Hebrew quarters of the Egyptian capital. If anyone was going to capture Uriah and keep him from escaping, it would have to be Daniel.

The ferry rounded the riverbend and the current turned back against itself in a whirlpool. It caught the bow and began spinning the boat in a slow circle. Daniel dived into the cold waters, pumping his arms and legs against the current. But it was nothing like the undertow he'd come against in the surf of the Great Sea. The river sucked him down, the swirling water closed in around him, and the light at the surface grew dim. He fought against the whirlpool, but his powerful arms couldn't pull him to the surface. The breath in his lungs was gone, and all he could see in the blackness was the vision of his father scolding his dead body as Elnathan hauled it back to Jerusalem. *"How many times did I warn you not to just dive in, Daniel? How many times . . . ?"*

Daniel shot out of the whirlpool, gasping for air, the ferry spinning a few cubits away and Uriah's horse leaning over the side with her nose in the water. Daniel shook his eyes open and coughed the water from his lungs. He'd been spared by the shifting current—or was it the serpent god of the water cave that saved him? He'd praise anything that had power to keep him alive.

Daniel stroked out into the channel. His arms were heavy, and his lungs burned with each breath, but he wouldn't turn back, not after two failed attempts to capture Uriah. He turned his head into the water, working his arms and legs and reaching each stroke toward the west bank. Uriah was not going to escape.

Not on Daniel's watch.

No one lived on the west bank of the Nile. Not on these steep, rocky shores that housed the graves of dead governors. The founding fathers of Elephantine buried their most beloved in large crypts. They were dark holes hacked out of the cliffs, like the entrances of a hundred caves dotting the rocky shore. Robbers had pillaged the gold and silver treasures over the years, but the gravesites were still shrines to the great dead men of Elephantine's past.

Daniel pulled himself out of the Nile and lay on a ledge of sandstone, heaving for breath. Above him was the opening to the lowest crypt, the only one under the chalk-white flood mark that ran along the river's bank. Water trickled from a crack in the cliff wall below the opening and muffled footsteps stirred above him.

Daniel slowed his breathing and turned his ear. Was it the sound of Uriah moving about in the crypt above him or the dripping of water? Daniel pulled himself up and climbed inside the musty-smelling tomb. Cobwebs blanketed his face and he brushed them away and stood in the entry, squinting. The sun had set, but there was enough light shimmering off the river to make out the shadows. It was a large cavern. The marks of a pickax scarred the ceiling above a long stone sarcophagus in the center of the chamber. The lid was missing and the sides were cracked, but Daniel didn't look inside; he wasn't looking for a dead man. He would bring Uriah back to Jerusalem alive. He stepped around the sarcophagus to the dark side when a sound drew his gaze to the opposite corner—or was it the echo of the water dripping off his own body and down the side of the stone coffin? He leaned over it, forcing his eyes to adjust to the shadows on that side and he was brushing the last cobwebs from his eyelashes when Uriah ran out of the shadows toward the entrance with the short sword waving from his hand. Daniel pushed the stone box off its moorings ahead of Uriah's stride. It hit the ground in a thunder of breaking stone, but it wasn't enough to stop Uriah. Daniel leaped at him, grabbing for his weapon arm, but Uriah pulled free and swung at him, just missing Daniel's flesh. They went to the ground and Daniel picked up a blunt stone as they rolled amid the broken remains of the sarcophagus. He swung it across Uriah's brow and the prophet fell limp in his arms. Daniel lay there, gasping for breath. He'd captured Uriah and the prophet wasn't a holy man, not by any measure. The fool had tried to stab Daniel with his own sword. He wasn't a man of God; he was a criminal and Daniel had risked his life to capture him.

Daniel dragged Uriah's body toward the entrance and laid him in the dim light. Blood poured from a wide gash in his brow. His eyes were open, but he lay unconscious. He was dressed in nothing but a kilt, his bare chest still covered with water from the swim and his fist still clutching the weapon. Daniel lifted Uriah's hand toward the opening. The soft light of dusk fell over it, but Daniel's short sword wasn't in his grasp. Uriah wasn't holding a weapon at all. He'd been fighting Daniel off with the gray tunic. It wasn't a heroic capture that would imress Elnathan, but at least it was a capture. And Daniel would let his mates believe he was armed. That was a tale that would make him a hero.

Or at least let him rise through the ranks of Laban's military.

CHAPTER 36

Aaron reined to the front of the caravan, thankful to breathe clean air. He'd spent the better part of four days choking on the dust of fifty camels, eighteen horses, twenty sheep, nine pack mules, three mule carts, and two goats. With so many animals, they were like Moses and the children of Israel—except that it had been a pillar of fire that went before the camp of Israel, not a cloud of dust. Aaron adjusted himself in the saddle, searching for any part of him that didn't ache after four days on the trail. Caravanning was different work than blacksmithing and he prayed for callouses to form in all the right places. If the Almighty had intended man to ride this far, he would have sent Aaron into the world with bowed legs. Even a long pair of leather chaps and a thick blanket thrown over the saddle couldn't keep the chafing from turning into a dreadful case of saddle sores, a malady not even the caravan cook could cure.

Before riding out of Beersheba this morning, Aaron purchased three bottles of fish oils from a merchant who claimed his remedy healed heart ailments, liver ailments, head pains, broken bones, cuts, bruises, hair loss, sore throats, bad eyesight, chapped lips, sunburn and, of course, saddle sores. But the merchant never explained if Aaron should swallow the potion or rub it on his legs. Beuntahyu jumped over a hole in the road and Aaron slipped in the saddle, almost falling to the ground. It was the fifth time he'd nearly fallen since rubbing the remedy over the most painful sores. He should have chased the ill-tasting stuff with three glasses of water instead of wearing it on his backside. Not even a bath in the clearwater springs during lunch cured him of the rash; and all he could do was keep riding and hope that Lehi was right, that once he'd been in the saddle a week, his sores would be gone. Standing on his head was the only other remedy.

Aaron left the caravan behind and rode down through the Besor River bed—five miles of twisting turns and sandy gullies—toward the coast. He eased off the reins and Beuntahyu broke into a gallop, chasing a sea breeze that blew up the narrow gorge. They turned past a stand of Joshua trees, out of the shadows, and onto the sun-swept plains of the Sinai desert. The blue waters of the Great Sea filled the horizon except where Raphia rose out of a sandy beachhead. Its red sandstone bluffs, heaven-reaching spires, and twisted rock columns stood beside the ocean like a temple built on the water's edge. It was an island shrine surrounded by a sea of white sand and bordered by blue waters.

Aaron raced across the strand, spurring seaside around the red rock to the empty beachhead. Raphia was nothing like Aaron's former port city home in Sidon where the bay was crowded with seafaring vessels, skyward reaching masts, and bustling shipyards. Here there was only a quiet, still beauty. He circled round through the tide, Beuntahyu kicking up a spray of seawater. That was still like Sidon: the scent of fish, the wash of brine, and the sputter of white foam washing over the dry sand at high tide.

Laman and Lemuel arrived on Aaron's heels and put to finding the well. Laman walked along the beachhead kicking at the dunes that had blown over the bedrock. He said, "We'll never find it under all this sand."

Lemuel got down on hands and knees next to Laman and they crawled along, sifting their hands through the sand, searching for the capstone.

The well at Raphia stood away from the shoreline where salt couldn't poison the water and gulls never dirtied it, as long as the capstone was sealed tight. It was the sweetest well on the desert leg of the trade route, without any mud coloring the water brown or the foul taste of stagnant water, made drinkable only with a shot of sour camel's milk. Raphia's water was sweet and flowing, fed by the underground aqueduct of the Besor River and filtered through miles of white sands before reaching the subterranean pool below the rocky bluffs of Raphia.

The well water beckoned to caravaneers: *Come, fill your skins here where the trade route transforms from a dependable byway through the mountains of Judah to a wandering of footprints over the shifting desert sands of the Sinai.* After Raphia, there were only four wells in the space of a hundred and fifty miles where there should be six to cover the distance safely, and that only if none had gone dry. Fresh-water wells were the only refuge on this last great obstacle separating Lehi's caravan from the kingdom of Egypt, a two-week crossing of the Sinai Peninsula that took Moses forty years.

Lehi rounded the northern face and spurred down along the bluffs. "Did you find it?" He reined in next to Laman.

"It's around here somewhere." Laman wiped a sand-covered hand over his brow. "Ride back and tell Sam to slow the herd until we draw the water."

"It's too late for that." Lehi came around. "The camels already have wind of the sea water."

Laman burrowed his arms deep into a dune but came up without the capstone. "There's never been this much sand covering the well."

Lehi spurred around them, his horse kicking up the sand. He rode in an ever-growing circle, the horse's hooves tapping the ground until the hollow echo of the well sounded. Lehi pulled up and said, "It's right here, boys. Now, start drawing the water before the herd clears the bluffs and chases into the sea."

They quickly uncovered the capstone and rolled it to the side.

Lehi dismounted and untied a bucket from his saddle. "Hurry, boys! Before the camels make themselves sick on the sea water." He shoved the bucket into the sand and began pushing it aside. "Clear off enough of the bedrock to hold the water."

Lehi waved to Aaron. "Ride around the point and help Sam and Nephi turn the caravan away from the sea. I don't want any of the animals getting saltwater sickness."

But it was too late. Sam had already cleared the farthest bluff, guiding the lead camel toward the well. He pulled hard on the bridle but the animal reared on its hind legs, snapping free of the rope and throwing its cisterns into the sand.

Lehi started toward them, waving his arms. He cried, "Stay seaside of him or he'll break."

Sam steered between the sea and the camel, but the animal reared again, this time pulling free and breaking rank. The stampede was on. The rest of the camels followed to the sea, their oil cisterns bouncing on their humped backs like a flotilla of fishing boats in a storm.

Aaron raced Beuntahyu across the beach to head them off, but with the sheep, mules, and goats running wild among the camels, he was helpless to keep them from getting into the salt water. Lehi arrived with Laman and Lemuel. They swung down into the surf, put their backs against the sides of the lead camel, dug their feet into the sandy bottom and pushed the large animal toward the shore, while Aaron slung a rope around its neck. Nephi and the caravan hands joined in the work, four to a camel, pushing and prodding the beasts one at a time out of the saltwater and over toward the sweet water of the well. It took the better part of the afternoon to guide them away from the surf.

Once the camels were watered and corralled in a ravine, Nephi began unlashing the oil cisterns from their backs. There were two strapped on each animal, brimming full with a homer of the highest-grade olive oil and sealed shut with yellow beeswax. Four were cracked and leaking beyond repair and Nephi changed out the oil into new vessels he carried on a mule cart for just such an accident. They'd only lost a few bath of oil, but Nephi was careful to note the loss in a ledger and report it to Lehi. They stored the oil cisterns in the shadows of a rocky outcrop with a canopy of animal skins to shade them. The oil would bring a high price in the market, though none of it was headed to the usual buyers. Every drop was already sold to Pharaoh Necho. One stop at his palace in Tanis and they'd be headed home with a cargo of gold.

Nephi finished covering the last cistern and asked, "How is the herd?"

Sam said, "Some of the animals are showing signs of sickness."

Lehi asked, "How bad are they?"

"Five or six drank their fill of sea water." Sam wiped the sweat from his brow and leaned against a cistern. "We could be here an extra day, maybe two."

"Then we put up the tent." Lehi gathered the caravan hands to a low spot between sand dunes, over where the wind didn't blow and torchlight wouldn't send a beacon out across the desert to invite unwanted guests. He untied the center stake from a pack mule, stabbed it into the sand and waited for Aaron to make his way over and steady it. It was a job he could do and he was happy to be part of the tent raising.

"Don't let go, son." Lehi stood beside Aaron and fastened the ceiling portion of the main tent to the long wooden pole. "If the center stake goes down we have to start over."

More than three hundred animal skins were sewn into the twelve tent compartments. The partitions rode on two mules, the pieces of the roof on another, and the poles, ropes, and stakes on a camel. Lehi directed the caravan hands as they laid out the tent in the sand around Aaron. It had the walls of a large circular center room for Lehi (and his wife when she traveled with him), a main entry to welcome visitors, and a dining room where the entire family could eat in times of bad weather, which meant hot weather—and in the desert that was usually the only weather. Four additions spread out from the center tent like spokes on a wagon wheel, each with its own entry room, though not as spacious as the main entrance. Like all desert sheikhhs, Lehi added to the size of his tent over years of caravanning, doubling it each time Sariah gave birth to another son. With four boys in the family, the tent had become a traveling mansion.

The servants raised the roof of the center tent first, tying it to the corner stakes and hoisting it into the air with one great heave-ho that echoed off the red rock bluffs. Laman's tent was the largest of the four additions and it was attached to the main tent beside the entry. The three smaller tents for Lemuel, Sam, and Nephi were raised at the back next to the dining compartment. When the entire family traveled, the servants slept under the stars, but it was rare to have Sariah and the girls on the trail, and Lehi invited Aaron and the other caravan hands to stow their gear and make their quarters inside.

When the sun fell below the horizon of the Great Sea, Raphia turned cold, colder than any other camp along the trade route. Aaron had believed the great desert of the Sinai Peninsula would be warmer than the mountains of Judah, but it wasn't and he remained alone at the fire after evening meal to warm himself. The rest of the caravan hands bedded down early after the day's ride. Even the cook hurried to pack his cart instead of lingering at the fire to pass out figs and tell tall tales. No one ever questioned his fiction except for the previous night when he tried to convince Aaron he'd been swallowed by a whale larger than the one that got the prophet Jonah. Aaron had lived by the Great Sea and knew better.

"Are you staying?" the cook asked and packed his bottles, jars and pans into his mule cart.

"A while," Aaron said. He took a handful of figs from a sack in the cart.

"Make sure you put out the fire. There are bedouins in these parts and I don't want my fire to be the reason we all wake up dead in the morning."

"This isn't another one of your stories, is it?"

"I wouldn't fool about something like that. The bedouins of these parts are no campfire tale."

Bedouins were peaceful people, staying put only as long as the desert brush supported their herds, then moving on to other pastures, green with winter foliage. But along this part of the trade route, the roving bands of bedouin robbers didn't tend sheep; they stole them. And Lehi's herd made a perfect target for plunder. At night the bedouin robbers searched out their prey, watching the horizon for campfires. The caravan hands hung bells around the camp this afternoon to warn of robbers, though a hundred bells weren't enough warning if a bedouin robber found the camp.

The cook rummaged through his cart until he found a long knife. "You don't take chances with bedouins." He pointed the weapon at the fire. "Why do you think I cooked dinner down in that pit?"

The lamb for evening meal was cooked a half mile away from the tent over a fire shielded by the bluffs, built down in a pit two cubits deep, and ringed with large stones. In the high country of southern Judah the cook used open fires, but here at Raphia he kindled them well below ground.

"Bedouins come out of the night without a sound." The cook stepped toward Aaron with his knife raised and his eyes open wide. "They hide in the crevices of rocks." He waved his knife toward the bluffs. The red rock had turned dark and cold with only the pale light of the moon casting a gray shadow over the outcrops. He inched Aaron beside the flames with his knife. "They come out of the desert night like a great mirage, and creep up to a sleeping man and slit his throat." He stepped aside from the fire and let the smoke filter down along the moon-swept beach and out over the rolling tides of the Great Sea.

Aaron stepped back. "I'll see that the fire is out."

"That's a good boy." The cook stuck his knife under his belt and started his mule toward camp, down along the base of the cliffs. His cooking things rattled about in the box of his cart and mixed with the sound of the surf.

Over near the cliffs, beyond the fire, Beuntahyu stood in the shadows pawing the ground and nodding. She was a spirited animal with a coat as white as the clouds of heaven. Despite her powerful young legs and forceful temperament, she dealt with Aaron in a gentle manner, always strict to obey his commands and willing to ignore his poor horsemanship. Somehow she understood Aaron was not like other men, and having her out here in the dark of night was a positive comfort.

Aaron hobbled over next to her and offered a handful of dates, but she pulled away and trotted beyond the reach of the fire's light, her ears up and her body rigid and pointed at the desert. She'd heard something with her ears that Aaron couldn't hear with his and she called to it, her powerful neck arched to the wind and whinnying into it like a wolf howling at the moon. She pawed the ground, raised on her back legs and kicked, then whinnied again. Aaron came to her side and stroked her mane. "What's riled you, girl?"

Beuntahyu stopped her spooking long enough for Aaron to see what she'd heard. It was a dark line on the horizon near the shore, a string of dark horses, four miles, maybe five out and headed toward camp at a good clip. If they were Bedouins, they were the wrong kind. Aaron smothered the fire with sand, pulled himself and his crutches up into the saddle and spurred toward camp at full gallop.

This was no campfire tale.

Aaron raised the tent flap for Lehi to come out into the night and see the swift-moving band of riders moving along the moonlit beach toward Raphia. The moon was setting over the Great Sea and its yellow light cast an eerie glow over the long line of men racing toward them. Lehi roused the caravan hands out of the tent and ordered them to light torches around the perimeter. He sent Sam and Nephi sprinting to the corral with five men, their shadows dancing over the bluffs like a hundred spirits. They were to hide the oil cisterns under camel blankets. If the night riders were a band of Bedouin robbers, they'd kill them for the oil. Laman and Lemuel stood at the entrance to camp flanked by men with swords drawn and torches raised, waiting to greet whatever evil came out of the darkness.

Lehi stepped to the edge of the light as the riders turned inland away from the surf, pounding up the beachhead, over the dune, and down into camp. Thick black smoke billowed from the oil-soaked rags and swirled around the lead rider. Captain Elnathan was the first to come into the light, riding a black steed. An ensign carrying the red and white royal banner of Judah rode on his right flank, and behind him were two lieutenants riding abreast before a double column of men. The captain's horse slowed to a stop and pawed the ground in front of Lehi.

Elnathan said, "We found what we were looking for and I have your son Laman to thank for leading us to him." He turned in the saddle toward the prisoner cart. It clattered to a stop at the back of the regiment, flanked by two horsemen. Uriah was cramped inside, his feet poking through the wooden bars of the back gate and the nape of his neck pressing against the front boards.

Elnathan said, "If you don't mind, we'll set up our camp down near the north face for the night. I'll need to use the well to get some water for my men and the horses."

Lehi braced himself against Aaron's crutch. He was not given to fear, but the sight of Uriah's bloodied body had power to make this strong man weak.

Elnathan said, "We'll only be resting a few hours. By sunrise we should be on our way. Do I have your blessing to draw water from the well?"

Lehi left Elnathan without answering and walked down past the sand-soaked cavalry. The horses flicked their tails at his head as he passed, but he didn't flinch. He came in behind the prisoner cart, held the iron bars with both hands and peered inside.

Aaron pulled a torch from the sand and followed next to him. The flickering light danced over Lehi's face and Aaron could see he was searching Uriah's body for movement, a breath, any sign that he was alive. He lay as a dead man would lie and Lehi's eyes filled with an emotion Aaron didn't know how to describe, but to say it was sadness and fear together. Lehi stood there, his cheeks pressed against the cold metal bars, his nose sticking between them and his eyes scanning the prophet's broken body. Uriah's beardless chin was caked with sand, his face drawn out and thin. Flies licked at a bloody gash on his forehead. His head was turned to the side, his mouth open and his arms spread awkwardly across his belly.

Aaron should have held the torch above Lehi's shoulder for him to see Uriah clearly, but instead he brought the flame around the side of the cart and let it stream through the bars onto Lehi's face. His gaze paused on the wound in Uriah's brow then moved down to the dried blood streaking his cheeks. The ugliness couldn't hide the innocent countenance of this young servant of God. Lehi shifted two bars over and leaned in for a better view. Uriah hadn't a whisker on his chin or a malicious bone in his body. Only thirty-one years old, with a young family waiting for him in Arim, and look at him. Lehi took a deep breath. He was still staring at Uriah, but his eyes filled with a faraway gaze as if he were looking beyond Uriah into the future, and Aaron understood that Lehi saw himself in Uriah's place.

Lehi pulled on the gate. The bars creaked in their wooden moorings, the lock rattled and the cart began to sway.

The driver spun on the stoop of the cart and snapped his whip overhead. "Back away."

Aaron raised the torch and cast a flickering glow over the driver's face. He knew the voice, and when the light rested on him, Aaron saw Daniel's dark eyes beneath a thick layer of dust. He was watching the back gate of the prisoner cart like a hawk watches a rodent. He jumped down and came around next to Lehi. "I said back away, sir." He stepped in front of the gate, but Lehi pushed around him and kept his vigil next to the cart, his hands firmly fixed around the bars. Daniel took Lehi by the shoulder and began pulling him back when

Aaron stepped between them. He said, "Leave him alone; he isn't doing any harm."

Daniel's face twisted into a scowl. He said, "What are you doing here?"

Aaron stood straight on his crutches. "I work for Lehi's caravan."

"Does Papa know?"

"I have his blessing."

"You're a fool." Daniel lowered his voice to a whisper. "These people will bring you nothing but trouble."

Captain Elnathan broke rank and trotted down the column. He pulled up beside the cart and dug in his horse's hooves, sending a spray of sand that should have turned Lehi's head. But Lehi kept his gaze fixed on the prophet and said, "Captain, I want you to give Uriah water before you see to your horses or your men."

"He doesn't drink." Elnathan leaned over the saddle. "He's been like that since we left Elephantine. Lies there as if he were dead or stares at the sky."

"He'll die if you don't give him water."

"It doesn't matter when he dies." Elnathan raised his voice. "The Elders are waiting to put him to death as soon as we arrive in Jerusalem."

Lehi turned from the cart and squinted up through the torch light at Elnathan. "Is that how you treat the men of God?"

"I have my orders." Elnathan spat in the sand. "I do what I have to do." He spurred around and started back to the front of the column. "Move out! We have a camp to set and water to draw."

Daniel climbed back onto the stoop and cracked the whip, sending the steeds lurching to the edge of the torchlight and out over the sandy beach of Raphia toward the well. Lehi followed, walking up the incline with Aaron on his crutches behind him. They stood together, watching the cart go into the night and listening to it clatter over the sand dunes. When it fell out of sight, Lehi turned his gaze heavenward to the starlit sky. His face was drawn out and a tear found its way down his cheek. He whispered, "Oh, God, uncover Thy hiding place."

Lehi's knees faltered and Aaron reached his arm around the man's waist and drew him in close. He leaned against Aaron, his body limp and listless. He was a strong man with a stronger will, but after seeing

Uriah like that, bloody, broken, and without hope, Lehi was filled with a fear that passed from his trembling body into Aaron's. They had seen the plight of a prophet of God, and Aaron feared they had seen a shadow of things to come.

Was Uriah's fate to be Lehi's future?

Dawn arrived too soon and Aaron wouldn't have gotten out of bed if it weren't for the stir of horses and the cries of men stowing their packs. He tied back the flap of the tent and found Lehi watching Elnathan and his men break camp. Lehi was dressed in a light blue tunic, a leather kilt, walking boots strapped to the knee and a water skin over his shoulder. It seemed a strange way to dress; he'd never seen Lehi in anything but a robe. He wore reading robes in his map room, working robes around the plantation, and a good traveling robe on the caravan. But there he stood, dressed in a kilt and a pair of boots, ready to strike out on foot.

Across the rise, Elnathan was riding out of Raphia. He took the point, flanked by his lieutenants and two straight lines of cavalry. Daniel pulled into formation at the rear, Uriah's body barely visible behind the bars of the cart. Lehi didn't move until it disappeared around the north face, then he started for the red-rock bluffs on a dead march toward the only place a man could get up past the steep face, over where the ridge flattened into a gentle slope. Aaron followed him up the rise to an overlook halfway up the bluffs. The soldiers snaked a long line across the last stretch of desert plains toward Judah's hill country. When the last horseman turned into the shadows of the Besor riverbed, Aaron said, "God be with Uriah."

"Amen." Lehi laid his hand on Aaron's shoulder and looked over the desert toward the capital city. "I told you once that these were dark days in Jerusalem."

"I remember." Aaron inched his crutches toward the edge.

"I fear they will grow even darker, son."

Lehi started up the face of the bluff, and Aaron asked, "Where are you going?"

Lehi pulled up and pointed toward the summit. "To get help for Uriah."

"Up there?"

"I must pray for him." Lehi hiked up the slope and disappeared over the ridge, vanishing into the pristine air of this secluded red-rock temple. Aaron watched long after Lehi was gone. What was he thinking? If he wanted to pray, he could have done it in the privacy of his tent; he didn't need a deserted hilltop. Aaron's feet wouldn't allow him to follow, and he wasn't going back to camp to tell Lehi's sons he'd let their father do such a foolish thing. He slumped down and pulled his feet in close. What Uriah needed was a host of men with swords, not a host of angels, and hopefully Lehi understood that. Aaron leaned his head against a rock.

Oh, let Lehi return with more than a prayer for Uriah.

Gulls hovered on a sea breeze and squawked at Lehi's intrusion into their world, high above the shores of the Great Sea. A morning fog blew in, shrouding his view of the shoreline below. This was the solace Lehi had come for, away from the cry of the camels and goats, and removed from the stir of camp. He leaned over the edge to see if his sons were awake now, drawing water from the well, feeding the animals, and preparing for their trek. The fog had yet to clear and he saw nothing but the uneven rock disappearing into the mists a few cubits below him. He should have been down there with his sons, gauging the health of the herd after taking in so much salt water yesterday, and reading maps of this barren part of the desert. That was the duty of a sheikh, and a less troubling task than seeking God's blessing for Uriah.

Lehi turned from the edge and walked across the summit to a flat sandstone rock that stood alone like an altar. He knelt beside it, turned his face up into the mists and prayed, "Dear God, please save Uriah." It was a selfish prayer, but it was the one he wanted most to pray. If Uriah lived, God wouldn't have need to raise up another prophet.

A bank of fog drifted over the bluffs, surrounding Lehi in a dark cloud so thick the water beaded up on his face and matted his hair against his scalp. There was a powerful force in the darkness, surrounding him, begging him to abandon his prayer and return down the bluffs to camp. No good could come of his prayer. There was nothing he could do for Uriah now. Shouldn't he be down preparing the caravan to cross the desert? Lehi gripped the rough sandstone ledge. Why did he lack the faith to keep praying? If there was a God in heaven, and he knew there was, the Almighty would hear his pleading. Lehi raised his voice to the darkness and said, "Oh, Lord God, who brought our fathers out of this wilderness to a land of promise, will you not save your prophet Uriah?"

Immediately dark mists gathered in around Lehi, so thick he couldn't breathe. His chest heaved for air, but he could get none. He wrapped his arms around his breast and fell against the stone altar, the rough sandstone tearing the flesh in his arms. The mists were like smoke, burning his lungs and suffocating the life from him. Was he going to die on this hilltop? Lehi turned on his side and lifted a bloodied arm into the darkness. With his breath faltering, he cried, "Oh God, Almighty, hear me!"

The darkness retreated from around his mouth, and though a thick fog still shrouded the hill, Lehi was released from the power of the adversary and lay gasping for breath.

A light gathered in the mists directly above him and it grew brighter until it pierced the darkness. It wasn't sunlight; the fog was too thick to let in its rays. It was like fire, a pillar of fire, brighter than the sun at midday. It rested on the stone altar and continued upward not more than five cubits before it disappeared into the mists like a pathway into heaven. The pillar grew until it was wide enough for a man to descend down through it and stand above the stone, his feet not touching the ground. He wore a robe of exquisite whiteness. His hands and forearms were bare as were his feet and ankles. The pillar of fire was brightest around the man's face, his countenance shining like lightning.

He extended his arm and said, "I am Yeshua the Anointed One."

Lehi lifted himself off the stone and knelt before the heavenly being. Was this the same vision given to Moses? For Moses spoke with God face to face as one man speaketh to another. But how could this be? Lehi wasn't Moses, he was an olive oil merchant and he wasn't about to lead any of God's people to a promised land.

Yeshua said, "Your mind is troubled because of Uriah, but be of good cheer. You will not suffer as he has suffered."

Lehi raised his hand to shield his eyes from the light. Standing before him was the God of Heaven who ruled over all men and yet He understood Lehi's fears; He knew the yearnings of his heart. The light cast a bright glow over Lehi, but there was no warmth on his skin, only a burning deep within him that chased away his doubts and immediately he understood the source of the light. It wasn't a pillar of fire; it was the love of God, and it filled Lehi's soul with a joy he had never known.

Lehi leaned forward over the stone and reached his hand toward Yeshua. He appeared like a man, with arms and legs and a voice. But how could that be if he were never born into the world?

"This is the body of my spirit." Yeshua's voice was like the wind, and each word he spoke had power to shake the ground. He understood Lehi's questions before he asked them and He lifted his hands from his sides, hands as perfect and whole as his entire body. "All the holy prophets have testified of me, that I lived before my coming in the flesh." He pointed beyond Lehi into the mists swirling about them, and said, "I will be born six hundred years from now to suffer for the sins of men and rise again, the firstfruits of the resurrection." Yeshua lowered his hands to his side. "The time is at hand for you to preach of my coming and call the people of Jerusalem to repent in my name and be saved."

"Will you not spare Uriah to do that work?"

"Fear not, for I will be on your left hand and on your right hand." Yeshua's voice softened. "Now, go. See after Uriah and I will make you mighty to defend him."

"He's guarded by many soldiers."

"Your words will be mightier than their swords." Yeshua raised his voice, and it was like a great rush of wind, though the air around them was still. He said, "Your enemies will not prevail against you." He began to walk upward, the conduit of light a stairway leading Him into another place Lehi could not see with his natural eyes. The pillar of fire gathered around him and he said, "I will visit you again in a dream." Then He was gone.

Vanished into the thick fog that hung over Raphia.

Aaron leaned back against the rock, searching for a little shade. Where was Lehi? Had he returned to camp another way? Aaron was about to make his way down when loose soil and rock streamed over the bluffs and covered him in dust. It was Lehi, and he traversed the incline above Aaron with the nimbleness of a young man, though the hair around his ears and along his temple was anything but youthful. He had aged twenty years in the time he was gone. The edges of his hairline had gone as white as the saltwater line along the beaches of the Dead Sea.

"We're leaving," Lehi said and continued past Aaron, down the gentle incline toward camp. "I'm sending my sons home with the caravan and I want you to come with me."

Aaron swung his body between his crutches to keep up. "What about the olive oil shipment?"

"Pharaoh will have to wait another day." They reached the beach and Lehi strode along the sand toward the tent. "Tell the servants to start breaking camp while I speak with my sons."

"We're going right now?"

"The Almighty has commanded it."

Aaron reached his crutches further ahead with each step and still couldn't match Lehi's brisk strides. Aaron asked, "The Almighty has commanded what?"

Lehi checked his stride and Aaron stabbed the ends of the crutches into the sand behind him, his body swinging between the poles like a carpenter's plumb.

Lehi said, "We're going to save Uriah."

CHAPTER 37

Laban carried a large leather sack over each shoulder and hefted the contents across the courtyard to the main steps of Solomon's Temple. He lost his grip on the right one and quickly swung his arm over the top to brace it against the side of his head. The metal edge of a breastplate pressed through the sack and lodged against his chin. The tunics and kilts weren't difficult to carry, but the ten pair of boots, and the swords and breastplates weighed more than any two men he'd thrown across a wrestling pit, and it was all dead weight.

The quartermaster wouldn't find the military dress missing from the commissary anytime soon, and with the coronation tomorrow and the celebrations that followed he'd have time to return them before it caused a stir. The sack over Laban's left shoulder began to slip and he dropped it down under his arm and held it on his hips, against his ribs. Why did Shechem want ten of his men disguised as soldiers? The man had no idea how much trouble this was. It should only require two of his finest—three at the most—to deal with the princes and their mother.

Laban picked his way around the large urns sprouting with palm branches and sidestepped the potted jasmine and poppies that dotted the courtyard. Why so many decorations? He never should have allowed the palace servants to bully the temple priests into allowing it. He was in charge of security for the coronation and this extravagance would only get in the way. Laban could ill afford the obstructions if the murders were to come off as planned. He'd make sure the grounds keepers cleared a path to the temple steps first thing in the morning. The way had to be free of these pots and urns if Shechem were to get to Zedekiah and escape before any of the royal guard could rescue the king.

A noise stirred behind Laban and he spun around, the bags shifting to one side and nearly tipping him off balance into an urn. Laban pushed aside a palm, expecting to see Shechem and his men, but it was only the ensigns that hung over the mezzanine. They slapped against the wall on a cool breeze, unfurled and ready to greet tomorrow's guests with the red, white, and black-striped colors of the tribes of Judah and Benjamin. Cursed things! It wouldn't be long before the blue and white banners of Joseph and the colors and patterns of the tribes of Ephraim and Manasseh replaced them. Laban would see to that once he was crowned.

The seven flames of the menorah danced yellow shadows over Laban's path, shifting with the breeze that blew through the palm branches. He leaned into his stride and stepped around a row of flower pots; the shadows moved and his foot caught the brim of the last one, knocking it from its tripod. The pot crashed over the stone floor and sent broken pieces of clay and uprooted poppies in every direction. Foolish decorations! Laban would have the gardeners sweep up the mess at first light. He kept walking toward the temple steps when the watchman came sprinting into the courtyard, his sword drawn. He stood beneath the archway leading from the front gates and scanned the yard; when he saw someone walking among the vegetation, he said, "Who goes there?"

"Put that away." Laban stepped from behind the urns into the full light of the moon.

"Captain Laban?" The watchman sheathed his sword. "What are you doing here, sir?"

Laban crossed the distance between them as quickly as his heavy load allowed. "I'm securing the grounds."

"It's been done." The watchman pointed to the galleries and swept his arm across the expanse of the courtyard where ten thousand noblemen and women of Judah would gather, come morning, to witness the coronation. He said, "Fifty men checked every door, searched behind every pillar and under every bench." He patted himself on the chest. "I had the priests check the sanctuary three times before they locked the temple doors and left for the night."

"Did you see anything unusual?"

"Nothing out of the ordinary, sir." The watchman motioned toward the large sacks Laban carried. "Can I help you with those?"

"I'm quite able." Laban pulled away and the metal inside clanged. "I'll take care of them myself."

"Whatever you say, sir."

"Why don't you go home and get some sleep."

"But, sir . . ."

Laban started the watchman walking back under the arch toward the main gates. "I'll take care of things here."

The soldier stopped in mid-stride. "I'm assigned to the night watch."

Laban unlocked the gate and let him into the street. "I'm telling you to go home, now."

"But . . ."

"You're dismissed. Now off you go."

Laban locked the gate behind the watchman and marched across the yard to the temple steps. He climbed to Zedekiah's throne, set the heavy sacks beside the legs and raised his boots onto the matching mahogany footstool. Thank heavens the menservants brought the chair over from the palace court before sunset. A throne was a fine place to rest and wait for Shechem to knock at the gate. He was late, but Shechem never was the disciplined sort. He came and went as he pleased, whenever he pleased, and it was no wonder his band had never overpowered any of Laban's forces, in any region of the country. Laban leaned back in the throne and stretched his powerful arms behind his head. The days of chasing robbers were gone now, replaced by a new order since Zadock introduced Laban and Shechem to more friendly terms. It was much simpler to do business with Shechem than it was to hunt him. Laban sank low in the throne and folded his arms across his chest. The chair was crafted in mahogany, with the head of a lion etched into the wood and a blue silk cushion stretched over the seat. It would have been a comfortable place to repose if not for the rigid backrest that pressed into Laban's spine, and the armrests that were nailed too high. Laban's first royal act would be the renovation of this chair to fit his powerful frame instead of Zedekiah's long, bony body.

A voice echoed off the walls of the temple. It was a voice Laban knew well and he lowered his boots from the footstool. The moon had sneaked behind a bank of thin clouds and he could barely make out the form of Shechem seated in the gallery's last row, his thick frame flush with the back wall. How did he get inside dressed like a robber? There were hundreds of soldiers patrolling the streets, another fifty stationed about the temple, and Laban the only one with a key to the gates.

"That chair suits you." Shechem's breath pulsed from his mouth like steam from a pot beginning to boil and his voice echoed across the large courtyards and off the limestone temple walls.

"Not so loud." Laban straightened in the throne.

"What are you worried about?" Shechem jumped from the gallery onto the courtyard proper and his long hair fell over his bare shoulders like a cape over a soldier's breastplates. "This is *our* kingdom now."

"Where are your men?"

"Don't you see them?" Shechem raised his arms and swept them over the expanse of the empty courtyard.

"Don't play me for a fool. You were supposed to bring them here tonight." Laban jabbed the toe of his boot into the leather sacks and let the metal breastplates clang against the swords. "That's what this meeting is about."

"Behold, Captain." On Shechem's signal, two, three, then finally ten longhaired men appeared from behind the temple's pillars and entrances and walkways. Out of the shadows they came, flanking Shechem and stealing across the courtyard, their leather-shod feet not making a sound. They were dressed as Shechem, a loincloth about the waist, boots strapped up to the knee, bows over one shoulder, and daggers stuck under their belts.

Laban said, "Two or three men would do."

"You want a show, don't you?" Shechem stepped aside and let Laban see them clearly. They were mighty men, with thick arms and powerful legs. "I bring you my finest showmen."

Laban pushed the packs toward them with his feet and the contents spilled out onto the steps. There were gray military tunics, long leather kilts with silver studs clasped to the end of each pleat, brass helmets, and broad swords and scimitars to replace the daggers Shechem's robbers hid under their kilts.

Shechem picked out a tunic and held it to his bare chest. "Why must we disguise ourselves at all?"

"Your men are easier to hide dressed as soldiers."

"You were going to have the palace cleared of everyone but the queen and her sons.

"I can't dismiss the palace help till morning." Laban issued the tunics to Shechem's men. "If they're going to stay the night in the palace along with two hundred servants, I want them disguised." He circled the robber band again and stopped at the foot of the throne. "They're not to dress as robbers until they appear on the queen's balcony tomorrow." He spread his arm out over the vast temple courtyards. "Then all in attendance will know that robbers have killed the heirs to the throne, along with their mother."

Shechem took out his dagger and tapped it against the footstool. "Is this where Zedekiah will kneel?"

"You're to use my sword."

Shechem reached for the weapon at Laban's hip.

"Not this one, you fool." Laban pulled away. "The relic."

"Where is it?"

"I never carry the blade with me." Laban walked in behind the throne. "My servant Zoram will be standing here, behind Zedekiah. He'll have the sword inside a wooden case. It shouldn't be any trouble wrestling it from the lad. He isn't a strong boy, spends his time in my treasury reading and writing and keeping my accounts."

"What about the king's guards?"

"I've called in two thousand from the field."

Shechem waved the dagger in Laban's face. "Those are poor odds, Captain."

"Most of them will be in the streets, keeping the peace." Laban raised his arm to the farthest reaches of the courtyard. "I've assigned three hundred inside the temple grounds. They'll be standing along the back wall." He walked down to the first bench at the bottom of the steps, directly below the throne. "You'll be sitting here with the priests. By the time my men see you, you'll be finished with Zedekiah and on your way out those doors." He faced an obscure priest's entry along the west wall that emptied into a side alley. "I'll see that it's unlocked."

Shechem sauntered to the edge of the landing, his loose-fitting loincloth sagging at his hips, and studied the small door that would be his escape. "There are easier ways to do this."

"It's to be done during the coronation."

"Ah yes, a public murder."

Laban raised the fingers on his right hand. "Five murders."

Shechem pointed his dagger at Laban and said, "What about my disguise?"

The cedar doors of the priest's quarters swung open and Zadock walked out. The hem of his robe slid across the courtyard, clinging to the mist-covered stone like a rag mopping the floor. He circled around the band of robbers, his pale complexion taking on the yellow reflection from the menorah and his dark-eyed gaze fixed on Shechem. "These are yours. And make sure you fit all your hair under the cap. I don't want any trouble with the priests." He handed Shechem a pleated white robe, a belt of rubies, and a mortar cap. "Keep your face covered and don't speak to any of them when they gather at the Gihon Spring for the washing ceremony." Zadock sat in the throne Laban had kept warm for him and looked out on the front bench. "You shouldn't have any trouble walking with them in the procession to the temple grounds as long as you get a seat at the front. You need to be as close to Zedekiah as possible."

"What about my men?"

"Have them come with me." Laban led Shechem's men to the doors near the back of the temple that emptied onto the loading docks of the palace. On the way past the decorations, he tore a frond from one of the palms and let it flutter to the ground. At least the preparations for the king's coronation weren't to be a complete waste. Royal funeral rites required as good a supply of greenery as did coronations. He unlocked the gate and let the robbers file across the alley to the palace kitchens and into the back stairwell. Zadock and Shechem went out by the same door, leaving the temple grounds silent and without a watch. But there was no reason to have one.

Laban was responsible for the royal family's safety.

Ruth tucked the leather satchel that held Mulek and Miriam's coronation robes under her arm and hurried up Milo Hill toward the government district. The sun had yet to rise over the Mount of Olives and burn the frost off the ground, but it wouldn't be long. The sun would crest over the summit earlier than it had in weeks, but it was such a slight change that the winter solstice would pass unnoticed by most of Jerusalem's residents. The water clock confirmed Ruth's calculations last evening, and this morning's dawn would be the first day of the New Year. She reached the top of Milo Hill and found her way through the empty market. There were no merchants preparing to barter away their wares today, not with all of Jerusalem waking to a coronation.

Today was the first day of the reign of Zedekiah, King of Judah, and Ruth prayed that the robes she'd woven would pass the public inspection of the coronation guests. She paused in the shadows cast by the archway separating the market from the government district and checked the robes one last time. Mulek's cuffs were large now, large enough to hide his toys. She'd done a good job disguising the long seams between a run of pleats. And Miriam's collar turned out better than expected. The jewels sewn into the cloth would come high around her cheeks, an elegant style Ruth created to complement Miriam's long neck. No telling the stir it would cause among Jerusalem's noblewomen. There had never been a garment with such a collar, but these were changing times and Ruth was daring enough to try a new style.

Ruth retied the bow on Miriam's sash and folded it into the leather case before stepping from the shadows of Market Street and heading toward the government archway. She had permission from the queen to pass and the officer in charge waved her through the army of palace servants scurrying about King Street with baskets of olives and dates, grapes and raisins, nuts and figs, and the king's favorite, fresh pomegranate. They diced and chopped and stirred them into a thousand breads and sauces, and prepared whole platters of the fruit, ready for eating. Table after table they filled to overflowing with more than enough food to rival the greatest coronation feasts of any king, so many tables Ruth couldn't count them. Why, she couldn't even see the last from the first. The tables lined both sides of the street from the Citadel steps, along the east wall of the temple and up to the palace gates before disappearing around the corner. A host of young boys ran about waving long plumes over the food to shoo away the flies.

An army of two hundred cooks tended the fire pits with eight hundred skewered lambs angled over hickory smoke. The crackle and smell of them filled the air with the celebration of a coronation. A caravan of donkeys filed down between the rows of tables with a load of fresh wines. Menservants unloaded the drink and sent the pack animals back for another load—one hundred homer of wine that required a good many donkey trips from the palace storehouse. Tradition bade the king make a feast for the people, and a feast he had made. The coronation guests would eat well today.

Ruth made her way past the last table of pomegranates and nuts, stepped around three servants carrying baskets of olives on their heads, and started down an obscure alley along the south wall of the palace toward the back entrance. She was about to hail the guard to open the gate and let her in when a woman stepped out from the shadows pulling a mule behind her. The animal was packed with saddlebags as if she were a farmer's daughter bringing food to the coronation, but her silver-threaded traveling robe was far too elegant for a commoner. She paused a moment before unveiling her face. It was Rebekah, and her long brown locks fell around her shoulders.

She said, "Tell Aaron I forgive him." Her voice was low and she turned her head down.

"Rebekah?"

"I didn't get a chance to tell him myself." Her lips began to tremble.

Ruth touched Rebekah's arm. "You can dear, once he returns from Egypt."

"Please tell him." Rebekah began to cry, her shoulders rising and falling with each flurry of tears. She took the mule by the reins and hurried down the alley toward her home.

Ruth would have gone after her, but the guard appeared at the gate and asked, "What are you doing here?" His voice was sharp enough to cut the iron bars he scowled through.

"I have a delivery for the queen," Ruth said.

"No one passes until after the coronation." The guard shooed her away with the back of the hand. "This isn't like any other morning." He folded his arms across his chest. "You can't come and go as you please."

Ruth stepped back and glanced at the catwalks atop the palace walls. There should have been ten soldiers perched and watching over the royal residence, but today there were none. The front entry was without its usual sentries and there were no soldiers wearing a path between the columns and canopies of the garden doors. A light breeze picked dried leaves off an oriental maple and swirled them about the trunk. There were no gardeners sweeping the paths and no maidservants batting dust from carpets. The palace stood abandoned without even a sparrow flying between the eaves. Except for the guard on the opposite side of the gate glaring back at Ruth, there was not another of Laban's men to watch over the queen and her sons.

Ruth opened the leather case and showed him the coronation robes. "Miriam and Mulek will need these before the ceremonies begin."

"I have my orders. The palace was cleared hours ago and no one is allowed back inside until after the coronation is finished."

Ruth asked, "Who sent them away?"

"Captain Laban, of course."

Laban? Why had he sent the palace guards away, to say nothing of the maidservants, menservants, cooks and butlers? Ruth pressed her cheeks against the metal bars and peered up along the west wall, toward Miriam's bedroom. The balcony was empty and the curtains drawn. "Is the queen in?"

"She's up there with her sons."

Ruth pulled back the sleeves of her robe and stepped one foot onto the metal bar at the base of the gate.

The guard said, "What are you doing?"

Ruth gripped the metal bars. "Either you open and let me deliver these robes or I shall climb over with or without your blessing."

"You try my patience, woman." The guard swung open the gate and said, "Come back this way as soon as you finish."

"Is there any reason to hurry?" Ruth returned the sleeves of her robe down to her wrists. "The coronation doesn't begin for hours."

"Do as I say." He pushed the gate shut behind her and locked it. "I don't want any trouble from Captain Laban. You never know what could go wrong, and then I'd be blamed for it."

Ruth hurried up the steps and inside the deserted kitchens. The cooks were gone, there were no maidservants preparing tea, and the ovens were cold. It was a peculiar silence on a day when the palace help should have been preparing for a multitude of guests. She quickly skirted past the chopping tables and around the pantry shelves to the back stairs leading to the royal residence on the fifth floor. She always came this way to avoid the palace guards. They asked too many questions, while the cooks never bothered her; why they didn't even notice her many trips through the kitchens.

Ruth turned the latch on the stairwell door and when it swung open a soldier stared at her out of the shadows. He was dressed in a gray military tunic that hardly fit his robust frame. A helmet covered his head, and locks of long hair fell out the back and down his neck. A single oil lamp cast a dim light over the soldier's companions. They were dressed as he was, with long swords and leather kilts that were far too small to cover the hips. It was a motley troop of men to be guarding the palace for a coronation, but at least they were a troop and she wasn't about to question their choice of watchplaces. If they believed a musty corridor at the back of the palace kitchens was the best place to protect the royal family, who was she to deny them their post?

The soldier took a deep breath and the gold chains pulled taut around his throat. His language was without the formality of other palace guards and he growled in low, rasping tones when he spoke. He rested his hand on the hilt of a dagger and said, "You shouldn't be in here, woman."

"I'm sorry, sir." Ruth held the robes close and backed a step. "I didn't know there would be soldiers guarding this part of the palace."

"How'd you get in here? The palace was cleared for the day." He waved to the other men over his shoulder. They had finished dressing and came up behind him.

"I was ordered to bring this for the queen and her son." Ruth opened the satchel and showed the robes. "They need them for the ceremony."

"I'll see that the queen gets them." He reached out for the robes, but Ruth pulled them back and said, "The queen's expecting me."

The soldier pulled a dagger from his hip and immediately Ruth knew she'd said the wrong thing. She quickly added, "Captain Laban sent me." Ruth caught her breath. Why had she said such a thing? She'd not even thought to say those words, but they rushed out of her before she could stop them, as if an unseen power were speaking for her.

The soldier stuffed his dagger under his belt and asked, "Laban sent you?"

"That's right."

But it wasn't right, not right at all. Ruth lowered her head. She had nothing to do with Laban and his orders. She raised her head to explain that it wasn't really on Laban's orders, at least not directly, but a feeling deep within her told her to keep silent and she obeyed.

The soldier covered his dagger with the end of his tunic and said, "You'll have to take the main stairs. I can't let you pass this way."

The door slammed shut and she offered silent thanks for the thick cedar planks that came between them. They were soldiers assigned to protect the palace and for that she was grateful, but they were like no other soldiers she'd seen about the palace in all her comings and goings. Ruth gathered the skirts of her robe and hurried out of the kitchens, down the corridor to the main hall, and up the stairs. The palace halls were empty, the front doors locked, but without a watch, and the anteroom deserted. Not a single maidservant scurried about dusting tables or putting out fresh flowers.

Ruth was nearly to Miriam's bedroom when the door flew open and four-year-old Benjamin rounded the corner. He pulled the hem of his sleeping robe up around his neck, wadded the garment into a ball of cloth and threw it on the ground, sprinting toward her with nothing but a loincloth of white linen about his middle. Ruth gathered him in her arms, walked him back to his sleeping robe and dressed him in it, pulling the hem back down around his legs and threading his arms through the armholes. His laughter filled the empty hall as his mother came out after him. He was playing, but by the stern look on Miriam's face she was not amused.

"Thank heavens you're here." Miriam took Benjamin from her. "I didn't think anyone was going to help me." The boy began to squirm and Miriam set him down and let him run back into the bedroom.

Ruth asked, "Where are the other boys?"

"Inside." Miriam reached for the satchel. "Do you have the robes?"

Ruth handed them over. "I added a collar to yours, and Mulek has larger cuffs."

"That should please him." Miriam hurried back to the bedroom. "Now, if I only had some help getting the boys dressed."

Ruth followed Miriam inside and found the princes in their sleeping robes. Eight-year-old Dan parted the portico curtains and stood in full view of the temple courtyard. What was the boy thinking? Did he not know it was a bad omen for a prince to be seen in public before his father's coronation? Ruth quickly pulled him back before anyone saw, and closed the curtains.

Mulek stood by the bedpost, playing with the ball and cup and catching it on every toss.

Miriam took the toy and helped him out of his sleeping garment. "I don't know where the help has gone. I expected Hannah and the others to be here hours ago, but I can't find any of them. The entire palace is deserted." She ran her hand over the braids in her hair. "I did these myself. Do they look presentable to you?"

Ruth said, "Something isn't right."

"Will you fix it?"

"Oh, not your hair, the braids are fine." Ruth stood behind Miriam and ran her fingers over them. Should she bother the queen with her concerns? Ruth tightened the last two braids and retied the bow that had come lose. Miriam had more pressing things to fret about than the dress and demeanor of the palace guards hiding in the back stairwell, but she couldn't keep from saying, "It's the palace. There's no one here except for a troop of—

"Benjamin! Close that curtain!" Miriam ran to the balcony and pulled her youngest away from the opening. She came back and stood beside Ruth. "I'm sorry, go on, what was it you were saying?"

Ruth took Miriam by the hand. She didn't need to worry the queen further. Miriam had enough on her mind and Ruth said, "I can help you get the boys bathed and dressed for the ceremony."

Ruth carried Benjamin toward the bath in the other room and Miriam followed with Mulek and Dan. This was to be a glorious time for the royal family, and Ruth wasn't about to darken it for Miriam.

She wouldn't let anyone spoil the day for Miriam.

Zoram stood a few strides from the edge of Gihon Spring holding Laban's sword case in one hand and the reins to King Zedekiah's donkey in the other. The animal was without decorations, no saddle and nothing that would distinguish it above any other creature except that its coat was pure white—white as the snow on Mount Hermon's peak. The donkey lifted its head, chomped on the bit, then sidled in next to Zoram. He stroked her mane and patted her side. She was a fine animal for the king's procession. Her body was high enough to keep Zedekiah's feet from dragging along the streets and she didn't have a mean streak that would make the task of riding her from here to the temple a chore for the king. The animal was as the prophecies required. The new king was to ride on the back of an unspotted ass the same way the Messiah would make His triumphal entry into Jerusalem. It was a cold winter's morning and Zoram wouldn't have to wait with the donkey much longer. Zedekiah would dip himself quickly in the frigid waters of the Gihon Spring and get on with the processional.

Captain Laban hovered over Zoram, bent over the saddlehorn. He should have been over with his men guarding the king as he bathed, but he had the sword to protect and he stayed close. The donkey tugged on the reins and reached for a clump of dead grass, nearly tipping the sword case out of Zoram's hands.

Laban lurched in the saddle. "Careful son."

"I have it, sir." Zoram kept a firm grip on the case and let out the slack for the donkey to eat. It was the first time Laban had allowed Zoram to remove the sword from the treasury. He never mentioned why it was missing these past weeks and Zoram didn't ask; he didn't want Laban to know he'd gone behind the purple curtain and found it gone. Zoram played his fingers over the case until he found the brass latches. They clicked open, and immediately Laban's head turned toward the sound. Zoram could never ask the captain why he went to his father in Anathoth to have Jeremiah anoint the blade. No good could ever come of the answer. A fly lighted over the case and Zoram shooed it away with the back of his hand before pulling back the silk that covered the blade. The finely smithed steel shimmered in the morning sun against the case's red silk backing and Laban reined a circle around Zoram, drawing the attention of the crowd that had gathered to witness the first rite of the coronation. Jews thronged the east gate and lined the road down past the Gihon Spring to the Hinnom Valley and back up the Mount of Olives opposite the gate. It was Laban's sword and all of Israel would see its bright sapphired hilt with emeralds and jade shining in the sunlight, and know that Laban was the last living heir of Joseph, the first royal blood of the Hebrews.

Laban's men circled the spring three horses deep and held a tight line. Zoram was the only one allowed close enough to see past the animals' stomping and pawing. Zedekiah stepped from the cold spring waters and dried with a towel. He had a thin tall frame that did not fit well into clothing, though his coronation robe went over his shoulder easily and it covered his leg, just the right length to keep the hem from getting soiled along the coronation route. Tradition dictated it be a simple garment. There were no pleats, no double cuffs or collars.

Zedekiah appeared from behind the line of horses to the cheering of the crowd. He took the reins of the donkey from Zoram and started up the incline toward the city gate as a troop of trumpeters went in ahead of him with their shofar horns raised to the sky and their blasts wailing out the arrival of the king. A crowd of jugglers and three lines of maidens followed the trumpeters through the gate, dancing to the music of three harpists and a drummer. The temple priests were the last to go in ahead of Zedekiah. They dressed in white robes, with silk sashes and mortar caps covering their hair, at least all of them but one, and Zoram stepped around the king's donkey to get a better view of him. He was taller than the others and he filled out his robe more like a brick mason than a holy man. What sort of priest had such a powerful stature? His hair was stuffed beneath his mortar cap, but there was so much that it bulged at the sides and stuck out along the base of his skull. He was a priest who didn't look anything like one and he didn't even bear a vessel of sacred olive oil for the coronation ceremony. He was out of place among these holy men and he walked behind them so that no one noticed; no one but Zoram.

Zedekiah sat as straight as a man of his constitution could on the back of a donkey and he waved to the crowd as he rode out from under the shadows of the east gate. Zoram kept in stride behind the king's donkey with the sword case held high. His arms tired after the first two blocks down Main Street and he rested it on his chest, until Laban reined past and ordered him to raise it back again. The captain wanted every Jew in the streets to get a good view, and who was Zoram to deny him his royalty?

The procession reached the corner of Milo Hill, down near Josiah's firing yard and when Zoram turned that way to show the sword to the crowd on his right hand, he spied Rebekah, Elizabeth's friend. She wore a dark traveler's robe and her hair was tied back and covered with a hood. What was she dressed like that for? Certainly the potter could afford to dress her in something better. He was a wealthy artisan and he could have clothed her in robes befitting a princess. On a day like this, she should have been wearing jewels around her neck and a perfume strong enough that he could catch the scent from this distance, not carrying a saddlebag over her shoulders. He rested the sword case on his turbaned head and waved to her, but before she could return the gesture Laban came alongside, his Arabian's large body obscuring Zoram's view of Rebekah.

Laban pulled past him, up beside the longhaired priest and leaned over to whisper in his ear before spurring back to his watch behind Zoram. The priest immediately left the procession. He mixed into the crowd standing in front of the bakery and stole down along the street, dodging quickly through the crowd.

He was headed for Rebekah.

Mima tipped the delivery boy a shekel and let him out with his cart through a side door. He'd never get through the crowd that lined the streets in front of the main gate, not with the king's procession passing by. The delivery boy thanked her and waited with his palm out for her to tip him three more shekels. The boy was a brazen fellow, but she paid him just the same and sent him on his way. The kilnmaster had used too much wood in the kiln last night and there would not be nearly enough stacked against the north side of the potter's estate to burn it down if she hadn't convinced the woodcutter's son to deliver more. He charged twice the usual amount for a delivery on the day of the coronation, but there would be little need to explain the expense to Josiah once the day was out.

The servants were gone to the coronation and the kilnmaster left Mima to tend the fire. She was the only servant who volunteered for the job, and since the kilnmaster didn't want to miss the festivities, he deemed her fit for the task. She stocked the fire with more than the kilnmaster would have ever allowed. The crackle of flames echoed through the air vents and filled the firing yard with the pop of burning logs. Mima covered the stacks of wood alongside the house in oil and hid the jars. Then she went inside to serve the potter and Rebekah their last breakfast.

The main dining hall of the potter's estate had a thick cedar door that locked from the outside, and no windows. It was a perfect place to trap someone with a fire. It stood in the center of the home and smoke would fill the room before anyone could escape.

Mima carried a tray with lamb, fresh bread, and fruits from the kitchen, but when she came around the corner she found Josiah seated at the table, alone. She set the tray down and asked, "Where's Rebekah?"

Josiah said, "She's outside watching the procession."

"She hasn't eaten."

"You know that girl; she eats like a sparrow. Her mother was the same way."

"She needs a good breakfast."

Mima hurried from the dining room and left Josiah with the uncut bread. She ran across the yard, pulled open the gate and found Rebekah standing on the corner.

"Rebekah!" Mima cupped her hands to her mouth. "Come inside girl."

Rebekah stepped down through the crowd and said, "I'd like to stay and watch a while longer."

Laban rode past and reined up in the street, just down from the potter's gate, his gaze following a priest dressed in white robes and a mortar cap over his long, bulging hair. The priest pushed a man and his wife out of his way, dodged a child, and headed toward Rebekah.

Mima stepped into the street and took Rebekah by the arm, pulling her back to the gate. "Come inside, girl."

"I want to watch a while longer." Rebekah pulled free.

"I said, come now!" Mima grabbed Rebekah with one hand and took hold of the latch with the other. She quickly pulled it shut, but before it banged against the post, she saw a dagger flash beneath the priest's robes. He pulled back, losing himself in the crowd, but Mima locked the gate just the same.

Mima escorted Rebekah to the dining hall and sat her at the foot of the table across from her father.

Josiah asked, "Did you enjoy the procession?"

Rebekah took the plate of fruit from Mima. "What I saw of it."

Mima said, "I insisted she come inside."

"I don't see why I couldn't have stayed a while longer." Rebekah held a fig and stared at it.

"It isn't safe for a young girl to be in the streets."

Rebekah set the fig down. "It's the middle of the morning."

Josiah finished his milk and turned to Mima. "Do you have it?"

Mima reached under the table and pulled up the end of a burlap sack. It was a rather large bag and the contents rattled about inside. "I believe I have two, but it was dark last night and I couldn't tell exactly what I was doing."

"Where did you get them?"

"In the pauper's field."

"From the oldest section?"

"I would never disturb the fresh ones." Mima shook her head and her large arms began to sway at her side. "That wouldn't be proper."

Josiah opened the sack and peered inside. "Did anyone see you?"

"There was not another soul out that late, sir."

"Very well, see that it's left here by the table."

Mima gathered the plates into a stack. "Good luck today, sir."

Rebekah looked up from her plate. "Mima?"

"Yes, girl?"

"Thank you."

"I thought you were out of patience for me this morning."

"I'm sorry. I'm just a bit anxious. That's all."

Mima leaned over and kissed Rebekah on the forehead. "You behave yourself, girl." She left them in the dining room to finish their meal.

Mima had a fire to tend.

Ruth sat Benjamin in her lap and held him until he stopped fidgeting. She had bathed him in perfumed soaps, washed his hair in jasmine powders and prayed the hot bath water had power to calm his unsettled spirit, or at least tire it for a moment so she could dress him in his robe. She led his arms through the sleeves and pulled the collar over his wet hair, and when his face popped out the head hole he grinned up at her and said, "I see you." His nose was red from the bath and his cheeks soft as a rose petal.

Ruth touched her finger to his face and said, "And I see you." She stood him on the chair in front of her and arranged the pleats down his front. For such a young boy he fitted into a robe well. Most four-year-olds would have looked like an overripe melon ready to pop. Young boys' bodies were given more to a kilt above the knee than the formal dress of a coronation robe, but Benjamin had a long body like his father and he carried the robe like a prince should.

Dan stood beside Ruth's chair and pulled his robe on without her help. He allowed her to latch his sandals after he tried twice and couldn't get them to stay, and when his fingers fumbled with the bow, Ruth was happy to tie it and let him believe he was old enough to dress himself. His deep brown eyes followed her hands over the silk and when she finished with the bow he said, "You tie pretty knots."

Ruth ran the pearl teeth of an Egyptian comb through his sandy brown hair. They were bows. Knots were for rope makers and seafaring men, but she kept these details silent and said, "Thank you Dan, I tie my prettiest knots for a prince."

Mulek stood beside the curtain, peering out over the temple courtyard through a slit. The sash to his robe hung over his shoulder and the end of it danced above the floor. Something in the yard had gained the boy's interest and he leaned forward, his shoulders hunched and his head bobbing like a piece of driftwood on the tides of the Great Sea. Ruth stepped to his side to tie the sash in place when Mulek spun around, the silken sash flying out of her hands. His body went straight as a board and his face white as the lace in the curtains. He cried, "Fire! The potter's home has caught fire!"

Ruth pulled back the curtain. He was right. A thick black plume gathered over the lower city, and bright yellow flames danced from the roof of the potter's estate.

Miriam burst through the door of her dressing room with the pleats of her new robe fleeing from before her hurried stride. "What is it?"

"It's a fire mama, a fire at the potter's home." Mulek nestled his head in his mother's robe. "Will Josiah be all right?"

"Pray for him, son." Miriam pulled the curtains shut. She quickly untied her veil and handed it to Ruth. "Watch my sons until I return."

"You can't leave; the coronation ceremony will begin soon."

"I need to know if the potter is safe." Miriam slid her wrists out of the narrow cuffs and untied the sash at the back. "Put this on and give me your robe."

"But . . ."

"Someone has to sit here."

Miriam undressed beside her throne. It was carved of the same blackwood used in her husband's, though the backrest was not as high and the armrests not as thick. Servants had hauled it up to her room and set it on the balcony yesterday and now it was positioned for Miriam to sit in and observe the coronation ceremony in the temple grounds below.

Ruth said, "I can't do that."

"Please." Miriam carefully lifted the delicately crafted collar over her head. "If I'm not here to sit on that throne when my husband arrives with the procession, Laban will grow suspicious and he'll come looking for me." She laid the garment in Ruth's arms and stood in her white linen under robes, waiting for Ruth to change clothes.

"This isn't wise." Ruth untied the sash on her robe and pulled her arms through the sleeves. "Something awful could happen."

"Something awful has already happened." Miriam dressed in Ruth's plain, light brown robe. "I must go to the potter." She kissed each of the princes on the cheek and said, "Be good you princes of Judah, listen to Ruth, and I'll be back before anyone misses me."

Miriam disappeared into the hallway and Ruth closed the door behind her. She kept hold of the latch and leaned her brow against the thick walnut planks in the door. What was she to do with Miriam gone and the coronation about to begin? Benjamin began to cry and Ruth gathered him in her arms to keep him from turning the latch and following after his mother. And what about the princes? She couldn't pretend to be their mother. Not in front of ten thousand coronation guests. Benjamin tried to wiggle free and Ruth sat him with his brothers, and draped her arms around them, pulling them in close. These three princes were her charge now, and until Miriam returned she would see they were kept safe. And there was nothing she could do for the queen but keep a prayer in her heart for Miriam's safe and swift return.

Godspeed, Queen of Judah.

Miriam's quick steps echoed down the empty corridor. There was not a soul in the halls of the west wing, but she pulled the hood of Ruth's robe over her face and hurried out the garden doors, down through the maze of paths. The palace guard sat with his back against a post and his legs propped up on a low-growing bush. When he saw Miriam approach he stood and asked, "Does it take that long to deliver robes?"

Miriam lowered her head and didn't answer. The moment she uttered a word, the man would know she wasn't Ruth. She stood in front of the gate that emptied into the alley behind the palace and waited for him to let her into the street, and when he slammed the metal bars shut, she didn't dare let the sound turn her gaze back toward him. She was away without being found out and she took the back road that ran behind the Citadel and came out at the base of Milo Hill behind the carpentry shop.

The potter's servants had formed a water brigade, passing buckets down the Main Street from the water shaft to the estate. Twenty soldiers and their captain stood near the gates. None of them were helping to put out the fire and Miriam hurried over. She held the hood close to her face and spoke through the cloth. She said, "Do something before it's too late."

"It's already too late, woman." The captain leaned against the gatepost. "The home is lost."

"Someone could still be alive."

"Inside there?" The soldier turned to the flames leaping from the collapsed roof. "I doubt that."

"Please!" Miriam pulled on his sleeve. "At least do something to save what's left of the home."

The soldier pulled free. "I have my orders."

"Orders?" Miriam said the word slowly.

"Captain Laban rode by here at the first call of fire. He said we shouldn't risk injuring our men."

"What about the potter and his daughter?" Miriam turned away to hide the tears that filled her eyes, but her voice was firm and unfaltering. She said, "Did Laban leave orders to let them die?"

The fire had consumed the Joshua trees growing up the side of the now charred north wall. The hearth stood alone in the center of the estate, its square mantle and heaven-reaching chimney the only recognizable shape inside the flames. The furniture, hallways, and railings were burned away, the back walls fallen over and the upper floors collapsed under the weight of the burning and broken roof beams. Miriam checked the servants' quarters at the back of the estate for some sign of Josiah and Rebekah, but it was empty. All the potter's men were putting out the fire. She hurried up and down the water brigade and found Mima passing buckets, her wide shoulders and bulky arms swaying with each bucket she hefted.

Miriam removed the hood from in front of her face and asked, "What happened?"

"My lady?" Mima's glance flitted between her and the soldiers at the front gate. "What are you doing here?"

"Is the potter safe?"

Mima ushered Miriam into the shadows over behind the kiln, away from the burning estate. "We can't be seen together."

"Where are Josiah and Rebekah?"

Mima lowered her head. "They're gone."

"Oh, Mima, I'm so sorry." Miriam wrapped her arms around the large woman, but she didn't return the gesture. She stood still and stiff. Miriam said, "Tell me what happened. Are you certain they were inside?"

"You should never have come here." Mima spoke in a low monotone. "It isn't safe for either of us." She started Miriam toward the gate. "You must go."

"But . . ."

"Go now!" Mima pushed her gently, but Miriam didn't leave the yard immediately. She covered her face, walked around the kiln and stood in the shadows of the smoke. The front facade of bricks began to sway and the men in the water brigade pulled back, calling for everyone to clear away. Miriam didn't heed the warning. She held her ground as the front wall collapsed in a thunder of falling brick. The rush of hot flames seared across her face and lifted the hem of her robe about her legs. Rebekah and Josiah were gone and there was nothing she could do to bring them back. She took a bucket from a servant and tossed the water at the fallen wall. It sprayed into a thousand droplets and boiled into a mist of vapor on the hot rubble.

Rebekah and Josiah were dead.

Ruth sat on the throne, set her elbows on the armrest and listened to the gathering crowd beyond the curtains. Where was Miriam? It didn't take that much time to get to the potter's home and back and she could only assume she was helping Josiah cope with his loss. Fires were a dreadful waste of good property. Ruth straightened the sleeves of Miriam's robe. They ballooned from the shoulder to just above the wrist where they came to a blossom of white bows. Thanks be to heaven she wore the same size robe as the queen. Only the most observant guests would see she was impersonating her royal highness—a crime that could get her thrown into prison. She primed the cuffs up past her wrist and let the white and purple silks cascade down on her arms. The delicately sewn collar rose up around her neck and hid her cheeks, but they could never reach high enough to hide the fear that gripped her soul. The pleats flowed down her front and the train cascaded over the armrests and wrapped around the wooden legs of the throne. Mulek and Dan tucked the train underneath and stood on either side of the throne, resting their hands on hers and waiting on her as if they were her sons. It was their duty to open the curtains and introduce her to the coronation ceremony on the third sounding of the shofar horns.

Ruth gathered Benjamin on her lap and tried to sit as a queen should sit, her head held high and her spine flush against the backrest, though keeping the boy from wiggling about was anything but dignified.

The trumpets blared and Ruth held Benjamin close. It wasn't out of nervousness for the guests who would be watching her once the curtains opened; she could endure their curiosity without panic. This was a deeper, darker dread. It passed over her like the angel of death passing over the children of Israel, and filled her with the impression that the princes' lives were in danger. What danger? The palace was well guarded and there was nothing to fear except being found an imposter. Ruth turned her gaze to Dan standing at her left hand. His sandy brown hair curled over his brow and about his ears. He had narrow lips like his mother and large eyes like his father and when he felt her gaze on him, he turned to Ruth telling her with the touch of his hand that all would be well. Ruth adjusted the collar around her face, and glanced at Mulek standing at her right hand. He was a noble-looking boy with his father's brow and wide shoulders. He stood straight and tall, the neatly pressed and pleated coronation garment flowing over his young body. The garment added ten years to his age. He nodded slowly, telling her he was ready to open the curtains and introduce her to the guests in the courtyards below.

The second round of the shofar horns sounded and the fear passed through Ruth again, this time with such force she could not deny it. The princes were in danger. From what, she didn't know, but there was no mistaking the feeling: Ruth was to protect them.

The third round of trumpeting sounded in the courtyards and the stir of the crowd silenced. The guests were in their places, the procession had filed inside the gates, and the trumpeters were sounding the arrival of the king. Mulek and Dan stepped toward the curtain, raised their hands to the slit and were about to pull it open when Ruth said, "Leave it closed!"

Mulek glanced over his shoulder. "What is it?"

Ruth set Benjamin down and stood, her train sweeping past the legs of the chair. "We must hide."

Mulek let go of the curtain. "This isn't a time for games."

"A game!" Benjamin ran a circle around the throne and wrapped himself in the long skirts of Ruth's robe. "I will hide and you can find me." He peered out from beneath the hem. "I see you."

"We're not going to hide." Ruth pulled Benjamin out from between her legs. "We're going to . . ."

What were they going to do? Ruth glanced around the room until her gaze fell on the bedroom door. They should run out into the hall and down the backstairs. They'd be safe among the soldiers. But from whom were they running? Ruth stood in the middle of the bedroom, halfway between the door and the throne. What was she doing there? She should be sitting at the throne with the curtains drawn open. Was she wrong about the danger? She gathered the princes around her, took one long gaze at the empty throne, then turned her back on it and started for the bedroom door. They were nearly to the threshold when Ruth halted, Benjamin and Dan running up against her legs.

Mulek asked, "Where are we going?"

"I don't know." Ruth held her hand to her brow. With every decision she made, her mind fell deeper into confusion. She pressed her fingers against her temple and . . .

Where was it she was taking the princes?

Dan tugged on the hem of her robe. "I can get you some water and some of mama's powders, the ones she drinks when she doesn't feel good in the head." His soft smile and wide eyes peered up at her and she was grateful for his concern, but she didn't need a drink of herbs right now, she wasn't losing her mind. Didn't he understand that? She was trying to save them from . . .

"I'll go and get some help." Mulek started into the hall.

"No, not that!" Ruth's voice caught in her throat. She grabbed him by the shoulder and forced him back into the bedroom. "I don't need any help!"

Mulek lowered his head and his voice faltered. He said, "I'm sorry."

"Oh, Mulek." Ruth wrapped her arms around his neck and drew him in close. "It isn't you, son." She wiped a tear from his eye before brushing away tears of her own. She glanced at the other boys. Benjamin's lower lip began to tremble. He stared down at his feet and rubbed his fingers together. Dan stood beside him and held his hand.

Mulek asked, "Why are you doing this?"

Ruth closed her eyes, took a deep breath, and saw immediately in her mind what she should do. And as soon as she determined to follow that course, a sweet, peaceful feeling pierced the stupor of her thinking like the rays of sun after a storm. She leaned her head in next to Mulek and asked, "Do you remember the day you told me the story of your charm?"

Mulek dried his eyes on Ruth's sleeve. "You mean about Moses saving the children of Israel from serpents?"

"Well yes, that." Ruth dabbed her cheeks dry on the silk cloth of the other sleeve. "But you also told me you could trust me."

Mulek's head shot up and his eyes brightened. "Mama taught me to listen to the still small voice."

"That's why we're doing this." Ruth took Benjamin's robe by the hem and pulled it up over his head, undressing him and leaving him standing in a white linen loincloth. "I want you to get out of your robes."

"But why?" Mulek stepped back.

"I've not gone mad." Ruth held Benjamin's robe between her hands and ripped it across the shoulders. It came apart in her hands and she threw it on the floor near the throne. "Just do as I'm doing." She undressed Dan next and tore his robe into pieces.

Mulek took a deep breath and rent the robe off his body, ripping away the long sleeves first, then the pleated front, and let the back of the robe fall to the ground behind his feet, leaving him dressed like Benjamin and Dan, in nothing but kilts of white linen. The boys began to shiver and Mulek drew his brothers in close. They huddled there, watching Ruth as she stripped down to her under robes. She held the coronation garment out in front of her for a moment. It was the finest robe she'd ever sewn and when she tore it, she tore away a bit of herself with it. The jeweled collar came away first. She kept the gems, but let the sash fall to the floor, the threads in the seams sheared into ugly spindles. She couldn't leave the precious stones—not if this were to look like the work of thieves. And that's exactly what the spirit whispered to her: make this appear as a theft.

The shofar horns in the temple grounds sounded again and Ruth said, "Over there." She steered the boys toward the two tapestries gracing the far wall. She lifted the largest one away from the stone and helped the princes shuffle behind it. It hung from a brass rod less than a cubit from the wall, but it provided enough room to stand unnoticed.

Benjamin asked, "Is this part of the game?"

"That's exactly what this is," Ruth said and stepped in behind the tapestries next to him. "And the way you play is to stay so still and quiet that no one ever finds you." She patted his head. "Can you do that?"

Benjamin didn't answer, but Ruth could feel his head bobbing in the darkness. He was telling her he'd already begun to play and Ruth prayed that they would all win this game. The bedroom fell quiet and there they stood half naked behind the tapestry. They had left their robes in rags on the floor, the throne empty, the curtains closed, and suddenly the sharp sting of embarrassment shot through Ruth. What had she done? How would she explain the danger if there was none? She was a fool and she was about to abandon their hiding place when the latch rattled and the door creaked open. It was a slight sound, hardly audible from behind the tapestries.

Ruth inched her head out and peered through the golden tassels along the hem. The door swung open and a man rushed into the room. He held a dagger in one hand and a raised sword in the other. He wore a loincloth around his waist and soft leather boots laced up to the knee that silenced the sound of his footsteps on the stone floor. His long hair twisted about his shoulders as he dashed to the empty throne. More men dressed like him poured into the room, each one bearing a dagger. They were robbers—Shechem's robbers—and Ruth understood why she was directed to hide the princes. The robbers moved about the bedroom, their leather-shod feet not making a sound. They scanned every corner and checked the side rooms and passageways.

The lead robber picked up the queen's robe and examined the torn cloth. "Keep searching the rooms." He turned his head and Ruth could see him clearly. He was the soldier from the back stairwell. Ruth's entire body began to tremble and she removed her hand from the tapestries to keep the wall hanging from shaking, but it was too late. The robber stepped toward her. His breath was steady and his footsteps light. She could hear him standing in front of the adjacent tapestry. A slight breeze streamed down along the wall, and the tapestry beside them nudged toward the wall. The robber was poking at it, searching for them, and Ruth could only pray that when he found no one behind it, he would end his search and leave them in peace. She huddled the princes together as far away from the edge of the light as she could. The drafting air slowed and then the sharpened blade of a dagger flashed in the shadows along the hem of their hiding place. It came in behind the thickly woven fringes and slowly lifted the tapestry away from the wall. The edge of the light crept toward Ruth and she bent away from it, wrapping her body over the boys. She was their last protection, their only shield against the robber's weapon and she offered the only silent prayer she could think to offer.

God of Israel, be our hiding place!

Zoram carried the sword case through the temple gates and the sound of the iron bars grinding in the pivot stones turned the heads of five thousand men. He stopped at the archway beneath the overhanging galleries, hidden in the shadows of the giant pillars that kept aloft the women's court above. Must he walk past so many nobles and be the object of their attention? It was the arrival of Laban's relic, not Zoram himself, that caused the stir among the coronation guests. He stayed in the shadows until the captain reined through the gate, got down off his horse, and handed the reins to a groundskeeper.

Laban marched in behind Zoram. "What's keeping you, son?"

Zoram didn't turn back to face him. He said, "There are so many, sir. And hardly any of them from Jerusalem."

Laban said, "It's a coronation, boy. Now, be off with you."

The temple priests turned past the gate with Zedekiah following behind on his white donkey.

Laban said, "You're to go first." He gently pushed Zoram in the back with both hands and started him walking toward the coronation guests.

The Elders of Jericho were dressed in black robes with pointed turbans and they looked like the Elders of Jerusalem, except that long vents were cut into the sides of their robes and their hems didn't come all the way to the ground, showing far too much of their dusty sandals to be from the capital city. Jericho was a hot place and these Elders' clothes were tailored to endure the long summers. Down from them stood the priests of Shilo in their white dress, and they brought with them the finest gift a priest can give a king. They bobbed their heads and whispered prayers as quiet as the gentle breeze that passed over the silent crowd, begging heaven to look kindly upon Zedekiah and his court. Mixed among the crowd were merchants from every house of business in the kingdom: gold traders from Shilo bearing a chest of cups and chains and bracelets, perfume sellers from Hebron with bottles of frankincense, horse traders from Megiddo with a stallion for the king and three more for the princes, and the famous wine merchants of Beersheba with a cart of their finest, bottled and corked and ready to celebrate the day.

The coronation guests stood shoulder to shoulder in a sea of silk turbans and hooded heads and when Zoram started down through them, they parted as if he were Moses, leading the children of Israel through the Red Sea. But Moses never saw as many gold rings and silver amulets on his journey to the promised land as did Zoram on his crossing of the courtyard toward the temple steps. He moved out from under the shadows, and the women in the galleries above leaned over to see him pass. There were five thousand, dressed in blue and white linens with matching veils draped from ear to ear and their hair braided about the shoulders. So many wore earrings that when they turned their heads toward Zoram, there was a faint chorus of chiming gold. The faint aroma of women's perfumes filtered down from their perch. It was frankincense and myrrh, rose petals and poppy, and it scented the air with the presence of many women.

The foreign guests stood near the front of the courtyard and Zoram made his way around them. The first royal he recognized was the boy dressed in blue silk robes with ten servants standing beside him, fanning him with palm branches. It was the son of Necho, Prince of Egypt, sent by his father to offer a gift to the new king of Judah. The boy's head was shaved except for a ponytail down one side, and his eyebrows were carefully trimmed. The viceroy of Babylon stood opposite the Egyptians as far away as the bench seat allowed. Their two countries were at war, and though they had yet to sling a bow or throw a spear in battle, the tension spanned the wooden bench. The viceroy folded his arms across his chest like a pouting child. Enemies made the worst guests. The viceroy was dressed in a deep blue robe, cut high around his cheeks and embroidered with the face of Nebuchadnezzar. The Babylonians had little art worthy of mention, and their weavers were almost as poorly trained. Who would want the bearded head of the king of Babylon emblazoned across the chest?

Zoram climbed the steps and stood behind Zedekiah's high-backed throne. There was more than enough hardwood to shelter him from the glances of so many rich and powerful noblemen.

The trumpeters emerged from behind the temple pillars and stood beside Zoram, announcing the arrival of Captain Laban with a volley of high-pitched, staccato blasts. The captain entered from under the archway, flanked on either side by his commanders, all of them dressed in military capes on this cold winter day and none as thick or as warm as the one Laban wore. It wrapped around his body like a blanket and came together over his right shoulder with a large gold clasp. Laban didn't come up the temple steps and stand at the front with Zoram. He headed through the crowd toward the back wall where three hundred soldiers stood in double-file lines, their swords raised to greet their captain and their brass breastplates clanging allegiance.

The trumpeters formed a double column down the steps of the temple and raised their instruments like a musical archway leading to the throne. The trumpets were crafted out of the horns of rams and when they sounded the second call—a series of long, low-pitched notes—it was a forlorn sound, a longing for deliverance, in contrast to the bright garment worn by the high priest who entered the grounds on cue with the trumpet call. He was the first holy man through the gate, his colorful robes lifting on the breeze. He wore a white underrobe that showed at the cuffs and collar beneath a purple outer robe. His breastplate was inlaid with precious stones set in rows of three, one for each of the twelve tribes of Israel and his labored stride was due more to the jewels' weight than his advancing years. He held his white miter cap in place as he walked toward the temple steps, followed by a host of white-robed priests.

Zoram tipped the sword case, shifting the weight to his left hand and straining around the backrest of the throne to find the longhaired one among the priests. He was taller than the others and he walked with a quick stride and pushed his way past his fellow priests, nearly running to the head of the group. He held the arm of one priest, stepped in front of another, and blocked two more on the way to his seat on the front bench at the base of the steps directly below the throne. He sat down immediately as he arrived, straightened his robe over the bench, and fixed his gaze on Zoram's sword case. And when he felt the weight of Zoram's gaze on him, he adjusted his mortar cap forward, shielding himself from Zoram's curiosity.

The trumpeters raised their horns a third time and played a resounding fanfare of startling harmonies as Zedekiah entered on the back of his white donkey. He was more comfortable on the animal's back now than he had been at the east gate, and he managed to smile and wave to the crowd without losing his balance. He dismounted without a misstep and when he handed the reins to a servant, he breathed an audible sigh. He climbed to the throne with his usual vigorous stride and turned his gaze to the palace balcony to wait with the coronation guests for Queen Miriam and the princes to join the ceremony.

The curtains moved slightly on the breeze but they remained closed. Why didn't Miriam have the princes part the curtain and step onto the balcony? Tradition bade she come out of her room, wave to the crowd and then sit with her sons. At least that's what the priests had rehearsed with Zoram and he couldn't go on with the coronation and present the sword to the high priest for the anointing of Zedekiah, not without Miriam. The Hebrews had never crowned a king without the queen present, except for David who had so many that none of the palace scribes knew which one to record present, so they left the record without any mention of her.

Zedekiah motioned for the trumpeters to repeat the fanfare. The echo of the shofar horns died on the temple walls and still no sign of Queen Miriam.

Laban left his soldiers at the rear of the grounds and hurried through the guests. He passed the front bench and the longhaired priest glanced up at him, but Laban kept walking, his gaze fixed on the queen's balcony. He climbed the steps and stood beside Zedekiah. He said, "Wait on the ceremony, sire. I'll see to your wife and sons." Without waiting for Zedekiah to speak, Laban hurried back down the steps and disappeared through the passage leading to the palace loading docks.

Zoram pulled the red silk over the blade and tucked the end beneath the hilt. Not another delay. He'd have to stand there with ten thousand souls watching him. But at least he shared that discomfort with Zedekiah and the high priest. Zoram locked the brass latches of the sword case and lowered the weapon under his arm. For all the anticipation he'd endured these past weeks leading up to the coronation, it was nothing short of tedious.

Were the ceremonies of royals always this dull?

Ruth huddled over the princes, her arms around their necks, and her hands pressing against their chests. She could feel Mulek's racing heart and Dan's quick breathing. Benjamin leaned into her thigh as the robber pulled the tapestry away from the wall and the edge of the light began to creep down along the stone toward them.

"What's the meaning of this?" It was Captain Laban's voice and it rang in the bedroom chamber like the crack of thunder. There was no mistaking it. Ruth had heard his low, powerful voice before and she'd never forget it. It had haunted her since the day she met him by the east gate. And she would have hated the sound of it still, if it didn't have power to save them.

The robber let go of the tapestry and it fell back into place against the wall, shrouding her and the princes in darkness. Ruth crept back down along the wall and peered out from behind the tassels.

Laban said, "Where are the bodies?" He snatched up a piece of torn robe. "You were to wait until the curtains were opened so the crowd could see!"

"There was no one here when we arrived."

"What?" Laban dropped the cloth to the floor.

"We found the room empty."

Laban circled the throne, the heels of his boots digging into the shreds of cloth strewn over the floor. He came around to the front of the chair and when his feet passed over Miriam's collar, he picked it out from among the remnants and ran his hand over the seams where Ruth had torn out the jewels. Why did God want her to do that? She didn't know, but she'd been directed of heaven to make it appear as if thieves had stolen the jewels she'd taken from the robe and kept in her palm.

Laban turned the collar over in his hand before he threw it to the floor. He said, "Get out of here before she sees us together."

"Who?"

"The queen, you fool! She *knows*." Laban ripped away the gold clasp holding his cape to his shoulder. "She has to know."

"We can search the palace for them."

"It's over." Laban went to the balcony curtains and peered through the slit. "Get out before I have to order my men to chase you out."

"But—"

"I said, get out now!"

The lead robber marched over to Laban, his long hair jumping about his shoulders. "What about Shechem?"

"He's no fool." Laban widened the slit and kept peering out into the courtyard. "He knows when to stay alive and return to fight another day."

Laban followed the robbers into the hall and the bedroom quieted, but Ruth kept the princes behind the tapestry until long after their footsteps fell silent.

Benjamin stirred about her knees, and through the darkness he whispered, "Did we win?"

Ruth lowered herself to the floor, her legs weak and limp. She curled up against the wall and gathered the princes against her breast. And though she tried to fight back her relief, the tears streamed down her face and onto their heads. Her shoulders lifted and pressed against their small bodies in great sobs. By the grace of God they were spared.

Between her tears Ruth said, "Yes, Benjamin, we won."

Zoram switched the sword case from under his left arm to his right. How long did Laban require to draw open two curtains? He shifted his weight to the other foot and leaned his shoulder against the throne. He wasn't the only one put out by the delay. A murmur began to filter through the crowd and the longer the curtains remained closed, the more the guests turned about to face the balcony; everyone but the longhaired priest.

He pushed the mortar cap back off his brow as Zoram switched the sword to the other arm. And when Zoram stepped back from the throne, the priest shifted his gaze with each of Zoram's slow steps. He had narrow eyes that peered over an even narrower nose. The scar on his cheek was a hook that disappeared under his mortar cap, along his sideburns.

Zoram ran his fingers over the brass clips of the sword case. They were set in place, but to be sure he placed the pin. He couldn't take any chances with the sword. What if the priest were a . . .?

Stop thinking foolishness! The man wasn't a thief. At least Zoram didn't think he meant any harm until he threw his mortar cap to the ground, his long black hair falling down around his shoulders. He tore away his robe and stood in nothing but a loose-fitting kilt. He bolted up the steps, his powerful legs pushing him forward and his thick arms swinging wildly. He didn't attract the attention of the guests; he didn't even make a sound, his soft leather boots carrying him up the steps like a ghost from hell. He didn't scream like a wild beast to scare Zoram or twist his face into a scowl as he bore down on him. He didn't need to do anything to frighten Zoram. He was Shechem, king of robbers, and his name was fear.

Zoram reached for the sword, but the pin was set and he couldn't get the case open. Why had he ever locked it? The case fell from his hands, the rosewood cracking on the stone. He ripped away the broken lid and reached inside, feeling for the hilt, but Shechem was on him. Sweat coursed down his wild-eyed face and his naked chest heaved. He swung a powerful fist and Zoram's head snapped back like the end of a mule whip. Pain fractured through his face and blood sprayed into his eyes. He would have surrendered to the man if his hand hadn't felt the hilt of the sword between the broken pieces of wood. God was with him! Zoram tightened his grip around the hilt and rolled over, snatching the sword from the splintered case. He came over onto his back with the weapon raised at Shechem and blood spattering from his lips. He cried, "Back away."

A woman on the terrace above began screaming, and the soldiers at the back of the courtyard lunged toward the front of the steps, but the crowd surged back away from the danger, and Laban's men were helpless to get past the mob.

Shechem hovered over Zoram, his wide-shouldered frame rising and falling with each breath. He said, "You fool," and reached for the blade, but Zoram pulled it back, and sliced through his flesh.

Shechem held his bleeding hand. "I'll see you pay for this," he said, and sprinted out the small side door and into the alley.

Zoram stayed on his back and let the sword fall to the ground beside him. Blood streamed down his cheek and he touched the gash in the side of his face. The swelling would go down in a few days, but he'd have to live with a nasty scar that would mar his face for . . .

Why was he worried about a scar? He was alive wasn't he?

King Zedekiah stepped to his side, the hem of his plain white robe brushing over Zoram's feet. He offered his hand and said, "You're a brave man."

"I wasn't trying to be brave, sir." Zoram stood. "I didn't have time to think about that."

"You saved my life and for that I thank you." Zedekiah wrapped his arms around Zoram and pulled him in close. The king's body was shaking. The danger had passed, but the man was still frightened and with good reason. The robber could have killed them both, and immediately Zoram understood how near the new monarch had come to death. He embraced the king as a troop of soldiers surrounded them. They raised their swords to the crowd, scanning the yard for more robbers, but there were none.

They were safe, for now.

Elizabeth stepped from her father's darkened shop into the evening rainstorm. It was an awful downpour, but Elizabeth would not turn back into the shelter of the smithy despite the heavy load she carried wrapped in a piece of leather and tied with cords. She locked the shop door behind her and hung the brass key around her neck. She couldn't lose it, not if she didn't want Papa to suspect her of taking these from the shop. The heavy package was difficult to carry and she held it against her breast with both hands. Papa could never know why she was stealing from him. She would have asked his consent, but he would want to know why and that was a question she couldn't answer. Better to let him believe a thief had robbed them until he was able to hear her reasoning, and God willing there would come a time when he was able. She raised a shawl overhead and continued up the street toward the upper city. The driving rain beat against her cheeks and the wind threatened to pull the shawl from around her neck. She didn't believe as Zoram believed, at least she wasn't certain she did. But she had to deliver this package to him, and there was no better excuse than to see him after he'd been attacked by the robber Shechem. She wouldn't wait another moment and listen to Jonathan's report of Zoram's bravery in the face of certain death. The coronation was hours old, but she had to find out for herself if Zoram was safe. She climbed to the top of Milo Hill and made her way past the bakery on Market Street and around to the back entrance of Captain Laban's treasury.

A lone guard stood under the only ledge along the wall, keeping out of the rain. Elizabeth walked to the edge of the lamplight that shone from a sconce above the guard. She said, "I've been summoned to see the keeper of the keys." What she didn't tell him was that she'd summoned herself.

The soldier held his coat collar close around his neck to keep the rain from running down his back and said, "Are you the nursemaid?"

Elizabeth stepped into the full light of the lamp. "Was he hurt badly?"

"There was a good deal of blood spilt, and he fainted three times from the loss of it." The soldier reached for the heavy satchel she carried in both hands. "Is that a delivery of medicines for him?"

Elizabeth turned away from his reach. "I need to get this to Zoram immediately."

"He's off with the doctor right now." The soldier stepped out from under the ledge and shielded his eyes from the driving rain. "I'll see that he gets it."

Elizabeth said, "I'll wait for him if you don't mind."

"In this storm?" The guard shook his head and water spilled from the brim of his helmet. "You've lost your mind, woman."

Elizabeth moved under the thin branches of an acacia tree and huddled against the locked gate that led to the treasury, but there was no shielding herself from the fear that Zoram was hurt worse than Jonathan had led her to believe. Her hair matted against her brow and fell in ratted thatches over her shoulders. Her robe took on enough water to flood the Jordan and the bow in her sash sagged about her hips, but she was not leaving until she was certain of Zoram's condition. She wrung what water she could from the sleeves and pulled the cloth away from her body, but the rain fell in sheets and stuck the robe to her like the skin of a dried date. The street was dark and the sound of rain beating down on the cobblestones filled the night, or was it the echo of footsteps off the high brick walls? She raised her gaze to find a troop of soldiers marching out of the shadows. Their swords were raised and they formed a slow-moving shield around Zoram. Elizabeth stood on her toes to get a better view. Zoram carried a broken sword case under his arm and the weight of it burdened his stride, but at least he could stride under his own power and Elizabeth breathed a sigh. If only she could see his face and the soft smile she'd come to adore since the day they first met, then she would know if he was well. But a blood-soaked bandage sagged over his brow and she could only assume he was too weak to raise his head to met her gaze.

Elizabeth brushed her matted hair off her brow and shook the drenched pleats of her robe. The cloth was limp in her hand and all she could do was let it hang from her shoulders like a saddle blanket on the flank of a pack mule. What was she thinking coming here on a night like this? It wasn't a proper time to pay a visit, and she was hardly presentable, but Zoram would want someone to share the events of the day, and she prayed that someone would be her. She retied her sash and stepped away from the tree toward the company of men.

The soldiers fanned out between them, their swords pointed at Elizabeth and the captain cried, "Stand down, woman!"

Zoram's head came up, his bloodied bandage falling down over his left eye from the sudden movement. He said, "She's with me."

"I'm sorry, sir." The captain ordered his men to stand down.

"What are you doing here?" Zoram pushed the bandage up and winced as his fingers touched the wound.

"Don't speak." Elizabeth pressed her palm against his uninjured cheek. "It must have been awful. All of Jerusalem is talking about what happened."

"I didn't do anything, really." Zoram turned toward his escorts. "Nothing they wouldn't have done to save the king."

"Sir, you were to see the sword is safely put away." The captain slapped his heels together. "Captain Laban's orders."

Zoram turned back to Elizabeth and held up the case. The finely carved surface was splintered, and pieces of wood were missing. "I have to take this to the treasury."

"I'll leave you to do your work." Elizabeth pulled the wet shawl close around her face. "I only came to see that you were safe."

"Don't go." Zoram blurted out the words so quickly Elizabeth smiled at his childishness. "I mean, will you come inside and wait while I see to the sword? I'd like to speak with you for a moment."

Elizabeth let the shawl fall down over her shoulders and the rain cascaded in large drops down her cheeks. "I suppose I could wait for a moment."

Zoram lived in a small two-room dwelling within Laban's estate, a few paces beyond the treasury door. It was built of rose-colored mud bricks and attached to the outside wall like a brick mason's afterthought. Elizabeth waited by Zoram's living quarters while he unlocked the treasury and disappeared into the underground vault with the soldiers and bolted the door behind him. There were no lights filtering through the window of Zoram's residence and when she tried the latch, the door came open in her hand. The least she could do was light a lamp to brighten the damp evening. She stepped inside and felt along the wall to the hearth. There was a lamp on the mantle and a flint beside it. She lighted the lamp and its glow spread across the small room. The hard-packed dirt floor was covered with a ragged throw rug, and two cedar chairs sat around a small table, the only furniture in the room except for the shelves along the far wall, stocked with scrolls from floor to ceiling. She got three logs from the wood box, set a fire in the hearth, and knelt beside the flames to take the chill out of her bones. Her eyes watered at the sudden warmth and she sneezed.

"Bless you." Zoram stood in the open door.

Elizabeth turned away from the fire, but stayed by the warmth of the flames. "My father says you're a brave man to save the king as you did."

"I was lucky, that's all. Lucky to be alive."

Elizabeth quickly stepped to his side. "Don't ever do that again."

"I couldn't let Shechem have a weapon; he would have used it to kill us both."

"All he wanted was the sword." Elizabeth placed her hands on her hips. "Didn't anyone ever teach you that about robbers? Give them what they want, and they'll leave you in peace."

"How is it that you know so much about the mind of Shechem?"

"You'd be surprised what I know."

Zoram smiled, his white teeth shining against his dark skin. "Laban ordered his men to stay with me through the night and keep Shechem from carrying out his threat."

Elizabeth held his arm. "He threatened you?"

"It's only a precaution; he was after the sword and Laban believes he may try again."

Zoram placed the lamp on the table and let the light cast an orange-red glow over a large plate of brass, nearly four hands wide and six long. There were no markings or engravings on it, the edges were cut straight and ground to a smooth finish, and the polished surface shimmered in the flickering light.

"It's for my father," Zoram said in answer to Elizabeth's staring. "I've smithed two of them, but I'm out of ore."

Elizabeth set her heavy leather package on the table next to the brass plate. She untied the cords and pulled back the shards covering five bars of pure copper and two more of silver. They were squared at the corners, purified in a smelter and ready to be mixed together in a rich concentration of brass. She asked, "Will this help?"

Zoram turned the bars in his hand. "Where did you get these?"

"That doesn't matter; they're yours now."

"I thought you were against helping my father and me."

"I was until . . ."

Zoram reached across the table for her hand. "Until what?"

"I'm not doing this for you or for your father." Elizabeth took back her hand and held it over her breast. "I'm doing this for myself." She pushed the lamp aside and cleared the view between them. "Moses promised that if we obey God we will know that He is life, and the length of our days." She ran her hand over the polished brass plate that lay on the table between them. "I'm bringing you this ore because I want to know if your life should be my life and the length of your days, my days also."

CHAPTER 38

Ruth stood by the kitchen window trimming the lamps for evening, the larger ones for the main room and the smaller ones for the bedrooms. She didn't normally allow Joshua to sleep with a lamp, but he refused to go to bed without one burning in his room. She tipped the jar and let the thick oil flow into the holding bowl. The boy had used nearly two shekels' worth of oil since the coronation, and despite the expense, Ruth allowed him the luxury. She filled his lamp to the brim and set the wick in the center spout. Odd, Joshua never had trouble falling asleep in the company of his older brothers. But Aaron was on his way to Egypt, Daniel on his way to who knew where, and she didn't know when either of them would return to comfort the boy. How quickly her roost had emptied, and of her two absent sons she worried most over Daniel. Would he return her son or a soldier, versed in the ways of Captain Laban's men? She tipped the oil flask on end and filled another lamp for Sarah's room. The girl was older than Joshua and she should have fallen asleep in the dark, but she couldn't deny Sarah the soothing light, not when the third small lamp was for Ruth. She filled it full and set it alongside the others. Jonathan complained that their home would burn in flames as the potter's had, but Ruth ignored his objection and slept with the light burning beside her. With each passing night, Daniel was closer to capturing Uriah and the lamp brought some light to that dark thought.

Ruth began filling the large lamp for the kitchen when a soldier from the Citadel marched through the gates. The sun was nearly set and the shadows had spread across the courtyard, but it wasn't difficult to see that he was one of Zadock's special guards. He wore striped red and black knickers that ballooned over his thighs and tied below his knees. A matching vest hung on his shoulders, its silver buttons jingling as he walked toward the house. When he saw Ruth standing in the window, he stopped below the sill, stabbed the end of his long spear into the ground and said, "I have a message for the blacksmith."

"Tell me what it is." Ruth set down the oil flask. "I'll see that he gets it."

The guard removed his plumed helmet and held it at his side. "Your husband is wanted immediately."

"At this hour?"

"He's to meet Zadock and the other Elders at the execution grounds. Tell him to come as soon as possible; the prisoner Uriah will be arriving presently."

Uriah at the execution grounds? Ruth pushed aside the lamps, and the oil spilled over the sides of the holding bowls. Not this, not after enduring the evil of the coronation. Why must she suffer the shame of her son aiding in Uriah's capture, after she'd endured in silence Laban's attempt to murder Miriam and her sons for spying? But she had no other choice than to keep quiet her knowledge of Laban's doings; she had promised Miriam to tell no one, not even Jonathan. She pressed her knees against the wall and leaned over the windowsill. If it became known that Miriam was the palace informant, it could mean something worse than death for all of them. Ruth steadied her trembling hands on the window ledge. At least Daniel didn't bring the captain of the guard into their home and force Ruth to live with the constant threat of Laban lurking about. Miriam's burden was incomparable. Ruth let go of the sill and folded her arms across her apron. No. It wasn't a mere burden; it was a game of chance, and life or death the only prize.

The guard asked, "Is there something wrong?"

"Nothing, nothing at all." Ruth shook her head. "I'll tell my husband. Is there anything more?"

"That should do, my lady." The soldier spun on his heels and marched out the gate, carrying his spear like a shepherd carries his staff.

Ruth gathered Jonathan's black council robe from a hook on the wall, took down the turban from the rack and got the headshawls he kept folded on the shelf. She went out the back door and found Jonathan at the washbasin behind the house. He was stripped to the waist and scrubbing with cedar soap and a cloth. He splashed cool water over his shoulders, his body shaking like a leaf in the cool winter breeze. It was just like him to wash outside in the winter. He had a stubborn streak and he wouldn't let the cold evening drive him inside. He'd wait until the washbasin froze over before he considered cleaning up beside a warm fire. Jonathan dunked his head in the basin and when he came up for air he asked, "Why do you bring me those?"

Ruth held out his council robes. "You've been summoned."

Jonathan dried his face with a towel. "Did the messenger leave word why?"

Ruth dabbed a drop of perfumed oil below Jonathan's chin and rubbed it over his skin, but she wouldn't look at him. How could she tell him that he was to attend the execution of an innocent man? No, this wasn't an execution. It was murder and it cut against the deepest feelings in her soul. If there was a way to remind the Council thou shalt not kill, tonight was the night and she prayed Jonathan would have the courage to be the messenger. She placed the turban on his head and laid the white headshawl over it, covering Jonathan's dark hair that was showing a streak of gray above the ears. Odd, she'd never noticed that before. Was he mellowing with the years or was it the strain of these past weeks that aged him before his time? She lined the white headshawl up with his brow and turned the hem back to his hairline. That hadn't receded as much as she hoped his stubbornness would. The hem of the black headshawl lay three fingers back from the edge of the white one and she arranged the trailing ends around his ears and onto his shoulders.

Jonathan asked, "What does Zadock want now?"

Ruth corked the perfume bottle and set it aside. "It isn't one of your usual meetings." She fitted the flowing black robe over his shoulders and primed the pleats around his feet. "You never told me the Council voted to execute Uriah."

Jonathan pulled back from her primping. "Have they captured him?"

Ruth nodded. "Zadock expects him to arrive this evening."

"Where?"

Ruth leaned forward against the washbasin and gently stirred her hand through the cold water. Ripples formed around her fingers and slowly moved outward to the edges of the basin. One small movement created such a stir. "I never thought it would come to this."

"Come to what?" Jonathan pulled up the sleeves of his robe until the white cuffs showed.

"You're to meet Zadock at the execution grounds."

Jonathan gathered his hood close around his neck and straightened his cuffs. "There's no reason to rush this."

"You could speak to the other Elders, tell them how you feel" Ruth took her hand from the washbasin. "Reason with them, see if they'll reconsider."

"I can't do that."

"And why not?"

"I won't risk our standing in the community for a, a . . ."

"An innocent man?" Ruth asked. She stepped back and peered up into his eyes, searching for the mercy she knew was locked deep in his soul, buried by his obsession to build a successful blacksmith shop.

Jonathan said, "The Council found him guilty."

"Did you vote with them?"

"Uriah committed treason during the war."

Ruth turned away and faced the shadows. "You don't know that."

"I couldn't go against the rest of the Council. I would have been the only one." Jonathan raised his arm in the air and the long black sleeves flapped like the wings of a raven. "What would Zadock think?"

Ruth spun around to face him. "It's you I need to trust, not him."

"We owe our shop to Zadock." Jonathan adjusted his turban.

"We've started a blacksmith shop without his help before."

"I don't understand your thinking." Jonathan wiped his brow on his sleeve. "What has Uriah ever done for this family?"

What had he done? Ruth walked around to the other side of the washbasin, the water dividing the distance between them. If only she could tell Jonathan what she knew of the Rekhabites, recount the blessed doctrines she had learned from Miriam and Mulek, then he would understand what glorious things the prophet Uriah and others like him had done for her and the children. Aaron knew the sweetness of their teachings. The Almighty had softened his heart like a farmer plows his field, furrowed with the pain of his injured feet and ready to receive the seed of her new faith and nurture it in his soul. Elizabeth was beginning to understand; not completely, but she'd felt the swellings in her breast, testifying of the Anointed One. Ruth troubled the water with her hand, this time splashing it up against the sides of the washbasin. If only Jonathan knew Laban as she knew him, then it would be a simple thing to tell him that the prophets were men he should trust. But Jonathan was a member of the Council and it was impossible to know if he would hear her as an Elder or as her husband. For now, she'd keep secret her knowledge of the Rekhabites and not answer his question about Uriah until he had the faith to bear her reply.

Ruth asked, "Will you be late this evening?"

Jonathan pulled up his sleeves. "Don't wait up for me." He started around the house, toward the front courtyard.

"Jonathan, wait." Ruth hurried to his side. "Please reconsider your vote?"

"It's too dangerous." Jonathan continued down along the side of the house with Ruth hurrying beside him, taking two steps for each of his. He said, "I'll not put our lives at risk."

Ruth tugged on his sleeve. "There is no one else who will."

Jonathan turned into the front courtyard before he stopped and Ruth ran up against him. His body was tense and his hands were fists at his side. He said, "Why must anyone risk their life for Uriah?"

Ruth lowered her head and didn't answer.

"Not you too, Ruth." Jonathan took her by the arm. "Tell me you haven't taken to Aaron's way of thinking."

She pulled away and walked slowly toward the house.

Jonathan raised his voice. "What are you keeping from me?"

Ruth opened the front door and went inside to find the kitchen as dark and cold as her conversation with Jonathan. The light of dusk lingered on the windowsill like a departing guest, and she could hear the gate swing open, then shut. Jonathan was gone. She felt her way to the table and moved her hands about until she touched the lamp.

The flint lay beside it, but she didn't strike a spark and light the wicks. There was no room in her soul for that kind of cheer right now. She sat in the darkness, staring at the window that framed the night sky. There were thick clouds obscuring the stars and the faint howling of a dog filtered over the rooftops and echoed against the sill.

If Jonathan wouldn't defend the prophet Uriah, who would?

Jonathan carried the incense burners under his council robes and turned down the alley behind the Citadel building toward the execution grounds. He'd smithed the silver vessels with the purest grade silver. They were polished with resin oils and ready for the potter's funeral. Jonathan trimmed them with jasmine and hyssop powders before leaving the house and they would make a fine tribute to Josiah.

The incense burners rattled against Jonathan's thigh and he took out the slack in the gold chain and held them close against his bosom. Hopefully Josiah and his daughter were taken by the smoke before they felt the flames. Fire must be a painful way to leave this life, but the Almighty didn't allow men to choose their demise and the potter didn't have any more sway with heaven than did Jonathan. Poor man. There were hardly any remains left of the potter. The servants found a few charred bones in the ruins of the dining room and they could have carried them in the funeral procession fitted into a small leather satchel. But the Chief Elder insisted Josiah and his daughter receive a funeral befitting the Second Elder. Zadock had paid the embalmers four pieces of silver to wrap the remains with linens soaked in wild gum seed oils, he had sent five more pieces of silver to a troupe of wailers, and he had sent not a shekel shy of ten silver coins to the carpenter for a casket of hardwood, nearly three cubits long. They couldn't lay what was left of the potter and Rebekah in a tomb, not without something to hide the nothingness that remained of their corpses.

A blast of strong wind lifted near the gate and blew dust over Jonathan's robes as he entered the execution grounds. Dried leaves swirled past him and skittered across the yard toward the group of Elders gathered in a half circle around the execution block. They were watching the tall wooden gates for Elnathan and his men to arrive with Uriah, and when they saw it was only Jonathan, they turned back to their quiet deliberations to discuss whatever men discuss when they wait to execute a man. Jonathan was the last Elder to arrive and he crossed the dimly lit grounds, rubbing his hands and stomping his feet as he sidled in next to Zadock. The sun had set and the cool of the winter evening descended over him like a deep frost, chilling him to the very soul.

"I smithed these in my shop." Jonathan handed over the incense burners. They were fashioned of silver and shaped like a potter's bowl. Three air vents lined the sides, and a long neck sprouted out the top like a chimney.

"That's kind of you blacksmith, but Uriah won't need them." Zadock held the incense burners up by their long chains. "Traitors don't get a funeral." He clucked his tongue. "A procession through the streets is far too expensive an extravagance for a traitor." He peered at Jonathan over the end of his long nose, his eyes as dark as the shadows shrouding the execution grounds. "Do you have any idea how much mourners and wailers charge for their work?"

"It was very kind of you to pay for that luxury."

"I didn't pay a shekel for Uriah's funeral. His body will be carted to his family in Arim when this is finished and that will be the end of his treason."

"The incense burners weren't meant for Uriah." Jonathan spoke softly. "I smithed them for the funeral of Josiah the potter."

"I'd forgotten about that." Zadock let go of the chains, and the incense burners fell to the ground. "How clumsy of me."

Jonathan picked them out of the dust. "I thought it would be a kind gesture from the Council if you were to have them carried at the front of the procession."

"That's very noble of you, blacksmith." Zadock leaned his head in. "I don't usually speak ill of the dead." His eyes narrowed and he pressed his lips together as he spoke. "But you should know that Josiah was a Rekhabite." He clucked his tongue, this time louder than before. "It's true, and all along we trusted him like family." He patted Jonathan on the back. "But that's been taken care of now, hasn't it? And there's nothing but charred bones to bury."

"Who took care of what, sir?"

"It's best the potter died this way without us having to expose his treason. No one need know otherwise." Zadock adjusted the robes on his shoulder. "In life he was an Elder and I'll see that he's buried as one." He leaned in to brush the dust off the incense burners. "Have your eldest son carry these in the funeral procession."

"Aaron's in Egypt."

Zadock turned his head, the shawls of his turban lifting off his shoulders with his sudden movement. "Egypt?"

"He's riding with a caravan of olive oil merchants."

"That's a fine thing. There's good money to be made in the oil trade." Zadock checked the gates then turned his gaze back to Jonathan. "I understand he was fond of the potter's daughter."

"I wouldn't use that word." Jonathan quickly hid the incense burners under his robe. "They spoke a few times, nothing more."

Zadock sighed. "She was a beautiful girl."

"I think he was taken by that."

"It's best this way." Zadock patted Jonathan on the arm. "She won't influence your son for the worse. It wouldn't have been a good marriage."

Marriage? Aaron hardly knew the girl.

Zadock said, "You'll be sure to see that someone carries the incense burners, won't you?"

"I'll find someone."

"You should be commended for your thoughtfulness."

"Thank you, sir."

Jonathan bowed and slowly backed away. He circled around behind the other Elders and came out beside the execution block. The torchlight cast long shadows over the thick slab of limestone that stood no higher than a man's waist. It was fitted with ankle and wrist chains and the dried blood streaked the sides of the coarse stone like a stained winepress.

The chill of winter bit at Jonathan's feet, and he began to pace. It was the frost in the ground, wasn't it? It certainly wasn't guilt that turned his limbs frigid. Uriah was a traitor and Jonathan had voted as the law required; treason was punished by death in this kingdom. Jonathan stomped his feet, the worn leather sandal slapping against the ground. It was the cold that chilled his blood; it had to be. Only frail men suffered from guilt and Jonathan was not a weak-minded soul. He curled his toes under, and on his third trip past the block he stopped beside the executioner. He was polishing his scimitar, a blade curved like a half moon. It was as wide as three men's hands and heavier than a millstone.

"It's perfect for this kind of work," the executioner said in answer to Jonathan's staring. He rubbed the chamois along the length of the blade. "You need a good first stroke to cut through a man's neck."

Jonathan blew warm air over his hands. Why was a boy of his young age doing the work of killing? He couldn't be any older than Daniel. "You do this a lot, do you?"

"It's my first time, but I've been trained well. The commander down at the training grounds, he knows how it's done and he showed me how to hold the sword." The executioner pressed the chamois hard against the metal. "He had me practice on melons."

"I didn't think there was an art to this."

"There is, sir." The executioner turned the blade over and began polishing the other side. "I only hope I do it right the first time. They say it isn't a pleasant sight if you do it wrong."

Jonathan stepped to the block. He set his hands on the weathered bloodstains and looked beyond the executioner, past the Elders who were milling about in conversation, out over the empty, windblown grounds. He said, "Killing a man hardly seems pleasant no matter how right you get it."

"It's painless, sir."

"Did your commander teach you that as well?"

"That's right. It's all in a good first stroke." The soldier raised the scimitar with both hands and brought it down, stopping the edge of the blade just above the surface of the block.

Jonathan quickly pulled his hands out of the way. "Have you ever asked a dead man what it felt like?"

The executioner slung the chamois over his shoulder. "I thought all the Elders were in favor of this."

"We are."

"Then why do you ask these questions?"

Jonathan folded his arms over his pleated robe and stomped the frost from his feet. "It's a cold evening, isn't it?"

The executioner set the sword down on the block. "No colder than any other, sir."

Jerusalem at last! Daniel turned the prisoner cart up Milo Hill, cracking the whip above the ears of four steeds. This was his finest hour and he leaned forward on the stoop, searching for the crowd. No maidens stood in the balconies ready to swoon over him and no curious folk had come to see him ride through the streets. There was no one with torch held high and voice ringing in a triumphant welcome. Only the clatter of wooden wheels and the pounding of thirty iron-shod horses filled the emptiness along Main Street.

Captain Elnathan rode beside the prisoner cart, his head rising and falling below the stoop. He'd warned Daniel not to expect a soldier's welcome. On Laban's orders, they were to arrive quietly after dark and proceed directly to the execution grounds. But Daniel could hope, couldn't he? He'd captured Uriah and there should at least be a small crowd of well-wishers, though he didn't need them. He'd earned the right to wear officer's stripes and if he had to return the criminal Uriah to meet his fate in the private shadows of evening instead of the full light of praise, so be it. Daniel was destined to rise through the ranks of the military, no matter how empty the streets, or how silent his glory.

The horses began to lag and Daniel cracked the whip again. He held the reins in one hand, bent over the side of the cart, and peered between the bars. Uriah lay still in his cell, his body curled up on the floor. He'd groaned once since they watered the horses at Hebron, something about the wrath of God, but the man's speech was so slurred he couldn't make out any more of his idle cursing. His hair was matted with dried blood and his eyes sunk deep into his fractured skull. Why did the Elders want the man dead? He didn't seem to have any enemies. At least not any who cared enough to come out this late at night to shake their fists, curse his name, and spit through the bars.

A stray dog howled outside the gate of the execution grounds and two guards waved Daniel through, ahead of the rest of the company. He pressed the steeds around the gatepost, forcing the inside wheels up off the street and raising a cloud of dust about the cart. The grounds stood empty except for a circle of black-robed Elders standing near the execution block. Daniel strained to see Jonathan among them. Papa would be impressed with Daniel's success, but the only men he could make out through the settling dust were the two who hurried over as he reined beneath the torchlight. The Chief Elder was dressed in his council robe with a black turban gracing his head and a gold amulet around his neck. Laban was vested in a leather kilt with silver studs sewn into the end of each pleat. His thick breastplates and arm guards readied him for battle, but Uriah was hardly an enemy worthy of so much armor. He hadn't eaten since Hebron and was so weak they had to feed him by hand this afternoon to keep him alive.

Daniel tied the reins to the rail and slid down from the stoop. "I captured him, sir. Just as you ordered."

Laban stood to the metal bars and peered in at Uriah. "Is he alive?"

"He's been that way most of the journey." Daniel rattled the bars until Uriah turned over and Laban could see the gash in his head.

"Who did this to him?"

"I did, sir. He tried to escape."

Elnathan reined in next to them. "You should thank the boy for what he did. If it wasn't for Daniel, we would never have caught him." He took a drink from his water skin. "Daniel will make a fine officer."

"I'm counting on that," Zadock said as he picked his way around the cart, careful to lift the hem of his robe. He started down the row of Elnathan's cavalrymen. The horses snorted, and the air pulsing through their nostrils lifted the hair that poked out from under Zadock's turban. He reached the last horse, glanced about the yard and then came back down the line of horses and stood beside the prisoner cart. He pulled on the iron bars, rocking the bed on its wheels. He said, "Fetch the king and tell him we're ready."

Miriam got out of bed, draped a shawl over her sleeping robe, and took the back stairs to the kitchens. A sip of tea seemed the only solution to rid herself of the visions of Uriah's headless body. She wouldn't sleep any longer and allow the nightmare to haunt the furthest retreats of her rest. Why did Zadock insist on an immediate execution? He could keep Uriah in the dungeon for a few days, long enough for Miriam to devise some way to help him escape. She rounded the last flight of stairs, pushed open the back doors to the kitchen and found the lamps still burning long after the evening meal had been cleared away. The cook stood at the hearth, boiling a pot of water over the fire. She mixed in ground tea leaves, a sprig of mint, and a few drops of honey before straining the brew through a linen cloth and into a cup.

Miriam ducked around the pots hanging from hooks above the cutting board. "You couldn't sleep either?"

"My lady." The cook spun around. "You gave me a start." She lost her grasp on the cup, but caught it with both hands before it fell. "What are you doing awake at this hour?"

"It's Uriah." Miriam came around the cutting board. "Is there any word?"

"None yet." The cook stirred in a spoonful of goat's cream. "I'm preparing a spot of tea for your husband. Poor man. He's fretting about this. Will you be joining him?"

"Thank you, my dear." Miriam filled a second cup and warmed her hands around it.

"I don't mean to be unkind." The cook peered about the kitchen before she spoke another word. "I'm pleased neither you nor your husband can sleep." She shook her head. "Your husband's late brother never had a conscience, God rest his soul. I worked in these kitchens from the day he was made king and he never fretted a minute when they did away with the other prophets. I think he rather enjoyed the awfulness."

Miriam took the tray from her. "You go to bed, now. I'll take this to my husband."

"I'm sorry if I've offended you; I didn't mean anything by it."

"No offense taken." Miriam touched her on the arm. "Now, off you go to bed."

"Yes, my lady." The cook put out the oil lamps and hurried toward the servants' quarters.

The crackle of a roaring fire filled the hallway outside the reading room, and orange light from the hearth flickered out the door and over the stone floor of the west wing. Miriam entered quietly and stood a few paces off from Zedekiah's reading chair. He didn't see her, or if he had, he didn't give her reason to believe so. He sat low in the chair, his shoulders pushed against the backrest and his legs sprawled toward the fire. She wanted to go to him and tell him of her fear of Laban, that he pursued her like a hunter hunts its prey, but she couldn't. If he learned how she had spied for the Rekhabites, his life would be in jeopardy along with hers. Better to let him live in darkness while she suffered quietly in Laban's shadow. Ignorance would keep her husband safe from the captain.

Zedekiah stared into the flames and Miriam came around beside the armrest, her arrival still unnoticed. He was lost in his thoughts and the light danced over his furrowed brow, half hidden behind the brim of his crown. He'd pushed it forward and it sat awkwardly on the front of his head, covering his eyes. He never wore the headpiece, but tonight was his first official act as king and Miriam was without a word of comfort for him. What could she say that would bring solace to this sorrow? He was king now, and despite suffering the horrors of the coronation, she prayed he had the courage to be a good king. His right hand propped up his chin and his left hand hung limp over the armrest with a scroll in it. It was a tally written in the Chief Elder's short, choppy script recording the vote on Uriah's guilt. There were eleven in favor of beheading and none to stay the executioner's blade. If Josiah the potter had voted, Uriah would live. But the potter was dead and Zadock had his unanimous vote to kill a prophet of God.

"You should be in bed," Zedekiah said and sat up. He'd caught Miriam staring and she leaned over and righted the crown on his head. She said, "As should you." She sat in the matching chair, the small tea table filling the distance between them.

"There's no word, yet." Zedekiah rubbed where the crown had left an impression on his brow.

"You're king now; you could change this."

"You don't understand."

"What's there to understand?" Miriam inched to the edge of her chair. "Uriah is an innocent man."

"I wish this were only about him." Zedekiah slouched further into his chair. "I was a fool to believe that by gaining the throne I would have the respect of the Elders and nobles of the city."

"You don't need their respect." Miriam inched the tea closer to his hand. "All you need is their allegiance."

Zedekiah removed the crown and held it in his hands. "This piece of gold does not have that kind of power."

"You're not siding with the Elders on this matter, are you?"

"There's nothing I can do. They have the law on their side."

Miriam took the crown and knelt before him. "You make the laws in this kingdom." She shook the gold headpiece. "You can walk into that execution ground, stand in front of Laban and the Elders and tell them . . ."

Miriam spied Laban standing in the doorway. She quickly placed the crown on Zedekiah's brow, pulled her shawl close around her shoulders, and walked to the hearth.

"Tell us what?" Laban sauntered into the reading room and the smell of strong wine came with him. How could he drink on a night like this? The captain had started his merrymaking well before it was wise to celebrate the execution. His brightly polished brass armor glimmered in the firelight. He came around in front of Zedekiah's chair and stood at attention. "It's time, Sire." He turned to Miriam. "Will you be joining us?"

"They don't allow women at an execution." Miriam kept her gaze on the fire's flame.

"We could make an exception for the queen." Laban came up behind her and she could feel his breath on her neck. It was the same presence she'd endured when she'd crouched behind the water trough and torn her veil on the stable door the night of Prince Jesse's reception.

"I prefer to keep my distance, Captain." Miriam lifted the hem of her sleeping robe and stepped along the mantle away from him.

"Forgive her, Captain." Zedekiah sat straight against the backrest. "Her mind has found no ease since the trouble at the coronation."

Miriam remained facing the fire. She said, "I'm curious, Captain. With all your preparations, how is it that Shechem was able to get so close to the king?"

"He was disguised as a holy man." Laban spoke quickly, his words barely audible.

Miriam stirred the fire with a poker. "He could have murdered my husband."

"We can't allow ourselves to distrust everyone, my lady."

"There are very few whom I trust." Miriam stabbed a smoldering log and turned it back into the flames. "You should be as careful."

"Your family wasn't harmed."

"No thanks to you or your men. You couldn't even keep thieves from lurking about the palace." Miriam dropped the poker and it clanged on the stones. And thanks be to heaven Laban didn't have his men in the palace. It was the only way Ruth could have concocted the story of thieves to cover what she found out about Laban. He was a murderer, and he would stop at nothing to rid the palace of the informant. Miriam held her hand to her neck where the jewels in her coronation robe would have reached, and said, "Where were you, Captain, when the thieves ransacked my room and made off with my jewels? If we hadn't hidden in the wine cellar, there's no telling what would have become of us."

"I'm sorry, your highness." Laban picked up the poker and returned it to her. "I'll not rest until we've captured the thieves."

Miriam hung the poker from a hook on the mantle. "That will be all, Captain."

Laban reached to help Zedekiah out of his chair. "Shall we go, Sire?"

Zedekiah remained seated. "I'm not going."

"You must." Miriam hurried to stand by his reading chair. "You have to hear Uriah's defense."

"There is no defense for this." Zedekiah walked to the hearth with the tally of votes on Uriah's guilt. "I've heard all I want to hear on the matter." He threw the papyrus into the fire. It burst into flames and the smallest bits of ash filtered up the chimney. "Let Zadock preside. I haven't the stomach for this."

Laban asked, "Is that your last word, Sire?"

"Go and leave me in peace." Zedekiah steadied his hand on the mantle, his brow pressed into his sleeve.

Laban nodded and he was gone.

When the west wing doors latched behind him, Miriam took Zedekiah by the arm and said, "Is there nothing you can do for Uriah?"

Zedekiah sank back into his chair. "I have no reason to offer mercy."

The flames roared in the hearth and filled the reading room with the crackle of a great fire, but all Miriam could hear were the prayers of her heart.

Dear God, send my husband a reason.

Jonathan moved behind the black-robed Elders until he could see between them and get a view of Daniel. His son stood beside the prisoner cart, head held high, feet together, and hands clasped behind his back, waiting for his next order. His tunic was soiled with earth, but he didn't look to have suffered any injuries. He was in good health, though it was hard to see his color through the dust that hid his complexion and salted his black hair a shade lighter. He started over to welcome Daniel home, but Laban entered the grounds from the palace, marched to Daniel's side and said, "Chain Uriah to the block."

Daniel unlocked the back gate and stepped aside to let the executioner lift Uriah out. He carried him up the steps, laid him belly first over the bloodstained limestone and cuffed his wrists in chains. Uriah's trembling hands were the only sign of life in his limp body. He was alive, but he would only have breath for a few moments more. Uriah's eyes shot open as the executioner pulled his head back by the hair and marked his neck with a piece of coal. It was the executioner's line, and it sat on his neck from ear to ear like a hangman's noose.

Zadock stepped in front of the Elders. "Are you all agreed to this?"

Stillness settled over the yard, and Jonathan could hear the beat of his heart. If he were to save Uriah, this was the moment. But how could he be certain Uriah wasn't guilty? Beside him stood the noblest princes of the city, men without any reason to want Uriah dead, except to follow the law. Laban was his most trusted customer and Zadock had given him the very shop where he made his smithing business. How could he speak against them? It was Zadock who had instructed him with regard to Uriah's guilt during the trial and

Jonathan kept silent his request to stay the execution, and stood hidden behind the perfume merchant and the gold trader.

The executioner adjusted his grip on the sword. He aligned the blade with the mark on Uriah's neck as two horses spurred through the gates and raced toward the execution block, kicking up a cloud of dust as they came.

Aaron was the only rider Jonathan recognized. He sat high in the saddle, his crutches tied to the saddlebags and his white bandages covered with dust. His blue-eyed gaze was fixed on the form of Uriah chained across the execution block. What was Aaron doing here? He should have been halfway across the Sinai, but there he was slowing his horse's stride to let his companion come up alongside him. Aaron was in the company of an older man Jonathan could only assume was Lehi, the olive oil merchant. He had a tanned, wind-blown complexion, penetrating green eyes, and a narrow chin with a small tuft of beard at the end. He rode calmly atop his steed, his body upright and his head leaning into the horse's stride as he reined in front of the Chief Elder.

Zadock pushed the muzzle of Lehi's horse aside. "What is the meaning of this, sir?"

"I am Lehi, the olive oil merchant."

"I know who you are." Zadock's voice echoed off the courtyard walls.

Lehi dismounted and the hem of his sand-covered riding robe spread over the cobblestone. "I wish to speak in Uriah's defense."

Zadock turned his back. "The time for that has passed."

Lehi tied his horse to a post and walked to the execution block. He knelt across from Uriah and stroked his blood-soaked hair. The prophet's eyes opened, and when he saw Lehi he said, "Glory to God." Uriah's voice was muffled, his lips pressed against the limestone. But his prophetic praise silenced the murmurings of the Elders. Uriah raised his hands toward Lehi, the chains stopping his reach and clanging about his wrists. "Mine eyes behold the one who will preserve the covenants and knowledge of the Anointed One." He passed his tongue over his parched lips. "Blessed art thou, Lehi. Through you, my children will come to know what great things the Lord has done for their fathers."

"You'll see them again, I'll see to that." Lehi ran his hand over Uriah's fractured brow. "Now rest a moment, my friend." He laid Uriah's head back on the stone. He turned to Zadock and said, "I left my caravan at Raphia on the shores of the Great Sea to ride here and ask that you free this man."

"Impossible. The Council has voted." Zadock shook his head, the ends of his black and white shawl flapping about his cheeks. "You can not beg for that kind of mercy."

"It is you, not I, who should beg for Uriah's freedom."

"Are you threatening me, sir?"

Lehi came around the block and stood in front of Zadock. "If you take Uriah's life, God will send the Babylonians to destroy this city and carry away this people captive."

"Blasphemy! God would never allow His Holy City to be destroyed." Zadock removed his turban and let the shawls fall from his head and come down around his neck. "It was Uriah's threats of war that got him sentenced to death and if you're not careful with your words, you will suffer the same fate."

"This is my homeland, the land of my fathers before me." Lehi raised his hands. "I seek only to keep us from the ugliness of war."

"Guards." Zadock shook a long bony finger at Lehi. "Take this man, and see him out of the grounds with his horse."

"I'll not go." Lehi gripped the chains holding Uriah to the block. "Not until I've spoken for Uriah."

Three soldiers pulled Lehi from the execution block when a voice rang out of the shadows, over behind the Elders. A man walked through the darkness toward the edge of the light. The torches cast a murky haze over his purple cape swirling behind his legs. He carried a rod that sparkled in the light and his head was capped in gold. When he stepped from the shadows, Jonathan recognized the scepter in his hand, the crown on his head, and the men at his side. King Zedekiah had slipped into the execution grounds through an unlighted passage with a small contingent of guards. The palace crier called out, "Hail Zedekiah, King of Judah!"

Zedekiah's straight hair lifted off his brow and flirted with the gold crown as he strode to the block. He took the scimitar from the executioner and when he pointed the end of it at Zadock, his silver-threaded cuffs fell down around the hilt. He said, "I will hear Lehi's defense."

Zedekiah had been king for three days, but tonight was the first time Jonathan had seen him act the part. He stepped in next to Lehi and it seemed the olive oil merchant's dark olive skin and his green eyes had taken on an unearthly brightness, brighter than the orange light that flickered from the torches. Not that his face was a different color, but it had a luster, an unexplainable glow.

Lehi said, "I have prayed on behalf of this people, that someone among us would have the courage to defend Uriah." He ran his hand over the limestone block. "While I prayed, a pillar of fire came out of heaven and dwelt upon a rock, and in the light stood the Holy One of Israel—the Anointed One the Rekhabites call Yeshua." Lehi held his hands out toward the king. "The God of Heaven has spoken: Let my prophet go."

Zadock said, "You're a fool. No man has seen God." He quickly walked to the king's side. "Must we endure this man's lies? He's an olive oil merchant, not Moses."

Lehi set one hand on the edge of the execution block and raised the other toward Zadock. "I have seen what I have seen and heard what I have heard, and I will not deny it."

King Zedekiah stuck his scepter under the chains strapped to Uriah's wrists and pulled out the slack. The metal clanged and mixed with the resounding echo of his voice. He said, "Release this man."

"But, Sire?" Zadock said. "He's our prisoner."

Zedekiah motioned to Laban's soldiers. "Take Uriah to the dungeons until I can arrange for a trial."

Zadock came around in front of him. "We've already judged him guilty."

"Not in my court, you haven't." Zedekiah adjusted his crown high on his head. "Or did you forget that I am the final judge in this kingdom?" He turned back toward the palace gate, his guards following close behind, but there was no mistaking his resolve.

Uriah was to be spared for now.

Laban came up behind the Chief Elder, leaned his head over the execution block, and said, "We need to talk."

"Not now." Zadock was watching Lehi mount his brown horse and rein a circle around Aaron's mount. Her white coat glistened in the torchlight and her strong legs pawed the ground. She had a thick flank and sleek long legs, one of the finest frames Zadock had ever seen on a horse. How had Aaron, the son of a blacksmith, ever come to own such an animal? He had yet to pay the blacksmith for his work.

Laban said, "That horse the boy is riding: it came from the same herd as mine."

"That's impossible."

Laban came around the execution block. "You heard what Lehi said, didn't you?"

"I don't believe a word of it. He's lying to save Uriah."

"Lehi knows." Laban took out a bottle of wine from under his cape and picked open the cork. "And now he's playing a game with me." He pointed the lip of the wine bottle toward the entrance where Lehi was turning out of the yard and down the alley toward King Street. Lehi paused at the entrance, looked back over the grounds and then he was away at a full gallop.

"He's after my sword and brass plates." Laban rubbed the lip of the bottle against his thin line of beard. "That's why he's lying about his vision. It's my relics he's after."

Zadock said, "You shouldn't be drinking here."

"A good wine has power to calm the soul."

"When did you ever worry about your soul?" Zadock turned from the putrid smell of Laban's breath. "You've had too much."

"I'll be the judge of that." Laban took another, longer drink and steadied himself against the execution block. "Lehi knows everything, I'm sure of it."

Zadock took the wine bottle from him. "How many have you had?"

"Two, maybe four." Laban ran his hands through his hair. "I don't remember."

"Go home, Captain, and get a good night's rest. Once this wine is out of you, you'll come to your senses." Zadock took Laban by the arm and ushered him toward the gates, but he pulled free.

Laban said, "Nothing will change come morning. Lehi will still be my cousin when I wake."

Zadock dropped the half-empty wine bottle. It shattered on the cobblestone and sprayed red wine over the ground. "Why didn't you tell me this before?"

"Lehi didn't know about his lineage until now."

"How did he find out?" Zadock bit on his upper lip.

"Uriah." They reached the gates of the execution ground and Laban leaned against the posts. "That's why we must see him dead."

"You fool." Zadock stuck his fingers under Laban's breastplate and raised him away from the gatepost. "Find out what Lehi knows."

"What about Uriah?"

"He's not going anywhere until the king convenes a trial." Zadock started back across the grounds, but pulled up when Laban asked, "Where are you going?"

"There's one more problem."

"The blacksmith?"

"Not him." Zadock pulled the skirts of his robe close around legs. "His oldest son."

Aaron cantered slowly past the execution block toward Daniel and Jonathan. They were gathered beside the prisoner cart on the path that led to the entrance, and Aaron couldn't get past without speaking to them no matter how much the gates beckoned for him to leave quickly. This was not to be a simple reunion. Why did Lehi have to speak about his vision in front of Jonathan? He had come down off the summit at Raphia a changed man, but a vision of God? Lehi should have quoted the prophets. No one ever took offense at the words of dead men. And if that didn't work, he could have begged Zadock to show mercy on Uriah, anything but tell the Elders of his vision. Papa wanted nothing to do with that sort of talk. It was too much like the Rekhabites. And though Lehi had little to do with the sect, Jonathan would count him among their number. Aaron fixed his gaze on Beuntahyu's mane and reined in beside his father. Jonathan's head came up and his face furrowed into a scowl. Daniel stood beside him, his hands braced on his hips and his shoulders hunched forward away from the empty prisoner cart. This wasn't going to be a reunion at all. It was a trial and Aaron was without anyone to defend him.

Jonathan came around in front of Beuntahyu and held the bridle. "You never should have come here."

"Don't you mean, I never should have come here with Lehi?"

Jonathan pulled Beuntahyu's head down and peered between his ears. "You should be in Egypt."

"I had to come back." Aaron tipped his head toward the execution block. "Didn't you hear what Lehi said? Uriah is an innocent man."

"What I heard was a fool babbling on about some sort of vision."

Aaron said, "Tonight was the first I heard of it."

Daniel stepped alongside Aaron. "You don't believe what he said, do you?"

"I won't deny it."

Daniel said, "You're going to make fools of us all."

Aaron sat up in the saddle. "I was there, on the bluffs above Raphia when he came down from speaking with God. He didn't say a word about it, but he didn't need to. I knew he was a changed man the moment I saw him."

Zadock crossed the grounds to them and immediately Aaron fell silent. The Chief Elder was the last man he wanted to hear their conversations about Lehi's vision.

Zadock said, "It appears you have a reunion with your sons."

Jonathan said, "It was unexpected, sir."

"I suggest you have a few words with the eldest boy." Zadock reached to stroke Beuntahyu on the nose, but she jerked her head away and whinnied.

"What sort of words, sir?"

Zadock didn't answer. He turned toward the gate with his head down and his turban leaning into the wind. He was a good ten cubits away when he spun around. The hem of his robe swirled about his feet as if he were standing in the air above the ground like a dark angel, his eyes drawn half shut and his stance firm against the gusting breeze. He said, "Get your house in order, blacksmith."

Zadock marched out the gate.

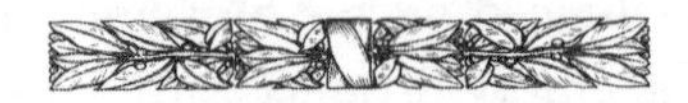

Aaron arrived home from the execution grounds well ahead of Daniel and Jonathan. He eased himself down from the saddle, untied his crutches, and walked Beuntahyu through the gate and into the courtyard. The light of an oil lamp filled the kitchen window, so bright its glow spilled into the darkened courtyard. Nothing had changed since he left home. The water clock still hung from the center roof beam as it had when he left and the branches of the olive trees were grown over the outside steps. That would never change, yet everything had changed. He walked Beuntahyu behind the house and tied her to a post beside the stable then slowly made his way back around to the front door. He swung it open and found Ruth at the kitchen table with Elizabeth, Sarah, and Joshua lighting the lamps for bed. Joshua set his down and ran to Aaron's side. "He's home, Aaron's home."

Sarah pressed her small body against his long-legged frame. She hardly came up past his hip and her long black curls fell down around his thigh. She tugged on Aaron's sleeve and asked, "What did you bring us from Egypt?"

"I didn't get there."

"You didn't what?" Elizabeth walked a lamp into the main room. Her hair was in braids and she was dressed in her sleeping robe. "Where have you been all this time?" She held the lamp to his face and the warmth of the flickering flame flashed across his cheeks.

Ruth hurried to Aaron's side, took his crutches and helped him to the bench seat. She said, "Look at you, tired and dusty. I'll get you something to drink."

"I'm fine, Mama, really."

"But your bandages, they're dirty." Ruth reached for them. "I'll get a washbasin to bathe your feet. And you'll need a change of clean linens."

"Not right now." Aaron leaned against the backrest and closed his eyes. "Stay and speak with me for a moment."

"What is it, son, are you hurt?"

"Papa will be back from the execution grounds with Daniel any moment and he isn't pleased with me."

"You were there?"

"Uriah's alive. They put him in the palace dungeons until the king convenes another trial."

Ruth closed her eyes and softly said, "It's a miracle."

"It was Lehi, Mama." Aaron held Ruth by the hand. "I can hardly wait to tell Rebekah."

"Oh, Aaron." Ruth took back her hand and held it to her mouth.

"What is it? I thought you would be pleased."

"There's something I need to tell you." Ruth began to pace in front of the bench. "While you were gone there was an accident."

"Was anyone hurt?"

Ruth leaned against the armrest. "It was a fire, son. A terrible fire."

"Where, Mama?" Aaron inched to the edge of the bench. "Where was the fire?"

Before Ruth could tell him more, the door swung open and Daniel marched in. His hair stood on end, blown up off his forehead from driving the prisoner cart through the hills of southern Judah. His face was burned red from the sun and his eyes were bloodshot from the wind. He hadn't had a bath in days and the smell of his sweat filled the room. He said, "Hello, Mama."

"Hello?" Ruth wrapped her arms around his thick neck. "Is that all you can say?"

Jonathan came in behind Daniel. He stopped in the doorway, removed his turban and let the cool breeze sweep the white and black shawls off his head and onto his shoulders. He patted Sarah on the back of her head and took Joshua by the hand. "It's time for both of you to go to bed."

"But, Papa . . . ?" Sarah frowned. "We haven't seen Aaron or Daniel for such a long time."

"I want you to go to bed now."

They gathered their lamps from the table, covering the small flames with the hollow of their hands, and slowly scaled the steps to their rooms. When they disappeared, Aaron stood on his crutches and said, "I'm sorry if I've made things difficult for you. I was only doing what Lehi asked of me."

Jonathan said, "You've made things difficult for all of us." He reached under his robe and took out the incense burners. The lamplight danced over the silver bowls. They were forged to a round sphere, the rough places ground out and the intricate latticework polished to a gleam. "There's to be a funeral tomorrow and I want you to carry these at the front of the procession."

Ruth said, "Not like this, Jonathan. Don't tell him like this."

Jonathan raised his hand to silence her. "Aaron needs to know that what he's done tonight could bring the same fate on our family."

"Jonathan!" Ruth gasped. "What are you saying?"

"These are dangerous times." Jonathan dropped the incense burners on the ground in front of Aaron. "I don't want us to end up dead like the potter and his family."

"Dead?" Aaron leaned on his crutches. "What are you talking about?"

Ruth took Aaron by the hand. "I'm sorry, son."

Jonathan said, "The estate went up in flames. Rebekah and her father were caught inside."

"It isn't so. She's not dead. You're wrong." Aaron picked the incense burners off the floor and held them to his chest. It wasn't true; these weren't for Rebekah's funeral. He backed his crutches toward the door.

"I saw her just before it happened." Ruth brushed away the tears, but that didn't stop more from streaming down her cheeks. She said, "Rebekah wanted you to know she forgave you. It was the last thing she asked of me."

Aaron threw his crutches down and spun around, the scars in his feet tearing against the stone floor. He hobbled out into the night and let the door bang shut behind him. They were wrong. Rebekah was still alive and he'd go to her and see that it was so. Aaron started around the house toward the stable, his scars ripping open with each step and the blood oozing from under the bandages. Months of healing wasted in one angry moment. The pain shot up his legs and he stumbled to the ground at Beuntahyu's hooves. She stuck her nose against his body, prodding him to get up in the saddle and off his feet, but he could hardly see the reins through his tears. He mounted up and drove his heels into her haunches, staining her white coat with his blood and spurring toward Rebekah's home at full gallop.

The scent of burned wood hung in the street outside the pottery yard. But there was no smoke pouring from the kilns. Aaron couldn't see the estate roof that should have filled the sky above the wall. The owl that made her home on the kiln stoop had taken up residence in the singed branches of a cedar. The bird hooted at him, telling him that things were not as they once were.

The gate to the yard stood ajar and Beuntahyu pushed at it with her hoof. It creaked open and the outline of Rebekah's home came into view. Moonlight streamed through the burned structure. The hearth was left standing, but the chimney had fallen over, its bricks strewn across the ground. The few stones remaining in the north wall were charred black. The second floor had caved into the dining hall and the roof beams stuck out of the rubble like barbs on the branches of a thorn bush. Why couldn't he ride below Rebekah's window, call her name and have her answer him and tell him that everything was as it was when he left for Egypt. That's all he'd prayed for. Didn't God owe him at least that?

Aaron dismounted and said, "Rebekah, where are you?"

Only the owl returned his cry. He picked his way through the ash, his mind numb to the pain that screamed at his feet. He said, "Rebekah, answer me!" Aaron held the incense burners to his heart, the ornate brasswork cutting into his chest. Must he carry these cursed things at Rebekah's funeral tomorrow riding on a horse? He never honored her in life by walking at her side with two whole feet. And in death he would shame her twice.

A cloud of ash picked up on a breeze and swirled around the half-fallen chimney. Aaron walked through the rubble of the ruined home. Fine black powder clung to his bloodied bandages and worked its way under the linens into the burns. With each step, the ash stung his wounds, infecting his feet, but he would not turn back. He knelt in the ruins and ran his hand through the soot, searching for some sign that Rebekah had escaped the destruction, but ash was all that was left of her.

Rebekah was gone.

CHAPTER 39

Laban poured himself a mug of wine and sat at the table in the shadows of the Jawbone Inn, farthest from the early morning sunlight. The rays filtered through the narrow windows and came together in a pillar of light near the front door. The innkeeper ran a broom over the floor, sweeping around the legs of Laban's chair and raising such a flurry of dust the captain sent him away. It was a good excuse to get rid of the man. He couldn't let him stay and hear what he was about to say. The innkeeper disappeared into the wine cellar as the front door swung open and the sunbeams scattered around the form of Lemuel. He stood beyond the light, his tall, thin frame rising between the doorposts. He had long, sandy-brown hair that fell down over his brow and when he shook it from in front of his eyes, his body was a thin shaft of harvest wheat.

Lemuel peered across the darkness and said, "Captain Laban, are you here, sir?"

"Where's your brother?"

Lemuel squinted into the shadows. "He couldn't come."

"He comes when I say he comes." Laban knocked his mug over, spilling wine over the table.

"It's our father." Lemuel stepped around the light and crossed the murkiness to Laban. "He's ill."

"How bad is it?"

"He may not make it through the night." Lemuel righted the mug and cleaned away the spilt wine with a rag. "No one knows what's wrong with him, not even the doctors. He's been unconscious for nearly three days." He set aside the wine-soaked rag. "You didn't have anything to do with this did you?"

"And if I did?"

"You gave your word." Lemuel straightened his narrow shoulders and pushed his long bangs up off his brow. "You said you'd leave us alone as long as we did as you asked."

Laban filled his mug to the brim. "I'd keep that promise if you hadn't told your father about his lineage."

"Lehi doesn't know anything about that."

Laban gripped the mug with both hands. "How do you explain his vision?"

"What does that have to do with my father's lineage?"

"Uriah is the only other man who knows about it and now your father's lying to keep him alive. Seems a rather odd thing, doesn't it?"

Lemuel's glance flitted over the bright pillar of light pouring through the window. "My father fancies himself a religious man."

"I don't care what he fancies himself. Only a fool would tell the Elders that he speaks with God face-to-face—and your father is no fool."

"Something happened to him at Raphia." Lemuel found a chair and pulled it to the table, his stomach pressed against the edge. "Whatever it was, it changed him."

"What kind of fool do you think I am?"

"Call it a dream, a harmless dream." Lemuel leaned over the table. "That's all it was."

"You want me to believe that your father learned about his lineage in a dream." Laban took a long drink.

"He didn't learn about it anywhere. I told you, he knows nothing of his lineage."

"It was either Uriah who told him . . ." Laban downed the last of the wine and wiped his lips on his sleeve. ". . . or it was you and your brother."

"We didn't tell him!" Lemuel leaned away from the table and pressed his shoulders against the backrest.

"You'd better pray that's true." Laban jabbed his finger at Lemuel. "If you or your brother so much as whisper a claim to my birthright, you'll wish you were dead."

Lemuel stood and pushed the chair aside, tipping it over as he walked past. He stopped beside the pillar of light, but none of the rays touched his gaunt frame. It was close enough that he could have reached out and touched the light, but he stayed in the shadows, his face shrouded in darkness, and Laban could only hear the seriousness in his voice. "My brother and I will take care of this."

Jonathan sat at the kitchen table waiting for the smells of morning to drive away his sleep. He'd spent the night in the company of unpleasant dreams and now he nodded between sense and senselessness, dozing at the table while Elizabeth cut the bread for breakfast. She leaned over the cutting board and pressed the blade through the center of the loaf, her long black hair unpinned and hanging at her shoulders. Joshua quietly came down the steps from his bedroom, tiptoed past the cold hearth and hid behind the wood stack before reaching for a piece of bread.

Elizabeth raised her knife and said, "You'll lose your fingers."

Joshua scurried out the door screaming for mercy and left Jonathan to doze a while longer. His eyes crept shut, his head bobbed forward and just as he was about to nod off, he righted himself and found Ruth sitting across the table from him. She wasn't there a moment before and it was as if she had appeared out of nowhere like an angel, with dark black hair pinned behind her head and her gaze turned down into her work. She was peeling the pomegranate she had purchased in the market yesterday. It was the first fresh fruit of the season, brought in from the coast, and the scent started Jonathan's stomach growling. He took a deep breath and let the smell of cold lamb on the plate in front of him mix with the pomegranate and warm bread. It was his first pleasant sensation since tossing and turning through last night's vision of Aaron chained to the wall of the palace dungeons, and Zadock burning their home to the ground and driving their family from Jerusalem. Why did he let his mind wander into such foolishness? These were good times, with plenty of work and more money than Jonathan could ever have hoped to earn. His good fortune certainly didn't merit the foolish worry that spilled over into his rest last night. Zadock's money was going to save this family.

Sarah parted the blanket that divided her sleeping quarters from the rest of the loft. Her hair hung in clumps about her shoulders, and her freckles—the ones Jonathan told her would disappear in a few years when she was old enough to be kissed by a boy—shone against the backdrop of her pale morning complexion. She skipped down the steps two at a time, dipped a spoon in the honey jar and headed for the door.

Ruth set down the paring knife. "Where are you going with that, young lady?"

"It's for Joshua; he likes honey."

"Wait right there." Ruth came around the table and took the spoon from her. "You're not going to put this in his hair like yesterday, are you?"

"He deserved what he got."

"Why don't you stay inside and help Elizabeth with the bread." Ruth placed the spoon back with the honey jar. "I'll be the judge of what Joshua deserves."

Daniel appeared at the top of the stairs. He stretched his arms and leaned over the railing. He was never at his best in the morning and the military hadn't changed that. His eyes were half closed and he would have fallen from the loft if not for the sturdy railing that held back his stout frame.

Jonathan said, "Wake your brother and have him come down for breakfast."

Daniel yawned and set his elbows on the railing. "He's gone."

"Where did he go?"

Ruth gathered the cut pomegranate into a bowl. "Aaron was up early tending to his feet."

"He's a foolish boy." Jonathan scratched his fingers through his hair. "Why he went to the Potters' yard without his crutches, I'll never understand."

Ruth said, "He pulled open a good number of the scars. There was so much blood on the bandages when he removed them, I couldn't see any of the . . ."

Ruth picked up the bowl of pomegranate and stood behind her chair. Her head was down and she quickly brushed the tears from the end of her chin.

Jonathan said, "What is it?"

"The infections are back and his feet have already swollen larger than I've ever seen them."

"He never should have walked through the ash of the potter's home. We may have to call for the surgeon. He's only going to suffer the same pain as before."

"It isn't his feet that are hurting right now."

"Rebekah's dead." Jonathan stared at the cold lamb. "There's nothing that he or any of us can do about that."

"You didn't have to tell him the way you did." Ruth came around the table and stood beside his chair.

"Zadock wants him to carry the incense burners in the funeral procession—that's all I was doing." Jonathan pushed away the plate of lamb.

"Aaron's heart is broken."

"It's too dangerous for him to associate with Lehi. The boy needs to understand that."

"What could be more dangerous than his infected feet?"

"I'll have a look at them," Jonathan said.

"You may want to look at his heart first." Ruth set the bowl of pomegranate in front of Jonathan next to the plate of lamb. "That may be his most painful injury."

The side door to the kitchen swung open and Joshua came flying in from outside. He said, "Aaron's saddling his horse. Can I ride it, Papa, before he goes?"

Jonathan turned to Ruth and in answer to his piercing glance she said, "Aaron's worried about Lehi."

"He's not to see the man."

Ruth arranged the bread under a white cloth sprinkled with water to keep it moist. "Aaron didn't sleep last night for the worry. He's already lost one friend and he doesn't want to lose another."

"Does he think Lehi will be the next corpse?"

"That's a question you'll have to ask him." Ruth dried her hands on a cloth. "He's determined to go to Beit Zayit this morning."

"Not without my blessing, he isn't." Jonathan shot up from the table, knocking his chair to the floor.

"Jonathan, please." Ruth took him by the arm. "He's going to speak with you about it before he leaves."

"There's nothing to speak about. He doesn't work for Lehi anymore!" Jonathan started for the side door leading to the stable when a knock sounded from the front.

"Would you answer that?" Ruth held Jonathan by the arm. "Please?"

Jonathan crossed the main room, pulled open the door and found a beggar peering at him from under the hood of a tattered brown robe. What poor timing. Did the man not collect enough alms beside the east gate that he had to beg at their door? Jonathan looked past him and saw a fine horse in the yard. How could a beggar afford a mighty brown steed with a new leather saddle? He hadn't bothered to tie it up to the post and it milled about the courtyard, sniffing the grape arbor and pawing at the dirt around the base of the olive trees. The animal was nosing into the water cistern when the muffled voice of the beggar drew Jonathan's gaze back to him. He spoke through the cloth of his hood, his words barely discernible. He said, "May I come in?"

"This isn't a good time."

The beggar pulled the hood tight around his face. "You must hear me."

"Whatever you're selling, I don't want to buy it." Jonathan stood in the doorway, his elbows touching the posts on either side, blocking the entrance.

"It's about your son, Aaron." The beggar leaned over and tried to see past Jonathan into the main room. "Is he here?"

"What do you want with him?"

"Your son had an interest in a young woman named Rebekah."

"Who told you that?" Jonathan stepped out the door and pulled it closed behind him. That was the same question Zadock asked at the execution grounds. Could the Chief Elder have sent this beggar to investigate further? Jonathan said, "If you're trying to stir up trouble for my son or for my family, you can take your leave."

The beggar's face was lost behind the hood of his robe with only his eyes visible through the shadows. He said, "Rebekah loved Aaron."

"I don't speak for the dead and I think it wise if you didn't either."

"I'm not dead, Jonathan." The beggar pulled back his hood and revealed the balding head of Josiah the potter. His face was caked with dust from his ride, but he was as alive and pink-faced in death as he was in life.

Jonathan said, "You're alive."

"I was never dead." Josiah stepped closer. "But dying was the only way to save myself and my daughter." He pulled the large hood down onto his shoulders and told a tale Jonathan did not want to hear. When the fire started at the potter's home, Josiah saddled two horses and packed the saddlebags with enough supplies and water to survive in the desert. He and his daughter slipped unnoticed out the back of the estate after placing a bag of bones from the pauper's field amid the flames to give the appearance of two burned corpses. Josiah said, "I would never have risked coming back to tell you this if it weren't for my daughter." He wiped the dust from his brow. "My wife's dying wish was that Rebekah marry a worthy man."

"Why do you haunt me with this?"

"I believe your son is that man."

Jonathan shook his head slowly. Did the potter really think that his untimely resurrection would coax Jonathan into agreeing to such an arrangement? He could never allow Aaron to marry the daughter of a criminal. "Zadock warned me about you." Jonathan shook his finger at Josiah. "He said you were a Rekhabite."

"I won't deny that."

"Then leave my house before I call for the soldiers."

"Please." Josiah reached for Jonathan's hand. "At least let me speak to Aaron and give him hope that he will see Rebekah again."

"It's best Aaron think your daughter dead."

"You don't mean that."

"I do." Jonathan's voice was absolute and the potter could not mistake his resolve. "Those who live in my house side with the Elders." He jabbed his finger against Josiah's chest. "If my son discovers that your daughter is anything but dead, I'll see that you join Uriah in the dungeons. Now leave my home, and cease to haunt me further."

Jonathan stepped to open the gate and let Josiah into the street when Aaron rounded the corner from behind the house. His feet were wrapped in fresh linens and the edges were already beginning to show dark red bloodstains. Ruth was right about the swelling. The bandages bulged around his feet more than they had in months. Aaron's hair was slicked back, and his face was washed. He slumped his shoulders forward. His head was down and he limped badly on his crutches as he led Beuntahyu toward them.

Jonathan whispered, "Cover your head, don't look back, and don't utter a word to my son."

Aaron stopped a good ten cubits away from them. He was looking at the ground as he spoke. "Papa, could I have a word with you?"

Jonathan stepped around Josiah, his stout body blocking Aaron's view of the man. "Where do you think you're going?"

Aaron touched the chains of the incense burners draped over his shoulder. "There's a funeral today."

"That isn't until evening, son."

"I'm riding to Beit Zayit first." Aaron stepped closer, tugging on the reins and pulling Beuntahyu with him. "I'm not sure why, but I have this feeling that something isn't right with Lehi."

"You'll be back before the funeral procession begins?"

Aaron didn't answer Jonathan's question; he didn't even hear it. He kept his head down and spoke his mind. "I know you don't approve, but I'm going to Beit Zayit with or without your blessing." He slumped on his crutches. "I thought I should tell you before I went. That's the least I could . . ."

"You have my blessing."

Aaron's head came up. "But last night . . . ?"

"I've changed my mind." Jonathan glanced over his shoulder to see that Josiah hadn't turned around. He was still facing the other way, his body hunched forward and his hood shaking slowly back and forth. Jonathan said, "I should never have allowed you to go to Beit Zayit the first time, and I shouldn't allow it now, but you've suffered enough loss."

Aaron pulled himself up into the saddle and winced as he fitted his feet into the stirrups.

Jonathan said, "Make sure you return in time for the procession."

"I could never miss Rebekah's funeral, Papa." Aaron grimaced when Beuntahyu breathed and her sides touched his feet.

Jonathan asked, "Will you be all right?"

Aaron came around and headed Beuntahyu toward the gate. He said, "I don't know if I'll ever be all right."

Jonathan stayed between Aaron and Josiah as he rode across the courtyard and into the street. It was sheer luck the boy didn't inquire after the stranger standing behind him. But Aaron had other things on his mind than visitors, and thank heaven for that. The gate swung closed behind him, latching shut against the post, just as Jonathan would lock away from Aaron what he knew about Rebekah. He could never know that she was alive. That was a gate that must be kept closed.

Forever.

Aaron did little to coax Beuntahyu around the steep switchbacks. She knew well the winding trail that snaked up the western hills. They were headed home and her stride quickened through the narrow corridor of rock walls at the summit and out onto the sunbathed hillsides of Beit Zayit. They raced down through the empty groves where not a single servant grafted branches into the trees and no one tended the fields of newly sprouted winter wheat.

There were no gardeners sweeping away the dead leaves that skittered across the paths of Lehi's estate, and there was no one to plant flowers in the baskets for spring. The yards were empty of grandchildren at play, and the clapping of Beuntahyu's hooves against the courtyard stones echoed unchallenged in the second-floor balconies. Aaron pulled up in front of the gate, but didn't swing down from the saddle. There was little reason with the windows covered and the gates locked. Where had everyone gone? Lehi and his family were nowhere to be found. Aaron swung Beuntahyu around and started toward the pressing yards when the front door swung open and Nephi stepped onto the porch. His hair was unkempt, a strange thing since Sariah made certain he was always well groomed. He had bloodshot eyes and his face was drawn out and pale. He came down the path with his gaze fixed on the incense burners Aaron carried over his shoulders. The silver balls dangled at the ends of silver chains like giant amulets and they sparkled in the bright sunlight.

"How did you know?" Nephi passed through the gate. "We didn't send word with anyone." He came around Beuntahyu and reached over her neck for the incense burners. "Father would have wanted you to be with us at a time like this."

"At a time like what?"

Nephi ran his fingers over the intricate patterns inscribed into the sides of the incense burners. "You must know about . . ."

Nephi fell silent when he saw Aaron's blood-soaked bandages.

"I hurt them last evening." Aaron swung his legs to one side of the saddle. "Will you help me down?"

Nephi wrapped his powerful arms around Aaron's waist, hoisted him to the ground and got his crutches from the saddlebag. They started slowly toward the house and Nephi said, "I haven't gotten much sleep these past few days." He showed Aaron into the main hall. "No one has."

Nephi led Aaron to the parlor across from the map room and they stood beside the opened hardwood doors. Sam milled about inside, trying to cheer his sisters and the daughters of Ishmael. They were dressed in plain black robes, all of them. And they sat in chairs near the warmth of the hearth and spoke in hushed tones. When they saw Aaron, they fell silent for a moment before continuing their quiet deliberations. Laman stayed in the shadows below the window. There was no light coming through the opening. It was covered with Lehi's colorful Egyptian reading robe, the one he always wore in the map room. Laman was without the usual company of Lemuel, and when he saw Aaron he turned away from the parlor door and stared at the shroud that was his father's robe.

Sariah sat in a large cushioned chair in the center of the room. She was dressed in a black robe like the other women, but she wore a black veil laced with silk threads and when she saw Aaron through it she raised her hands to greet him. They trembled slightly and she immediately placed them back down on the armrests and turned her head away. Ishmael stood on one side of her and on the other was an empty chair, Lehi's chair. It was the one he kept in the map room, hewn from the dull yellow olive wood of sick and dying plantation trees. At the foot of the chair were Lehi's sandals, carefully placed side-by-side with the latches untied. These were the rituals of death, the signs of a man passing; and Aaron glanced about the room, searching for Lehi, but he was nowhere to be found.

"Where's your father?"

"He's with the doctor."

Aaron lowered his voice to a whisper. "What's happened?"

Nephi closed the parlor doors and showed Aaron to the upper floor. He said, "When Lehi returned from the execution grounds three days ago, he was exhausted. We hadn't returned with the caravan yet and mother tried feeding him, but he wouldn't have anything to do with food. His body was weak and his limbs cold. Mother said he nearly threw himself down on his bed, fell into a deep sleep, and we haven't been able to wake him since."

Lehi's bedroom was the first one at the top of the stairs overlooking the main lobby. Two blue Egyptian urns with palm leaves graced either side of the open door and the manservant attending the entrance stepped aside to let them pass. Lehi's bed stood beneath an open window, the cool air filtering over his limp body. He lay on his back under a thin, linen sheet. His hair was matted against his scalp, his lips were chapped and his skin as pale as the sheet beneath his head. The doctor stirred a yellow powder into mineral water and slowly spoon-fed the mixture into Lehi's mouth. A nursemaid fussed on the other side of the bed, bathing Lehi's arms in cold water.

Nephi said, "We'd like to be alone for a moment."

The doctor nodded and put away his medicines, and the nursemaid carried the water basin out into the hall and closed the door behind them.

Aaron limped to the bed and stared down at Lehi's body. Not even his breathing raised his chest enough to tell if he were alive. His eyes were pressed shut and he'd lost the coloring in his face. How could this happen? Aaron was supposed to watch over Lehi. That was his promise. He was to be healed so that he could save the life of a prophet, and not just any prophet. He was to save the life of Lehi the prophet. He reached over the bed, drew back the linen sheet and held Lehi's hand. It was cold and lifeless. Not three days ago Lehi stood before the Elders in the execution grounds and declared he had seen

God face-to-face. He was strong then, his words filled with the power of heaven. Aaron kept hold of Lehi's hand. How quickly things had turned for the worse.

Nephi whispered, "Pray with me." He set Aaron's crutches aside and together they knelt beside the bed. Aaron kept hold of Lehi's hand while Nephi laid his thick arms over his father's body and nestled his head against his side. He said, "O God, hear the prayer of our hearts and lengthen the days of my father."

Nephi was only a fifteen-year-old boy, but he spoke with the conviction of a much older, much wiser man. He said, "My father is a righteous man and he will serve thee faithfully if it be thy will to . . ."

Nephi stopped his prayer and pulled away from Lehi's body. "Did you feel that?"

Aaron nodded. He'd felt the movement. It was slight, but Lehi's limbs had moved. His head turned to the side, his cheek falling against the pillow. His hand twitched in Aaron's grip and his eyes came open. He blinked twice and focused his gaze on Nephi and then Aaron, and a glimmer of a smile passed over his lips. He said, "I have seen the Council of Heaven." His voice was low and rasping, but his eyes were alive and filled with light. "The very Council where the Almighty and His holy angels dwell."

Nephi wrapped his arms around his father's neck. "Papa, you're alive."

Lehi reached out and took Aaron's hand. There was no mistaking the power in his grip. His strength was returning quickly and his hand was warm. He said, "While I slept, I was carried away in a vision and I have read from the book of heaven and I know that the Messiah, the one who will be called Yeshua the Anointed One, shall redeem this people if they will repent." He sat up in bed, leaned up on one elbow and Nephi helped him with a drink of water. He cleared his throat and his voice grew stronger. "Great and marvelous are the words of the Lord. His throne is high in the heavens and His power, and goodness, and mercy are over all the inhabitants of the earth; and, because He is merciful, He will not suffer those who come unto Him to perish."

Aaron peered up at him from where he knelt. He said, "You're a prophet. I knew it the first time we met."

"I wasn't then, son." Lehi held Aaron's hand to his chest and he could feel the beating of his heart.

"But you're a prophet now, aren't you?"

Lehi pulled back the linen, swung his feet to the floor and stood over Aaron's kneeling frame. His knees gave slightly and he balanced himself on the bedpost until the cherry red color flooded his face. He laid both his hands on Aaron's head and in the name of Yeshua the Anointed One, said, "Take off your bandages, rise up and walk."

Aaron slowly pressed his right foot against the floor. There was no pain, not even a twinge of what he'd felt dismounting Beuntahyu in the courtyard. He tested his left foot. Again there was no pain. He ripped away the bloody wraps and exposed the bare skin. It was as pink and smooth as a newborn's without any sign of pus. The open burns and ugly scars that had haunted him were gone. He stood, placing the full force of his weight on his feet. There was no pain, not the slightest and he slowly took his first step. He walked stiffly at first, his joints not accustomed to bearing him up, but after a few strides, he moved about the room without a hitch in his gait. No longer would he walk bent over like a beggar. He walked as an eighteen-year-old man should, with shoulders back and head held high. He spun around and started back to Lehi, thinking to shout his thanks to the man who had healed him, but instead he fell to his knees and offered a silent prayer, to God. By His grace and almighty power he'd been healed. Aaron could now honor Rebekah at her funeral and carry the incense burners at the head of her procession—on feet made whole by the power of God.

Lehi wrapped his arms around Aaron and held him close, his graying hair pressed against Aaron's neck. He was still an oil merchant with a sturdy frame and leathered hands, but he was also newly appointed by God, ordained by angels and called by the Council of Heaven to preach repentance.

Lehi was a prophet of God.

HISTORICAL NOTES

AUTHOR'S NOTE: *Pillar of Fire* is a fictional work based on events recorded in the opening chapter of the *Book of Mormon: Another Testament of Jesus Christ.* The story, settings, and, in some instances, the plot lines were developed from historical research of the period. Though it is impossible to review all the sources that contributed to the preparation of this novel, the following notes summarize the historical basis of elements in the story.

PROLOGUE

The story of Joseph interpreting Pharaoh's dream is taken directly from the Old Testament, Genesis chapter 41. Much of the dialogue comes from the scriptural account, as well as the description of the dream and the giving of a ring and amulet by Pharaoh to Joseph. However, there is no record in the Old Testament of a sword and brass plates being given to Joseph's sons as symbols of their Hebrew birthright.

Birthright treasures, or treasures of inheritance, were commonly passed from father to son in the royal families of both the Old Testament and Book of Mormon and usually included an inheritance of land as well as the authority to preside. Based on scripture and the diaries of early LDS church members who were with the prophet Joseph Smith when he discussed the sword of Laban and the brass plates, it is likely that Joseph who was sold into Egypt prepared these treasures for his sons before his death and that they served to designate Ephraim and Manasseh as his heirs, who were worthy of a royal birthright (Brett L. Holbrook, "The Sword of Laban as a Symbol of Divine Authority and Kingship").

According to Jewish tradition, Methuselah slew demons with a wonderful sword. It was the same weapon that Abraham is said to have inherited and passed on to Isaac who, in turn, gave it to Esau, only to have *his* brother Jacob take it from him for a mess of pottage. If Joseph did impart a sword to his sons, Ephraim and Manasseh, then early LDS sources suggest it may have been inscribed with the words mentioned in this prologue (Daniel N. Rolph, "Prophets, Kings, and Swords: The Sword of Laban and its Possible Pre-Laban Origins").

Moses freed the Hebrew slaves and brought them out of Egypt. The tribes of Judah and Benjamin settled the lands near the capital city of Jerusalem. The remaining ten tribes settled the lands northward. Near the end of King Solomon's reign, the prophet Ahijah declared that one of the king's generals, a man named Jeroboam, would rule over Israel. Jeroboam was head of the house of Joseph, which included the tribes of both Ephraim and Manasseh, two of Israel's most powerful political groups. When Solomon heard the prophecy that one of his own military officers would be given the kingdom instead of his son, he sought to take the man's life. General Jeroboam fled to Egypt and remained in exile until the death of Solomon, when he returned and led the northern ten tribes to secede from the kingdom over the issue of high taxation (*Old Testament Student Manual: 1 Kings-Malachi).* The tribes of Ephraim and Manasseh were part of the newly formed Northern Kingdom and it is likely that Joseph's sword and plates of brass were kept by the king in the capital city of Samaria (Rolph, "Prophets, Kings, and Swords: The Sword of Laban and its Possible Pre-Laban Origins").

Excavations around Samaria concur with the writings found on a stone tablet left by the son of the conquering king, Sargon II. He claimed to have constructed ramparts of earth, brought up battering rams, and dug tunnels to penetrate the city's fortifications. He also took as prisoners over two hundred thousand people from the ten tribes, along with their livestock (*Old Testament Student Manual: 1 Kings-Malachi).* During the war, some twenty thousand refugees fled to Jerusalem, doubling the population of the southern kingdom's capital city (*Great People of the Bible and How They Lived).* It is possible that both the sword of Joseph and the brass plates found their way to Jerusalem at this time. It is not certain if Hoshea, the last king to rule over the Northern Kingdom, escaped during the kingdom's fall, but he and his family may have been part of this vast migration of Jews and could have transported the national treasures to Jerusalem (Rolph, "Prophets, Kings, and Swords: The Sword of Laban and its Possible Pre-Laban Origins").

If Hoshea and his sons did escape to Jerusalem, we do not know if they were given an estate in the upper city or deeded property. Based on the relative status and wealth of Hoshea's descendants as recorded in the Book of Mormon one hundred and twenty years later, it is possible that he and his sons were well received by the King of Judah.

Many scholars suggest that the sword and brass plates Laban kept guarded in his treasury were national treasures, and the Babylonians would have attempted to confiscate them as a sign of conquest over Judah just as the Egyptians carried the arc of the covenant back to Tanis after their invasion of the kingdom (Rolph, "The Sword of Laban as a Symbol of Divine Authority and Kingship").

The succession of kings in the Northern Kingdom was accomplished more by murder and assassination of fathers by sons than by other less-violent means (*Old Testament Student Manual: 1 Kings-Malachi*). The fictional account of Laban obtaining the treasures from his father and brothers is not out of line with what we know about the military captain's nature. The Book of Mormon indicates that Laban was prone to acts of violence in protecting his wealth and powerful standing among the Jews.

Chapter One

The majority of this historical novel takes place over a period of six months, opening in August of the year preceding Lehi's family's departure from Jerusalem. The footnotes in the Book of Mormon indicate the year for the beginning of this novel should be *about* 601 B.C. More precise dating has determined the most likely year to be 598 B.C., with Lehi and his family escaping from the land of Jerusalem a year later. A casual reading of the Book of Mormon may cause confusion since the date in the scripture's footnote is an approximation: "about 600 B.C." For that reason, the opening of this novel in 601 B.C. is dated to coincide with the approximate date listed on page one of the Book of Mormon rather than the precise year, 598 B.C., when these events took place.

The smallest linear measurement among the Hebrews at the turn of the sixth century before Christ was a barleycorn. The next largest was the width of a finger, equal to two barleycorns laid end to end. Four fingers equaled a palm length. Three palms laid end to end were called a span, and two spans equaled a cubit, or about eighteen inches. The Egyptian cubit measured two inches more than the Hebrew cubit, about twenty inches, because the pharaoh who adopted the use of the cubit for measure had a larger palm than the standard used among the Jews. A short cubit was often used in Hebrew measurements. It was five palms, rather than six (*Old Testament Student Manual: 1 Kings- Malachi*).

About eight months prior to the fictional move of Jonathan's family to Jerusalem, the nation of Babylon declared war on Israel. It was a short three-month war, ending with the fall and surrender of Jerusalem. The Babylonians took the seventeen-year-old king named Jehoiachin and his family captive and brought them back to Babylon as a symbol of their conquest, but the conquerors were not interested in ruling the kingdom. They appointed the boy-king's uncle, Zedekiah, as a vassal king with the stipulation that he pay a tribute tax each year of about one quarter of the gross national product (*Great People of the Bible and How They Lived*). They also took captive all of Jerusalem's blacksmiths, uprooting whole families and leaving their property without a legal birthright heir. Blacksmiths were the foundation of a strong army, and no intelligent general went to war without a host of them to mend swords and breastplates. Before the Babylonian army left the city in April, 601 B.C., they ran roughshod through Jerusalem's blacksmithing district to keep the Israelites from rebuilding their military might.

Jonathan the blacksmith and his son Aaron are fictional characters, but their trade and expertise as blacksmiths are historically based. The first labor unions were among ancient Phoenician blacksmiths who united themselves into guilds to protect their secrets. Of all the smiths in the ancient world, none were more acclaimed for their secrets than the Phoenicians living along the northeast coast of the Mediterranean Sea, in what is now Lebanon. Phoenician blacksmiths refined the art of steelmaking, a secret they kept closely guarded and one that garnered them a great deal of wealth. Centuries before the opening of this novel, King Solomon hired blacksmiths from Sidon, a famous port city along the Mediterranean coast, to assist him in building the temple in Jerusalem (William J. Hamblin, "Sacred Writings on Bronze Plates in the Ancient Mediterranean").

Zadock is a fictitious character with a historical basis in what scholars call metonymic names or what could be called a nickname (Gordon C. Thomasson, "What's in a Name?"). Anciently, Jews used personal names as titles much the same way we call people by the name of famous personalities i.e.: a good student is an Einstein, a good batter a Babe Ruth, a good playwright a Shakespeare. The Jews were expert at the use of metonymic names. The name Elias, for example, is a personal name as well as a title given to men who act as forerunners (John the Baptist was an Elias because he was a forerunner to Christ). Zadock was a famous Chief Elder or chief priest presiding over the Council of Elders at Jerusalem. His name was used to refer to men who followed in his place, a sort of title given to those equated with the greatness of the original Zadock. His name became synonymous with Chief Elder, and a good Jew in Old Testament times would understand the name to mean a respected head of the Council of Elders of the Jews at Jerusalem.

After the Babylonian invasion, our Zadock may have been more powerful than the monarchy. King Zedekiah was appointed by the Babylonians, which diminished his political power in the eyes of many prominent Jews. Into this political vacuum stepped Zadock who held sway with the princes and nobles of the city and who influenced Israel's government from his position that today would be akin to the mayor of the city council, but with far more sweeping powers.

Captain Yaush was a historical character who governed the city-fort at Lakhish. His authority extended across the mountainous regions south of Jerusalem and his palace-fort sat high above the southern leg of the trade route. Any caravaneer trading between Israel and Egypt passed by way of Fort Lakhish. It is not certain what part Yaush played in the pursuit of the prophet Uriah. It appears he may have been unwilling and is depicted as such in this chapter. He did, however, play a significant role (Nibley, "Dark Days in Jerusalem").

Uriah was a historical character who lived south of Jerusalem in a small town near Fort Lakhish. The Old Testament and the Lakhish letters tell us that he was a prophet of considerable reputation. In this chapter he quotes Proverbs 10:2. Events from his life are recorded throughout this novel.

CHAPTER TWO

From the ancient ruins of Fort Lakhish come the only known written records of Jerusalem during the time period of 600 B.C., apart from the Book of Mormon and Jeremiah's writings in the Old Testament. The Lakhish letters are a collection of messages and orders sent between the military commander in Jerusalem (possibly Captain Laban) and Captain Yaush at Fort Lakhish. Both Laban and Yaush were historical figures: Laban mentioned frequently in the Book of Mormon, and Yaush in the Lakhish letters. The communications between the two men indicate that some soldiers in Laban's army and possibly Commander Yaush himself may have vacillated between loyalty toward Laban and support of Uriah the prophet. The King of Judah, Zedekiah, is silent in all this, deferring much of the decision making to his generals. The collection of Lakhish letters, written on potsherds, were excavated from the ruins of Fort Lakhish in the area believed to be a secret and highly secured guard station, which explains why they may have survived after the fort was destroyed in the second Babylonian invasion. Hugh Nibley suggests the letters were part of a military investigation and court marshal of military personnel involved with the circumstances surrounding the prophet Uriah's insurrection (Nibley, "Dark Days in Jerusalem").

The courier Hosha Yahu is a historical character and was considered a high military official. He was in charge of the kingdom's mail delivery system in southern Judah and was suspect in the military investigation surrounding the leak of sensitive information from the Lakhish letters to the prophet Uriah. The Lakhish letters indicate that the mail headed to the fort passed through Hosha Yahu's hands (Nibley, "Lakhish letters," 380-406).

Shechem was a historical character who lived in the hills surrounding Jerusalem, but in a different time period than Lehi. Anciently, robbers wore extremely long hair out of the desire to be regarded as possessing similar physical strength to Samson. Jewish tradition indicates that many robbers wore long hair. Robbers were recruited from every walk of life: the poor, the rich, the adventurous, the outcast. They appointed their own priests, fostered their own religious creeds, and made oaths to conceal their misdeeds. Some members of robber bands were citizens of Jerusalem, holding high office in government. A robber's aim was not simply monetary; they sought power as well. Their goal was to control the kingdom by gaining control of the throne, not by revolt, but by placing men in high position on governing councils. To this conspiring end, robbers did not shrink from committing murders. It was not uncommon for robbers to sneak into Jerusalem during large feast celebrations and murder government officials who refused either to join their order or to cooperate in promoting members of their band placed in government positions. Though Shechem was not contemporary with Lehi, robber bands like his were, and they practiced traditions similar to the Gadianton robbers described in the Book of Mormon. It is clear from the Book of Mormon that Lehi wished to leave behind those wicked traditions when he left Jerusalem (2 Nephi 1). However, the similarities between the Gadianton Robbers and Shechem's Robbers indicate that Lehi was not as successful as he had hoped. The oaths, practices, and beliefs of old-world robbers found their way to the Americas either in the written record of the brass plates, or in the memory of someone in Lehi's company familiar with the traditions of ancient robbers. It is important to note that upon their arrival in Bountiful, Nephi accused his older brothers of conspiring to murder their father in the same manner as robbers (1Nephi 17:44; also John W. Welch, "Theft and Robbery in the Book of Mormon and Near Eastern Law,"; also Nibley, "Dark Days in Jerusalem").

Although Ruth is a fictional character, the struggles she witnessed between the prophets and the leaders of government in Jerusalem around 600 B.C. are historically based (Nibley, "Dark Days in Jerusalem"). Each side sought public support for their religious and political ideas in a fight that crossed social, religious and political lines. The prophets preached that the only way to avoid another war was accommodation and peace with Babylon, but the Elders wanted nothing to do with that. Most of the princes of the city, the members of the council of Elders, etc. were businessmen and the only way to get rich in Jerusalem was to trade with Egypt, not with Babylon. It was a troubling debate with no clear winner since Egypt and Babylon were at war, and Israel was the geographic buffer between the two (Nibley, "Israel's Neighbors"). The Elders went so far as to declare the prophets traitors, particularly Jeremiah and Uriah. They were branded spies for no other reason than preaching peace with Babylon. The struggle was bitter enough to divide father against son and mother against daughter (Nibley, "The Jerusalem Scene").

From the time of his appointment as king, Zedekiah vacillated between the prophetic call for peace on one side and the Elders of the Jews' desire to normalize relations with Egypt on the other. It was because Zedekiah finally succumbed to the Elders of the Jews and stopped paying tribute to Babylon (about nine years after Lehi left Jerusalem) that the Babylonian army returned to Judah and leveled the city to the ground. The Book of Mormon tells us (2 Nephi 1: 3-4) that when Lehi reached the New World he was given a vision of the destruction of Jerusalem, which began Israel's seventy-year captivity recorded in the last books of the Old Testament (*Great People of the Bible and How They Lived;* also Nibley, "The Jerusalem Scene").

Chapter Three

Most inner courtyards of the homes in Jerusalem were used to grow some sort of food, usually grapes or olives. Because food was always a concern for city dwellers, no open space went uncultivated.

The family of Jonathan the blacksmith is fictional. Daniel's desire to join the army and prove himself through his wrestling skills is very much in line with what we know about military training during this time. After the war with Babylon, the Jewish military began rebuilding their forces, and joining the army was a quick way to earn money. The Jews adopted a Greek military model for training their soldiers that included tests of strength, the final test being a wrestling match. It was not uncommon for the captains of the army to also be the finest wrestlers. It should be noted that by this time the fame of Hercules, a military wrestler in Athens, had spread through the Mediterranean region, into Egypt and beyond (Guidance Associates Video Reproduction, "The Ancient Games").

CHAPTER FOUR

The Old Testament indicates that the art forms depicting a serpent were used at various times by the Hebrews to designate the Messiah who would redeem Israel. The symbol was employed by various factions within Judaism. Moses smithed a serpent out of brass and held it up before the camp of Israel, telling them to "look upon it and be saved." The brasswork was kept in the temple with the Ark of the Covenant and thought lost until it was discovered by King Josiah in the temple along with some missing temple scrolls around 610 B.C. It is believed that Moses's brass serpent was taken with other spoils of war in the last Babylonian conflict ten years after Lehi left Jerusalem. More information concerning the use of the serpent as a symbol for Christ is found in the historical notes for chapter twenty (Wallace E. Hunt, Jr., "Moses' Brazen Serpent as it Relates to Serpent Worship in Mesoamerica").

The prophet Uriah is a historical character who made his home in Qiryat Ye'arim, the same town where his extended family, father, mother, and siblings resided. The exact timing of Uriah's escape is not certain since scholars disagree on the Old Testament record of who was actually king at the time, Zedekiah or his older brother, Jehoiakim. Most scholars agree that one of the prophet Jeremiah's scribes, possibly Baruch, incorrectly recorded in the Old Testament that Uriah's escape took place under the rule of Zedekiah's brother (Nibley, "The Jerusalem Scene"). In this novel, Uriah is depicted as having escaped during Zedekiah's rule despite the chronology implied in the Old Testament (Jeremiah 26: 21-23). It should be noted that the historical characters from the Book of Mormon were intimately connected to the prophet Uriah of the Old Testament and that he was one of the *many prophets* referred to by Nephi (1 Nephi 1: 4).

Two records give us a picture of the events portrayed in this chapter. The Old Testament indicates that Uriah avoided imprisonment by escaping. The Lakhish letters tell us that the commander of the military in Jerusalem (possibly Laban) wrote to Commander Yaush at Fort Lakhish, telling him that he was concerned about the effect Uriah's preaching had on the morale of his soldiers. Uriah's preaching "weakened the hand" or was a concern for the morale of his army. Yaush was finally ordered to apprehend Uriah since the prophet lived in the town near the fort. The first attempt failed and a second attempt was made to capture him (Nibley, "Dark Days in Jerusalem").

CHAPTER FIVE

The old city of Jerusalem was built almost entirely on hills, and any resident who got around the city did so by climbing rather steep inclines.

The climb began at the south end in the city of David (lower city) and moved north up the hills of Solomon's City (upper city) onto the slopes of the temple mount. Today Jerusalem is famous for three hills. The first is the site where Abraham bound Isaac as sacrifice, and where he was subsequently delivered by an angel. The second is the temple mount; the third, Golgotha, where Jesus Christ was crucified. In 600 B.C. only the first two hills held special significance. They were inside the city gates proper. Golgotha was located outside the walls of the old city.

Chapter Six

Scholars of textiles indicate that the kilts worn by men of the Scottish highlands, as well as the plaid patterns used in their clothing to establish clan membership, may have been adopted from the ancient Israelites. The common dress for boys and young men in ancient Judah and Egypt was a kilt. Some were made of cloth and others of leather. Each of the twelve tribes of Israel had its own distinct cloth pattern that they wove into blankets and clothing. It is possible that the traditional cloth patterns and kilts of the Scottish clans are modern vestiges of Ancient Israelite dress (Florence E. Petzel, *"Textiles of Ancient Mesopotamia, Persia and Egypt")*.

The Egyptian foot loom was invented about 620 B.C. and was gaining popularity in Mediterranean countries about the time Lehi left Jerusalem. The introduction of the foot loom saved enormous amounts of time as well as allowing weavers to use more intricate patterns that had previously required far too much labor to be practical. An Egyptian foot loom is displayed as part of the Rameses exhibit of the Egyptian National Archives and Museum Authority (Petzel, *"Textiles of Ancient Mesopotamia, Persia and Egypt")*.

The London Museum of Natural History displays a replica of the only known Egyptian water clock in existence today. The original is in the Egyptian Museum in Cairo (*Great People of the Bible and How They Lived)*. It is a large clay bucket with markings on the inside. It is unclear exactly how the Egyptians calibrated their readings, but there are numerous references to its use in the ancient world. When the Book of Mormon was first published by Joseph Smith, scholars claimed that Israel had few ties to Egypt, and it was ridiculous to believe Lehi and his family would have known the language of the Egyptians, or that members of Lehi's family (Nephi and Sam) would have had Egyptian names. During the last forty years, however, archaeologists and linguists have uncovered numerous evidences that Israel and Egypt were closely connected through trade agreements as well as cultural exchange. The use of the water clock in this chapter is an attempt to show the close relations these two cultures shared around the turn of the sixth century B.C.

Archaeologists have uncovered a clay figurine in digs around Jerusalem dating to the time of Lehi that shows children playing leapfrog. Children in ancient times may have played many of the intuitive games of contemporary children (*Great People of the Bible and How They Lived*).

The wealthy scented their clothes and bathed in expensive perfumes imported from the frankincense and myrrh groves of southern Arabia. However, most women settled for crushing the scent out of wild flowers to prepare a perfume for their robes and bath water. Though flowers did not retain their scent for as long as the expensive perfumes, they were an inexpensive alternative (*Great People of the Bible and How They Lived*).

Prince Mulek is a historical character. The Old Testament does not mention any of the sons of Zedekiah by name; however, the Book of Mormon makes numerous references to one son named Mulek. The Lakhish letters refer to the prince with the letters NKD. Students of Semitic languages will recognize these letters as a term of affection and endearment meaning "little king" (Nibley, "The Jerusalem Scene").

Queen Miriam is a fictional character in the sense that we do not know the name of Zedekiah's wife or what role she may have played. Hugh Nibley suggests that she was most likely responsible for saving her son Mulek from execution by the Babylonians eight years after Lehi left Jerusalem (Nibley, "Dark Days in Jerusalem"). That Zedekiah was married we are sure, but the written records are silent with regard to details about the Queen of Judah. She likely played a central role in rearing Mulek and her other sons.

CHAPTER SEVEN

King David and the prophet Ezekiel both attempted to standardize weights during their lifetime. Complete uniformity, however, was never achieved. Unscrupulous people took advantage of the lack of standardization by using incorrect measures of weight, often keeping in reserve two sets of measures. To guard against unfairness, individuals commonly carried their own weights with them in a bag. The need for this practice brought strong rebukes from the prophets because it was a symptom of the spiritual erosion rampant among the Israelites. This chapter begins with a description of weights and measures because their misuse was the principal sign of selfishness among Jews and signaled the loss of charity among the people. Perishable and nonperishable items were bartered among the Jews including foodstuffs, livestock, household goods, tools, clothing, copper, silver, and gold. It wasn't, however, until about one hundred years prior to the opening of this novel that a system of silver and gold coins became part of the bartering system. A system of coins and a system of barter coexisted as means of exchange, which may explain why the names of coins were also the names of measures of weight. For example, a gerah, the smallest measure of weight had the same name as the smallest silver coin. Though gold coins shared some of the names of weight measures, for example a talent of weight and a talent of gold, gold had a much greater value and was not tied as closely to the names of weights as were silver coins (*Old Testament Student Manual: 1 Kings-Malachi)*.

The prophet Jeremiah is a historical character about whom we know a great deal from his writings in the Old Testament. He was born and raised in the small village of Anathoth about five miles northeast of Jerusalem. Considered an uneducated hayseed by the princes of the city, Jeremiah was never fully accepted in Jerusalem. He was declared a traitor for preaching peace with Babylon, but he had enough of a following among Jerusalem's residents that the Elders feared any direct punishment. Sometime before Lehi left Jerusalem, Jeremiah was banished from the capital for his political meddling, though it is believed he continued coming to the city in disguise. It was mistreatment of Jeremiah and other prophets, possibly Uriah, which may have fostered Lehi's concern for the holy men described in the first chapter of the Book of Mormon.

From the Lakhish letters we learn that the Hebrew slang *piqqeah*, translated into English as visionary, dreamer, or one whose eyes have been opened by God, may have been used as a derogatory reference to the prophets in Jerusalem at 600 B.C. Though it is not certain how vulgar the term was, high-ranking military and government officials used the word in derision and it could be equated with obscenities common in the modern world. The Book of Mormon (1 Nephi 2:11) tells us that Laman and Lemuel blamed the forfeiture of their property, riches, and comfortable lifestyle on the fact that their father was a visionary man. It may have been that they used the derogatory slang *piqqeah* to verbalize their insinuations against their father (1 Nephi 17:21-22). The Book of Mormon also records (1 Nephi 5:1-4) that when Sariah complained to Lehi about her sons' absence after returning to Jerusalem for the brass plates she called him a visionary man. Lehi's response was stern and so strikingly out of character from what we know of his normal treatment of Sariah, it is possible that in her anguish she employed the word piqqeah derogatorily. In Lehi's rebuttal to Sariah he may have referred to himself using the more respectful usage of the word, ha-piqqeah. He told her that he knew he was a visionary man and blessed of God to have seen a vision of their sons' safe return and of obtaining a future land of promise (Nibley, "The Jerusalem Scene"). Other scholars have suggested there are other Hebrew word forms that could have been used in reference to Lehi as a visionary man (John A. Tvedtnes, "Was Lehi a Caravaneer?").

CHAPTER EIGHT

Ancient communities in Israel had a council of Elders that governed on political and religious matters. The Book of Mormon refers to the council in Jerusalem as the The Elders of the Jews (1 Nephi 4:22-27). The Hebrew term is Sarim Council. It is possible that the Old Testament phrase "princes of the city" used by Jeremiah is also a reference to this same Council. The Council was a brotherhood of Jerusalem's elite, composed of wealthy men of considerable standing in the community. They enacted laws and passed judgment on both secular and religious matters. There is little information about the selection of Elders. They were required to be not less than forty years old. It is assumed that when a vacancy occurred, the head of the council selected a new member.

The custom of finalizing the sale of land by offering the sole of one's sandal, face down, was a common practice in Israel, and is still practiced by some orthodox Jews today. If the seller agrees to the terms, he is obliged to return the sandal, face up (*Great People of the Bible and How They Lived)*.

This chapter describes the professions of Jerusalem's wealthy citizens. Silk trade from the Orient went through the port at Aqaba, a city about one hundred fifty miles south of Jerusalem on the inlet off the Red Sea known as the Gulf of Aqaba. Lehi referred to this gulf as the fountain of the Red Sea (1 Nephi 1:8-9). King Solomon built the docks at Aqaba six hundred years prior to the beginning of this novel and began the first ocean trade between the nations of the Orient. After Lehi escaped Jerusalem, his company may have camped for up to three years in the hills on the outskirts of Aqaba before heading farther south (Lynn M. and Hope Hilton, *In Search of Lehi's Trail)*. The gold trade in Jerusalem was tied to Egypt, the region's largest gold producer. Hebrews traded foodstuffs, skilled labor, and animals in exchange for Egyptian gold. Moneychangers were the most vilified of all merchants since they charged a percentage of any sale to verify the weights of products and to change precious metals or foreign currencies into Hebrew money. Moneychangers were known for charging far more than what was considered legal and in some cases making dishonestly high assessments of weights in order to increase their profits. It was Jesus who cleansed the temple by casting out the moneychangers who had made the house of God a house of business, and in the case of moneychangers, often a less than honest business (*Great People of the Bible and How They Lived;* also *Old Testament Student Manual: 1 Kings-Malachi).*

CHAPTER NINE

Hugh Nibley indicates that in Lehi's day many people escaped into the desert to find religious freedom and renew covenants they believed had been lost among the Jews. (Nibley, "More Voices From the Dust," 239-244). Many groups took their wives and children into the desert to prepare for the coming Messiah and to escape persecution at the hands of the official religion. The Old Testament refers to one such group in the Book of Jeremiah as Rekhabites (Jeremiah 35).

The Old Testament and the Book of Mormon describe the world of the Rekhabites and sectaries of the desert (Jeremiah 35). Nibley explains that from earliest times, communities of faithful Jews withdrew to bide their time in the wilderness. The prophet Jeremiah and other prophets of his time were not typically associated with any religious faction within Judaism, but they did champion the cause of Rekhabites and others who shunned the popular religious and political fads of their day and called for a return to strict observance of the Law of Moses in anticipation of the coming of the Messiah. The Rekhabites were, in essence, a "Church of Anticipation" (Nibley, "Dark Days in Jerusalem," 380-406).

A religious group similar to the Rekhabites called themselves Covenantors. They believed the Jewish religion had gone astray from the true teachings of Judaism and they wanted to worship according to what they called covenants. Among other things, they believed in continuing revelation, this life as a probation, pre-mortal existence and resurrection, and dispensations of the gospel with periods of falling away and restoration. They had a book of covenants called the *Manual of Discipline*. They believed strongly in prophets, priesthood, eternal marriage, and eternal progeny. A group of these religious dissenters lived at the historic community of Qumran and left us the now famous Dead Sea scrolls, dating back as far as 400 B.C. and ending about 73 A.D. Hugh Nibley suggests that the Covenantors' society may have started long before the scrolls were written, possibly as early as seven to eight hundred years before Christ (Nibley, "More Voices From the Dust"). It is possible that the religious refugees of Lehi's day, the Rekhabites, were some of the founders of the group that wrote the Dead Sea Scrolls and who lived on the shores of the Dead Sea.

Josiah the potter is a fictional character based on the life of a historical figure who was responsible for founding the community at Qumran. He claimed divine guidance for his people, taught them what he knew about the Messiah, required strict observance of the Law of Moses and introduced among them the idea of baptism, a sacrament or holy supper, and many other doctrines previously thought to have emerged after the advent of Christ. Some ancient Near Eastern scholars explain that phenomenon by suggesting that Jesus Christ and his cousin, John the Baptist, must have been associated with or educated by the descendants of these people who lived at Qumran up until it was destroyed by the Roman army about 72 A.D. Another possibility, rejected by many, is that the people at Qumran were guided by revelation from God, since their doctrines and organization parallel other dispensations of the gospel as revealed to prophets over the centuries. Among the writings in the Dead Sea Scrolls are numerous references to a man who either founded the community of Covenantors at Qumran or who was revered by them enough to be considered their leader. His teachings are part of the *Manual of Discipline*. As prolific as the writings are, there is no mention of his name. The only title given him in the written record of the Dead Sea Scrolls was Teacher of Righteousness, a code name used to protect the man from persecution and discovery (Nibley, "More Voices From the Dust").

The Bible and other ancient Hebrew writings mention the use of baskets and rope as a means of escape (2 Corinthians 11:33). During wartime siege, residents of Jerusalem escaped over the walls in baskets to find food (*Great People of the Bible and How They Lived).*

CHAPTER TEN

Among ancient blacksmiths, there were two secrets that allowed for the smelting of high-quality steel. The first was the purifying of fuel. Pieces of hard coal, or what modern steelmakers call ingots, burn at higher temperature than black coal. Ingots allowed ancient smiths to heat their smelting ovens to a temperature hot enough to refine iron ore into steel. The ingots were prepared by burning the impurities out of coal until only hard ingots remained. The hard coal did not catch fire quickly, but once lit, it burned at extremely high temperatures.

Sam and Nephi are historical characters. The first two books of the Book of Mormon were authored almost entirely by Nephi. Book of Mormon scholars generally agree that he wrote the history of his family's departure from Jerusalem from memory when he was about forty years old and living in the Americas. At the time Nephi left Jerusalem, he was likely about fifteen years old and Sam a few years older, possibly seventeen. The name Sam was the most common name given to Egyptian boys at the turn of the sixth century B.C. It was also the name of a popular pharaoh. Nephi, or Nafai as the Egyptians write it, was a prince in Egypt and, though not as common a name as Sam, it was also a popular name for a boy (Nibley, "Lehi in the Desert").

CHAPTER ELEVEN

It was common architectural practice in the royal and government buildings of Lehi's day to leave out windows in the bottom floors as a deterrent to robbers. The most famous building in Israel incorporating this design was the Citadel in Jerusalem. The Jews borrowed the design from the palace in southern Arabia's capital city of San'a in what today is the capital of Yemen. At night, when the lights in the palace were lit, the building appeared to float above the ground, due to the lack of light on the windowless floors. To Bedouin desert dwellers and commoners, the large floating palace at San'a represented the evils of riches and power. If Lehi was a caravaneer, he could have traveled to San'a and seen firsthand the floating palace and been aware of the Bedouins' dislike for the worldliness it represented, much the same way the Citadel building's architecture may have represented the oppression of the Elders of the Jews. In Lehi's dream, recorded in the Book of Mormon, the Lord may have chosen to represent the world as a large and spacious building floating above the ground because of Lehi's familiarity with those buildings. It is important to note that Joseph Smith Senior was given a dream similar to the one received by Lehi. They differed in that Lehi saw a representation of things he would have been familiar with, mists of darkness over deep rock canyons, a floating building, etc., while Joseph Smith Sr. saw a log cabin, a trail leading into a deep dark woods, etc. (Nibley, *Since Cumorah).*

Two of the more prominent prophets in Jerusalem during this time period were Jeremiah and Uriah. Scholars of religion are not certain if the prophets at 600 B.C. had any contact with each other. The general consensus is that they received their calling from God, each one delivering his message without collaboration with the other. They were, however, aware of one another's work and though it is impossible to rule out contact among them, it is unlikely they collaborated in any organized group (John W. Welch, "Lehi: The Calling of a Prophet").

CHAPTER TWELVE

The Jawbone Inn is a fictitious setting based on what we know about inns in Jerusalem at 600 B.C. Drinking establishments were usually family-owned cooperatives, each with their own clientele which, in Jerusalem, was determined by location. Upper city inns catered primarily to the noble class while lower city inns were frequented by commoners. It could have been that some inns catered to specific groups like soldiers or artisans, though there was no law or practice dictating who could or could not patronize a particular inn; it was understood where one should go to drink. There could have been as few as twenty inns in Jerusalem during Lehi's day or as many as a hundred such establishments (*Great People of the Bible and How They Lived)*.

Laman and Lemuel are historical characters. We are not certain of their age, though most scholars conclude they would have been in their early twenties at the time Lehi left Jerusalem. There is no historical basis for Laman and Captain Laban having similar appearances, though evidence from the Book of Mormon suggests that they were related and could therefore have shared some physical characteristics (1 Nephi 5:14-16). Clues to their relationship stem from Lehi's comments recorded in the Book of Mormon when he read the brass plates. They had been Laban's property and his genealogy was recorded therein. This same genealogy informed Lehi that he was a descendant of Joseph (1 Nephi 5:14). For Lehi to make that connection he would have had to have some close relative named in the genealogy, since it is apparent that he did not know he was descended of Joseph prior to reading the brass plates (Nibley, *Since Cumorah)*.

CHAPTER THIRTEEN

The trade route passed by Jerusalem on the plateaus about four miles west of the city. The capital sat on the crest of three hills and was surrounded by narrow valleys. Caravanners did not risk driving their soft-cloven hoofed camels over the narrow, rocky trails leading to the city gates. Instead, mules were the animal of choice to pack wares into the city. For that reason, the archways in the capital were designed lower than usual and the streets more narrow, since there was no need to make room for camels or elephants (Hilton, *In Search of Lehi's Trail)*.

It is not certain if the royal herd was branded, even less with the head of a lion, but brands were used anciently to verify ownership much as they are today. Since the reign of King David, the symbol of the royal house of Judah was the head of a lion. It appeared as an insignia on walls, pottery, and clothing (*Great People of the Bible and How They Lived)*.

Joseph Smith tells us that Lehi had daughters older than Laman who married the eldest sons of Ishmael long before they left Jerusalem. It is possible that Lehi and Sariah were grandparents before their exodus. Ishmael was a cousin or close relative to Lehi and, in ancient times, it was common for second cousins to intermarry. Lehi and Ishmael may have arranged the marriages of their sons and daughters long before they left Jerusalem and when the sons of Lehi returned to bring them into the desert, it was a perfectly logical step to keep alive those marriage arrangements (Sidney B. Sperry, "Did Lehi Have Daughters Who Married the Sons of Ishmael?"). A reprint is available through the F.A.R.M.S. Sperry Archive.

CHAPTER FOURTEEN

The fate of the sword of Laban at the time of the first Babylonian incursion into Judah—eight months prior to the opening of this novel—is unclear. There is evidence supporting two possibilities. First, the sword was protected in Laban's treasury from the Babylonian soldiers. The second possibility suggested by Book of Mormon scholars, and the one preferred for developing the characters in this novel, is that the Babylonians confiscated the sword as part of the spoils of war. We do know that ancient armies seized religious and political relics after their conquests, and it could be that the sword was one of those spoils the Old Testament tells us were carried off to Babylon. As suggested in this chapter, scholars indicate that if the sword was taken by the Babylonian army, another sword would have been smithed as a replacement. Based on these conclusions, the sword of Laban could have been an original or a replica of one of the national treasures (Rolph, "Prophets, Kings, and Swords: The Sword of Laban and its Possible Pre-Laban Origins").

CHAPTER FIFTEEN

The art of juggling was firmly established as a form of entertainment in Persia around 600 B.C. and traveling showmen carried the art into Mediterranean countries. It was not uncommon for these entertainers to pass through Jerusalem or for locals to learn the art. Unlike today, where juggling is often associated with clowns, in the ancient world it was done by highly skilled performers employing derring-do routines. Ancient clay art depicts jugglers performing for royalty (*Great People of the Bible and How They Lived).*

For centuries Bethlehem has been known for large farmers' markets where produce from the vineyards of southern Judah can be found in plenty and at a much lower cost than in Jerusalem. Bethlehem was always considered the home of the common man's market while Jerusalem was the wealthy man's market. The soil around Bethlehem and surrounding vineyards is a deep red color and very distinctive to the darker soils around Jerusalem (*Great People of the Bible and How They Lived).*

The shofar horn, or rams horn, was used to announce Moses' return off Mount Sinai with the revelations from God that included the Ten

Commandments. Since that day, the sounding of the shofar horn has been equated with the reception of revelation from God. The blowing of trumpets cited by John in the New Testament indicate the delivery of revelation by an angelic messenger in the last days. It is this symbolism that is also portrayed in statues of the angel Moroni blowing a trumpet from the rooftops of many Latter-day Saint temples (Lenet Hadley Read, "Joseph Smith's Receipt of the Plates and the Israelite Feast of Trumpets").

Zoram is a historical character found in the Book of Mormon. It is highly unlikely that he was related to or had significant contact with Jeremiah the prophet, but their relationship in this novel makes the story line more efficient. We do know that Zoram was employed in Laban's treasury and that Nephi recognized him as the keeper of the keys (1 Nephi 4:20).

The Old Testament records that God warned Jeremiah that the Jews of his day had become so wicked he should not raise children among them. Some Bible scholars suggest that Jeremiah never married or fathered children, while others insist that this passage of scripture is a simple allusion to the wickedness of the day, without any correlation to Jeremiah's marital status. In this novel, the prophet Jeremiah is portrayed as a married man with Zoram as his only adopted child.

Joseph Klauser of the Hebrew University in Jerusalem points out the advent of a prophet called Messiah Ben Joseph recorded in Hebrew scripture. He is to be raised up in the last days of the earth. He will be clothed in prophecy and will be a restorer of covenants that were lost. His name is understood to mean one descended from the House of Joseph. His work is to be done in preparation for the coming of Messiah Ben David, or the Anointed One descended from the House of David. Latter-day Saints interpret this Jewish prophecy as evidence of Joseph Smith's role in restoring the gospel of Jesus Christ in the latter days (Alan H. Richardson, *"One Thousand Evidences for The Church of Jesus Christ of Latter-day Saints").*

In this fictional account of Zoram and Jeremiah, the importance of preserving information regarding eternal covenants is portrayed. The title page of the Book of Mormon tells us that one of the book's main objectives, in addition to testifying of Christ, is "to show unto the remnant of the House of Israel what great things the Lord has done for their fathers; and that they may know the covenants of the Lord, that they are not cast off forever." Lehi prophesied that the brass plates would "go forth unto all nations, kindreds, tongues, and people who were of his seed," and that they should "never perish; neither should they be dimmed any more by time" (1 Nephi 5:18-19). It may be that Joseph Smith fulfilled Lehi's words in the publication of the Book of Mormon since much of what was written in the brass plates was also rewritten into the gold plate record Moroni prepared for translation by Joseph Smith. The brass plates served a very important purpose for Lehi's descendants. They preserved the written language as well as providing a hard copy of religious covenants and doctrine. The title page of the Book of Mormon indicates that the covenants were of eternal consequence and that by not knowing them a man could be cast off forever. It may be that some important insights regarding temples or temple covenants were preserved in the brass plates and, if so, would have assisted Nephi when he built a temple after Lehi's colony arrived in the Americas about 580 B.C. (Ludlow, "The Title Page").

The principal purpose of this chapter is to emphasize the title page of the Book of Mormon written by the prophet Moroni. In it he reiterates the eternal gospel theme of turning the hearts of the fathers to the children and the hearts of the children to their fathers so that the earth is not cursed. It is the same message the prophet Malachi recorded in the Old Testament, and Joseph Smith recorded in the Doctrine and Covenants and it is a consistent message whenever God has established His gospel among His children (Ludlow, "The Title Page"; also Joseph F. McConkie, "Pre-mortal Existence, Foreordinations and Heavenly Councils," 173-198).

CHAPTER SIXTEEN

Men of considerable wealth built treasuries into their estates to guard their most valuable possessions. To guard against thieves and robbers, the estates were surrounded by high walls, and the treasuries themselves were often built below ground in the foundation walls of the building. Only the most trusted family servants were employed there and given keys to the doors. The keys were similar to the modern skeleton key and were usually made of iron or brass *(Great People of The Bible and How They Lived).*

Ancient records written on papyrus were subject to decomposition in less than a hundred years. Parchment scrolls were records written on animal hides, and proved much more resilient than papyrus records. Potsherds, or pieces of broken pottery were used as tablets to scratch in writings that were disposable—much like what we call "scratch paper" today. More permanent records were imprinted in soft clay that hardened and could be stored—indefinitely if the clay were fired in a kiln. The fired clay tablets could break, but they did not decay like papyrus, parchment, or unfired clay tablets. Metal plates were a recording medium that could withstand the test of time. They were a tedious but purposeful means of preserving in writing the sacred rituals of ancient communities, their laws, religious doctrine of a prophetic nature, and their histories. They were bound together with rings much like pages in a book and were referred to as a codex. Ancient kings, monarchs, and religious leaders used them to record the most sacred or important documents and histories (Hamblin, "Sacred Writings on Bronze Plates in the Ancient Mediterranean").

The Book of Mormon records that after Nephi and his brothers returned to their camp south of Jerusalem with the brass plates of Laban, Lehi gave thanks and then read them in their entirety (1 Nephi 5:10). Lehi informs us that they contained the first five books of Moses, similar to the first books of the Old Testament that give the account of the creation of the world and the biography of Adam and Eve, the parents of the human family. Scholars of religion suggest that the first books of Moses written on the brass plates would have been in a less altered state than the books of the Old Testament, since they would not have endured centuries of abridging and rewriting. The brass plates also included a history of the Jews from the beginning down to the reign of King Zedekiah (1 Nephi 5:11-12). Lehi was surprised to find the prophecies of Jeremiah already inscribed into the plates since he was still alive and living near Jerusalem at the time (1 Nephi 5:13). This chapter was inspired by the idea that someone would have had to include Jeremiah's writings in the record before it was taken from Laban's treasury. It is plausible that Zoram played some role in recording the prophetic words of Jeremiah on the brass plates.

Some of the prophecies recorded in the brass plates found their way into the Book of Mormon. Jacob, Nephi's brother, records the allegory of the olive tree written by the prophet Zenos who most likely lived in the Northern Kingdom (Jacob 5). For that reason it is believed that the brass plates were kept for a time by the kings and prophets of the Northern Kingdom of Israel, possibly Laban's forebears.

CHAPTER SEVENTEEN

The sixth century B.C. was a time of great men. Plato, Socrates, Zoroaster and many others were contemporaries with Lehi. Hugh Nibley suggests that it was a time when the Lord placed great thinkers on the earth in preparation for great events in the same way the world was prepared for the restoration of the gospel during the renaissance. Hercules is a well-known historical figure mentioned in this chapter. He lived a hundred years prior to Lehi, about 720 B.C., but his fame as a wrestler was still alive among people living around the Mediterranean. The most famous wrestling hold attributed to Hercules was the flying mare. He used it to win the Olympic games in Athens. He became a heroic figure to Athenians and soldiers across the ancient world (Nibley, "The Lesson of the Sixth Century B. C."; also Guidance Associates, "The Ancient Games").

Chapter Eighteen

Anciently, carbon-rich black ash was used by blacksmiths to make steel. Iron ore was full of carbon, but in far too great a quantity to form strong bonds in the metal. The smelting process burned away virtually all the carbon, but by adding just the right amount back into the molten ore, the correct molecular bonds formed during the cooling process. The ancient blacksmith did not understand the science of his art, but by trial and error he discovered the secrets that allowed him to smith the metal called steel. Clay molds were used to melt the iron ore. The mold was not the precise shape of the desired object, but the blacksmith forged, ground, and polished the piece to achieve the final product.

The scene in which Ruth describes her feelings that her family is being pulled apart is indicative of the social forces operating in Jerusalem at the turn of the sixth century B.C. Hugh Nibley suggests that families were divided along political and religious lines, some family members siding with the party of the prophets and others siding with the party of the Elders (Nibley, "The Jerusalem Scene").

Ishmael is a historical character who Joseph Smith tells us was a cousin to Lehi. Before the opening chapter of the Book of Mormon, Ishmael's two eldest sons may have already been married to Lehi's two eldest daughters. It is possible that they worked in the same profession and lived in or around the same area. From Joseph Smith and the Book of Mormon, we learn that the two families were intimately connected before the scriptural account begins (Sperry, "Did Lehi Have Daughters Who Married the Sons of Ishmael?"). A reprint is available through the F.A.R.M.S. Sperry Archive.

Chapter Nineteen

Ancient potters first fired their pottery in pits. With the advent of large indoor kilns, potters could fire at higher temperatures and began developing glazes and ceramic-like pottery that was more durable and more expensive. Pottery was stacked in the kiln and fired over five to seven days. Because of the large amount of wood required, it was rare for a potter to fire his kiln more than once a month. For that reason, he built large kilns that would accommodate a good deal of pottery.

Chapter Twenty

The children of Israel were afflicted by flying, fiery serpents in the Sinai Desert (Numbers 21:6). Biologists indicate that today there are snakes in regions of that desert with deadly venom, bright colorful skin, and tremendous leaping ability, and small wings or flaps extending from the side of their body with which they can hurl themselves from rock outcrops and tree branches (Hunt Jr., "Moses' Brazen Serpent as it Relates to Serpent Worship in Mesoamerica"). The Lord instructed Moses to smith a brass image of a serpent and hold it up on a pole, promising his people that if they would look toward it after being bitten they would live (Numbers 21:8). Among ancient Jews the serpent came to symbolize faith in the Messiah or Anointed One to whom all Israel should look in order to find salvation. Even Satan himself, the greatest beguiler of all, has attempted to pass himself off as the one symbolized by the brass serpent. The brass relic smithed by Moses remained with Israel's other sacred symbols; its final known resting place was in Solomon's temple alongside the Ark of the Covenant. It was once thought lost, until King Josiah found it with some forgotten temple scrolls in 620 B.C. and began a reformation of Judaism that lasted only until his death at 610 B.C. It is believed that in the Babylonian war depicted in the prologue, the brass serpent was taken as part of the spoils of war. Factions within Judaism have used the mark of the serpent as a secret sign of membership in their movement much the same way early Christians used the mark of the fish to secretly identify themselves to believers.

The Jews had holy names for God that were never spoken out loud in order to keep them from becoming common or profane, as well as more commonly uttered names that were not profane to speak aloud. The word or title *ha-Mashiakh* is the Hebrew basis for the word Messiah the Anointed One. *Jesus* is the Greek translation for the Hebrew name *Yeshua*, its English translation being *Joshua*. That name and title spoken together, *Yeshua ha-Mashiakh,* when translated into English is *Joshua the Anointed One* and that same translation in Greek is the basis for the name and title, *Jesus the Christ.* If Rekhabites knew the name of Jesus Christ during Lehi's day, the use of a common given name like *Yeshua*, paired with the name of God, *ha-Mashiakh,* most likely would have infuriated the religious hierarchy.

CHAPTER TWENTY ONE

There is no detailed record of the exact size of Laban's sword or what jewels, if any, were inlaid into its hilt. Nephi records that the blade was made of the most precious steel and the hilt of gold. The phrase "fine workmanship" in 1 Nephi 4:9 could be a reference to the hilt or to some other characteristic of the blade, i.e. the manner of smelting, the forging, or the workmanship of the hilt (Hamblin, "Sacred Writings on Bronze Plates in the Ancient Mediterranean").

It was common practice to loan servants to assist with the gathering of crops or other tasks related to a man's livelihood and it would not be entirely out of order for Laban to loan out the help of his servant Zoram as part of an agreement between households (*Great People of the Bible and How They Lived*).

A gold talent was the largest coin in the Hebrew monetary system. The coins were worth a great deal and were rarely used in common exchange. They were usually used to keep in reserve excess wealth, much like a bank or an investment in today's economy (*Old Testament Student Manual: 1 Kings-Malachi*).

Chapter Twenty Two

Prince Jesse is a fictional character; however there was a prince of Phoenicia who may have been an ally of the Queen of Judah. Nibley indicates that about ten years after this first volume ends, Mulek and his mother may have been saved from death at the hands of the Babylonians by members of the royal family of Phoenicia (Nibley, "Dark Days in Jerusalem").

It was common for young boys to carry secret messages into closely guarded areas, past soldiers, and in and out of city walls. They were not perceived as a threat and could pass unnoticed by soldiers. The Lakhish letters indicated that the captain of the guard at Jerusalem and the general at Fort Lakhish both suspected a boy by the name of Mulek of carrying messages for the prophets (Nibley, "Dark Days in Jerusalem").

Chapter Twenty Three

During the reign of King Hezekiah (about 721 B.C.), more than half of the population of Jerusalem lived outside the walls. Hezekiah began a massive construction project to extend the walls of the city to the west and bring that portion of the city under protection. As part of the construction efforts, a two-thousand-foot tunnel was dug from the Gihon Spring outside the east gate to the Pool of Siloam inside the walls in the lower city. Tunnelers, using pickax and shovel, began digging from both ends to meet somewhere in the middle. They were led by fissures in the stone and, near the end of the project, by listening through the bed rock for the sounds and voices of the other tunnelers. In 1964 a plaque, written by the original construction crew and detailing their work, was found inside the tunnel. For many years modern archeologists believed that the Pool of Siloam was the only access to the spring water inside the walled city, though there were references to a water shaft, dug high in the upper city, that allowed citizens to climb down into the tunnel to get water. In 1953 archeologists unearthed the water shaft that had been filled in over the centuries. Though the water shaft is not used today, Hezekiah's tunnel is and it is possible to walk from the head waters at the Gihon Spring in knee-deep water through the two-thousand-foot underground tunnel and come out at the Pool of Siloam (*Great People of the Bible and How They Lived*).

CHAPTER TWENTY FOUR

It is not certain how many Elders were on the Council. The number may have varied from a few men to as many as forty, depending on the population of Jerusalem at any given time and the dictates of the leadership. It is certain that the Council was originally intended to represent the people of the city. There was a hierarchy, but exactly how it was determined is unclear. It could have been according to seniority or by some other criteria, such as wealth (John Bright, *A History of Israel*). Elders were usually forty years old. Some references from the Old Testament as well as ancient Near Eastern scholars suggest that the word Elder, which originates from the Hebrew word for beard, were older, or at least to the age of wearing a beard. It was from that association that the wearing of a beard in ancient Israel became associated with wisdom and the authority to rule (Tvedtnes, "The Elders at Jerusalem in the Days of Lehi").

Flute playing and dancing were common forms of entertainment in royal courts and important gatherings. They added a refined and dignified prelude to events such as that depicted in this chapter (*Great People of the Bible and How They Lived*).

CHAPTER TWENTY FIVE

The Pool of Siloam served as the main watering place in Jerusalem between 710 B.C. and into the middle ages. It is still a clear-flowing source of water fed by the Gihon Spring (*Great People of the Bible and How They Lived*).

CHAPTER TWENTY SIX

The term "at Jerusalem" in ancient times was intended to mean the city proper and all the outlying areas that fell under the city's jurisdiction. Even the city of Bethlehem, five miles south of Jerusalem, was considered to be part of the city-state of Jerusalem since it fell under the watch of the captain of the guard at Jerusalem. It would be proper for Nephi, then, to say that Christ was to be born at Jerusalem when in fact he was born in Bethlehem. For this reason it is possible that Lehi and his family could have *lived* "at Jerusalem" all their days, but actually *lived* outside the walls of the city in the surrounding countryside.

Beit Zayit was selected as the location for Lehi's home in this novel since it is close enough to Jerusalem to fall within the capital city's jurisdiction. Some scholars have suggested that Lehi maintained a second home or property within the city walls, but most conclude that the estate where he lived with his family was located somewhere outside Jerusalem. The Book of Mormon tells us that when his sons gathered together their gold and silver to trade with Laban for his plates of brass, they had to go down to the land of their inheritance (1 Nephi 3:22), meaning outside the city walls, to get their wealth. Beit Zayit is situated beyond the hills west of Jerusalem. It has numerous hillsides for olive culture, a good water supply, and access to the three major trading destinations of the southern peninsula: Egypt, Aqaba, and Arabia by way of both the southern desert and the Dead Sea (Hilton, *In Search of Lehi's Trail;* also U.S. Army Map Service, "Jerusalem Southwest Asia," 1:250,000, AMS K502, Sheet NH 36-4, 1958).

The Book of Mormon does not directly mention Lehi's profession, but it does give important clues. He was a wealthy man, most notably evidenced by the gold and silver in his personal treasury. He owned land on which he grew food. We know he lived outside the city of Jerusalem from quotations in the Book of Mormon telling us that he "went down" to his house from Jerusalem, an ancient Hebrew reference to going outside the walls of the city or out into the countryside. Lehi was experienced in desert travel and he owned a tent. Owning a tent in ancient times was a substantial investment, since it required a good number of animal hides sewn together over a period of years. For Lehi to escape Jerusalem with little notice and take with him a tent, meant that he most likely had traveled often enough to justify owning one. The Book of Mormon tells us in the first chapter that "Lehi went forth," a possible reference to travel along the known trade routes of the ancient world (Nibley, "Lehi in the Desert"; also Hilton, *In Search of Lehi's Trail).*

In this novel, Lehi is characterized as a caravaneer and olive grower. Some Book of Mormon scholars have suggested that Lehi's major source of income was blacksmithing or some form of metal working, due to Nephi's fascination for and description of Laban's sword and his ownership of a steel bow among other things (Tvedtnes, "Was Lehi a Caravaneer?"). Others have concluded that the evidence points to caravanning and the olive oil trade. For the purposes of this novel, Lehi is portrayed in that profession. This conclusion is based, in part, on what we know about the major sources of wealth in sixth-century Jerusalem. Most wealthy men of the day owned and operated merchant businesses, trading and caravanning olive oil, wine, wheat, and gold with the nations of the Mediterranean, principally Egypt. The names of Lehi's sons support the theory that Lehi owned a caravan operation. It is possible Sam and Nephi were born after he had established himself as a caravaneer to the nation of Egypt (Nibley, "Lehi in the Desert"; also Nibley, "The Jerusalem Scene"; also Nibley, "Dark Days in Jerusalem").

Sariah is one of the prominent women in the Book of Mormon. Her faithful support of her husband Lehi is evident throughout the opening chapters of First Nephi. Though she may have been accustomed to a wealthy lifestyle, she seemed equally able to adjust to the rigors of life on the trail. This idea is compatible with the assumption that she was not always a wealthy woman, but garnered her wealth during the course of her married life with her husband. The only complaint registered to her husband in the Book of Mormon was with regard to the safety of her children, not with other difficulties they encountered.

The Romans were the first agriculturalists to standardize and write a manual for the growing and production of olives. Olive culture, however, flourished in Israel long before the Roman rise to power and their subsequent fascination for olive production. Ancient Jews were familiar with the olive tree and the tasks associated with its care. The Old Testament and Book of Mormon are replete with references to olives and olive oil production (John Gee and Daniel C. Peterson, "Graft and Corruption: On Olives and Olive Culture in the Pre-Modern Mediterranean").

Truman Madsen writes of the symbolism of the olive press as a type for Christ's atonement since it required great amounts of pressure to extract oil from olives, and the mule or ox that was used to push the pressing stone around the vat was prodded by a stinging whip in a way that prefigured Christ's mistreatment. Madsen also suggests that the feast of new oil, which required anointing in olive oil, and which symbolized the redeeming of the olive crop, also reminded Jews of the atonement, which provides redemption for mankind. Christ walked halfway up the Mount of Olives to a garden where olives were pressed and there He suffered for the sins of the world. Geth (*gat* in Hebrew) means "press" and semane (*shemen* in Hebrew) means "oil." The Garden of Gethsemane refers to the garden of the olive press (Truman G. Madsen, "The Olive Press: A Symbol of Christ").

Anciently, one leg of the trade route north of Jerusalem followed along the eastern shores of the Mediterranean Sea until it turned inland around the coastal mountain called Mount Carmel. King Solomon built Fort Megiddo at the top of the pass and stabled more than a thousand horses there. Some of the stables can still be seen in excavations at the site. When the Northern Kingdom was formed, the royal herd may have been divided among the tribes of Israel, some of the animals going to the royal family of Judah, while others were taken by the governing families of the remaining tribes (*Great People of the Bible and How They Lived).*

The Egyptian name Sam was the most popular given name among boys in Egypt. It was the name of a popular Egyptian God as well as a great general warrior (Nibley, *Since Cumorah).*

In the Book of Mormon, Nephi records that his record consisted of the language of his father, which he further explains to be the learning of the Jews and the language of the Egyptians (1 Nephi 1:2). Scholars are beginning to understand the influence Egypt had on Israel around the turn of the sixth century B.C. In addition to the exchange of goods like textiles, olive oil, gold, and wine, the Egyptians exported their language to Israel. Necho, the pharaoh of Egypt during this time, indicated that Egypt was the greatest nation on the earth because of its language, which like English today, had become the language of business. Egyptian teachers made their living tutoring the children of wealthy businessmen in Israel. In this chapter, Memphis is a fictional character, but it is possible that Lehi hired an Egyptian teacher to educate his sons in the language of the Egyptians, which at that time was an abbreviated form of hieroglyphic known as demotic or reformed Egyptian (Nibley, *Since Cumorah).*

CHAPTER TWENTY SEVEN

The dialogue for Zadock's speech to the Sarim Council (Elders of the Jews) was adapted from information taken from the Lakhish letters. They indicate that Uriah's preaching of peace with Babylon was "weakening the hands of the soldiers" and in order to resolve the problem, Uriah and Jeremiah should be considered spies (Nibley, "The Jerusalem Scene").

During the reign of King Zedekiah, the Elders of the Jews had sweeping powers and made decisions of national import without regard to the rule of the king. Most kings preferred to stay out of common law matters and rarely interfered with the rule of the princes of the city or Elders. The first scene in this chapter shows the Elders voting on a matter without first consulting the throne. It was a time of political upheaval that saw Zedekiah's power diminished by the Elders and other political groups (Nibley, "The Jerusalem Scene").

Elnathan is a historical character mentioned in both the Old Testament and the Lakhish letters. He was assigned the mission to seek out the prophet Uriah and return him to Jerusalem for speaking out against the government as did other prophets. Both the Old Testament and Lakhish letters provide a short but succinct account of his mission from start to finish (Jeremiah 26: 21-24). The Old Testament tells us that Captain Elnathan and others were sent to Egypt to bring back Uriah the prophet after he fled the country prior to the reign of Zedekiah. Bible scholars, however, point out that based on other historical information, Baruch, Jeremiah's scribe, incorrectly recorded the event and that Elnathan was most likely sent during the reign of Zedekiah. More details regarding this event can be found in the historical notes for chapter four. What we do know is that Uriah was very likely one of the prophets referred to in the first chapter of the Book of Mormon (Nibley, "Dark Days in Jerusalem").

Very few Jews owned horses and it would have been uncommon for a boy such as Daniel to have had any experience with the expensive animals or to be familiar with how to ride one (*Great People of the Bible and How They Lived).*

CHAPTER TWENTY EIGHT

Lehi is a historical character who is a prophet in the Book of Mormon. In this chapter, however, Lehi has not yet received a call from God. This scene between him and Aaron, however, shows that he was a visionary man, close to the spirit of God. Nibley indicates that Lehi was a dreamer and a poet as were many of the sheikhs and caravaneers of his day and that they received much of their inspiration and personal revelation through dreams (Nibley, "The Jerusalem Scene"; also Nibley, *Since Cumorah;* also Welch, "Lehi: The Calling of a Prophet"). Scholars agree he was in his middle to late forties at the time he left Jerusalem. The scriptures leave us scant information regarding his physical appearance, but we have enormous amounts of information regarding other characteristics (Hilton, *In Search of Lehi's Trail).*

The prophets Nahum, Zephaniah, Habakkuk, Uriah, and Jeremiah are the only prophets mentioned by name in the Old Testament who were contemporary to Lehi. The Book of Mormon tells us that there were other prophets as well, but their names are not mentioned (1 Nephi 1:4). At times of coronation it was common for the Lord to raise up many prophets. It is not surprising that prior to the time of Zedekiah's coronation the Lord would send so many men, including Lehi, to preach His will to the people of Jerusalem (Nibley, *Since Cumorah;* also Welch, "Lehi: The Calling of a Prophet").

The peace offering can be compared to a family gathering with religious overtones. It contained the elements of a party-feast to celebrate the completion of a family milestone, marriage, birth, or some other important event.

Chapter Twenty Nine

The rules governing who could and could not enter the courtyards of Solomon's temple changed over time. It was usually dependent upon the political hierarchy. A woman may have been permitted in the courtyard at specific times and only under supervision from an authority figure.

The famous menorah of Solomon's temple was intended to burn continuously until the Messiah came. The Jews called it the eternal flame and took great care to keep it lit. There is no record that the flame was ever extinguished up until the temple was destroyed about ten years after this novel ends.

Chapter Thirty Four

We cannot be certain how close the relationship between Laban and the royal bloodline of Joseph who was sold into Egypt may have been without the genealogy recorded in the brass plates, but we do know that such a relationship did exist. By virtue of his ownership of the relics Laban was most likely a very close blood relative (Rolph, "Prophets, Kings, and Swords: The Sword of Laban and its Possible Pre-Laban Origins"). The Book of Mormon tells us that Laban and his family kept the brass plates (1 Nephi 5:16) and the sword. Joseph Smith told the early saints that the sword was a symbol of kingship in ancient Israel and was anointed by prophets as such (Rolph, "Prophets, Kings, and Swords: The Sword of Laban and its Possible Pre-Laban Origins"). Swords were intended to symbolize the mantle of royal authority. It is likely that the sword of Joseph was used in the coronation ceremonies of Northern Israel's kings, much like monarchs of the middle ages used crowns. Because Laban possessed this heirloom, it is possible that he was part of the direct father-to-birthright-son bloodline of Joseph and had a strong claim to some sort of kingship.

Chapter Thirty Five

Exactly where Uriah was captured is not certain. Some scholars suggest he was hiding in the western mountains of Judah for some time and for that reason Uriah is shown to have visited Lehi at Beit Zayit before leaving for Egypt (Nibley, "Dark Days in Jerusalem"). The Old Testament records that Captain Elnathan, along with others, was sent down to Egypt to capture him. Though no mention is made of Elephantine, it is possible that he would have found refuge among other Jews living in southern Egypt. When Jerusalem was destroyed ten years later, Jeremiah and a group of Jews escaped to Elephantine to find refuge from the Babylonian army.

Scholars believed for many years that the Hebrews built only one temple and that to suggest they had others was sacrilege. More recent excavations at the island city of Elephantine indicate that members of the Jewish colony built a second temple for their worship and religious rites. It was not as large or as ornate as Solomon's temple in Jerusalem, but it served the purpose of the military men and their families stationed there. It is interesting to note that one of the first criticisms launched against Joseph Smith after publishing the Book of Mormon was the statement that Nephi built a temple after the manner of Solomon's Temple. Since the discovery of a Hebrew temple in Egypt, that point against the validity of the Book of Mormon has been dropped by most critics (Nibley, *Since Cumorah*).

CHAPTER THIRTY SIX

There were six standard liquid measures used among the Hebrews, the smallest being an *auphauk* equal to six cubic inches. Next, a *log* equal to a half pint, then a *hin* measuring about a gallon, a *seah* at two gallons, a *bath* at just under six gallons and the largest liquid measure was a *homer* equal to fifty-eight gallons, the typical size of a cistern used by caravaneers. A camel could caravan two homer over the desert. Lehi's caravan of fifty camels would have hauled nearly six thousand gallons of olive oil (*Old Testament Student Manual: 1 Kings-Malachi).*

Caravaneers wove their tents from the skins of animals. As each child was born, a room was added to the tent to accommodate the growing family (Hilton, *In Search of Lehi's Trail).*

Sour camel's milk was used to cure the bad taste from otherwise drinkable water. It didn't remove germs, but it did take the edge off the worst-tasting water and make drinking on the desert more palatable (Hilton, *In Search of Lehi's Trail).*

Wells on the trade route of the ancient middle east were usually dug as far as a camel could travel in one day, usually no more than twenty to twenty-five miles. The trade route was determined by where the wells could be dug and no caravaneer set out without a firm understanding of where each well was located. To cross the desert without such knowledge was to risk death (Hilton, *In Search of Lehi's Trail).*

It was common practice for desert travelers to hang bells around the perimeter of their camp to protect from Bedouin robbers. Dr. Hugh Nibley indicates that the practice is still in use today as a deterrent to theft and robbery (Nibley, *Since Cumorah*).

The Book of Mormon tells us that, "My father, Lehi, as he went forth prayed unto the Lord, yea, with all his heart, in behalf of his people" (1 Nephi 1:5). In ancient times the phrase, as he "went forth" or to "go forth" was understood to mean that a man had gathered supplies and means, usually camels, mules, or horses to travel a good distance from his home. To "go forth" to the market or to draw water from a well is not as likely a usage as is to "go forth" on the trade route or to "go forth" on a journey to a distant city. There is evidence to support the conclusion that something spurred Lehi on this particular journey to pray since he did not "go forth" with the intent to be alone where he could pray, but was instead enroute on a journey when some event inspired him to seek the Lord in behalf of his people (Hilton, *In Search of Lehi's Trail*; also Welch, "Lehi: The Calling of a Prophet"). Because Lehi was particularly concerned about the treatment of the prophets, this novel employs the historical account of Uriah's capture and return from Egypt as the watershed event in Lehi's life that causes him to pray earnestly enough that he was given a glorious vision. Though it is not likely that Lehi encountered Uriah on the trade route, he would have been acutely aware of his capture, and it seems appropriate to use the account to spur Lehi to pray over the events occurring in Jerusalem.

The Book of Mormon records that there came a pillar of fire that dwelt on a rock before Lehi. Ancient Hebrew prophets often referred to the light associated with the appearance of heavenly personages as fire. To ancient prophets, fire was the best description of the brightness associated with such apparitions. Nephi does not record who or what his father saw in this first vision, only that what he saw caused him to tremble because of it. Religious scholars indicate that this may have been a vision similar to the one Joseph Smith had in the Sacred Grove when God the Father and His Son Jesus Christ appeared to him (Welch, "Lehi: The Calling of a Prophet"; also McConkie, "Pre-mortal Existence, Foreordinations and Heavenly Councils," 173-198). Verse six of the first chapter of the Book of Mormon may be a reference to Lehi's first vision, with more revelation coming at a later time as indicated in verses seven through fourteen. This follows the same pattern as Joseph Smith who received more revelations after his first vision experience and recorded them in the Doctrine and Covenants.

Chapter Thirty Seven

A common feature among ancient civilizations, which still exists today, is the idea of kingship. Scholars conclude that kingship is a dominant concept combining governance and religious belief in societies as diverse and isolated as Egypt, Mesopotamia, Persia, China, Italy, northern Europe, and pre-Columbian Mexico. All ancient societies "trace the line of kings to the first king, a supreme cosmic deity who founded the kingship rites. . . . The accounts of the creation speak of a creator, a first man, and a first king—all referring to the same cosmic figure" (Cyril J. Gadd, *Ideas of Divine Rule in the Ancient Near East*, 21).

The ritual most associated with kingship is that of the coronation and its various rites. The similarities between Jewish coronations and those of other cultures suggest they sprang from a common source (Frederick H. Borsch, *The Son of Man in Myth and History,* 87-88). Among other rituals, Judah's kings were washed and anointed, and they participated in a procession usually for their subjects to pay homage or for the king to tour his realm. They wore a special garment and crown, and among their regalia they typically carried a sword as a symbol of their power (Stephen D. Ricks, and John J. Sroka, "King, Coronation, and Temple: Enthronement Ceremonies in History," 236-271).

Most ancient societies crowned their kings sometime after the winter solstice, once it was determined that the shortening of days had ended and the sun was to remain longer in the heavens. Today, we call this the New Year, and many cultures in the Northern Hemisphere celebrate religious and pagan holidays during this time of the year. The return of the sun was a central theme in coronation rites. One common tradition was the procession that began in the eastern portion of the kingdom, or at the east side of the temple, holy place, or city and followed the route of the sun, west, to the place of enthronement. For that reason the procession detailed in this novel begins at the east gate and moves west-by-northwest through Jerusalem toward the temple grounds (Ricks and Sroka, "King, Coronation, and Temple: Enthronement Ceremonies in History").

When Israel did away with the rule of prophets, they replaced them with the rule of kings as was the custom among their gentile neighbors. The adoption of kingship in Israel may have also been accompanied by the performance of the coronation immediately after the occurrence of the winter solstice. In this novel, the coronation of Zedekiah is timed to coincide with the lengthening of days in early January, around the time of our modern New Years celebration. This New Year coronation rite should not be confused with the Jewish New Year, or Rosh Hashannah, which is a religious holiday celebrated in late September or October. Anciently, Rosh Hashannah was known among Jews as a dual celebration, the Feast of the Trumpets and the Day of Remembrance. When Moses came down from mount Sinai having received covenants from God by revelation, the Israelites blew their shofar horns, and to a good Jew in ancient days, the sounding of those trumpets was synonymous with the receipt of revelation from heaven. When Moses initiated the Law among Israel, he introduced three autumnal celebrations to help the people remember the covenants they had made with God—the first being the Day of Remembrance which began a ten-day period over which Jews were given to deep personal reflection in the spirit of repentance and which culminated in the second celebration, the Day of Atonement. The Day of Remembrance came to be celebrated on the same day as the Feast of Trumpets, and for centuries in ancient Israel it was a day for personal reflection, repentance, and for remembering the covenants God had established among His people through the prophet Moses. On that day the prayers offered by the priests called for Jews to remember their covenants with God, and for God to remember His covenants with Israel. Though modern Jews refer to the day as a Jewish New Year, it does not appear to have ties to the coronation rites practiced after the winter solstice. Both the Jewish and Gentile New Year holidays have assimilated traditions from each other over the years, each containing some elements of repentance in the form of goal setting, personal reflection, as well as homage or honor paid to a religious leader or king. The Feast of the Trumpets, however, and its roots in the receipt of revelation from heaven and the making and keeping of revealed covenants have not endured as a powerful component of the Jewish New Year celebration (Lenet Hadley Read, "Joseph Smith's Receipt of the Plates and the Israelite Feast of Trumpets").

The coronation feasts depicted in this chapter are based on the lists of food detailed in the Old Testament for similar coronations. It was not uncommon for the king to feed more than twelve thousand people on the day of his coronation *(Great People of the Bible and How They Lived).*

CHAPTER THIRTY EIGHT

Uriah may have been one of the prophets who caused Lehi enough concern that as he went forth he prayed in behalf of the people of Jerusalem (1 Nephi 1:6, 20).

CHAPTER THIRTY NINE

The Book of Mormon tells us that after Lehi saw a pillar of fire, he returned home, threw himself on his bed and had a marvelous vision of heaven (see 1 Nephi 1:8-15). Scriptures record numerous other occasions where men and women have had similar experiences in which they have essentially fallen into a deep sleep for a period of time. In most cases, the duration was about three days, during which time they beheld visions. The Book of Mormon does not tell us how long Lehi was asleep or even if he was asleep on his bed; however, since other prophets have had sleep visions lasting three days, in this work Lehi is depicted as having such a vision. Alma the younger (Mosiah 27:19-22), Paul (Acts 9:3-9), and King Lamoni (Alma 18: 40-43), provide us with some of the most detailed accounts of such visions.

There were three forms or patterns of prophetic calls issued in Lehi's day. First, a vision of the throne of God; second the vision of the Heavenly Council; and third a pattern in which the prophet meets God, is commissioned, offers objections, is reassured, and is given a sign (Moses 6; also Welch, "Lehi: The Calling of a Prophet"; also McConkie, "Pre-mortal Existence, Foreordinations and Heavenly Councils"). Prophets in Lehi's day were called with any one or a variation of patterns. According to the account of Lehi's call as a prophet, it appears that he may have experienced all three patterns or forms. We do not know exactly what Lehi saw in the pillar of fire, though a pillar of fire was anciently associated with what Joseph Smith called a pillar of light. Lehi may have seen God the Father and His Son, Jesus Christ, as did the prophet Joseph Smith. What we do know, is that whatever he saw caused him to quake and tremble and he may have objected at that time only to be reassured in the vision that followed after he returned home. During his vision experience, he saw God sitting upon his throne surrounded by numberless concourses of angels as well as other manifestations that gave him confidence in his ability to serve as a prophet of God (Welch, "Lehi: The Calling of a Prophet"; also McConkie, "Premortal Existence, Foreordinations and Heavenly Councils").

LIST OF REFERENCES

Borsch, Frederick H. *The Son of Man in Myth and History,* (Philadelphia: Westminster, 1967).

Bright, John. *A History of Israel,* (Philadelphia: Westminster Press, 1981).

Church Educational System (The Church of Jesus Christ of Latter-day Saints), *Old Testament Student Manual: 1 Kings-Malachi,* second edition (1982), 33-34.

Gadd, Cyril J. *Ideas of Divine Rule in the Ancient Near East,* (London: Oxford University Press, 1948).

Gee, John and Peterson, Daniel C. "Graft and Corruption: On Olives and Olive Culture in the Pre-Modern Mediterranean," in *The Allegory of The Olive Tree* Steven D. Ricks and John W. Welch, eds., (Salt Lake City: Desert Book and Provo: F.A.R.M.S., 1994), 186-247.

Great People of the Bible and How They Lived, (Pleasantville NY: Readers Digest Association, 1974).

Guidance Associates, "The Ancient Games," in *ABC Television Special Feature: The Munich Summer Olympics,* 1972.

Hamblin, William J. "Sacred Writings on Bronze Plates in the Ancient Mediterranean," F.A.R.M.S. preliminary report, 1994.

Hilton, Lynn M. and Hope. *In Search of Lehi's Trail, (*Salt Lake City: Deseret Book, 1976).

Holbrook, Brett L. "The Sword of Laban as a Symbol of Divine Authority and Kingship," *Journal of Book of Mormon Studies,* vol. 2, no. 1, 39-72.

Hunt, Wallace E. Jr. "Moses' Brazen Serpent as it Relates to Serpent Worship in Mesoamerica," *Journal of Book of Mormon Studies,* vol. 2, no. 2, 121-31.

Ludlow, Daniel H. "The Title Page," in *The Book of Mormon: First Nephi,*

The Doctrinal Foundation, papers from the second annual Book of Mormon Symposium. Monte S. Nyman and Charles D. Tate, eds., (Provo: Brigham Young University, 1986), 5-11.

Madsen, Truman G. "The Olive Press: A Symbol of Christ," in *The Allegory of the Olive Tree: The Olive, The Bible, and Jacob 5.* Stephen Ricks and John W. Welch, eds., (Salt Lake City: Deseret Book and Provo: F.A.R.M.S., 1994).

McConkie, Joseph F. "Pre-mortal Existence, Foreordinations and Heavenly Councils," in *Apocryphal Writings and the Latter-day Saints.* ed. C. Wilford Griggs, (Provo: Brigham Young University Religious Studies Center, 1986).

Nibley, Hugh W. "Dark Days in Jerusalem: The Lakhish letters and the Book of Mormon," in *The Prophetic Book of Mormon* [The Collected Works of Hugh Nibley, vol. 8], (Salt Lake City: Deseret Book and Provo: F.A.R.M.S. 1989).

_______ "Israel's Neighbors," F.A.R.M.S. Reprint, 1984.

_______ "Lakhish letters" in Noel B. Reynolds and Charles D. Tate, eds., *Book of Mormon Authorship: New Light on Ancient Origins,* (Provo: Brigham Young University Department of Religious Studies, 1982).

_______ "Lehi in the Desert," in *Lehi in the Desert/The World of the Jaredites/There Were Jaredites.* ed. John W. Welch [The Collected Works of Hugh Nibley, vol. 5], (Salt Lake City: Deseret Book and Provo: F.A.R.M.S., 1988).

_______ "More Voices From the Dust," in *The Old Testament and Related Studies.* [The Collected Works of Hugh Nibley, vol. 1], (Salt Lake City: Deseret Book and Provo: F.A.R.M.S., 1986).

_______ "The Jerusalem Scene," F.A.R.M.S. Reprint, 1980.

_______ "The Lesson of the Sixth Century B. C.," F.A.R.M.S. Reprint, 1984.

_______ *Since Cumorah,* second edition, ed. John W. Welch [Collected Works of Hugh Nibley, vol. 7], (Salt Lake City: Deseret Book and Provo: F.A.R.M.S., 1988).

Petzel, Florence E. *Textiles of Ancient Mesopotamia, Persia and Egypt,* (Corvallis Oregon: F.E. Petzel, 1987).

Read, Lenet Hadley "Joseph Smith's Receipt of the Plates and the Israelite Feast of Trumpets," *Journal of Book of Mormon Studies* vol, 2, no. 2, 110-20.

Richardson, Alan H. *One Thousand Evidences for The Church of Jesus Christ of Latter-day Saints,* (Salt Lake City: Hawkes Publishing, 1994).

Ricks, Stephen D. and Sroka, John J. "King, Coronation, and Temple:

Enthronement Ceremonies in History," in *Temples of the Ancient World.* ed. Donald W. Parry, (Salt Lake City: Deseret Book and F.A.R.M.S., 1994).

Rolph, Daniel N. "Prophets, Kings, and Swords: The Sword of Laban and its Possible Pre-Laban Origins," *Journal of Book of Mormon Studies,* vol. 2, no. 1, 73-79.

Sperry, Sidney B. "Did Lehi Have Daughters Who Married the Sons of Ishmael?" *Improvement Era 55,* Sept. 1952, 642. A reprint is available through the F.A.R.M.S. Sperry Archive.

Thomasson, Gordon C. "What's in a Name?" *Journal of Book of Mormon Studies,* vol. 3, no. 1, 1-27.

Tvedtnes, John A. "The Elders at Jerusalem in the Days of Lehi," in *The Most Correct Book: Insights from a Book of Mormon Scholar,* (Salt Lake City: Cornerstone, 1999), 59-75.

_______ "Was Lehi a Caravaneer?" in *The Most Correct Book: Insights from a Book of Mormon Scholar,* (Salt Lake City: Cornerstone, 1999), 76-98.

U.S. Army Map Service, "Jerusalem Southwest Asia," (AMS K502, Sheet NH 36-4, 1958).

Welch, John W. "Lehi: The Calling of a Prophet," in *The Book of Mormon: First Nephi, The Doctrinal Foundation, papers from the second annual Book of Mormon Symposium* Monte S. Nyman and Charles D. Tate, eds., (Provo: Brigham Young University, 1986).

_______ "Theft and Robbery in the Book of Mormon and Near Eastern Law," F.A.R.M.S. Reprint, 1992.

PRONUNCIATION GUIDE

Zadock	ză′-dŏk
Hosha Yahu	hōsha-yah′-hoo
Shechem	shĕk′-ĕm
Necho	nĕ′-kō
Lakhish	lah-hēsh′
Arim	ah-rēm′
Yaush	yah-oosh′
Elnathan	ĕl-nŭ-tahn′
Beit Zayit	bait-sī-ēt′
Piqqeah	pē-kay′-ah
Sarim	sah-rēm′
Beuntahyu	bē-ŭn′-tuh-you

NORTH
E
S
W

ASSYRIA

ISRAEL
SIDON
MOUNT CARMEL
FORT MEGIDO
SAMARIA
ANATHOTH
QUMRAN
QIRYAT YEARIM
JERUSALEM
HEBRON
FORT LAKISH
Besor River
JUDAH
AQABA

GREAT SEA

RAPHIA
SINAI DESERT
PELUSIUM
TANIS
NILE DELTA
MEMPHIS
NILE RIVER